Mike Ashley is a full-time writer, editor and researcher with almost a hundred books to his credit. He has compiled over fifty Mammoth books including The Mammoth Book of Historical Crime Fiction, *The Mammoth Book of Perfect Crimes and Impossible Mysteries*, *The Mammoth Book of Historical Detectives* and *The Mammoth Book of Locked Room Mysteries and Impossible Crimes*. He has also written a biography of Algernon Blackwood, *Starlight Man*. He lives in Kent with his wife and three cats and when he gets the time he likes to go for long walks.

THE MAMMOTH BOOK OF

Dark Magic

Edited by Mike Ashley

ROBINSON

RUNNING PRESS
PHILADELPHIA · LONDON

Constable & Robinson Ltd.
55–56 Russell Square
London WC1B 4HP
www.constable&robinson.com

First published in the UK as *The Mammoth Book of Sorcerer's Tales*
by Robinson, an imprint of Constable & Robinson Ltd., 2004

This edition published in the UK as *The Mammoth Book of Dark Magic*
by Robinson, 2013

A copy of the British Library Cataloguing in Publication
Data is available from the British Library

UK ISBN: 97-8-178033-991-7 (paperback)
UK ISBN: 978-1-78033-992-4 (ebook)

First published in the US as *The Mammoth Book of Sorcerer's Tales*
by Carroll & Graf Publishers, an imprint of Avalon Publishing Group, Inc., 2004

This edition published in the US as *The Mammoth Book of Black Magic*
in 2013 by Running Press Book Publishers, a Member of the Perseus Books Group

US ISBN: 978-0-7624-4815-9
US Library of Congress Control Number: 2012942540

9   8   7   6   5   4   3   2   1
Digit on the right indicates the number of this printing

Running Press Book Publishers
2300 Chestnut Street
Philadelphia, PA 19103-4371
Visit us on the web!
www.runningpress.com

Printed and bound by CPI Group (UK) Ltd, Croydon, CR0 4YY

CONTENTS

COPYRIGHT AND ACKNOWLEDGMENTS

FOREWORD: SPELLBOUND

What is it about sorcerers and wizards that has kept us fascinated for nearly a thousand years, all the way from Merlin to Gandalf?

The answer's simple.

Power.

The ability to have power over things – over time, the weather, other people. Over you.

It's that ultimate wish fulfilment. How many times have we wished to make ourselves invisible, or to fly, or to create something out of nothing, or zap someone out of existence? It's that desire to have control over anything – everything.

That's what these stories are about. Power and control. Either the discovery of strange powers or being on the receiving end of them and realizing it isn't all fun. Being kept spell-bound!

It's highly unlikely, I would imagine, that anyone who found they had some incredible power would use it for good. They might, to start with. But come on, admit it, that desire to try something a little different, a little naughty, a little evil, would engulf us all in the end, I'm sure. After all, we're only human. Mind you, if we had magical powers perhaps we wouldn't be human, and that's another element of these stories, the tension between controlling human morals or ethics or otherwise letting evil reign. Because, if we ever did have control over magic, it would be a constant battle between order and chaos. It's been hard enough over these last fifty years keeping the lid on the nuclear threat and now on terrorism. Just imagine if a nation mastered magic.

Each of these stories explores the tensions and dilemmas in

dealing with magic. Don't expect any cutesy stories here of benign old wizards in pointy hats. There's none of those. In many of the stories magic has led to corruption and evil. You won't find them much nastier than the witch in Tim Pratt's "The Witch's Bicycle" or the mages in Tim Lebbon's "Forever".

There are those who try to put magic to good, such as the girl in James Bibby's "The Last Witch" or Ogion in Ursula K. Le Guin's "The Bones of the Earth", or the forensic sorcerer helping the police in a case of child abduction in "The Rite Stuff", but even they find it difficult controlling their power. It's far from easy to make magic work without it corrupting.

Magic may take many forms. I don't try to define a sorcerer. Here you will find wizards, witches, warlocks, enchanters – there's even computer magic in Doug Hornig's story. You'll find control over time in John Morressy's story, control over dragons in Tom Holt's, and the ultimate control over human destiny in Peter Crowther's powerful finale. Stories are set in this world or others, in this time or another.

As always I've brought together a mixture of new stories and rare reprints. Six of the stories have been specially written for this anthology and have not appeared anywhere else. These are by James Bibby, Peter Crowther, Tom Holt, Michael Kurland, Tim Lebbon and Richard Lupoff. There are also some unusual reprints, most far from readily available in print elsewhere. My thanks to Hugh Lamb, Stefan Dziemianowicz, Mark Owings and those on the < Horrabin Hall > internet chat group for their suggestions for stories. I only wish I had space for more.

From here on, though, all understanding of reality ceases. Watch your step.

Mike Ashley

TEN THINGS I KNOW ABOUT THE WIZARD

Steve Rasnic Tem

Steve Rasnic Tem (b. 1950) has been writing fantasy and horror fiction for over twenty years and has had stories published in Weird Tales, The Horror Show, Twilight Zone *and scores of other magazines and anthologies. He's published over 200 stories and you'll find a fair selection in* City Fishing *(2000), plus a whole load of intrigue in the multimedia CD* Imagination Box *compiled with his wife Melanie Tem. His stories have won both the British Fantasy Award and the World Fantasy Award. He gets our anthology under way with a story that is not as straightforward as it may seem.*

One: That He Has a Beautiful Daughter

Clarence first met Amanda in the marketplace when she stole several fruits from his vending cart. He'd been completely entranced by her: her long, silky black hair falling loosely to her shoulders, her narrow face and full lips. And her eyes, like emeralds on snow. He was watching those eyes when he should have been watching her hands. It was only as she started to turn away that he saw her slipping the fruit into the front pockets of her dress.

He stood in complete bewilderment a moment – by her clothes she'd seemed well off – before jumping over the side of his cart and bounding after her, heedless of the fruit being spilled and retrieved by eager passersby behind him.

The girl was fast, and Clarence had a difficult time of it just keeping her fleeting form in sight. She seemed to know well the lanes and back alleys – surprising for someone of her bearing – and it took all of Clarence's experience not to become lost himself.

But finally she made a wrong turn, and Clarence found himself face to face with the beautiful maiden, her back to a dead end. He had her. But she smiled much too engagingly, he thought, for a thief caught in the act.

He stared at her for some time: she examined him with those emerald eyes just as intently. Clarence knew how to handle the ordinary thief; he had a great deal of experience in the market-place. But he had no idea how he should speak to a lady, even if she were a thief.

"You took my fruit!" he finally blurted out.

She merely smiled and nodded.

"You didn't pay!"

She laughed out loud.

"But why?" he asked.

"Why . . . I was hungry," she replied in a soft and musical voice.

Two: That He Has a Very Unusual Daughter

Clarence spent the following weeks with the maiden, whose name was Amanda, in considerable mental and emotional confusion. He was never quite sure what she was thinking, or what she meant by some of her bizarre statements.

"Where do you come from?" he would ask her.

"Past the moon and beneath the tavern floor," she would reply.

Such nonsense . . . but he found her utterly fascinating. He couldn't control himself. He couldn't stay away from her.

More than once he had to stop her from stealing something from a local shop. She didn't really need to do such things: she simply enjoyed the challenge, she had told him. But still she persisted, and more than once they had some close calls together. Many of the local merchants were quite capable of handling their affairs without benefit of law. Clarence found himself constantly afflicted with aches and pains acquired during Amanda's escapades.

She was prone to marked swings in mood. One moment she might be laughing with him and the next screaming. He could never predict how she was going to react to anything he said. So any indication of a mood shift made him anxious.

It soon became obvious to him that Amanda had grown fond of him as well. Even though she complained about his inability to talk back to her, to be more forceful, she wanted to spend most of her time with him, she said. And despite her strange ways, he felt the same. "But my father is a wizard," she told him. "And you must meet him first, and impress him if we are to marry. That may prove difficult, Clarence my love. He is a strange man, but he's of course responsible for my existence." She laughed.

Clarence didn't know quite what to say.

Three: That He Lives in a Dark, Secluded House by the Sea

Clarence could not fathom the materials the wizard used to build his house; they seemed to be an amalgam of contradictory substances. The house was part of a granite cliff, with trees and other vegetation so mixed in that they appeared to be part of the structure itself. A large cypress melded into the roof line. A boulder formed the central portion of one of the countless chimneys. Clay and steel and cement supported one of the outside walls. There were circular doors, rectangular doors, and triangular doors. Vines covered some oddly-shaped windows and uncovered others. Strange animals nested in the oddly-angled nooks and crannies. The lines of perspective appeared contradictory.

And one section of the house seemed impossibly dark, even in the morning light, as if that section of the house had been fashioned of night itself.

It had taken them two days' journey to get there, and Clarence had wondered the entire time why it was worth the effort. Amanda complained about her father constantly: how he attempted to control her life, how he had adamant opinions on almost any subject, how he inflicted "silent rages" upon anyone who dared disagree with him.

But when Clarence had questioned their going, Amanda had lashed out at him with unexpected viciousness. "Because he's my father!" she had cried. "It's for me to decide whether to visit him or not!"

So they'd made the trip, through wastelands and mysterious, dream-like landscapes Clarence had never known existed. The wizard was indeed isolated; there seemed to be no other dwellings as far as the eye could see. Clarence couldn't understand why anyone would even want to live out there.

"You grew up in this place?" Clarence asked as they stood below the wizard's cliff-dwelling.

"I did. . . ." Amanda said quietly.

"I don't understand. Who were your friends? Who did you play with as a child?"

She turned to him with a slight frown. "I didn't have any friends," she said flatly. "Any companions I had my father made for me out of dust and swampwater."

With that, she turned and guided him to the steep staircase climbing the cliffside to the wizard's house.

Four: That He Is Very Old

The wizard sat behind an immense table piled high with books. He was difficult to see behind the dusty volumes: only a purple-sleeved arm at the side now and then, white and fish-like hands, or the top of his head, nearly bald and intricately veined.

"Father . . ." Amanda said with a nervous edge to her voice. There was no answer.

"Father, I've come home to visit. I've brought a friend."

Clarence heard a chair scrape, a dry cough, and then a small, wizened figure crept around from behind the table. Clarence relaxed a bit at the wizard's appearance: he seemed to be only five feet tall or so, and quite frail. Who could fear a man like that?

But the wizard suddenly straightened up, his back unbending, shoulders broadening, head pulling erect so that he was quickly over six feet in height and fixing Clarence with large, bloodshot eyes.

Clarence stepped back and allowed Amanda to approach her father.

"This is Clarence, father. My friend."

The wizard stepped forward out of the dim light so that Clarence was able to see his features more clearly. His skin was so white it appeared to be luminous, his bald head like an oval of light. What little hair he had was white and cropped closely, making a band above his ears. He also had a short white beard which covered his chin. His eyes seemed terribly mobile in contrast to the rest of his features. His mouth was a rigid line. Although his features did not in and of themselves seem ancient, his entire aspect was one of incredible age. Clarence sensed that the wizard was the oldest creature he had ever met.

The wizard did not speak to Clarence.

"It has been a long time between visits, Amanda," the wizard said to his daughter.

"I . . . I've been away." For the first time, Clarence saw Amanda avert her eyes in embarrassment. He had never thought before that she could feel such a thing.

There was an awkward silence during which Amanda seemed to be struggling to find something to say. Her father waited impatiently.

"How has your health been?" she finally asked.

"Well enough," he said. Then, "You may spend a few days here, Amanda, but I have my work and will need solitude thereafter." He turned and left.

Amanda stood there quietly, and Clarence could not approach her.

Five: That He Is a Shape-Shifter

That first day in the wizard's house proved to be a long one for Clarence. Amanda was sullen and irritable with him much of the time, and the wizard seemed to be ignoring them.

But when he had questioned Amanda about her father's absence, she had lashed out at him. "Open your eyes, can't you! He's watching us both constantly! He doesn't even make an effort to hide it!"

Clarence looked around uneasily. "I . . . don't see . . ."

"Look! There he is now!" she cried, pointing to a corner of the room.

Clarence looked where she had pointed but saw nothing but an untidy pile of clutter. "Where? I don't see him."

"The mouse! The mouse, you fool."

Clarence stared. There was a mouse there, a small gray one. It wrinkled its nose at the two of them, then scurried into a small hole in the debris

"Your father?"

"Of course . . ."

Six: That He Is Not Really Bad, Just Arrogant

Clarence saw many other animals, and one time a small dwarf with an immense red nose, all of whom seemed to observe him with a bit too much intensity, a bit too much interest for normal creatures of that type. He began to feel watched constantly. Amanda told him there were no pests or animals of any type in residence at the house normally – the wizard used a charm to keep them away – so any other creatures or personages found there were the wizard himself. Clarence encountered a cat, a dog, a small wren, a caterpillar, a spider, a cricket, and a moose (which he was startled to discover in his bedroom one evening) in just his first two days in the wizard's home. He became particularly careful of his actions when he was around Amanda.

This angered Amanda greatly, and twice she pulled Clarence close for an embrace when one of these creatures was in the room. Clarence sputtered and tried to pull away, a nervous eye on the creature.

"Coward!" Amanda screamed. She began hitting Clarence across the chest. "Spineless idiot!"

But the rest of the time she was distant, preoccupied. She seemed to want to have little to do with Clarence.

The wizard did not do anything which might have been called bad; even Amanda's many complaints about her father did not seem to add up to the evil man Clarence had first visualized. The wizard was merely headstrong and arrogant; he was daily exposed to the temptation of great power, and obviously he often gave in to it. He enjoyed using power, and used it extensively. Who could really blame him for that?

"So many . . . like my father . . . they start thinking they're gods in their old age," Amanda had said to him. But as far as he could tell, the wizard had not gone that far.

One of the wizard's most disturbing amusements was his habit of producing ghosts from the past, either replicas of Amanda's childhood companions he'd manufactured previously, or figures from Clarence's own childhood. Clarence felt as if he were constantly dreaming, confronted daily by his long-dead parents, the pet lizards he'd once owned, his long-dead sister's three-year-old self, and assorted young friends mostly long-forgotten.

Amanda's "ghosts" were a bit more exotic. A giant spider with bright red eyes and eighteen legs. A large, fat, jelly-like creature with one thick leg. Two sets of siamese twins. A large bird with a bell around its neck. And a few a bit more disturbing: a hideous, deformed head that talked, a small subhuman which bled from its ears constantly and impossibly, and a furry creature which screamed piteously in constant pain.

Amanda was on edge, her eyes darting, her hands dry and raw from rubbing them together. Clarence could not understand why the wizard, whom neither had seen for more than a few minutes in his true form, would do this to his own daughter. What was he thinking of?

Seven: That He Has a Separable Soul

Clarence discovered that after several days he was growing increasingly angry with both Amanda and her father. The wizard was needling him almost constantly, sending all manner of apparitions into his room to disturb him. And the wizard's presence was almost constant. Many times Clarence did not know whether a particular presence was the wizard in disguise or one of his manufactures.

So, surprisingly, he found himself talking back to Amanda with more fervor, not letting any of her small jibes past him.

He had actually expected she would like him better that way, of course. But that wasn't her reaction.

"You're getting to be just like him!" she screamed at Clarence. "You have an opinion about everything, and you think you're the only one who knows the truth!"

One day, Clarence and Amanda sneaked into the wizard's

study when they knew he was out in the woods. It was unusual for him to be away. He spent hours here, working long into the night with little or no sleep. The study was an immense, drafty chamber, filled with books, manuscripts, odd statues and carvings, jars full of substances, preserved animals, and all sorts of mechanical instruments. Clarence did not like the place and wanted to leave, but Amanda wouldn't permit it.

"I think he's keeping some important secrets from us; I want to find them."

She began to rummage through all the strange articles. Clarence stood watching nervously. Then he heard a bird cackle, and jumped. He sought the source of the sound in the darkness.

"It's only Janalai," she said, chuckling. When Clarence still looked puzzled, Amanda grabbed him by the hand and pulled him into one of the corners. She lit a small candle and a yellow glow illuminated the objects there.

A bird sat in its nest atop several old barrels and large books. The column looked unstable, but the bird seemed content enough. It had a long neck and a bright green head. Ragged purple feathers protruded from its sides helter-skelter, looking as if the bird had been in a serious accident.

Amanda walked over to the bird, clutched its neck, and pulled it roughly out of its nest. A silver egg lay within.

"See," Amanda gestured with her other hand, "Janalai guards my father's soul."

"His soul?"

"Many wizards are able to remove their souls," Amanda said. "They hide it somewhere, as in this egg. You can't destroy a wizard until you find the hiding place of his soul, actually. It makes them almost indestructible."

"But why does he leave it in such an open area? Someone could come in here and steal it!"

"He moves it to another hiding place periodically, although there has been no need of late to do so. No one comes here anymore. My father is not an active enough opponent for anyone to want to kill."

Clarence looked again at the egg and shuddered, imagining it falling to the hard rock floor.

Eight: That He Is in Complete Control

On the fifth day, Clarence discovered he could not leave the wizard's house. He'd simply wanted some fresh air, then found that there were no more doors to the outside, and that all the windows were bolted. When he went to Amanda to tell her about this, she shrugged. "So, what did you expect?" she said.

As a child, Amanda had once told him, she'd thought her father could do anything. He'd always seemed to know what she was thinking. And when she'd misbehaved, she'd believed that he had paralyzed her because she'd been unable to move with the consequent fear. He knew what was right and wrong, and had the power of life and death over her. He was in complete control.

There was no escaping him.

Nine: That He Has a Test for Me

On his last day at the wizard's house, Clarence woke up on the floor of a great dark hallway, a place he had never seen before. He stood up and began to walk down the length of the hall when the walls started to shift, sending him scrambling madly to avoid being crushed by the moving stone.

He found himself in a small room with the walls slowly closing in on him. He had to move the heavy table around quickly so as to wedge the walls apart.

Suddenly the floor dropped out from under him and he found himself on the table and sliding down an immense stone ramp where the floor used to be. He had to leap off before the table smashed into a wall at the bottom of the ramp.

Then all the creatures he'd met from Amanda's past began chasing him, and no matter how fast he ran he seemed to get no farther away from them.

Suddenly he was in the same long corridor he began in, but the walls were lined with pictures now, and as a floating ball of light descended by each one he was able to examine them. They seemed to be several pictures of Amanda, a picture of the wizard, and one of another woman whom Clarence had never seen before.

Ten: That a Wizard's Daughter Is Hard to Love

The wizard was suddenly at his side, seeming impossibly tall. "My wife . . ." the wizard said, gesturing toward the picture of the unknown woman.

"My mother . . ." he said, pointing toward one of the pictures Clarence had thought to be of Amanda. Clarence started to protest involuntarily, but was able to control himself.

"Amanda . . ." the wizard said, pointing to the next picture, ". . . and her sisters. . . ." He swept his arm across the length of the hall, and the descending lights illuminated countless other portraits, all looking exactly like Amanda's.

The wizard turned to him. "I never knew my mother; my father was a great magician who took her away from me. But still she did not have to go; she did not have to leave me. Each time I have lost Amanda, one such as you has brought her back to me. I keep remaking her, her companions, and yet she is ungrateful . . . still she leaves me . . ."

Clarence ran through the hallway, through the doors, up winding staircases. The wizard put nothing more in his way. Clarence did not slow down until he reached Amanda's door.

He heard her crying within. He opened the door slowly.

Amanda was playing with her companions: the small subhuman bleeding, the little furry thing crying, the deformed bodiless head talking with maddening animation.

Amanda was beginning to fade, as her companions were beginning to fade. Somehow she looked older even as she began to disappear but Clarence could not be sure. He remembered what she'd said so long ago: "He is of course responsible for my existence . . ."

And then she was gone completely. A gray mouse scurried out from under the bed, staring at Clarence as it wiggled its nose. Then it became a ferocious-looking silver cat that ran out the door screeching.

Clarence knew that Amanda would soon be appearing in the room again, a new and different Amanda for the wizard to love.

But he did not wait.

VILLAGGIO SOGNO

Richard A. Lupoff

Richard Lupoff (b. 1935) is always experimenting. His fascination with the works of the creator of Tarzan led to his first book Edgar Rice Burroughs: Master of Adventure *(1965) but since then he has produced fiction in the mode of H.G. Wells with* Nebogipfel at the End of Time *(1979),* Jules Verne *with* Into the Aether *(1974),* Conan Doyle *with* The Case of the Doctor who Had No Business *(1966) and works that don't really fit into any category such as* Sacred Locomotive Flies *(1971) and* Sword of the Demon *(1976) – that one was a Japanese fantasy. That's what's so great about his work, every one is a surprise. The following story, written specially for this anthology, struck me that it might have elements of Robert W. Chambers's* The King in Yellow, *but it has all the Lupoff style. With luck he is considering developing the idea presented here into a series of stories or a novel.*

"YOU'LL HAVE TO PAY the toll if you want me to drive into the city," the driver said, "or you could walk across the bridge and save some coins." His name was Signore Azzurro. His passengers were two girls, Margherita and Francesca. It was not clear which girl he addressed, and in fact he probably didn't care. As long as he collected his fare and a nice tip – surely these two nice girls would give him a nice tip – they were pretty much interchangeable to him.

They put their heads together and conferred, examined the contents of their purses, and decided to be extravagant.

The driver whipped up the big bay horse and clicked his tongue. The beast moved forward in a cheerful trot, the *carrozza*'s wheels rattling noisily over the rough gravel roadway. The River Fiume roared beneath the stone bridge, its foam and spray reaching the bridge, an occasional splatter of icy water reaching even to the *carrozza*. When this happened the girls shrieked in mock horror and alarm.

The city rose above white stone cliffs on the other side of the River Fiume. Buildings three and even four storeys tall, banners, noise, people speaking many languages, people whose skins were of many colours, wagons and carriages drawn by horses and horses ridden by handsome bravos and even a few actually ridden by women, barking dogs running among them – Villaggio Sogno was a place of marvels and of dreams.

Villaggio Sogno was a city of whitewashed plaster and wood. The buildings were roofed in copper and turquoise. When the sun glinted off the walls and the roofs, as it did this day, Villaggio Sogno rose to the sky like a dream. Old Allegra Chiavolini, the teaching woman, spoke of such wonders and warned the children of *un fascino*, the glamour, the magical spell that could give a repulsive old man the appearance of a handsome young wrestler, a hovel the appearance of a lovely cottage, a pig the appearance of a beautiful roe.

"You can sometimes defeat *un fascino*," Signora Chiavolini taught them, "with this piece of music." And she whistled a tune. The children of the town all learned to whistle the tune, and Margherita in time learned to play it as well. She had doubts about the old teacher's story, she had doubts that there was such a thing as the glamour, but it was thrilling, on occasion, to awaken late at night when the whole household was in bed and asleep, and imagine that some frightening creature was at large, disguised as a harmless animal or person. Margherita whistled the tune then, that Allegra Chiavolini had taught her, and went back to sleep feeling safe.

The two girls had been there before, brought for special treats by their respective families, but today was a special day. They were permitted to visit Villaggio Sogno without adult supervision. Their parents had fretted, Margherita's mother in particular, but twelve years old was almost grown up, or at least beginning to be grown up, and before much longer they would be going to the higher school and having parties with boys at them.

So each girl, with her savings in her purse (and with some forbidden lip-rouge and daring eye-shadow as well) was permitted to go off for the day with her best friend.

"Where shall I drop you off, young ladies?" Signore Azzurro asked over his shoulder.

The girls conferred again. Then Margherita said, "Over there. In front of the department store." This, they both knew, was not *un fascino*. Their parents had bought things for them in this emporium and they had taken them home to admire and to use.

Signore Azzurro pulled to the edge of the road and turned with his hand out. He received his payment and a tip. "When shall I pick you up for the ride home?"

Another hasty conference, even though the matter had been discussed in private and in meetings with both families, and the girls had given their solemn promise in this regard.

"When the clock in the Great Tower sounds the end of work and mechanical figures emerge to give their show."

"Very good, young miss."

The girls dismounted.

The driver watched them until they disappeared into the crowd, a wistful smile on his face. Perhaps he was a father himself, or perhaps it was simply his nature.

Margherita and Francesca stood in front of the great store. It rose three storeys into the air and its front was as long as three houses set end to end. There was a sign mounted atop the building giving the name of the establishment: *Mercato Monumentale*. The front of the store was made up of a series of show windows displaying the most marvellous clothing. The girls had seen it on their earlier visits to Villaggio Sogno, but their parents had hurried them past, intent on whatever errands occupied the minds of stodgy adults. Now they could study the contents of the windows to their hearts' content.

They could also use the polished window-glass as a mirror, and they stood side by side applying red to their lips and blue to their eyelids. They wore similar braids, Margherita's a rich, dark brown colour that approached blackness; Francesca's, red. Margherita's eyes were a blue that could also be mistaken for black; Francesca's, brown.

When they had finished applying the forbidden cosmetics they inspected each other's handiwork, approved, and entered the store.

In an hour they emerged carrying packages and wearing hats. Margherita's was striped green and yellow, with a yellow feather rising from it. She wore it tilted to one side. Francesca's was a bright red beret.

They left *Mercato Monumentale* and set out looking for a place to get some food. As they wended their way they passed street vendors and artisans who had set up shop on the sidewalk. They stopped to study the wares of a craftsman who made miniatures in silver. Francesca bought a tiny silver pin in the form of a book for her friend Margherita. Margherita bought a tiny silver pin in the form of a piccolo for her friend Francesca. They attached the ornaments to each other's blouses and exchanged a fond hug. Then they resumed their search for a meal.

They considered one place that smelled delicious but was filled with rough-looking men. Another seemed to appeal mainly to ancient women in their thirties and forties.

Finally they found a restaurant called Honshu Kekko Ryori. They had a delicious meal, unlike anything they had ever eaten at home. Each dish was arranged like a bouquet. There were tender meats with delicate flavours, mushrooms of varieties new to the girls, vegetables and noodles in steaming broth. Most memorable was a bright green condiment that made both girls cry until they laughed. The meal was served by a beautiful woman of Honshu wearing a lovely silk kimono. Margherita and Francesca couldn't get over how lovely the woman was, or how delicious the food had been. They managed to eat with chopsticks, while sitting on straw mats without their shoes. It was like being in a different world. They agreed that someday they would visit Honshu and see how people lived there.

But after lunch they decided it was time to do what they had come to Villaggio Sogno to do. Margherita's father was going to have a birthday soon and the girls were here to buy him a gift. He was a big man who seldom spoke. When he was not at work he loved to read. Margherita had consulted her mother about the best gift for her father, and they decided together that a book would be the best present. Margherita thought that a beautiful new book would be the best choice, but her mother surprised her by saying that an old book would make Father happiest.

"It's the thought that counts," Mother said. "He'll be happy to be remembered and will love anything you get him. But I happen to know that he loves best, books by an old writer named Jacopo Mursino. He wrote an epic poem in sixteen volumes, detailing the history of the universe from its creation to its end. Without your father's knowledge," Mother continued, "I have consulted the town scholar about Signore Mursino's poem. He says that only fifteen volumes are known to exist. The missing book is referred to in several others. Even its name is known. It is called *Lavori di Hipocrita*. By report, it tells the story of the Last Great Era, before the universe ends in volume sixteen. No copy of volume fifteen is known to survive in any library, anywhere, or in any scholar's collection."

Mother frowned in concentration.

Margherita knew her father's two great loves. One was to spend time in the bosom of his family. They walked the woodland near home taking note of every bird, animal, and flower that they encountered. They had formed a family orchestra. Father played a fiddle, Mother a miniature hip-harp, Margherita's brother Ottavio a brass horn, and Margherita herself a silver flute. The flute was the oldest and most precious possession in the family. It had been crafted by Mother's mother's father's uncle-in-law, the greatest silversmith in their town. Even after these years – generations – Alceo the Silversmith was remembered and spoken of with awe. Metalworkers to this day considered it the highest compliment to be called, "Another Alceo." The flute was said to have supernatural powers, but the only power that Margherita had evoked from it was the power of beautiful music.

The family orchestra performed in the evenings for their own pleasure, and on holidays in the town square for the entertainment of the community.

Father's second great love was his books. When he was not with his family, he was locked in his study with his books. When he was with his family he would tolerate any prank. He was a broad-shouldered man, heavy-bearded and muscled. He could lift Mother, Ottavio, and Margherita off the ground at once. As a young man, family legend had it, he and another had been rivals for the affection of the town's greatest beauty.

Father and his rival, a lad named Farruccio Farruli, had agreed to wrestle for the right to court the beauty, and a space had been selected for their match on the bank of the River Fumio. After an hour of struggle the two young men were both covered with a mixture of blood, mud, and grass, and were down to their last resources of strength. At this moment Father had charged at his rival, hoisted him bodily into the air, and thrown him so far into the river that a boat had been sent to bring him back to shore, for fear that he would drown if left to his own resources.

When Father turned back to face the beauty, she said, "You have beaten your rival. Now you may try to win my love. A good start would be to wash yourself off and put on a decent outfit."

Father pressed his suit successfully.

Margherita's earliest memories included lying on the carpet near the hearth on a winter's night, and Father lifting her as if she weighed no more than his fiddle, carrying her to her cradle and kissing her goodnight. He always murmured something before he kissed her but she could never understand what he said.

Even now, almost a woman (or so she told herself), she would sometimes lower her head and close her eyes near the fire, and Father would lift her and carry her to her bed, and murmur something before he kissed her. She had yet to understand his words. He never realized that she only pretended to fall asleep.

Father's second favorite author, after the poet-historian Jacopo Mursino, was the story-writer Carla Zennatello. If Mursino's greatest (and sole surviving) work was his sixteen-volume history of the universe, the creations of Carla Zennatello were far more brief. Each "book" consisted of a single riddle, written in Zennatello's personal calligraphy, preceded and followed by pages of beautiful, colourful illustrations showing noble men, lovely women, playful children, muscular horses, swift roes, dogs, cats, and birds. Each book was bound in the tough leaves of a plant that grew deep in the woods, tanned to a strength and stamina greater than that of leather, for Carla Zennatello would neither kill any sentient being nor use the product of such a killing.

Each such book could fit into the hand of an infant. Carla

Zennatello would invent a riddle and create one of his little books each time a child was born in the community, and give it to the new mother to be held in trust until the child was old enough to be entrusted with such a treasure.

Carla Zennatello. never revealed the answer to any of her riddles. She told the parents of each child who received one of her books that when that child had solved her special riddle, she would know her destiny.

Now Carla Zennatello had been dead for two hundred years, almost as long as Jacopo Mursino had been dead. A few of her riddle-books were known to exist, but none of the solutions of her riddles were remembered.

Margherita and Francesca knew there was a store in Villaggio Sogno that sold new books, but they hoped to find one where they might find an old book to please Margherita's father. They walked until they heard a boy's voice crying the news. They followed their ears until they saw him, a boy somewhat younger than themselves, dressed in worn but clean trousers and blouse. He held a stack of printed sheets at his side and with the hand not so occupied he waved a single copy.

Francesca craned her neck to get a proper look at the printed sheet. Its title was *Il Popolo di Sogno*. There was a picture of a vainglorious looking man on it. He was waving to an admiring throng.

Margherita asked the boy if he knew where they might buy an old book.

The boy looked at the two girls, puzzled. "Who would want an old book?" he asked. "Better to buy a new one. Best of all, buy a copy of *Il Popolo* and get a portrait of our glorious leader for no extra money. Learn of yesterday's kicking match, learn of bodies found in alleys, learn of armies marching and of politicians arguing."

He took up his cry again.

A passer-by bought a news sheet.

Francesca tugged at the boy's elbow and Margherita said, "We want to buy an old book. Does anyone sell them in Villaggio Sogno?"

The boy said, angrily, "Go see Signore Malipiero."

"How do we find him?"

"He'll be in his shop."

"Where is that? You are not being at all helpful!"

"And you are not helping my business!" He stopped to sell another news sheet.

"Where is Signore Malipiero's shop?"

Angrily the boy turned to face the two girls. He pointed a finger and told them to proceed to the town square, to turn at the tavern displaying a sign that read *Il Ubriacone* and a giant painted mug of *birra*, to continue until they came to a dressmaker's establishment, they could not miss the dressmaker's establishment unless they were even more stupid than they seemed, to turn again (and he pointed to show them which way to turn) and they would surely see the establishment of Signore Malipiero or they could come back and he would refund their fee.

"If I am not here, merely ask for me. Guglielmo Pipistrello. Now goodbye."

He held out his hand.

Francesca put a coin in it.

Signorino Pipistrello turned away and resumed shouting the news.

Margherita and Francesca followed his directions faithfully. They stopped in the town square. A statue stood there. Its title was embossed on a copper plate, green with age: *Chaos Giving Birth to Order*. To Margherita the statue looked like a great fish or dolphin vomiting up a globe of the world. The name of the sculptor also appeared on the copper plate, and the year of the statue's creation, long ages ago. Couples strolled in the sunlight and children ran among them playing ball or eating sweets. The Great Tower stood above the square, a clock on its face and iron doors waiting to open at the end of the day.

The tavern was where Guglielmo Pipistrello had said it would be.

The dressmaker's establishment was where he had said it would be, also.

The two girls halted in the street before a shop with a wooden trough filled with old books in front of it, and glass windows so obscured with cobwebs and dust that they could not see through them. The trough of books bore a hand-written sign that gave the price of the books as a small coin for one, two small coins for three, and a large coin for an armload.

Above the door of the shop was a sign, not merely painted but carved into wood: *Ettore Malipiero, Purveyor of the Rare and Precious.*

Margherita and Francesca stared at each other.

"The boy said we could get an old book from Signore Malipiero."

"And he said that we would find Signore Malipiero's shop near the dressmaker."

"And there is a trough of cheap books outside the shop."

Margherita bent over the trough of books. She picked one up, that seemed to be promising. She had learned to read at an early age, learning to read music and learning to read words at the same time. Her earliest books had mixed pictures and music and stories. Her mother had been her teacher. Her brother, Ottavio, could already read when Margherita was learning. It was competition with Ottavio that spurred her to develop both her skill with books and her talent with her silver flute until she surpassed Ottavio's performances with his horn.

The book looked, felt, and smelled old. Its cover was battered and the title could not be read. Margherita opened it to the title page and read, *Three Voyages in Distant Lands*, by Sylvio di Filippo. She had never heard of the author, but then, she realized, she had never heard of many authors. She knew of Jacopo Mursino and of Carla Zennatello because Father spoke of them. He had read all but one volume of Mursino's great poetic history of the universe and longed above all things to read the missing volume. In this, he had said many times over family meals, he was but one of many. He said that he wished he had been able to obtain two of Zennatello's works. They had become known as blessing books, and there was competition for the few known to survive. If he had been able to obtain two of them he would have made birth-gifts of them to his own two children, Ottavio and Margherita, but had instead laid a precious fiddle in Ottavio's cradle and the silver flute made by Margherita's ancestor Alceo in her crib, so that the children should grow up with the instruments as their earliest possessions and familiar companions.

Next to *Three Voyages in Distant Lands* Margherita found a copy of a book she already knew, Claudia Belluzzo's *Tunes and Rhymes for Little Ones*. She had loved that book, with its colourful pictures of tiny animals, birds, tortoises, and bears. Each picture was accompanied by a little poem and a simple musical lesson. Margherita had played those melodies on a miniature child's flute – this was before she was old enough to play Alceo's silver flute – and the creatures in the book had danced to her tune. Or so it seemed to her. And Mother gave her testimony that it was indeed so.

A shriek interrupted Margherita's concentration on the trough of books. It was Francesca who had shrieked. She was clutching a book to her chest. "*Minuscolo-Minuscolo!* I used to love this book! I slept with it beneath my pillow! I read my copy until it fell to pieces. Now I see another copy."

The two girls prepared to enter the store. Behind them was a narrow cobblestone street. It was unlike the broad thoroughfare where Signore Azzurro had left them, nor was there the colour and bustle of the town square with its statue and great tower. Instead the street was dark. The buildings were old and their upper storeys seemed to lean toward each other, covering the cobblestones and blotting out the bright sky and warm sunlight of the day.

Something sleek in shape scurried past on one side of the street. It was a dark shade, maybe green but more probably gray-black. It appeared to be covered with a scaly or leathery skin. An armadillo in Villaggio Sogno? A snake? But it had legs, Margherita thought. Surely it moved too rapidly to be a terrapin. A small crocodile, such as the Gypsies said lived in the swamps alongside the River Nile in their homeland?

Whatever it was, it dived into a dark, narrow opening between two buildings.

An old woman, her bonnet hiding her face and long sleeves concealing her hands, scuttled by on the other side of the street, then disappeared into another street. A cart rolled past, pulled by an ox as tall as a man and as wide as a shed. The driver wore a broad-brimmed hat. His shoulders were as massive as two hogs.

Carrying the three books with them, Margherita and Francesca entered the store. As they set foot upon the doorstep they were confronted by a man so tall that he had to stoop to leave the shop. He was as thin as a stick and his height was added to by a pointed cap of purple felt. He growled at the girls and elbowed them aside, shoving between them and scurrying away from the shop.

Inside the establishment the girls confronted a boy who could not be more than fifteen years of age. His hair was the colour of ground barley, his eyes the shade of the River Fiume. His ears stuck out from the sides of his head like the wings of a raven. His bones protruded through the shoulders and elbows of his dust-coloured shirt. The sleeves of the shirt were too short for his arms and his wrists stuck out like two knobs.

"Signorine," the boy addressed the girls, "what can I do for you? You wish to purchase books?" He ogled the volumes that Margherita and Francesca had brought from the trough. "Let me see your choices, please." The boy stepped behind a wooden counter, darkened by years and rubbed smooth by countless hands and books.

The girls laid their choices on the counter.

The boy turned them over, nodding his approval.

Francesca gave another shriek. Really, Margherita decided, she would have to talk with her friend about that. It was humiliating to be with someone who reacted to each little surprise as if a winged angel had suddenly appeared in the sky, surrounded by a nimbus of flame.

"What was that?" Francesca gasped.

Margherita turned in time to see a dark form disappear behind a curtain covering a doorway in the back of the store. "It is just – it was—"

"It was—" Francesca waved her hands at the level of her face.

The boy behind the counter leaned across the wood, craning his neck. "That's just Nero."

"Who?"

"Nero. The store dog. Signore Mallpiero's dog. That's all. He lives in the store."

"No." Francesca shook her head. "That was no dog. It had skin like a lizard."

"No." Margherita shook her head. "It had feathers. It was shaped like a dog but it was covered with feathers. Maybe it was a – what do you call it – a gryphon."

"No such thing as a gryphon," Francesca said. "I've heard of gryphons, read about them and seen pictures. They are imaginary beasts."

"Oh, really." Margherita was annoyed. "I suppose it was a big India-bird, then."

"Not with skin like that."

"Feathers."

The boy with the too-short shirtsleeves came out from behind the counter. He stood facing the curtained doorway. "Come on, Nero. Nero, come to Peppino."

The curtain shook, then a nose appeared, or was it a beak, followed by a four-legged creature. It was a gryphon, Margherita thought, with clawed feet and feathers like a bird. She squeezed her eyes shut, then opened them again. It was an ordinary dog with short dark fur and a squarish face that it shoved into the skinny boy's hand.

Margherita turned to Francesca.

Francesca had dropped one hand and held the other to her mouth. "I thought it was a lizard," she said, "but I see, it's only a dog." She squatted on the creaking wooden floorboards and put her arms around Nero's neck.

The skinny boy reached behind the counter and brought out two bits of biscuit. He handed one to each girl. "Give him a treat and he'll be your friend."

Each girl, in turn, fed her bit of biscuit to the creature. Nero wagged his tail gratefully.

"Your name is Peppino," Margherita addressed the boy.

"At your service." Peppino made a silly bow. "Peppino Campanini. Apprentice bookseller and student of manuscripts and wonders."

Margherita and Francesca introduced themselves.

"So, you wish only these treasures from our bargain bin." The boy heaved an exaggerated sigh. "My master will be displeased with me if I cannot sell you something better than these." He lifted the three books and his eyebrow and said, "But I admit that they are a good choice. Oh, you found the *Minisculo-Minisculo*. Is that what brought you in? Signore Malipiero always salts the bargain trough with a few little treasures. I think you two ladies have cleaned us out today. *Minisculo, Tunes and Rhymes, Tre Viaggi* – everything else outside is trash. Surely you will not insist on buying these three treasures for a single coin."

"That's what your sign says."

"Of course, of course, but we do not count on a customer so sharp-eyed as you and your companion are."

"What else do you have?"

Peppino Campanini put the heels of his hands to his eyes as if to keep himself from crying. Then he dropped his hands. "You are too smart. I cannot deal with you."

He leaned over the counter again, impossibly far. Margherita half expected him to lose his balance and fall to the floor at the feet of herself and her friend, but he managed to hang on. "Signore Malipiero! Signore Malipiero! Customers to wait on, please."

Nero had sat on his haunches throughout the exchange. Now he stood up and trotted to the curtained doorway. He reappeared tugging by the cuff an old man, red faced and grey haired, wearing round spectacles, very dirty, making Margherita wonder how he saw through them and why he bothered to use them. He wore a pale shirt patterned with large black dots and trousers of a colour so long-ago faded that it was impossible to identify. Nero had his teeth in one shirt cuff, in the other hand he held a tattered, oversized book. Slips of paper curled from between its pages and the old man had crooked his forefinger to save his place and his middle finger to save another.

He blinked at the skinny boy. "Peppino, why do I pay you? Why do you call me whenever there is a customer?"

Without waiting for his helper to respond, the old man turned toward Margherita and Francesca. He bowed deeply. He had a round stomach and he made a sound something like "Oof!" as he stood back up. "You wish a powder, a potion, something to help you to learn without studying, something to make your boyfriends chase you, something—"

He stopped and studied them. "My apologies. Two beauties such as you need no help to make your boyfriends chase you. You have boyfriends? You want something else? Talent? No, I can see that you both have great talent. What do you want?"

Francesca said, "My friend wants a birthday gift for her father."

The old man nodded. "Ahh."

Margherita said, "He loves books."

"Ahh," the old man said again. "Well, you have come to the right place. My name is Ettore Malipiero and this is my establishment. As you can see, I have books."

He made a sweeping gesture that included all of the store and seemed also to include Nero, Peppino, the mysterious realm behind the curtained doorway, the street outside and very likely all of Villaggio Sogno.

"And what are your names, young *signorine?* And what does your father wish to receive for his gift? You must ask yourself. What will make my beloved father happy on this day?"

"He loves old books," Francesca said.

"Very old books," Margherita said. "And other old things, but best of all, old books."

"Good, good," the old man said. "The old books are the best books."

Nero snuffled at Margherita's hand. He was looking for another biscuit but she had no more. She bent to apologize to the dog, and as she did so she could detect Signore Malipiero from the corner of her eye. There was something strange about him, something that did not agree with his cheerful and friendly manner. She straightened but he was just an old man, smiling at two girls and his dog. And from the corner of her eye, Margherita caught another glimpse of Nero, and he was not a friendly dog but something else once again, something that he ceased to be when she looked more closely at him.

"How much money do you have?" the old man asked.

Margherita and Francesca conferred. They had started the day with their savings but they had paid Signore Arruzza for the ride into Villaggio Sogno and had tipped him to make sure that he would return for them at the end of the day. And their meal at Honshu Kekko Ryori had cost them a pretty penny and then some. And they even bought a news sheet from Guglielmo Pipistrello just to get him to pay attention to them long enough to get directions to the bookstore.

To Ettore Malipiero, Francesca said, "Not very much."

"Not very much, eh? Then why did you come to my store? Don't you know this is the finest establishment in Villaggio

Sogno for the purchase of rarities of this type? Perhaps your father, Signorina, would like a powder instead. How old is he? Do you think his powers are waning? Something to restore the strength and energy of a man of some years. I can make you a very good price, and your father will be grateful. As will your mother, I assure you."

"No, a book."

"Ah, well." Signore Malipiero scratched his head. Margherita was almost certain that she saw sparks fly from his hair when he scratched, and the sound that accompanied them was unlike anything she had ever heard before.

"Perhaps," he said, "a new book would please your father. There are many talented authors even today, Signorina. Does your father read Cesare Zampieri? Very fine, his writings inspire the reader to deeds of courage and nobility. I even knew a man who had been unhappily married for many years but did nothing save put up with a nagging wife and a demanding daughter, pardon my candour, Signorine, I am an old man, you must forgive me, until he read a copy of Zampieri's fine book, and then he set his mind to awaken him one night after the entire household was soundly sleeping and—"

He stopped and smiled as if ashamed of himself. "I am so sorry. This matter is too delicate for the ears of two such young ladies as yourselves. No, I would not recommend Zampieri. Perhaps a better choice would be the meditations of Oreste Ronga. Yes, I think Ronga might be the perfect gift for the father of a lovely young lady like yourself." He turned to Francesca. "I think your friend's father would enjoy Ronga. Do you know Oreste Ronga? A very talented writer. No? You do not know Ronga? There is a store not far from here that sells new books. I send customers there every day. *Libri e Libretti*. Just step outside my shop and turn – what is it, Signorine?"

They were both frowning.

"An old book!" Margherita said.

"An old book!" Francesca echoed.

The old man sighed. "If you insist. Well, come with me, I will see if I can find something, perhaps a codex whose binding is lost, water-stained, foxed, tilted, missing a signature. I'll try and find you something."

Something scratched Margherita's hand and she looked down and caught a glimpse of a clawed foot moving away. But it was only Nero. "I think he wants another biscuit," she told Peppino.

"It's almost his dinner time," the boy said. "I don't know if it's such a good idea."

Nero stood on his hind legs. He was tall enough to reach the counter and he scratched its surface, leaving a row of parallel tracks. For a common dog he had very long, very sharp claws, more like those of a hunting bird than a house pet.

Signore Malipiero said something softly to his assistant and the boy grew pale. He reached under the counter for a biscuit and tossed it to Nero.

"Come." Ettore Malipiero stood in the curtained doorway to the second room.

"Come with me, young ladies, and we will see what we can find to make a suitable gift for your father's birthday gift. You are sisters?"

Francesca said, "No, we're neighbours and friends."

"Ah, good." The man led them into a second room. Like the first, it held many, many bookshelves. It was a very odd room, with five walls instead of the customary four. Two of the walls were filled with books from floor to ceiling; two, from ceiling to floor; and one, starting at the level of Margherita's blue eyes, was filled in both directions, to the ceiling and to the floor.

There were a number of cabinets in the room, each with many small drawers. The cabinets were of wood. The drawer-pulls, by their appearance, were of rare ivory. If this were the case, the ivory would have been imported from distant Abyssinia.

The centre of the room was clear, save for two wooden chairs.

Oil lamps and candelabra stood on the cabinets. When they entered the room only a single lamp was burning, casting dark shadows in the room. The flickering flame of the lamp made the dark room seem double dark, but Signore Malipiero lit a straw from the burning lamp and used it to light more lamps and candles.

"Sit yourselves down," Signore Malipiero told the girls. "I will bring you some books. Oh, I have been in this business for a very long time, young signorine. I have been buying and selling books and other things for more years that you can imagine. I do know my stock. Oh, yes."

He went to one wall and stood studying the bookcases, one hand to his chin, which had clearly not seen the glint of his razor for some days, the other upraised tentatively as if he were about to reach for this book – no, this one – no, this. At last he gave a satisfied sigh and pulled a volume from the shelf. He did not carry it to the two girls, but instead walked to a wooden cabinet and laid the book on its back so that the light of a candelabrum flickered across its reddish cover.

Margherita noticed that the flames of the candles and the lamps were wavering as if in a breeze, and in fact she did feel a chilly flow of air passing over her face and her shoulders. She looked at Francesca and saw a wisp of her friend's hair flutter in the current of air.

Signore Malipiero crossed the room and knelt to reach the bottom row of books. He pulled a volume in a brown cover from the shelf, studied it for a time, then slipped it back into its place. "No, no," the girls heard him mutter, "that one will never do. Not for one's father, not for one's father's birthday." He pulled another volume from the shelf, one with a yellow cover that bore the signs of great age. "Ah, this one, this one will please such a man as could be the parent of such a daughter."

He laid the yellow book on the cabinet beside the red one.

Once more he crossed the room. At the wall where he now stood, a ladder rose. Margherita's gaze had followed the old man since they entered the room. Now she watched him climbing the ladder. It appeared to be old, everything in the store appeared to be old except for the helper, Peppino Campanini.

Margherita watched the old man climb the old ladder until it disappeared into darkness. How tall was this room? Margherita wondered. How high did the bookshelves rise? How high would Signore Malipiero climb?

Sounds of scuffling and of grunting came from high above. The ladder shook. Margherita feared that it would fall, that Signore Malipiero would tumble from the heights and break his neck when he landed. What would happen then?

But eventually the old man's feet reappeared covered in scuffed and worn boots, then his legs, then his torso, then the back of his head. When he reached the floor he turned to face Margherita and Francesca. He was covered in dust or soot, it was not possible to tell which. He held clutched in his arms a huge volume, its binding hiding his entire torso. In fact, it reached from his knees to his shoulders.

Signore Malipiero staggered beneath its weight, struggling to cross the room and lay the huge, black-covered volume on the cabinet.

He bent and opened a drawer in the cabinet, removing from it an old pair of bellows. He closed the drawer once again, then walked to the far side of the cabinet where he directed the bellows at the three books he had pulled from the shelves. He pumped the bellows once, twice, thrice; at the red book, the yellow book, the black book.

A cloud of dust arose from each of the books and was carried on an air current to the centre of the room. Margherita was startled and gasped in surprise, not a wise thing to do, for she found that she had inhaled the dust. She heard Francesca gasp as well, and realized that her friend had also inhaled the dust. It had formed a cloud, the three colours blending and whirling about one another, and in the cloud Margherita saw another place, a terrible place.

It was a room larger than any she had seen in her life, a room the ends of which she could not see. The floor was of stone, the stone covered with a deep layer of grey dust. Pillars as large around as the largest tree rose from the floor only to disappear in darkness above. Row upon row the pillars stretched in all directions, so that Margherita turned about, unsure whether she was in the bookstore or in this other place, trying to get her bearings. Instead she felt her head beginning to whirl. Everything about her was grey, fading in the distance to blackness. The air was cold and had a stale odour in her nostrils and a foul, choking flavour in her mouth.

She turned her face and peered upward. She could not see the tops of the pillars, nor the roof above her. There was only blackness. Something cold and very light landed on her face; she brushed it away and found a tiny smudge on her fingertip, as if she had brushed away a small snowflake made of floating dust rather than frozen water.

Rows of blocks stood between the pillars, each as tall as her waist, as long as a wagon and as wide as a bed. Something lay atop each block, covered with what appeared to be a soft cloth.

Everything was grey.

Ettore Malipiero was there, but he was not the kindly, gruff-mannered man of the bookshop. He was something different, something frightening and evil. He was the creature she had seen from the corner of her eye. Nero was at his side, but it was not Nero the friendly hound but Nero the terrible animal she had glimpsed so briefly.

She tried to reach for her friend Francesca's hand but a cold lethargy had stolen away her power of movement.

The creature who was Ettore Malipiero loomed over Margherita and Francesca, the three books balanced in his arms. Even Signore Malipiero was seen through a film of grey, but the books retained a suggestion of their colours. He dropped the red volume on Francesca's lap and the yellow volume on Margherita's. He still held the black book himself, but instead of a feeble old man who could hardly manage to balance the huge volume in his arms, he had become a giant. He was bigger than Margherita's brother Ottavio, bigger than Margherita's father. His skin was not that of an old man, but he was manlike enough to hold the book open before him as easily as a child holds her first reader.

His face was not that of a man. It was more like that of a lizard, and when he opened his mouth to reveal rows of gleaming teeth his tongue flicked out, a tongue forked like that of a snake, and his voice was half the voice of a man and half the hiss of a snake. He turned away and opened cabinet drawers, and Margherita wondered briefly how cabinets had appeared among the great columns, but her attention was drawn back by the sight of this changed Malipiero hooking ivory pulls with curving, razor-like claws. He scooped powder from the drawer and half-spoke, half-hissed words while he dropped powder into the burning candles of the candelabrum. As he did so coloured columns mushroomed up from the candles, yellow and red and black in this new grey world.

He took a shallow bowl and filled it with powder and stood over Margherita and Francesca and blew the powder at the girls. His breath was cold and stank of rancid oil.

Margherita tried not to breathe the powder that the creature that was Signore Malipiero blew at her, but it swirled around her head while she held her breath until finally she could hold her breath no longer and had to inhale the powder. She felt herself lifted. She could not tell if she was floating into the cold, stale air or if Signore Malipiero was lifting her in his scaly arms. She felt a pressure inside her head as if her brain was going to explode. She shut her eyes and tried to think only of Mother, Father, Ottavio, Francesca.

When she opened her eyes she knew she was in that other world, the grey world of huge columns, rectangular blocks, dust-covered stones and distant blackness. Now she could see the ends of the giant room. Far, far from her the pillars came to an end, as did the rows of blocks, beyond them was blackness and a few very distant stars. A few flakes of the grey, unclean snow drifted from the heavens.

The creature that was Signore Malipiero bent over a block. The cloth that lay over it moved as if lifted by a wind, but Margherita felt no wind. It moved as if what lay beneath it was moving feebly. Signore Malipiero lifted the cloth and lowered his face over what lay on the block. Clearly Margherita saw that the block was on stone, but Signore Malipiero's form prevented her from seeing what lay beneath the cloth.

She raised her eyes. The cloths on other blocks moved as if stirred by the wind or by what lay beneath them. The silence of the great place was nearly complete, but there was some sound, Margherita was certain of this, some faint and strangely sorrowful sound.

The shapes of the things beneath the grey cloths were similar to the lizard-snake Malipiero, yet some of them were smaller than he, and in a strange way made Margherita think that they were the shapes of girls. She shut her eyes, trying to understand what had happened, but when she opened them again she understood no more than she had. Malipiero moved to another block, drew back another cloth, bent sorrowfully over another girl-lizard-snake.

This was a world of death, she thought, and these were the daughters of the creature she had seen as Ettore Malipiero. Monster though he was, he was a father. He wished to save his daughters. He wished to bring his daughters into Margherita's world.

This must be the meaning of the powder, the yellow and red

and black powder. She had been deceived by *un fascino*, a glamour. There was no Signore Malipiero, no human Signore Malipiero. There was only the horrid snake-lizard creature of this world of the dead, and the two snake-lizard daughters of the creature. Somehow, Margherita realized, the father had managed to cross from this dead world into her own, into Margherita's beautiful living world. But he could not abandon his two daughters. He was not a human father but in his own horrid way he was some kind of man, some kind of father.

With a start, Margherita realized that she felt a terrible pity for the snake-lizard Malipiero and an aching kinship for his two snake-lizard daughters. They were girls, unlike Francesca and herself and yet like them, too. What had become of their mother? Did she occupy another block of stone, did she lie beneath another grey cloth? There was no way that Margherita could know. And what would become of Margherita and her friend Francesca now?

The snake-lizard Malipiero loomed over Margherita and Francesca, and over the blocks where lay his two snake-lizard daughters. He held something that might be the great black book and bowl that must contain the coloured powders that he had burned in the bookshop. If it was a bookshop! What if the whole shop had been a glamour? What if it was a deceptive extension of this world of death into her own world?

With a whir of wings more faint that that of an insect approaching on a summer's night, a tiny speck appeared. It moved through the distant blackness, through the dark night and the dusted snow beyond the farthest pillars. It moved toward Margherita and the others, growing as it approached, walking upright like a man or a snake-lizard thing, but it was neither.

The thing that was Ettore Malipiero rose to its full height and stood facing the newcomer. The newcomer halted. He smoothed the cloth over one girl-figure, then the other. He placed his hand on Ettore Malipiero's shoulder and drew him toward himself. Margherita thought that the newcomer was trying to comfort Malipiero, but Malipiero seized him in his great claw-tipped hands and hurled him against the nearest pillar.

The newcomer collided with the pillar and crashed to the floor sending up a cloud of gray, choking dust. He leaped to his feet but

Malipiero was upon him, slashing with his claws, biting with his rows of shining teeth. The two rolled on the floor, wrestling as Francesca's father and his rival had wrestled so long ago for her mother's favour, but this struggle was for something other than love.

What would happen to Margherita and Francesca once the two struggling figures had settled their dispute? Margherita decided that Signore Malipiero had found a way to bring her and her friend to this world and was determined to leave them here to spend eternity lying on blocks of stone, covered with heavy cloths, while slow layers of cold dust drifted down upon them. He would return to the world of Villaggio Sogno with his own girls, giving them the places of Margherita and Francesca.

The two fighters, Ettore Malipiero and the newcomer, rolled and thrashed in clouds of dust.

Margherita grasped Francesca by the arm. She pursed her dry lips and tried to whistle the tune that old Allegra Chiavolini had taught the children of the town long ago. Her mouth was dry and tasted of dust and death. All that emerged was a meaningless *whoosh* of air. She wished desperately for her silver flute, the wonderful flute of her ancestor Alceo, but that was at home in her own room. In a flash she reached for the decorative piccolo she had pinned to Francesca's bodice. With trembling fingers she retrieved her gift and placed it against her lips.

Was it a real silver flute, however tiny? Could she draw a tune from it? The finger holes were dreadfully close together but they were placed properly. She blew through the mouthpiece one time, then gave her all to playing the tune that Allegra had taught the children, the tune that the aged woman claimed would dissolve any glamour and reveal the truth behind it.

She managed to evoke Allegra's tune, shrilly and softly, but each note emerged from the instrument accurately and danced away through the cold air.

The dead world disappeared.

The massive pillars, the stone blocks, the shrouded figures, the distant blackness and stars and snow-of-dust disappeared.

Margherita was back in the shop, Francesca at her side. Or was she? She blinked. She was not seated in the five-sided room of *Ettore Malipiero: Purveyor of the Rare and Precious*. She was seated beside Francesca in a shop where dummies stood with half-finished gowns held in place by pins. Pictures of clothing of various sorts adorned the walls. Two, no, three seamstresses sat in a circle chattering busily as they tended to their work. An older woman, clearly the owner of the business, stood with a customer, showing her samples of cloth.

Margherita could not help but take note of the work of the three seamstresses nor to overhear the conversation that took place among them. Each was working on a lovely gown, each gown of a different colour. One was yellow and gay; one, red and daring; one, a sombre black but brightened with a pattern of glittering diamonds and onyxes.

The first seamstress was saying, "I trust that Signorina A. will be pleased with this golden gown, to wear on her honeymoon journey. I know she will be happy with her new husband."

The second seamstress said, "I hope that Madonna B. will approve of her crimson gown, to wear on her triumphal tour of the concert halls. I know it will draw the attention that a great diva craves."

The third seamstress, smiling, made her contribution. "I know that *La Duchessa* C. will be pleased with her so-dark gown. So young and energetic a woman, to be married to *Il Duca*, so aged and fragile a man. She ordered the gown herself, giving orders that *Il Duca* was not to see it or even know that *La Duchessa* was thus preparing for the inevitable."

Margherita clutched the hand of her friend and tried without success to stifle a giggle.

The older woman looked around, startled. "Who are you two girls? What are you doing in my shop? I didn't see you come in."

She spoke to the seamstresses, calling them by name. "Did any of you see these two girls come in? Do any of you know them?" The seamstresses all shook their heads. No, Madonna. No, Madonna. No.

The woman spoke angrily to Margherita and Francesca. "Did my rival send you here? Have you come to spy on me, to see my new patterns, to steal them from me?"

The girls started to protest, the woman did not wait. "Get out! Get out of my shop! Get out of here or I'll call my son Peppino and have him beat you with a broomstick! Go back where you came from and tell her to get patterns of her own if she wishes to compete with me!"

Chased by the angry woman, Margherita and Francesca stood outside the shop. The sign above the door was carven and painted. It read, *Eleanora Pampanini: Purveyor of Lovely Gowns and Useful Garments.*

Margherita and Francesca clutched each other and set out to retrace their footsteps to the town square. As they turned one corner and another they came upon an establishment called *Libri e Libretti.* Inside they inquired, without much hope, for Mursino's *Lavori di Hipocrita* or for one of Carla Zennatello's riddle books. The merchant smiled a wry smile. "Not in all my years selling books, young ladies. Not in all my many years." They purchased a new book instead, as a gift for Margherita's father, and left the shop.

As they did so, a very tall figure who had been concealed in a shadowed nook followed them. In the street outside, strangely, he managed to place himself ahead of them in their path.

The two girls halted, gazing up into the face of the very man who had brushed past them as he left the shop of Ettore Malipeiro. He smiled down at them from beneath his pointed cap.

"I could not but hear your request at *Libre e Libretti.*"

"Please, Signore, we are on our way home."

"Of course, of course, Signorina, I would not wish to inconvenience you. But if you seek the books of Signore Mursino or the great Carla Zennatello, I might be able to help you." He bowed and introduced himself. "I am called Ragno Distruttore."

The tall man seemed to arch over the heads of the two girls, like a willow tree arching over a pond.

Francesca said, "Do you have such books?"

"Alas, Signorina, not just now. But books come to me from time to time, as do many other rarities and wonders. If you would care to visit my establishment, I would gladly guide you there right now."

Francesca made to follow the man, but Margherita placed her hand on the arm of her friend. "Look at the sky. It's late. Signore Azzurro will leave without us."

"Yes, yes." Francesca said, "I'm sorry, Signore Distruttore, we cannot."

"Well then, may I extend an invitation. You will find my place of business as well as my home in the Piazza Campo Sereno."

"I do not know that place."

"Ah, surely you can find it. Ask anyone at all. If they do not know the piazza, surely they know it by the monument to the great soprano Lucrezia Spina di Rosa, the famous singing statue of Villaggio Sogno. Once there, you will find my house, as tall among its neighbours as I am tall among other men. Come by day or night. I suffer, you see, from an inability to sleep. You will see the lantern flickering in my window to all hours. It is the burden I bear."

"Come, Francesca! We must go!" Margherita was tugging at her friend's sleeve.

"But, Margherita, Signore Distruttore—"

"We must go!"

"But—"

"Signore Distruttore, addio!" Margherita dragged her friend away from the sticklike man. He reached a long, skinny arm and long, clawlike fingers after them, but Margherita dodged from his grasp, dragging Francesca along with her. Ragno Distruttore pursued them, his long legs covering ground in great strides, but he seemed to tire quickly and soon fell behind. The girls ran until they were out of breath, then stood, feeling more secure in the midst of a crowd of jolly women and men.

By this time the sun was surely setting. The streets of Villaggio Sogno were as busy as ever, but now they were filled with workers making their way home and with celebrants arriving for an evening of revelry. The two girls stopped outside a music hall. From within they could hear musicians tuning their instruments and singers preparing their throats for the evening's performance.

"Why did you drag me away from Signore Distruttore?" Francesca demanded.

"I do not trust that man. He frightened me."

"But he said he might help us find the books."

"We have a book already. Father will have to do without Mursino or Zennatello. I do not know what Signore Distruttore had in mind, but I'm sure we would have been sorry if we had gone with him. You are too trusting, Francesca. Far too trusting."

Francesca snorted. "After this day, I will not be afraid of anything. We escaped from monsters, Margherita. I would not be afraid of a mere skinny man."

Margherita felt the need to change the subject. "I feel sorry for Signore Malipiero."

Francesca agreed. "And for his daughters," she added. "Especially for the daughters. I wonder if they had names. I wonder what became of them." She shook her head. "Surely, they died. Their world was nothing but a world of death. Their father was trying to rescue them, trying to make an exchange."

"Us for them," Margherita said.

"Yes, us for them. But instead, it was them for us."

They stood for a few moments, crowds of men and women passing them on all sides, busily heading for whatever destination they had chosen for themselves.

On their way back to *Mercato Monumentale*, Margherita and Francesca passed by Guglielmo Pipistrello, still peddling copies of *Il Popolo di Sogno*. He smiled at them this time. They raised their noses in the air and walked past him.

Signore Azzurro was waiting for them in front of the great department store. "You are ready to go home?" They climbed into the *carrozza*. He whipped up his horse and whistled and the carriage creaked and rattled away from the curb, toward the high bridge, toward the River Fiume, toward home.

"I wish I could have found the missing Mursino volume that Father longs for," Margherita said, "or one of Carla Zennatello's riddle books." The present she had found for her father at *Libri e Libretti* lay in her lap, brightly wrapped and tied with a birthday ribbon.

"Now do you think we should have gone with Signore Distruttore?" Francesca asked.

Margherita shook her head. "Absolutely not!"

"You say that now," Francesca said. "You say that now. But we will return to Villaggio Sogno. I would like to see the statue of the great Lucrezia Spina di Rosa. Surely you agree with me."

"Perhaps."

As the *carrozza* left the high bridge over the River Fiume and turned toward home the girls glanced back at Villaggio Sogno. The sun had disappeared behind the walls and spires of the town, the sky had darkened and stars were shining from the heavens. Other lights twinkled in the piazzas and in the buildings of the town, where families were gathered at dinner, players performed comedies and tragedies upon the stage, couples exchanged gifts or courted over meats served with wine, ale, or mead. One of them might even be the lantern in Signore Distruttore's window. Someday, Margherita thought, she would leave her family home and make her own way, perhaps in Villaggio Sogno, perhaps in the great world beyond. She might even see the land of Honshu with its soft-spoken people, its lovely costumes and its strange ways.

Margherita felt herself growing sleepy. She knew that Signore Azzurro would deliver her and Francesca safely to their families, and dropped her head to her best friend's shoulder and dozed.

THE GAME OF MAGICAL DEATH

Doug Hornig

Doug Hornig (b. 1943) is probably better known for his private eye novels than for his fantasy. Most feature Vietnam vet Loren Swift the first of which, Foul Shot *(1984), was nominated for an Edgar Award. But he's written much else besides, including poetry, a book about the 1975 World Series and even a song. None of which will prepare you for the following in which we encounter computer magic.*

"I DON'T WANT TO eat my salad," Billy Sampson said. "I don't like salad. Besides I've got a lot to do. May I be excused, please?"

His parents were so out of it. They didn't know a CPU from a BMW. It was useless talking to them. In the electronic age, they were dinosaurs.

"Billy," his mother said, "we don't care what kind of fancy computer program you have to write tonight. If you don't get enough vitamins, you won't be able to write your own name. Now eat."

He pushed the salad around his plate. A bunch of soggy vegetables. There was no point in attempting to explain that when you were the first kid to get a new game, you had to try it out right away. That there were matters of status involved. Not to mention the excitement of the unknown. The only thing to do was humor them. Somehow he got down most of the salad, nearly gagging in the process.

"Now may I be excused, please?"

"Don't you want any dessert, Billy?"

"Maybe later."

"All right. Try to get to bed at a decent hour, will you?"

Billy went quickly to his room and shut the door. That was one thing his parents were good about. They respected his privacy. If his door was closed, they wouldn't disturb him unless he invited them in.

His IBM Personal Computer sat on the desk, inert, mere potential. It wasn't the best micro on the market; in fact, considering what you got for the money, it was one of the worst. Still, because of the I-B-M on the nameplate, it was clobbering the competition. More new stuff was being written for its operating system than for any other. That's why he'd traded up and gotten one. Some of his friends in the local hacker network had done the same. Others had decided to hold on to their Apples and CP/M machines for a while. That way, the group as a whole covered the field.

Carefully, lovingly, he removed the new disk from its protective sleeve. It had come into his possession by pure chance, so he was sure none of the other guys had it yet. He'd been reading *Computer World*, as he did every week, and had idly glanced at the Employment section, something he rarely did. There he'd found a tiny box ad that someone had presumably placed in that section by mistake. It read: "THE GAME OF MAGICAL DEATH, for IBM PC and compatibles, NEW from Personal Computer Odysseys, Homer, AK 99603, $59.95." Billy Simpson had never heard of Homer, Alaska, much less of Personal Computer Odysseys. That wasn't surprising. The new companies came and went faster than you could keep track of them. Now here was one with a brand-new game. It was a bit pricey, but if he scooped the gang, it'd be worth it. Billy had sent off his check the same afternoon.

The game arrived in five days. Peculiar. How long did it take the mail to get to Alaska and back, anyway? Certainly more than five days. And then there was the three-line printed note that was packed with the disk: "Personal Computer Odysseys, Prompt Personalized Service Our Specialty, Thank You For The Anticipated Order." Whatever that meant.

But Billy didn't like to dwell on things over which he had no control. If it was a strange company, so what? There were

a lot of strange people in the field. The thing that mattered
was the quality of the product. He slotted the disk into one of
the PC's drives and booted up. Then he loaded his new
game.

GOOD DAY. MR. SAMPSON, the screen said. DO YOU WISH TO PLAY
THE GAME OF MAGICAL DEATH? IF SO, HIT "RETURN."

It knows my name, eh? Now *that's* personalized service.

He pressed the "Return" key. The next screen appeared.

SELECT LEVEL OF PLAY.

LEVEL 1: RANDOM DEATH

LEVEL 2: MULTIPLE DEATH

LEVEL 3: INTERPERSONAL DEATH

LEVEL 4: CREATOR DEATH

LEVEL 5: PERSONAL DEATH

ABORT

Great. A decent game had to have levels of play. The working
assumption was that the lower levels would be too easy for him.
Billy excelled at games. He always started at a higher level than
anyone else. He was the best. So he entered a "5." Bypass the kid
stuff.

ACCESS DENIED.

Nervy of it. Oh well. He tried a "4," then a "3" and a "2."
Same result in each case. Finally he settled for a "1."

RANDOM DEATH. YOUR OPPONENT IS:

There was a ten-second pause before the name "JEFFREY HIGH-
PORT" appeared. Then, SELECT THREE WEAPONS, followed by a
menu of about two dozen choices.

Billy was going to like this game. There was no accompanying
instructional booklet. Therefore he had no idea of how the
weapons had to be used or what his opponent was armed with.
That was a neat touch. He'd have to feel his way along, learn by
doing.

He selected "Impenetrable Umbrella," "Evasive Action," and
"Heat-Sensitive Laser." One offensive weapon, one defensive,
one that could go either way. A good mix.

OPPONENT HAS INGESTED A MIND-ALTERING CHEMICAL THAT
GIVES GREAT DETERMINATION BUT DIMINISHED MOTOR ABILITY.
HIS VEHICLE IS PURSUING AT A HIGH RATE OF SPEED AND WILL
IMPACT YOU IN X SECONDS. YOUR RESPONSE:

An elementary trap, unworthy of Billy's abilities. The Umbrella would be something they'd let him use only once, otherwise he could hide behind it indefinitely and the game would stalemate. If he activated it too early, his opponent would likely just go around it and his defenses would be seriously compromised. The trick would be to set the Umbrella at a time when the pursuing vehicle's momentum would carry it to destruction. For now, just slow it up.

He typed: "Heat-Sensitive Laser."

x = 30. VEHICLE PARTIALLY DISABLED, IMPACT IN X SECONDS. SINGLE TRAJECTORY MISSILE LAUNCHED. YOUR RESPONSE:

So far, so good: 30 seconds would have been plenty of time to avoid the Umbrella. He'd scored a hit with the laser, and his opponent's coordination was impaired because of the drug. Assuming they'd started with roughly equal weaponry, it was time to seize the advantage.

"None."

x = 35. MISSILE WIDE OF TARGET. VEHICLE SELF-REPAIRING. IMPACT IN X SECONDS. YOUR RESPONSE:

Billy had him now. The self-repair feature would have been a defensive weapon. The guy would probably have only one more. It was time to suck him in for the kill.

"Evasive Action."

x = 10. VEHICLE IGNITING AFTERBURNER. IMPACT IN X SECONDS. YOUR RESPONSE:

Since there was no way of telling whether they were operating on clock time, Billy punched in his response immediately.

"Impenetrable Umbrella."

x = 3. IMPACT, VEHICLE DESTROYED. OPPONENT NEUTRALIZED. YOU WIN, BILLY SAMPSON.

And then the screen went blank. No return to the original menu, no further instructions, nothing. Billy tried every technique he could think of, but was unable to coax a response from the machine. He even turned the PC off and started from scratch. Still nothing.

What the hell? This wasn't fair. It was an interesting game, sure. But he hadn't paid $59.95 for something that conked out at Level 1. By the time he went to bed. Billy had composed in his mind a very nasty letter to the people at Personal Computer

Odysseys.

The second disk arrived the following day. It was waiting when
he got home from school.

So the game was played on sequential diskettes. Very interesting. Perhaps the last one would reactivate the first, so that
someone else could play. That would be O.K.

He put the game away. He'd play it later. Build up his
anticipation first.

After dinner his father said, "Billy, can I talk to you seriously
for a couple of minutes?"

"Sure, Dad."

Here it came again. How he was wasting his time with that silly
computer, how his schoolwork was suffering etc. He'd learned to
let it in one ear and out the other without really listening.

They settled themselves in the living room.

"Now Son," his father began, "in a couple of months, you'll be
getting your driver's license. I guess you know what a responsibility that's going to be."

"I sure do, Dad." This didn't look so bad after all.

"Billy, I don't know if you drink. Do you drink, Son?"

"I have a beer now and then. You know, with the guys."

"Well, thank you for being honest. I don't condemn it, of
course. I like the occasional cocktail myself, as you will have
observed. But there's one thing I'd like you to promise me."

"What's that, Dad?"

"Your mother and I have talked it over. We'd like you to
promise that, after you get your license, if you've ever had one
beer too many, you'll call us. And we'll come bring you home. It
doesn't matter what time it is. Just call before you drive. We'd
rather you got us out of bed than take the chance of . . . well, of
something like this."

Billy's father handed him the afternoon paper. On the front
page was a three-column photo. The crumpled remains of an
unidentifiable car.

"Such a young fella, too," Billy's father said. "Just a year older
than yourself. Will you promise us, Son?"

"Sure, Dad. No problem." He didn't drink that much, anyway.

"Thank you. We appreciate it."

Billy gave the story accompanying the photo a quick scan: "Jeffrey Highport, 17, of Crozet, was killed yesterday evening when he lost control of his vehicle and struck a concrete bridge abutment on Interstate 64, Police said the youth was returning home from a party in Charlottesville at which there had been some drinking, although it was not immediately . . ."

Then he stopped and looked again at the name. He stared at it. Jeffrey Highport.

Very slowly, he set the newspaper down on the sofa. His mouth was suddenly dry. He ran his tongue over his lips.

"What is it, Son?" his father asked.

"Uh, that's a terrible story, Dad. You won't have to worry about that with me. No, uh, not me."

Billy got up, went to his room, and closed the door.

No.

It was a coincidence. It had to be. There was no way . . .

For an hour he sat on his bed, turning the new floppy disk over and over in his hand, wondering what to do. It was a coincidence. Those kinds of things happened all the time. Guy goes fishing, catches a big bass, opens it up, and there's the wedding ring he dropped in the lake twenty years earlier. It happens.

No, it doesn't. Not like this. There was only one explanation. Billy Sampson had somehow caused the death of a local teenager he'd never even met. It was insane, but there it was. Jeffrey was indisputably dead.

He thought about it some more, slowly realized that he was wrong. There was another possibility. That was that Jeffrey had always been going to die. He had always been going to be drinking, his car had always been going to crash, on that specific day. And what the game had done was to open a window somewhere that gave Billy a fleeting glimpse of the future.

In that case he bore no responsibility. Except to try to use what he had discovered for some positive purpose.

There was only one thing to do, of course, despite all of the agonizing. Not one person in a thousand would have done any differently. He booted up the PC and activated the new diskette.

WELCOME BACK, MR. SAMPSON. DO YOU WISH TO CONTINUE THE GAME OF MAGICAL DEATH?

He hit "Return."

The familiar menu appeared. Billy felt that he now understood the rules, but he tried "1," "3," "4," and "5" anyway. Unsurprisingly, access was denied. The game was consistent. He entered a "2."

MULTIPLE DEATH. YOUR OPPONENTS ARE:

Pause.

ROBERT ARCHER, BELINDA ARCHER, SALLY ARCHER, COOKIE ARCHER. SELECT FOUR WEAPONS.

The menu was entirely different this round. Billy examined it, searching for a pattern. The first time, he'd selected casually and had won with his play. As he moved to higher levels, the game was apt to be less forgiving. He'd need more than proper timing; appropriate firepower would be essential.

He made his choice.

OPPONENTS ARE BARRICADED IN FORTRESS PREPARING POISON GAS. GAS IS IRRESISTIBLE WHEN COMPLETED. YOU HAVE 15 MINUTES. YOUR RESPONSE:

This time he was expected to make the first move. He thought about it. After ten minutes he decided that they'd figure him to be setting up a diversion. So he fired his best shot first.

"Fire Arrow."

OPPONENT FAILED TO RAISE PROTECTIVE SHUTTERS IN TIME. FORTRESS ON FIRE. SPRINKLERS ACTIVATED. YOUR RESPONSE:

"Horse."

OPPONENT ATTACK WITH CROSSBOW INEFFECTIVE. POISON GAS EXPLOSION BEFORE FIRE EXTINGUISHED. FORTRESS DESTROYED. YOUR RESPONSE:

That should have been it. The gas had blown up, he was at a safe distance, it ought to be over. What was wrong?

Of course. He typed quickly.

"Armor."

Assuming the gas itself wasn't counted, the opponents had used three of their four weapons. Leaving them one. That wouldn't matter unless there was someone to use it.

SURVIVING ARCHER'S SPEAR NEUTRALIZED BY ARMOR. YOUR RESPONSE:

"Hand Ax."

ALL OPPONENTS NEUTRALIZED. YOU WIN, BILLY SAMPSON.

The screen went blank. This time, Billy didn't attempt to revive it. He went to bed, where he tossed and turned, succumbing to nightmares whenever he drifted off.

The third diskette showed up on Saturday. Billy had spent the previous two days in bed in his room, dreading its arrival. He'd gone home sick from school the day he heard about the Archer family. They had lived in the Belmont section of town, Robert and Belinda and their two daughters. Robert worked for the phone company. The night Billy was playing Level 2 of the game, the gas main in the Archers's house ruptured. Enough gas eventually accumulated that the stove's pilot light ignited it. Three members of the family burned to death in their home. The fourth, Sally, was the older sister, and her bedroom was farthest from the site of the explosion. She jumped from her second-story window before the flames got to her. When she landed, she pitched forward and hit her head on a stone. The blow split her skull and killed her.

At seven in the evening, Billy's father came into his room.

"Son," he said, "I know how poorly you've been feeling, but do you think you could get along without your mother and me for a couple of hours? There's this durn cocktail party. At David's over on High Street. And, well, it's important to the business that we be there. Think you'll be O.K.?"

"Sure, Dad."

"Thanks. I'll make it up to you."

In truth, Billy wasn't unhappy that his parents were going out. He couldn't tell them what was happening. They'd immediately phone the university clinic and make an appointment with the head of Psychiatry. Despite being sick with fear, Billy knew that he would proceed to Level 3. It was probably best done alone.

WE MEET AGAIN, MR. SAMPSON, the screen said this time. ARE YOU SURE YOU WISH TO CONTINUE WITH THE GAME OF MAGICAL DEATH?

Billy hesitated, but only for a moment, before firmly striking the "Return" key. Then he entered "3." This time there was no pause by the machine.

INTERPERSONAL DEATH. YOU ARE DEFENDING: MR. AND MRS. WILLIAM SAMPSON. SELECT TWO WEAPONS.

Oh God. They'd changed the rules on him. And he could make only two choices out of twenty-four.

The sweat ran off him. Was he in real time and was the clock running? He couldn't guess. He studied the menu, his brain a maze of rapidly shifting deductive-logic circuits.

Then he had it. It was simple. This time he had one big advantage. *He knew where his parents were.* Given that, there weren't so many possibilities. Or were there? Car wreck, poisoned canapes, acts of God? No. He'd stick with his original conclusion. He chose.

DEFENDANTS ARE ACCOSTED BY GANG OF STREET TOUGHS ARMED WITH KNIVES. YOUR RESPONSE:

Piece of cake. The game was forcing him to make the initial response for the second time in a row, but he'd anticipated that as well as the nature of the threat. One weapon was all he really needed. He typed the words without hesitation.

"Black and white."

STREET TOUGHS DISPERSED BY POLICE CRUISER. DEFENDANTS UNHARMED. YOU WIN, BILLY SAMPSON.

Blank screen.

Billy chucked the diskette into the wastebasket. He was finished being sick, too. He was on top of things now. The best.

Half an hour later he had to endure his parents' recounting of their harrowing experience. He feigned wide-eyed interest and profound relief that they'd come through it all unscathed. That night he slept like the dead.

The fourth diskette came with the next mail. Billy was ready for it. The game was a challenge once again. He raced through dinner, even eating his salad, then hurried to his room.

"My son, the computer genius," Billy's father said sarcastically to his mother. "No time for us common folk."

But by then Billy was staring at the latest screen.

DO YOU WISH TO ENGAGE ME IN THE GAME OF MAGICAL DEATH, MR. SAMPSON?

He hit "Return," then spent a long time contemplating the Level menu. Level 4 was "Creator Death." What did that mean? Surely he wasn't gaming with God. The Creator of the game, then? That must be it. The message *had* said: "Do you wish to engage *me* . . ."

And what could the outcome be? His own life wouldn't be on the line; Personal Death was level 5. If it was the Creator's life, what would happen if that were lost? Was it the end of the game?

Billy considered typing in "Abort." But he just wasn't sure what would happen then. It might mean that he'd never be allowed to play again. And in spite of everything, he didn't want the game to end. He punched "4."

CREATOR DEATH. SELECT 6 WEAPONS.

That was it. No indication of who was fighting whom for what. The menu was the usual length, but six selections meant that some very complex action sequences were possible. Billy chose carefully, hoping to mislead the game as to his intentions. When he finished, the machine typed, YOUR RESPONSE:

All right, that was fair. If the Creator was indeed fighting for its life, it deserved to be able to maximize its chances. So it was making the first move, but demanding that Billy respond before he knew what that move was.

Billy reasoned that in his first move at the two previous levels, he'd taken his best shot. The game might thus reason that he'd try to trick it by doing that a third time. But then it would reason that he knew that and would keep his good stuff in reserve. Finally, at this level of complexity, it would have to assume that Billy would double back once more and end up where he'd started, taking the big step after all. Primary defense would thus be activated at once. So Billy used one of his lesser weapons.

"Air Strike."

AIRCRAFT DESTROYED BY HEAT SEEKING MISSILES. YOUR RESPONSE:

He'd been wrong. The game had precisely anticipated his first move, using neither more nor less than it needed to counter. It would now attack, thinking that Billy wouldn't expect so logical a move.

"Land Mines."

ASSAULT TANKS LOST IN MINEFIELD. YOUR RESPONSE:

They were neck and neck. This was the moment, Billy knew. He knew it suddenly and with perfect clarity. He *knew* that the game was going to make a secondary move of some kind. It was time to blast away. He passed up "Indestructible Shield" and typed: "10-Megaton Thermonuclear Device."

ELECTROMAGNETIC SCATTERING INSUFFICIENT DETERRENT TO THERMONUCLEAR BOMB. COMMAND HQ DESTROYED. YOU WIN, BILLY SAMPSON. THANK YOU FOR PLAYING THE GAME. GOOD-BYE AND GOOD LUCK.

Once again the blank screen.

He'd done it.

The story was on the front page of the afternoon paper. An earthquake had rocked Alaska's Kenai Peninsula. A savage one. Homer had been particularly hard hit. Much of it was now rubble. There was no telling how many lives had been lost, or what the true extent of property damage was.

Billy was stunned. He knew without doubt who one of the casualties was. The Creator had been playing for keeps.

Yet, even more surprising was the arrival of the fifth diskette in the afternoon mail. Billy hadn't expected that. He'd thought that if the Creator lost at Level 4, there would never be a Level 5.

Now he was looking at the Level menu. It had come up without an opening message. It was either "5" or "Abort." There were no other choices left.

"Personal Death." What did that mean? His death? Or the death of some unknown number of persons. How would the battle be fought? If he won, was there a reward? There must be. The stakes were too high to think otherwise. What could be worth his life? The permanent gift of future sight? The screen offered no help.

His finger hovered over the key-board. Life or death? Life *and* death? Whose? It dropped onto the "5."

The message came up.

AN INCURABLE PLAGUE THREATENS ALL HUMAN LIFE ON THE PLANET, NO TREATMENT POSSIBLE. The message faded. EITHER "A" OR "B" NEUTRALIZES THE THREAT AND SUCCESSFULLY COMPLETES THE GAME. Fade. ENTER "A" OR "B" TO TERMINATE THE GAME. YOUR RESPONSE:

A fifty-fifty chance. No clues.

Billy Sampson began to scream. He screamed and screamed and could not stop. He stared at the message and screamed.

Billy's father rushed into the room, grabbed Billy around the shoulders, shook him.

"Son," he said, "what is it? What *is* it?"

Billy continued to scream.

Billy's father looked at the computer screen.

"Oh, for God's sake," he said, and punched "A."

Along the Carenage, in the city of St. George's, Grenada, an island nation occupied by foreign powers, the first child, a girl, age seven, went into convulsions.

THE INFESTATION

Tom Holt

I've written so many introductions to new stories by the ever reliable Tom Holt (b. 1961) in my anthologies over the last decade that I can't think of anything new to say. For that matter the author of over thirty books from Lucia in Wartime *(1985) to* In Your Dreams *(2004) hardly needs any introduction.*

I ARRIVE AT THE docks half an hour late. How anyone is supposed to know this escapes me, because there is no clock in the dockyards; in fact, there aren't any clocks in the whole of Ap'Escatoy, apart from the one-handed old wreck in the bell-tower, which stopped twenty-seven years ago and hasn't run since. But the way everyone looks at me tells me, with absolute precision, that I'm late, and that my default has been noticed.

"You're late," the boss says. He's a short, slim, elderly man with hair growing in his ears, and he doesn't like me. He hired me because I was qualified and cheap, and his contract with the herring people stipulates that every consignment he sends must be examined for latent corruption and supernatural infestation by a qualified magician, in accordance with Guild regulation 344/7c.

Heaven bless regulation 344/7c, because without it there'd be a lot of barely competent wizards going hungry in this city. You hear people talking about how regulations and red tape will be the death of our mercantile economy, but as far as I'm concerned, they're the pinnacle of our achievement as a civilisation. Guild regs make work for the otherwise unemployable, of whom I am one.

The boss doesn't like me, and I don't blame him. He's a shrewd, hard-headed businessman; when it comes to paring overheads to the bone, he's an artist. The sight of me, an untrimmable overhead, makes his palms itch. He'd have fired me years ago, only he knows he couldn't find anybody who'd work for the money.

"Sorry," I say, looking at my boots; I've been trained to stare down basilisks and manticores, but I find it hard to maintain eye contact with the boss. "Traffic. Two carts wedged head-on in Tannery Row. Had to go round by the fish market."

Which was actually true. All my excuses are always true, and he knows it. But they're still excuses, a commodity he has no interest in. "Well, you're here now," he says. "Shed fifteen, see the foreman. That lot's got to be on board the Unicorn for the dawn tide, so you'd best get a move on."

I nod, and escape. Shed fifteen is right down the far end of number seven quay. I know it well. It's dark and it smells of fish, and rotten vegetables, and wet jute. This is going to be a long day.

The foreman must be new, because I don't know him. That's no surprise; the boss doesn't keep foremen long for some reason. This specimen is pretty much like the others; big, strong, miserable, with a polished bald head and tufts of sandy hair over his ears. He may last three months, if he's lucky.

"You'll be the wizard," he says. "You're late."

"Sorry," I say. As my eyes adjust to the gloom, I'm looking at row on phalanxed row of five-by-four blackened oak barrels, thousands of the things. They're divided into four blocks, with three narrow aisles running longwise between them. My job is to scry each barrel, one by one, for latent corruption and generic evil. "Which lot's ours?"

He grins at me, a foreman's grin. "All of them."

"What?" I've given the foreman his treat for the day; he has a fine palate for other people's pain. "But there's thousands—"

"Better get started, then," says the foreman, and there's no arguing with that. I sigh, slump and wriggle out of my coat. He's still grinning; but let him. He'll be gone in three months, and I'll still be here, thanks to my guardian angel, 344/7c.

Here's what I have to do. The essence of our craft is the ability to see. Imagine – this isn't me, this is what they told us on our first day at the Seminary – imagine you've been blind all your life, and suddenly you wake up, and you can see. Now imagine that you live in the proverbial country of the blind, where vision is such a remote concept that most people don't really believe it's possible. Imagine, then, that you – and maybe a few dozen others each year, out of a population of two million – have woken up on this fine spring morning, and you find yourself in a world crammed with wonders and horrors you couldn't possibly have understood a few hours ago. That's the gift we few share; lucky us.

And then you go to the Seminary, as I did; and you sit at the feet of beings who look and sound like ordinary men and women, but who have knowledge and power that totally redefines their existence. For the first few terms, you look at them and think, "That'll be me one day"; and you do the work, read the set books, go to the tutorials, and you realise two things. The first is that the only worthwhile occupation, the only existence that makes any sense of the tragic farce of being alive, is magical research. To be a Fellow of the Seminary is to get up off the sea bed and walk up a mountain. These are the men who cut through the fetters of the human race, who prise knowledge out of its shell, who hold the ramparts against the constant furious onslaught of evil. The second thing you realise, at least if you're me, is that you simply don't have what it takes to be one of them. You could study all the rest of your life, know the books by heart, listen to the explanations a thousand times; but this is one anvil you can't lift, one shelf too high for you to reach. You aren't researcher material, and that's all there is to it.

For those of us who graduate but are not chosen to continue our studies, there's always commercial work. Fair enough. It's not alchemy or fighting evil, but it's useful, honest work and someone's got to do it. You can scry for minerals for a mining consortium, or cast integrity spells on bridges and towers to stop them falling down, or tend the salamanders at one of the major foundries; you can heal, always a highly respected vocation, or you can join the Arbitration Corps and read litigants' minds for a living; you can even, heaven help us, teach.

Or you can end up down at the docks, like me, scrying barrels twelve hours a day, in compliance with regulation 344/7c. In order to get into that particular line of work, of course, you have to have failed at absolutely everything else. It's hard, but it can be done. Look at me. I managed it.

Scrying's the first thing they teach you at the Seminary. Basically, all it means is looking at something, very hard. First you see the object itself. In first grade, year one, day one, they give you two eggs. You look at them, and (unless you're so hopeless you shouldn't even be there) eventually you see past the shell into the white and the yolk, and you can tell which is the rotten one and which is the good one. You can do it with eggs, or houses, or mountainsides which may or may not contain rich seams of valuable minerals; you can do it with people. If you're any good, you can see right down through all the layers to the very essence of a thing. And, of course, you can do it with barrels of pickled herrings. It's not difficult, in the sense of being complex or ambiguous, or requiring intelligence to interpret what you see. But it's hard – bloody hard – in the sense that after a bit it makes you feel dizzy and faint and gives you a headache. This may explain why qualified magicians prefer not to do it for a living, if they have the choice.

What qualified magicians prefer to do is the next stage up in the curriculum; having seen the fault or problem, fixing it. This may involve changing one thing into another, or moving things by the power of pure thought, or subtly deflecting the interplay of conflicting forces to achieve the required result. But I was never terribly good at that sort of thing. I could do it, well enough to scrape through my final exams, but pretty well everybody in my year could do it a whole lot better. Hence me being in shed fifteen, with all those barrels.

Some technical terms explained. Latent corruption is just where the stuff in the barrel – herrings, usually – has gone bad. The buyer doesn't want to prise off the lid and get a faceful of foul-smelling gas. You get a lot of latent corruption in the herring business. Supernatural infestation, also known as generic evil, is much, much rarer, I'm delighted to say. Currently, I believe, we're turning up one case every fifteen years, in the whole of the Armat peninsula. But wonderful 344/7c requires exporters to scry for it because one case every fifteen years is still very bad, just as one catastrophic earthquake with accompanying volcanic eruption and triple-strength tsunami every fifteen years would wipe out an entire civilisation. Supernatural infestation is when one of Them hitch-hikes a ride in a harmless-looking container. And They're clever (they have to be, with all those super-intelligent research fellows on their tracks all the time), and They're resourceful, and They're extremely good at what they do.

I'll give you an example. When I was a kid, we went to visit my aunt and uncle on Spatha Island. The ferry goes round the tip of Cape Fortune, and it's a long, dreary ride because there's nothing to see on the cape apart from bare black rock and a few crumbled stubs of walls. But forty years ago, Ap'Ischun on Cape Fortune was twice the size of Ap'Escatoy – until one of Them sneaked in there, hidden inside a cask of nails, and found a sufficient source of nourishment to allow It to pupate and hatch. It was shortly after the destruction of Ap'Ischun that the Guild brought in regulation 344/7c; and not a moment too soon.

So here I am. The foreman's gone off to shout at people. I have a lamp, not that I need it, and all these barrels to peer into. This is my life. I'm thirty-two years old, I live in one room out back of a wheelwright's shop in the grotty quarter, I eat in the drovers' diner under the aqueduct arches and I have just enough left over at the end of the month to pay for not quite enough cheap red wine to bomb myself into oblivion. I studied four years to get here. I'm a wizard.

It's hard to describe the feeling of scrying through the side of an oak barrel. It's a bit like punching your hand through a sheet of ice, a bit like reaching for something inside a clump of brambles; and once you're in, it's a bit like lifting up a heavy sack of grain with one hand and holding it at arm's length for a whole minute. You get used to it. Actually, that's a black lie. You don't get used to it, but after a while you figure out how to take your mind off it. The best way is to think of something nice; food, sex, good music, the greyhound races. Mostly I think about being a proper wizard, transmuting elements and battling evil. I'm a sad bugger.

Today, as I peer my way through a billion herrings, I'm trying to solve Etzel's ninth paradox. Nobody's ever managed to do it, except presumably Etzel himself, and he died before he could publish the proof; either that, or his widow found it in an old trunk and snipped off the end of the parchment, where he'd written "This doesn't bloody work," before handing it in to the Seminary authorities. Etzel's Ninth is a steel rose pushing up through the cracks in a glacier, while the skies rain blood. It's a teaser, no doubt about that; but if you think it's nuts, you should see Etzel's Eighth, and he won an award for that.

I'm thinking hard about the steel rose; because it so happens that I have a friend who's a blacksmith, and one of the trade tests before they let you go off and bash horseshoes on your own is to make a steel rose – thin curled sheets for the petals, hammer-welded onto a bit of bar for the stem, and I can't remember offhand how they do the thorns. My friend showed me the one he made, and it's a delicate thing; hellish hard to make, because when you're welding it all up together, you have to get the heat just right or the whole thing'll melt into a horrible fused blob. Anyway; could this, I ask myself, be the key to Etzel's notorious riddle? If it'd been a steel carrot or a copper delphinium, there could be scope for ambiguity, but a steel rose – hardly a coincidence. If the steel rose is the dividing line between aspiring and mastery, let's call that wisdom for the sake of argument, then where does that leave the glacier, and what price the skies raining blood? But if we let x be the moment of fusion when the petals weld together – I stop. I've seen something. I'm annoyed, because the barrel I've seen it in is three rows up and two rows in. I'm supposed to mark any dicky barrels I come across with a big red chalk cross, and I really don't fancy clambering up into the stack and reaching across to make my chalk-mark.

I go back, and look again. I'm not absolutely sure what it is I've seen. Something; when you've seen the insides of as many herring-barrels as I have, you know when something's wrong long before you've identified the actual problem. But it doesn't look like any of the usual forms of latent corruption. It's not the slimy black rot, or the grey feathery mould, or rancid oil or a dead rat in the pickle or anything I can see. But it's something. So I have to stop, try and clear my head, actually think for the first time in I don't know how long. There's whole lot of things you can find in a herring-barrel that aren't snagged by 344/7c. There's caulking sheen, for instance, which is where the wizard (some poor dropout like me) who applied the sealing spell to keep it fresh was a touch heavy-handed with the influence. It doesn't do any harm, but the top inch of the brine glows a little, and sometimes there are little sparkly bits floating in it. 344/7c has no problem with caulking sheen; but it's not that. There's fellow-travellers; which means small, inoffensive supernatural creatures, like nixies or sand-sprites, stowing away in the barrel. Fellow-travellers are a good thing, usually, because their benign presence has preservative qualities, and some people reckon it gives the herrings a delicate smoky flavour. There's also bulking charms and weight spells, creating a false illusion of full measure; both of them are unethical and somewhat illegal, but 344/7c doesn't refer to them, so they're none of my business.

Well; I've ruled out latent corruption, and supernatural infestation's so incredibly rare that whatever the thing is, it's bound not to be that. A sensible man, who still has several thousand barrels to do, would mouth "sod it" and move on. But a sensible man doesn't daydream about battling evil, and maybe he's never sailed past Cape Fortune. I go back, and look again.

None of the above; no glow, no luminous blue vapour-trails in the brine, no anomalous inconsistencies of weight or volume. If I'm going to do this by ruling out every damn thing it could be, I'll be here all night. Better to try and ascertain whether it's the one thing I'm supposed to be looking for; and if it's not, move on to the next barrel. Trouble is, looking for infestations isn't an exact science. There aren't any characteristic symptoms, tell-tale marks or – it slams into my head like a hammer, something I've never encountered before but recognise immediately; because it wants to be noticed. The quarry and the predator both hide, but the predator calls it an ambush.

It's in there; and for a long moment it holds me, tight as a snare. The one thing all the authorities agree on is how perfectly fascinating They are, when you come across one. It's not horror you feel, they say, or fear, or disgust or anger. The first, over-poweringly strong reaction is amazement; I've never seen anything like that before. The shape of the thing, which isn't like any shape you've ever imagined; the colour, which is so amazingly different; the way it seems to hum and crackle with the most astounding vitality; and the sheer beauty of it, of course, because nothing in the world is as beautiful to look at as They are. You know perfectly well what it is, no doubt about it, but somehow none of what you know about it matters. At times, the books say, They've been worshipped as gods by people who should know better; though not, needless to say, for very long.

That's what they say, and they're right. It's fascinating, and lovely, and so advanced, so perfect, so stunningly complex and yet so simple; all I want to do is stand and marvel at it, that such things should actually exist in this tacky little world. It's so different that once you see it, it's like – here I am again, first day at school – it's like up to that moment you've been blind, and suddenly you can see. Just being in its presence makes me believe I could possibly get to understand all the things that never could be forced to make sense. All the times I asked "Why?"; here's the answer. Right in front of me.

They warn you about this, of course. Don't allow yourself to fall under its spell. Which is a bit like telling a man who's just gone off the edge of a cliff to stop falling, right now, or you'll go to bed with no dinner. Don't allow yourself – and they go on to say how you need to call on your inner reserves of perception and understanding in order to deny its glamour and confront its dark purpose. Fine; except that I have no inner reserves. If I had inner reserves I wouldn't be here, I'd be scrying for gold in the Baec delta, on fifteen thousand a year. I am totally unequipped to deal with this situation – which, perversely, is what gives me the boost I need to tear myself away; because I know I'm not equipped, no, let's be honest about it, not worthy to stand before this Thing in all its manifold splendour. I'm embarrassed to intrude on it. Sure, it's smiling at me, calling to me, but I know who I am, so I know it's only being polite. Really, it wants me to go away and fetch a grown-up.

I back away, one step at a time, until I bump up against the barrels on the other side of the aisle. The touch of that solid oak on my neck and shoulders hooks me out of the circle of its radiance. I drop the lamp (fire risk; what the hell) and run.

Outside the fresh air hits me, and my legs melt. I lean against the doorframe and slide down, like a raindrop on a windowpane. And I think.

There is a procedure. Thank God, there is a procedure. In the event that you identify an infestation, immediately contact the Warden's office. Good, I'll do that. I know how to do that; and then my part in this is over, and I'm free and clear.

Getting in touch with the Warden's office is no big deal. All you need is a properly-attuned seeing-stone; and regulation 344/7c – thrice-blessed and immeasurably wonderful 344/7c – stipulates that any facility used for the storage and transhipment of bulk commodities must have a properly-attuned and regularly inspected stone no further than one hundred yards from the main gate. The boss had to pay for it, out of his own money (no grants, no subsidies; all this red tape is bleeding the economy dry) and once a month I go up to it, rub it diffidently with my rather shabby sleeve, and speak to a nice middle-aged woman who works in a building on the other side of the city, but whose face appears for a minute or so in the cloudy-brown glass of the stone. I ask her if she can hear me and she says yes, she can hear me just fine; I tell her the registration number of the stone, she ticks it off her checking list, and that's my fleeting contact with the ruling elite over for another month. So yes, there is a stone; and yes, I know it works and how to use it; which means, in this context, yes, there will be a sunrise tomorrow and we'll all still be here to see it.

I run. On the way, I nearly run into the boss, who grabs hold of me and snarls, "Where are you going?"

Not now, I mutter to myself, please – "Emergency," I tell him. "Got to use the stone."

"The what?"

God, he probably thinks I'm talking about the toilet. "The seeing-stone," I tell him. "Got to call the Warden's office. Emergency."

A tiny drop of that trickles in through a crack in his wrought iron skull. "Here," he says, tightening his grip, "what the hell's going on? What's the matter with my shipment?"

I could stop and explain; but the regulation uses words like "immediately" and "top priority" and "by any means necessary", and – forgive me – I'm going to enjoy this.

"Please let go," I say. "I'm in a hurry."

"Not till you tell me what—"

I try and keep it gentle, just a light shove with my inner force;

but I was always lousy at force modulation in third grade, always either too little or too much. This time, too much. A lot too much; the boss is lifted off his feet and shot backwards, like a man kicked by a very strong horse, and crashes up against the fence; it splinters all round him (been rotten for years, but he was too tight to have it replaced) and he flumps to the ground in a heap, covered in chunks of smashed paling. My reward, I suppose, for following regulations to the letter.

I run. Here's the stone. It's masked under a grubby old canvas cover, to protect it from fallen leaves and bird-poo. The string the cover's tied on with is mouldy and the knot's gone tight. My fingernails break on it, so I take out my knife and cut it. You can get away with that sort of thing when you're on vital official business.

"Warden's office."

It's not the nice middle-aged woman this time. It's a thin-faced man, early fifties, big grey eyebrows. I pull myself together.

"I need to report an infestation," I say. "I'm at the north dock, and the infestation's in a barrel in shed fifteen, number seven quay. The barrel's sixteen down the second aisle, that's down from the door end, three rows up, two rows in. I can't really describe it for you, because – well, I can't."

There, I've done it; now it's up to them, though really it's me who's just saved the city. They'll come and deal with the Thing in the barrel, but they're the experts, it's what they're paid for. I'm the one who's acted above and beyond the call – "What level would you put it at?"

For a moment, I can't think what he's talking about. Then I remember. They classify the horrible things by levels of destructive potential, level one to level twelve. As I recall, the one that took out Ap'Ischun was a level three.

"No idea," I said. "You'll be able to judge for yourself when you get here."

He looks at me. "There's a problem," he says.

Terror. Actually, it's the first time I've actually felt it myself – read about it, of course, in books, enough to recognise it for what it is. Not just fear, which I know very well. Fear makes you go cold, digs fingers into your inner tubes and twists, loosens your bowels. Terror freezes you, so you don't feel anything at all.

"Problem?" I say.

He looks at me through the cloudy glass. "How far advanced is it? Has it begun to form rudimentary wings?"

"I don't know, I'm not a bloody scholar," I snap. "Sorry," I add, because he's from the Warden's office, and it's entirely possible to be scared of two things at the same time. "I don't know. I didn't notice any wings, but—"

"They don't look like wings to start off with," he interrupts. "More like little purple buds, in between the seventh and eighth dorsal vertebrae."

"Sorry," I say. "Didn't see."

He frowns. His frown tells me it's not my fault, but nevertheless I'm part of the problem. "How about the nasal membranes?" he says. "Have they started scintillating?"

"No idea. Look, what's the problem?"

He closes his eyes, just for a moment. He looks out of his depth. Cue more terror. "This isn't the only report we've received today," he said. "In fact, we've had seven—"

"Seven?"

He nods. "Unprecedented," he says. "Frankly, we haven't got a clue what's going on. The point is, I can't send anybody, because there's nobody to send. They're all out, I'm on my own here."

That's not good at all. "Can you come?"

"Me?" I'm almost expecting him to burst out laughing. "Fat lot of good that'd do. I'm not a qualified man, I'm just a clerk. No, you're a wizard, you're going to have to deal with it," he hesitates. "You are a wizard, aren't you?" he asks. "I mean, you're qualified and everything?"

"Well, yes," I say. "But—"

"That's all right, then. Report in as soon as the situation's stabilised. I'll try and send someone out as soon as anybody's available, but I can't even guess at when that'll be."

"Hang on," I yelp. "Yes I'm qualified, but I was bottom of my year, I can't handle something like this. I do commercial work, I scry cargo for 344/7c infringements."

"But you're qualified."

"Yes, but look—"

"So you passed demonology and pest control?"

"Yes, but I only just scraped through. Forty-seven per cent in demonology, and that's just because I happened to revise apostrophic impulses the night before it came up in the exam." I could hear myself babbling, couldn't stop. I had to make him understand –

"You passed, though. So you're qualified. You know what to do."

"Look, I knew ten years ago. But I haven't even looked at a grimoire since. I'm just not competent to handle something like this, it'd be begging for a disaster – " He shrugs. "It's you or nobody," he says. "And there's no use getting stressed with me, there's absolutely nothing I can do. If there was, I'd do it. You don't think I'm happy, do you, leaving the defence of the city to you? But we haven't got any choice, either of us, so get out there and deal with it, before it's too late. If you leave it till it's shed its secondary wing sheaths, you can kiss goodbye to civilisation as we know it."

That's me told. Accordingly, a few minutes later, I'm back in warehouse fifteen, facing something I was never meant to face, without the faintest idea how to cope, with no support and nothing in reserve. It's still there. I'd been hoping that when I got back there'd be nothing to see, no sign of any infestation, figment of my overheated imagination. As I walked down the quay I'd been writing the dialogue for my next chat with the clerk from the Warden's office; the bit where he calls me a stupid, time-wasting disgrace to the Fellowship, strikes me off the roll and forbids me to practise magic ever again. I wouldn't have minded that one little bit. Instead, here I am, still a wizard, in fact the sole representative of my craft in the battle of the millennium.

Not good.

"Hello," I say.

He's grown while I've been away. I'm not quite sure how I know this, because They don't inhabit perceivable space in the same way we do. It's one aspect of the fact that They don't belong here; They come here precisely because the rules here are so much more flexible, as far as They're concerned. It's like when you were a kid and you played at pirates and marines with your friends. When you found you were losing, you changed the rules. "You can't kill me," you say, when your little chum lands one fair

and square on you with his wooden sword, "I'm wearing in-
vulnerable armour." "Well, I've got an invincible sword," your
friend replies, and so it escalates, until you're a couple of gods
pelting each other with thunderbolts. You make it up as you go
along, being anything you want to be; and that's how They are,
over here. Nice for them; not so good for us, when we've got to
play with them.

"Hello yourself," He says, and yawns; I can hear him inside my
head. "I don't know you. What are you?"

I'm afraid to say; I'm ashamed of how small and fatuous I am.
"I'm – " Too scared to speak, is what I am. There are so many
things I mustn't say. Mustn't tell Him my name, or He can
possess me, move into my body like the bailiff's men. Mustn't lie
to Him, or He'll be able to read my mind. Mustn't tell Him I'm a
wizard, or He'll raise all His shields straight away, and a surprise
attack's my only hope. Pretty well anything I tell Him, He can use
against me; oh yes, and I can't refuse to answer, or He'll be able to
answer for me, and anything He says will become true. Is it
possible that that's why He asked the question in the first place?

"Sorry," He says, "I missed that. What are you?"

"I'm very well, thank you," I say, and the words come out of
their own accord, like the last residual twitch in a dead limb.
"How about you?"

"Very comfortable, thank you," He says. "But you didn't
answer my question. I said what, not how."

Never thought I'd get away with it. "I'm a human mortal," I
say.

"That much I'd already guessed. Are you a wizard?"

Can't lie. But didn't the Senior Tutor himself once tell me I'd
never make a wizard? "What a question to ask," I say. "Do I look
like one?"

He laughs; and in my mind's eye, I see Him in the form of a
huge and mighty dragon. His wings are only partly formed, but
his magnificent coat of scales glitters like fire reflected in the sea,
each scale a perfect mirror. I know this; across ten years of wasted
time, I can hear myself patiently and painfully forcing the facts
into my overflowing memory, like someone packing a very small
suitcase, sitting on the lid to make it shut. I'm revising, the night
before the exam; "The first trial is the ordeal by reflection,"

chants that unsatisfactory young student; "he will try and subdue me by showing me myself at the precise moment when I truly was myself."

Interesting, in a way; so that's who I am, who I've always been: the student, desperately out of my depth in a station I was born to, which I never chose. Remarkably, the realisation brings me comfort rather than distress. I have no illusion about myself for Him to shatter. He can't hurt me here, in the place where I suffered the most.

"I think you're a wizard," He says, "but not a very good one. Do you know who I am?"

I nod to myself. "I think you're an infestation," I say.

"Good heavens," He replies. "What a thing to say. But that's just a word. What does it mean?"

The second trial is the ordeal by definition. "You're a leak," I say. "Like a perforated ulcer, or a breach in the sea wall. You're a spot where the darkness seeps through into the light, and you don't belong here."

He laughs. "Why ever not? Go on, that's just what your schoolbooks say, it's not what you really think. You think I'm beautiful and wonderful and strange. Are you going to let them make up your mind for you, or are you going to decide for yourself?"

I know the answer to that one. "I'm not worthy to decide," I reply, with feeling. "Fortunately, my superiors in the craft know better, and they've taught me the truth."

He's not a dragon any more. In my mind's eye he's a deer, a young fawn with his first soft coat starting to grow through. His deep, dark eyes meet mine and we share the loneliness of the forsaken, the hunted. "I'm all alone here," he says (the ordeal by compassion; I always had trouble remembering that one), "I'm lost and abandoned and a little bit frightened. Do you have to be my enemy? You haven't even asked me what I'm doing here."

Without realising it, I'm reaching out to touch his neck, where the fur is soft and deep. I pull my hand away just in time. "If you're lonely," I say, "why don't you go back to where you came from?"

He acknowledges the right answer with a slight nod, respectful. "We understand each other," He says, "that's good. If we understand each other, we've got a foundation to build on. You see? We're talking to each other like grown-ups now."

I'm lost; I can't remember what comes next, after compassion, and I don't recognise it from what He's trying to do. Think, think; I must have remembered in the exam, or else I'd have failed and I wouldn't be here now. Reflection, definition, compassion –

"Well?" He says. "What about it? Isn't it better, talking to each other instead of fighting?"

Got it. The fourth trial is the ordeal by communication; and there he is, standing in front of me, a tall, slim young man with his right hand extended in a gesture of open friendship; if we can just talk things over, straight from the shoulder, surely we can settle our differences like civilised people. Can't we?

"No," I say.

"Up to you," He replies. "But I think you're making a mistake. Think about it, why don't you? I mean, let's just go back over what we've already established. Here's me, a breach in the sea-wall was the image you used, all that force and power bursting to get through; and here's you, the perpetual student, trapped forever in the night before your finals. Hardly a fair fight, is it?"

There are five trials, and the fifth is the hardest; beware the ordeal by truth. "No," I say, "it's not. I shouldn't even be here. The rules say, all I'm supposed to do is notify the Warden's office and they send along a special task force, with all the gear. All I'm supposed to do is check the barrels for rotten fish."

"Absolutely," He says. "It's not your fault. You can't be expected to stand up to something like me. Wizards ten times your strength just shrivel up and die when I so much as scowl at them; what the hell do they expect you to do, on your own, no backup, nothing? It'd be pointless, you'd be throwing your life away for no reason. What've they ever done for you that makes them deserve such devoted loyalty?"

"Nothing," I say. "They've always treated me like rubbish."

"Exactly," He says. In my mind's eye I see Him as a kind, gentle old man, reaching out an arm to comfort me. Nobody else understands, but He does. That's why they taught me to hate Him; because He's the only one who understands, who knows what I'm really like. "Exactly. They're not on your side, so why on earth should you be on theirs? Isn't it time you realised who your real friends are?"

Beware the ordeal by truth, because there's no defence against it. But (so they taught us in fifth grade; I spent that lecture looking out of the window, because it was mid-winter, and the first snow was just beginning to fall) in the fifth trial, the best defence is no defence at all. It's always the strongest wizards who fail the fifth trial; like knights in a bog, dragged down by the weight of their armour. The ones who survive are the ones with no armour at all.

"That's all right," I say. "I don't deserve their friendship, or their respect. I'm a piss-poor wizard and a disgrace to the profession, and all I'm fit for is scrying herrings under regulation 344/7c. If I die here, it doesn't matter, I'm no great loss. What matters is stopping you."

The next bit I never had any trouble remembering.

He comes at me like the jaws of a vice, crushing me from all sides as the screw tightens. I can feel his unimaginable strength all about me, the strength I'd wantonly chosen to reject, when I could so easily have joined with it. I can feel the strain on my bones; if I'd only paid attention in Physics, I could probably calculate how much time I've got left, before the pressure exceeds the tensile strength of bone and sinew. There's nothing I can do, I can't push back in all directions at once. Goes without saying, He's so much stronger than I am, and I can't deflect Him, or throw Him like a wrestler. In fact, the only thing I've got going for me is a tiny, slender thread of memory that joins me to a cold, hungry, miserable young student huddled over a candle, reading the same words over and over again as the time before the exam starts dwindles away. That thread's my lifeline, but it's painfully brittle; if I tug too hard it'll snap, and then I'm screwed. Instead, I've got to pull gently, reel it in like a giant fish, until –

"Where's the point," He says, in a voice as compassionate as an angel, as contemptuous as my father, as infinite in its wisdom and forgiveness as both together, "where's the point? You've seen me, and you've seen you; you've got to realise it can only end one way. Why get yourself squashed when all you need to do is reach out, and I'll take your hand and pull you through, to my side?" He smiles. "You'd like it here, things are very different. Face it, you're a waste of time and resources on your side, but over here—"

"You almost sound," I say, "like you're sorry for me."

"Oh, I am," He says. "I pity you with a depth of understanding you could never begin to imagine. Like I said, we understand one another, just as we're both misunderstood by all the rest of them. We could be—"

He's squeezing my heart. Imagine you're holding a ripe plum, and you crush it until the stone starts to dig into the web between your fingers. "Friends?" I say.

"Well, maybe not. But we could respect each other. Who is there on your side who's ever respected you?"

"Screw you," I say. "Just kill me and come on over."

He sounds shocked. "But I don't want to," He says. "We're not killers. We come in peace. Far better that you should understand."

It occurs to me that all I've got to do is let go, and the pain will stop. It'd be the sensible thing to do. I've never had much to do with pain, I'm delighted to say, never been seriously ill or anything like that; so handling it isn't one of my few skills. Giving up, though, I've always had a knack for.

"All right," I say, and I gather a loop of the thread round my left hand. "Point taken. I give up."

"You won't regret it." He sounds so kind. "Come through."

"I can't quite –"

"Here," He says, "take my hand."

"Got you!"

I pull; the line holds. I snap the box shut, jump up and sit on the lid. I can feel Him, His furious struggles as He pounds against the sides of the box, but I'm not going to budge; because I know that so long as I keep my bum on this lid He can't get out. So blatant, really, so obvious; but for all Their strength, They're simple creatures, and They fall for it every time. All you've got to do, once you've recognised Their strength and your weakness, and you've acknowledged your common ground, how you're both lonely outcasts in a hostile world – it's so easy, when you've forged that bond of common ground between you, to turn the tables: and next thing you know, He's in the box and you're sitting on the lid, laughing like a drain.

(I was hopeless at all that stuff at the Seminary – went over my head like geese going south for the winter – but I still passed. Borrowed a friend's revision notes. Odd how some things stay with you, years later.)

Eventually, they come and take over; five men from the Warden's office. They don't look so mighty and proud now, not after a very long, hard day at the office. They look drawn and grey and bleached, and when they see me sitting on the lid of the box, grinning, you can see them slumping with relief. "You handled it all right, then?" they say. I nod.

"No bother," I reply.

They come and put their seal on the box, concentrating hard on the job in hand (it'd be a disaster if He got out now, after all my hard work). Then they tie a rope round the box to carry it with, and they stop for a moment. "Thanks," they say.

"You're welcome," I reply.

"It's been a bitch of a day," they tell me. "Nine of the bloody things, all at the same time. It's a record. The most there's ever been in one day was six, and that was 500 years ago."

I shake my head. "Bad business," I say.

"Bad business," they agree. "Still, we coped."

I smile. "That we did."

They leave. I don't. I'm not going anywhere. I still have 3,000 barrels of pickled herrings to peer into before I can go home, because I have work to do, and the boss pays me to keep 433/7c off his back, not save the world.

I get finished just in time; as I'm leaving, the foreman's turning up with the loading crew. I yawn as I wish him good morning.

"You're cutting it fine," he says. "What happened? Fall asleep?"

He wouldn't understand. "Something like that," I say.

He grins. "Almost forgot," he says. "Boss wants to see you. Something about pushing him over in the yard."

"Oh yes," I say. "That."

His grin widens, like a breach in a sea wall. "Don't suppose I'll be seeing you round here again," he says.

"Don't suppose you will," I reply. "Well, it's all yours. Good hunting."

I take my coat and head over to the boss's office, to face a different sort of demon of pure evil, one I'm not going to be able to deal with quite so easily. At least I know my limitations.

(In case you were wondering, the answer to Etzel's Ninth is entropy. Guessing the answer is dead easy. It's proving it that drives wise men crazy.)

THE WITCH'S BICYCLE

Tim Pratt

*Tim Pratt (b. 1976) is a poet, author and reviewer who hails
from Oakland, California. He currently works as an associate
editor at* Locus, *the news magazine of the science-fiction field,
and co-edits the little magazine* Flytrap. *Although still quite
new to the game his work is being noticed. The title story of his
first collection,* Little Gods *(2003), was nominated for the
Nebula Award presented by the Science Fiction & Fantasy
Writers of America, and he's been shortlisted for the Campbell
Award for best new writer.*

The title of the following story, which is also in Little Gods,
*may conjure up an image of the wonderful Margaret Hamilton
as the Wicked Witch of the West at the start of the 1939 film
version of* The Wizard of Oz, *but no matter how nasty you
thought she was, the witch in the following story is a thousand
times more evil.*

E VEN HER BICYCLE WAS evil.
    A heavy black chain wrapped around the frame and front
tire secured the bicycle to an iron lamppost in front of Antiquities
and Tangibles, a cramped and jumbled antique store downtown.
The bicycle seemed to strain against the chain like a half-starved
greyhound, skeletal and ferocious. It was a heavy bike with
wheelguards that had been new in the 1950s. The frame was a
dusky red, the color of rubies from a long-forgotten treasure
trove. The handlebars curled like ram's horns. A headlamp on the
front glittered in the afternoon sunlight, throwing bright flashes.

The seat was pitted black leather, and the spokes were bright, shiny chrome. The pedals were spiked to grip the soles of shoes, and cut anyone foolish enough to try and pedal the bicycle barefooted.

The bicycle's owner emerged from the antique store. Her hair and her dress were the same red as the bike frame, like faded silk roses, her black leather beret matched the seat, and chrome rings flashed on her fingers. Her eyes, before she put on her sunglasses, were as bright and reflective as her bicycle's headlamp. She carried a plastic bag with a real drawstring, and something inside the bag rattled and clattered. Something old and obscure, surely, as it had come from Antiquities and Tangibles, the Sargasso Sea of the antiques trade, the place where only the most marginalized and unappreciated remnants of the past fetched up.

She unlocked the chain and wrapped it around her waist like a belt, then fastened it, spinning the combination lock into nonsense numbers. She dropped her bag in the chrome basket behind the seat and mounted the bicycle. Her boots were leather, with chrome buckles. She cooed to her bicycle, and it seemed almost to steady itself, as if some gyroscopic mechanism kept it upright. As she pedaled away down the sidewalk, she sang, and the hum of the smoothly oiled bicycle chain and the rasp of the fat tires on the pavement seemed to sing with her.

She sang "What Is This Thing Called Love?"

Behind her, in the basket, the bag's contents shifted and clattered, not at all in time with the song.

Cory sat out behind the high school, throwing rocks at a sewer grate, waiting for the bus to come back. Because his school was overcrowded, there were two separate bus schedules. First load left right after school, and went fully-loaded. The second load made it back about forty minutes later, each bus picking up a dozen or so leftover students. For some reason Cory's subdivision had drawn second-load status, and now he had to suffer through this empty after-school time. He *had* to get a car next year, or at least make friends with someone who drove. The other people who rode his bus were out behind the gym smoking pot, probably. Even *they* didn't want to have anything to do with him. At least they weren't violent – just stupid. Unlike some –

"Look who's here," a smooth voice said from his left. Cory hunched his shoulders. School had only been in session for three weeks, and he'd already grown to hate that voice. He didn't even know the kid's name, the leader of the vicious little trio. He didn't have any classes with him, and in a high school of 2,000 students it wasn't surprising that he never saw him during the day. But this kid – Cory thought of him as "Rocko" because he looked like a young and pugnacious version of Edward G. Robinson, though his voice was surprisingly pleasant – this kid rode second load on one of the other buses, and apparently had nothing better to do in these forty dead minutes after school than look for people to torment. His little trio – the other two Cory had dubbed "Angel" and "Curly," after Rocko's hench-man from the movie *Key Largo* – usually hung around by the vending machines, harassing the freshmen who emerged from after-school band practice to get sodas or chips. Cory had run afoul of them once and gotten away with no worse than a shoving, and since then he'd spent his time reading outside or in odd corners of the school, occasionally slipping away when he heard them approaching. It could be worse, he supposed – in lots of schools there were stabbings and shootings, but as his mom reminded him, this was a good school in a good area. Which meant only the risk of being beaten up by three guys – he wasn't likely to die.

Apparently the band kids had grown wary, and the trio had gotten bored and gone searching for new meat, because here they were. Cory had been so engrossed in stone-tossing that he hadn't heard them coming.

Rocko sat down beside him and slung an arm over his shoulder. Cory shrugged him off, and Rocko laughed, that pleasant, easy laugh. "You like throwing rocks, huh? You want to have a little rock-throwing contest?"

Cory started to stand up. Rocko grabbed the arm of his jacket and pulled him back down. Cory tried to jerk his arm away, but Rocko held him tight, not even moving from his place on the curb. "Just a friendly game," he said.

Cory glanced at Rocko's buddies. Angel and Curly lounged against a science classroom, watching him, sneering. Angel was black and Curly was Hispanic. Say what you would about Rocko, he wasn't a racist. As long as you were mean-spirited and servile, there was a place for you in his gang.

"No, thanks," Cory said. "I don't feel like playing a game."

Rocko ignored him. "The way I figure it, there's nothing too hard about throwing rocks into a grate. That's not any kind of a challenge, you know? Now, if you were aiming rocks at a person, and that person was trying to get away – that'd be challenging. Don't you think?"

Cory couldn't believe he was hearing this.

"We'd need bigger rocks, though," Rocko said thoughtfully.

Cory jerked his arm away again, and this time broke free.

"Ready to start running?" Rocko asked.

"What makes you be like this?" Cory asked, frowning at Rocko's froglike, smiling face. "Why do you do this?"

"I look at it like dogshit," Rocko said. "There's dogshit on your shoe, you scrape it off, right? I look at you, and I see dogshit, but I can't get rid of you, you just keep . . . hanging around. If I can't get rid of you, I can at least let you know you're dogshit, right? Make sure you don't forget it."

Cory just stared at him. He'd dealt with bullies in the past, and small-scale violence, but those had always been brutally stupid people, strutting for their friends. Rocko sounded so . . . *reasonable*.

"There's just this look about you," Rocko went on. "The way you walk around, all hunched up, the way you always look like you smell something bad. I see you in the halls and it *disgusts* me." He shrugged. "So I guess that's why I do this. Plus, my psychiatrist says I'm in a really explorative stage, that I'm testing my boundaries and trying to define myself."

Cory took a step backwards. Where could he possibly go? The school wasn't that big, and he had to come back here to catch the bus anyway. He couldn't outrun them if they decided to chase him.

"Anyway," Rocko said. "The place where I used to live, before I moved here, they had security guards everywhere, they had metal detectors, they had to lock down the classrooms a couple of times because of riots in the halls. Then I come to this place and there's no cops or anything. I can't believe it, I mean, I know it's the sticks, but *really*. So yeah, I guess I'm just . . . testing the boundaries." He stood up. Angel and Curly stood a little straighter when Rocko rose, like well-trained dogs. "I'm not going to *kill* you or anything," Rocko said. "But . . . you know . . . it's a long year. No telling what could happen." He glanced at Angel. "How long 'til the bus comes?"

"Fifteen minutes," Angel said. He did not have Rocko's orator's voice. His voice sounded like someone falling down a flight of stairs.

"I gotta get a sodding car," Rocko said, shaking his head. "This is just ridiculous. Another year until I turn sixteen, can you believe that?"

"You could always get a bicycle," Cory said. He wasn't sure why – it just popped out.

"What am I, ten years old?" Rocko said.

"Let's beat his ass," Curly said. "This talking's bullshit."

"Talking's not bullshit," Rocko said. "But there does come a time for talk to end. You've got ten minutes, guys. Have fun."

"We're not like him," Curly said, approaching. "We're not testing boundaries or anything."

"Nah," Angel agreed.

Rocko sat on the curb, seemingly oblivious to the impending violence picking up rocks and examining them.

Cory couldn't do much but run. Probably a couple of teachers were still hanging around the office, and if he got really desperate he could burst into the band classroom and take refuge there until the bus came. Everyone would think he was a pussy, but he'd rather be mocked than beaten. He backed up, trying to gauge the right time to dash. He could head for the dark covered area between the gym and the science buildings, the place everybody called "the Tunnel," and then break across the courtyard and get into the main building. Maybe they wouldn't catch him.

"What's up, guys?" a girl's voice said from the direction of the Tunnel. Angel, Curly, and Cory all looked.

The girl was tall and brunette, her hair pulled back in a messy ponytail. She wore a striped field-hockey uniform, and there were bits of grass stuck to her knees. She held a hockey stick, resting it across her shoulder, and for a moment Cory thought she looked like a particularly athletic incarnation of Death, armed with some kind of wooden practice scythe. "You guys waiting for the bus?" she asked, all innocence.

"We were just waiting for you, baby," Curly said, smiling widely and stepping toward her.

Cory, relieved to no longer be the focus of attention, relaxed, then immediately felt ashamed. Now they were going to give this girl shit, and he couldn't do anything about it – why should he feel better at *her* expense?

"I heard all you field hockey chicks are lesbians," Curly said, still smiling. "Wanna prove me wrong?"

She flipped her ponytail. "Oh," she said, in a bored voice. "I didn't realize you were assholes, or I wouldn't have bothered you."

Angel laughed.

She looked at him. "That was an inclusive comment."

"Bitch," Curly said. "I know—"

"Now, now," Rocko said, rising from his place on the sidewalk. "That's no way to talk to a lady."

"She shouldn't talk to me like she did," Curly said. "Nobody talks to me that way."

"Sticks and stones may break your bones," Rocko said. "And, as you might have noticed, she *does* have a stick, and you *do* have bones."

Curly snorted. "Shit. What's she going to do with that?"

The girl smiled at him. She had braces, but Cory still thought it was a beautiful smile, if a little nasty and malicious. She didn't move the stick, didn't thump it into her palm, nothing – just stood there, smiling.

"Shit," Curly said again. "Ugly bitch ain't worth the trouble." He turned his back and slouched away. Angel glanced at Rocko, then went with Curly, back toward the band practice rooms.

The girl glanced at Cory. "You're not saying much. Are you the ringmaster of this circus?"

"No," Rocko said. "That would be me. But I wish you wouldn't judge me by the company I keep. Good help's hard to find."

"So what are you doing here, then?" she asked Cory, ignoring Rocko.

"Just . . . waiting for the bus," he said.

She nodded. "Me, too. First time I've had to ride it. I used to ride home with a friend, but now practice has started . . ." She shrugged.

Cory was never good at talking to people, especially not to girls, especially not in front of Rocko.

"He's really not worth talking to," Rocko said. "He just asks a lot of stupid—"

"I think your friends are waiting for you," she said, glancing at Rocko. "Maybe you should go check on them, make sure they don't get lost or something."

Rocko frowned, then smoothed back his dark hair. "Which bus do you ride?"

"None of your fucking business," she said.

Rocko narrowed his eyes. "Just wondered if you were on mine."

She simply looked at him.

"Fine," Rocko said. "See you around." He glanced at Cory. "And you – I'll definitely see you around." He sauntered off.

"He's a little shit, isn't he?" the girl said, watching him go. She glanced at Cory. "I'm Heather."

"Cory."

"Those guys bother you a lot?"

He shrugged, uncomfortable. "Not really. Sometimes."

"Girls mostly just talk about each other. And that can get nasty, believe me. But they don't tend to . . . hit each other so much. I feel for you."

"It's no big deal. I can handle it."

"No doubt," she said, and though he was acutely attuned to sounds of sarcasm and contempt, he didn't detect either in her voice. "Which bus do you ride?"

"228."

"Hey, me, too. Where do you live?"

"In a subdivision called Foxglove."

"Cool," she said, nodding. "My family just moved there. We're the last house on the street, down by the circle, right up against the woods. I haven't met anybody else in the neighborhood."

He shrugged, looking off toward the road, unsure whether to be nervous or pleased to hear she was his neighbor. "There isn't really anybody else our age. Some little kids is all."

"Maybe we could play basketball or something. My dad put a hoop up over the garage."

"I'm not very good at basketball."

She shrugged. "So play with me and you'll get better, right?"

"Yeah, I guess so." She was a jock. She'd stomp him at basketball. Wouldn't *that* be fun? She hadn't laughed at him yet, but she would. Everyone did eventually.

The stoners came wandering from behind the gym, and a minute later the bus appeared.

Survived another day, Cory thought. He glanced at Heather. *Got rescued by a girl.*

He got onto the bus and took his usual seat halfway back, on the passenger side. He looked out the window at the parking lot.

Heather plopped down next to him. "This seat taken?"

She wanted to sit next to him? What did that mean? "No."

"You mind if I sit with you? I mean, I know there's lots of room and all, but it gets boring sitting by yourself."

"No, it's fine."

"So what do you do for fun?" She had her hockey stick in her hand, and she thumped it against the back of the seat in front of them while she talked.

He shrugged. "I watch a lot of movies. My dad has a big library of videos."

"Cool!" She said. "I saw *The Burning Witch* last week – have you seen it?"

He shook his head *The Burning Witch* was a horror movie – from the previews it looked to be mostly about a woman who cackled and set things on fire with her mind, and then some teenagers defeated her. It looked pretty dumb. "No, I haven't. I like mostly old movies. Black and white stuff."

She frowned. "Like *It's A Wonderful Life?*"

"No . . . like *The Big Sleep* and *Lady in the Lake* and *The Thin Man* . . ." She was looking at him blankly. "Um . . . *Casablanca? The Maltese Falcon?*"

"Oh, yeah," she said, nodding. "Wow. You like that stuff, huh?"

She didn't seem contemptuous, exactly, just . . . surprised. "Yeah, well, my Dad really likes them, so we watch them together sometimes. He likes Humphrey Bogart and Lauren Bacall a lot. We watched a movie called *Key Largo* a couple of weeks ago. There's a guy in that movie named Rocko who looks a lot like . . ." He trailed off.

"Like who?"

He sighed. "Like that guy back at school."

"So he looks like a smiling frog?"

Cory laughed. "Yeah." He glanced at her. She was nice. Not like most of the other girls, who always found something in him to laugh at – his shoes, his hair, the way he walked, the way he talked. It didn't much matter – they always found something. Even the ones who didn't tease him just ignored him.

"I haven't seen many old movies. Maybe we could watch one sometime?"

His dad would tease him so much if he brought a girl home! He'd mean it in a good-natured way, but Cory was already wincing at the thought. Still . . . if Heather thought the movies were cool, it could be worth a little teasing.

"Sure. I'd like that." He reached out and tapped the handle of her hockey stick. "Don't they usually keep these at school?"

She rolled her eyes. "I'm supposed to practise at home, try to get 'better control' the coach says. I've got a stick of my own, but it hasn't come from California yet. My parents have so much *stuff*, it's two big truckloads. My dad's driving back with the last of it this week."

"You're from California?"

"Monterey," she said. "Lived there my whole life."

Cory grimaced. "From California to North Carolina. Seems like a step in the wrong direction."

She shrugged. "All depends on the people, right? If I can make good friends here, it'll be just as good as home was."

She flashed him that braces-and-all smile, and just then Cory would have done anything for her.

Rocko watched bus 228 pull away, his face expressionless. His two associates had drifted off, probably to smoke in the bathroom. Rocko went back outside and sat on the curb. He picked up a rock and held it up to the light, watching the bright flecks flash. He thought about dissections.

Suddenly a bicycle was before him, its rider a woman with dusky red hair and a black leather beret. She was somewhere past young, but not all the way gone into middle aged. She looked like a hippie in her long dress and tights, but her boots were a biker's, and she wore chrome rings. She looked down at him from the bike's high seat. The bicycle seemed to complement her, and he realized its color matched that of her hair.

"Rocko," she said, her voice somewhere between a purr and a rasp.

He frowned. "That's not my name, lady." He didn't like sitting here, with her peering down at him – he felt vulnerable, like a frog in a dissecting pan. He started to get up.

"Frog in a pan," she said. "Nice image, Rocko. But now you're pithed."

He froze, his ass just inches from the concrete, stopped in the act of rising. His legs began to quiver immediately from the strain of holding him up. He felt his heart beating, but he couldn't blink, couldn't move. Like a live frog pithed for dissection, his spine pierced with a metal rod, everything but the most basic physical functions suspended. His fear even had a detached quality; it was wholly intellectual, with no emotional component. He wondered clinically – and he could be very clinical – whether his glands were working, whether adrenaline was pumping into his veins. He thought not.

"Sit down," she said, and his butt hit the curb. She leaned over, the rose curtain of her hair almost touching his face. "I call you Rocko because that's what the Boy calls you."

Rocko heard the emphasis she put on the word "Boy," knew that she meant it as more than a generic term. "This is about the Boy, and the Girl, so I'll call you what they do."

Rocko was trying to move his arms. He wanted to lash out at her, knock her over in a tangle of legs, skirt, chrome, and chain. He thought about his psychiatrist – "testing boundaries" – he'd never had boundaries as tight as this, trapped in his own body.

"But you can have a place in this, too, Rocko. You can be the Rival. You do like her, don't you? The Girl?"

Rocko growled – or tried to. He didn't make a sound.

She laughed. "She snubbed you, didn't she? And for that dogshit, that Boy you hate without reason."

Without reason? Rocko always had reasons, and that kid, that Cory.

What? Well, he was a piece of shit, always had his nose in a book, he slouched around, stank of cowardice, thought he was better than everyone else . . . There. Lots of reasons. A whole truckload of reasons.

That girl, though . . . she was something else. He had no doubt she'd have used that stick today, if she'd needed to. She was pretty, but not snotty, not afraid to get sweaty and play hard. Not like Cory, who'd probably never sweated in his life.

"Yes," the woman said, nodding. "You can be the Rival. You *are* the Rival." She crooked her finger and he jerked upright. It felt like a rope wrapped around his chest, pulling him to his feet.

She's a witch, he thought, with that same, intellectual fear.

"Would you like to kill the Boy, and win the Girl?" she asked.

Kill? Rocko had a certain interest in the subject, but killing anyone would be so *messy* in the particulars. Just like beating someone up – he didn't much enjoy that, though he often desired the consequences. That was so often a problem; to achieve a certain end, he had to resort to ugly means. If only he could skip those intermediate states, wave his hands and have someone die, or put them on the ground writhing in pain.

He looked at the woman (he had no choice, he couldn't even blink, but now he *looked*). She'd pithed him like a frog without even saying a word, and he suspected that she didn't need to hear him speak, because she could read his mind. Maybe he could learn power like that from her. The power of ends, and the circumvention of clumsy, inelegant means.

"Kill?" he said, and now his voice worked. The idea of killing lacked emotional color, too. He could kill someone easily, if he felt like this while doing it. "Sure. I could do that."

She grinned. "A will to kill is a wonderful thing. It means you always have a last resort. But you really just want the Girl, yes?"

Rocko grunted. He didn't want the girl to think he was nothing, that was for sure, and he couldn't stand to see her with a dogshit like Cory.

"So the best thing to do would be to humiliate the Boy, somehow, and let her find out about it, maybe even witness it.

Then she'd know he's nothing, and that you're clever, and brave, and much more worth her attention. Yes?"

Rocko could feel her eyes boring into him from behind her black glasses. "Yeah. Yeah, that would do it."

"You and your little friends can come up with something, can't you? Something suitable?"

"Something suitable for a shit like him," Rocko said, getting an idea. Of course. Everyone had to use the bathroom sometime, didn't they? "I think so."

"Good," she said. "It's better than murder, at least for now. If you've never buried a body, you don't know how much trouble it can be."

"Cory!" his mom called. "You have a visitor!"

Cory looked up from his homework – just a worksheet on ecology, boring as mud – and frowned. Who could—

Oh. His throat tightened a little. Could it be Heather? Already? "Coming, mom!" He stopped in front of the mirror, raking his fingers through his shaggy brown hair, then gave it up as a bad job. Heather'd seen him at very nearly his worst this afternoon, and she'd seemed to like him fine then.

He hurried downstairs, into the living room.

He hardly recognized the girl he found there. Heather had been sweaty, grass-stained, red-cheeked and mussed before. But this girl – she could be one of the prettiest girls in school. She had blue ribbons braided into her hair, and wore a plain white t-shirt tucked into khaki shorts. Her sneakers were clean, too, not the scuffed ones she'd been wearing before. He could faintly see the lace of her bra under the shirt, and he looked away, blushing.

"Heather tells me you met at school today," his mom said.

"Yeah," Cory said. "She just moved to the neighborhood."

"Welcome to town, Heather," Cory's mom said. "I'll have to go meet your parents sometime."

"Sure," Heather said. "My dad's not here yet, he's driving in another truck full of stuff. He'll be around next week, though."

"I'll make a point of introducing myself," she said. "There's brownies in the kitchen, if you guys want a snack. Would you like to stay for dinner, Heather?"

She glanced at Cory. He shrugged. Heather rolled her eyes at him. "Sure. That'd be great!"

"I'll leave you two alone," Cory's mom said, glancing at Cory with a small, secret smile – a smile that meant she'd be asking him about this nice new girl later on. She went into the kitchen.

"She bakes brownies and she makes dinner?" Heather said. "What, did you win the mom lottery? We eat Chinese and pizza most of the time at my house."

"Chinese and pizza sounds pretty good to me. Mom's a research assistant for a lawyer, and she works from home about half the time. She usually makes something for dinner on the days she's home."

"How come she doesn't pick you up from school?"

He shrugged. "She says just because she's home doesn't mean she's not working."

"Well, that's too bad. It means you get to keep me company on the bus, though." She twirled around, an impromptu ballerina. "How do I look?"

Cory had never dealt with a girl his own age in such proximity before. How did you answer that? What would she think if he said she looked pretty? Would she think he liked her? Did he like her? "You look fine," he said cautiously.

"Aren't you a charmer?" she said, but it was good-natured. "I was just going to come right over, but my mom's big on making good first impressions, she said I shouldn't meet the neighbors for the first time looking all grubby. She braided my hair and made me change – she wanted me to wear a *dress!* I don't even like wearing dresses to church."

Cory wouldn't have known what to think if Heather had shown up here in a dress – he certainly would have felt uncomfortable in his own jeans and t-shirt, even if this *was* his house.

"Want to see my room?" Cory asked.

"Sure." She followed him up the stairs. "You'll have to come to my house sometime, and check out the woods out back. They're really cool."

"I go back there a lot, actually. There's some really nice, quiet places. The woods are pretty big, too, bigger than you think at first."

"Ever get lost?"

He hesitated, always unwilling to make himself sound foolish. "Yeah, once. I finally came out of the woods about a mile away on the highway, and walked back from there."

"I haven't gone far enough to get lost yet, but I'm sure I will." It sounded like she relished the idea – like it would be more of an adventure than an embarrassment. Maybe, for her, it would be. And maybe if he went exploring with her, he could learn to look at getting lost in the same way.

He showed her his new computer, and the Bogart poster he'd gotten for Christmas. She really liked his microscope, sitting dusty on a shelf – seemed a lot more interested in it than he'd ever been, truthfully. "Oh, good books!" she said, looking over his row of Charles de Lint and Orson Scott Card. She tapped a copy of *Ender's Game* with her forefinger. "I read this in school last year." She pulled down one of his *Sandman* trade paperbacks. "I've never read these. Are they any good?"

"They're awesome."

"Let me borrow them sometime? You can raid my shelves, too, if you want."

"Sounds good." So what if she liked bad movies? She had good taste in books, at least.

They talked about books for a while, then played video games. She was better than him at killing zombies, but he excelled at racing futuristic cars through decaying cityscapes

Cory's dad got home right before dinner. He was nice to Heather – he was always nice to everyone. His parents mostly talked to Heather during dinner, asking about her old hometown, what her parents did, and so on. Cory learned a lot about her that way, and Heather seemed perfectly at ease around his parents. Dinner was chicken parmesan with salad and some kind of sun-dried tomato bread – a nicer meal than they would've had if they didn't have company over, Cory suspected.

After dinner, Cory walked with Heather out in the yard. "Sorry about that," he said. "My parents playing twenty questions with you that way."

"It's okay. They're parents, they do stuff like that. I didn't mind. As long as you can play the same game when you come to have dinner at my house."

Cory felt warm. For the first time since school had started, he began to think that this year wouldn't be horrible. It was possible Heather would meet other people, find out Cory wasn't exactly at the top of the social ladder, and drift away from him . . . but maybe she'd stick around and be his friend. That would make this year a lot better, even if they didn't have any classes together.

"Want to go down to the woods before it gets totally dark?" she asked. "There's this really cool spot by a stream, it only takes about five minutes to get there from my house . . ." Unselfconsciously, she reached out and took his hand, pulling him along. Her hand was warm, and Cory wanted to hold it forever.

Heather lived at the end of the street, and as they walked along, Cory noticed a woman riding toward them on a bicycle, moving in slow arcs, drifting from one side of the street to the other and back again, only incidentally making forward progress. She had long reddish hair, and dark glasses. She wore a long skirt, too, and Cory didn't see how she could pedal the bicycle without getting the fabric caught in the chain and the gears. The woman stared at them as she approached, slowing down. She rolled past them so slowly that it seemed like her bicycle should fall over from a lack of forward momentum. Her skirt matched the bike frame, and her boots seemed almost a part of the pedals – looking at her made Cory's eyes get blurry. The impression was hard for him to define, even to himself, but he had trouble telling where the woman left off and the bicycle began, like they were a single creature made of chrome and flesh, hair and leather.

Heather's hand tightened in his, and they stood still as she rolled past them, mere feet away. She grinned, and for an instant her teeth seemed to flash like chrome. Then she pedaled on, something in a bag clattering in the basket behind the bicycle seat, like pieces of metal clanging together.

Cory and Heather stood for a moment, watching her go. "Does she live around here?" Heather asked.

"Never seen her before in my life."

"Weird," Heather said decisively, and then squeezed his hand and started walking again.

That night, Cory woke in darkness. He sat up, disoriented. Something had awakened him, but he wasn't sure what. Some noise outside, maybe? He went to the window and looked down into the backyard.

Someone was pedaling a bicycle around a circle in the grass, a girl in a nightgown. Was that . . . Heather? It looked like her, still with the blue ribbon in her braid. He frowned, wondering what she was doing down there, wondering if he should go down himself. She just kept pedaling that big old-fashioned bike, going counter clockwise around the dogwood tree in the middle of the yard.

Cory pulled on his shoes, grabbed his jacket, and slipped quietly down the stairs, frowning. Was Heather okay? Just out for a middle-of-the-night adventure?

He went out the back door, closing it quietly, then down the steps across the grass toward Heather. "Hey!" he called softly, not wanting to wake his parents.

When he got within a few feet of the perimeter of her circle, he realized the rider wasn't Heather at all. He couldn't understand how he'd thought it was – she wasn't even wearing a nightgown, and she was an adult. That's when he began to think it might be a dream.

The bicyclist skidded to a stop in front of him. He stepped away, afraid, because this was the woman he and Heather had seen earlier, the one who seemed somehow *blended in* with her bicycle.

"Hello, my darling boy," she said, putting a funny emphasis on the last word.

"You shouldn't be here," he said. "This is private property."

"I'm here to help you. But if you want me to go . . ." She shrugged, and put her foot on the pedal.

"What do you mean?" He was cold despite his jacket, the night wind blowing straight through him. Would he be cold, if this was a dream?

"There's a boy at your school," she said. She didn't put any particular emphasis on the word "boy" that time. "You call him Rocko, yes?"

Cory nodded. It had to be a dream, but that didn't make it any more disturbing.

"He's going to do something nasty to you tomorrow afternoon, my Boy. He hates you, but that's not such a large thing – his kind is always full of hate, though he is rather more a monster than most bullies, I think. Today, though, he became *jealous* of you, too – he likes the Girl, the Girl who likes you. His jealousy is much more dangerous to you than his hatred. He'll want to do something about his jealousy, something to humiliate you."

"How do you know that? How do you know I call him Rocko?"

"Because I'm the good witch, my Boy, and I want you to defeat your Rival." She smiled, and the bag in the basket behind her shifted with a clatter.

"What's in that bag?" Cory asked.

She looked behind her, then back at him. "You'll find out soon enough. Have patience. I do. You won't need anything from that bag tomorrow. You'll just need a little bit of magic, a tiny spell . . . a *turnaround*. I'll teach you how to do it. It takes a little blood to start with, but that shouldn't be hard – I bet there will be blood tomorrow afternoon, your own blood, if you're not quick. After the blood is spilled, it's just the matter of a gesture, and a word, and certain . . . *patterns* . . . of thought. I'll show you how." She reached out toward his face, and he flinched away. "Shh, be a good Boy."

He wanted to turn and run, despite her claim to be a "good witch" – nothing about her reassured him, nothing made her seem good. He couldn't believe she had any human feeling, any more than . . . than a bicycle would.

He couldn't move, not a muscle, though, and oddly, he didn't feel afraid. He *thought* frightened thoughts, but panic didn't sing in his veins. The witch touched his face with her fingers, and with her chrome rings.

"You won't remember any of this, my Boy. Not until tomorrow, when you need to."

School the next day was the usual, everything pretty easy except for biology, where Cory struggled to understand what mitochondria did, and why on earth he should care. He'd agreed to meet Heather down by the office when she got done with classes. Earth Science was his last class, and thinking about seeing Heather again soon made it hard for him to think about "the ecology of the microcosm" that his earth science teacher kept talking about.

He didn't think about Rocko all day, until he started reading after school. He sat on a bench near the office and read *Good*

Omens, thinking it'd be pretty cool if he had the kind of powers the kid, Adam, had in that book. There were bullies in that story, but they were pretty harmless – you never got the sense the kids really worried about being beat within an inch of their lives by Greasy Johnson, like Cory feared Rocko and Curly and Angel. Maybe that was because *Good Omens* took place in England – maybe people just weren't as violent on the other side of the sea.

Cory stuck the book in his bag and wandered down the hall toward the bathroom so he could pee before meeting Heather.

He stepped into the bathroom, and rough hands grabbed him, slamming him against the wall. Angel and Curly had him by the arms, and before he could even think of pulling away they stepped on his insteps, crushing his toes, pinning his feet so he couldn't kick or thrash. "Hiya," Curly said. "No girls with sticks here to save you today, huh?"

"We're still not testing boundaries," Angel said. "So don't worry about that."

Rocko sauntered out of a toilet stall. "I didn't think you'd ever come to take a piss, kid," Rocko said, zipping up his pants. "I figured the place to find a shit like you would be right here, in the toilet, but then you made me wait. I'm a busy guy. It's not right, me having to wait for you."

Cory thought about the old movies he'd seen, about Bogart's effortless aplomb, the way he'd casually disarmed the gunsel from *The Maltese Falcon*. But even Bogart got beaten up sometimes, especially when two or three guys came for him at once. And Cory was no Bogart. He wanted to spit in Rocko's face . . . but what if they just planned to scare him? Wouldn't spitting make them do something much more nasty?

Curly ground his foot into Cory's instep, and Cory bit back a shout of pain. He could try to keep from blubbering like a baby, at least.

Rocko looked at his watch. "Are you meeting your girlfriend this afternoon. dogshit?"

"Leave her alone," Cory said, without thinking.

Curly and Angel laughed, one right into each of Cory's ears.

"I think he's in love," Angel said.

"I think he just wants to screw her," Curly said sagely.

"I thought that's what *you* wanted to do," Angel said.

"True," Curly agreed.

"Does this make you feel tough, three against one?" Cory said.

"No," Angel said. "But it's more fun this way, and I usually feel pretty tough anyway. Do you think I *couldn't* kick your ass on my own?" He ground down with his foot, and Cory couldn't stop himself from yelping.

"Well, we don't want you to keep you from meeting Miss hockey-sticks-and-sunshine," Rocko said. "So we'll get this over with and then let you go." He paused. "Punch him in the bladder a couple of times, first, let's see if we can make him wet himself."

Cory clenched his teeth. Curly hit him just above the pelvic bone, and it made a sharp bolt of pain jolt through him, but he kept control of his bladder.

"That's a little too close to his dick for me, man," Angel said. Curly scowled.

"Fair enough," Rocko said. "I guess it doesn't much matter, anyway. Bring him over." Rocko walked to the far stall, the one that was always out of order, that didn't flush properly. He pushed open the door, and a horrible stink wafted out. "We all took turns filling the pot," Rocko said. "There's some shit, and some piss, and some more shit."

Cory started to struggle then, wrenching his arms as hard as he could. Curly and Angel grunted and held on tight, dragging Cory across the floor toward the stall. Knowing he couldn't break free, Cory opened his mouth to scream –

—and Rocko shoved a wad of balled-up toilet paper in his mouth, making him gag. "Shut up," Rocko said quietly. "I can keep you from screaming – you see that, right? So no one's going to come help you. I'm going to take that toilet paper out of your mouth, and if you try to bite me, I'm going to do something a lot worse to you than I already have planned." He grinned. "I want your mouth cleared out, so you can taste my shit and piss in there, but if I have to, I'll keep you gagged. I'll just swish the next wad of paper around in the toilet bowl first. Can you be quiet?"

Terrified, helpless, Cory nodded. Rocko reached to pull out the paper.

Blood, Cory thought. The thought came with nothing else, no context, no mental referents, but he acted on it all the same, biting Rocko's finger.

Rocko jerked his hand back with a hiss, and Cory saw the flecks of bright blood on his forefinger. "You shit!" he cried. "God damn you, I'm going to *get* you for that!"

Something welled up in Cory when he saw the blood – words to be said, certain movements to be made with his fingers, and a strange twisting in his mind. He didn't know where the impulses came from, but he followed them, because he somehow knew his salvation lay that way.

Everything blurred. His vision dimmed, and he felt as if he'd been dropped down an elevator shaft, a sensation of things whipping past at high speed. *Turnaround*, he thought. An interval of time went by – he couldn't be sure how long – but when he came back to his normal awareness, things had changed.

Rocko was kneeling before the filthy toilet, his head inside the bowl, and Cory had his foot pressed down on the back of Rocko's neck. He stumbled back, horrified – what had he done? He'd only wanted to get *away*!

Curly and Angel were leaning against the wall, bleeding from split lips, looking groggy. "Fuck," Angel said, his voice slurred. "That's some kind of kung-fu shit."

Rocko lifted his head, and turned to look at Cory. The things smeared on his face made Cory gag, and it didn't help that they'd planned to shove *his* face into the toilet bowl; that didn't make it any less horrible.

"Get him!" Rocko snarled. "Get him and kill him!"

"To hell with you!" Angel said. "Did you see what that motherfucker *did*? I'm not messing with him!"

Curly nodded his assent, and the two of them went stumbling out of the bathroom.

"How did you do that?" Rocko said softly, still kneeling on the floor. "You little bastard, that wasn't kung-fu, that was fucking impossible."

"Just leave me alone," Cory said, his voice hoarse. He felt horribly on edge, and he wasn't sure he'd be able to keep from crying. He backed away. "Just stay away from me, I don't want anything to do with you, leave me alone!"

He ran from the bathroom, stumbling toward the office. He slowed down and took deep breaths. Rocko wouldn't be coming after him, not right away – he had to clean his face off first. What had *happened* back there? How had he done . . . whatever he'd done?

Turnaround, he thought. The thought came in a woman's husky voice, but that didn't make any sense, either.

"Cory?" Heather said. "Are you okay?"

She came hurrying down the hallway, hockey stick in hand.

Cory shook his head. "I . . . Rocko and his friends tried to mess with me again, in the bathroom."

She scowled. "Are you okay?"

"Yeah. I got away." He didn't want to go into details, not least of all because he couldn't *remember* the details. "I'm okay."

She put her hand on his shoulder, and Cory realized he was shaking. "Take it easy. It'll be okay. Let's catch the bus."

"Yeah. Okay. It just . . ."

"It's adrenaline," she said. "You're still all jazzed-up from it. You'll feel better soon. Come on."

"You sure buggered that up, didn't you?"

Rocko jerked his head up from the sink, where he'd been washing his face for the tenth time. He looked in the mirror, but didn't see anyone behind him. He turned around, and there was the woman, the witch from yesterday. Standing – with her *bicycle* – by one of the toilet stalls.

Rocko wondered for a moment if he was going insane. Witches and their malevolent bicycles didn't usually hang out in high school bathrooms. What would his psychiatrist say if Rocko told him about *this*?

"That piece of shit had some kind of trick." Rocko said through clenched teeth.

"Looks like you're the piece of shit, now."

He took a step toward her threateningly, then stopped, remembering the pithed feeling from yesterday.

"It's not too late, though," she said. "You tried humiliation, and if failed . . . turned around on you, in fact – *you* were humiliated instead."

"So what do you suggest?" he asked, trying to stay cool. "Your last advice didn't help me much."

"As I said, the will to kill is a wonderful thing. You shouldn't do it here at school, though . . . we wouldn't want you to get expelled."

"So where?"

She shrugged. "An opportunity will present itself, Rocko. Opportunities always do."

"And what should I kill him *with*?"

"This," she said, and took the bag from the basket on her bike. She opened it so he could look inside.

"That's a pretty weird suggestion," he said after a moment.

"Not the sort of weapon a ninth grader would be expected to use, though, my little Rival. And you don't own one, and it's not something you can pick up in the hardware store, so it's unlikely to be traced back to you. As long as you keep it clean of fingerprints and ditch it after you're done."

"What do you care? What's in this for you?"

"I'm the good witch, and I'm a big believer in the power of true love. I think you and that Girl could be beautiful together, if we get the Boy out of the way."

Rocko didn't believe her for a moment, but it didn't matter. He hadn't wanted to kill Cory before, not really, but now, after what he'd done to him in the bathroom today . . . "Can you make me like I was yesterday? So that when I . . . when I do it . . . I don't feel anything?"

"Oh, my little Rival," she said. "I think that's something you can learn to do on your own. Maybe you can even learn to *enjoy* the killing."

He thought that over. She was right. And whether he enjoyed it, or felt nothing, or whatever, he could still *do* it. "I can't carry that out of here," he said, nodding toward the bag. "It's not exactly inconspicuous."

"Would you believe me if I told you it will be near to hand when you need it?"

He looked at her for a moment, then nodded. "Yeah. From you, I believe it."

Cory and Heather sat together again on the way home. "Do you have Mr. Troublestone?" she asked.

"Yeah, seventh period, for Earth Science."

"Me too, but I've got him fifth. Do you have to do that micro-ecology thing?"

"Yeah. Seems like a pretty simple report."

"Simple, but *boring*. I was thinking it would be fun to write the report about something in the real world."

"Like what?"

"Like that stream in the woods behind my house. There's flies and frogs and reeds and even little fish . . ." She shrugged. "I thought we could study that. You know how Mr. Troublestone's always talking about old-time naturalists, drawing pictures of animals and flowers and stuff. I bet if we did something like that for the stream, learned about its ecology, we'd get a good grade. And it's more fun than just reading about the stuff."

"That sounds good. You should do that."

"*We* should do it. I bet he'd let us work together, since we'd be doing more than just a report – we'd have drawings and an observation journal and stuff." She shrugged, and didn't look at him. "You know, if you want to." She kept her voice neutral.

She's afraid I'll laugh! Cory realized. *Afraid I'll make fun of her, or think she's a geek!* It was a revelation, to realize that she could fear something like that from him, and it made him like her even more. "It sounds great," he said. "I'd love to do that with you."

She grinned. "Hope you don't mind getting a little mud on your face."

"I can think of worse things."

They went down to the stream that afternoon and sat looking into the water. It would have been easier to do this project in the spring, when there'd be tadpoles and things, but they could still find interesting stuff to write about. After a while they just sat, tossing stones into the water, already easy and peaceful together.

"I had a weird dream last night," Heather said, leaning back on her elbows, looking at the leaves overhead. "About that woman we saw ride by on the bicycle yesterday. She had a measuring tape, and she kept walking around me, asking me to hold out my arms and stuff, and she took my measurements. She said she thought I'd be a good fit, and when I asked her if she was going to make a dress for me, she just laughed. She said I'd make one for her." She frowned. "No . . . she said 'You'll make a good dress for me. You'll fit like a glove.'" She shook her head. "Weird. It freaked me out a little, I don't know why. Scared me bad enough to wake me up."

Cory didn't say anything, because now he began to remember his own dream – or had it been a dream at all? "I dreamed about her, too."

Heather looked at him. "No. Really?"

"I think so," he said, nodding. "I dreamed she was riding her bicycle around and around the tree in my backyard. Only it wasn't her at first, the – the woman." He'd almost said "the witch." Had she called herself a witch, a good witch? He couldn't quite recall.

"It wasn't her? Who was it?"

"It . . . I thought it was *you*, first, and then it turned into her." Saying those words chilled him, as if he'd dropped his heart into the autumn stream running at their feet. To begin as Heather, and *turn into* that witch, what a horrible idea!

But Heather was grinning at him. "You're having dreams about me, huh?"

He blushed, then laughed, forgetting his fear. "Yeah, well, it was a *bad* dream, so don't be too flattered."

"I knew you were a charmer from the first moment I met you," she said. "I should get going – it's almost dinnertime. Want to come back here tomorrow, and start on this project for real?"

The next day was Saturday. "Sure. What time should I come over?"

"Oh, whenever. My parents usually make a big breakfast on Saturdays, but I don't know if mom will, since dad's still out of town. Come over around ten, I guess, just to be safe."

They made their brief farewells, and Cory walked farther into the woods, taking the scenic route in the general direction of his house.

Something moved in the bushes. He paused, listening. Probably it was just somebody's dog, but there were deer, sometimes, and he always enjoyed getting a glimpse of those. He looked toward the source of the sound, in a thick tangle of underbrush.

Something pushed out of the tangled vines and branches – something red, and black, and chrome.

It was the bicycle, the witch's bicycle, pushing its way through the woods. Its headlamp seemed to consider him, multi-faceted as a fly's eye.

The witch was nowhere to be seen.

Cory, frightened beyond all reason, turned and fled the woods, racing for home.

That night, as the Boy and the Girl and the Rival all slept unquietly, the witch rode her bicycle through their neighborhood. Bad dreams drifted from her like vapors, and she sang "Love is a Many Splendoured Thing," her bicycle tires humming along. The day before the transference always woke romantic thoughts in her – for without love, without the ancient dance of Boy Meets Girl, how would she keep her youth forever?

She rode her bike through the Girl's yard, her bicycle not bumping at all as it went over the grass, not slowing as it went into the trees, its headlamp dark. She had no need of the light – both she and the bicycle could see perfectly well in the dark.

She'd left off her black beret tonight, and had instead braided her hair with a bit of blue ribbon. Otherwise she looked the same as always, not yet ready to completely give up her resemblance to the bicycle in order to fully assume her resemblance to the girl. That could wait until tomorrow, when her mind would be fully loosened.

She looked around the stream for a likely spot. The location was a good one, really – in her girlhood, when this little play had been acted out the *first* time, it had taken place in a dark wood, by a little stream not unlike this one. Her young lover (whose name she'd forgotten long ago – she just thought of him as the First Boy) had faced off against his Rival for her affection while she stood by, watching, horrified . . . and fascinated. They had both stolen their father's dueling swords, planning to fight for her like grown men. The Rival's blade had snapped against the Boy's, breaking in half. The Boy had stabbed the suddenly disarmed Rival in the heart . . . and when she saw the blood, the Girl who would become the witch understood. This murder over a Girl was not an isolated event, it was an ancient thing, enacted time and again in various guises throughout the ages. There had to be power in that, she knew, in that timeless repetition, a power that could be awakened and directed and sealed by the spilling of blood.

She took the bag from the basket and opened it. She drew out the Boy's sword and jammed it point-first into the dirt by a tree. It was a dueling épée, old but newly sharpened. It had taken her ages to find a set that looked even *close* to being right. Then she removed the Rival's sword, identical to the Boy's. She took a rasp file from her bag and sat in the dirt with the Rival's sword across her knees. She filed away at the blade halfway down its length, humming as she did so. Her bike stood nearby, seeming almost wary, standing upright even though the kickstand hadn't been put down.

She'd discovered the secret of eternal youth – one of the secrets, anyway; she supposed there must be many ways, for those willing to walk beyond the lighted paths. She survived so long, rejuvenating herself, by staging reenactments of that first fight, when she'd been a young thing in the first bloom of womanhood. She never let her hair turn gray, and in recent decades she rode her bicycle, to make herself seem young. She'd worked with this bicycle for so long that blood and magic had washed over it, making it into something more than a disguise and a conveyance – making it into something alive, something almost like a familiar. She resembled the bicycle, too, dressing to match it, and that further confused the question of her identity. To-morrow she would drink a potion to loosen her mind, to loosen the threads mooring her spirit to this body. She would put a blue ribbon in her hair, and dress herself to match the new Girl.

But that was only preliminary business, nothing more than clearing the way. The meat of her magic required other people, young people – and blood. Every few decades she found a new Boy and Girl and Rival, and put this little passion-play into motion. Making sure the Boy and Girl got together, seeing the Rival humiliated, driving him to murder. The Boy would face the Rival, and kill him, while the Girl looked on. When the blood spilled, a sacrifice to ignite the spell, the witch would *become* the new Girl, sliding easily into the young body, crowding out the resident mind – taking her place in this new variation on the old drama of love and murder. That was the power of imperative resemblance, the magic of recurring situations – she would become young, as she'd been at that first duel. Her old body would be left behind in the woods, and would cause a stir when discovered, but nothing would come of it.

The witch turned the sword over and rasped at the other side of the blade. She'd have to smear it with dirt so the marks wouldn't be noticeable. She would have a little trouble in the Girl's body, of course. She wouldn't have the girl's memories, or access to her mind – her mind would go wherever such things went when they were crowded-out, probably nowhere, into oblivion. The witch would have trouble dealing with the Girl's parents. In the past, she'd had to kill parents, but things were easier in this day and age. Now, she only had to tell someone in authority that her parents touched her inappropriately, that they invited their *friends* to touch her inappropriately. The witch could press lit cigarettes into her new young thighs, and show the burns to the teachers or the police – that should take care of any disbelief.

The witch hummed happily as she rasped, moving the file in time to her song. Finally she put the file back in her bag, satisfied. She put the filed sword into the dirt on the other side of the stream, half-hidden by a bush. She thought a duel across the water would be very picturesque. She wondered if the Girl would faint at the first sight of blood. That's what the last girl had done, and it had made the transition to her mind *much* easier. No resistance at all, just a simple expulsion.

The witch climbed onto her bicycle and rode out of the woods, into the dark. Tomorrow she would be young again. It had been too long – it had *always* been too long.

Rocko woke up Saturday morning after a round of awful dreams, in which he'd tried to stab a boy by a stream while a dark-haired girl looked on, wide-eyed and helpless. He'd felt strong in the dream, like a conqueror . . . but the next thing he knew he was dying, his blood running into the water.

He woke, shivering.

His parents weren't awake yet. Good. He slipped into the kitchen and ate a cold biscuit out of the fridge. Then he dressed, thinking about Cory, about finding the right time to strike.

When he went out the side door, he found the witch's bicycle leaning against his house. He approached it warily, but it seemed harmless and inert. He touched the curved handlebars. Just metal. He looked around for the witch, and didn't see her anywhere.

"You know the way to his house?" Rocko asked.

The bike just sat there.

Rocko took the handlebars and moved the bicycle into the yard. He climbed on and started pedaling the heavy bicycle, wondering how he would know which way to go.

The handlebars tugged under his hands, toward the left, and Rocko went with them. *Like the planchette on a ouija board*, he thought, *moving under my fingers.*

For some reason, even though he was not the type of boy to sing aloud, he found himself shouting the half-remembered words to "Love Me Tender" as he pedaled.

After about a mile, the bike started pedaling itself.

Cory walked to Heather's house with his notebook under his arm, thinking about his dream last night. He found Heather in her front yard, smacking balls with her hockey stick, driving them into one of those portable netted goals. She wore jeans and an untucked blue shirt. Her hair was mussed, and her face was red from exertion. She was altogether beautiful.

"Want to take a few swings?" she asked, seeing him.

"Maybe later."

"Any time. Want to head for the stream?" She picked up her bookbag from where it rested by a flowerbed.

"Sure."

"Mom said she'll make lunch for us. She wants to meet you."

That both pleased him and made him nervous. "You told her about me?"

She laughed. "I had to tell her something when I went to your house. She made me braid my hair, remember?"

"Right, right." They ambled into the woods. She swung her hockey stick at pine cones.

"Did you have any—"

"—weird dreams last night?" she finished. "Yeah. No witch, though, just watching a couple of kids I'd never seen before try to kill each other."

"I dreamed I stabbed somebody. There was a girl there, too . . . and she came over and stared down at the kid's blood while it ran into the water. She hardly seemed to notice me, even though I tried to get her attention."

"That's so messed up," she said. "Very weird."

"I saw something yesterday . . ."

"What?"

"I thought . . . I thought I saw that woman's bicycle in the woods. Not her, just the bike, with no one riding it. But that's crazy. Right?"

"I don't know. I just wish the dreams would stop. If it keeps up, I'll be afraid to go to sleep."

They got to the stream and started talking about their project, both of them glad to have something besides bad dreams to pay attention to.

The bicycle took Rocko into a subdivision after about an hour and a half of riding. He hoped the bicycle would be around to take him *back*, because he didn't remember the way. "That sword better be here," he said to the bicycle when it began slowly coasting toward the woods at the end of the subdivision. "Not to mention that dogshit Cory."

The bicycle did not respond, but a short distance into the woods, it stopped moving, and started to fall over. Rocko stepped off and stood still, listening. He heard water, and, maybe, voices. Did Cory have friends? It didn't seem possible. But if he did . . . well, Rocko would do what he had to when the opportunity presented itself, as opportunities invariably did.

He crept through the woods, toward the voices . . . and saw Cory and Heather, right across a stream.

Heather. Shit. He hadn't expected her to be here. Still . . . maybe it was a good thing. Cory had surely told Heather how he'd made a fool of him, driven off his friends and left him face-down in a shit-filled toilet bowl. They'd probably *laughed* about it, when it should have been *Cory* she laughed at.

Well, he'd show her now, wouldn't he? Show her that he couldn't be messed with that way, not without consequences. She'd *see*.

He glanced around.

And right there, driven point-first into the soil, was the sword. He pulled it out and held it. It felt good in his hand – it felt *natural*.

No feelings, he reminded himself. *Just do what needs to be done.* He started across the creek.

"Did you hear something?" Cory asked.

"I don't—" Heather began.

The next things happened very fast.

Rocko came out of the bushes on the far side of the stream, holding something long in his right hand – was it a *sword*? He wasn't scowling, or cursing, or smiling, just hurrying toward the stream with a fixed, intent expression on his face. Cory instinctively stepped between Rocko and Heather.

"Are you crazy?" Heather shouted, falling back. Cory didn't know which of them she was talking to.

Cory retreated too, banging his elbow on a tree. He glanced that way – and saw a sword, driven point-down into the dirt by the tree trunk.

What he had to do seemed obvious. He'd done it last night in his dream, hadn't he?

He pulled the sword out of the dirt and held it before him. He'd never held a sword before, but he knew how; it felt like second nature.

Rocko stood on the other side of the stream. "This is for my humiliation," he said. He nodded toward Heather. "And for the Girl."

"You can't have her," Cory said, not sure where the words came from. "You'll have to come through me."

"So be it," Rocko said, and jumped across the stream. Cory waited in *en garde* position, his mind curiously blank. These events seemed to have little to do with him – they were almost formalities, somehow, but essential nonetheless.

Rocko raised his sword, and his face finally betrayed expression – a snarl of total, concentrated rage.

Then Heather hit Rocko with her hockey stick, snapping his sword and driving the broken pieces into his chest. A look of comical surprise crossed Rocko's face, and he looked toward Heather. She hit him in the side of the head with the flat of the stick, and he stiffened, then stumbled backwards and fell in the stream, still holding the hilt of his sword.

"Jesus," Heather said, breathing hard.

Then, off in the bushes, the witch screamed.

What had the Girl *done*? Her place was to stand to one side and watch the bloodshed, not intercede! The witch had loosened the moorings of her mind, dressed in jeans and a blue shirt to match the Girl, put a ribbon in her hair. She was ready to *become* the Girl, waiting only for the Boy to spill the Rival's blood and ignite the spell – and that had been ruined!

She ran out of the woods where she'd been watching. "Bitch!" she yelled. "You little whore, you little interfering whore!"

It might not be too late. If she could make the Rival bleed, maybe this tableau was still close enough to the original – the imperative resemblance hadn't totally broken down. She was too far away, though, she'd never get to him and kill him in time, especially with the Girl still standing there, fierce as an Amazon, her hockey stick in hand.

But her bicycle – it was closer.

Rocko sat up, groggily, and saw the witch coming, screaming. He looked at the shattered remnant of sword in his hand, and suddenly understood the essentials, if not the particulars, of the situation.

The witch had set him up. She'd meant for him to die here, and had given him a useless sword. She'd probably been behind Cory's impossible feat of strength and speed in the bathroom, too.

He would *kill* her. He struggled to his feet.

Then he saw the bicycle bearing down on him, and froze, pithed by fear.

The bicycle came out of the trees, lumbering slowly at first but then building speed. Rocko stared at the witch's bicycle as it raced toward him. Heather held her hockey stick across her chest, but she was looking at the witch, who was dressed like Heather and grinning horribly.

The riderless bicycle was going to pass by Cory. He saw its ram's-horn handlebars, only they'd twisted, so their points aimed forward, like bull's horns. They would gore Rocko easily, and his blood would pool in the stream . . .

In one smooth motion, with thoughtless ease, Cory tossed his sword point-first toward the bicycle as it passed him. His sword flew neatly into the spokes on the back tire. The rotation of the wheel slammed the sword against the frame, binding the spokes and making it impossible for the wheel to turn. The bicycle slalomed, and the witch screamed again. The bike skidded for several feet before it fell, then slid into the stream, stopping by Rocko's feet.

Rocko looked down at it, then at the witch, who stood clutching her hair and shouting incomprehensibly.

Rocko grinned. He reached down and snatched the sword from the bike's spokes. The bicycle's wheels spun, but it couldn't seem to right itself. Cory cursed softly. Rocko was going to come after him, and this time he didn't have a weapon of his own. He couldn't run, either, not if that meant leaving Heather to Rocko's mercy, and to the witch.

Rocko lifted the sword and shouted. His face held plenty of expression, now – fury, and delight.

He didn't run for Cory. He ran past Heather, straight for the witch. She hardly seemed to see him – just stared at Heather, and pulled on her hair, and wept.

Rocko plunged the sword into the witch's stomach, driving it in to the hilt, then put his hand on her chest and shoved. The witch fell over backward, her body sliding off the blade. Rocko lifted the sword high, then drove it down into her throat.

He left it there, sticking up, not unlike the way Cory had found it, sticking up from the ground. Rocko looked at Cory and Heather, his eyes glazed, breathing heavily.

"Don't come near us," Heather said, moving close to Cory, clutching her stick.

"Shit," Rocko said, his voice thick. "I'm not messing with either of you. I took care of what I needed to do." He frowned. "Almost, anyway." He approached, and Heather stepped in front of Cory – protecting him, as he'd moved to protect her.

Rocko didn't come much closer to him, though. He veered back toward the stream, and the bicycle. "*This* thing. I don't know how it works . . . but it's got a mind of its own. It might even have *her* mind." He looked at Heather. "Get that stick over here, and smash this thing up, would you? I'll get a rock."

"He's right," Cory said. "I don't know what happened, but . . . the bicycle is part of it. We have to break it."

"Don't mess with us," Heather said. "Don't mess with Cory."

Rocko shrugged. "He proved he was worth something. He saved my life." He flashed a sick grin at Cory. "If Heather hadn't ambushed me, though, and if I hadn't been stuck with a second-rate sword, I'd have finished you."

"We've seen what you can do," Heather said, looking at the witch's body, then away.

Rocko looked at the witch's body and nodded. "Yeah. I crossed a boundary there, didn't I? I wonder what my psychiatrist will say when I tell her I killed her because she was a witch?"

Cory and Heather didn't say anything. They just went to work on the bike with the stick and some rocks, shattering its headlamp first, then pounding its wheel hubs into shapelessness Rocko bashed at the seat until it came off. Halfway through their destruction they heard shouting and footsteps.

"Who—" Cory said, alarmed.

"Grown-ups," Rocko grunted. "Those builders of boundaries. They heard all the screaming, probably. Let's finish this before they get here."

They worked faster, and when they finished, the bicycle was just bits of junk glittering in the stream.

"So much for the micro-ecology," Heather said. "The water will probably be poisoned forever."

A woman came into the clearing, followed by another woman and a man. "Heather!" the first woman shouted. "What—" She saw the witch's body. "Oh my God!" she cried, covering her mouth with both hands.

"I killed her," Rocko said, stepping forward. He looked over his shoulder at Cory, then favored Heather with a smile. He turned back to the grown-ups. "I killed her because she was a witch."

The adults looked at one another.

Heather grasped Cory's hand, hard. He squeezed hers just as tightly. This was going to be a long afternoon, and long days ahead . . . but maybe, on the other side of it, he would still be able to hold Heather's hand.

THE SAGE OF THEARE

Diana Wynne Jones

I often think, why should children get all the best books. I'm not sure that many adults are adventurous enough to see what children are reading. Maybe the Harry Potter books are changing that, but I think adults need to check out the children's section in the bookshop a little more often. They will then discover the brilliance of Diana Wynne Jones, because her books deal with adult themes and will be enjoyed by all ages. Her first book appeared in 1973, Wilkins' Tooth, *followed rapidly by the brilliantly funny* The Ogre Downstairs *(1974),* Eight Days of Luke *(1975) and* Cart & Cwidder *(1975), the first book of hers that I discovered and the first of her series set in the world of Dalemark. With* Charmed Life *(1977) she began her other popular series featuring Chrestomanci. Imagine if magic worked, someone would have to regulate it to make sure it does not get out of hand. In many countries that means bureaucracy. That's the fun of the Chrestomanci series. Chrestomanci (pronounced Krest-oh-Man-See) is the most powerful of all enchanters set in place by the government to control the use of magic. But, of course, it's never that simple.*

THERE WAS A WORLD called Theare in which Heaven was very well organised. Everything was so precisely worked out that every god knew his or her exact duties, correct prayers, right times for business, utterly exact character and unmistakable place above or below the gods.

This was the case from Great Zond, the King of the Gods, through every god, godlet, deity, minor deity and numen, down to the most immaterial nymph. Even the invisible dragons that lived in the rivers had their invisible lines of demarcation. The universe ran like clockwork. Mankind was not always so regular, but the gods were there to set him right. It had been like this for centuries.

So it was a breach in the very nature of things when, in the middle of the yearly Festival of Water, at which only watery deities were entitled to be present, Great Zond looked up to see Imperion, god of the sun, storming towards him down the halls of Heaven.

"Go away!" cried Zond, aghast.

But Imperion swept on, causing the watery deities gathered there to steam and hiss, and arrived in a wave of heat and warm water at the foot of Zond's high throne.

"Father!" Imperion cried urgently.

A high god like Imperion was entitled to call Zond Father. Zond did not recall whether or not he was actually Imperion's father. The origins of the gods were not quite so orderly at their present existence. But Zond knew that, son of his or not, Imperion had breached all the rules. "Abase yourself," Zond said sternly.

Imperion ignored this command too. Perhaps this was just as well, since the floor of Heaven was awash already, and steaming. Imperion kept his flaming gaze on Zond. "Father! The Sage of Dissolution has been born!"

Zond shuddered in the clouds of hot vapour and tried to feel resigned. "It is written," he said, "a Sage shall be born who shall question everything. His questions shall bring down the exquisite order of heaven and cast all the gods into disorder. It is also written—"

Here Zond realised that Imperion had made him break the rules too. The correct procedure was for Zond to summon the god of prophecy and have that god consult the Book of Heaven. Then he realised that Imperion *was* the god of prophecy. It was one of his precisely allocated duties. Zond rounded on Imperion. "What do you mean coming and telling me? You're god of prophecy! Go and look in the Book of Heaven!"

"I already have, Father," said Imperion. "I find I prophesied the coming of the Sage of Dissolution when the gods first began. It is written that the Sage shall be born and that I shall not know."

"Then," said Zond, scoring a point, "how is it you're here telling me he *has* been born?"

"The mere fact," Imperion said, "that I can come here and interrupt the Water Festival, shows that the Sage has been born. Our Dissolution has obviously begun."

There was a splash of consternation among the watery gods. They were gathered down the hall as far as they could get from Imperion, but they had all heard. Zond tried to gather his wits. What with the steam raised by Imperion and the spume of dismay thrown out by the rest, the halls of Heaven were in a state nearer chaos than he had known for millennia. Any more of this, and there would be no need for the Sage to ask questions.

"Leave us," Zond said to the watery gods. "Events even beyond my control cause this Festival to be stopped. You will be informed later of any decision I make." To Zond's dismay, the watery ones hesitated – further evidence of Dissolution. "I promise," he said.

The watery ones made up their minds. They left in waves, all except one. This one was Ock, god of all oceans. Ock was equal in status to Imperion and heat did not threaten him. He stayed where he was.

Zond was not pleased. Ock, it always seemed to him, was the least orderly of the gods. He did not know his place. He was as restless and unfathomable as mankind. But, with Dissolution already begun, what could Zond do?

"You have our permission to stay," he said graciously to Ock, and to Imperion: "Well, how did you know the Sage was born?"

"I was consulting the Book of Heaven on another matter," said Imperion, "and the page opened at my prophecy concerning the Sage of Dissolution. Since it said that I would not know the day and hour when the Sage was born, it followed that he has already been born, or I would not have known. The rest of the prophecy was commendably precise, however. Twenty years from now, he will start questioning Heaven. What shall we do to stop him?"

"I don't see what we can do," Zond said hopelessly. "A prophecy is a prophecy."

"But we must do something!" blazed Imperion. "I insist! I am a god of order, even more than you are. Think what would happen if the sun went inaccurate! This means more to me than anyone. I want the Sage of Dissolution found and killed before he can ask questions."

Zond was shocked. "I can't do that! If the prophecy says he has to ask questions, then he has to ask them."

Here Ock approached. "Every prophecy has a loophole," he said.

"Of course," snapped Imperion. "I can see the loophole as well as you. I'm taking advantage of the disorder caused by the birth of the Sage to ask Great Zond to kill him and overthrow the prophecy. Thus restoring order."

"Logic-chopping is not what I meant," said Ock.

The two gods faced one another. Steam from Ock suffused Imperion and then rained back on Ock, as regularly as breathing. "What *did* you mean, then?" said Imperion.

"The prophecy," said Ock, "does not appear to say which world the Sage will ask his questions in. There are many other worlds. Mankind calls them if-worlds, meaning that they were once the same world as Theare, but split off and went their own ways after each doubtful event in history. Each if-world has its own Heaven. There must be one world in which the gods are not as orderly as we are here. Let the Sage be put in that world. Let him ask his predestined questions there."

"Good idea!" Zond clapped his hands in relief, causing untoward tempests in all Theare. "Agreed, Imperion?"

"Yes," said Imperion. He flamed with relief. And, being unguarded, he at once became prophetic. "But I must warn you," he said, "that strange things happen when destiny is tampered with."

"Strange things maybe, but never disorderly," Zond asserted. He called the water gods back and, with them, every god in Theare. He told them that an infant had just been born who was destined to spread Dissolution, and he ordered each one of them to search the ends of the earth for this child.

("The ends of the earth" was a legal formula. Zond did not

believe that Theare was flat. But the expression had been unchanged for centuries, just like the rest of Heaven. It meant
"Look everywhere.")

The whole of Heaven looked high and low. Nymphs and
godlets scanned mountains, caves and woods. Household gods
peered into cradles. Watery gods searched beaches, banks and
margins. The goddess of love went deeply into her records, to
find who the Sage's parents might be. The invisible dragons
swam to look inside barges and houseboats. Since there was a god
for everything in Theare, nowhere was missed, nothing was
omitted. Imperion searched harder than any, blazing into every
nook and crevice on one side of the world, and exhorting the
moon goddess to do the same on the other side.

And nobody found the Sage. There were one or two false
alarms, such as when a household goddess reported an infant that
never stopped crying. This baby, she said, was driving her up the
wall and, if this was not Dissolution, she would like to know what
was. There were also several reports of infants born with teeth, or
six fingers, or suchlike strangeness. But, in each case, Zond was
able to prove that the child had nothing to do with Dissolution.
After a month, it became clear that the infant Sage was not going
to be found.

Imperion was in despair, for, as he had told Zond, order meant
more to him than to any other god. He became so worried that he
was actually causing the sun to lose heat. At length, the goddess of
love advised him to go off and relax with a mortal woman before
he brought about Dissolution himself.

Imperion saw she was right. He went down to visit the human
woman he had loved for some years. It was established custom for
gods to love mortals. Some visited their loves in all sorts of
fanciful shapes, and some had many loves at once. But Imperion
was both honest and faithful. He never visited Nestara as anything but a handsome man, and he loved her devotedly. Three
years ago, she had borne him a son, whom Imperion loved almost
as much as he loved Nestara. Before the Sage was born to trouble
him, Imperion had been trying to bend the rules of Heaven a
little, to get his son approved as a god too.

The child's name was Thasper. As Imperion descended to
earth, he could see Thasper digging in some sand outside Nes-

tara's house – a beautiful child, fair-haired and blue-eyed. Imperion wondered fondly if Thasper was talking properly yet. Nestara had been worried about how slow he was learning to speak.

Imperion alighted beside his son. "Hello, Thasper. What are you digging so busily?"

Instead of answering, Thasper raised his golden head and shouted. "Mum!" he yelled. "Why does it go so bright when Dad comes?"

All Imperion's pleasure vanished. Of course no one could ask questions until he had learned to speak. But it would be too cruel if his own son turned out to be the Sage of Dissolution. "Why shouldn't it go bright?" he asked defensively.

Thasper scowled up at him. "I want to know. *Why* does it?"

"Perhaps because you feel happy to see me," Imperion suggested.

"I'm not happy," Thasper said. His lower lip came out. Tears filled his big blue eyes. "Why does it go bright? I want to know. Mum! I'm not happy!"

Nestara came racing out of the house, almost too concerned to smile at Imperion. "Thasper love, what's the matter?"

"I want to *know*!" wailed Thasper.

"What do you want to know? I've never known such an enquiring mind," Nestara said proudly to Imperion, as she picked Thasper up. "That's why he was so slow talking. He wouldn't speak until he'd found out how to ask questions. And if you don't give him an exact answer, he'll cry for hours."

"When did he first start asking questions?" Imperion inquired tensely.

"About a month ago," said Nestara.

This made Imperion truly miserable, but he concealed it. It was clear to him that Thasper was indeed the Sage of Dissolution and he was going to have to take him away to another world. He smiled and said, "My love, I have wonderful news for you. Thasper has been accepted as a god. Great Zond himself will have him as cupbearer."

"Oh not now!" cried Nestara. "He's so little!"

She made numerous other objections too. But, in the end, she let Imperion take Thasper. After all, what better future could there be for a child? She put Thasper into Imperion's arms with all sorts of anxious advice about what he ate and when he went to bed. Imperion kissed her goodbye, heavy-hearted. He was not a god of deception. He knew he dared not see her again for fear he told her the truth.

Then, with Thasper in his arms, Imperion went up to the middle-regions below Heaven, to look for another world.

Thasper looked down with interest at the great blue curve of the world. "Why—?" he began.

Imperion hastily enclosed him in a sphere of forgetfulness. He could not afford to let Thasper ask things here. Questions that spread Dissolution on earth would have an even more powerful effect in the middle-region. The sphere was a silver globe, neither transparent nor opaque. In it, Thasper would stay seemingly asleep, not moving and not growing, until the sphere was opened. With the child thus safe, Imperion hung the sphere from one shoulder and stepped into the next-door world.

He went from world to world. He was pleased to find there were an almost infinite number of them, for the choice proved supremely difficult. Some worlds were so disorderly that he shrank from leaving Thasper in them. In some, the gods resented Imperion's intrusion and shouted at him to be off. In others, it was mankind that was resentful. One world he came to was so rational that, to his horror, he found the gods were dead. There were many others he thought might do, until he let the spirit of prophecy blow through him, and in each case this told him that harm would come to Thasper here.

But at last he found a good world. It seemed calm and elegant. The few gods there seemed civilised but casual. Indeed, Imperion was a little puzzled to find that these gods seemed to share quite a lot of their power with mankind. But mankind did not seem to abuse this power, and the spirit of prophecy assured him that, if he left Thasper here inside his sphere of forgetfulness, it would be opened by someone who would treat the boy well.

Imperion put the sphere down in a wood and sped back to Theare, heartily relieved. There, he reported what he had done to Zond, and all Heaven rejoiced. Imperion made sure that Nestara married a very rich man who gave her not only wealth and happiness but plenty of children to replace Thasper. Then, a little sadly, he went back to the ordered life of Heaven. The exquisite organisation of Theare went on untroubled by Dissolution.

Seven years passed.

All that while, Thasper knew nothing and remained three years old. Then one day, the sphere of forgetfulness fell in two halves and he blinked in sunlight somewhat less golden than he had known.

"So that's what was causing all the disturbance," a tall man murmured.

"Poor little soul," said a lady.

There was a wood around Thasper, and people standing in it looking at him, but, as far as Thasper knew, nothing had happened since he soared to the middle-region with his father. He went on with the question he had been in the middle of asking. "Why is the world round?" he said.

"Interesting question," said the tall man. "The answer usually given is because the corners wore off spinning around the sun. But it could be designed to make us end where we began."

"Sir, you'll muddle him, talking like that," said another lady. "He's only little."

"No, he's interested," said another man. "Look at him."

Thasper was indeed interested. He approved of the tall man. He was a little puzzled about where he had come from but he supposed the tall man must have been put there because he answered questions better than Imperion. He wondered where Imperion had got to. "Why aren't you my Dad?" he asked the tall man.

"Another most penetrating question," said the tall man. "Because, as far as we can find out, your father lives in another world. Tell me your name."

This was another point in the tall man's favour. Thasper never answered questions: he only asked them. But this was a command. The tall man understood Thasper.

"Thasper," Thasper answered obediently.

"He's sweet!" said the first lady. "I want to adopt him." To which the other ladies gathered around most heartily agreed.

"Impossible," said the tall man. His tone was mild as milk and rock firm. The ladies were reduced to begging to be able to look after Thasper for a day, then. An hour. "No," the tall man said mildly. "He must go back at once." At which all the ladies cried out that Thasper might be in great danger in his own home. The tall man said, "I shall take care of that, of course." Then he stretched out a hand and pulled Thasper up. "Come along, Thasper."

As soon as Thasper was out of it, the two halves of the sphere vanished. One of the ladies took his other hand and he was led away, first on a jiggly ride, which he much enjoyed, and then into a huge house, where there was a very perplexing room. In this room, Thasper sat in a five-pointed star and pictures kept appearing around him. People kept shaking their heads. "No, not that world either." The tall man answered all Thasper's questions, and Thasper was too interested even to be annoyed when they would not allow him anything to eat.

"Why not?" he said.

"Because, just by being here, you are causing the world to jolt about," the tall man explained. "If you put food inside you, food is a heavy part of this world, and it might jolt you to pieces."

Soon after that, a new picture appeared. Everyone said "Ah!" and the tall man said, "So it's Theare!" He looked at Thasper in a surprised way. "You must have struck someone as disorderly," he said. Then he looked at the picture again, in a lazy, careful kind of way. "No disorder," he said. "No danger. Come with me."

He took Thasper's hand again and led him into the picture. As he did so, Thasper's hair turned much darker. "A simple precaution," the tall man murmured, a little apologetically, but Thasper did not even notice. He was not aware what colour his hair had been to start with, and besides, he was taken up with surprise at how fast they were going. They whizzed into a city, and stopped abruptly. It was a good house, just on the edge of a poorer district. "Here is someone who will do," the tall man said, and he knocked at the door.

A sad-looking lady opened the door.

"I beg your pardon, madam," said the tall man. "Have you by any chance lost a small boy?"

"Yes," said the lady. "But this isn't—" She blinked, "Yes it *is*!" she cried out. "Oh Thasper! How could you run off like that? Thank you so much, sir." But the tall man had gone.

The lady's name was Alina Altun, and she was so convinced that she was Thasper's mother that Thasper was soon convinced too. He settled in happily with her and her husband, who was a doctor, hard-working but not very rich.

Thasper soon forgot the tall man, Imperion and Nestara. Sometimes it did puzzle him – and his new mother too – that when she showed him off to her friends she always felt bound to say, "This is Badien, but we always call him Thasper." Thanks to the tall man, none of them ever knew that the real Badien had wandered away the day Thasper came, and fallen in the river, where an invisible dragon ate him.

If Thasper had remembered the tall man, he might also have wondered why his arrival seemed to start Dr Altun on the road to prosperity. The people in the poorer district nearby suddenly discovered what a good doctor Dr Altun was, and how little he charged. Alina was shortly able to afford to send Thasper to a very good school, where Thasper often exasperated his teachers by his many questions. He had, as his new mother often proudly said, a most enquiring mind. Although he learned quicker than most the Ten First Lessons and the Nine Graces of Childhood, his teachers were nonetheless often annoyed enough to snap, "Oh, go and ask an invisible dragon!" which is what people in Theare often said when they thought they were being pestered.

Thasper did, with difficulty, gradually cure himself of his habit of never answering questions. But he always preferred asking to answering. At home, he asked questions all the time: "Why does the kitchen god go and report to Heaven once a year? Is it so I can steal biscuits? Why are invisible dragons? Is there a god for everything? Why is there a god for everything? If the gods make people ill, how can Dad cure them? Why must I have a baby brother or sister?"

Alina Altun was a good mother. She most diligently answered all these questions, including the last. She told Thasper how babies were made, ending her account with, "Then, if the gods bless my womb, a baby will come." She was a devout person.

"I don't want you to be blessed!" Thasper said, resorting to a statement, which he only did when he was strongly moved.

He seemed to have no choice in the matter. By the time he was ten years old, the gods had thought fit to bless him with two brothers and two sisters. In Thasper's opinion, they were, as blessings, very low grade. They were just too young to be any use. "Why can't they be the same age as me?" he demanded many times. He began to bear the gods a small but definite grudge about this.

Dr Altun continued to prosper and his earnings more than kept pace with his family. Alina employed a nursemaid, a cook and a number of rather impermanent houseboys. It was one of these houseboys who, when Thasper was eleven, shyly presented Thasper with a folded square of paper. Wondering, Thasper unfolded it. It gave him a curious feeling to touch, as if the paper was vibrating a little in his fingers. It also gave out a very strong warning that he was not to mention it to anybody. It said:

> Dear Thasper,
> Your situation is an odd one. Make sure that you call me at the moment when you come face to face with yourself. I shall be watching and I will come at once.
> Yrs,
> Chrestomanci

Since Thasper by now had not the slightest recollection of his early life, this letter puzzled him extremely. He knew he was not supposed to tell anyone about it, but he also knew that this did not include the houseboy. With the letter in his hand, he hurried after the houseboy to the kitchen.

He was stopped at the head of the kitchen stairs by a tremendous smashing of china from below. This was followed immediately by the cook's voice raised in nonstop abuse. Thasper knew it was no good trying to go into the kitchen.

The houseboy – who went by the odd name of Cat – was in the process of getting fired, like all the other houseboys before him. He had better go and wait for Cat outside the back door. Thasper looked at the letter in his hand. As he did so, his fingers tingled. The letter vanished.

"It's gone!" he exclaimed, showing by this statement how astonished he was. He never could account for what he did next. Instead of going to wait for the houseboy, he ran to the living-room, intending to tell his mother about it, in spite of the warning.

"Do you know what?" he began. He had invented this meaningless question so that he could tell people things and still make it into an enquiry. "Do you know what?" Alina looked up. Thasper, though he fully intended to tell her about the mysterious letter, found himself saying, "The cook's just sacked the new houseboy."

"Oh bother!" said Alina. "I shall have to find another one now."

Annoyed with himself, Thasper tried to tell her again. "Do you know what? I'm surprised the cook doesn't sack the kitchen god too."

"Hush dear. Don't talk about the gods that way!" said the devout lady.

By this time, the houseboy had left and Thasper lost the urge to tell anyone about the letter. It remained with him as his own personal exciting secret. He thought of it as The Letter From A Person Unknown. He sometimes whispered the strange name of The Person Unknown to himself when no one could hear. But nothing ever happened, even when he said the name out loud. He gave up doing that after a while. He had other things to think about. He became fascinated by Rules, Laws and Systems.

Rules and Systems were an important part of the life of mankind in Theare. It stood to reason, with Heaven so well organised. People codified all behaviour into things like the Seven Subtle Politenesses, or the Hundred Roads to Godliness. Thasper had been taught these things from the time he was three years old.

He was accustomed to hearing Alina argue the niceties of the Seventy-Two Household Laws with her friends. Now Thasper suddenly discovered for himself that all Rules made a magnificent framework for one's mind to clamber about in. He made lists of rules, and refinements on rules, and possible ways of doing the opposite of what the rules said while still keeping the rules. He invented new codes of rules. He filled books and made charts. He invented games with huge and complicated rules, and played them with his friends.

Onlookers found these games both rough and muddled, but

Thasper and his friends revelled in them. The best moment in any game was when somebody stopped playing and shouted, "I've thought of a new rule!"

This obsession with rules lasted until Thasper was fifteen. He was walking home from school one day, thinking over a list of rules for Twenty Fashionable Hairstyles. From this, it will be seen that Thasper was noticing girls, though none of the girls had so far seemed to notice him. And he was thinking which girl should wear which hairstyle, when his attention was caught by words chalked on the wall:

> IF RULES MAKE A FRAMEWORK FOR
> THE MIND TO CLIMB ABOUT IN,
> WHY SHOULD THE MIND NOT CLIMB RIGHT OUT?
> SAYS THE SAGE OF DISSOLUTION

That same day, there was consternation again in Heaven. Zond summoned all the high gods to his throne. "The Sage of Dissolution has started to preach," he announced direfully. "Imperion, I thought you got rid of him."

"I thought I did," Imperion said. He was even more appalled than Zond. If the Sage had started to preach, it meant that Imperion had got rid of Thasper and deprived himself of Nestara quite unnecessarily. "I must have been mistaken," he admitted.

Here Ock spoke up, steaming gently. "Father Zond," he said, "may I respectfully suggest that you deal with the Sage yourself, so that there will be no mistake this time?"

"That was just what I was about to suggest," Zond said gratefully. "Are you all agreed?"

All the gods agreed. They were too used to order to do otherwise.

As for Thasper, he was staring at the chalked words, shivering to the soles of his sandals. What was this? Who was using his own private thoughts about rules? Who was this Sage of Dissolution? Thasper was ashamed. He, who was so good at asking questions, had never thought of asking this one. Why should one's mind not climb right out of the rules, after all?

He went home and asked his parents about the Sage of Dissolution. He fully expected them to know. He was quite agitated when they did not. But they had a neighbour, who sent Thasper to another neighbour, who had a friend, who, when Thasper finally found his house, said he had heard that the Sage was a clever young man who made a living by mocking the gods.

The next day, someone had washed the words off. But the day after that, a badly printed poster appeared on the same wall.

**THE SAGE OF DISSOLUTION ASKS
BY WHOSE ORDER IS ORDER
ANYWAY??
COME TO SMALL UNCTION
SUBLIME CONCERT HALL
TONITE 6.30**

At 6.20, Thasper was having supper. At 6.24, he made up his mind and left the table. At 6.32 he arrived panting at Small Unction Hall. It proved to be a small shabby building quite near where he lived. Nobody was there. As far as Thasper could gather from the grumpy caretaker, the meeting had been the night before. Thasper turned away, deeply disappointed. Who ordered the order was a question he now longed to know the answer to. It was deep. He had a notion that the man who called himself the Sage of Dissolution was truly brilliant.

By way of feeding his own disappointment, he went to school the next day by a route which took him past the Small Unction Concert Hall. It had burnt down in the night. There were only blackened brick walls left. When he got to school, a number of people were talking about it. They said it had burst into flames just before 7.00 the night before.

"Did you know," Thasper said, "that the Sage of Dissolution was there the day before yesterday?"

That was how he discovered he was not the only one interested in the Sage. Half his class were admirers of Dissolution. That, too, was when the girls deigned to notice him. "He's amazing about the gods," one girl told him. "No one ever asked questions like that before."

Most of the class, however, girls and boys alike, only knew a little more than Thasper, and most of what they knew was second-hand. But a boy showed him a carefully cut-out newspaper article in which a well-known scholar discussed what he called "The so-called Doctrine of Dissolution". It said, long-windedly, that the Sage and his followers were rude to the gods and against all the rules.

It did not tell Thasper much, but it was something. He saw, rather ruefully, that his obsession with rules had been quite wrong-headed and had, into the bargain, caused him to fall behind the rest of his class in learning of this wonderful new Doctrine. He became a Disciple of Dissolution on the spot. He joined the rest of his class in finding out all they could about the Sage.

He went round with them, writing up on walls:

DISSOLUTION RULES OK.

For a long while after that, the only thing any of Thasper's class could learn of the Sage were scraps of questions chalked on walls and quickly rubbed out.

WHAT NEED OF PRAYER?

WHY SHOULD THERE BE A HUNDRED ROADS
TO GODLINESS, NOT MORE OR LESS?

DO WE CLIMB ANYWHERE ON THE STEPS
TO HEAVEN?

WHAT IS PERFECTION: A PROCESS OR A STATE?
WHEN WE CLIMB TO PERFECTION

IS THIS A MATTER FOR THE GODS?

Thasper obsessively wrote all these sayings down. He was ob-sessed again, he admitted, but this time it was in a new way. He was thinking, thinking. At first, he thought simply of clever questions to ask the Sage. He strained to find questions no one had asked before. But in the process, his mind seemed to loosen, and shortly he was thinking of how the Sage might answer his questions. He considered order and rules and Heaven, and it came to him that there was a reason behind all the brilliant questions the Sage asked. He felt light-headed with thinking.

The reason behind the Sage's questions came to him the

morning he was shaving for the first time. He thought, *The gods need human beings in order to be gods*! Blinded with this revelation, Thasper stared into the mirror at his own face half covered with white foam. Without humans believing in them, gods were nothing! The order of Heaven, the rules and codes of earth, were all only there because of people! It was transcendent.

As Thasper stared, the letter from the Unknown came into his mind. "Is this being face to face with myself?" he said. But he was not sure. And he became sure that when that time came, he would not have to wonder.

Then it came to him that the Unknown Chrestomanci was almost certainly the Sage himself. He was thrilled. The Sage was taking a special mysterious interest in one teenage boy, Thasper Altun. The vanishing letter exactly fitted the elusive Sage.

The Sage continued elusive. The next firm news of him was a newspaper report of the Celestial Gallery being struck by lightning. The roof of the building collapsed, said the report, "only seconds after the young man known as the Sage of Dissolution had delivered another of his anguished and self-doubting homilies and left the building with his disciples."

"He's not self-doubting," Thasper said to himself. "He knows about the gods. If *I* know, then *he* certainly does."

He and his classmates went on a pilgrimage to the ruined gallery. It was a better building than Small Unction Hall. It seemed the Sage was going up in the world.

Then there was enormous excitement. One of the girls found a small advertisement in a paper. The Sage was to deliver another lecture, in the huge Kingdom of Splendour Hall. He had gone up in the world again. Thasper and his friends dressed in their best and went there in a body. But it seemed as if the time for the lecture had been printed wrong. The lecture was just over. People were streaming away from the Hall, looking disappointed.

Thasper and his friends were still in the street when the Hall blew up. They were lucky not to be hurt. The Police said it was a bomb. Thasper and his friends helped drag injured people clear of the blazing Hall. It was exciting, but it was not the Sage.

By now, Thasper knew he would never be happy until he had found the Sage. He told himself that he had to know if the reason behind the Sage's questions was the one he thought. But it was more than that. Thasper was convinced that his fate was linked to the Sage's. He was certain the Sage *wanted* Thasper to find him.

But there was now a strong rumour in school and around town that the Sage had had enough of lectures and bomb attacks. He had retired to write a book. It was to be called *Questions of Dissolution*. Rumour also had it that the Sage was in lodgings somewhere near the Road of the Four Lions.

Thasper went to the Road of the Four Lions. There he was shameless. He knocked on doors and questioned passers-by. He was told several times to go and ask an invisible dragon, but he took no notice. He went on asking until someone told him that Mrs Tunap at No. 403 might know. Thasper knocked at No. 403, with his heart thumping.

Mrs Tunap was a rather prim lady in a green turban. "I'm afraid not, dear," she said. "I'm new here." But before Thasper's heart could sink too far, she added, "but the people before me had a lodger. A very quiet gentleman. He left just before I came."

"Did he leave an address?" Thasper asked, holding his breath.

Mrs Tunap consulted an old envelope pinned to the wall in her hall. "It says here, 'Lodger gone to Golden Heart Square', dear."

But in Golden Heart Square, a young gentleman who might have been the Sage had only looked at a room and gone. After that, Thasper had to go home. The Altuns were not used to teenagers and they worried about Thasper suddenly wanting to be out every evening.

Oddly enough, No. 403 Road of the Four Lions burnt down that night.

Thasper saw clearly that assassins were after the Sage as well as he was. He became more obsessed with finding him than ever. He knew he could rescue the Sage if he caught him before the assassins did. He did not blame the Sage for moving about all the time.

Move about the Sage certainly did. Rumour had him next in Partridge Pleasaunce Street. When Thasper tracked him there, he found the Sage had moved to Fauntel Square. From Fauntel Square, the Sage seemed to move to Strong Wind Boulevard, and then to a poorer house in Station Street. There were many places after that.

By this time, Thasper had developed a nose, a sixth sense, for where the Sage might be. A word, a mere hint about a quiet lodger, and Thasper was off, knocking on doors, questioning people, being told to ask an invisible dragon, and bewildering his parents by the way he kept rushing off every evening. But no matter how quickly Thasper acted on the latest hint, the Sage had always just left. And Thasper, in most cases, was only just ahead of the assassins. Houses caught fire or blew up, sometimes when he was still in the same street.

At last he was down to a very poor hint, which might or might not lead to New Unicorn Street. Thasper went there, wishing he did not have to spend all day at school. The Sage could move about as he pleased, and Thasper was tied down all day. No wonder he kept missing him. But he had high hopes of New Unicorn Street. It was the poor kind of place that the Sage had been favouring lately.

Alas for his hopes. The fat woman who opened the door laughed rudely in Thasper's face. "Don't bother me, son! Go and ask an invisible dragon!" And she slammed the door again.

Thasper stood in the street, keenly humiliated. And not even a hint of where to look next. Awful suspicions rose in his mind: he was making a fool of himself; he had set himself a wild goose chase; the Sage did not exist. In order not to think of these things, he gave way to anger. "All right!" he shouted at the shut door. "I *will* ask an invisible dragon! So there!" And, carried by his anger, he ran down to the river and out across the nearest bridge.

He stopped in the middle of the bridge, leaning on the parapet, and knew he was making an utter fool of himself. There were no such things as invisible dragons. He was sure of that. But he was still in the grip of his obsession, and this was something he had set himself to do now. Even so, if there had been anyone about near the bridge, Thasper would have gone away. But it was deserted. Feeling an utter fool, he made the prayer-sign to Ock, Ruler of Oceans – for Ock was the god in charge of all things to do with water – but he made the sign secretly, down under the parapet, so there was no chance of anyone seeing. Then he said, almost in a whisper, "Is there an invisible dragon here? I've got something to ask you."

Drops of water whirled over him. Something wetly fanned his

face. He heard the something whirring. He turned his face that way and saw three blots of wet in a line along the parapet, each about two feet apart and each the size of two of his hands spread out together. Odder still, water was dripping out of nowhere all along the parapet, for a distance about twice as long as Thasper was tall.

Thasper laughed uneasily. "I'm imagining a dragon," he said. "If there was a dragon, those splotches would be the places where its body rests. Water dragons have no feet. And the length of the wetness suggests I must be imagining it about eleven feet long."

"I am fourteen feet long," said a voice out of nowhere. It was rather too near Thasper's face for comfort and blew fog at him. He drew back. "Make haste, child-of-a-god," said the voice. "What did you want to ask me?"

"I-I-I—" stammered Thasper. It was not just that he was scared. This was a body-blow. It messed up utterly his notions about gods needing men to believe in them. But he pulled himself together. His voice only cracked a little as he said, "I'm looking for the Sage of Dissolution. Do you know where he is?"

The dragon laughed. It was a peculiar noise, like one of those water-warblers people make bird noises with. "I'm afraid I can't tell you precisely where the Sage is," the voice out of nowhere said. "You have to find him for yourself. Think about it, child-of-a-god. You must have noticed there's a pattern."

"Too right, there's a pattern!" Thasper said. "Everywhere he goes, I just miss him, and then the place catches fire!"

"That too," said the dragon. "But there's a pattern to his lodgings too. Look for it. That's all I can tell you, child-of-a-god. Any other questions?"

"No – for a wonder," Thasper said. "Thanks very much."

"You're welcome," said the invisible dragon. "People are always telling one another to ask us, and hardly anyone does. I'll see you again." Watery air whirled in Thasper's face. He leaned over the parapet and saw one prolonged clean splash in the river, and silver bubbles coming up. Then nothing. He was surprised to find his legs were shaking.

He steadied his knees and tramped home. He went to his room and, before he did anything else, he acted on a superstitious impulse he had not thought he had in him, and took down the household god Alina insisted he keep in a niche over his bed. He put it carefully outside in the passage. Then he got out a map of the town and some red stickers and plotted out all the places where he had just missed the Sage.

The result had him dancing with excitement. The dragon was right. There was a pattern. The Sage had started in good lodgings at the better end of town. Then he had gradually moved to poorer places, but he had moved in a curve, down to the station and back towards the better part again. Now, the Altuns' house was just on the edge of the poorer part. The Sage was *coming this way!* New Unicorn Street had not been so far away. The next place should be nearer still. Thasper had only to look for a house on fire.

It was getting dark by then. Thasper threw his curtains back and leaned out of his window to look at the poorer streets. And there it was! There was a red and orange flicker to the left – in Harvest Moon Street, by the look of it. Thasper laughed aloud. He was actually grateful to the assassins!

He raced downstairs and out of the house. The anxious questions of parents and the yells of brothers and sisters followed him, but he slammed the door on them. Two minutes' running brought him to the scene of the fire. The street was a mad flicker of dark figures. People were piling furniture in the road. Some more people were helping a dazed woman in a crooked brown turban into a singed armchair.

"Didn't you have a lodger as well?" someone asked her anxiously.

The woman kept trying to straighten her turban. It was all she could really think of. "He didn't stay," she said. "I think he may be down at the Half Moon now."

Thasper waited for no more. He went pelting down the street.

The Half Moon was an inn on the corner of the same road. Most of the people who usually drank there must have been up the street, helping rescue furniture, but there was a dim light inside, enough to show a white notice in the window. ROOMS, it said.

Thasper burst inside. The barman was on a stool by the window craning to watch the house burn. He did not look at Thasper. "Where's your lodger?" gasped Thasper. "I've got a message. Urgent."

The barman did not turn round. "Upstairs, first on the left," he said. "The roof's caught. They'll have to act quick to save the house on either side."

Thasper heard him say this as he bounded upstairs. He turned left. He gave the briefest of knocks on the door there, flung it open and rushed in.

The room was empty. The light was on and it showed a stark bed, a stained table with an empty mug and some sheets of paper on it, and a fireplace with a mirror over it. Beside the fireplace, another door was just swinging shut. Obviously somebody had just that moment gone through it.

Thasper bounded towards that door. But he was checked, for just a second, by seeing himself in the mirror over the fireplace. He had not meant to pause. But some trick of the mirror, which was old and brown and speckled, made his reflection look for a moment a great deal older. He looked easily over twenty. He looked—

He remembered the Letter from the Unknown. This was the time. He knew it was. He was about to meet the Sage. He had only to call him. Thasper went towards the still gently swinging door. He hesitated. The Letter had said call at once. Knowing the Sage was just beyond the door, Thasper pushed it open a fraction and held it so with his fingers. He was full of doubts. He thought, Do I really believe the gods need people? Am I so sure? What shall I say to the Sage after all? He let the door slip shut again.

"Chrestomanci," he said, miserably.

There was a *whoosh* of displaced air behind him. It buffeted Thasper half around. He stared. A tall man was standing by the stark bed. He was a most extraordinary figure in a long black robe, with what seemed to be yellow comets embroidered on it. The inside of the robe, swirling in the air, showed yellow, with black comets on it. The tall man had a very smooth dark head, very bright dark eyes and, on his feet, what seemed to be red bedroom slippers.

"Thank goodness," said this outlandish person. "For a moment, I was afraid you would go through that door."

The voice brought memory back to Thasper. "You brought me home through a picture when I was little," he said. "Are you Chrestomanci?"

"Yes," said the tall outlandish man. "And you are Thasper. And now we must both leave before this building catches fire."

He took hold of Thasper's arm and towed him to the door which led to the stairs. As soon as he pushed the door open, thick smoke rolled in, filled with harsh crackling. It was clear that the inn was on fire already. Chrestomanci clapped the door shut again. The smoke set both of them coughing, Chrestomanci so violently that Thasper was afraid he would choke. He pulled both of them back into the middle of the room. By now, smoke was twining up between the bare boards of the floor, causing Chrestomanci to cough again.

"This would happen just as I had gone to bed with flu," he said, when he could speak. "Such is life. These orderly gods of yours leave us no choice." He crossed the smoking floor and pushed open the door by the fireplace.

It opened on to blank space. Thasper gave a yelp of horror.

"Precisely," coughed Chrestomanci. "You were intended to crash to your death."

"Can't we jump to the ground?" Thasper suggested.

Chrestomanci shook his smooth head. "Not after they've done this to it. No. We'll have to carry the fight to them and go and visit the gods instead. Will you be kind enough to lend me your turban before we go?" Thasper stared at this odd request. "I would like to use it as a belt," Chrestomanci croaked. "The way to Heaven may be a little cold, and I only have pyjamas under my dressing-gown."

The striped undergarments Chrestomanci was wearing did look a little thin. Thasper slowly unwound his turban. To go before gods bareheaded was probably no worse than going in nightclothes, he supposed. Besides, he did not believe there were any gods. He handed the turban over. Chrestomanci tied the length of pale blue cloth around his black and yellow gown and seemed to feel more comfortable.

"Now hang on to me," he said, "and you'll be all right." He took Thasper's arm again and walked up into the sky, dragging Thasper with him.

For a while, Thasper was too stunned to speak. He could only marvel at the way they were treading up the sky as if there were invisible stairs in it. Chrestomanci was doing it in the most matter of fact way, coughing from time to time and shivering a little, but keeping very tight hold of Thasper nevertheless. In no time, the town was a clutter of prettily lit dolls' houses below, with two red blots where two of them were burning. The stars were unwinding about them, above and below, as if they had already climbed above some of them.

"It's a long climb to Heaven," Chrestomanci observed. "Is there anything you'd like to know on the way?"

"Yes," said Thasper. "Did you say the gods are trying to kill me?"

"They are trying to eliminate the Sage of Dissolution," said Chrestomanci, "which they may not realise is the same thing. You see, you are the Sage."

"But I'm not!" Thasper insisted. "The Sage is a lot older than me, and he asks questions I never even thought of until I heard of him."

"Ah yes," said Chrestomanci. "I'm afraid there is an awful circularity to this. It's the fault of whoever tried to put you away as a small child. As far as I can work out, you stayed three years old for seven years – until you were making such a disturbance in our world that we had to find you and let you out. But in this world of Theare, highly organised and fixed as it is, the prophecy stated that you would begin preaching Dissolution at the age of twenty-three, or at least in this very year. Therefore the preaching had to begin this year. You did not need to appear. Did you ever speak to anyone who had actually heard the Sage preach?"

"No," said Thasper. "Come to think of it."

"Nobody did," said Chrestomanci. "You started in a small way anyway. First you wrote a book, which no one paid much heed to—"

"No, that's wrong," objected Thasper. "He – I – er, the Sage was writing a book *after* preaching."

"But don't you see," said Chrestomanci, "because you were back in Theare by then, the facts had to try to catch you up. They did this by running backwards, until it was possible for you to arrive where you were supposed to be. Which was in that room in the inn there, at the start of your career. I suppose you are just old enough to start by now. And I suspect our celestial friends up here tumbled to this belatedly and tried to finish you off. It

wouldn't have done them any good, as I shall shortly tell them."
He began coughing again. They had climbed to where it was
bitterly cold.

By this time, the world was a dark arch below them. Thasper
could see the blush of the sun, beginning to show underneath the
world. They climbed on. The light grew. The sun appeared, a
huge brightness in the distance underneath. A dim memory came
again to Thasper. He struggled to believe that none of this was
true, and he did not succeed.

"How do you know all this?" he asked bluntly.

"Have you heard of a god called Ock?" Chrestomanci coughed.
"He came to talk to me when you should have been the age you
are now. He was worried —" He coughed again. "I shall have to
save the rest of my breath for Heaven."

They climbed on, and the stars swam around them, until the
stuff they were climbing changed and became solider. Soon they
were climbing a dark ramp, which flushed pearly as they went
upwards. Here, Chrestomanci let go of Thasper's arm and blew
his nose on a gold-edged handkerchief with an air of relief. The
pearl of the ramp grew to silver and the silver to dazzling white.
At length, they were walking on level whiteness, through hall
after hall.

The gods were gathered to meet them. None of them looked
cordial.

"I fear we are not properly dressed," Chrestomanci murmured.

Thasper looked at the gods, and then at Chrestomanci, and
squirmed with embarrassment. Fanciful and queer as Chrestomanci's garb was, it was still most obviously nightwear. The
things on his feet were fur bedroom slippers. And there, looking
like a piece of blue string around Chrestomanci's waist, was the
turban Thasper should have been wearing.

The gods were magnificent, in golden trousers and jewelled
turbans, and got more so as they approached the greater gods.
Thasper's eye was caught by a god in shining cloth of gold, who
surprised him by beaming a friendly, almost anxious look at him.
Opposite him was a huge liquid-looking figure draped in pearls and
diamonds. This god swiftly, but quite definitely, winked. Thasper
was too awed to react, but Chrestomanci calmly winked back.

At the end of the halls, upon a massive throne, towered the mighty figure of Great Zond, clothed in white and purple, with a crown on his head. Chrestomanci looked up at Zond and thoughtfully blew his nose. It was hardly respectful.

"For what reason do two mortals trespass in our halls?" Zond thundered coldly.

Chrestomanci sneezed. "Because of your own folly," he said. "You gods of Theare have had everything so well worked out for so long that you can't see beyond your own routine."

"I shall blast you for that," Zond announced.

"Not if any of you wish to survive," Chrestomanci said.

There was a long murmur of protest from the other gods. They wished to survive. They were trying to work out what Chrestomanci meant. Zond saw it as a threat to his authority and thought he had better be cautious. "Proceed," he said.

"One of your most efficient features," Chrestomanci said, "is that your prophecies always come true. So why, when a prophecy is unpleasant to you, do you think you can alter it? That, my good gods, is rank folly. Besides, no one can halt his own Dissolution, least of all you gods of Theare. But you forgot. You forgot you had deprived both yourselves and mankind of any kind of free will, by organising yourselves so precisely. You pushed Thasper, the Sage of Dissolution, into my world, forgetting that there is still chance in my world. By chance, Thasper was discovered after only seven years. Lucky for Theare that he was. I shudder to think what might have happened if Thasper had remained three years old for all his allotted lifetime."

"That was my fault!" cried Imperion. "I take the blame." He turned to Thasper. "Forgive me," he said. "You are my own son."

Was this, Thasper wondered, what Alina meant by the gods blessing her womb? He had not thought it was more than a figure of speech. He looked at Imperion, blinking a little in the god's dazzle. He was not wholly impressed. A fine god, and an honest one, but Thasper could see he had a limited outlook. "Of course I forgive you," he said politely.

"It is also lucky," Chrestomanci said, "that none of you succeeded in killing the Sage. Thasper is a god's son. That means there can only ever be one of him, and because of your prophecy he has to be alive to preach Dissolution. You could have destroyed Theare. As it is, you have caused it to blur into a mass of cracks. Theare is too well organised to divide into two alternative worlds, like my world would. Instead, events have had to happen which could not have happened. Theare has cracked and warped, and you have all but brought about your own Dissolution."

"What can we *do*?" Zond said, aghast.

"There's only one thing you *can* do," Chrestomanci told him. "Let Thasper be. Let him preach Dissolution and stop trying to blow him up. That will bring about free will and a free future. Then either Theare will heal, or it will split, cleanly and painlessly, into two healthy worlds."

"So we bring about our own downfall?" Zond asked mournfully.

"It was always inevitable," said Chrestomanci.

Zond sighed. "Very well. Thasper, son of Imperion, I reluctantly give you my blessing to go forth and preach Dissolution. Go in peace."

Thasper bowed. Then he stood there silent a long time. He did not notice Imperion and Ock both trying to attract his attention. The newspaper report had talked of the Sage as full of anguish and self-doubt. Now he knew why. He looked at Chrestomanci, who was blowing his nose again.

"How can I preach Dissolution?" he said. "How can I not believe in the gods when I have seen them for myself?"

"That's a question you certainly should be asking," Chrestomanci croaked. "Go down to Theare and ask it." Thasper nodded and turned to go. Chrestomanci leaned towards him and said, from behind his handkerchief. "Ask yourself this too: Can the gods catch flu? I think I may have given it to all of them. Find out and let me know, there's a good chap."

TIMEKEEPER

John Morressy

Those of you who have read my comic fantasy anthologies will know John Morressy (b. 1930) for his light-hearted stories of Kedrigern the Wizard, several of which have been collected in book form, starting with A Voice for Princess *(1986), but he's written a lot more besides. There's his epic fantasy series Iron Angel, which began with* Ironbrand *(1980), and his science-fiction novels including the intriguing* The Mansions of Space *(1983). Plus plenty of short stories of which the following introduces quietly and effectively what may be the most powerful enchanter of all.*

A SINGLE LANTERN WAS the only source of light in the shop. Two men stood in the center of the room, spilling out broadening shadows across the floor and against the counter and the empty walls.

The shorter and heavier of the men, the bearer of the lantern, moved. Shadows swooped, and the floor creaked under his weight. He pushed a box into place, stepped on it, and reached up to hang the lantern from a hook depending from the ceiling. This done, he took a few steps to the counter. He blew a swirl of dust from the glass top and rubbed the surface clear with his handkerchief.

"It's only dust, Mr. Bell," he said. "If you decide to take this place, we'll have it spotless before you move in."

The taller man said nothing. With the light behind and above him, only a slight distance over his head, his face was obscured, and his expression could not be seen. The other man continued.

"You won't find a better location in this town, Mr. Bell. You have two nice rooms upstairs for your living quarters, and a large room in back for storage or a workshop. And there's the big display window on the street," he said earnestly.

"I'll take it, Mr. Lockyer," the tall man said.

"A wise decision, Mr. Bell. There's no property in this town more suitable for a jeweler's shop."

"I'm not a jeweler, Mr. Lockyer," Bell corrected him.

Lockyer shook his head vigorously and waved his hand as if to brush away his error. "No, of course not. You're a clockmaster. You mentioned that. Sorry, Mr. Bell."

"I make and repair timepieces. I do not deal in trinkets."

"You're certainly needed here, Mr. Bell. Do you know, if anyone wants a clock or a watch repaired, he has to take it all the way down to Boston? That's a long trip, and, more often than not, it's a waste of time."

"I never waste time, Mr. Lockyer."

"People are going to be mighty glad you came here. And you will be, too. You'll do well here, Mr. Bell," the smaller man said. He paused, smiling at the dark outline of the other, then he went on, "As a matter of fact, I have a watch you might look at when you're all set up. It was my grandfather's originally. Kept perfect time for nearly a century, that watch did, but last year I dropped it on the stone floor down at the railroad station, and that was the end of it. I took it to the best jeweler in Boston, and those people held on to it for nearly six months, and then told me they couldn't do a thing; it was beyond repair."

"Bring it to me."

"Do you think you might be able to replace the works?"

"I'll repair it, Mr. Lockyer," Bell said. "Take it to your office tomorrow."

"I will, Mr. Bell. I'll have the lease all ready for your signature. My men will get to work here first thing tomorrow morning. You'll be able to move in by the end of the week."

"I'll do my own cleaning and move in tomorrow. Just give me the keys."

Lockyer looked uncomfortable. "Well now, it's always been our policy not to turn a place over to a tenant until it's spotless," he said, looking around at the dusty surfaces and cobwebbed corners. "I appreciate your hurry, but I just wouldn't feel right giving you a place in this condition. It needs a good cleaning."

"I always do my own cleaning. Let me have the keys, and I'll be open for business tomorrow afternoon," the tall man said.

"You'll never manage that, Mr. Bell," said the other. "There's too much to be done."

"I know how to make the best use of time, Mr. Lockyer. Come by at six tomorrow, and your watch will be ready."

Lockyer entered the shop a few minutes before six the following evening. He was astonished at the changes that had been wrought in a single day. The windows, the glass countertop, and the display case were all spotless. The floors and woodwork gleamed freshly polished. The shelves were filled with an assortment of clocks. Some were quite ordinary; others were like none that Lockyer had ever seen before.

Bell was not in the shop. Lockyer went to the display case and stooped for a closer look at the clocks behind the glass front. The hour struck, and he was immersed in a medley of sound. Tiny chimes tinkled like tapped crystal; deep-tolling bells and rever-berant mellow gongs vied with chirps and whistles and birdsong in a brief fantasia. Scores of tiny figures came forth to mark the hour each in its own way.

Lockyer found himself drawn to the capering figures of a Harlequin turning handsprings, one for each of the six peals of the little silver bell at the very top of the clock. The figure was smaller than his thumb, yet it moved with supple smoothness, free of the awkward lurching of the clock figures he had seen so many times before. At the sixth stroke the Harlequin turned its final handspring, bowed, and retreated inside a pair of gaily painted doors that shut firmly behind it. Lockyer leaned close, stooping, his hands on his knees, fascinated by the tiny figure's grace. He started at the sound of the clockmaker's voice and straightened quickly to find Bell standing behind the display case.

"I'm sorry if I startled you," the tall man said.

"I was watching. . . . I was fascinated by this," said Lockyer, his eyes returning to the clock now placidly ticking its way to another hour and another performance. "I've never seen a clock like this . . . like any of these."

"You must come again when the hour is striking, and see the others. Some are quite unusual."

"They must be very expensive."

"Some are priceless. Others are less expensive than you might think."

Lockyer leaned down to look more closely at the Harlequin clock. He touched his pudgy fingers to the glass of the case in a childlike gesture, and drew them back quickly in embarrassment. Looking at Bell, he said, "How much is that one?"

"That one is not for sale, Mr Lockyer. I've been offered a great deal of money for it, but I'm not prepared to let my little Harlequin go."

"It's a marvelous piece of work. Everything in the shop is marvelous . . . and you've set it all up so quickly!" Lockyer said with a frank, ingenuous smile. "It's incredible that you accomplished so much in less than a day."

"Would you like your watch, Mr. Lockyer?"

"Oh, surely you haven't had enough time. . . ." Lockyer broke off his protest as Bell drew out his grandfather's watch, bright and new-looking, and held it up for Lockyer to hear. The watch was ticking very softly. Lockyer took it, looked at it in amazement, and held it to his ear again.

"It will keep time for your grandchildren, Mr. Lockyer. And for their grandchildren, too."

Lockyer's expression grew somber, but only for an instant. He asked, "How did you do it? The watchmaker in Boston told me it was ruined. He said no one could fix it."

"There are very few things that can't be fixed. Perhaps I've had more experience than others."

Looking from the watch to Bell in silent wonder, Lockyer said after a time, "It looks brand-new. I must admit, I didn't think you could fix it."

"It was a pleasure, Mr. Lockyer."

The smaller man looked at his watch again, held it to his ear, and shook his head bemusedly. He tucked the watch into his vest pocket and reached for his wallet. "How much will it be?"

Bell raised his hand in an arresting gesture. "There is no charge."

"But you must have put a lot of time and work into this."

"I never charge my first customer."

"You're very generous." Lockyer looked at the shelves behind the display case. "Perhaps . . . you mentioned that some of your clocks are not too expensive, and perhaps . . . I'm sure my wife would be pleased with a nice clock for the mantel."

"Then we shall find one to her liking," Bell said. He walked slowly down the length of shelves, paused, retraced his steps, and at last stopped to take down a clock mounted atop a silver cylinder embellished with enameled swans on a woodland lake. He placed it on the countertop. The clock was silent; its hands were fixed at a minute before twelve.

"It's waiting for its proper owner," he explained.

He touched something at the back, and the clock began to tick. When the hands met at twelve, the cylinder opened, and, to the accompaniment of a sweet melody, a little dark-haired ballerina stepped forth, bowed, and began to dance. Lockyer stared at the figure in astonishment and murmured the single word "Antoinette."

At the last stroke, the tiny dancer withdrew, and the cylinder closed around her. Lockyer continued to stare for a moment, then he rubbed his eyes and looked up at Bell.

"It's uncanny," he said, his voice hushed and slightly hoarse. "We had a daughter. She loved to dance. We hoped that she'd be a ballerina, but it wasn't to be. She died of pneumonia two years ago."

"I'm very sorry, Mr. Lockyer. I hope I've not caused you pain."

"No! Oh no, Mr. Bell. That little dancer is the image of Antoinette as she was when we lost her."

"Then you have your daughter back. Every time the hour strikes, she will dance as she once did."

"My wife would be so happy," said Lockyer, his eyes fixed on the clock. He spoke like a man voicing his private thoughts. "She's never gotten over it, really. She seldom leaves the house anymore. But that clock. . . . I know it must be very expensive, but I'll manage to pay for it somehow."

Bell stated the price. Lockyer gaped at him, and at last cried, "But that's ridiculous! You could sell this clock for a hundred times that much!"

"I choose to sell it to you for exactly that price, no more and no less. Will you have it?"

"I will!"

"Then it is yours," the clockmaster said. He made a quick adjustment at the back, turning the hands to the proper time, and then he took up the clock and handed it back to Lockyer. "It's properly set now. It will require no further adjustment. I hope it brings pleasure to you and your wife."

"It's certain to do that. Thank you, Mr. Bell," Lockyer said as he backed from the counter, the clock cradled in his arms.

The Clockmaker's shop soon became a point of interest in the town. Schoolchildren and idlers clustered outside the window to observe the hourly spectacle. Customers came in increasing numbers, some to bring a watch or clock for repair or adjustment, and some to buy one of the timepieces that Bell sold at such modest prices. All who entered the shop stayed long, entranced by the marvels of workmanship that filled the display case and lined the shelves.

Lockyer was a regular visitor. At least once each week, usually more than that, he showed up at Bell's shop to report on the remarkable accuracy of his watch, to thank Bell for the ballerina clock, and then to examine the latest product of Bell's workshop. He was awed by the speed with which the clockmaker could create his marvelous mechanisms. Every week brought something new.

Late in the year, when Lockyer stopped in the shop on a rainy afternoon, Bell was placing a new clock in the display case. At the sight of Lockyer, the clockmaker smiled and set the clock on the glass top, extending his hand in welcome.

"Would you care to see it work?" he asked.

"Yes, Mr. Bell," said Lockyer eagerly. He put his umbrella in the stand by the door and came to the display case.

He saw a dark sphere, about the size of a cannonball. It appeared to be of crystal, so deep blue that it was almost black. Atop the opaque crystal was a small white-and-gold clock no bigger than a child's fist. The hands of the clock stood at one minute to twelve.

Lockyer studied the crystal, and could distinguish nothing within but darkness. The clock was exquisite, the crystal flawless, but this seemed a disappointingly simple timepiece to come from one who was capable of the intricate and subtle mechanisms that filled the shop.

As if he had read Lockyer's thoughts, Bell said, "It is not quite so simple as it appears." Lockyer glanced sharply up in embarrassment. Bell smiled and set the clockwork going.

It appeared to Lockyer that by the time the hands had met, the darkness in the crystal had softened somewhat. At the first stroke of twelve, a light appeared at the center. With each successive stroke, a new light glowed somewhere in the crystal, and all grew steadily brighter. The outer lights moved about the central one, brightest of them all, and smaller lights, hardly more than pinpoints against the rich blue that now suffused the sphere, circled some of the outer lights. Silent and serene, they moved in stately procession around the bright center. At the ninth revolution, the lights began to fade and the darkness deepen. When the twelfth revolution was completed, only the faint glow at the center of the crystal remained, and then suddenly it was gone, and all within was darkness once again.

"That's marvelous! It's . . . it's the universe!" Lockyer blurted.

"Only a representation of one small part," said Bell, lifting the sphere and placing it in the case.

"It's incredible, Mr. Bell. Incredible. Those lights . . . and the way they move . . . how did you do it?"

"I have my secrets. I thought you'd enjoy seeing this one, Mr. Lockyer. It will not be here after today."

"Are you actually selling that? Who could afford such a—" Lockyer silenced himself abruptly, more embarrassed than before. Bell's dealings were no one's business but his own; if he undervalued his own work, the fact did not seem to trouble him, or to do him any harm.

"I charged a fair price. And the woman who ordered this very special clock for her husband can well afford it."

"Sutterland. It can only be Elizabeth Sutterland." Bell

nodded, but said nothing, and Lockyer went on, "Well, maybe I shouldn't say this, but it hurts me, Mr. Bell, it really hurts me, to think of a beautiful piece of workmanship like this clock being in the hands of a man like Paul Sutterland. He doesn't deserve it."

"Mrs. Sutterland seems to think he does."

"Elizabeth has forgiven him a hundred times, taken him back when he's done things. . . ." Lockyer stopped himself. He gestured angrily, and stood with reddened face, glaring at the dark sphere.

"Perhaps she loves him, Mr. Lockyer."

"If she does, she's a fool. I'm not a prying man, but I can't help hearing things, and if only a fraction of the things I hear about Paul Sutterland and that crowd of his friends are true, Elizabeth should have left him long ago."

"Things may improve, Mr. Lockyer. People do change."

Bitterly, Lockyer said, "Some people do. I know Sutterland, and I know that he'll never change, not if he lives to be a hundred."

"We must hope."

Lockyer nodded impatiently and went to the door. He took his umbrella, put his hand on the doorknob, and then turned to Bell. "Look, Mr. Bell, I'm sorry. I had no right to say the things I said. I got angry for a moment. Elizabeth is an old friend. A lot of people in this town respect her."

"It's perfectly all right, Mr. Lockyer."

"It isn't all right. That's what troubles me. Sutterland is cruel to his wife and children. He treats his servants brutally. And to think of her giving him something so exquisite. . . ." He gestured helplessly.

"As I said, we must hope. Perhaps this anniversary present will mark a turning point for the Sutterlands."

Mrs. Sutterland arrived late that afternoon. She was a beautiful woman, her fine features almost untouched by time, her thick hair a glowing auburn; but years of unhappiness had left their mark in other ways. Her manner was cool and formal, and there was a tautness in her voice that served as a barrier to all but essential conversation.

The sight of the clock changed her. She folded back her veil and looked with unfeigned delight at the motion of the tiny worlds within the sphere. When the last light faded, she turned eagerly to the clockmaker, her eyes aglow, her expression animated.

"Mr. Bell, this is a wonder! I've never seen anything to rival it. My husband will be overwhelmed!" she said exuberantly.

"I'm happy to see you so pleased, Mrs. Sutterland."

"I'm delighted. It's quite beyond anything I expected, Mr. Bell." She placed her gloved hands on the crystal and looked into its dark depths, and as she looked, her expression hardened and weariness seemed to enfold her like a shadow. When she addressed him again, the barrier was in place. "If by any chance the clock should be damaged, Mr. Bell – we will, of course, take the greatest care of such a delicate mechanism, but children and servants can be clumsy – if some mischance should occur—"

"I will repair it," said Bell.

This town, like all towns, had its share of idlers and wastrels. Some of them were frequent observers of the noontime display in Bell's shop window, but, being the sort of men to whom punctuality was not so much a virtue as an imposition, they did not become patrons. Nearly a full year passed from his arrival before one of them visited the shop, and he came only to amuse himself at the clockmaker's expense.

His name was Monson, and he was given to this kind of amusement. He was a portly, florid-faced man with handsome features and a confident manner, well-dressed and well-spoken. He belonged to a prominent and prosperous family, though he himself showed no signs of industry or concern for good repute. He came to the shop one morning, spent a quarter hour examining the clocks on display, and then introduced himself to Bell. "People say you repair damaged clocks and watches," he went on.

"I do," said Bell.

"I've heard that you can repair any watch, no matter how badly it's been damaged."

"People have been satisfied by my work. Perhaps they exaggerate."

"Well, if you're as good as they say, I have a little job for you. It should be no trouble at all for a man of your abilities." Monson drew a dirty rolled-up handkerchief from his pocket, laid it on the countertop, and unfolded it to reveal a jumble of wheels, springs, and tiny bits of metal, a cracked dial; and a bent and battered watchcase. All were encrusted with dried mud, and the case was scored and scratched. When Bell remained silent, Monson said, "Too much for you?", and favored him with a bland smile.

"Perhaps not, Mr. Monson," said Bell.

Monson's smile wavered in the face of this calm response, but he quickly recovered. "It slipped from my fingers and rolled into the roadway. A horse trod it into the dirt, and the wagon wheels rolled right over it. I thought it was beyond fixing, but this watch has sentimental value to me, and so I kept the pieces. Then, when I heard everyone in town singing your praises, I told them I'd bring the watch to you and let you show how good you really are." His smile was a mocking challenge.

"Come back tomorrow at four," Bell said, taking up the handkerchief full of fragments.

"So soon, Mr. Bell? You work fast."

"I do not waste time, Mr. Monson, neither mine nor other people's," Bell replied.

Monson left, and when he joined the friends who had waited for him outside, their laughter could be heard inside the shop. The next day all three came at the appointed hour. Three other men, all well-dressed and in very high spirits, were also present, having entered only a few minutes earlier. They joined the others around Monson when he greeted the clockmaker, placed his palms on the top of the display case, and said boldly, "My watch, if you please, Mr. Bell."

"Your watch, Mr. Monson," said the clockmaker. He placed a small box on the glass and opened it. Inside was a spotless white handkerchief – Monson's own, as the monogram attested – which he unfolded to reveal a watch in excellent condition. The hands were at two minutes past four.

"No, no, Mr. Bell. You must have misunderstood me. I want my own watch, not a replacement," said Monson, shaking his head.

"This is your watch."

Monson took up the watch and inspected it front and back. After a time he said, "It may be my watchcase . . . either the original or a damned clever imitation . . . but even if it is my own, the rest of it. . . ." He put the watch down and shook his head emphatically. "I didn't authorize you to replace the works, I told you to repair them, and you said you would."

"I replaced only those parts that were missing," Bell said. "I repaired your watch, Mr. Monson."

"Nobody could have repaired that watch," said Monson flatly. "I handed you a lot of junk."

"You did indeed. Nevertheless, I repaired the watch. Do you want it, Mr. Monson?"

"Of course I do. It's my watch, isn't it? You said so yourself. But if you think you're going to charge me some outrageous price, you'd better think again. I'm on to that trick."

Bell quoted the price of his repairs. The men with Monson grinned at one another. One of them laughed. Whether Monson, or Bell, or the situation in which they found themselves, was the source of their amusement was not clear, but Monson did not appear to share their feelings. He took the coins from his pocket and dropped them with a clatter on the glass top. He took up the watch, turned, and stalked from the shop without another word.

Later that week, two of the men who had been with Monson came to Bell's shop. They looked over the clocks on display carefully and critically, and finally informed Bell that they intended to buy a clock for their clubroom at the hotel. Nothing on the shelves or in the display case was precisely what they had in mind, one of them explained further, but there were three that might be acceptable, provided the price was low enough. They pointed out the three, and when Bell told them the prices, they gaped at him in astonishment.

"What do you mean, asking prices like those?" one demanded. "There's nobody in this town can pay that kind of money for a clock!"

"I hear that if you like people, you sell them a clock for practically nothing. What's wrong with us that you ask so much? Do we look like fools?" said the other angrily.

"My prices vary," said Bell. "You saw how little I asked from your friend."

"Well then, treat us the same way, if you don't want trouble," said the second man.

Bell did not reply at once. Then, as if he had not heard the threat, or had chosen to ignore it, he said, "You gentlemen have chosen three of the most expensive clocks in my shop. I have others that cost much less."

"If we wanted a cheap clock, we'd go to the general store. We're willing to pay good money for good workmanship, but we won't be gouged."

"Perhaps I can show you something else. The clocks you selected are very delicate. I may have others more suitable for a gentlemen's clubroom," Bell said.

They blustered a bit, but were mollified by what they took as his apology. He went to his storeroom and brought out several sturdy clocks set in brass and polished mahogany, with deep-resounding bells to mark the hour. The price of these clocks was absurdly low. The men examined them and selected one; but even as Bell was packing it carefully in a box for them, one of the men looked longingly at the first clock they had chosen.

"That clock with the little acrobat is still my favorite. Will you reconsider the price?" he asked.

"I set my prices very carefully, gentlemen. It is impossible for me to bargain."

"How does that acrobat work?" asked the other. "That's what fascinates me. I didn't see any wires."

"I didn't see wires on any of them. Be damned if I can figure out how those little people operate. What's your secret, Bell?"

Bell smiled, but said nothing.

"Probably just as well for us to get a good, sturdy clock and not one of those others. They're interesting, but they wouldn't last long once things got boisterous down at the club," said one of the men. The other laughed, and said, "Even a good, solid clock like this one may not last long. What do you say, Bell – if someone bounces this off a wall, will it keep on telling proper time?"

"If anything happens to this clock, come to me," Bell said.

Elizabeth Sutterland revisited the clockmaker's shop in the spring. Bell was at the door, awaiting her arrival, and she waved to him as her carriage pulled up. She entered the shop with the light step of a girl. Folding back her veil, she looked around the shelves and turned to Bell, beaming.

"Mr. Bell, I came at a perfect time – you have a score of new creations on your shelves!" she exclaimed.

"I trust the clock you purchased last year is performing satisfactorily?"

"It hasn't lost a second. And it's such a pleasure to watch. It seems to be just a bit different every time it strikes. The children love it, and Mr. Sutterland is absolutely fascinated by it. He keeps saying that he intends to come here himself and tell you how much pleasure he's gotten from it."

"I look forward to his visit, Mrs Sutterland."

"Well, I hope he gets to it soon. He seems so very tired lately."

"These are busy times," said Bell, ushering Mrs. Sutterland to the counter and seating her.

"Oh, it isn't overwork. He just seems weary. It's almost as if he's gotten much older in the last few months," she said, looking up at the shelves.

Bell did not reply. He followed her gaze, and then reached up to take the clock that had attracted her eye. He set it on top of the counter. She leaned closer, examined it, then looked at him and smiled expectantly. "It's a lovely scene, Mr. Bell. So peaceful. I can't imagine what I'll see when it strikes."

The hands stood at two minutes to three. The clock face was set in a gold dome that canopied a woodland scene; a still pond surrounded by willows. A rowboat about the size of a child's little finger floated near the center of the pond. In it was a figure in a straw hat, dangling a fishing pole in the water. All was serene. When the first chime struck, the fisherman pulled up a tiny fish, unhooked it, and cast his line again, to land a fish at each stroke. The three fish flopped and thrashed in the bottom of the boat. The fisherman took them up and dropped them back into the water. As the ripples spread and faded, he settled in his seat, tilted his hat against the declining sun, lowered his line, and returned to his fishing.

Mrs. Sutterland clapped her hands together in an innocent gesture of sheer delight. "That's wonderful, Mr. Bell!" she exclaimed.

"Thank you, Mrs. Sutterland," he said, taking up the clock to replace it on the shelf. "Is there any other you'd like to see?"

"I love them all, Mr. Bell, but I'm really here to look for something suitable for my mother's birthday."

"Have you a special clock in mind?"

"I was hoping you might have another clock like the one I bought for my husband."

"Alas, no. Each clock is unique," said Bell. "But let me think. I may have something more suitable." He swept the shelves with a slow, searching gaze, then studied the contents of the display case. He stood for a time, frowning, a finger pressed to his lips; then, excusing himself, he withdrew to his workroom. Some minutes later he emerged bearing a delicate white vase that contained twelve red rosebuds.

"A clock, Mr. Bell?" she asked.

He nodded, pointing to a small dial near the base, its hands at one minute to twelve. He set the clock going and placed it before Mrs. Sutterland. As the clock struck, a rosebud opened at each stroke, and a growing fragrance filled the air. She exclaimed softly in wonder and delight.

"Oh, Mr. Bell, it's absolutely perfect!" she said when the last rose was full-blown. "My mother adores roses. I couldn't give her a nicer present."

"I completed this clock only yesterday, Mrs. Sutterland."

"Just in time for Mother's birthday!"

"Exactly on time, it appears," Bell said.

Late in the summer, Paul Sutterland died quietly at his home. He was in his early forties, and showed no evidence of disease; but in his last days, he was a shrunken white-haired man, drained and feeble in body and mind. His widow mourned him sincerely, but there were many in town who counted her fortunate to be free of him.

In the fall, on a dark, rainy day of empty streets, Monson and two of his friends brought their damaged clock to Bell's shop. Monson stood it on top of the display case and stepped back, laughing. The others joined in as Monson pointed to the shattered face.

"One of the lads fancies himself a marksman, Bell. How long will it take you to fix this one?" he asked.

Bell took up the clock and examined it, turning it in his hands. His expression was grave.

"Well, how long? We want it tomorrow. You're a fast worker, aren't you?" said one of the men, glancing at his companions and laughing.

"Too much for you, Bell?" asked Monson. "If you can't fix it, we'll take another one to replace it. A fancy one, one of your special models this time," he added, gesturing toward the shelves.

"Those clocks are not for sale," Bell said.

"You're a hell of a businessman, Bell. You don't want to sell your best goods, and what you do decide to sell, you sell at crazy prices."

"He makes enough on the ones he sells to rich women. Is that it, Bell?" one of Monson's companions asked.

"Yes, what are you up to with Liz Sutterland?" Monson asked. "She spends a good bit of time here, some people say. Don't get any ideas about her, Bell, do you hear me?"

"Leave my shop," said Bell.

"Leave? We're customers, Bell. You're a shopkeeper, and you'll treat us with respect. We want to look over these precious clocks of yours, all these not-for-sale treasures you're hoarding, and you'll show us what we tell you to show us."

"Leave my shop," Bell said once again, his voice level and unchanged. He put down the ruined clock and took a step toward them.

"How about this one?" said Monson, moving swiftly to the shelves and picking up a creation of gold and porcelain and brightly enameled metal on which a single uniformed guardsman stood smartly at attention. "Don't do anything to upset me, now, Bell. I might drop it."

Bell's voice was calm and icy cold. "Put down the clock and leave my shop."

Monson looked at his two friends and grinned. He cried sharply, "Oops! Careful, now!", and feigned dropping the clock, laughing loudly. At his motion the figure was jarred and fell to the floor. Monson quickly replaced the clock on the shelf. "I didn't mean to do that. You should have just kept quiet, Bell. We didn't intend any harm."

"Of course you intended harm. And you've accomplished it."

The atmosphere in the shop had changed in an instant. Bell seemed to loom over the three men; and they, though all of them were more powerfully built than he, and some years younger, now shrank from him. He bent, very gently took up the fallen figure, and raised it close to his eyes.

"You can fix it, Bell," one of the men said.

"Yes, you can fix things like that easily," said the other. "It's not as if we hurt anyone."

"Don't bother about the clock we brought in. It was a joke. Just a joke," said the first.

Monson stepped forward and thrust out his jaw defiantly. His voice was forced and unnaturally loud. "Just a minute. Bell can fix that clock of ours, and there's no reason why he shouldn't. If I did any damage – any real damage – I'm willing to pay for it, as long as it's a fair price. We have nothing to apologize for. We'll pay, and that's the end of it."

Bell raised his eyes from the broken figure in his hand. "I will calculate the proper payment," he said.

The disappearance of Austin Monson and two of his cronies was a matter of general discussion and much speculation around town in the following months. Explanations of all sorts, from the ridiculous to the lurid, circulated for a day or two, then gave way to newer. But as time passed, interest waned, and soon the three vanished men were spoken of only by their friends.

In the year that followed this cause célèbre, Bell's clientele grew to include nearly everyone in town. Even the poorest family, it seemed, could afford to own a clock from his shop. And all his clocks, whatever the price, however simple or elaborate, kept perfect time. No customer was ever dissatisfied.

Bell was always available to a customer or a casual visitor, always willing to demonstrate some ingenious new timepiece. By this time, Lockyer and his wife had become regular weekly visitors; and every week, Bell had a new clock to display, ever more ingenious, sometimes close to magical. When the hour struck, one might see birds take wing or porpoises leap from a miniature sea or bats fly from a ruined belfry; woodsmen felled trees, skaters swooped and spun and cut intricate figures, a trainer put tiny lions and tigers through their paces, jugglers tossed Indian clubs smaller than a grain of rice, archers sent their all but invisible arrows into targets smaller than a fingernail; a sailor danced a hornpipe, a dervish twirled in ecstasy, a stately couple waltzed serenely while a quintet of periwigged musicians played. And never were the movements of these little figures awkward or mechanical, but always smooth and natural; no wires or levers of tracks could be seen, only graceful and disciplined motion, time after time.

Bell seemed to sell his clocks as quickly as he could make them. Even those that were not for sale left the shop, to be replaced on the shelves by new ones. Only a few were permanent. The little Harlequin whose acrobatics had captivated Lockyer on his first visit to the shop was still in place. The fire-breathing dragon on his hoard of gold and precious gems and skeletons in armor was still in a corner of the window, slouching forth every hour to the terror and delight of all the children. And a trim little pavilion of gold and porcelain and bright stripes of red and blue enameled metal, before which a single uniformed guardsman marched and counter-marched every hour while a piper and a drummer marked the beat, stood where it had been for as long as Lockyer could recall; a year, at the very least.

During the holiday season, Bell's shop was a crowded, busy place, cheerful and lively. Those few townspeople who did not yet own one of his clocks were finally about to make a purchase, and others wished to buy one as a special gift for a relative or a friend. How he managed to do it no one knew, but Bell met the increased demand and even produced a magnificent new clock, a lighted cathedral with carolers before its steps and a choir of angels hovering over its spires. He placed it in the window three days before Christmas, and every passerby stopped to marvel.

In the cold, dark days of the new year, the mood of the town changed. No one criticized Bell or his work, or complained of his prices, but now the shop was often empty, no customers visiting for two or three days running. The Lockyers still came regularly, sometimes bringing their infant daughter. They noticed no change in Bell's manner and heard no word of complaint from him, but they sensed a difference that they could not explain to one another.

New rumors had begun in the clubroom where Monson's friends still gathered. Here they drank, and brooded, and their idle minds dwelt on the still-unexplained disappearance of their old companions. As rumors do, their stories fed on themselves, and interwove one with another, corroborating exaggeration with misstatement and validating both with falsehood. In time they became firmly convinced of their own imaginings.

Bell was the culprit, said the rumormongers. Why? Envy, of course. That was plain to anyone who knew the facts. Monson had shown him up, made him look foolish. The ridiculous clockmaker had thought himself a rival for the widow's affections – fancy a woman like her wedded to a shopkeeper! – and when he learned of her preference for Monson, jealousy added to envy had pushed him to desperation. Monson had put him in his place, and he had sought revenge. It was obvious. Just what he had done to his rival, and how, and why he had included others in his deed, was not clear – Bell was too crafty to leave evidence that would give him away; no one questioned his shrewdness – but he was the guilty party, that was plain to any reasonable person, and he must be brought to justice.

At first the townspeople laughed at these wild tales, considering their source and their probable motive. But they heard them again and again, and in time a tiny seed of something – not quite doubt, but perhaps a vague and reluctant uncertainty – took root in their minds. What was said so often, so earnestly, could not be completely without foundation, they told themselves. Not that they believed a word of it – but Bell was a mysterious man; no one would deny that. Where had he come from, and why had he come to this town? How could a man price his wares so erratically and stay in business, even prosper? Who bought those expensive clocks, and what became of the ones that were not for sale but nevertheless vanished from the shelves? How could anyone produce mechanisms of such delicacy and precision so quickly and yet so perfectly, and still turn out sturdy, serviceable clocks at bargain prices? And if it was indeed true that Monson and his friends had been talking about visiting Bell on the very day of their disappearance, then the clockmaker owed the town an explanation. No amount of good workmanship, not even genius, exempted a man from the common judgment, said the good citizens. The rumors grew more insistent, the issue more troublesome, the questions more pointed, as spring drew near.

One evening, when the shop was closed and the streets empty, Lockyer tapped at the clockmaker's back door. Bell was in his workroom, as he usually was in the evening hours, and he opened the door after a short delay.

"Mr. Bell, you must seek protection." Lockyer said without preamble when the door opened.

"I need no protection," Bell replied.

"You do," Lockyer insisted. "You must know the stories that are going around town."

"I have heard foolish rumors," Bell conceded.

"You and I know that they're foolish, but others in town are beginning to believe them. There's talk of coming to your shop and demanding an account of Monson's disappearance."

Bell's voice was unperturbed. "My shop will be open at the usual hour. I have always been willing to answer reasonable questions. Will you come in, Mr. Lockyer?"

"No, no, I can't," said Lockyer, drawing back. "But you must do something to protect yourself. Monson's friends are behind this, and they want to hurt you. They may break in on you in the night."

"Will the townspeople permit this?"

Lockyer hesitated, then lamely replied, "No one wants anything to happen to you. But Monson's friends have everyone confused. They have a lot of influence in this town; some of them do, anyway. And the people have heard so many stories that they don't know what to believe. They're confused."

"So I must fear the actions of a lawless mob."

"I'm afraid that's the case. You must protect yourself."

"I will, Mr. Lockyer," said Bell. Without another word, he closed the door. Lockyer heard the bolt slide into place.

They came to the shop later that night, eleven men strong. Others waited outside, at front and back. Several had been customers at one time or another, and some had come on occasion to observe the clocks as they struck the hour, or watched the display in the window. Three who had been present when Bell had presented Monson with his repaired watch were the leaders. The others did not speak.

"We're here to find out what you did to our friends, Bell. We're not leaving until we're satisfied," said one, planting himself in front of the clockmaker.

"Why do you blame me?" Bell asked, looking calmly down on him.

"They said they were coming here. We all heard them say that. And then we never saw them again. You're the one behind their disappearance, all right."

"Just admit it, Bell. We can make you tell us everything, if you force us to," one of the others said. He raised a walking stick and tapped it on the glass top of the display case.

"We can smash this place to bits, and you with it," said the first. "Now, tell us what you did to our friends."

Bell looked down at him, then at the man with the walking stick, then at such others as met his glance. He raised his hand and pointed to the door. "It is best that you leave my shop," he said.

"Best for you, that's certain. But we're not leaving," said the first man, and several of the others, under the challenge of his ferocious gaze, murmured their agreement.

"Don't try to bluff us, Bell. You've bluffed this whole town for too long. Answer our questions, or it's going to get mighty unpleasant," said the second. He brought his stick down sharply. The glass cracked.

Then, suddenly, at exactly nine minutes past the hour of one, all the clocks in the shop began to strike in unison. Deep gongs and crystalline chimes, resonant bells and the sound of tiny drums and trumpets, music and birdsong and a din of indistinguishable pealings and tollings and clangings, all blended to engulf the intruders in a wave of sound; and on and on they struck, twelve times and twelve more and twelve times twelve more, rapidly at first, and then steadily diminishing in volume and rapidity, fading as if they were receding at a steady rate, becoming ever fainter until they could be heard no more.

The men stood benumbed by the assault of sound. They felt no pain and sensed no restraint by external force. Not one of them carried any trace of physical harm as a result of that night. Their breath came freely; they could move their eyes and hear every sound. But their bodies were held, as if the air had grown viscid and glutinous, clinging to them, dragging at them like thick mud or heavy snow, but a thousand times more inhibitive than mud or snow because, invisible and insensible as it was, it clung not only to their feet and legs, but to their hands, arms, heads, and bodies. They felt as if time itself had crawled almost to a halt, congealing and trapping them within it like insects in amber.

Those who spoke of that night – and few of them ever did so, and those few reluctantly, after long silence, and still fearful of ridicule – agreed on several points. Bell, they all said, was untouched by the phenomenon. He removed the clocks from the shelves and the window and the display case, one by one, carefully and lovingly, and took them into his workroom. This process took some time, several hours at least, but none of the men felt the pain or cramping that such a long period of enforced immobility, or near immobility, would be certain to cause. Bell worked methodically, ignoring the intruders, his attention confined to his clocks.

On these facts all agreed, but each had his own particular memory of that night. According to one man, the shop grew steadily darker; another said that the light remained constant, but Bell himself moved ever more swiftly, until at last he moved too fast for the eye to follow, and vanished from sight; a third man claimed that Bell grew more insubstantial and wraithlike with each timepiece he removed, and at last simply faded into nothingness. One man recalled a sight of a fly that passed before his face so slowly that he could count the beats of its wings. The fly progressed no more than a foot; and yet the man swore that its passage consumed three hours, at the very least. One of his companions spoke of the disturbing sight of ash fallen from the cigar in the hand of a man standing near him: it fell to the ground so slowly that in all the time he stood confined, no less than four hours by his calculation, it had not reached the floor. Two other men mentioned their awareness of each tick of a clock, separated by an agonizing interval. One claimed a full hour's space, while the other spoke only of "a horrible long wait" between one tick and the next.

Whatever happened on that night, however it happened, when the men could move – and their immobility ended in an instant, without warning – Bell and all the clocks were gone.

Five men fled the shop in terror the instant they had command of their legs. Those who remained did so more from fear of showing fear than from courage, or even anger. They looked to one another uncertainly, awaiting direction, and finally someone said, "We have to go after him."

The workroom was dark and empty. They drew the bolt on the

back door, and one shouted to the others waiting outside, "Did you see him?"

A man carrying a pick handle emerged from the shadows. "Didn't see nobody. Nobody's come out that door."

"Are you sure?"

"Of course we're sure, damn it!" called an unseen voice near at hand. "What happened? Bell get away from you?"

They did not reply. They returned to the shop, and noticed something that had escaped them in the first shock of freedom. The shop was thick in dust, and cobwebs hung from the ceiling and rounded the upper corners of the shelves. The air was stale, like that of a room long sealed. As they looked around them, the clock in the town hall struck the quarter hour. One man looked at his watch and announced in a hushed voice, "One-fifteen."

No one ever learned what became of the clockmaker. No clocks like his were ever seen again by any of the townspeople, even those who traveled widely and took an interest in such things. Those that he sold have been passed on through three or four or even five generations. They keep perfect time, and have never required repair.

THE DOUBLE SHADOW

Clark Ashton Smith

Clark Ashton Smith (1893–1961) was alleged to read a dictionary most days for relaxation, delighting in the more obscure and magical sounding words. I don't know how true that is, but it wouldn't surprise me. Every time you read a Smith story you need to keep the dictionary handy. Why call someone a wizard when he could be a thaumaturge? Why have a shadow when it could be an adumbration? The words maketh the story, and in the eyes of Smith, who began his literary career as a poet, before becoming engulfed by the wonder of weird fiction, the words created the worlds. Although his writing life spanned fifty years, most of his weird fiction was concentrated into a decade from about 1928–1937 when there was a phenomenal outpouring of strange and exotic stories, mostly for the greatest of all pulps, Weird Tales. *Stories set in Atlantis, Xiccarph, Zothique, Hyperborea or Averoigne – the very names conjure up the magical and the mystical. His work has been collected in several volumes published by Arkham House, including* Out of Space and Time *(1942),* Lost Worlds *(1944),* Genius Loci *(1948) and* Tales of Science and Sorcery *(1964), with a more recent "best of" selection,* A Rendezvous in Averoigne *(1988).*

When I was compiling this anthology and testing out ideas for stories with other enthusiasts, Clark Ashton Smith was the one name that everyone suggested as the premier writer of sorcerous tales. I thought so, too. And Smith regarded "The Double Shadow" as his best weird tale, so here's the best from the best.

M Y NAME IS PHARPETRON, among those who have known me in Poseidonis: but even I, the last and most forward pupil of the wise Avyctes, know not the name of that which I am fated to become ere tomorrow, therefore, by the ebbing silver lamps, in my master's marble house above the loud sea, I write this tale with a hasty hand, scrawling an ink of wizard virtue on the gray, priceless, antique parchment of dragons. And having written, I shall enclose the pages in a sealed cylinder of orichalchum, and shall cast the cylinder from a high window into the sea, lest that which I am doomed to become should haply destroy the writing. And it may be that mariners from Lephara, passing to Umb and Pneor in their tall triremes, will find the cylinder; or fishers will draw it from the wave in their seines; and having read my story, men will learn the truth and take warning; and no man's feet, henceforward, will approach the pale and demon-haunted house of Avyctes.

For six years I have dwelt apart with the aged master, forgetting youth and its wonted desires in the study of arcanic things. We have delved more deeply than all others before us in an interdicted lore; we have called up the dwellers in sealed crypts, in fearful abysses beyond space. Few are the sons of mankind who have cared to seek us out among the bare, wind-worn crags; and many, but nameless, are the visitants who have come to us from further bourns of place and time.

Stern and white as a tomb is the mansion wherein we dwell. Far below, on black, naked reefs, the northern sea climbs and roars indomitably, or ebbs with a ceaseless murmur as of armies of baffled demons; and the house is filled evermore, like a hollow-sounding sepulcher, with the drear echo of its tumultuous voices; and the winds wail in dismal wrath around the high towers but shake them not. On the seaward side the mansion rises sheerly from the straight-falling cliff; but on the other sides there are narrow terraces, grown with dwarfish, crooked cedars that bow always beneath the gales. Giant marble monsters guard the landward portals; and huge marble women ward the strait porticos above the surf; and mighty statues and mummies stand everywhere in the chambers and along the halls. But, saving these, and the entities we have summoned, there is none to companion us; and liches and shadows have been the servitors of our daily needs.

Not without terror (since man is but mortal) did I, the neophyte, behold at first the abhorrent and tremendous faces of them that obeyed Avyctes. I shuddered at the black writhing of submundane things from the many-volumed smoke of the braziers; I cried in horror at the gray foulnesses, colossal, without form, that crowded malignly about the drawn circle of seven colors, threatening unspeakable trespass on us that stood at the center. Not without revulsion did I drink wine that was poured by cadavers, and eat bread that was purveyed by phantoms. But use and custom dulled the strangeness, destroyed the fear; and in time I believed implicitly that Avyctes was the lord of all incantations and exorcisms, with infallible power to dismiss the beings he evoked.

Well had it been for Avyctes – and for me – if the master had contented himself with the lore preserved from Atlantis and Thule, or brought over from Mu. Surely this should have been enough: for in the ivory-sheeted books of Thule there were blood-writ runes that would call the demons of the fifth and seventh planets if spoken aloud at the hour of their ascent; and the sorcerers of Mu had left record of a process whereby the doors of far-future time could be unlocked; and our fathers, the Atlanteans, had known the road between the atoms and the path into far stars. But Avyctes thirsted for a darker knowledge, a deeper empery. . . . And into his hands, in the third year of my novitiate, there came the mirror-bright tablet of the lost serpent people.

At certain hours, when the tide had fallen from the steep rocks, we were wont to descend by cavern-hidden stairs to a cliff-walled crescent beach behind the promontory on which stood Avyctes' house. There, on the dun, wet sands, beyond the foamy tongues of the surf, would lie the worn and curious driftage of alien shores and trove the hurricanes had cast up from unsounded deeps. And there we had found the purple and sanguine volutes of great shells, and rude lumps of ambergris, and white flowers of perpetually blooming coral; and once, the barbaric idol of green brass that had been the figurehead of a galley from far hyperborcal isles. . . .

There had been a great storm, such as must have riven the sea to its last profound; but the tempest had gone by with morning, and the heavens were cloudless on that fatal day; and the demon winds were hushed among the black crags and chasms; and the sea lisped with a low whisper, like the rustle of gowns of samite trailed by fleeing maidens on the sand. And just beyond the ebbing wave, in a tangle of russet sea-weed, we descried a thing that glittered with blinding sun-like brilliance.

And running forward, I plucked it from the wrack before the wave's return, and bore it to Avyctes.

The tablet was wrought of some nameless metal, like never-rusting iron, but heavier. It had the form of a triangle and was broader at the widest than a man's heart. On one side it was wholly blank, like a mirror. On the other side many rows of small crooked ciphers were incised deeply in the metal, as if by the action of some mordant acid; and these ciphers were not the hieroglyphs or alphabetic characters of any language known to the master or to me.

Of the tablet's age and origin we could form no conjecture; and our erudition was wholly baffled. For many days thereafter we studied the writing and held argument that came to no issue. And night by night, in a high chamber closed against the perennial winds, we pondered over the dazzling triangle by the tall straight flames of silver lamps. For Avyctes deemed that knowledge of rare value, some secret of an alien or elder magic, was held by the clueless crooked ciphers. Then, since all our scholarship was in vain, the master sought another divination, and had recourse to wizardry and necromancy. But at first, among all the devils and phantoms that answered our interrogation, none could tell us aught concerning the tablet. And any other than Avyctes would have despaired in the end . . . and well would it have been if he had despaired, and had sought no longer to decipher the writing.

The months and years went by with a slow thundering of seas on the dark rocks, and a headlong clamor of winds around the white towers. Still we continued our delving and evocations; and farther, always farther we went into the lampless realms of space and spirit; learning, perchance, to unlock the hithermost of the manifold infinities. And at whiles Avyctes would resume his pondering of the sea-found tablet, or would question some visitant regarding its interpretation.

At length, by the use of a chance formula, in idle experiment, he summoned up the dim, tenuous ghost of a sorcerer from prehistoric years; and the ghost, in a thin whisper of uncouth, forgotten speech, informed us that the letters on the tablet were those of a language of the serpent-men, whose primal continent had sunk eons before the lifting of Hyperborea from the ooze. But the ghost could tell us naught of their significance; for, even in his time, the serpent-people had become a dubious legend; and their deep, antehuman lore and sorcery were things irretrievable by man.

Now, in all the books of conjuration owned by Avyctes, there was no spell whereby we could call the lost serpent-men from their fabulous epoch. But there was an old Lemurian formula, recondite and uncertain, by which the shadow of a dead man could be sent into years posterior to those of his own lifetime, and could be recalled after an interim by the wizard. And the shade, being wholly insubstantial, would suffer no harm from the temporal transition, and would remember, for the information of the wizard, that which he had been instructed to learn during the journey.

So, having called again the ghost of the prehistoric sorcerer, whose name was Ybith, Avyctes made a singular use of several very ancient gums and combustible fragments of fossil wood; and he and I, reciting the responses of the formula, sent the thin spirit of Ybith into the far ages of the serpent-men.

And after a time which the master deemed sufficient, we performed the curious rites of incantation that would recall Ybith. And the rites were successful; and Ybith stood before us again, like a blown vapor that is nigh to vanishing. And in words faint as the last echo of perishing memories, the specter told us the key to the meaning of the letters, which he had learned in the prehuman past. And after this, we questioned Ybith no more but suffered him to return unto slumber and oblivion.

Then, knowing the import of the tiny, twisted ciphers, we read the tablet's writing and made thereof a transliteration, though not without labor and difficulty, since the very phonetics of the serpent tongue, and the symbols and ideas, were somewhat alien to those of mankind. And when we had mastered the inscription, we found that it contained the formula for a certain evocation which, no doubt, had been used by the serpent sorcerers. But the object of the evocation was not named; nor was there any clue to the nature or identity of that which would come in answer to the rites. And, moreover, there was no corresponding rite of exorcism nor spell of dismissal.

Great was Avyctes' jubilation, deeming that we had learned a lore beyond the memory or prevision of man. And though I sought to dissuade him, he resolved to employ the evocation, arguing that our discovery was no chance thing but was fatefully predestined from the beginning. And he seemed to think lightly of the menace that might be brought upon us by the conjuration of things whose nativity and attributes were wholly obscure. "For," said Avyctes, "I have called up, in all the years of my sorcery, no god or devil, no demon or lich or shadow which I could not control and dismiss at will. And I am loath to believe that any spirit or power beyond the subversion of my spells could have been summoned by a race of serpents, whatever their skill in necromancy and demonism."

So, seeing that he was obstinate, and acknowledging him for my master in all ways, I agreed to aid Avyctes in the experiment, though not without misgivings. And then we gathered together, in the chamber of conjuration, at the specified hour and configuration of the stars, the equivalents of sundry rare materials that the tablet had instructed us to use in the ritual.

Of much that we did, and of certain agents that we employed, it were better not to tell; nor shall I record the shrill, sibilant words, difficult for beings not born of serpents to articulate, whose intonation formed a signal part of the ceremony. Toward the last, we drew a triangle on the marble floor with the fresh blood of birds; and Avyctes stood at one angle, and I at another; and the gaunt umber mummy of an Atlantean warrior, whose name had been Oigos, was stationed at the third angle. And standing thus, Avyctes and I held tapers of corpse-tallow in our hands, till the tapers had burned down between our fingers as into a socket. And in the outstretched palms of the mummy of Oigos, as if in shallow thuribles, talc and asbestos burned, ignited by a strange fire whereof we knew the secret. At one side we had traced on the floor an infrangible ellipse, made by an endless linked repetition of the twelve unspeakable Signs of Oumor, to which we could retire if the visitant should prove inimical or rebellious. We waited while the pole-circling stars went over, as had been prescribed. Then, when the tapers had gone out between our seared fingers, and the talc and asbestos were wholly consumed in the mummy's eaten palms, Avyctes uttered a single word whose sense was obscure to us; and Oigos, being animated by sorcery and subject to our will, repeated the word after a given interval, in tones that were hollow as a tomb-born echo; and I, in my turn, also repeated it.

Now, in the chamber of evocation, before beginning the ritual, we had opened a small window giving upon the sea, and had likewise left open a high door on the hall to landward, lest that which came in answer to us should require a spatial mode of entrance. And during the ceremony, the sea became still and there was no wind, and it seemed that all things were hushed in expectation of the nameless visitor. But after all was done, and the last word had been repeated by Oigos and me, we stood and waited vainly for a visible sign or other manifestation. The lamps burned stilly; and no shadows fell, other than were cast by ourselves and Oigos and by the great marble women along the walls. And in the magic mirrors we had placed cunningly, to reflect those that were otherwise unseen, we beheld no breath or trace of any image.

At this, after a given interim, Avyctes was sorely disappointed, deeming that the evocation had failed of its purpose; and I, having the same thought, was secretly relieved. We questioned the mummy of Oigos, to learn if he had perceived in the room, with such senses as are peculiar to the dead, the sure token or doubtful proof of a presence undescried by us the living. And the mummy gave a necromantic answer, saying that there was nothing.

"Verily," said Avyctes, "it were useless to wait longer. For surely in some way we have misunderstood the purport of the writing, or have failed to duplicate the matters used in the evocation, or the correct intonement of the words. Or it may be that in the lapse of so many eons, the thing that was formerly wont to respond has long ceased to exist, or has altered in its attributes, so that the spell is now void and valueless."

To this I assented readily, hoping that the matter was at an end. And afterward we resumed our habitual studies, but made no mention to each other of the strange tablet or the vain formula.

Even as before, our days went on; and the sea climbed and roared in white fury on the cliffs; and the winds wailed by in their unseen, sullen wrath, bowing the dark cedars as witches are bowed by the breath of Taaran, god of Evil. Almost, in the marvel of new tests and cantraips, I forgot the ineffectual conjuration; and I deemed that Avyctes had forgotten it.

All things were as of yore, to our sorcerous perception; and there was naught to trouble us in our wisdom and power and serenity, which we deemed secure above the sovereignty of kings. Reading the horoscopic stars, we found no future ill in their aspect; nor was any shadow of bale foreshown to us through geomancy, or such other modes of divination as we employed. And our familiars, though grisly and dreadful to mortal gaze, were wholly obedient to us the masters.

Then, on a clear summer afternoon, we walked, as was often our custom, on the marble terrace behind the house. In robes of ocean-purple, we paced among the windy trees with their blown crooked shadows; and there, following us, I saw the blue shadow of Avyctes and my own shadow on the marble; and between them, an adumbration that was not wrought by any of the cedars. And I was greatly startled, but spoke not of the matter to Avyctes, and observed the unknown shadow with covert care.

I saw that it followed closely the master's shadow, keeping ever the same distance. And it fluttered not in the wind, but moved with a flowing as of some heavy, thick and purulent liquid; and its color was not blue nor purple nor black, nor any other hue to which man's eyes are habituated, but a hue as of some darker putrescence than that of death: and its form was altogether monstrous, seeming to move as if cast by one that trod erect, but having the squat head and long, undulant body of things that should creep rather than walk.

Avyctes heeded not the shadow, and still I feared to speak, though I thought it an ill thing for the master to be companioned thus. And I moved closer to him, in order to detect by touch or other perception the invisible presence that had cast the adumbration. But the air was void to sunward of the shadow; and I found nothing opposite the sun nor in any oblique direction, though I searched closely, knowing that certain beings cast their shadows in such wise.

After a while, at the customary hour, we returned by the coiling stairs and monster-flanked portals into the house. And I saw that the strange adumbration moved ever behind the shadow of Avyctes, falling horrible and unbroken on the steps and passing clearly separate and distinct amid the long umbrage of the towering monsters. And in the dim halls beyond the sun, where shadows should not have been, I beheld with terror the loathly, distorted blot, having a pestilential hue without name, that followed Avyctes as if in lieu of his own extinguished shadow. And all that day, everywhere that we went, at the table served by specters, or in the mummy-warded room of volumes and books, the thing pursued Avyctes, clinging to him even as leprosy to the leper. And still the master had perceived it not; and still I forbore to warn him, hoping that the visitant would withdraw in its own time, going obscurely as it had come.

But at midnight, when we sat together by the silver lamps, pondering the blood-writ runes of Hyperborea, I saw that the shadow had drawn closer to the shadow of Avyctes, towering behind his chair on the wall. And the thing was a streaming ooze of charnel pollution, a foulness beyond the black leprosies of hell; and I could bear it no more; and I cried out in my fear and loathing, and informed the master of its presence.

Beholding now the shadow, Avyctes considered it closely; and there was neither fear nor awe nor abhorrence in the deep-graven wrinkles of his visage. And he said to me at last: "This thing is a mystery beyond my lore: but never, in all the practise of my art, has any shadow come to me unbidden. And since all others of our evocations have found answer ere this, I must deem that the shadow is a very entity, or the shade or sign of an entity, that has come in belated response to the formula of the serpent-sorcerers, which we thought powerless and void. And I think it well that we should now repair to the chamber of conjuration, and interrogate the shadow in such manner as we may."

We went forthwith into the chamber of conjuration, and made such preparations as were both needful and possible. And when we were prepared to question it, the unknown shadow had drawn closer still to the shadow of Avyctes, so that the clear space between the two was no wider than the thickness of a necromancer's rod.

Now, in all feasible ways, we interrogated the shadow, speaking through our own lips and the lips of mummies and statues. But there was no answer; and calling certain of the devils and phantoms that were our familiars, we made question through the mouths of these, but without result. And all the while, our mirrors were void of any presence that might have cast the shadow; and they that had been our spokesmen could detect nothing in the room. And there was no spell, it seemed, that had power upon the visitant. So Avyctes became troubled; and drawing on the floor with blood and ashes the ellipse of Oumor, wherein no demon nor spirit may intrude, he retired to its center. But still, within the ellipse, like a flowing taint of liquid corruption, the shadow followed his shadow; and the space between the two was no wider than the thickness of a wizard's pen.

On the face of Avyctes, horror had graved new wrinkles; and his brow was beaded with a deathly sweat. For he knew, even as I, that this was a thing beyond all laws, and foreboding naught but untold disaster and evil. And he cried to me in a shaken voice, and said:

"I have no knowledge of this thing nor its intention toward me, and no power to stay its progress. Go forth and leave me now: for I would not that any man should witness the defeat of my sorcery and the doom that may follow thereupon. Also, it were well to depart while there is yet time, lest you too should become the quarry of the shadow . . ."

Though terror had fastened upon my inmost soul, I was loath to leave Avyctes. But I had sworn to obey his will at all times and in every respect; and moreover I knew myself doubly powerless against the adumbration, since Avyctes himself was impotent.

So, bidding him farewell, I went forth with trembling limbs from the haunted chamber; and peering back from the threshold, I saw that the alien umbrage, creeping like a noisome blotch on the floor, had touched the shadow of Avyctes. And at that moment the master shrieked aloud like one in nightmare; and his face was no longer the face of Avyctes but was convulsed and contorted like that of some helpless madman who wrestles with an unseen incubus. And I looked no more, but fled along the dim outer hall and through the portals giving upon the terrace.

A red moon, ominous and gibbous, had declined above the

crags; and the shadows of the cedars were elongated in the moon; and they wavered in the gale like the blown cloaks of enchanters. And stooping against the gale, I fled across the terrace toward the outer stairs that led to a steep path in the waste of rocks and chasms lying behind Avyctes' house. I neared the terrace-edge, running with the speed of fear; but I could not reach the topmost outer stair: for at every step the marble flowed beneath me, fleeing like a pale horizon before the seeker. And though I raced and panted without pause, I could draw no nearer to the terrace-edge.

At length I desisted, seeing that an unknown spell had altered the very space around the house of Avyctes, so that none could escape therefrom. So, resigning myself to whatever might befall, I returned toward the house. And climbing the white stairs in the low, level beams of the crag-caught moon, I saw a figure that awaited me in the portals. And I knew by the trailing robe of sea-purple, but by no other token, that the figure was Avyctes. For the face was no longer in its entirety the face of man, but was become a loathly fluid amalgam of human features with a thing not to be identified on earth. The transfiguration was ghastlier than death or decay; and the face was already hued with the nameless, corrupt and purulent color of the strange shadow; and its outlines had assumed a partial likeness to the squat profile of the shadow. The hands of the figure were not those of any terrene being; and the shape beneath the robe had lengthened with a nauseous undulant pliancy; and the face and fingers seemed to drip in the moonlight with a deliquescent corruption. And the pursuing umbrage, like a thickly flowing blight, had corroded and distorted the very shadow of Avyctes, which was now double in a manner not to be narrated here.

Fain would I have cried or spoken aloud: but horror had dried up the font of speech. And the thing that had been Avyctes beckoned me in silence, uttering no word from its living and putrescent lips. And with eyes that were no longer eyes but an oozing abomination, it peered steadily upon me. And it clutched my shoulder closely with the soft leprosy of its fingers, and led me half swooning with revulsion along the hall, and into that room where the mummy of Oigos, who had assisted us in the threefold incantation of the serpent-men, was stationed with several of his fellows.

By the lamps which illumed the chamber, burning with pale, still, perpetual flames, I saw that the mummies stood erect along the wall in their exanimate repose, each in his wonted place, with his tall shadow beside him. But the great, gaunt shadow of Oigos on the wall was companioned by an adumbration similar in all respects to the evil thing that had followed the master and was now incorporate with him. I remembered that Oigos had performed his share of the ritual, and had repeated an unknown stated word in turn after Avyctes; and so I knew that the horror had come to Oigos in turn and would wreak itself upon the dead even as upon the living. For the foul, anonymous thing that we had called in our presumption could manifest itself to mortal ken in no other way than this. We had drawn it from fathomless deeps of time and space, using ignorantly a dire formula; and the thing had come at its own chosen hour, to stamp itself in abomination uttermost on the evocators.

Since then, the night had ebbed away, and a second day has gone by like a sluggish ooze of horror. . . . I have seen the complete identification of the shadow with the flesh and the shadow of Avyctes . . . and also I have seen the slow encroachment of that other umbrage, mingling itself with the lank shadow and the sere, bituminous body of Oigos, and turning them to a similitude of the thing which Avyctes has become. And I have heard the mummy cry out like a living man in great pain and fear, as with the throes of a second dissolution, at the impingement of the shadow. And long since it has grown silent, like the other horror, and I know not its thoughts or its intent. . . . And verily I know not if the thing that has come to us be one or several; nor if its avatar will rest complete with the three that summoned it forth into time, or be extended to others.

But these things, and much else, I shall soon know: for now, in turn, there is a shadow that follows mine, drawing ever closer. The air congeals and curdles with unknown fear; and they that were our familiars have fled from the mansion; and the great marble women seem to tremble visibly where they stand along the walls. But the horror that was Avyctes, and the second horror that was Oigos, have left me not, and neither do they tremble. With eyes that are not eyes, they seem to brood and watch, waiting till I too shall become as they. And their stillness is more terrible than if they had rended me limb from limb. And there are strange voices in the wind, and alien roarings upon the sea; and the walls quiver like a thin veil in the black breath of remote abysses.

So, knowing that the time is brief, I have shut myself in the room of volumes and books and have written this account. And I have taken the bright triangular tablet, whose solution was our undoing, and have cast it from the window into the sea, hoping that none will find it after us. And now I must make an end, and enclose this writing in the sealed cylinder of orichalchum, and fling it forth to drift upon the sea-wave. For the space between my shadow and the shadow of the horror is straitened momently . . . and the space is no wider than the thickness of a wizard's pen.

THE RITE STUFF

Michael Kurland

When Michael Kurland (b. 1938) appeared as a character in Chester Anderson's The Butterfly Kid, *he came back with his own sequel* The Unicorn Girl *(1969), which established his reputation. At the time Kurland was the editor of the music paper* Crawdaddy. *Although he continues to write the occasional science-fiction novel, such as the alternate-history escapade* The Whenabouts of Burr *(1975) and the interplanetary adventure* Star Griffin *(1987), he has been drawn more to mystery fiction in recent years. Fortunately Kurland is able to blur the borders between mystery and fantasy so that his novels of Sherlock Holmes's nemesis James Moriarty, which began with* The Infernal Device *(1979), and his continuation of the Lord Darcy stories of Randall Garrett,* Ten Little Wizards *(1988) and* A Study in Sorcery *(1989), will be enjoyed by fantasy and mystery fans alike. The same goes for the following.*

In this infinite continuum with its complex multiplicity of universes and dimensions all things are possible. This is one of those things.

T HE DAY WAS CLEAR and cold, as it often is in early March in San Francisco. A muckle of fog was rolling in from the ocean, squatting like a vast, misshapen troll on the hills to the west, and flicking its many tongues at me as I walked down Polk Street toward the old Victorian where Jonathan Stryk lived and worked.

A box hedge stirred with the breeze as I passed, and further along the street some wind chimes above a doorway jingled melodically at my approach. But the air around me was still. I paused. A newspaper in the street ahead of me ruffled its pages, and the branches stirred on the California Pine at the curb. Was I being followed by a wind elemental? Such things were not random. Was someone interested in my comings and goings? I am Inspector Peter Frey, a detective in the Impossible Crimes Division of the San Francisco Police Department, and it is neither desirable nor safe for my comings and goings to be monitored by an outside agency.

I turned the corner on to California Street, where the square brownstone monastery of the Brothers of Eternal Damnation stands cater-corner from the black concrete structure of the Brothers of Perpetual Torment. A line of men stood patiently outside the Damned Brothers' wicket gate, a few cringing under the glare of the great stone head of T. Leseaux peering over the wall by the gate. They were awaiting the three o'clock bell, when the gate would be opened long enough to admit them, and have the men sorted out according to their abilities and their desires. The great majority of them would leave tomorrow morning sorely disappointed, but one or two perhaps would be told that they had some trace of Power that might be cultivated. They would then have to decide whether the prize, a highly-developed ability to use some possibly arcane mantic skill, was worth the price: ten years of poverty, shaven head, strict obedience to some rather arbitrary rules, a ridiculous-looking monks' get-up, a diet of corn meal mush and termites (so I have been told), and praying to some gods, the names of which most of us would rather not say aloud.

When, back in the 1860s, T. Leseaux discovered the principles upon which magic worked, he could have had no idea of the great changes he – or his discovery – would have on our society. The great Polish mathematician Thomasoni believes that the reason nobody discovered how magic works before T. Leseaux is because magic *didn't* work before sometime in the middle of the Nineteenth Century – or perhaps it did only somewhat and sporadically. He believes that some basic physical constants of our universe have changed, or the sun has moved into a sector of the universe with slightly different rules, or something. And he has the equations to prove it.

It's interesting how many people still refuse to believe in magic, with the evidence of it all around them. A magician transports himself from here to there, clearly unsupported by anything. "It's a trick," they exclaim. A sorceress turns a man into a pig. "Mirrors," they insist. A necromancer predicts the future with eighty percent accuracy. "Why not a hundred?" they ask. But are they any worse than those who believe that sorcery will solve all their problems? "My brother had his leg taken off at the knee by a threshing machine," one says. "Witch it back." Sure. Although I have heard of some theoretical sorcerers in Germany – but I digress.

I hurried down the street to Stryk's building. He had recently had it painted a deep forest green with a sombre brown trim, and it now fit in better with the other buildings along the block. But somehow, even in its new coat, it still spoke of mysterious comings and goings and secrets that were better not said. The brass plaque on the door had been recently polished:

Jonathan Stryk, D.Th.
Mantic Investigations

I pushed the button and heard nothing from within, but shortly the heavy oak door swung open on silent hinges, revealing an ill-lit corridor of some dark wood. There was no one in sight.

"I hate that!" I said. "Show yourself!"

The sound of girlish laughter filled the doorway, and Melisa appeared before me. Without even a *poof* or a clap of thunder – just appeared. One second empty corridor, the next, the slender, dark-skinned, white-haired waif was standing there in a green dress, barefoot, arms akimbo, laughing at me. "Greetings, Peter my love," she said, "Himself will see you shortly, he's finishing up an incantation, or possibly a breakfast muffin, at the moment."

"Ah, Melisa," I said, following her into the house. "I wish you meant that." I took off my hat and coat and hung them on the coat-rack just inside the door.

She looked up at me quizzically. "The incantation or the breakfast muffin?" she asked.

"I meant the 'Peter my love' part," I told her.

"You're forgetting the Seventh Law of Magic," she told me, dancing ahead of me down the corridor.

"Not being a magician," I reminded her, "I've never learned the Seventh Law of Magic."

"Be very careful what you wish for," she said, "is the Seventh Law."

"What are the other six?"

"There are well over a hundred by now," she told me, a serious expression on her pixie face. "And they keep changing places."

We went into the parlour, which is the first room on the left, and she pointed at the couch. "Sit," she said. "Help yourself to coffee, Jonathan will be down directly; he's been expecting you."

"But I told no one I was coming," I said.

"Nonetheless he's been expecting you. The coffee's on the sideboard. I have a task, and will return when it is done." She crossed to the door to what had once been a sitting-room or perhaps a music room, but was now hung with dark drapes and lit with red candles. "No more than twenty minutes," she said. "Perhaps, if I am not fortunate, much less."

I poured myself a demi-flagon of the thick, black, sweet liquid that Stryk calls coffee and settled down to wait. A copy of last month's *Genii*, the magazine about magic and magicians was on the table and I picked it up. This was the issue that had an article by Har Janif, an East Coast magus, blasting forensic magic and calling all its practitioners gulls or frauds; and saving special scorn for Jonathan Stryk. His credentials, according to Janif, were suspect, and his accomplishments merely smoke and mirrors. "This sort of magic on demand," said Janif, "violates the very rules of magic, and is best left to charlatans and humbugs like Stryk."

I had asked Stryk about the article when it appeared, and he had merely smiled and said, "Who knows, he may be right." It was like Stryk, with his colossal ego and his even larger sense of humour, to leave that very issue of *Genii* on the table in his parlour.

After a while, attracted by the melodic murmurings that I

could hear from the next room, I put the magazine aside and approached the door, which Melisa had left open.

The elfin waif was settled cross-legged on the deep strangely-figured rug that covered the floor, holding an oversized crystal of some milky-white substance in the air in front of her with her right hand. In her left hand she held what appeared to be a child's jumper, made of light brown corduroy, and was running it through her fingers, twisting it this way and that. She was chanting something something softly to herself; the sound was melodious, but I couldn't make out the words, or even tell what language they were in.

As I watched, the crystal seemed to clear, and then to glow with an inner light. I could discern figures moving about inside it, and once a hand, or claw, seemed to reach toward me and then be yanked back sharply. For which, I admit, I was grateful. Through all this Melisa remained frozen, except for her left hand, which continued worrying the bit of fabric. After perhaps five minutes she let out a little cry, perhaps of pain. Her arm dropped, and the crystal fell from her hand and rolled away on the carpet, its inner light extinguished. For a few seconds she was motionless and mute, then she folded in on herself, arms and legs and bowed head, and began rocking back and forth and whimpering softly.

"What is it?" I approached, but hesitated touching her, since I didn't know whether I would help or harm.

Melisa looked up. "Why can the crystal never show pleasant, attractive scenes of happiness and light?" She began shuddering as one might if caught naked in a snowstorm, and I wondered what it was that she had seen.

"Because that is not what we ask of it," said a deep, sombre voice. I turned and saw the tall, gaunt, red-robed form of Jonathan Stryk striding into the room from an inner door. He gathered Melisa up in his arms and held her until the shuddering had passed.

"But you were in your studio," she said.

"I heard you and so I came," he told her, carrying her back into the parlour and setting her down softly on the couch that I had just vacated.

"Through three floors, furniture and all?" she asked with a tentative smile.

"Through ten miles of solid granite of the Mount of Sorrow, if need be," he said, smiling gently back at her.

I sighed, or was it a grimace? Why couldn't I talk to women like that? For that matter, why didn't I have a woman to talk to like that? And could he really have heard her through ten miles of solid granite? And where was the Mount of Sorrow anyway? Perhaps it would be wise not to demand an answer to the last question.

Stryk looked at the crystal and the balled up garment where they lay on the floor. "What did you find?" he asked her.

"It's the jumper from the Langford child," she said. "I was skrying using the incantation you devised."

"The Langford kidnaping?" I interrupted. "You're working on that now?"

My astonishment must have shown in my voice. Stryk nodded at me. "Senator Langford asked for my help. He did not want it known publicly."

"You mean he didn't want the police to know," I said bitterly. "Is it any wonder that we can't solve crimes when nobody trusts us to solve crimes?"

"Come now," Stryk said. "It happened in far-off Chicago, and is of little concern to the San Francisco Police. And I believe the Chicago department is cooperating with Senator Langford's desires in the matter. It is, after all, his daughter."

"And what can you be doing from here that the Chicago Police can not do better?" I asked. "Wave your magic wand and make the child reappear?"

Stryk smiled grimly. "I'm a sorcerer," he said, "not a miracle worker. The senator sent me a telegram asking for my assistance in locating the child, or at least ascertaining whether she is still alive. I replied that he should send some clothing that little Deborah had worn, or a favourite toy. He sent both, putting the package on the Sandusky and Western yesterday. We received it this morning."

"Ah!" I said. "And?"

"I devised an incantation for Melisa to use in skrying for the child with the lesser crystal," Stryk said. "I do not yet know the result." He turned to Melisa, who was sitting up on the couch.

"I saw the child," she said softly. "I was on the third recitation and had skryed only restless spirits and an angry djinn, when all at once the mist turned silver-white and Deborah's jumper felt ice cold under my hand. And I saw her. Several – beings – interposed themselves between me and her, as though they were aware of my seeking, but I saw her. She was in Hell."

"Dead?" asked Stryk. "What a pity. But why would one so young and innocent be condemned . . ."

"No, no," said Melisa. "She is not dead. I could see that clearly. Nonetheless she was in Hell."

"What does that mean?" I asked.

She looked at me, her brown eyes wide. "I do not know," she said. "The images I see are not reality, but a warped vision occluded by mists and distorted by the minds of unearthly beings."

I made the sign of protection with my left hand; always a good idea when such things are spoken of. "And what do you do next?" I asked Stryk.

"Use the great crystal to verify and perhaps amplify Melisa's skrying, and then report to Senator Langford," Stryk said. "Our brief goes no further."

"Actually . . ." I began.

"And you, Peter," Stryk said, without noticing that he was interrupting. "What can we do for you?"

"I thought you knew that I was coming," I said.

"Yes," Stryk agreed, "but not why."

"Ah!" I said, shaking my finger at him. "Then it was yours!"

"It what?"

"The wind elemental that's been following me about town."

"Ridiculous," said Stryk.

"Silly," said Melisa.

"Perhaps," I said, "but it's there. Probably right outside this building at this very moment. I assume you have protective spells to prevent its entering."

"Sometimes," said Stryk, "a wind is just a wind."

"'Just winds' don't follow one about," I told him.

"Interesting," said Stryk. "Let us see." He retreated to the inner room for a moment and returned with a small, lacquered box. Wrapping his deep red robe even more firmly around him, he stalked toward the front door. I followed at a reasonable distance, not wishing to come between Stryk and whatever he was about to do. Melisa was behind me.

Stryk opened the door and muttered several short phrases which may have included the phrase "Umjum Gumball," or may not, and opened the lacquered box. Holding it carefully at arm's length by the thumb and forefinger of his left hand, he gently shook it. A red powder wafted out like smoke from a lazy fire. It headed down the stoop away from the house, spreading as it went. In a short while it was – how to say it – taken up by this unseen creature made of the very air, until it permeated its windy body and made visible the twenty-foot tall wind elemental.

"See?" I said. "Sometimes a wind is – that!" I pointed to the puffy insubstantial monster whirling and throbbing and assuming new and ever more grotesque shapes before us.

Stryk pulled a small pointed wand from his sleeve and gestured toward the airy beast. He muttered a couple of words under his breath and then said "Explain yourself!" to the air in front of him in a deep, commanding voice.

"I am what I am," came the faint whisper in reply.

"Why are you following Inspector Frey?" Stryk demanded.

After a while came, "Because . . . Yes."

"Because yes?" I asked. I know one can't expect much from a bundle of air, but . . .

Melisa frowned and pursed her lips. After a few seconds a wide smile spread across her pixie face and she suppressed a giggle.

"Funny?" I growled.

She stood on tiptoe and murmured "It was a two-part answer," in my ear.

"Two part?"

She nodded. " 'Why?' – 'Because.' 'Are you following Inspector Frey?' – 'Yes.' "

Stryk sketched a figure in the air with his wand. Blue sparks inhabited the creature and somehow pulled it together until it was smaller than it had been and seemingly more dense. "Who energized you?" he demanded.

"I," the creature began, stretching the sound out and out in a windy sort of way, "am a registered elemental of the *Daily Call-Bulletin*."

"Damn!" I said. "A newsy snoop!" I advanced toward the

thing shaking my fist, an admittedly useless gesture against this bagless bag of wind. "Begone!" I said firmly.

"I can't," the thing complained in its whiney windy voice. "I'm tied to you by a spell cast by the city editor."

"We'll see about that," Stryk said. He thrust the small wand before him like a midget épée and intoned, "I sever whatever ties hold this elemental force of nature and invoke the geas of Paracelsus!"

A red bolt of lightning emerged from the tip, looked around for a place to go, and zapped into the streetlight standard some twenty yards away.

The air creature pulsed with an internal light. "Free?" it asked. "Free," it decided. "Free!" And it sped away down the street, blowing leaves, bushes, and the lids off a couple of garbage cans along the way.

"It worked!" said Stryk, sounding a little surprised.

"Shouldn't it have?" I asked.

Stryk shrugged. "A strange being," he said. "Too airy to be held by a spell, but with too little intellect to know that it isn't. So it does what it's told."

"So that 'Paracelsus' business?"

"One of the Names of Power. Pen name of a Swiss alchemist from half a millennium ago," Stryk said. "Should mean nothing to a wind elemental. But yon windy beast didn't know that."

"And if it hadn't worked?"

Stryk smiled. "I held Paracelsus's real name in reserve."

"His real name?"

"Phillippus Aureolus Theophrastus Bombastus von Hohenheim."

I nodded. "That would have done it," I agreed.

"Especially," said Melisa, "the 'Bombastus' part."

"Now," said Stryk, "come back inside and tell me what's on your mind."

I complied. "It's odd," I said when I was settled once more comfortably on the drawing room couch. "I didn't know you were working on the Langford kidnaping."

"What's odd about it?" Stryk asked.

"I came here to ask you to work on the Langford kidnaping."

Stryk leaned back in his chair. I had surprised him. I cherished the moment. "What have the San Francisco police to do with a Chicago kidnaping?" he asked.

"The kidnappers got in touch with Senator Langford late last night," I told him. "They instructed him to take the Midnight Express to San Francisco, check into the St. Barnabas, and wait for their call. The Chicago police telegraphed us, and my boss sent me to you."

"I'm honoured," Stryk said.

"The senator asked for you," I told him. "I guess he doesn't read the magazines."

"Peter!" Melisa said reproachfully.

Stryk smiled unperturbedly and his shoulders moved. Perhaps he was suppressing a laugh.

"Sorry," I said. "We probably would have called you in anyway. You know that. What does this Janif fellow have against you anyway?"

"If you ever meet Dr Janif," Stryk said, "do not shake his hand. If you must do so, count your fingers afterward and wash immediately with a strong disinfectant soap. He exudes a venomous pus."

"Well," I said. "I take it you're not friends, then?"

"He discovered his Power early," Stryk said grimly. "It is the ability to make certain insects march in rows. He opened a cockroach circus, but it was not a great success."

"You're joking!" I said.

"Yes," he agreed. "Now let us see what we can do to help Senator Langford. He should be arriving around four this afternoon. We'd best get to the hotel well before then. Give me twenty minutes to glance into the great crystal to see what I can make of what Melisa has seen, and then we'd best be off."

"I'll use the time to change," Melisa said, and darted off.

It was no more than twenty minutes later when we three left the house and leapt aboard one of the ubiquitous double-decker cable cars heading downtown on California Street. Stryk was in an unusually sombre mood and would not discuss what he had seen in the crystal, if anything. He was wearing what he calls his "gentleman's disguise": a light pink double-breasted wool suit with a wide foulard cravat, carrying a dark dragonskin briefcase holding an assortment of those items that no magician leaves home without. He might have been a banker or a diplomat.

Melisa was dressed in a dark blue schoolgirl skirt and jacket with a ruffled white blouse and black shoes. Her white hair had somehow turned dark brown, as it did when she wished to remain unnoticed. Whether by magical artifact, or some powder or liquid I know not, but within five minutes of returning home it would be white again.

When we arrived at the St Barnabas, Stryk and Melisa went off by themselves to inspect whatever aspects of the hotel that sorcerers would choose to inspect. I awaited them in the Webster Tea Room, an ornate gilded and mirrored Victorian chamber that had actually once hosted President Daniel Webster. I believe that most of the mirrors were replaced after the big quake, but the rest of the furnishings were original. It was easy to lose track of time in a room like this, which was essentially timeless. I imagined women in narrow-waisted gowns coming through the door accompanied by men in black tie and tails, talking in hushed tones about the Rebs firing on Fort Sumter, or burning New York, or the balloon assault on Atlanta, and ordering rum punch or brandy and hot water.

Stryk and Melisa joined me after about half an hour and I told them of my fancy, and Stryk stroked his short beard thoughtfully. "Time travel utilizing the Law of Similarity," he said. "An interesting notion."

"It was just a random thought," I said.

Stryk patted me on the back and pulled up his chair. "You must learn to cultivate such thoughts," he said. "One such thought could make you immortal."

The waiter came over. I ordered a scotch and spring water, Stryk ordered coffee, and Melisa requested a buttered scone and lemonade. They still call it a tea room, but only visiting Canadians drink tea.

"Turmoil!" Melisa said suddenly.

We looked at her. "What?" asked Stryk.

"Turmoil." She made an indefinite gesture with her hand. "Somewhere around us. It is like a piercing yellow light in my mind."

"Directed at us?" Stryk asked.

Melissa closed her eyes for a moment. "No," she said finally.

"Then let us await events," said Stryk.

"Speaking of awaiting events, what shall we do to prepare for the senator?" I asked Stryk.

"What is being done?" he asked.

"Nothing," I said. "We're permitted to guard him but not to otherwise interfere. At the senator's request. He's afraid that our 'heavy-handed approach' will endanger his child's life."

The bitterness must have shown in my voice, for Stryk looked at me sharply. "Accept what is," he advised me, "and don't carry what was around on your shoulders."

"Is that some of your sorcerers' philosophy?" I asked him sacrcastically.

"It's a quote from 'The Wisdom of Yi,'" he said.

"Who's Yi?" I asked.

"Ah! That's the question." Stryk explained.

A sombre looking man in a dark red double-breasted suit trotted into the room and looked around. He whispered something to the headwaiter, who pointed to our table. A few seconds later he was standing there, looming politely over us. "Inspector Frey?" he asked cautiously, looking from Stryk to me.

I nodded. "I am he. What can I do for you?"

"My name is Pierson. I am the manager of the St Barnabas." He leaned forward so that he could lower his voice. "We've had an, er, incident on the third floor. If you wouldn't mind coming with me—"

"What sort of incident?" I asked.

"Well—" he hesitated and lowered his voice even more. "A murder," he whispered.

"That is an incident," I admitted. "Have you called the police?"

"You are the police," Pierson said.

I made an annoyed gesture with my hand. "The local precinct," I said. "It'll be their case. To start with, anyway. Send them a citygram."

"The city telegraph isn't working at the moment. I sent a boy to the precinct station," Pierson said. "I didn't want to go yelling on the street for the nearest copper. What would the guests think?"

"I understand," I said. "Bad for business, a murder in the hotel."

"Indeed," he agreed. "Particularly a mysterious killing with no apparent explanation."

"Really?" I said. "How so?"

"He was a guest," Pierson said. "Named, ah—" He took a card from his breast pocket and consulted it. "Lundt." He spelled it. "Paul Lundt. From Chicago. Our floor man heard the sound of a shot from inside his room and went to investigate. The door was locked from the inside. After calling and receiving no answer, he sent for the security officer, who broke it in. Mr Lundt was on the bed – dead. There was no one else in the room. I searched the room myself, and no one was concealed anywhere. And I've left our security man at the door to make sure nothing is disturbed."

I swivelled around to stare up at the plump hotel manager. "Don't tell me," I said. "There's no other exit from the room."

"I do tell you that," Pierson said. "There is no other door and the window opens on a three-storey drop to the service yard in back of the hotel."

I sighed and got up. "It sounds like it's going to become my case anyway." I turned to Stryk and Melisa. "If you wouldn't mind assisting . . ."

"Not at all," Stryk assured me, rising.

Melisa floated to her feet. "Murder," she said. "Turmoil."

"Probably," Stryk agreed.

I explained briefly to Pierson who Stryk and Melisa were, and that I would require their assistance, and we headed for the elevator.

"Who does your protective spells?" Stryk asked as the elevator boy lurched us toward the third floor.

"The WCHMORC," Pierson said.

"Efficient and reasonably priced," Stryk said. " 'The West Coast Holy and Mystical Order of the Rosy Cross' – the local Rosicrucian guild. They stand behind their product."

Pierson nodded. "We were using the Associated Theosophists," he said. "But they make such a big deal about everything."

The third floor corridor was deserted except for a large man in a white suit and Panama hat who was lounging against the frame of the open door to room 312. A cigar jutted from his mouth and he wore an air of stolid disdain for the world around him, and especially the corpse in the room behind him.

"Gores," I said.

The big man took the cigar from his mouth. "Frey," he answered. "You got here fast."

"I was here," I told him. "Let's take a look."

"Stryk," he said, looking behind me. "Melisa." He jammed the cigar back in his mouth. "You must have been having a convention."

"You touch anything?" I asked him, looking into the room.

"Only the door," he told me. "I kicked it in."

As the house detective, or as the hotel liked to call him, the Director of Security Services, Gores would be one of the few people unaffected by the protective spell on the door. It was all a matter of intent. Most people trying to break into a hotel room would have felt increasingly dizzy or nauseate, and would have collapsed before they succeeded. The spell somehow recognized that Gores was *supposed* to be there. Don't ask me how an inanimate weaving of forces can recognize anything; that's how it's been described to me, and there you have it.

Pierson peered into the room and hiccuped nervously at the sight of the corpse. "Well, I'll just leave you gentlemen to your work," he said, and headed back toward the elevator.

The corpse, a well-groomed white male about 35 years old, was slumped over the edge of the bed in his shirt sleeves, with his cravat untied and hanging loosely around his neck. He may have been leaning over the open suitcase that was beside him on the bed. His suit jacket was hung neatly over a chair by the bed. There was a bloody hole in the collar of his white shirt, right below the throat, and the suitcase as well as the area around him on the bed and the floor were all basted in blood. The protective spell seemed to have been disrupted by the broken door, since I felt scarcely a twinge of nausea as I entered the room. I was careful not to touch anything myself, and squatted by the body. "Locked from the inside, eh?" I asked Gores.

"Bolt thrown," he said. "See for yourself." He indicated the splintered wood and bits of lock still clinging to the door and the bits of lock mechanism and shards of wood on the floor around the door.

"Maybe we'd better do a reconstruction," I said, "just for the record."

Gores snorted. "Please yourself," he said. "But I know when a door's locked, and when it's not locked."

"Nonetheless . . ."

Melisa had come into the room, and was probing the air with outstretched fingers, her eyes closed. "Funny," she said, "I find no residue of malice or fear in the room."

"So somebody without malice shot him," I ventured. "Maybe a professional hit man. And he was caught by surprise – no time to feel fear."

Stryk quickly set up the tools of his trade: a small charcoal brazier on a tripod, a leather case containing a double row of glass phials filled with a variety of those things that sorcerers fill their glass phials with, and a wand, thick around as a roll of quarters at the base and tapering to a point about a foot and a half out; like a fat midget pool cue. He poured a little liquid into the charcoal and lit it with a gesture.

Gores backed away from the doorway. *Never meddle in the affairs of wizards,* as the old saw has it. Particularly when they're playing with fire.

Stryk took a small leather-bound book from his briefcase and looked through it thoughtfully. Finding the page he wanted, he ripped it out with exaggerated care, folded it into quarters, and fed it to the fire. A puff of black smoke emerged from the brazier, and turned bright green as it rose. Stryk traced a figure in the smoke with his wand and then touched the tip to the spot on the door where the lock had been torn away.

Splinters of wood on the door frame vibrated. Fragments of wood on the floor stirred and jiggled. Then, slowly and deliberately, all the pieces that had been part of the door lock and frame rose, crept, twisted, slid, or flew back into place, and the door that had been emerged from the wreck of the door that was.

I went over to inspect it when the smoke had cleared. The bolt was clearly thrown, jutting out like a tongue from the face of the lock. "It was thus?" I asked Stryk.

"I affirm it," he replied, putting a brass cap over the fire on the brazier.

"Well, that's settled," I said. "We do have a 'locked room' mystery here."

"Damn!" Gores said, inspecting the newly-restored lock. "The door is fixed now, is it?"

"No," Stryk told him. "The attraction is temporary. It should go back to the way it was in a few hours."

Gores shook his head. "Damn!" he said again.

"In the context, perhaps not a good expression," Stryk said. He straightened up and came over to the bed. "May I?" he asked, gesturing toward the corpse.

"Please," I said.

He stooped over the corpse and made poking and prodding motions with his hand and wand, although he never actually touched the body. "Hmmm," he said. "Haaa," he said.

He took what looked like a bit of crystal on the end of a string and held it by the string end at various places around the body. In some spots the crystal went in a circle, in some it swung back and forth, and in one spot it tugged at the string as though it would get away and go off on its own. "So," he said.

"What?" I asked.

"Shot," he said.

"I knew that," I told him.

"Better to be sure," he said. "Lead slug entered the body right below the neck and fragmented. Bits and pieces of it are scattered from his stomach to his brain. Nasty."

"Anything else?" I asked.

"Look," he said, pointing down toward the open suitcase.

I went over and peered down. The suitcase was empty, and the bottom and sides were black and charred. It looked as though the insides had been burned out, and the contents, whatever they had been, were now crumbling bits of carbon and ash. "Damn!" I said.

Stryk shook his head. "Please," he said. "There are – beings – that might be close to us even now that might take that term seriously."

"Yes," I agreed, resisting the impulse to duck my head under my arm and recite a protection spell. "Are you saying," I whispered hoarsely, "that it was a demonic fire that burned out the inside of this case?"

"Notice," Stryk said, "that the bed under the suitcase isn't even singed. How would you account for that?"

"The so-called 'cold fire' of teleportation," I suggested. "It leaves a residue like that, I believe."

"And what would you say was teleported?" he asked.

"I wouldn't," I said. "That's where you and Melisa come in."

Stryk went slowly around the room, poking into this and that; Melisa stood in one corner of the room with her eyes closed, palping the air with her slender fingers; I searched the dead man's pockets, removing everything I found and making a pile of his effects on the top of the desk across from the bed.

There was some small change; a ticket stub to a Chicago Hurlers baseball game dated last Saturday; a clasp knife with two blades, one dull and the other duller; an ivory toothpick in a leather case, a small phial of water with a sticker on it saying it had been blessed by Bishop Langeurt of the Cicero Old Rite Order of the Druid Assembly of North America; a wallet that didn't want to open, and three keys on a gold key ring in the shape of a pyramid. On each of the four faces of the pyramid was a single letter from some alphabet I was unfamiliar with.

"Can either of you identify this?" I asked, holding up the pyramid.

Melisa opened her eyes and focused on the little object. "Seekers of the True Mu," she said. "The four sides have four letters from the Muvian alphabet: *Akka*, *Pokka*, *Tikka* and *Hum*. They stand for Inner Growth, Harmony, a large black beetle, and Universal Awareness."

"Beetle?" I asked.

"The beetle stands for—"

"Never mind," I said. "Is there anything about these Seekers I should know?"

"There's one born every minute," Stryk said from the window, which he had pulled open and out of which he was peering.

"Is this some bizarre coincidence," asked a gravelly voice from the doorway," or does it concern us?"

A skinny, bald guy named Godfrey, who happened to be the Chief of Detectives for the City of San Francisco, was standing there, hands on his waist, glaring into the room.

"Ask not for whom the bell tolls," Stryk intoned, bringing his head back inside the window and pulling it closed.

"Chief," I said. "What are you doing here?"

"Senator Langford is due any minute now," Godfrey said. "I came along to make sure that he was properly received; station some men in appropriate places; see what you and your magical, mystical friends there had planned to do. And I'm greeted by the news that there's a stiff on the third floor."

"That's funny, you know," Stryk said thoughtfully.

"There's nothing funny about a murder," Godfrey said. "Even if the corpse is from Chicago."

"Not that," Stryk said. "The senator didn't ask you to keep your men away, or at least out of sight?"

"Nothing like that," Chief Godfrey told him.

"Then the kidnapper doesn't seem to care if the whole San Francisco Police Force is out trying to stop him. He seems awfully sure of himself."

"Now that you mention it . . ." Godfrey said.

Stryk stuck his wand in his belt. "Let's go downstairs," he said," I think we're done here."

"Giving up on solving the locked-room mystery already?" Godfrey asked Stryk, but he was looking at me. Chief Godfrey didn't believe in this new-fangled business of hiring forensic magicians to investigate a crime scene. Oh, sure they could measure this and conjure that, and tell you that the murderer had white shoes and a brown moustache, but it took that good old-fashioned police sense to actually solve a crime. Or so he had insisted to me several times.

"Oh, no," Stryk answered, pausing in packing up his apparatus. "I know how it was done; clever, but fairly obvious. As a matter of fact, I wonder – " he shook his head. "But we have to discover the who and the why. I think the 'why' will give us the 'who.' But the answer isn't in this room."

"You do?" Godfrey asked. "How . . ."

"Downstairs," Stryk repeated, hefting his briefcase and rising to his feet.

"Before we go," I said, grabbing Lundt's wallet from the table. "Would you open this for me? It's got some kind of protective spell on it."

"Bring it with you," he growled.

We trooped back to the elevator and rang the bell.

"I need to know," Chief Godfrey insisted, "whether this has anything to do with Senator Langford and the kidnaping."

"Of course it does," Stryk told him.

"Sometimes a wind is just a wind," I reminded Stryk.

"Not when it blows in from Chicago," he told me. The elevator door opened, and three uniforms from the local precinct stepped out. Godfrey gave them instructions to guard the door to room 312 until further notice, letting Gores go back to his normal job of looking for sneak thieves, cutpurses and trollops. We got into the elevator ourselves, and someone said "Lobby."

"Darn!" the elevator boy said, closing the door. "And I had been planning to go cross town."

Chief Godfrey poked Stryk in the chest. "How do you know," he demanded, "that this isn't just a random room robbery?"

Stryk shook his head. "The room's protective spell is still in place, for one thing. Whoever did it was invited into the room. And when he left Lundt was still alive."

Godfrey looked at Stryk intently, as though he were trying to get the joke. "Still alive?"

"Yes. You might say he killed Lundt after he left the room."

I snapped my fingers. "The Monkey's Paw!" I exclaimed.

They all looked at me. Even the elevator boy turned to look at me. "I read this book," I explained. "It was about this case in Germany where the murderer animated a monkey's paw and left it behind in the victim's house. And then, after he had left and gone to establish an unbreakable alibi, the monkey's paw crawled over and strangled the victim."

They all kept looking at me. "This victim was shot," Godfrey reminded me.

"This monkey's paw had a gun," I suggested.

The elevator door opened, and we spilled out into the lobby. Chief Godfrey went off to speak to a small cluster of men in brown suits that I recognized as being from the plainclothes protective division of the force. Stryk headed over to the room clerk's counter and I followed. "I'd like to see your registration book," he told the clerk, a young man with a prominent nose and watery blue eyes. The clerk looked over at the manager, who nodded, and he pulled the oversized sign-in book from beneath the counter. Stryk opened it and leafed through the last few pages. "I'm interested in anyone who has come in from Chicago recently," he told the clerk.

The clerk helped him look. There were four Chicagoans in the last three days. The victim, Mr Lundt had checked in yesterday. I was tempted to make a pun about when he had checked out, but decided not to. The other three were a husband and wife named Gilgum who were here for a schoolteachers' convention and a Mr Bianchi who traveled in salamanders. "One of our regulars," the clerk assured us. "Salamanders, horned toads, asps. And several sorts of insects. We don't let him keep his livestock here, of course."

"Of course," I murmured.

The clerk nodded. "Just his samples."

Stryk pointed to a little mark to the right of Lundt's signature. "What is that?"

The clerk peered. "Ah," he said. "Mr Lundt checked a piece of luggage in our check room."

"He did, did he? And where is your check room?"

"Well, actually, you check the bag with me and I take it to the check room," the clerk said.

"Will you get the Lundt luggage for us, please?"

"Well, under the circumstances – certainly. If you'll just wait a minute," he bobbed his head a few times and headed toward that private land behind the counter where only room clerks may go.

As the room clerk departed I pulled Lundt's wallet from my jacket pocket and waved it at Stryk. "Open," I said. "Please."

Stryk sighed and took the wallet. He mumbled a few magical words and tried to pry it open. His hands slid around it as though it had just been buttered.

"Ha!" Stryk said. "I see!" He put the wallet on the counter and contemplated it for a minute. Then he pulled his wand from his belt, intoned a few words and tapped the wallet twice with the back end of the wand. He then flipped the wand over, said, "Exaultet Magnificat!" in a loud clear voice, and tapped the wallet with the tip of the wand.

The wallet flew open, scattering papers and cards and coins all over the counter top and the nearby floor. I gathered them up as best I could, as many as I could find, and looked them over.

There were a couple of ones, threes and tens, and a twenty-five dollar bill; the return half of a round-trip ticket from Chicago to San Francisco, good for a year from the date of purchase, which was last Friday; a driver's licence from the State of Illinois, stamped for both electric and steam vehicles, and a membership card in the American Amateur Conjurers' Society.

"He was one of you," I told Stryk, tossing him the card.

He turned it over in his hand and flicked it with his fingernail. "Prestidigitation," he said. "Card tricks, coin tricks, box tricks."

"Box tricks?"

Stryk shrugged. "Lady gets into box, conjurer spins box around and it falls open – no lady. Not magic – a clever illusion."

"Music hall stuff?" I asked.

"Exactly," Stryk agreed. "Some of their tricks simulate the Power, but they're all just tricks."

Chief Godfrey came up to join us. "The senator will be here in a minute," he told us. "What are 'just tricks'?"

I explained.

"So these 'conjurers' have not the Power?" asked Godfrey.

"Some do," said Stryk." As you know, the Power comes in many guises, partly dependent upon some inner spirit that we do not yet understand, and partly upon the training or practice of the adept or the order he or she is a member of. Sometimes a magician with one limited Power will use some of these conjurers' tricks to enhance his reputation, to seem more powerful than he is."

Chief Godfrey shook his head. "Such deceit," he said.

"It is sad," Stryk agreed. "Would you like to see a card trick?"

"I think not," said Godfrey.

The room clerk came scurrying up from the back, with Pierson, the manager, a few steps behind. "They don't know how it happened," the room clerk blurted. "It's very strange."

"What is?" I asked.

"Mr Lundt's luggage – it's not there!"

"Really?" Stryk asked. "Fascinating! Who took it?"

"Nobody knows," the manager said, putting his arms on the counter wearily. "The chit – the little metal disk we give in exchange for the luggage, has been returned, but nobody remembers receiving it or giving out Mr Lindt's piece of luggage."

"What did it look like?" I asked.

"It's a little brass disk with a number stamped on it," the room clerk said.

"The luggage," Stryk said. "What did the luggage look like?"

"Oh." The clerk put his hands wide apart. "About this wide. It was a sort of trunk, I remember. Rectangular with brass – you know – fittings and things. Like a steamer trunk, but not as big."

"So a trunk this wide," Stryk spread his hands apart, "just disappeared?"

"Maybe the night man—" Pierson began. A little bell behind the counter trinkled, and he jumped. "The bell!" he said. "That's the doorman. Senator Langford's cab has arrived. I must see to things." An expression of grave concern crossed his face, and he scurried out from behind the counter.

About five minutes later the senator and his wife, three or four aides, and a bevy of cops crossed the lobby, Pierson walking backward in the lead, making little nervous hand gestures as he talked to the senator. A large luggage cart took up the rear, filled with a large amount of luggage. A large man with the look of a cop stayed with the luggage cart, which was being pushed by two bellhops. His overcoat marked him as having arrived from Chicago with the senator.

Half the group took the first elevator up, half the second, and the luggage cart with its hefty escort, the third. "I think they're preparing to pay a ransom," I said. "And I think it's in that cart."

"There's certainly something of value in their luggage," Stryk agreed.

Melisa made a slight whimpering sound. Stryk dropped his hand on to her shoulder. "Be brave," he said.

"There is a – a – blackness following those people," she said. "I have never felt anything like that before."

"Could it have been from that luggage cart?" Stryk asked.

"It could," she said. "But I'm not sure. It was like an emptiness – I don't know how to put it. Not pleasant."

"The senator's going to want to see you right away," Chief Godfrey told Stryk. "Let's go up."

"Give them a few minutes to get settled," Stryk said.

"I don't think Senator Langford is interested in getting settled," I said.

Stryk sighed. "You're right, of course. But I'm afraid this isn't going to turn out well."

Chief Godfrey looked at him sharply. "Listen," he said. "If you fail, you fail."

"Oh, I won't fail," Stryk said.

The senator was in the President Huey Long suite on the fifth floor. Uniformed policemen were guarding each entrance to the corridor, with a few extra scattered about for fill. When we walked in the senator, a tall, distinguished-looking man with a great shock of gray-brown hair, was yelling, "Just leave everything where it is. When I want to unpack, I'll tell you to unpack," at his aides, helpers and factotums. They dispersed without argument to the corners of the room and stood in different postures of discontent, or sat down on whatever was available, leaving the great pile of luggage in the middle of the floor. The two bellboys were standing by the door with the luggage cart, waiting for their tip. Manager Pierson gave them a "scat" sign with the back of his hand, and they scatted sulkily, pulling the cart behind them.

Senator Langford's wife Mary, an attractive woman despite the lines of grief that currently etched her face and the spiritless slump of her shoulders, was sitting on a white couch to the right of the door, her hands folded over the purse on her lap, staring into space. Langford went to sit beside her and put his arm around her. "We'll have our little girl back soon, Mary," he promised. Upon which Mary burst out sobbing and, pulling a small white handkerchief from her purse, covered her face.

A self-important looking gentleman with a brush moustache and a receding hairline stalked over to us and extended his hand in the general direction of whoever wanted to take it. "Harold Fenster," he said. "Senator Langford's legislative aide. Would one of you be Dr Stryk?"

"That would be me," Stryk said.

Fenster aimed the hand more directly at Stryk. "Glad to meet you," he said. "Come speak with the senator."

The senator stood up as we approached. "Stryk?" he asked. "Have you discovered anything?"

"Deborah is alive," Stryk told him. "Or at least she was a couple of hours ago."

"Where is she?" Langford demanded, reaching forward as though he would clutch Stryk's jacket, and then drawing his hand back. "Could you tell where she is? Is she all right? What have they done with her?"

"She was alive and unharmed physically," Stryk told him. "She is surrounded by dark forces. There is sorcery at work here, clouding my attempts to see better."

"But she was alive?"

"Yes."

"Thank god!" Langford turned to his wife. "Mary, she's alive."

Mary nodded without looking up. "Bring her to me," she sobbed.

"I will, I will," Langford told her. "As soon as we get further instructions." He turned back to Stryk. "They've asked – who-ever they are – for two million dollars, all in twenty-five dollar bills. I have it here. They are going to let me know how to deliver it."

I did a quick calculation. "That's eighty thousand bills. Quite a big stack."

"It's a trunkful," Langford said, pointing to the pile of lug-gage. "That black trunk there. Two million. It'll just about wipe me out, but of course that doesn't matter if we get Deborah back."

He couldn't help it, of course. Our research on him had shown that he was worth between ten and fifteen million dollars, in these days when a family of four can live well and keep two servants and an electric – or even a horse and buggy – on sixty dollars a week. One would think that, for a man worth at least ten million, losing two million would be a major insult but only a minor inconve-nience. But it isn't so. It really hurt. It really felt like he was losing almost everything. He would brood and cry about the loss of ten percent of his worth more than you or I would about losing our life savings and our favourite hunting dog. During the crash of '32 plutocrats were jumping out of office windows because they were down to their last two or three million. But again I digress.

Fenster pulled the black trunk free of the pile of luggage and took a square of parchment out of his jacket pocket. He held it in his left hand with his right on the trunk and began mumbling something in Latin. By some of the words, I recognized it as the release on a protective spell on the trunk – think of it as the key for a specific lock. Otherwise the person using the spell would have to carry the magician around every time he wanted to get into the trunk.

When he was done mumbling he folded the parchment up and put it back in his pocket. Then he produced a heavy brass key from another pocket, turned the lock, and lifted the trunk lid.

Stryk and Melisa passed a look between them, but I could not tell what it portended.

"Two million dollars," Fenster said. "In twenty-five dollar bills, all used and non-sequential. That's what the kidnappers want, and that's what they shall have. May each and every bill burn their fingers whenever they touch it."

We looked. A five-by-six array of portraits of President Roosevelt stared back. The first woman president and head of one of the most influential Wiccan covens on the East Coast, Eleanor Roosevelt had presided over the passing of the most far-reaching social legislation yet seen. She – and it – were the reason that congress had passed the strict laws against any sorcerer, warlock, wizard or witch holding public office or any position of trust in the government. It must have been witchcraft, the Tories had decided. And they weren't going to put up with a willful woman again, if they could help it.

Fenster closed the top and relocked it. A good thing, because the sight of that much money all in one place gave me a throbbing sensation in the back of my head, right above the neck.

"How are you going to deliver it?" Chief Godfrey asked.

"They'll tell us," Senator Langford said. "They'll be in touch any time now."

"How?" I asked.

"They didn't say."

There was a knock at the door and we all jumped. Well, I know I jumped; I wasn't really looking at what everyone else was doing. A white envelope had been pushed under the door, and it was just sitting there smirking at us. Pierson, who was right by the door, jerked it open and hopped into the hall like a great rabbit. Then he turned back to us. "Nobody here," he said. "The hall is empty."

Several people rushed into the hall to verify what he said. It was so.

"The senator's name is on the envelope," Pierson said.

"Here, let me look at it," said Godfrey, taking the envelope. He poked at it, peered at it, probed it, sniffed it, wrinkled it, listened to it, and finally handed it to Senator Langford.

The senator took a deep breath and slit it open. There were two folded sheets of paper inside. He unfolded them. Several of us peered over his shoulder as he read. The first one contained a message in printed block letters. It said:

BELOW IS A COPY OF THE CHALDEAN RITE OF TRANSFERENCE. RECITE IT, PRONOUNCING THE WORDS AS THOUGH THEY WERE WRITTEN IN ENG-LISH. EVERYONE IN THE ROOM MUST SAY THE RE-SPONSES. THEN PLACE THE PAPER ON TOP OF THE TRUNK CONTAINING THE MONEY AND SET IT AFIRE. YOUR DAUGHTER WILL BE INSTANTLY RETURNED TO YOU.

Langford turned to the next sheet. There were about forty lines of "Chaldean." Just to give you the flavor of it, here are the first four:

MANAY TIKEY FONDO DIN PRATE ORG KANDO MU
RESPONSE: TONDO LU TIMMIT
TISSA YUBIT STIPPA ROOG BISTA MEM KOOKRA BIM
RESPONSE: TONDO LU TIMMIT

Langford passed the page over to Stryk. "What do you make of it?" he asked. "It looks like gibberish to me."

"I've never seen anything like it," Stryk confessed. "But then ancient Chaldean isn't my specialty. I must admit that many magical incantations and rites seem like gibberish to the lay person."

Langford took the page back and stared at it for a long time, looking pained and bewildered.

"Do it, Tom, do it," his wife urged from her seat on the couch. "Whatever it is, do it."

Fenster said. "Might as well, sir. Look, it's the same response each time. I'll just make some copies and hand them around so we can all respond together."

"What's supposed to happen?" Senator Langford asked.

"I have no idea," Stryk confessed.

Langford shrugged. "What the hell," he said. "I've never felt so helpless." He turned to Fenster. "Make those copies."

"Yes, sir," Fenster said. He took some scraps of paper and hurriedly wrote "TONDO LU TIMMIT" on each one, then he passed them around.

Senator Langford stood up and coughed. "Don't anybody laugh," he said. "Whatever else this is, it isn't funny."

He recited the seeming gibberish in a clear, loud voice, and we all responded at the proper times. Then Fenster took the page from him, put it on top of the trunk, and struck a match.

A thin stream of black smoke lofted toward the ceiling as he applied the match to the paper. Then it grew to a cloud of black smoke. Then Fenster leapt back as the smoke itself seemed to catch fire, and burned with a bright blue light that filled the room for a few seconds, and then went out with an audible "pop."

"That's it?" Godfrey asked.

"What happened?" Senator Langford asked.

Fenster took his brass key and put it in the lock and lifted the trunk lid. A cloud of residual smoke billowed into the room. Someone coughed. "The money's gone," Fenster said.

"What do you mean, 'gone'?" demanded Langford, advancing toward the trunk.

"Gone!" Fenster repeated stubbornly.

I peered over the edge of the trunk and saw that, indeed, the five-by-six rectangle of stacks of twenty-five dollar bills had disappeared, its place taken by a charred, black empty space. And beneath it . . .

"Oh, my good lord," Fenster said as the smoke cleared. He reached inside the trunk and lifted out a small, unconscious girl child.

"Deborah!" her mother called, and in a second she had the child in her arms. Another second and Langford was holding both of them, and then we were all surrounding the mother and child and saying inane things, or laughing, or crying.

"She won't wake up," Mary said after a minute, and instantly we were all silent, and looking down at the motionless little girl.

"Look at her face!" cried someone.

Deborah's face contorted into a look of pain and horror, and then shifted to a look of wild fear, and all the while her eyes were closed, her body was motionless, her breathing was even and shallow, and she was silent.

"Let me," said Stryk, and he took the child and brought her over to the couch and lay her down. He examined her face closely for a minute, holding a finger to her throat to check her pulse and raising an eyelid to stare at an eye that refused to stare back. Then he lifted his head. "Melisa," he called. "I think this is a task for you."

The waif knelt by the couch, placing one hand on Deborah's forehead and the other on her knee, and closed her eyes. For a minute or so they were both motionless, although it seemed, I cannot say how, that some sort of energy seemed to be flowing from Melisa to the little girl. And then, so gradually that we thought it an illusion at first, Deborah began to rise above the couch, until she was floating perhaps a foot and a half in the air. She remained so for some seconds, and then dropped back to the couch.

Melisa stood up, visibly drained. "She is sleeping," she said. "She will wake up in an hour or so."

Jonathan Stryk turned to the senator and his wife. "I would suggest that Melisa stay with the child for at least a week or so," he said. "She will need psychic guidance and care to recover from her ordeal."

"Is this some sort of ploy to get a bigger fee?" Langford demanded harshly. "I can't see that you have been of much use here; you couldn't even understand the kidnappers' magic."

"Don't take your anger out on me," Stryk said mildly. "There has been little magic here. There was a spell cast on little Deborah back in Chicago to remove her Ka – her soul, if you will – and cast it into some nether world of demons and wraiths; probably the only nether world of which the warlock who did this knew. She has been residing there for the past days, and it was not a pleasant place to be. If Melisa, who is the strongest empath I know, had not been here to bring her out of the spell right away, her mind might have been lost in this labyrinth of horror for good."

"Why would anyone do such a thing?" I asked.

"To prevent us from determining the girl's location by skrying or spell-casting. And they must have had a strong reason for doing so, since such determinings are tenuous at best."

"What do you mean, no magic?" Langford asked. "Why, we saw with our own eyes—"

"What you were meant to see," Stryk told him. "A trunk full of money when there was no money – or precious little – and a girl appearing in a puff of smoke when she was actually there all the time."

Langford looked at him with obvious disbelief. "Explain yourself," he said.

Stryk looked around the room. "Sit down," he said in a voice that commanded attention. "All of you. I'll tell you just what happened – and why."

Chief Godfrey dropped into his chair. Several of those in the room without nearby chairs settled cross-legged on the floor.

"This was carefully thought out," Stryk said, adopting his "I am the teacher" mode, with appropriate gestures. "There were at least three people involved – maybe more. First the girl was kidnapped – on her way home from school, I believe?" he looked questioningly over at Mrs Langford, who nodded agreement.

"Then a competent, but thoroughly heartless and unprincipled warlock put a spell on her, sending her Ka into some sort of limbo. This was done both to keep her body unconscious and to prevent a forensic sorcerer – me – from being able to follow her movements, even in a broad, general fashion."

"Why?" Senator Langford asked.

"For the best of reasons," Stryk told him. "So that you wouldn't know that she was being moved from Chicago to San Francisco. It happened two days ago, and she was moved in that very trunk," he continued, pointing dramatically at the offending piece of luggage.

"The person who brought the trunk, a man named Lundt, put it in the check room of this hotel, with Deborah unconscious inside, and went up to his room on the third floor, where he was promptly murdered."

Chief Godfrey leaned back in his chair and stared intently at Stryk. He wasn't convinced yet; but he wanted to be. "How?" he asked. "And why?"

Stryk nodded. "A slight digression," he said, "to explain an impossible crime." Was it a trick of the light, or did his eyes seem to glow slightly as he glanced around the room?

"As to why I can only guess," Stryk said. "Perhaps, after he brought the trunk in, the plotters had no further need for him. Perhaps he didn't know the real plan, and they were afraid he'd talk when he found out. As to how, it was not magic, although it was made to look like an 'impossible crime' so that we'd think that it was – part of the misdirection to get us to accept magic as the explanation for what was to come."

"If it wasn't magic—" Chief Godfrey began.

"He was shot from within the opened suitcase on the bed," Stryk said. "Probably by a mechanical gun set to go off when he opened it."

"Then what happened to the gun?"

Stryk pointed a long finger at Pierson, the hotel manager. "He took it," he said.

Pierson jumped to his feet. "Excuse me?" he yelped.

"The inside of the suitcase was singed to make us think of teleportation," Stryk said. "But it was singed *beforehand* – the residue was jumbled, showing the case has been moved. Therefore the weapon was removed by hand – human hand – and the only hand in the room after the killing, by your own admission, was yours."

"That's nonsense," Pierson barked. "Nonsense, nonsense! I protest!"

The protest was because two of the plainclothes cops had come up behind Pierson and shoved him back down in his seat.

"Now," said Stryk, "back to the story of the trunk. At some point this trunk was substituted for the trunk full of money. A thin layer of bills was put on a paper frame at the top, the bills and the frame having been soaked in a liquid that would cause them to burn up almost instantly when a flame was applied. Some more singeing was put around the trunk to enhance the 'cold fire of teleportation' effect, which our minds would already be primed for by the singed suitcase in the murdered man's room."

"Why such an elaborate scheme?" asked Chief Godfrey.

"Misdirection," Stryk told him. "If you think of magic, you won't think of a simple, non-magical substitution. That's also why I was involved."

"But I, ah, involved you myself," Senator Langford said.

"Did you?" Stryk asked. "At whose suggestion?"

"Um, well; Fenster, it was you, wasn't it? You told me about this article you had read . . ."

"I don't think so, boss," Fenster said.

"Ah but it was," said Stryk. "Would it interest you to know, Senator, that the article he read claims that I'm a charlatan and a fraud? Just what they needed for their scheme; an incompetent forensic sorcerer who would be awed by the supposed presence of powers far greater than his own."

Senator Langford stared at his legislative aide, and Fenster looked away. "How was it done?" Langford asked. "The switch, I mean."

"I'm not sure," said Stryk, "but the perfect time would have been when your luggage was downloaded in front of the hotel and put in that high-sided luggage cart."

"Yes!" Mrs. Langford said. "I remember. Fenster helped unload the luggage, and I wondered about it. I've never seen him go out of his way to lift anything before."

"Fenster and Pierson," Chief Godfrey said. "A perfect pair of scoundrels"

"I wouldn't have done anything to hurt the girl," Pierson whined.

"No," Stryk agreed. "You needed her alive to work the scheme. Can't have a phoney transference rite without having someone to transfer. But you didn't care much what shape she was in."

Fenster suddenly made a leap for the door. Stryk produced a wand from his sleeve and snapped it like a whip, and Fenster was suddenly frozen in mid-air.

"Grab him," Stryk said.

Two burly cops took hold of the frozen Fenster, and Stryk waved his wand again. Fenster slumped into the arms of the law.

"Charlatan, am I?" Stryk muttered. He turned to Chief Godfrey. "That trunk with the two million in it is somewhere in this hotel. I'd suggest that you put some men on to finding it, before someone stumbles on it by accident."

"Good idea," the chief said.

"Shall we go now?" Stryk asked Melisa.

"I'll stay with the girl for a while," Melisa told him. "Just to be sure she wakes up without fear."

"Good idea," said Stryk.

MASTER OF CHAOS

Michael Moorcock

Michael Moorcock (b. 1939) is one of the true grand masters of fantasy. Since the 1960s he has created an incredible body of work, remarkable as much for its ingenuity and creativity as for its sheer volume. Although for a period Moorcock was producing something like a book a month, his storytelling power was such that the books lost none of their quality. In the fantasy field he is best known for his huge cycle of books about the Eternal Champion, which began in the early sixties with his stories about the albino sorcerer Elric of Melniboné but has since grown to include just about all of Moorcock's fascinating characters such as Corum, Dorian Hawkmoon and even that wildly unpredictable Jerry Cornelius. Even the following story, which was originally a one-off way back in 1964, was subsequently woven in to the eternal tapestry. Yet it's still a story not many may know, so I'm more than happy to resurrect one further reflection of the Eternal Champion, Earl Aubec of Malador.

F ROM THE GLASSLESS WINDOW of the stone tower it was possible to see the wide river winding off between loose, brown banks, through the heaped terrain of solid green copses which blended very gradually into the mass of the forest proper. And from out of the forest, the cliff rose, grey and light green, up and up, the rock darkening, lichen-covered, to merge with the lower, and even more massive, stones of the castle. It was the castle which dominated the countryside in three directions, drawing the eye from river, rock or forest. Its walls were high and of thick granite, with towers; a dense field of towers, grouped so as to shadow one another.

Aubec of Malador marvelled and wondered how human builders could ever have constructed it, save by sorcery. Brooding and mysterious, the castle seemed to have a defiant air, for it stood on the very edge of the world.

At this moment the lowering sky cast a strange, deep yellow light against the western sides of the towers, intensifying the blackness untouched by it. Huge billows of blue sky rent the general racing greyness above, and mounds of red cloud crept through to blend and produce more and subtler colorings. Yet, though the sky was impressive, it could not take the gaze away from the ponderous series of man-made crags that were Castle Kaneloon.

Earl Aubec of Malador did not turn from the window until it was completely dark outside; forest, cliff and castle but shadowy tones against the overall blackness. He passed a heavy, knotted hand over his almost bald scalp and thoughtfully went towards the heap of straw which was his intended bed.

The straw was piled in a niche created by a buttress and the outer wall and the room was well-lighted by Malador's lantern. But the air was cold as he lay down on the straw with his hand close to the two-handed broad-sword of prodigious size. This was his only weapon. It looked as if it had been forged for a giant – Malador was virtually that himself – with its wide cross-piece and heavy, stone-encrusted hilt and five-foot blade, smooth and broad. Beside it was Malador's old, heavy armor, the casque balanced on top with its somewhat tattered black plumes waving slightly in a current of air from the window.

Malador slept.

His dreams, as usual, were turbulent; of mighty armies surging across blazing landscapes, curling banners bearing the blazons of a hundred nations, forests of shining lance-tips, seas of tossing helmets, the brave, wild blasts of the warhorns, the clatter of hooves and the songs and cries and shouts of soldiers. These were dreams of earlier times, of his youth when, for Queen Eloarde of Lormyr, he had conquered all the Southern nations – almost to the edge of the world. Only Kaneloon, on the very edge, had he not conquered and this because no army would follow him there.

For one of so martial an appearance, these dreams were surprisingly unwelcome, and Malador woke several times that night, shaking his head in an attempt to rid himself of them.

He would rather have dreamed of Eloarde, though she was the cause of his restlessness, but he saw nothing of her in his sleep; nothing of her soft, black hair that billowed around her pale face, nothing of her green eyes and red lips and her proud, disdainful posture. Eloarde had assigned him to this quest and he had not gone willingly, though he had no choice, for as well as his mistress she was also his Queen. The Queen's Champion was traditionally her lover – and it was unthinkable to Earl Aubec that any other condition should exist. It was his place, as Champion of Lormyr, to obey and go forth from her palace to seek Castle Kaneloon alone and conquer it and declare it part of her Empire, so that it could be said Queen Eloarde's domain stretched from the Dragon Sea to World's Edge.

Nothing lay beyond World's Edge – nothing save the swirling stuff of unformed Chaos which stretched away from the Cliffs of Kaneloon for eternity, roiling and broiling, multicolored, full of monstrous half-shapes – for Earth alone was Lawful and constituted of ordered matter, drifting in the sea of Chaos-stuff as it had done for aeons.

In the morning, Earl Aubec of Malador extinguished the lantern which he had allowed to remain alight, drew greaves and hauberk on to him, placed his black-plumed helm upon his head, put his broadsword over his shoulder and sallied out of the stone tower which was all that remained whole of some ancient edifice.

His leathern-shod feet stumbled over stones that seemed partially dissolved, as if Chaos had once lapped here instead of against the towering Cliffs of Kaneloon. That, of course, was quite impossible, since Earth's boundaries were known to be constant.

Castle Kaneloon had seemed closer the night before and that, he now realized, was because it was so huge. He followed the river, his feet sinking in the loamy soil, the great branches of the trees shading him from the increasingly hot sun as he made his way towards the cliffs. Kaneloon was now out of sight, high above him. Every so often he used his sword as an axe to clear his way through the places where the foliage was particularly thick.

He rested several times, drinking the cold water of the river and mopping his face and head. He was unhurried, he had no wish to visit Kaneloon, he resented the interruption to his life with Eloarde which he thought he had earned. Also, he too had a superstitious dread of the mysterious castle, which was said to be inhabited only by one human occupant – the Dark Lady, a sorceress without mercy who commanded a legion of demons and other Chaos-creatures.

He reached the cliffs at midday and regarded the path leading upwards with a mixture of wariness and relief. He had expected to have to scale the cliffs. He was not one, however, to take a difficult route where an easy one presented itself, so he looped a cord around his sword and slung it over his back, since it was too long and cumbersome to carry at his side. Then, still in bad humor, he began to climb the twisting path.

The lichen-covered rocks were evidently ancient, contrary to the speculations of certain Lormyrian philosophers who asked why Kaneloon had only been heard of a few generations since. Malador believed in the general answer to this question – that explorers had never ventured this far until fairly recently. He glanced back down the path and saw the tops of the trees below him, their foliage moving slightly in the breeze. The tower in which he'd spent the night was just visible in the distance and beyond that, he knew, there was no civilization, no outpost of Man for many days' journey North, East or West – can Chaos lay to the South. He had never been so close to the edge of the world before and wondered how the sight of unformed matter would affect his brain.

At length he clambered to the top of the cliff and stood, arms akimbo, staring up at Castle Kaneloon which soared a mile away, its highest towers hidden in the clouds, its immense walls rooted on the rock and stretching away, limited on both sides only by the edge of the cliff. And, on the other side of the cliff, Malador watched the churning, leaping Chaos-substance, predominantly grey, blue, brown and yellow at this moment, though its colors changed constantly, spew like the sea-spray a few feet from the castle.

He became filled with a feeling of such indescribable profundity that he could only remain in this position for a long while, completely overwhelmed by a sense of his own insignificance. It came to him, eventually, that if anyone did dwell in the Castle Kaneloon, then they must have a robust mind or else must be insane, and then he sighed and strode on towards his goal, noting that the ground was perfectly flat, without blemish, green, obsidian and reflecting imperfectly the dancing Chaos-stuff from which he averted his eyes as much as he could.

Kaneloon had many entrances, all dark and unwelcoming, and had they all not been of regular size and shape they might have been so many cave-mouths.

Malador paused before choosing which to take, and then walked with outward purposefulness towards one. He went into blackness which appeared to stretch away forever. It was cold; it was empty and he was alone.

He was soon lost. His footsteps made no echo, which was unexpected; then the blackness began to give way to a series of angular outlines, like the walls of a twisting corridor – walls which did not reach the unsensed roof, but ended several yards above his head. It was a labyrinth, a maze. He paused and looked back and saw with horror that the maze wound off in many directions though he was sure he had followed a straight path from the outside.

For an instant, his mind became diffused and madness threatened to engulf him, but he battened it down, unslung his sword, shivering. Which way? He pressed on, unable to tell, now, whether he went forward or backward.

The madness lurking in the depths of his brain filtered out and became fear and, immediately following the sensation of fear, came the shapes. Swift-moving shapes, darting from several different directions, gibbering, fiendish, utterly horrible.

One of these creatures leapt at him and he struck at it with his blade. It fled, but seemed unwounded. Another came and another and he forgot his panic as he smote around him, driving them back until all had fled. He paused and leaned, panting, on his sword. Then, as he stared around him, the fear began to flood back into him and more creatures appeared – creatures with wide, blazing eyes and clutching talons, creatures with malevolent faces, mocking him, creatures with half-familiar faces, some recognizable as those of old friends and relatives, yet twisted into horrific parodies. He screamed and ran at them, whirling his huge sword, slashing, hacking at them, rushing past one group to turn a bend in the labyrinth and encounter another.

Malicious laughter coursed through the twisting corridors, following him and preceding him as he ran. He stumbled and fell against a wall. At first the wall seemed of solid stone, then, slowly it became soft and he sank through it, his body lying half in one corridor, half in another. He hauled himself through, still on hands and knees, looked up and saw Eloarde, but an Eloarde whose face grew old as he watched.

"*I am mad*," he thought. "*is this reality or fantasy – or both?*"

He reached out a hand, "*Eloarde!*"

She vanished but was replaced by a crowding horde of demons. He raised himself to his feet and flailed around him with his blade, but they skipped just outside his range and he roared at them as he advanced. Momentarily, whilst he thus exerted himself, the fear left him again and, with the disappearance of the fear, so the visions vanished until he realized that the fear preceded the manifestations and he tried to control it.

He almost succeeded, forcing himself to relax, but it welled up again and the creatures bubbled out of the walls, their shrill voices full of malicious mirth.

This time he did not attack them with his sword, but stood his ground as calmly as he could and concentrated upon his own mental condition. As he did so, the creatures began to fade away and then the walls of the labyrinth dissolved and it seemed to him that he stood in a peaceful valley, calm and idyllic. Yet, hovering close to his consciousness, he seemed to see the walls of the labyrinth faintly outlined, and disgusting shapes moving here and there along the many passages.

He realized that the vision of the valley was as much an illusion as the labyrinth and, with this conclusion, both valley and labyrinth faded and he stood in the enormous hall of a castle which could only be Kaneloon.

The hall was unoccupied, though well-furnished, and he could not see the source of the light, which was bright and even. He strode towards a table, on which were heaped scrolls, and his feet made a satisfying echo. Several great metal-studded doors led off from the hall, but for the moment he did not investigate them, intent on studying the scrolls and seeing if they could help him unravel Kaneloon's mystery.

He propped his sword against the table and took up the first scroll.

It was a beautiful thing of red vellum, but the black letters upon it meant nothing to him and he was astounded for, though dialects varied from place to place, there was only one language in all the lands of the Earth. Another scroll bore different symbols still, and a third he unrolled carried a series of highly stylised pictures which were repeated here and there so that he guessed they formed some kind of alphabet. Disgusted, he flung the scroll down, picked up his sword, drew an immense breath and shouted:

"Who dwells here? Let them know that Aubec, Earl of Malador, Champion of Lormyr and Conqueror of the South claims this castle in the name of Queen Eloarde, Empress of all the Southlands!"

In shouting these familiar words, he felt somewhat more comfortable, but he received no reply. He lifted his casque a trifle and scratched his neck. Then he picked up his sword, balanced it over his shoulder, and made for the largest door.

Before he reached it, it sprang open and a huge, manlike thing with hands like grappling irons grinned at him.

He took a pace backwards and then another until, seeing that the thing did not advance, stood his ground observing it.

It was a foot or so taller than he, with oval, multi-facetted eyes that, by their nature, seemed blank. Its face was angular and had a grey, metallic sheen. Most of its body was comprised of burnished metal, jointed in the manner of armor. Upon its head was a tight-fitting hood, studded with brass. It had about it an air of tremendous and insensate power, though it did not move.

"A golem!" Malador exclaimed, for it seemed to him that he remembered such manmade creatures from legends. "What sorcery created *you!*"

The golem did not reply, but its hands – which were in reality comprised of four spikes of metal apiece – began slowly to flex themselves; and still the golem grinned.

This thing, Malador knew, did not have the same amorphous quality of his earlier visions. This was solid, this was real and strong, and even Malador's manly strength, however much he exerted it, could not defeat such a creature. Yet neither could he turn away.

With a scream of metal joints, the golem entered the hall and stretched its burnished hands towards the earl.

Malador could attack or flee, and fleeing would be senseless. He attacked.

His great sword clasped in both hands, he swung it sideways at the golem's torso, which seemed to be its weakest point. The golem lowered an arm and the sword shuddered against metal with a mighty clang that set the whole of Malador's body quaking. He stumbled backwards. Remorselessly, the golem followed him.

Malador looked back and searched the hall in the hope of finding a weapon more powerful than his sword, but saw only shields of an ornamental kind upon the wall to his right. He turned and ran to the wall, wrenching one of the shields from its place and slipping it on to his arm. It was an oblong thing, very light and comprising several layers of cross-grained wood. It was inadequate, but it made him feel a trifle better as he whirled again to face the golem.

The golem advanced, and Malador thought he noticed something familiar about it, just as the demons of the labyrinth had seemed familiar, but the impression was only vague. Kaneloon's weird sorcery was affecting his mind, he decided.

The creature raised the spikes on its right arm and aimed a swift blow at Malador's head. He avoided it, putting up his sword as protection. The spikes clashed against the sword and then the left arm pistoned forward, driving at Malador's stomach. The shield stopped this blow, though the spikes pierced it deeply. He yanked the buckler off the spikes, slashing at the golem's leg-joints as he did so.

Still staring into the middle-distance, with apparently no real interest in Malador, the golem advanced like a blind man as the earl turned and leapt on to the table, scattering the scrolls. Now he brought his huge sword down upon the golem's skull and the brass studs sparked and the hood and head beneath it was dented. The golem staggered and then grasped the table, heaving it off the floor so that Malador was forced to leap to the ground. This time he made for the door and tugged at its latch-ring, but the door would not open.

His sword was chipped and blunted. He put his back to the door as the golem reached him and brought its metal hand down on the top edge of the shield. The shield shattered and a dreadful pain shot up Malador's arm. He lunged at the golem, but he was unused to handling the big sword in this manner and the stroke was clumsy.

Malador knew that he was doomed. Force and fighting skill were not enough against the golem's insensate strength. At the golem's next blow he swung aside, but was caught by one of its spike-fingers which ripped through his armor and drew blood, though at that moment he felt no pain.

He scrambled up, shaking away the grip and fragments of wood which remained of the shield, grasping his sword firmly.

"*The soulless demon has no weak spot,*" he thought, "*and, since it has no true intelligence, it cannot be appealed to. What would a golem fear?*"

The answer was simple. The golem would only fear something as strong or stronger than itself.

He must use cunning.

He ran for the upturned table with the golem after him, leapt over the table and wheeled as the golem stumbled but did not, as he'd hoped, fall. However, the golem was slowed by its encounter and Aubec took advantage of this to rush for the door through which the golem had entered. It opened. He was in a twisting corridor, darkly shadowed, not unlike the labyrinth he had first found in Kaneloon. The door closed but he could find nothing to bar it with. He ran up the corridor as the golem tore the door open and came lumbering swiftly after him.

The corridor writhed about in all directions and, though he could not always see the golem, he could hear it and had the sickening fear that he would turn a corner at some stage and run straight into it. He did not – but he came to a door and, upon opening it and passing through it, found himself again in the hall of Castle Kaneloon.

He almost welcomed this familiar sight as he heard the golem, its metal parts screeching, continue to come after him. He needed another shield, but the part of the hall in which he now found himself had no wall-shields – only a large, round mirror of bright, clear-polished metal. It would be too heavy to be much use, but he seized it, tugging it from its hook. It fell with a clang and he hauled it up, dragging it with him as he stumbled away from the golem which had emerged into the room once more.

Using the chains by which the mirror had hung, he gripped it before him and, as the golem's speed increased and the monster rushed upon him, he raised this makeshift shield.

The golem shrieked.

Malador was astounded. The monster stopped dead and cowered away from the mirror. Malador pushed it towards the golem and the thing turned its back and fled, with a metallic howl, through the door it had entered by.

Relieved and puzzled, Malador sat down on the floor and studied the mirror. There was certainly nothing magical about it, though its quality was good. He grinned and said aloud:

"The creature *is* afraid of something. It is afraid of itself!"

He threw back his head and laughed loudly in his relief. Then he frowned. "Now to find the sorcerers who created him and take vengeance on them!" He pushed himself to his feet, twisted the chains of the mirror more securely about his arm and went to another door, concerned lest the golem complete its circuit of the maze and return through the door. This door would not budge, so he lifted his sword and hacked at the latch for a few moments until it gave. He strode into a well-lit passage with what appeared to be another room at its far end – the door open.

A musky scent came to his nostrils as he progressed along the passage – the scent that reminded him of Eloarde and the comforts of Lormyr.

When he reached the circular chamber, he saw that it was a bedroom – a woman's bedroom full of the perfume he had smelled in the passage. He controlled the direction his mind took, thought of loyalty and Lormyr, and went to another door which led off from the room. He lugged it open and discovered a stone staircase winding upwards. This he mounted, passing windows that seemed glazed with emerald or ruby, beyond which shadow-shapes flickered so that he knew he was on the side of the castle overlooking Chaos.

The staircase seemed to lead up into a tower and when he finally reached the small door at its top, he was feeling out of breath and paused before entering. Then he pushed the door open and went in.

A huge window was set in one wall, a window of clear glass through which he could see the ominous stuff of Chaos leaping. A woman stood by this window as if awaiting him.

"You are indeed a champion, Earl Aubec," said she with a smile that might have been ironic.

"How do you know my name?"

"No sorcery gave it me, Earl of Malador – you shouted it loudly enough when you first saw the hall in its true shape."

"Was not *that*, then, sorcery," he said ungraciously, "the labyrinth, the demons – even the valley? Was not the golem made by sorcery? Is not this whole cursed castle of a sorcerous nature?"

She shrugged. "Call it so if you'd rather not have the truth. Sorcery, in your mind at least, is a crude thing which only hints at the true powers existing in the universe."

He did not reply, being somewhat impatient of such statements. He had learned, by observing the philosophers of Lormyr, that mysterious words often disguised commonplace things and ideas. Instead he looked at her sulkily and over-frankly.

She was fair with green-blue eyes and a light complexion. Her long robe was of a similar color to her eyes. She was, in a secret sort of way, very beautiful and, like all the denizens of Kaneloon he'd encountered, a trifle familiar.

"You recognize Kaneloon?" she asked.

He dismissed her question. "Enough of this – take me to the masters of this place!"

"There is none but me, Micella the Dark Lady – and I am the mistress."

He was disappointed. "Was it just to meet you that I came through such perils?"

"It was – and greater perils even than you think, Earl Aubec. Those were the monsters of your own imagination!"

"Taunt me not, lady."

She laughed. "I speak in good faith. The castle creates its defenses out of your own mind. It is a rare man who can face and defeat his own imagination. Such a one has not found me here for two hundred years. All since have perished by fear – until now."

She smiled at him. It was a warm smile.

"And what is the prize for so great a feat?" he said gruffly.

She laughed again and gestured towards the window which looked out upon the edge of the world and Chaos beyond. "Out there nothing exists as yet. If you venture into it, you will be confronted again by creatures of your hidden fancy, for there is nothing else to behold."

She gazed at him admiringly and he coughed in his embarrassment. "Once in a while," she said, "there comes a man to Kaneloon who can withstand such an ordeal. Then may the frontiers of the world be extended, for when a man stands against Chaos it must recede and new lands spring into being!"

"So that is the fate you have in mind for me, sorceress!"

She glanced at him almost demurely. Her beauty seemed to increase as he looked at her. He clutched at the hilt of his sword, gripping it tight as she moved gracefully towards him and touched him, as if by accident. "There is a reward for your courage." She looked into his eyes and said no more of the reward, for it was clear what she offered. "And after – do my bidding and go against Chaos."

"Lady, know you not that ritual demands of Lormyr's Champion that he be the Queen's faithful consort? I would not betray my word and trust!" He gave a hollow laugh. "I came here to remove a menace to my Queen's kingdom – not to be your lover and lacky!"

"There is no menace here."

"That seems true . . ."

She stepped back as if appraising him anew. For her this was unprecedented – never before had her offer been refused. She rather liked this stolid man who also combined courage and imagination in his character. It was incredible, she thought, how in a few centuries such traditions could grow up – traditions which could bind a man to a woman he probably did not even love. She looked at him as he stood there, his body rigid, his manner nervous.

"Forget Lormyr," she said, "think of the power you might have – the power of true creation!"

"Lady, I claim this castle for Lormyr. That is what I came to do and that is what I do now. If I leave here alive, I shall be judged the conqueror and you must comply."

She hardly heard him. She was thinking of various plans to convince him that her cause was superior to his. Perhaps she could still seduce him? Or use some drug to bewitch him? No, he was too strong for either, she must think of some other stratagem.

She felt her breasts heaving involuntarily as she looked at him. She would have preferred to have seduced him. It had always been as much her reward as the heroes who had earlier won over the dangers of Kaneloon. And then, she thought, she knew what to say.

"Think, Earl Aubec," she whispered. "Think – new lands for your queen's Empire!"

He frowned.

"Why not extend the Empire's boundaries further?" she continued. "Why not *make* new territories?"

She watched him anxiously as he took off his helm and scratched his heavy, bald head. "You have made a point at last," he said dubiously.

"Think of the honors you would receive in Lormyr if you succeeded in winning not merely Kaneloon – but that which lies *beyond!*"

Now he rubbed his chin. "Aye," he said. "Aye . . ." His great brows frowned deeply.

"New plains, new mountains, new seas – new populations, even – whole cities full of people fresh-sprung and yet with the memory of generations of ancestors behind them! All this can be done by *you*, Earl of Malador – for Queen Eloarde and Lormyr!"

He smiled faintly, his imagination fired at last. "Aye! If I can defeat such dangers here – then I can do the same out there! It will be the greatest adventure in history! My name will become a legend – Malador, Master of Chaos!"

She gave him a tender look, though she had half-cheated him.

He swung his sword up on to his shoulder. "I'll try this, lady."

She and he stood together at the window, watching the Chaos-stuff whisping and rolling for eternity before them. To her it had never been wholly familiar, for it changed all the time. Now its tossing colors were predominantly red and black. Tendrils of mauve and orange spiralled out of this and writhed away.

Weird shapes flitted about in it, their outlines never clear, never quite recognizeable.

He said to her: "The Lords of Chaos rule this territory. What will they have to say?"

"They can say nothing, do little. Even they have to obey the Law of the Cosmic Balance which ordains that if man can stand against Chaos, then it shall be his to order and make Lawful. Thus the Earth grows, slowly."

"How do I enter it?"

She took the opportunity to grasp his heavily-muscled arm and point through the window. "See – there – a causeway leads down from this tower to the cliff." She glanced at him sharply. "Do you see it?"

"Ah – yes – I had not, but now I do. Yes, a causeway."

Standing behind him, she smiled a little to herself. "I will remove the barrier," she said.

He straightened his helm on his head. "For Lormyr and Eloarde and only those do I embark upon this adventure."

She moved towards the wall and raised the window. He did not look at her as he strode down the causeway into the multicolored mist.

As she watched him disappear, she smiled to herself. How easy it was to beguile the strongest man by pretending to go his way! He might add lands to his Empire, but he might find their populations unwilling to accept Eloarde as their Empress. In fact, if Aubec did his work well, then he would be creating more of a threat to Lormyr than ever Kaneloon had been.

Yet she admired him, she was attracted to him, perhaps,

because he was not so accessible, a little more than she had been
to that earlier hero who had claimed Aubec's own land from
Chaos barely two hundred years before. Oh, he had been a man!
But he, like most before him, had needed no other persuasion
than the allurement of her body.

Earl Aubec's weakness had lain in his strength, she thought. By
now he had vanished into the heaving mists.

She felt a trifle sad that this time the execution of the task given
her by the Lords of Law had not brought her the usual pleasure.

Yet perhaps, she thought, she felt a more subtle pleasure in his
steadfastness and the means she had used to convince him.

For centuries had the Lords of Law entrusted her with Kaneloon and its secrets. But the progress was slow, for there were
few heroes who could survive Kaneloon's dangers – few who
could defeat self-created perils.

Yet, she decided with a slight smile on her lips, the task had its
various rewards. She moved into another chamber to prepare for
the transition of the castle to the new edge of the world.

SEVEN DROPS OF BLOOD

Robert Weinberg

Robert Weinberg (b. 1946) has one of the largest collections of old pulp magazines in the world, which makes me very envious. He first made his name as a bookdealer and collector – he also has a phenomenal collection of original pulp art – but he began to sell short fiction as far back as 1969. Those who remember the old magazine Worlds of If, *with its feature for new writers, may recall that Weinberg was a treasured "If first" in the May 1969 issue. He also compiled several books of reference, including the indispensable* A Biographical Dictionary of Science Fiction and Fantasy Artists *(1988), plus several anthologies before his first novels appeared. These included the series of occult mysteries that began with* The Devil's Auction *(1988). Out of that grew a number of short stories featuring the occult detective Sidney Taine. In the following, Taine is on the trail of the Holy Grail.*

"I WANT YOU TO locate," said the man in dark glasses, his voice intent, "the Holy Grail."

Not exactly sure how to reply, Sidney Taine, known through-out Chicago as the "New Age detective," stretched back in his chair and stared across the desk at his client. The speaker was a short, stocky man, impeccably dressed in a grey pin-stripe suit and charcoal tie. His sharp, almost angular features appeared cut from solid rock. A full black beard covered most of his jaw.

Heavy dark eyebrows flowed together above his glasses, giving his features a sinister turn. His wide nose jutted out from the center of his face like the sharp beak of some massive bird of prey. He looked and sounded like a man accustomed to getting his own way.

Ashmedai was the name he used, not indicating whether it was first or last or both. His smooth, confident motions entering Taine's office made it quite clear that the eyes behind the black lenses were not those of a blind man. What secret those glasses actually hid, the detective was not sure he wanted to learn. According to ancient Hebrew tradition, Ashmedai reigned as king of demons.

"I'm not King Arthur," said Taine slowly, measuring his reply. "Nor am I a member of the Round Table."

"I dislike fairy tales," replied the bearded man, a slight smile crossing his lips. "The Grail I seek is real, not folklore. And, it is presently lost somewhere in Chicago."

"In Chicago?" repeated Taine, rising from behind the desk. He felt uncomfortable staring at those dark lenses. Ashmedai's face remained a mystery. Taine firmly believed that the eyes reflected a man's soul. Ashmedai kept his hidden for a reason. The detective looked out the windows of his office onto Lake Michigan. He was a tall, muscular man, built like a linebacker on a football team, his every move reflecting the dangerous grace of a stalking cat. Clients who spoke in riddles annoyed him. Dark, threatening clouds hovered over the placid waters. Jagged streaks of lightning flared in the late afternoon sky, reflecting the disquiet Taine felt addressing Ashmedai.

"You are aware of the theory," said Taine, "that claims the Holy Grail is not the Cup of the Last Supper. That instead, it is the container that held the burial wrappings of Christ. Which, the same scholars who advocate this position, identify as the Shroud of Turin."

Ashmedai shrugged. "I've read *The Shroud and the Grail* by Noel Currer-Briggs. He raises some interesting points. But, much of his book is filled with idle speculation. Too often, he manipulates the translations of early legends to fit his hypothesis. Worse, he shows no understanding of the true purpose behind Joseph of Arimathaea's actions during and after the Crucifixion."

"Which is?" asked Taine, when Ashmedai hesitated. The

stranger spoke with convincing authority about the most mysterious of all occult traditions.

"Currer-Briggs dismissed as utter nonsense the legend that Joseph used the Grail to catch drops of Jesus' blood from the wound made in his side by the Spear of Vengeance," replied Ashmedai. "He let his modern sensibilities overcome his scholarly curiosity. Instead of searching for the reason behind Joseph's actions, the author shrugged off the entire episode as tasteless and revolting. Seeking another explanation for the stories linking the Grail and Christ's blood, Currer-Briggs fastened on the blood-stained burial wrappings used by Joseph and Nicodemus. The container containing those linens, marked with the same blood, he concluded was the true Grail. Extending his theory, he then identified the wrappings as the Shroud of Turin."

Ashmedai chuckled. "A wonderful mental exercise, but absolute nonsense. Joseph of Arimathaea knew exactly what he was doing when he caught the Savior's blood in the Grail. For all of his facts, Currer-Briggs refused to acknowledge the reality of the occult."

Taine inhaled sharply, suddenly understanding what Ashmedai meant. "Black magic relies on blood," said the detective. "The blood of Christ . . ."

"Would work wonders," concluded Ashmedai. "Especially when linked with Seth's Chalice."

Taine's eyes narrowed. Few people knew of the existence of that fabled Cup. The detective had learned of it only after years of studying the darkest secrets of the supernatural. Again, he wondered exactly who was Ashmedai? And what were his sources of information?

"According to *The Lost Apocrypha*," said Taine, "when Seth, the third son of Adam and Eve, traveled to the Garden of Eden he was given a chalice by the Lord as a sign that God had not deserted humanity."

"I'm glad to see your reputation is well deserved," said Ashmedai. "It's hard to believe a mere detective would know of such things."

"I'm not an ordinary detective," said Taine.

"If you were, I wouldn't be here," replied Ashmedai, chuckling softly. "A talisman of incalculable power, the Cup passed down through the ages, from generation to generation, held by only the greatest of mages. Until it was given as a gift to Jesus by one of his disciples. And became known ever after as the Holy Grail."

"Which you claim is now in Chicago?" said Taine, a hint of skepticism creeping into his voice.

"I *know* it is," said Ashmedai. The bearded man reached inside his jacket pocket. His hand emerged with a wad of money, held tightly together by a rubber band. Casually, he dropped the cash on Taine's desk.

"I'll pay you $5,000 to find the Chalice. It belongs to me and I want it back. No questions. If you need more money, just let me know."

Taine looked down at the cash, then up at Ashmedai. Down and up again, not saying a word.

"Nothing to worry about," said Ashmedai. "It's honest money. Over the years, I've invested in a number of long-term securities. They pay a handsome return. Money serves me merely as a means to an end."

Still, Taine made no move to pick up the package. Though he was not above bending the law for his clients when necessary, he held himself to a strict code of ethics which he refused to compromise. The notion of dealing in stolen religious artifacts crossed over that boundary.

"I need a few more details before I'll take the case," said Taine. "You state the Grail belongs to you. What's your claim to it? And how was it stolen?"

"Suspicious, Mr. Taine?" asked Ashmedai, a touch of amusement in his voice. "I assure you, *my right to the Chalice is more legitimate than most.*"

The bearded man hesitated, as if considering what to say next. "Details of what happened to the Cup after the Crucifixion are shrouded in mystery. Arthurian legend has Joseph traveling to England, taking the Grail with him. Several occult references place the Chalice in the hands of Simon the Magician. I've even read an account of the vessel surfacing in the court of Charles the Great, Charlemagne." Ashmedai shook his head, almost in dismay. "No one really knows the truth. Though I suspect it is much less colorful than any of those fables.

"The Grail and Joseph of Arimathaea disappeared shortly after Christ's burial. They vanished into the murkiness of ancient history. In time, both became enshrined in legend. In 1907, archaeologists at a dig outside of Damascus, Syria, uncovered a spectacular silver chalice, decorated in great detail with images of the Last Supper. Comparison to like pieces dated the Cup as belonging to the 5th century AD.

"After making discreet financial arrangements with certain government officials, the discoverers of the Chalice of Damascus offered it for sale to the highest bidder. A Syrian antique dealer, acting as agent for an American millionaire, bought the rarity for $700,000. Like hundreds of other pieces, it disappeared into the reclusive publisher's vast California estate."

"The Chalice of Damascus and the Holy Grail . . .?" began Taine.

"Were one and the same," finished Ashmedai. "Some enterprising smith concealed Seth's Cup beneath a sheath of finely crafted metal, both protecting and concealing the relic. The truth emerged only after exhaustive scientific testing performed at the millionaire's estate. Hidden under a silver lining was the Cup of the Last Supper. I tried for decades, without success, to purchase the Grail. The new owner refused to let it go. The more I offered, the more obstinate he became. After his death, his estate maintained the same position. Finally, this year, facing a huge tax increase and declining revenues due to unwise investments, they relented. It cost me a king's ransom, but the Grail belonged to me."

"Only to be stolen," said Taine.

"I never even saw the Cup," said Ashmedai bitterly. "Last night, two security guards flew in to O'Hare Airport, with the Grail in their possession. They departed the terminal shortly after nine in the evening, in a hired limo, bound for my estate in northern Illinois. That was the last anyone saw of them."

"The police?" asked Taine.

"They're waiting for a ransom note," said Ashmedai. "The fools are treating the disappearance as an art theft."

"And you don't?"

"The Grail is the most coveted magical talisman in the world," replied Ashmedai. "I thought no one other than myself knew its location. Obviously, I believed wrong. Someone stole the Chalice and intends using it for his own ends. What that purpose might be, I have no idea. But, knowing the power inherent in the Grail, I shudder at the thought."

Taine nodded. There was no mistaking the worry in Ashmedai's voice. Still, he had his doubts about the man. "And your plans for the Grail?"

"If I thought to use the Chalice for evil intent, I would have stolen it years ago," said Ashmedai. "Instead, I waited, biding my time, and acquired the treasure honestly. My intent was never criminal." He paused. "My collection of occult rarities is the greatest in the world. I am assembling it for a purpose that need not concern you. The Grail belongs there, well-guarded and protected, away from the schemes of little men." His voice grew icy cold. "I am not a man easily crossed, Mr. Taine. Whoever stole the Grail will pay – pay *severely*."

Taine considered that Ashmedai seemed not to care about the fate of the two bodyguards. All the bearded man wanted was the Grail. Nothing else mattered.

"I have a few ideas," said Taine, dropping back into his chair. "Some people to call." He slid a pad of paper and a pen across the desk. "Give me a number where I can reach you."

"Call me day or night," said Ashmedai, scribbling a phone number on the paper. He passed it over to Taine. "Let me know the instant you locate the Cup. I'll come at once."

"If it can be found," said Taine, "I'll find it."

"So I have heard," said Ashmedai. "That is why I hired you. Good luck."

Somehow, Taine had a feeling he'd need it.

Seven hours later, the detective wearily pushed open the door to the Spiderweb Lounge on Chicago's northwest side. None of his usual sources had provided a clue to the missing relic. Nor had his own investigations at the airport turned up anything the least bit useful. Much as Taine disliked the notion, the only remaining option was to enter the Spiderweb. And deal with its owner, Sal "The Spider" Albanese.

According to crime insiders, Albanese's nickname came from his involvement in every sort of illegal activity in Chicago. Stolen property, guns, prostitution, drugs, and murder were all part of his everyday business. Like a giant spider, the crime boss spun his deadly web across the Windy City.

Others assumed that the moniker derived from Albanese's appearance. An immensely fat man who favored dark clothing, the elderly gangster bore an uncanny resemblance to a gigantic arachnid. Sal's unwavering gaze and jet-black eyes did nothing to dispel that image.

Only a select group knew of Albanese's youthful encounter with the outer darkness. They had actually seen the incredible scars across the fat man's back and understood the full significance of the title, "The Spider." Sidney Taine, occult investigator, was one such man.

While not an admirer of the gangster, Taine belonged to a certain occult fraternity that included Albanese as well. Which was why he was admitted to the crime chief's office without any hassle.

"Taine," grunted Albanese, waving one huge hand at the detective. In his other, the Spider held a foot-long meatball sandwich. Albanese was always eating, feeding his bloated three-hundred-pound body. "Long time no see. Join me for a late snack?"

"No thanks," replied Taine, nodding to Tony Bracco and Leo Scaglia, Albanese's ever-present bodyguards. Tony, short but built like a fireplug, crinkled his eyes in recognition. Leo, tall and thin, who handled a knife with the skill of a surgeon, grinned and nodded. He worked out at the same gym as Taine, and he and the detective had boxed more than a few rounds in the sparring ring.

Albanese made short work of the sandwich. Reaching for the tray on his desk, he guzzled down a stein filled with beer, then raised a second meatball hero to his lips. The mobster ate three or four sandwiches at a time.

They chatted for a few minutes, discussing the Bulls, the Bears and the Cubs. Albanese followed all sports closely. Making book helped pay the bills. Finally, the gangster got down to business.

"Whatcha here for?" asked Albanese, biting deep into his third sandwich. Carefully, he wiped little drops of meat sauce off his shirt. "From your call I take it this ain't no social call. You working for the Brotherhood?"

"Not tonight," said Taine. "I'm investigating a robbery. My

client is willing to pay quite a bundle for the return of some stolen property. No questions asked. With *your* contacts, I thought you might be able to help."

"Always glad to help a frien'," said Albanese, taking another bite. "Whatcha missing?"

"A silver cup," said Taine. "A religious artifact known as the Chalice of Damascus."

Sal Albanese froze in mid-bite, his jaws gaping wide open. Seconds passed, and then, very carefully, he put his sandwich down on the desk. "Too messy," he declared, not very convincingly.

"About the Chalice . . .?" said Taine.

"Don't know nothing about no chalice," declared Albanese curtly. "None of my people had anything to do with robbing relics, Taine. That ain't my style."

The big gangster sounded angry. Black eyes glared at Taine defiantly, as if challenging the detective to say otherwise. However, behind the bluster, Taine sensed something else. Fear.

"Are you positive . . .?" Taine tried one more time.

"You doubting my word, Taine?" asked Albanese, his huge hands clenching into fists. "I don't like being called a liar."

"No offense, Sal," said Taine. It made no sense to antagonize the crime boss without good reason. "I just assumed that with all your connections you would have all the details about this theft."

"I ain't heard," said Albanese, unconvincingly. "Now clear out, Taine. I got business to discuss with the boys. Don't got any more time for idle chit-chat."

Taine turned to leave. In the corner of an eye, he caught a furtive gesture made by Leo Scaglia. The tall bodyguard, half-turned so that only Taine could see the signal, moved one hand as if to indicate, "later." The detective dipped his head acknowledgingly, then departed.

An hour later, back at his office, Taine picked up his phone on the first ring. Scaglia, his voice muffled and barely distinguishable, was on the other end.

"You wanted information on the Chalice?" asked the bodyguard, straight off, without any word of greeting. "I know where it is."

"Sal has it?" asked Taine, uncertain what to believe.

"Nah. He won't touch no religious stuff. You know him. But ain't nothing goin' on that Sal don't hear about. He was just too scared to say anything to you at the Club. Sal suspects that somebody's passing on all our secrets to those crazy Jamaicans. Bracco's been acting pretty odd lately, flashing a lot of money and making big talk. So the boss had me make this call, private like. Sal thought you'd want to know the truth. That lunatic, King Wedo, stole your precious chalice."

"King Wedo?" repeated Taine, taken by surprise. Though he had never met the mysterious Jamaican crime lord, he had heard quite a bit about him. In Chicago for less than a year, the gang leader had earned a reputation as a merciless, violent killer with a taste for the bizarre.

"Sal's frightened and with good reason," continued Scaglia. "Those Jamaican bozos working for King Wedo are crazy. They'd just as soon rip out your guts as look at you. Life is cheap, don't mean a thing to them. Bastards take a dislike to somebody, he's dead meat."

A note of fear crept into Scaglia's voice. "Joey Ventura made the mistake of crossing King Wedo. Got greedy during a coke delivery and swiped some goods he didn't pay for. Stupid idea. The Jamaicans pulled Joey right out of a restaurant at lunch time. Shot down three bystanders dumb enough to interfere. Like I said, life don't mean nothin' to them devils."

Scaglia's voice dropped to a whisper. "King Wedo planned a special finish for Joey. Called it a demonstration. The maniac cut off Joey's fingers and toes, one joint at a time, and forced him to swallow the pieces. It took the poor slob three days to die. Now you understand why Sal is cautious."

"Perfectly," said Taine. "Any clue to why King Wedo clipped the Chalice? Ransom perhaps?"

"Nothing definite. But King Wedo don't need no money, not with the dough he's raking in from the drug trade. Word on the street is that the Jamaican is heavy into black magic. Maybe he figures this chalice of yours will give him some sort of mystical powers. Who the hell knows with these crazy bastards."

"Sure," answered Taine, his mind racing. King Wedo and the Holy Grail added up to a dangerous mix. He had to retrieve the

Chalice. "Maybe I should talk to the King about returning the Cup. You have any idea where he holds court?"

"You're nuts, man. One wrong word to that geek and he'll carve out your heart. With his fingernails."

"Let me worry about that," said Taine. "Where's his main base?"

"On the near south side," replied Scaglia. "Around Twenty-Sixth and the railroad tracks." The bodyguard hesitated for a moment, then cursed. "The Jamaicans might let you enter their hideout, but they sure the hell won't let you leave. No chance you'll change your mind?"

"Can't," said Taine. "It's my job."

"Well, you'll need some backup," said Scaglia. "And I guess that means me. I'll meet you there in an hour. Corner of Twenty-Sixth and Rand. Don't be late, 'cause if you are, I might just lose my nerve."

"I'll be there," said Taine and hung up the phone.

Taine arrived at the designated location a few minutes after midnight. Amber-colored street lights cast an eerie glow on the otherwise deserted avenue. Huge old warehouses lined both sides of the street, towering into the night sky like ancient tombs. Soundlessly, Leo Scaglia beckoned from the doorway of a nearby building. After a quick check of the surroundings, Taine slipped out of his car and joined the mobster.

"What's the story?" whispered Taine.

"We're in luck," replied Scaglia, grinning. "King Wedo and his thugs are out celebrating. One of Sal's contacts spotted them a half-hour ago at the Kozy Klub. We should have no problem finding that chalice and making off with it before the Jamaican returns. Damned SOB is so sure of himself, I doubt he bothered leaving anybody on guard."

"Sounds too easy," said Taine, staring at Scaglia suspiciously. "Why are you so eager to help, Leo? I never knew you to take any unnecessary risks."

"Back off, Taine," said Scaglia, glancing around the deserted street. "Sal's pushing for King Wedo to take a fall. Wants me to lend you a hand. Anything that makes King Wedo look bad, makes Sal look good. I'm following the Capo's orders. Besides, we're friends."

Leo pushed open the door to the warehouse. "Follow me and don't make a sound. There might be a guard inside. King Wedo's office is in the rear of the building. That's probably where he's keeping the Chalice."

The two men crept silently. Taine moved with surprising grace for a man his size. Leo Scaglia slithered through the darkness like some giant snake, intent on its prey. Past rows and rows of massive crates filled with unknown goods they slipped, only the soft sound of their breathing breaking the stillness of the stale air. Finally, they reached the rear of the building.

"That's the place," Leo whispered softly in Taine's ear, pointing to the foreman's office located at the junction of two walls. "No lights on. Looks deserted."

Both men pulled out their guns. "You go first," said Scaglia. "You know what to look for. I'll cover you."

Carefully, Taine twisted the knob. It turned effortlessly, not locked. Taking his time, the detective inched open the door. It was as dark inside the office as without. Slowly, ever so slowly, he slipped inside.

And found himself staring at a slender black man, sitting behind a wide desk. King Wedo. Waiting with him, standing at his side, were two powerfully built Jamaicans. Both men held Skorpion machine gun pistols aimed at Taine's stomach.

"Mr. Taine," said King Wedo, with a faint smile. "How nice of you to drop by."

Behind Taine, the door swung open. "Sorry, buddy," he heard Leo Scaglia say, "but orders is orders." Then something hard and unyielding crashed down on his skull and he heard nothing else.

When Taine regained consciousness, he found himself securely bound to a heavy wood chair. He was in the same room, now brightly illuminated. King Wedo faced him on the other side of the wide desk. The two massive bodyguards stood behind their boss's chair. Leo Scaglia, arms folded across his chest, lolled against a large metal filing cabinet. "*You're* the informer! In Albanese's organization?" said Taine, disgusted by his own stupidity. "Not Bracco?"

"So what else is new?" said Scaglia, chuckling. "When I called the King and told him you were fishing for the Chalice, he ordered me to reel you in. Easiest assignment I ever had. You didn't suspect nothin'."

"I'm too naive for my own good," said Taine. Whoever had tied him to the chair had taken his gun as well as the knife sheathed to his ankle. However, they had missed the razor blade concealed in his shirt sleeve. Cautiously, he started sawing at the ropes binding his wrists. "For some reason, I still trust my fellow man."

"A bad habit, Mr. Taine, especially for a private investigator," said King Wedo. The Jamaican spoke softly but distinctly, with the barest trace of an English accent. "But, of course, you are no ordinary detective. That is why I instructed Leo to bring you here. You are going to prove very useful to me, Mr. Taine. Very, very useful."

Reaching into a drawer of the desk, King Wedo pulled out a plain wooden goblet. Though Taine knew the Chalice's origin dated back thousands of years, there was not a scratch on it. "The Holy Grail," said King Wedo, to no one in particular. "Stripped of that foolish silver decoration, it appears incredibly ordinary. But, as we all well know, looks can be deceiving."

King Wedo rose from his chair, casually balancing the Cup in one hand. A short, slender man with pleasant, even features, only his narrow, mad eyes betrayed the cruelty lurking within. "Consider me, for example," he continued, circling the desk so that he stood only a few feet away from Taine. "I am notorious as a crazy gangster. An image I work hard to cultivate. Fear serves me well, Mr. Taine. Still, none of my enemies, or my friends for that matter, suspect that I am also a master of black magic. Only a select few even realize that sorcery exists."

King Wedo chuckled. "In my youth, I attended school in England. My father, a wealthy plantation owner, had dreams of me continuing and expanding the family business. Even then, I had other plans.

"You can imagine my surprise when I discovered, quite by accident, that my history professor was a practicing black magician. Delivering a paper to his home, I stumbled on him placing a curse on one of his faculty rivals. Immediately sensing my interest in the dark art, he offered me the opportunity to become his apprentice." The Jamaican's eyes narrowed. "For a price, of course."

Taine grimaced. Sorcerers always demanded payment for their services. A fee paid in blood.

"I learned a great deal from Professor Harvey during the three years I studied with him. He taught me some rather unusual business methods. Tactics for success I have employed well. Still, the Professor and I parted on good terms nearly a decade ago. Never once during the intervening years did I hear from him."

Taine remained silent, busily sawing his razor blade into the ropes. Gangsters loved to brag about their accomplishments. King Wedo was consumed by a desire to display his brilliance. Surrounded by thugs and assorted lowlifes, the Jamaican reveled in the chance to show off for Taine. Which made it quite clear to the detective that the gangster planned murdering him afterwards. Dead men never betrayed secrets.

"That was why I was surprised, a week ago, to suddenly receive a call from him. No sentimentalist, Harvey's contact was strictly business. The old man told me of the Holy Grail and how it was being shipped to Chicago. The Professor requested my aid in stealing the relic, promising me fabulous riches for my cooperation. I agreed to help. But, my arrangements benefited only me.

"Using information supplied by Harvey, my men intercepted the Grail messengers, killed them both, and made off with the Chalice. Instead of turning it over to the Professor, I kept the Cup for myself. The old fool should have known better than to trust someone like me. I have plans for the Grail. Plans that concern you, Mr. Taine."

A cold chill swept through Taine. He did not like the sound of that remark.

"Why me?" asked the detective. Anything to stall for a little more time. Cutting the ropes was proving difficult. "What makes me special?"

"Sidney Taine, the psychic detective," replied King Wedo, his lips curling in a slow grin. "I know all about you, Mr. Taine. Those who practice the black arts like to keep close tabs on their adversaries. And, I believe that description fits you very well. *Adversary*."

Gently, King Wedo placed Seth's Cup on his desk. Crossing his arms across his chest, he shook his head in mock dismay. "If I am an evil soul, my friend, then by definition, are you not a good one? A righteous one?"

Taine shuddered. King Wedo's words struck a chord deep within his being. He finally understood what the Jamaican planned – an ancient rite of dark magic, of blood sorcery. Evidently the concern showed in his face. The gang leader chuckled.

"Seven drops of blood from a righteous soul," he recited, using words of frightening power, "if the Cup of Purity is thy goal."

King Wedo strolled back around the desk and dropped back in his chair. Smiling, he reached into a desk drawer and pulled out a plastic bag filled with white powder. "Coke," said King Wedo, confirming Taine's immediate suspicions.

"Good stuff," continued the Jamaican, "but not perfect. Not pure." The gang leader leaned forward, his gaze fastened on his prisoner. "The purer the dope, the better the hit. That's the story on cocaine. Even the dumbest crackhead knows it. Problem is that no system filters out all the impurities. No matter how fine you make it, the stuff ain't perfect. It's never totally pure."

"You don't intend . . .," began Taine, shocked by the Jamaican's plan.

"Ah, but I do, Mr.Taine," said King Wedo, nodding. "I do. According to all of the medieval legends, *the Holy Grail purifies whatever it touches*. The mere contact with the Cup changes water into wine, poor man's bread into cake. Well, we're going to see if those stories are true."

The Jamaican opened the bag holding the cocaine. "Think of the rush, Mr. Taine. Imagine the purest cocaine in the world – available only from me. I'll be able to name my price."

King Wedo beckoned Scaglia closer. "You got your knife handy, Leo?" he asked.

"Of course," said Scaglia, pulling out a six-inch switchblade. With a bare whisper of sound, the metal blade glittered in the harsh light. "Never go anywhere without it."

"Take the Cup," said King Wedo commanded. "And christen it with seven drops of Mr. Taine's blood."

"Whatever you say," said Scaglia, delicately balancing the

switchblade in one hand, the wooden Cup in the other. "You want me to cut his throat?"

"Leo, Leo, Leo," said King Wedo, sounding properly shocked. "How wasteful. The formula calls for the blood of a righteous man each time we perform the ceremony. We don't have an endless supply of righteous men in Chicago." The Jamaican's voice turned grim. "We must make Mr. Taine last a long, long time."

"You're the boss," replied Scaglia, shrugging his shoulders. Nonchalantly, he slipped the cold steel beneath the first button of Taine's shirt. With a flick of the wrist, the hood slashed through the thin material up to the detective's neck.

"Tough break, buddy," he muttered, bending close with the Cup of Seth. "But orders is orders."

Another slash of the knife. A thin red ribbon blossomed across Taine's chest. Carefully, Scaglia collected his bounty. "Seven drops," warned King Wedo. "No more, no less."

"Got 'em," said Scaglia. He straightened, holding the Cup before him. "Now what?"

The gang leader opened the plastic bag holding the cocaine. Using his pinky, he casually stirred the white powder. "From what I've read, the blood activates the magical properties of the Cup instantly. Let's see what it does with the coke."

Scaglia growled – a beast-like sound rising from deep within his chest. A mad noise that caught all of them by surprise. Taine's eyes blinked in shock as the grail-bearer's features twisted with sudden fury.

"You dirty son-of-a-bitch!" Scaglia shouted, and grabbed for his gun.

Weapons exploded and the room filled with the sound and smell of gunfire. Scaglia's body erupted in blood. Like a grotesque, drunken marionette, he staggered back and forth, driven by the fury of the bullets slamming into his torso.

"Be careful of the Cup!" shrieked King Wedo, standing, only his voice betraying any sign of panic. "Try not to hit it." Hot blood gushing from a dozen wounds, Scaglia should have been dead, but wasn't. Only his burning will kept him alive. Somehow, some way, he pulled his gun free and returned fire. Taine, not sure he understood what was taking place, wrenched hard on the last few strands of cord imprisoning his hands. The rope snapped, and the detective dropped to the floor. Unarmed, he was not crazy enough to attack either Scaglia or Wedo's cronies.

The shooting stopped as abruptly as it began. Silence echoed through the small office. Both bodyguards were down – one shot through the heart, the second man's nose a red ruin where a bullet crashed up and through to his brain.

Scaglia lay sprawled across King Wedo's desk, the Grail clutched tightly in one hand. Amazingly, a spark of life still flickered in his eyes.

"I don't like traitors, Leo," said King Wedo, rising up from the floor on the other side of his desk, a stiletto tightly gripped in one hand. He spoke calmly, without the least trace of malice. "You took my money to betray your boss. But, evidently, he paid you even more to double cross me." King Wedo shook his head. "Bad choice, Leo."

Scaglia raised his head. "You scum," he gasped out, his mad eyes burning with hatred. "No one paid . . ."

"Enough lies," said King Wedo. With a savage twist of the knife, he ripped the blade across Leo's throat. The gangster's body arched in agony as his life blood poured out onto the wood desk. One last gasp and he was dead.

"Don't try anything, Mr. Taine," continued King Wedo, a .45 automatic appearing in his hand as if by magic. He never even glanced at the dead man. "Please rise very slowly from the floor. And, keep both of your hands in plain sight."

Taine stood up. At this range, King Wedo couldn't miss. The Jamaican seemed unruffled by the violence that had taken place during the past few minutes.

"I never panic," said King Wedo, as if reading Taine's mind. Careful never to shift his eyes from Taine, the gang leader reached down for the Holy Grail. "That's why I always come out on top. That's why I'm the king."

Wrapping his fingers around the edge of the wood goblet, King Wedo pulled the Grail free of Scaglia's grip. "I thought I could trust Leo, but I guess not. No matter."

The muzzle of the automatic never wavered. "Two can keep a secret if one of them is dead, Mr. Taine," said King Wedo. "Good-bye."

Desperately, the detective flung himself to the side. One of the dead bodyguards still held a gun. It was a forlorn hope, but Taine's only chance. He scrambled for the weapon, expecting any second to hear the roar of King Wedo's automatic and feel the impact of a slug in his back. Surprisingly, nothing happened. Taine whirled, the dead man's weapon in hand. Then came to a sudden stop, caught completely by surprise.

King Wedo stood frozen in place. Sweat glistened on his forehead. Madness twisted his face in a grimace of incredible pain. The .45 automatic no longer threatened Taine. Instead, its muzzle touched right against the gangster's forehead. Wild eyes meet Taine's in a silent plea for help. But there was no time left. King Wedo's finger jerked hard against the trigger. The gun roared once, then fell silent.

"An interesting, if not surprising tale," said the man called Ashmedai. "Many legends refer to the Grail as the Cup of Treachery." He paused, and shook his head, as if in disappointment. "A title it has well earned. Too many men have been betrayed. I wonder if this King Wedo ever grasped the truth?"

"I think he did," said Taine, staring at the Holy Grail resting on the desk top between them. "In that last instant, I believe he realized the trap into which he had fallen. But, by then, holding the Cup, there was nothing he could do. In a way, it was a grim sort of justice."

Ashmedai shrugged and reached for the Cup. "The fools never understand that the Grail turns *all* that come in contact with it pure. Including those men foolish enough to hold it."

Taine nodded, his gaze fixed on the Chalice. "The conflict in their souls destroyed them both. Repentance was not enough. Scaglia could no longer serve evil, so he tried to destroy it. And King Wedo, overwhelmed by his monstrous crimes, resorted to suicide."

The detective paused. "Do you dare risk taking it? I carried it here in a box I discovered in King Wedo's office. I never touched it myself."

"The spell wears off quickly," said Ashmedai confidently, lifting the Grail. "Joseph was no fool when he covered the Cup in silver. No ordinary mortal could touch the Chalice and live with himself afterwards. No man is that pure."

The bearded man examined the Cup carefully, a wistful smile playing across his lips. "So many years – so many years."

"Now that you have it . . ." began Taine.

"The Grail goes into my collection," replied Ashmedai, his gaze still fixed on the Cup. "Where it will remain out of the sight of man until needed."

"You called it the Cup of Treachery?" said Taine, puzzled. In all of his studies of the occult, he had never encountered the phrase before.

Ashmedai lowered the Chalice to the desk. Unseen eyes stared at Taine from behind dark lenses.

"The Chalice was a gift to Christ from one of his disciples," said the bearded man. His voice sounded weary, terribly so. "One who doubted and thought to use the Grail as a final test. And thus began a tale of treachery – and eternal damnation."

Ashmedai sighed. "Now do you understand?"

"Yes," answered Taine, no longer curious to see the eyes behind those glasses.

TO BECOME A SORCERER

Darrell Schweitzer

There is a small but very select group of fantasy writers whom I regard as the inheritors of one of the greatest of all fantasists, Lord Dunsany. Dunsany was supreme at creating believable magical worlds inhabited not necessarily by heroes, but by villains, minor gods and mischief-makers. What's more he could invent names for these people that were so beautifully out of this world. Like the dragon Tharagavverug and the magician Allathurion in "The Fortress Unvanquishable, Save for Sacnoth". Many have tried to imitate Dunsany but few have succeeded. Amongst Dunsany's inheritors have been Jack Vance, Clark Ashton Smith (whom we met earlier), Michael Shea and today's supreme stylist, Darrell Schweitzer (b. 1952). Since 1991, Schweitzer has been producing an occasional series of stories about the sorcerer Sekenre. The following, which was the first, was nominated for a World Fantasy Award and was reworked to form the start of the novel The Mask of the Sorcerer *(1995).*

Surely Surat-Kemad is the greatest of the gods, for he is lord of both the living and the dead. The Great River flows from his mouth; the River is the voice and word of Surat-Kemad, and all life arises from the River. The dead return to Surat-Kemad, upon the waters or beneath them, borne by some secret current, back into the belly of the god. We are reminded of Surat-Kemad daily, for he made the crocodile in his own image.

I, Sekenre, son of Vashtem the sorcerer, tell you this because it is true.

1

That my father was a magician I knew from earliest childhood. Did he not speak to the winds and the waters? I heard him do so many times, late at night. Could he not make fire leap out of his hands, merely by folding and unfolding them? Yes, and he never burned himself, for the fire was cold, like river water in the winter.

Once he opened his hands to reveal a brilliant, scarlet butterfly, made of paper and wire but alive. It flew around the house for a month. No one could catch it. I cried when it died and the light went out of its wings, leaving it no more than a trace of ash.

He made a different kind of magic with his stories. There was one in particular that went on and on, about a young heron who was cast out of his nest by the other birds because he had short legs, and no beak or feathers. He could pass for human, for all that he wasn't. So he wandered in a lonely exile and had many adventures, in far lands, among the gods, among the ghosts in the land of the dead. Every evening for almost a year, Father whispered more of the story to me as if it were a special secret between the two of us. I never told it to anyone else.

Mother made things too, but not fire out of her hands, nor anything that truly lived. She built *hevats*, those assemblages of wood and wire and paper for which the City of the Reeds is famous, sometimes little figures that dangled from sticks and seemed to come alive when the wind struck them, sometimes great tangles of ships and cities and stars and mountains which hung from the ceiling and turned slowly in a vastly intricate, endless dance.

Then a fever came over her one summer and she spent weeks working on a single, articulated image. No one could stop her. Father would put her to bed but she would get up again in her sleep and work on the thing some more, until a vast snaky creature of painted wooden scales writhed throughout every room of the house, suspended on strings just below the ceiling. At last she put a face on it – half a man, half a crocodile – and even

I, six years old at the time, knew it to be an image of Surat-Kemad, the God Who Devours.

When the wind blew, the image writhed and spoke. Mother screamed and fell to the floor. Later, the thing was merely gone. No one would tell me what had become of it. When Mother recovered she could not recall anything that had happened to her.

One evening by a late fire, she explained that it had been a kind of prophecy, and when the spirit has departed, the seer is no more than an empty glove cast aside by some god. She had no idea what it meant, merely that a god had spoken through her.

I think even Father was frightened when she said that.

He told me one more installment of the story of the heron boy the same night. Then the spirit of that, too, left him.

Father must have been the greatest magician in all Reedland, for our house was never empty in the early days. People came from all over the city, and from the marshlands; some journeyed for days on the Great River to buy potions and philtres or have their fortunes told. Mother sometimes sold them *hevats*, sacred ones for devotions, or memorials for the dead, or just toys.

I didn't think of myself as any different from other boys. One of my friends was the son of a fisherman, another of a paper-maker. I was the son of a magician, just another child.

But in the story, the bird-boy thought he was a heron –

As I grew older, Father became more secretive, and the customers came no further than the door. Bottles were passed out to them. Then they stopped coming.

Suddenly the house was empty. I heard strange noises in the night. In the earliest hours of the morning, Father began to receive certain visitors again. I think he summoned them against their will. They did not come to buy. Then Mother, my sister Hamakina, and I were locked in the bedroom, forbidden to emerge.

Once I peeked out between two loose panels in the door and saw a bent, skeletal figure in the dim lamplight of the hallway outside, a visitor who stank like something long decayed and dripped with the water from the river below our house.

Suddenly the visitor glared directly at me as if he had known I was there all along, and I turned away with a stifled yelp. The memory of that horrible, sunken face stayed with me in my dreams for a long time.

I was ten. Hamakina was just three. Mother's hair was starting to go gray. I think the darkness began that year. Slowly, inexorably, Father became, not a magician who worked wonders, but a sorcerer, to be feared.

Our house stood at the very edge of the City of the Reeds, where the great marsh began. It was a vast place, which had belonged to a priest before Father bought it, a pile of wooden domes and sometimes tilted boxlike rooms and gaping windows fashioned to look like eyes. The house stood on log pilings at the end of a long wharf, otherwise not a part of the city at all. Walk along that wharf the other way and you came to street after street of old houses, some of them empty, then to the square of the fish-mongers, then to the street of scribes and paper-makers, and finally to the great docks where the ships of the river rested at their moorings like dozing whales.

Beneath our house was a floating dock where I could sit and gaze underneath the city. The stilts and logs and pilings were like a forest stretched out before me, dark and endlessly mysterious.

Sometimes the other boys and I would paddle our shallow boats into that darkness, and on some forgotten dock or rubbish heap or sandbank we'd play our secret games; and then the others always wanted me to do magic.

If I could, I refused with great and mysterious dignity to divulge awesome mysteries I actually knew no more about than they. Sometimes I did a little trick of sleight-of-hand, but mostly I just disappointed them.

Still, they tolerated me, hoping I would reveal more, and also because they were afraid of Father. Later, when the darkness began, they feared him even more; and when I wandered in the gloom beneath the city, paddling among the endless wooden pillars in my little boat, I was alone.

I could not understand it then, but Father and Mother quarrelled more, until in the end, I think, she too was afraid of him. She made me swear once never to become like my father, "never, never do what he has done," and I swore by the holy name of

Surat-Kemad without really knowing what I was promising not to do.

Then one night when I was fourteen, I woke up suddenly and heard my mother screaming and my father's angry shouts. His voice was shrill, distorted, barely human at times, and I thought he was cursing her in some language I did not know. Then came a crash, pottery and loose wood falling, and silence.

Hamakina sat up beside me in bed.

"Oh, Sekenre, what is it?"

"Quiet," I said. "I don't know."

Then we heard heavy footsteps, and the bedroom door swung inward. Father stood in the doorway, his face pale, his eyes wide and strange, a lantern in his upraised hand. Hamakina turned to avoid his gaze.

He remained there for a minute as if he hadn't seen us, and slowly the expression on his face softened. He seemed to be remembering something, as if he were waking up from a trance. Then he spoke, his voice faltering.

"Son, I've had a vision from the gods, but it is *your* vision, by which you will become a man and know what your life is to be."

I was more bewildered than frightened. I got out of bed. The wooden floor was smooth and cold beneath my bare feet.

Father was forcing himself to be calm. He clung to the edge of the doorway and trembled. He was trying to say something more, but no words came, and his eyes were wide and wild again.

"*Now?*" I asked without realizing what I was saying.

Father strode forward. He seized me roughly by my robe. Hamakina whimpered, but he ignored her.

"The gods don't send visions just when it's convenient. *Now.* You must go into the marshes *right now*, and the vision will come to you. Remain there until dawn."

He dragged me from the room. I glanced back once at my sister, but Father merely closed the door behind me and barred it from the outside, locking her in. He blew out his lantern.

The house was entirely dark and smelled of river mud and worse. There was a trace of something burning, and of corruption.

Father raised a trapdoor. Below floated the dock where all our boats were moored.

"Down you go. *Now.*"

I groped my way down, fearfully, shivering. It was early in the spring. The rains were nearly over, but not quite, and the air was cold and full of spray. Father closed the trapdoor over my head. I found my boat and got in, and sat there in the darkness cross-legged, my feet drawn up under my robe. Something splashed nearby once, twice. I sat very still, clutching my paddle firmly, ready to strike at I knew not what.

Slowly the darkness lessened. Out beyond the marshes, the moon peered through thinning clouds. The water gleamed silver and black, waves and shadow. And it was then that I made out what seemed to be hundreds of crocodiles drifting in the water around me, their snouts barely breaking the surface, their eyes sparkling in the dim moonlight.

It was all I could do not to scream, to keep silent. It was the beginning of my vision, I knew, for these beasts could easily have tipped over my boat and devoured me. In any case, there were too many of them for them to be natural creatures.

It was as I leaned over to slip off my mooring line that I saw, quite clearly, that they were not even crocodiles. Their bodies were human, their backs and buttocks as pale as the flesh of drowned men. These were the *evatim*, the messengers of the river god. No one ever saw them, I'd always been told, save when they are about to die, or else when the god wishes to speak.

So my father had been telling the truth. There was a vision. Or I was going to die, then and there.

I paddled a short distance off, very carefully. The *evatim* parted before me. The tip of my paddle never touched one. Behind me, in the darkness, I heard someone coming down the ladder onto the dock. Then something heavy splashed in the water. The *evatim* hissed, all as one. It was like the rising of a great wind.

I paddled for what felt like hours among the posts and pillars and stilts, groping my way with my paddle sometimes, until at last I came to open, deep water. I let the current take me a short distance, and looked back at the City of the Reeds where it crouched amid the marsh like a huge, slumbering beast. Here and there watchlamps flickered, but the city was dark. No one goes outdoors in the city at night: because the mosquitoes swarm in clouds at sunset, thick as smoke; because the marsh is full of ghosts who rise up out of the black mud like mist; but mostly for fear of the *evatim*, the crocodile-headed servants of Surat-Kemad, who crawl out of the water in the darkness and walk like men through the empty streets, their heavy tails dragging.

Where the city reached into deep water, ships lay at anchor, bulging, ornately-painted vessels come upriver from the City of the Delta. Many were ablaze with lights, and from them sounded music and laughter. The foreign sailors do not know our ways or share our fears.

In the City of the Reeds, all men who are not beggars wear trousers and leather shoes. Children wear loose robes and go barefoot. On the very few cold days they either wrap their feet in rags or stay indoors. When a boy becomes a man, his father gives him shoes. It is an ancient custom. No one knows the reason for it.

Father had hurried me out of the house without even a cloak. So I passed the night in quiet misery, my teeth chattering, my hands and feet numb, the cold air burning inside my chest.

As best I could, I steered for the shallows, in among the grasses and reeds, making my way from one patch of open water to the next, ducking low beneath vines, sometimes forcing my way through with my paddle.

A vision of sorts came to me, but all disjointed. I did not understand what the god was trying to say.

The moon seemed to set very suddenly. The river swallowed it, and for an instant moonlight writhed on the water like Mother's thousand-jointed crocodile image somehow glowing with light.

I set my paddle down in the bottom of the boat and leaned over, trying to make out the thing's face. But I only saw muddy water. Around me, dead reeds towered like iron rods. I let the boat drift. I saw a crocodile once, huge and ancient and sluggish with the cold, drifting like a log. But it was merely a beast and not one of the *evatim*.

A bit later I sat in a stagnant pool surrounded by sleeping white ducks floating like puffs of cotton on the black water. Night birds cried out, but I had no message from them.

I watched the stars, and by the turning of the heavens I knew it was no more than an hour before dawn. I despaired then and called out to Surat-Kemad to send me my vision. I did not doubt that it would come from him, not from some other god.

At the same time, I was afraid, for I had made no preparation, no sacrifice.

But Surat-Kemad, he of the monstrous jaws, was not angry, and the vision came.

The light rain had stopped, but the air was colder yet, and, trembling and damp, I huddled in the bottom of my boat, both hands against my chest, clutching my paddle. Perhaps I slept. But, very gingerly, someone touched me on the shoulder.

I sat up in alarm, but the stranger held up a finger, indicating that I should be silent. I could not see his face. He wore a silver mask of the Moon, mottled and rough, with rays around the edges. His white, ankle-length robe flapped gently in the frigid breeze.

He motioned me to follow, and I did, silently dipping my paddle into the water. The stranger walked barefoot on the surface, ripples spreading with every step.

We travelled for a long time through a maze of open pools and tufts of grass, among the dead reeds, until we came to a half-submerged ruin of a tower, no more than a black, empty shell covered with mud and vines.

Then hundreds of other robed, masked figures emerged from the marsh, not walking on the water as had my guide, but *crawling*, their movement a curious waddle, their bodies swaying from side to side as does that of a crocodile when it comes out on land. I watched in amazement as they gathered around us, bowing low at the upright man's feet, as if in supplication.

He merely spread his hands and wept.

Then I recalled one of my father's stories, about a proud king, whose palace was more resplendent than the sun, of whom the gods were jealous. One day a crocodile-headed messenger came into the glittering court and hissed, "My master summons you, O King, as he summons all." But the king, in his pride, bade his guards beat the messenger and throw him into the river whence he came, for the king did not fear the gods.

And Surat-Kemad did not care to be feared, only obeyed, so the Great River flooded the land, swallowing the palace of the king.

"That's not much of a story," I'd complained to Father.

"It is merely true," he said.

Now I looked on in awe, desperate to ask so many questions but afraid to speak. But the sky lightened, and the weeping of the standing man became merely the wind rattling in the reeds.

The sun rose, and the supplicants removed their masks and became merely crocodiles. Their robes were somehow gone in the shifting light. I watched their dark bodies sink into the murky water.

I looked to the standing man, but a long-legged bird remained where he had been. It let out a cry and took to the air, wings thundering.

The warm sun revived me. I sat up, coughing, my nose running, and looked around. The sunken tower was still there, a heap of dead stone. But I was alone. It was midday before I got back to the City of the Reeds.

The city is a different place in the daylight, bright banners waving from towers, houses likewise bright with hangings and with designs painted on walls and roofs. The ships of the river unload by day, and the streets are filled with the babble of tongues, while traders and officials and barbarians and city wives all haggle together.

It is a place of sharp fish smells and strange incense and leather and wet canvas and unwashed rivermen who bring outlandish beasts from the villages high in the mountains, near the birthplace of the river.

By day, too, there are a thousand gods, one for every stranger, for every tradesman, for everyone who has ever passed through or resided or merely dreamed of a new god during an afternoon nap. In the street of carvers one can buy idols of all these gods, or even have new images, made if one happens to be divinely inspired at the time.

At night, of course, there is only Surat-Kemad, whose jaws rend the living and the dead, whose body is the black water, whose teeth are the stars.

But it was by day I returned, making my way through the tangle of ships and smaller boats, past the wharves and floating docks, then beneath the city until I came out the other side near my father's house.

Hamakina ran to me when I emerged through the trapdoor, her face streaming with tears. She embraced me, sobbing.

"Oh Sekenre, I'm so afraid!"

"Where is Father?" I asked, but she only screamed and buried her face in my robe. Then I said, "Where is Mother?"

Hamakina looked up into my face and said very softly, "Gone."

"Gone?"

"*She has gone to the gods, my son.*"

I looked up. Father had emerged from his workroom, his sorcerer's robe wrapped loosely over soiled white trousers. He hobbled toward us, dragging himself as if he didn't quite know how to walk. I thought there was something wrong with his legs.

Hamakina screamed and ran out onto the wharf. I heard the front door bang against the outside of the house.

I stood my ground.

"Father, where is Mother?"

"As I said . . . gone to the gods."

"Will she be coming back?" I asked, hopeless as I did.

Father did not answer. He stood there for a moment, staring into space, as if he'd forgotten I was even there. Then he said suddenly, "What did you see, Sekenre?"

I told him.

He was silent again.

"I don't know," I said. "It didn't mean anything. Did I do something wrong?"

For once he spoke to me tenderly, as he had in the old days when I was very small.

"No, faithful child, you did nothing wrong. Remember that the vision of your life goes on as long as your life does; and, like your life, it is a mystery, a maze, with many turnings, many things suddenly revealed, many things forever hidden. The longer you live, the more you will understand what you have seen this night. Each new piece of the vast puzzle changes the meaning of all that has gone before as you draw nearer and nearer the truth . . . but you never reach your destination, not entirely."

The cold and the damp had given me a fever. I lay ill for a week, often delirious, sometimes dreaming that the masked figure in the vision stood at my bedside, barefoot on the surface of the black water while dead reeds rattled all around. Sometimes, as the sun rose, he took off his mask and a heron screamed at me, leaping into the air on thunderous wings. Sometimes it was my father beneath the mask. He came to me each dawn, put his hand on my forehead, recited words I couldn't make out, and bade me drink a sweet-tasting syrup.

After the fever had gone, I saw him very little. He retreated to his workroom, noisily barring the door. Hamakina and I were left to care for ourselves. Sometimes it was hard just finding food. We tried to assemble the leftover pieces of Mother's *hevats* but seldom got much for the results.

Meanwhile, lightning and thunder issued from the work-room. The whole house shook. Sometimes there were incredibly foul odors, and my sister and I would spend our nights outdoors, on rooftops among the beggars of the city, despite all the dangers. And once, as I crouched by the workroom door, terrified and holding back tears, Father spoke and I heard him answered by many voices, all of them faint and far away. One sounded like Mother. All were afraid, pleading, babbling, screaming.

At times I wondered where Mother had gone, and tried to comfort Hamakina. But in my worst fears, I knew perfectly well what had happened to her. I could not tell Hamakina that.

There was no one I could turn to, for now Father was the most feared of all the city's black sorcerers, and even the priests dared not anger him. Demons of the air and of the river regularly convened at our house. I heard them scratching, their wings and tails dragging, while my sister and I huddled in our room, or kept to the rooftops.

In the streets, people turned away when they saw us, made signs and spat. Then one day Father came to me, moving slowly and painfully, as if he were very old. He sat me down at the kitchen table and stared into my eyes for a long time. I was afraid to turn from his gaze. He had been weeping.

"Sekenre," he said, very gently, "do you love your father still?"

I could not answer.

"You must understand that I love you very much," he said, "and I always will, no matter what happens. I want you to be happy. I want you to do well in your life. Marry a fine girl. *I don't want you to become what I have become.* Be a friend to everybody. Have no enemies. Hate no one."

"But . . . how?"

He took me by the hand, firmly. "Come. Now."

I was terribly afraid, but I went.

There was near panic as he came into the city, yanking me along, walking in his strange way with his whole back writhing and rippling beneath his sorcerer's robe like a serpent trying to stagger on heavy legs.

People shouted and ran as we passed. Women snatched up their children. A pair of priests crossed their staves to make a sign against us. But Father ignored them all.

We came to a street of fine houses. Astonished faces stared down at us from high windows. Then Father led me to the end of an alley, down a tunnel, and into a yard behind one of the mansions. He knocked at a door. An old man appeared, by his garb a scholar. He gasped and made a sign to ward off evil. Father pushed me inside.

"Teach my son what you know," he said to the old man. "I will pay well."

That was how I became an apprentice to Velachronos the historian, scribe, and poet. I knew letters already, but he taught me to make fine ones full of swirls and beautiful colors. Then he taught me something of the history of our city, and of the river and the gods. I sat with him for long hours, helping to transcribe ancient books.

Clearly Father wanted me to become learned, so that I would dwell in honor among the people of the city, and know at least modest comfort, as Velachronos did. The old man remarked on this once, "You seldom see a rich scholar or a starving one."

But my sister was ignored completely. Once, when I came home after lessons and found Father outside of his workroom, I said, "What about Hamakina?"

He shrugged. "Take her along. It hardly matters."

So Velachronos had two apprentices. I think he accepted us out of fear at first. I tried to convince him we were not monsters. Gradually he acquiesced. Father paid him double. I labored over the books. Hamakina, too, learned to paint beautiful letters, and Velachronos taught her something of music, so she could sing the ancient ballads of the city. Her voice was very beautiful.

He was kind to us. I remember the time with him fondly. He was like a grandfather or a generous uncle. He took us to the children's festival that spring, and rose from his seat to applaud when Hamakina won the prize in the contest of the masks and the sparrow-headed image of the god Haedos-Kemad leaned forward and showered her with candy.

I felt too old for that sort of thing, yet Father had never taken me to the priests to declare me a man. It is a simple rite unless parents want to make it elaborate. There is only a small fee. I had already had my vision from the gods. Yet Father did not take me and I remained a child, either because I was somehow unworthy, or he merely forgot.

Meanwhile his sorceries grew more extreme. At night the sky flickered from horizon to horizon, and sometimes he came out onto the wharf in front of our house to speak with the thunder. It answered back, calling out his name, and, on occasion, my name.

The stenches from the workroom worsened, and there were more voices, more terrifying visitors in the night. But, too, Father would sometimes stagger about the house, pulling at his beard, flailing his arms like a madman, like someone possessed by a frenzied spirit, and he would seize me and shake me so hard it hurt and plead with me, "Do you love me, son? Do you still love your father?"

I could never answer him. It drove me to tears many times. I locked myself in my room and he would stand outside the door, sobbing, whispering, "Do you love me? Do you?"

Then came an evening when I sat studying in my room – Hamakina was off somewhere – and a huge barbarian adventurer climbed in through the window, followed by a little rat-faced man from the City of the Delta.

The barbarian snatched the book from my hands and threw it into the river. He took me by the wrist and jerked. My forearm snapped. I let out a little yelp of pain and the rat-faced man held a long, thin knife like an enormous pin to my face, pressing gently on one cheek, then the other, just below my eyes.

He whispered, flashing filthy teeth. His breath stank.

"Where's yer famous wizard da' who's got all the treasure? Tell us, brat, or I'll make a blind girl out of ye and tie yer guts fer braids—"

The barbarian merely grabbed me by the front of my gown in one huge hand and slammed me against the wall so hard that blood poured out of my nose and mouth.

I could only nod to my left, toward Father's workroom.

Later, when I returned to consciousness, I heard the two of them screaming. The screaming went on for days behind Father's door, while I lay feverish and Hamakina wiped my forehead but could do nothing more. It was only when the screaming faded to distant murmurs, like the voices I'd heard that one time before, like the voice that might have been Mother's, that Father came and healed me with his magic. His face was ashen. He looked very tired.

I slept and the barefoot man in the silver mask knelt on the surface of the water, sending ripples all around my bed. He whispered to me the story of the heron boy who stood among the flock in the dawn light and was left behind when the birds took flight, standing there, waving his graceless, featherless arms.

A few weeks later, Velachronos threw us out. I don't know what happened with him at the end. Perhaps it was just a rumor, or a culmination of rumors, or he might even have heard the truth about something I did not know, but one day, when Hamakina and I came for our lessons, he stood in the doorway and all but shrieked, "Begone! Get out of my house, devil-spawn!"

He wouldn't explain or say anything more. There was nothing to do but leave.

That night a vast storm came up from the mouth of the river, a black, swirling mass of clouds like a monster huge enough to smother the world, lumbering on a thousand flickering, fiery legs. The river, the very marshes, raged like the frenzied chaos-ocean that existed before the Earth was made, while the sky thundered light and dark; and for an instant you could see for miles across froth-capped waves and reeds lashing in the wind; then there was only utter blackness and stinging rain and the thunder once more, thunder calling out my father's name again and again.

He answered it, from within his secret room, his voice as loud as the thunder, speaking a language that did not sound like human speech at all, but shrieks and grating cackles and whistles like the raging wind.

In the morning, all the ships were scattered and half the city was blasted away. The air was heavy with the cries of mourners. The river ran beneath our house muddy and furious where before it had been mere shallows.

Many people saw the crocodile-headed messengers of the Devouring God that day. My sister and I sat in our room, almost afraid to speak even to each other. We could not go out.

From Father's workroom there was only silence that went on for so long that, despite everything, I began to fear for him. I met Hamakina's gaze, and she stared back, wide-eyed and dazed. Then she nodded.

I went to the workroom door and knocked.

"Father? Are you all right?"

To my surprise, he opened the door at once and came out. He steadied himself against the doorway with one hand and hung there, breathing heavily. His hands were gnarled, like claws. They looked like they had been burned. His face was so pale, so wild, that part of me wasn't even sure it was Father until he spoke.

"I am going to die," he said. "It is time for me to go to the gods." And, again despite everything, I wept for him.

"Now you must be a faithful son for the last time," he said. "Gather reeds and bind them together into a funeral boat. When you are done, I shall be dead. Place me in it and set me adrift, so that I shall come, as all men do, to Surat-Kemad."

"No, Father! It isn't so!"

When I wept, I was remembering him as he had been in my early childhood, not as he had become.

He squeezed my shoulder hard and hissed angrily, "Quite inevitably, it *is*. Go!"

So Hamakina and I went together. Somehow our house had lost only a few shingles in the storm, and the dock below the trapdoor was still there. My boat was too, but sunken and dangling from its line. We struggled to pull it up, dumped it out, and set it afloat. Miraculously, not even the paddles had been lost.

We climbed in and paddled in silence for about an hour, far enough into the marshes that the waters were again shallow and still and reeds as thick as my arm swayed against the sky like trees. With a hatchet I'd brought along for the purpose, I cut down several, and Hamakina and I labored throughout the day to make a crude boat. In the evening, we towed it back to our house.

I ascended the ladder first, while she waited fearfully below. For the first time I could remember, the door to Father's workroom was left open. He lay inside, on a couch amid shelves of books and bottles, and at a glance I knew that he was dead.

There was little to do that night. Hamakina and I made a cold supper out of what we could find in the pantry. Then we barred the windows and doors, and pushed a heavy trunk over the trapdoor, lest the *evatim* crawl up and devour the corpse, as they sometimes do.

I explored the workroom only a little, going through Father's books, opening trunks, peering into coffers. If he had any treasure, I didn't find it. Then I picked up a murky bottle and something inside screamed at me with a tiny, faraway voice. I dropped the bottle in fright. It broke and the screaming thing scurried across the floorboards.

The house was full of voices and noises, creakings, whispers, and sighs. Once something heavy, like a huge bird perhaps, flapped and scraped against a shuttered window. My sister and I stayed up most of the night, lanterns in our hands, armed with clubs against whatever terrors the darkness might hold. I sat on the floor outside the workroom, leaning against the door. Hamakina lay with her face in my lap, sobbing softly.

Eventually I fell asleep, and Mother came to me in a dream, leaning over me, dripping water and river mud, shrieking and tearing her hair. I tried to tell her that all would be well, that I would take care of Hamakina, that I would grow up to be a scribe and write letters for people. I promised I wouldn't be like Father. But still she wept and paced back and forth all night. In the morning, the floor was wet and muddy.

Hamakina and I rose, washed, put on our best clothes, and went to the priests. On the way, some people turned their backs to us while others screamed curses and called us murderers. In the square before the temple, a mob approached with knives and clubs, and I waved my hands and made what I hoped looked like magical gestures until they turned and fled, shouting that I was just as bad as my Father. In that single instant, I almost wished I were.

A whole army of priests followed us back to the house, resplendent in their billowing gold-and-silver trousers, their blue jackets, and their tall, scale-covered hats. Many of them held aloft sacred ikons of Surat-Kemad, and of the other gods too: of Ragun-Kemad, the Lord of Eagles, and Bel-Kemad, god of spring, and of Meliventra, the Lady of the Lantern, who sends forgiveness and mercy. Acolytes chanted and swung smoking incense-pots on golden chains.

But they would not let us back into the house. Two temple matrons stood with us on the wharf, holding Hamakina and me by the hand. The neighbors watched from a distance. fearfully.

The priests emptied out Father's workroom, breaking open the shutters, pouring bottle after bottle of powders and liquids into the river, dumping many of his books in after, then more bottles, then most of the jars, carvings, and strange specimens. Other books, they confiscated. Junior priests carried heaps of them back to the temple in baskets. Then it seemed the exorcisms went on for hours. They used so much incense that I thought the house was on fire.

In the end, the priests marched away as solemnly as they had come, and one of the matrons gave me a sword which had been my father's, a fine weapon, its grip bound in copper wire, its blade inlaid with silver.

"You may need this," was all she would say.

Fearfully, my sister and I ventured inside the house. The air was so thick with incense that we ran, choking, our eyes streaming, to open all the windows. Still, the burners hung everywhere and we dared not remove them.

Father lay on the couch in his workroom, bound in gauze. The priests had removed his eyes and placed amulets like huge coins in the empty sockets. I knew this was because they were afraid he would find his way back otherwise.

Hamakina and I had to get him down to the funeral boat. There was no one to help us. It was a terrible struggle. Hamakina was, after all, only eight, and I was fifteen. More than once I was afraid we would accidentally *drop* him. One of the gold amulets fell out. The empty socket gaped like a dry, red wound. I was almost sick when I had to put the amulet back.

The funeral boat was hung with gauze and charms. Incense

rose from a silver cup set in the prow. One of the priests had painted a symbol, a serpent swallowing its tail, only broken, on the stern.

In the twilight of evening, Hamakina and I towed the funeral boat out into the deep water beyond the city, among the crooked masts of the wrecked ships, and beyond. The sky faded gently from red to black, streaked with the purple tatters of the last few storm clouds. An almost frigid wind blew out of the marshes. The stars gleamed, multiplied upon the rippling water.

I stood in my shallow boat and recited the service for the dead as best as I knew it, for my father whom I still loved and feared and did not understand. Then Hamakina let loose the line, and the funeral boat began to drift, first downstream toward the delta and the sea; but in the darkness, just before it disappeared, it was clearly going *upstream*. That was a good sign. It meant the boat had caught the black current, which carries the dead out of the world of the living, into the abode of the gods.

I thought, then, that I had time to mourn. When we got back, the house was merely empty. For the first time in many years, I was not afraid. It was almost bewildering. I slept quietly that night, I did not dream. Hamakina, too, was quiet.

The next morning an old woman who lived in one of the first houses at the other end of the wharf knocked on our door and said, "Children? Are you well? Do you have enough to eat?"

She left a basket of food for us.

That, too, was a good sign. It meant that the neighbors would eventually forgive us. They didn't really think I was as my father had been.

I took the basket inside slowly, weeping half for joy. Life would be better. I remembered my promise to my mother. I would be different. The next day, surely, or the day after, Velachronos would take us back and we could resume our lessons.

Only that night Father came to me in a dream, and he stood before my bed wrapped in gauze, his face terrible behind the golden disks. His voice was – I cannot truly describe it – *oily*, like something dripping, something thick and vile; and the mere fact that such a sound could form itself into words seemed the greatest obscenity of all.

"I have delved too far into the darkness, my son, and my

ending can only come with the final mystery. I seek it. My studies are almost complete. It is the culmination of all my labors. But there is one thing I need, one thing I have come back for."

And in my dream I asked him, "Father, what is it?"

"Your sister."

Then I awoke to the sound of Hamakina screaming. She reached for my hand, missed, caught the edge of the bed, and fell with a thump, dragging the covers onto the floor. I always kept a lit lantern on the stand by the bed. Now I opened the little metal door, flooding the room with light.

"Sekenre! Help me!"

I stared incredulously for just an instant as she hung suspended in the air, dangling, as if an invisible hand had seized her by the hair. Then she screamed once more and seemed to fly through the window. For a second she grabbed hold of the sill. She looked toward me. Our eyes met. But before I could do or say anything she was yanked loose and hauled through. I ran to the window and leaned out. There was no splash; the water below rippled gently. The night was still. Hamakina was simply gone.

II

In the morning, the third after Father's death, I went to see the Sybil. There was nothing else to do. Everyone in the City of the Reeds knows that when the great crisis of your life comes, when there is truly no alternative but surrender and death and no risk is too great, then it is time to see the Sybil.

Fortunate is the man who has never called on her goes the old saying. But I was not fortunate.

She is called the Daughter of the River, and the Voice of Surat-Kemad, and the Mother of Death, and many other things. Who she is and what she is, no one has ever known; but she dwelt, fearsomely, the subject of countless terrifying stories, beneath the very heart of the city, among the pilings, where the log posts that hold up the great houses are thick as any forest. I had heard of the terrible price she was reputed to demand for her prophecies, and that those who visited her came away irreparably changed if they came away at all. Yet since time immemorial she had dwelt there, and for as long people went to listen to her words.

I went. For an offering, I had my father's sword, the silver one the temple matron gave me.

It was in the earliest dawn twilight that I slipped once more through the trapdoor beneath our house. To the east, to my right, the sky was just beginning to brighten into gray, but before me, toward the heart of the city, night lingered.

I paddled amid the wreckage left by the recent storm: planks, bobbing barrels and trunks, and, once, a slowly rolling corpse the *evatim* had somehow overlooked. Further in, a huge house had fallen on its supports, now awash and broken, its windows gaping like black mouths. Later, when the gloom lessened a bit, I came upon a capsized ship jammed among the pillars like a vast, dead fish caught in reeds, its rigging trailing in the black water.

Just beyond it, the dark, irregular mass of the Sybil's dwelling hung suspended, undamaged by the storm, of course.

There's another story they tell about her: that the Sybil was never young, but was born an old hag in the blood of her mother's death, and that she stood up in the pool of her mother's blood, in the darkness at the world's beginning; and she closed her hands together, then opened them, and columns of flame rose up from her palms.

My father used to do that trick, and once he grew terribly angry when I tried it, even though I'd just sat staring at my hands, opening and closing them without understanding or results. It was enough that I had made the attempt. He was perhaps even frightened at first, at the prospect that I might try again and eventually succeed. Then his face shifted from shock to cold fury. That was the only time in my life he ever beat me.

But when the Sybil made fire with her hands she rolled the flames into balls with her fingers. She breathed on one to make it dim, and released them both – the Sun and Moon. Then she drank long and deep of the Great River where her mother's blood flowed into it, stood up by moonlight, and spat out the sparkling stars. And by starlight the multitude of gods awoke along the banks of the river and beheld the Earth for the first time.

As I gazed upon her house, I could almost believe the story. No, I *did* believe it. The Sybil's house was more of an immense cocoon, like a spider's web filled to overflowing with debris and dead things, spun and accumulated since the beginning of time. It hung from the underside of the city itself, its outer strands a tangle of ropes and netting and vines and fibers stretching out into the darkness in every direction until I could not tell where the enormous nest began or ended.

But the core of it hung down almost to the water, like a monstrous belly. I reached up and tied my boat to it, slipped Father's sword under my belt, bound my robe up to free my legs, and started to climb.

The ropes trembled, whispering like muted thunder. Mud and debris fell in my face, splashing all around me. I hung on desperately, then shook my head to clear my eyes, and continued climbing.

Higher up, in complete darkness, I squeezed along a tunnel of rotting wood, sometimes losing my grip and sliding backwards for a terrifying instant before I found another hold. The darkness was . . . *heavy*. I had the impression of an endless mass of debris in all directions, shifting, grinding as I wriggled through it. Sometimes there was an overwhelming stench of decay.

I crawled over the upturned hull of a boat. It swayed gently beneath my weight. Something soft fell, then slithered against its side. All the while my hands and bare feet scraped desperately for purchase against the rotting wood.

Then came more rope, more netting, and in the dimmest twilight I was in a chamber where trunks, wicker baskets, and heavy clay jugs all heaved and crashed together as I crawled among them.

Serpents and fishes writhed beneath my touch amid reeking slime.

And yet again in utter darkness I made my way on hands and knees across a seemingly solid, wooden floor. Then the boards snapped beneath me and I tumbled screaming amid ropes and wood and what touch alone told me were hundreds of human bones. I came to rest on heaving netting with a skull in my lap and bones rattling down over my bare legs. I threw the skull away and tried to jump up, but my feet slid through the net and I felt only empty space below.

I dangled there, clinging desperately to the rope netting. It broke and I was left screaming once more, swinging in the darkness while an avalanche of bones splashed into the water far below.

One further story I'd heard came to me just then: that when someone drowns in the river, the *evatim* eat his flesh, but the bones go to the Sybil, who divines fortunes from them.

So it seemed.

At precisely this point she called out to me, and her voice was like an autumn wind rattling in dead reeds.

"*Son of Vashtem.*"

I clung tighter to the remnants of the net, gulped, and called up into the darkness.

"I'm here."

"*Sorcerer, son of sorcerer, I await your coming.*"

I was so startled I nearly let go.

"But *I'm* not a sorcerer!"

"*Sorcerer, son of sorcerer.*"

I started climbing once more, all the while telling her about myself in broken, panting speech. Still a few bones fell, suddenly out of the darkness, striking me on the head as if in sarcastic reply to what I gasped out. But still I told her how I had never done any magic myself, how I had promised my mother *never* to be like my father, how I was apprenticed to the learned Velachronos, how I was going to be a scribe first, then maybe write books of my own, if only Velachronos would take me back when this was all over.

Then the Sybil's face appeared to me suddenly in the darkness above, like a full moon from behind a cloud. Her face was pale and round, her eyes inexpressibly black, and I think her skin *did* glow faintly.

And she said to me, laughing gently, "Sorcerer, son of sorcerer, you're *arguing* with the dread Sybil. Now is that a brave thing to do, or just foolish?"

I stopped, swinging gently from side to side on the ropes.

"I'm sorry. I didn't mean to—"

"What you *mean* is not necessarily what you *do*, Sekenre. Whether or not you're sorry afterwards means nothing at all. There. I have spoken your name once. *Sekenre*. I have spoken it twice. Do you know what happens if I speak it three times?"

I said meekly, "No, Great Sybil."

"Sorcerer, son of sorcerer, come up and sit before me. Do not be afraid."

I climbed up to where she was. I could barely make out a

wooden shelf or ledge, covered with bones and debris. I reached out gingerly with one foot and my toes found, surprisingly, solid, dry planking. I let go of the ropes and sat. The Sybil reached up and opened the door of a box-lantern, then of another, and another. I thought of lazy beasts winking themselves awake.

Now light and shadow flickered in the tiny, low-ceilinged room. The Sybil sat cross-legged, a blanket with gleaming embroidery draped over her knees. A man-headed serpent with scales like silver coins lay curled in her lap. Once it hissed and she leaned low while it whispered in her ear. Silence followed. She gazed into my eyes for a long time.

I held out my father's sword.

"Lady, this is all I have to offer—"

She hissed, just like the serpent, and for an instant seemed startled, even afraid. She waved the sword away.

"Sekenre, you are interrupting the Sybil. Now, again, is that brave or just foolishness?"

There. She had spoken my name thrice. I felt an instant of sheer terror. But nothing happened. She laughed again, and her laugh was a human one, almost kindly.

"A most inappropriate gift, sorcerer, son of sorcerer."

"I don't understand . . . I'm sorry, Lady."

"Sekenre, do you know what that sword is?"

"It was my father's."

"It is the sword of a Knight Inquisitor. Your father tried to deny what he was, even to himself. So he joined a holy order, an order of strictest discipline, devoted to the destruction of all things of darkness, all the wild things, witches, sorcerers, even the wild gods. He was like you, boy, at your age. He wanted so much to do the *right* thing. For all the good it did him. In the end, he only had the sword."

"Lady, I have nothing else—"

"Sekenre – there, I said it again. You are very special. The path before you is very special. Your future is not a matter of how many times I speak your name. Keep the sword. You shall need it. I require no payment from you, not yet anyway."

"Will you require it later, Great Sybil?"

She leaned forward, and I saw that her teeth were sharp and pointed. Her breath smelled of river mud.

"Your entire life shall be payment enough. All things come to me in proper time, even as you, I think, come to me now, when your need is greatest."

Then I began to tell her why I had come, about Father, and what had happened to Hamakina.

"Sorcerer, son of sorcerer, you are lecturing the Sybil. Brave or foolish?"

I wept. "Please, Great Lady . . . I don't know what I'm supposed to say. I want to do the right thing. Please don't be angry. Tell me what to do."

"Sorcerer, son of sorcerer, everything you do is the correct thing, part of the great pattern which I observe, which I weave, which I prophesy. At each new turning of your life the pattern is made anew. All the meanings are changed. Your father understood that, when he came back from beyond the sea, no longer a Knight Inquisitor because he knew too much of sorcery. He had become a sorcerer by fighting sorcery. He was like a doctor who contracts the patient's disease. His knowledge was like a door that has been opened and can never be closed again. A door. In his mind."

"No," I said softly. "I will not be like him."

"Hear then the prophecy of the Sybil, sorcerer, son of sorcerer. You shall journey into the very belly of the beast, into the mouth of the God Who Devours."

"Lady, we are all on a journey in this life, and when we die—"

"Sorcerer, son of sorcerer, do you accept the words of the Sybil of your own will, as a gift given?"

I was afraid to ask her what would happen if I refused. It wasn't much of a choice.

"Lady, I accept."

"It is of your will then. If you stray from your path, if you step aside, that, too, changes the weaving of all lives."

"Lady, I only want to get my sister back and—"

"Then accept these too."

She pressed something into my hand. Her touch was cold and hard, like living iron. The serpent thing in her lap hissed, almost forming words. I held my open hand up to one of the lanterns and saw two grave coins on my palm.

"Sorcerer, son of sorcerer, on this day you are a man. Your

father did not raise you to manhood before he left you. Therefore I must perform the rite."

The serpent thing vanished into her clothing. She rose, her movement fluid as smoke. I could only see her face and hands, like lanterns themselves floating in the half-light. She took a silver band and bound my hair as the men of the city bind it. She gave me a pair of baggy trousers such as the men of the city wear. I put them on. They were much too long. I rolled them up to my knees.

"They used to belong to a pirate," she said. "He won't be needing them now."

She rummaged around among the debris and produced a single boot. I tried to put it on. It was nearly twice the size of my foot.

She sighed. "Always the pattern changes. I'm sure it's portentous. Never mind."

She took the boot from me and threw it aside.

Then she leaned down and kissed me on the forehead. The touch of her lips was so cold it burned.

"Now you are marked by the Sybil, sorcerer, son of sorcerer, and by that mark men will know you. Because you are marked, you may call on me three times, and I shall hear you and reply. But beware. If you ask my favor more than that, I shall own you, like all the things in my house. That is the price I ask of you."

She gave me a water bottle and a leather bag with food in it – cheese, bread, and dried fish – and told me to put the grave coins in the bag too so I wouldn't lose them. The bag had a long cord. I slipped it over my neck. I hung the bottle from the loose belt I wore outside my robe.

My forehead was numb where she had kissed me. I reached up and felt the spot. It was cold as ice.

"Now go, sorcerer, son of sorcerer, into the very jaws of the Devourer, of your own will. Go, as the Sybil has prophesied, *right now*—"

She stamped her foot once. I screamed as the floor swung away beneath me like a trapdoor and I was falling endlessly down amid glowing white bones and debris and the Sybil's tumbling lamps. I saw her face once, far above, streaking away in the darkness like a shooting star.

I hit the water hard and sank deep, but somehow reached the

surface again, lungs bursting. I started to swim. The sword cut my legs. The bag choked me. I almost threw them both away, but did not, and slowly, clumsily made my back to where I thought my boat waited. I looked around fearfully for the *evatim*, which surely haunted this place. Above, the house of the Sybil was silent and dark.

At last my feet touched soft mud and I stood up in the gloom. Faint light filtered among the ten thousand wooden legs of the city. I waded through thick mud, then into open water and fell in over my head and swam a short distance, struggling toward the light. Then my feet found a sand bank, and I climbed out of the water and rested.

A whole night must have passed then, for I slept through terrible dreams of my father in his sorcerer's robe, stalking back and forth at the water's edge, his face so twisted with rage that he hardly seemed to be my father at all. He would lean over, raise his hand to strike, then pause, startled, even afraid, as if he had seen something in my face he had never seen there before.

I tried to call out to him.

Suddenly I was awake, in total darkness. A footstep splashed nearby. Far away, the birds of the marshes sang to announce the dawn.

And my father's voice spoke.

"Sekenre . . . do you still love me?"

I could not answer. I only sat terribly still, shivering in the cold air, my knees drawn up to my chest, hands clasped tight to my wrists.

Daylight came as a gray blur. I saw a boat nearby, beached on the same sandbank. It was not my own, but a funeral boat, made of bound reeds.

For an instant I thought I understood fully what the Sybil had prophesied and I froze in terror, but I had known so much of terror in my life already that I had grown indifferent to it. I couldn't bring myself to care. I couldn't think coherently.

Like one bewitched, when the body acts of its own accord without the will of the mind, I pushed the boat out into open water, then climbed in and lay still among the scented corpse-wrappings.

I felt only resignation now. So it had been prophesied.

Almost on a whim, I reached into the leather bag and took out the two grave coins. I placed them over my eyes.

III

For a long time I lay still and listened to the water lapping against the side of the boat. Then even that sound faded, and I felt, very distinctly, the boat reverse direction, and I knew I was drifting with the *black current* now, out of the world of the living, into the land of the dead. The water was silent, as if the boat were gliding along a river of oil. I could hear the pounding of my own heart.

I lay awake and tried to make sense out of my adventure with the Sybil, reviewing every detail in search of some central thread by which all the parts would be connected, like beads on a necklace, assuming form and meaning. But there was nothing. I had expected as much. It is the way of prophecies: you don't understand them until they're about to come true, and then, suddenly, the whole pattern is revealed.

Even the silence of the river and the thunder of my heart were part of the pattern.

Even my sister's voice.

I thought it was just a ringing in my ears at first, but it formed words, very weak, very far away, at the very threshold of hearing.

"Sekenre," she said. "Help me. I'm lost."

I called back to her, either with my voice or my mind.

"I am coming, little one. Wait for me."

She sobbed hoarsely, sucking in breath as if she had been crying for a long time.

"It's dark here."

"It's dark here, too," I said gently.

She was too brave to say she was afraid.

"Hamakina – is Father with you?"

Something splashed in the water right next to the boat, and my father's voice whispered, inches from my ear.

"*Sekenre, if you love me, go back. I command you to go back! Do not come here!*"

I let out a yell and sat up. The grave coins fell into my lap. I twisted about, looking all around.

The boat slid past huge, black reeds. In the silent darkness, white herons stood in rows along the river's edge, faintly glowing as the Sybil's face had glowed. And in the water, the *evatim* watched me, rank upon rank of them like dead-white, naked men with crocodile heads, lying motionless in the shallows. But there was no sign of Father.

Above me, the sky was dark and clear, and the stars were not the stars of Earth, but fewer, paler, almost gray, arranged in the constellations of the dead, which are described in the Books of the Dead: the Hand, the Harp, the Jar of Forgetting, the Eye of Surat-Kemad.

Very carefully, I picked up the grave coins and put them back in my bag. I was thirsty and drank a sip from the water bottle. I could not drink river water here, for only the dead may drink of the water of the dead, and only the dead may eat the fruits of the land of the dead. That too is written in the Books of the Dead.

And so I gazed with mortal, uncovered eyes into the darkness that never ends. Far behind me, along the way I had come, there was a faint suggestion of light, a mere paling of the sky, as if way back there was an opening through which I had already passed. The living world drew farther and farther away with each passing instant.

The white herons rose as one and for a moment the air was filled with the utterly silent passage of their wings. Then they were gone. They too, like the *evatim*, were messengers of the God of the Dark River.

But for me there was no message.

I began to see ghosts among the reeds, sitting up in the mud as I passed, beseeching me to take them aboard my funeral boat so they might go properly into the final land. They were no more than wisps of smoke, suggestions of shapes glimpsed from the corner of the eye. When I looked directly at any one of them, I could not see it.

Some called out in languages I had never heard before. Only a few spoke of places and people I had known. I was afraid of these few. I did not want them to recognize me. I lay back down in the bottom of my boat and put the coins back over my eyes. I slept fitfully after a while and dreamed of my father. He paced back and forth on the surface of the black water, his trailing robe sending ripples as he walked, his face contorted with rage. Once he stopped and seemed to shake me furiously, saying, "No, my son, no. This is not what I wanted for you. I command you. I forbid you . . . because I love you still. Go back to Reedland. Go!"

But, in my dream, I only answered, "Father, I will go if you let me take Hamakina back with me."

He made no answer but continued to rage and pace, too furious even to ask if I loved him.

I awoke from my dream to the faint sound of singing like many voices carried on the wind from far away. I sat up once more, put the coins in my bag, and saw a vast trireme bearing down on me, its sail bellied full, its oars thrashing the water into foam.

Yet it was an insubstantial thing like the ghosts in the reeds, a shape of smoke. The voices of the oarsmen were muted, the throbbing of the pace-setter's drum like the failing thunder of a distant, dying storm. The stars shone through the hull and sail, and the foam of the oars was a phantom thing, the water around me still black and smooth and silent.

This was a wonder, but no mystery, for the Great River co-exists with the River of the Dead, for all that they flow in different directions. Sometimes the rivermen fleetingly glimpse the traffic of the dark current, faint shapes in the night. When they do, they reckon it a bad omen and make sacrifices to soothe the anger of whatever god might have been offended.

Now I, on the River of the Dead, saw the living as phantoms. The trireme loomed up, and then my boat passed through it. For a moment I was among the oarsmen and I could smell the reek of their laborings. Then a richly-furnished cabin swam around me. A great lord feasted, surrounded by his followers. I think it was the Satrap of Reedland himself. One lady of his company paused, cup in hand. Our eyes met. She looked more startled than afraid. She poured out a little of her wine, as if to make a libation to me.

Then the trireme was gone, and I lay back again, the coins on my eyes, my father's sword clutched against my chest.

I slept once more and dreamt once more, but my dream was only a confusion, shapes in the darkness, and sounds I could not make out. I awoke parched and famished, and took another sip from my water bottle, and ate a little of the food in the leather bag.

It was as I ate that I realized that the river was no longer flowing. The boat lay absolutely motionless in the middle of a black, endless, dead marsh beneath the grey stars. Even the *evatim* and the ghosts were gone.

I was truly afraid. I thought I would be left there forever. No, somehow I was *certain* of it. Somehow the Devouring God had tricked me, and the Land of the Dead would not accept me while I yet lived.

I forced down one last bite of bread, then closed the bag and called out, half sobbing: "*Sybil! Help me! I've lost my way!*"

And the sky began to lighten. I saw not merely reeds, but huge trees rising out of the marsh, stark and barren like ruined stone pillars.

Some of the stars began to fade. I thought the Moon was rising – how strange that I should be able to see the Moon here! – but instead the face of the Sybil drifted into the sky, pale and round and huge as the full Moon. She gazed down on me for a time in silence and I was afraid to speak to her. Then her face rippled, as a reflection does when a pebble is dropped into a still pool, and she was gone, but her voice came rattling through the reeds.

"*Sorcerer, son of sorcerer, you have called on me foolishly and have wasted one summoning. You are near to your goal and could have found your own way. Nevertheless, if you think you need a guide, reach down into the water and draw one up.*"

"Into the *water*?" I said. For an instant I was terrified that I had wasted a second summoning with that question. But the Sybil did not reply.

I reached down into the frigid water, wary of lurking *evatim*. I groped around, swinging my arm from side to side, my fingers outstretched. For an instant I lay there, half out of the boat, wondering if this were another of the Sybil's riddles. Then the water suddenly stirred, as if something were rising, and my fingers closed on something stringy and slippery like an underwater weed, and I pulled.

A hand broke the surfacè, then another. I let go of what I had been holding and scrambled back. The hands caught hold of the side of the boat and the boat rocked beneath the weight of that which climbed aboard. There was a sudden, overwhelming stench of decay, or rotted flesh. Long, muddy hair fell across a face that was more bone than anything else.

I screamed then, and kept on screaming when the thing opened its eyes and began to speak and I knew that it was my mother.

"Sekenre—"

I covered my face with my hands and merely sobbed, trying to remember her as she had been once, so very long ago.

"Sekenre –" She took hold of my wrists and gently drew my hands away from my face. Her touch was as cold as the Sybil's kiss.

I turned from her.

"Mother, I did not expect –" I could not say more, and broke into tears again.

"Son, I did not expect to see you in this place either. Truly, it is a terrible thing."

She pulled me forward and I did not resist, until I lay with my face in her lap, my cheek against her wet, muddy gown, while she gently stroked my forehead with a bony finger. I told her all that had happened then, of Father's own death, and his return for Hamakina.

"I am your father's sin, returning to him at last," she said.

"Did he—?"

"Murder me? Yes, he did. But that is the least part of his offense. He has sinned more against you, Sekenre, and also against the gods."

"I don't think he meant to do wrong," I said. "He says he loves me still."

"He probably does. Nevertheless, he has done great wrong."

"Mother, what shall I do?"

Her cold, sharp finger drew a circle around the mark on my forehead.

"It is time for us to resume our journey. The boat has served its purpose now. You must leave it."

I looked at the black water with ever-increasing dread.

"I don't understand. Are we to . . . *swim*?"

"No, beloved son. We are to walk. Get out of the boat now, and walk."

I slipped one leg over the side, one foot in the frigid water. I looked back at her uncertainly.

"Go on. Do you doubt this one small miracle, after all you have seen?"

"Mother, I—"

"*Go on.*"

I obeyed her and stood upon the water. It felt like cold glass beneath my feet. Then she stood next to me, and the boat drifted slowly away. I turned to watch it go, but she took me by the hand and led me in a different direction.

Her touch was like the Sybil's, a touch of living, frigid iron.

The channel widened, and the *evatim* were waiting for us. Here the water flowed almost swiftly, making silent waves and eddies and whirlpools behind the dead trees. Many ghosts waded in the shallows, but they did not call out to us. They merely stood there, turning as we passed. One of them was a man in full, gleaming armor, holding his severed head in his hands.

Then there were other boats around us, black and solid and silent, not phantoms of the living, but other funeral boats. We came alongside a long, sleek barge, its pointed ends rising high above the water, a lantern flickering inside its square cabin. The *evatim* crawled into this cabin and the barge rocked. I could hear them thrashing in there.

At last something huge and dark loomed before us, like a mountain, blotting out the stars. On every side I saw drifting funeral boats following our course, some of them twisting and turning among reeds. One caught on something, or else the *evatim* tipped it over. A mummy slipped into the water and drifted by, bandages trailing, so close I could have reached out and touched it.

The darkness closed around us very suddenly, shutting out the stars. I heard water rushing, and boats creaking and banging against one another.

"Mother!" I whispered. I reached forward and tugged at her gown. A piece of it came away in my hand. "Is this it? Is this the mouth of Surat-Kemad?"

"No, child," she said softly. "We have been in the belly of the beast for some time now."

And that, somehow, was even more terrifying.

IV

Nothing was clear any more, the whole adventure no more than an endless continuity of dream and waking, stark images and featureless mist, pain and terror and dull discomfort.

I had been on the river I knew not how long – hours, days, weeks – and at times it seemed I was inexpressibly weary, and at others that I was back home in my bed, asleep, that all of this was some crazed nightmare. But then I reached out, turning and stretching as one does when awakening – and I touched my mother's cold, wet, ruined body.

And the stench of decay was gone from her, and she smelled only of the river mud, like some long-sunken bundle of sticks and rags.

Sometimes there were herons all around us, glowing dimly in the utter darkness like smoldering embers, their faces the faces of men and women, all of them whispering to us, imploring, speaking names – and their voices blended together like a gentle, indistinguishable rustle of wind.

Mostly, we just walked in the darkness, alone. I felt the cold surface of the river beneath my feet, but there was no sense of motion, for all my legs moved endlessly.

Mother spoke. Her voice was soft, coming from the darkness like something remembered in a dream.

I don't think she was even addressing me. She was merely talking, her memories, her whole life rising into words like sluggish bubbles: scraps of unfinished conversations from her childhood, and, too, much about my father, and me, and Hamakina. For what might have been a very long time or only a few minutes, she sang a lullaby, as if rocking me – or perhaps Hamakina – to sleep.

Then she was silent. I reached out to assure myself that she was still there, and her bony hand found mine and squeezed gently. I asked her what she had learned about the Land of the Dead since she had come here, and she replied softly, "I have learned that I am forever an exile, without a place prepared for me, since I have come unprepared and unannounced into Surat-Kemad's domain. My place of exile is the river, along which I must wander until the gods die and the worlds are unmade."

I wept for her then, and asked if this was Father's doing, and she said that it was.

Then she asked me suddenly, "Sekenre, do you hate him?"

I had been so confident just then that I did, but I could not find an answer.

"I don't think he meant to do any harm—"

"My son, you must sort out your feelings toward him. That is where you have lost your way, not on the river."

Again we walked for a long time, still in utter darkness, and all the while I thought of my father and remembered my mother as she had once been. What I wanted, more than anything else, was merely for everything to be restored – Father, Mother, Hamakina, and myself, in our house by the edge of the City of Reeds, as all had been when I was small. Yet, if I had learned any lesson in life thus far, it was that you can't go back, that our days flow on as relentlessly as the Great River, and what is lost is never restored. I was not wise. I understood very little. But I knew that much.

The father I longed for was merely gone. Perhaps he, too, longed to be restored. I wondered if he knew it was impossible.

I tried to hate him.

The darkness and the silence of the river gave a sense of being in a tunnel, far underground, but were we not more than underground, deep in the belly of Surat-Kemad? We passed from darkness into darkness, always beginning as if through countless anterooms without ever finding the main hall.

So with our days. So with our strivings, I thought. Whatever we seek to understand yields only a glimmer, and a vast mystery.

So with my father—

Very suddenly, Mother took both my hands in hers and said, "I may only guide you a little way, my son, and we have come that little way. I cannot go where an exile is not welcome, where there is no place prepared –"

"What? I don't understand."

"I am not permitted into the god's house. I must leave you at the doorstep."

"But you said—"

"That we have been deep within his belly for some time. Yet we are at the doorstep of his house—"

She let go of me. I groped frantically for her, then found her again.

"Mother!"

She kissed both my hands very gently, and her lips, like the Sybil's, were so cold they burned.

"But you are a hero, my son, and you may take the next step, and the next. That is what is is to be brave, you know, merely to take the next step. I have always known that you were brave."

"Mother, I—"

Then she sank down into the water. I clung to her. I tried to hold her up, but she sank like a thing of stone, and I lost my grip. At the very last I found myself crawling absurdly about on the cold surface of the river, sliding my hands from side to side like a blind child who has lost marbles on a smooth floor.

I stood up, suddenly shivering, rubbing my arms with my hands.

She was wrong, I told myself. I wasn't a hero. I wasn't brave. I merely had no choice. The Sybil had seen that much.

Yet I never once thought of turning back. The road behind me was impassable, in more ways than one.

I wanted to call on the Sybil again, to tell her I had once more lost my way. In the darkness, without any point of reference except the sensation in my feet to tell me which way was down, I couldn't even tell if I was facing the way I was supposed to be going, or the way I had come.

In the end, it did not matter. I don't think direction is a physical thing in the belly of a god. Instead, it is a matter of degree.

Things began to happen swiftly once more. Lights rose around me, like lanterns drifting up from the surface of the water, then above me like stars. The water itself rippled, frigid, oily waves washing over my feet.

I started to run, afraid that whatever magic had held me up was leaving me, now that Mother had. Nothing, it seemed, could be more horrible than to be immersed in that river, there, in the belly of Surat-Kemad.

I ran, and the points of light moved with me, turning as I turned, swirling about me like burning motes on the wind. There was a sound. I thought it was indeed the wind, but then I realized that it was *breathing*, spittle hissing through teeth, and the lights were *eyes*, not reflecting light as a dog's will by a campfire, but actually glowing, like living coals.

The darkness lessened and I saw that I had indeed emerged from a tunnel. Jagged, fissured cliffs loomed on either side of the river, towering to unknowable heights. Far above, the grey stars of the deadlands shone once more.

And the *evatim* stood around me by the thousands, on the river, scrambling up the cliffs, some of them just standing at the water's edge, staring. By the light of their eyes and by the pale stars, I could see that I had come at last to the place where the Great River ended and truly began, a vast lake where the white-bodied, crocodile-headed ones paced back and forth, ankle-deep in thick grey mist, their long jaws bobbing up and down.

The *evatim* bore long hooks on poles, like boathooks, and as I watched one of them would occasionally pause, then reach down with his hook and draw up a human corpse, heave it onto his shoulder and depart, or just stand there, holding the dead in a lover's embrace.

I realized to my horror that I was standing on a vast sea of corpses. I looked down and I could make them out dimly beneath the water's surface, inches below my feet: faces, arms, bobbing chests and backs and buttocks jostling slowly in the black water like numberless fish in a net. I jumped back in revulsion, but there was nowhere to jump to.

I started to run again. Somehow, miraculously, the *evatim* seemed too busy with their tasks to notice me.

For the first time my footfalls made a sound, a heavy splashing and sucking, as if I were running through mud.

Truly this was the place I had read of in the Books of the Dead that Velachronos and I had copied, where the bodies and souls of the dead and the unborn are sorted out by the *evatim*, who are the thoughts and servants of the terrible god, and each person is judged, and carried to his rightful place, or cast out, or devoured.

I despaired then, for I knew that if Hamakina were *here*, I would surely never find her.

Yet I took the next step, and the next, and the next, slowing to a fast walk. If that is what it is to be brave, then I was. I continued. The mist swirled around my shins.

I seemed to be nearing the shallows. Reeds rose around me like bare iron rods. I passed one sunken funeral boat, then another, then a long stretch of boards and debris but no corpses or *evatim*.

A beach spread before me like a pale band on the horizon, like a white sunrise. The *evatim* struggled across it in an endless procession, dragging their burdens from the water.

I stood among the reeds and watched them for a time. Then I took a step forward, and cold water splashed around my knees. I gasped involuntarily at the sudden shock of no longer walking *on* the water, but in it. There was mud and sand beneath my feet.

I neared the beach, crouched down, trying to conceal myself among the last of the reeds. Gradually I could make out three huge doorways in the cliff-face beyond the end of the white sand. The crocodile-headed ones labored toward them, bearing their burdens through the doorways.

I didn't doubt that each doorway led to a different place, and that there the final judgement of the god was made. Yes, I was on Surat-Kemad's doorstep, in the anteroom of his great hall, forever beginning my quest.

But I didn't know which of the three doors to go through. Surely my Father waited beyond . . . one of them.

I took the next step, and the next, freely mingling with the *evatim*, who took no notice of me. We crowded toward one of the doors. I was hemmed in by cold, hard bodies. I let the movement of the great mass of them determine my direction.

The empty face of an old woman bobbed in front of my face, her corpse slung over the shoulder of her bearer, her open mouth black, frozen as if perpetually about to shout or kiss or devour.

Once more the cliffs rose around me. Once more some of the *evatim* scrambled up the jagged stones, their glowing eyes seeming to rise into the sky like stars. Those who had climbed, I saw, set their burdens down on ledges and began to feast.

I turned away quickly and stared at the ground, and at the almost luminously pale feet and legs of the *evatim*.

The sides of the great doorway were carven smooth, its iron gates flung wide. The gates resembled, more than anything else, enormous, gaping jaws.

I tried to peer ahead again, but I could not see over the mass of the *evatim*. I jumped up. I turned and looked back, but only masses of crocodile-faces stared back at me, like a swirling shifting cloud filled with burning eyes.

"Stop! You are not of the brotherhood of the *evatim!*"

I whirled around again. A pallid, black-bearded face hovered before me, its red eyes unblinking. It rose on the body of a snake, only stiff as a tree trunk and covered with glistening silver scales the size of my outstretched hand. As I watched, another face rose from the ground on such a glittering stalk, and another, bursting out of the sand, out of the stone of the cliff face until a forest of them blocked my way. The *evatim* drew aside.

"*You may not pass!*" one of them said.

"*Blasphemer, you may not enter our master's domain.*"

I got out my leather bag and struggled desperately with the drawstring, then poured the two grave coins into my hand.

"Wait," I said. "Here. These are for you."

The foremost of the man-headed serpent-things leaned forward and took the coins into its mouth. Its lips, like the Sybil's, like my mother's, were searingly cold.

But the coins burst into flame in the creature's mouth and it spat them out at my feet.

"*You are still alive!*"

Then all of them shouted in unison, "*This one is still alive!*"

And the *evatim* came writhing through the scaled, shrieking forest, free of their burdens, on all fours now, their great jaws gaping. I drew my father's sword and struck one of them, and another, and another, but one caught me on the right leg and yanked me to my knees. I slashed at the thing again and again. One of the glowing eyes burst, hissed, and went out.

Another reared up, closed its jaws on my back and chest, and pulled me over backwards. That was the end of the struggle. The great mass of them swarmed over me, while still the serpent-things shouted and screamed and babbled, and their voices were like thunder.

Teeth like knives raked me all over, tearing, and I still held the sword, but it seemed very far away and I couldn't move it—

A crocodilian mouth closed over my head, over my shoulders and I called out, my voice muffled, shouting down the very throat of the monster, "Sybil! Come to me again—!"

I cannot say what actually happened after that. I saw her face again, glowing like a distant lantern in the darkness below me, but rising, racing upward, while the *evatim* tore at me and crushed me slowly in their jaws.

Then I distinctly felt myself splash into water, and the viscous blackness closed around me and the *evatim* were gone. I sank slowly in the cold and the dark, while the Sybil's face floated before me and grew brighter until the darkness was dispelled and my eyes were dazzled.

"This time, you did well to call on me," she said.

I awoke on a bed. As soon as I realized that it was a bed, I lay still with my eyes closed, deliberately dismissing from my mind any thought that this was my familiar bed back home, that my adventures had been no more than a prolonged, horrible dream.

I knew it was not so, and my body knew it, from the many wounds where the *evatim* had held me. And I was nearly naked, my clothing in tatters.

But I still held my father's sword. I moved my right arm stiffly, and scraped the blade along hard wood.

This bed was not my bed. It was made of rough boards and covered not with sheets but with sand.

I started to sit up, eyes still closed, and gentle hands took my by the bare shoulders. The hands were soft and warm.

I was dizzy then. The sword slipped from my grasp. I opened my eyes, but couldn't focus. There was only a blur.

Warm water was being poured over my back. My wounds stung. I let out a cry and fell forward and found myself awkwardly embracing some unknown person, my chin on his shoulder.

I could see, then, that I was in a room stranger than any I had ever imagined, a place once richly furnished but now a wreck, turned on its side like a huge box rolled over, its contents spilled everywhere. Stained glass windows hung open above me, dangling, ornately worked with designs of glowing fishes. Books and bottles lay in heaps amid fallen beams, plaster, and bricks. There was a splintered staircase that coiled out and ended in midair. An image of Surat-Kemad had been fixed to the floor and remained fixed, but now it stuck out horizontally into space. A lantern dangled sideways from the grey-green snout.

My host pushed me gently back onto the bed and I was staring into the face of a gray-bearded man. He squinted in the half-light, his face wrinkling. For a moment the look on his face was one of ineffable joy, but it faded into doubt, then bitter disappointment.

"No," he said. "It is not so. Not yet."

I reached up to touch him, to be sure he was real and alive, but he took my hand in his and pressed it down on my chest. Then he gave me my father's sword, closing my fingers around the grip, and I lay there, the cold blade against my bare skin.

Then he said something completely astonishing.

"I thought you were my son."

I sat up and this time sat steadily. I saw that I was indeed almost naked, my clothing completely shredded, and I was smeared with blood. Suddenly I felt weak again, but I caught hold of a bedpost with my free hand and remained upright.

I blurted, "But you are not my father—"

"Then we are agreed," he said.

"I don't understand."

Wind roared outside. The room swayed and creaked, the walls visibly shifting. More plaster, wood, and a sudden avalanche of human bones clattered around us, filling the air with dust. Tiles rained over my shoulders and back. The window overhead clacked back and forth.

I thought of the Sybil's house. I looked to my companion with growing dread, but he merely shrugged.

"It'll pass. Don't worry."

When all was once again still, I said, "I am Sekenre, son of Vashtem the sorcerer."

He hissed and drew back.

"Then I fear you!"

"No," I said. "I'm not a sorcerer myself." I started to explain, but he waved his hand, bidding me to cease.

"You are a powerful sorcerer indeed. I can tell! I can tell!"

I concluded that the man was mad. What could be more natural, after all I had been through, than to meet someone who was mad? If he thought I was a sorcerer, there was no sense dissuading him.

I placed my father's sword across my legs, then folded my arms across my chest, and directed toward him what I hoped was a stern gaze.

"Very well. I, a sorcerer, command you to explain yourself."

He spread his hands and looked helpless. "Sorcerer, I don't know where to begin—"

"Why did you think I was your son?"

He moved over to the broken statue of a bird and sat on the flat space where the head had once been. He did not answer my question, but sat still for several minutes. I thought he had forgotten me and had fallen into some sort of reverie. I stared up at the dangling window, then toyed with the sword in my lap.

At last he sighed and said, "What do you know of where you are, sorcerer and son of sorcerer?"

I told him something of my history, and he only sighed again and said that I was a mighty sorcerer for all I was yet an ignorant one.

"Then teach me," I said.

"When your mother left you," he said, "that was because she could not pass beyond *Leshé*, the realm of dreams. Because she had never been prepared for burial, she could not truly enter the land of the dead. There are four realms; you must understand this. Earth is the realm of *Eshé*, the world of living men. But our dreams arise from the mists of the river, from *Leshé*, where the country of sleep borders the country of death. We see unquiet ghosts in our dreams because they linger in *Leshé*, as your mother does. Beyond is *Tashé*, the true domain of the dead, where all dwell in the places the god has appointed for them."

"And the fourth realm?"

"That is *Akimshé* – holiness. At the heart of the god, in the mind of the god, among the fiery fountains where even gods and worlds and the stars are born – that is *Akimshé*, holiness, which may not be described. Not even the greatest of the prophets, not even the sorcerers, not even the very gods may look on the final mystery of *Akimshé*."

"But it's still inside Surat-Kemad," I said. "I don't see how—"

"It is well that you do not understand. Not even Surat-Kemad understands. Not even he may look on it."

I said very quickly, "I have to continue on my way. I have to find my father."

And my companion said one more surprising thing.

"Yes, of course. I know him. He is a mighty lord here."

"You – you – *know* him –?" I couldn't say anything more. My thoughts were all a jumble.

"He dwells here in peculiar honor because he is a sorcerer," the old man said, "but he must remain here, unique among the servants of Surat-Kemad, but a servant nonetheless."

I got to my feet unsteadily. The remains of my trousers dangled. I wrapped them around my belt, trying to make myself at least decent, but there wasn't much to work with. I slid the sword under the belt.

I stood there, breathing hard from the exertion, wincing as the effort stretched my lacerated sides.

"You must take me to my father," I said.

"I can only show you the way." He shook his head sadly.

"Where?"

He pointed up, to the open window.

"There?"

"Yes," he said. "That way."

"But –" I walked across the room to a door now sideways in the wall, and opened it, lowering the door against the wall. I stared through at a dense sideways forest, the forest floor rising vertically to one side, the trees horizontal. There was a glowing mist among the trees, like fog at sunrise before it melts away. Brilliantly-plumed birds cawed and fluttered in the branches. Warm, damp air blew against my face and chest.

The gray-bearded man put his hand on my shoulder and led me away.

"No," he said. "You will never find your father through that door." He pointed to the ceiling again. "*That* way."

I started to climb, clumsily, my muscles aching. My right palm was numb where the guardian-serpent's lips had touched me.

I caught hold of the image of the god, hooking an arm over it. Then pulled myself up and sat there astride Surat-Kemad, my feet dangling.

"You never answered my question. Why did you think I was your son?"

"It is a very old sorrow."

I didn't command him. "Can you . . . tell me?"

He sat down on the edge of the bed and gazed up at me. "I was called Aukin, son of Nevat. I dwelt far beyond any land you ever knew, beyond the mouth of the Great River and across the sea among the people you would call barbarians. I had a wife. I loved her very much. Is that a surprising thing, even for a barbarian? No, it is not. When she died bearing my first son, and my son too was dead in her womb, my grief was without bounds. The gods of my homeland could not comfort me, for they are harsh spirits of the forest and of the hills, and they do not deal in comfort. Therefore I came into your country, first to the City of the Delta, where I prayed long before the image of Bel-Hemad and gave the priests much gold. But he did not answer me, and when I ran out of money, the priests sent me away. So I wandered all along the Great River, in the forests, on the plains, among the marshes. I tarried with holy men in the high mountains. From them I learned to dream. They thought they were teaching me content-ment, but no, I clung to my bold scheme. It was this: I would be the mightiest dreamer of all and travel beyond *Leshé* to the lake of *Tashé* and farther, and I would find my son who had tried but failed to enter the world, and I would bring him back with me. The dead have been truly reclaimed by the Devouring God, so there is no hope for my wife, but the *unborn*, I thought – I still think – perhaps will not be missed. So far I have succeeded only with the first part of my plan. I am here. But I have not found my son. When I saw you, *alive*, here, I had hope again, just briefly."

"This is the Sybil's doing," I said.

"Yes, I can tell that it is, by the mark on you."

"The mark on me?"

He got up, rummaged among the debris, and handed me a broken piece of mirrored glass.

"Didn't you know?" he said softly.

I looked at my reflection. The spot on my forehead where the Sybil had kissed me was glowing as brightly as had the eyes of the *evatim*.

I handed the glass back to him, and it was then that I noticed that my hands, too, gave off a faint light where my mother had touched them at the very end. Where the guardian-serpent's lips had touched me when it took the coins, the skin was seared and healed into a smooth white scar.

I sat still, staring at my hands.

"If I really am a sorcerer," I said, "I'll try to help you. You don't have to be afraid of me."

He offered me a cup. "Here, drink this."

"But I can't. If I drink anything here, I'll–"

The old man sighed. "You are still an ignorant sorcerer. *This* water is from *Leshé*, from the river where it is filled with dreams. It will give you many visions. It will truly open your eyes, but it will not bind you to the dead. The waters of *Tashé* will do that, but not those of *Leshé*."

"Do I need to see visions?"

"I think you do, to get where you're going."

"This is the Sybil's doing again," I said.

"Yes, it is. Drink."

I drank. The water was very cold and, surprisingly, sweet. My whole body trembled with it. Only in the aftertaste was it bitter.

"Now go," said Aukin, son of Nevat, who had lost his own son.

I stood up, balancing myself precariously on the image of the god, and caught hold of the window-ledge, then heaved myself up. For a moment I dangled there, looking down at the old man. He waved me on. I heaved again and felt a blast of hot wind against my face and chest, and sand stung me, as if I had crawled out into a sandstorm.

Then I was falling, not back into the room, but *down*, away from the window as directions somehow reversed. The window receded above me and was gone as I tumbled head over heels through hot, blinding, blowing sand.

Visions came to me:

As I fell, I saw the whole of *Tashé* spread out before me. I saw that each dead person there dwelt in a little space formed out of some memory from life, either a pleasant one, or, if some guilty memory tormented him, an endless terror. So the domain of *Tashé* was an incongruous tangle, a jumbled mass like the inside of the Sybil's house.

And as I fell, I was in many places at once. I walked on soft moss to the edge of a pool, deep in a forest suffused with golden light. Three young girls sat by the pool, washing their hair. A young man, scarcely older than myself, sat by them, strumming on a lyre. All around them, the forest seemed to go on forever. Pale white fishes drifted through the air among the trees.

Then I took one step back from the pool, and the forest was gone.

I ran beneath the pale stars over an endless expanse of bricks so hot that they burned my feet. Bricks stretched glowing to the black horizon. I wept with the pain and began to stagger. It was all I could do not to sit down. Smoke and flame hissed out of fissures. Still I ran on, gasping for breath, streaked with soot and sweat, until I came to a window set horizontally in the ground, in the bricks as if in a wall. The window was open. A curtain blew straight up at me on a searing gust. Still, somehow, I had to look.

I swayed dangerously, then dropped to my hands and knees, screaming aloud at the new pain. I crept to the edge, peered in, and beheld a king and his courtiers below me, all sitting solemnly at a banquet table. Yet there was no feast before them, and each face was contorted in unimaginable agony. Their bodies and clothing were transparent, and I could see that the hearts of these men and women were white hot, like iron in a forge.

And again, I saw a girl in a pleasantly lit room, singing and spinning forever. A man sat at her feet, carving a piece of ivory into a form that was somehow infinitely ornate and beautiful but never complete.

And I lay, naked as I was, in a frigid stream amid snowbanks. A blizzard made the sky featureless white.

And crowds babbled in a marketplace; and I was alone in endless, silent halls thick with dust; and I walked on water to a ruined tower where men in white robes and silver masks awaited my coming; and a resplendent pirate paced back and forth end-lessly on a single deck suspended in the middle of the air. He looked up, startled, as I plummeted by.

And I saw into memories, into the lives of all who dwelt in that land of *Tashé*, and I knew what it meant to be a king, and a slave, and in love, and a murderer, and I knew what it was to be old and remember all these things vaguely, as in a fading dream.

And I found my sister, Hamakina.

I fell amid swirling, stinging sand, and suddenly the sand became millions of birds, flapping their soft wings against me to hold me up. All these birds had my sister's face, and they spoke with my sister's voice.

"Sekenre, I am here."

"Where?"

"Brother, you have come for me."

"Yes, I have."

"Brother, it is too late."

I wasn't falling anymore, but lay choking in a heap of cold, soft ashes. I sat up, spitting out ash, trying to wipe ash from my eyes.

In time, tears and spittle gave me enough moisture to clean my face, and I could see. I was in a garden of ash. Fading into the distance in all directions, white, bare trees stood in neat rows, leafless, yet heavy with round, white fruit. Ash rained from the sky, the ash, the sky, and the earth all featureless gray, until I could not tell where earth and sky met.

I stood up amid dead flowers with stalks like winter reeds – huge, yet delicately preserved in every colorless detail.

The ash fell heavily enough that I could feel it striking my shoulders in clumps. I was coated with it, until I too seemed a part of this place. I held my hands over my face, struggling to breathe and to see, while making my way along a path amid sticks that might have been the remains of hedges, the ash cool and soft and knee-deep.

The overwhelming smell in the air, the odor of the ash, was intensely sweet, unpleasantly so, strong enough that I felt faint. But I knew I could not stop here, could not rest, and I took one step, and the next, and the next . . .

In an open place, which might have been the center of the garden, a wooden shelter stood half-buried amid drifts, a domed roof atop squat pillars. The roof was shaped into a wide-mouthed, staring face, the mouth already clogged as if the thing were vomiting gray powder.

Hamakina sat waiting for me there, on a bench beneath that strange roof. She too was barefoot and in rags, plastered with ash. But her cheeks were newly streaked with tears.

"Sekenre . . ."

"I've come to take you back," I said gently.

"I can't go. Father . . . tricked me. He told me to eat the fruit, and I—"

I waved a hand toward one of the white trees.

"*This?*"

"It didn't look like this then. The trees were green. The fruit was wonderful. It smelled wonderful. The colors were . . . *shining*, changing all the time, like oil on water when the sun touches it. Father told me to, and he was angry, and I was afraid, so I ate . . . and it tasted dead, and then suddenly everything was like you see it now."

"*Father* did this?"

"He said it was part of his plan all along. I didn't understand a lot of what he said."

"*Where is he?*"

I drew my sword, clutching it tightly, furious and at the same time aware of how ridiculous and helpless I must have seemed. But it was *my* sword now, no longer my father's, given to me by the Sybil for a specific purpose –

"Sekenre, what will you do?"

"Something. Whatever I have to."

She took me by the hand. Her touch was cold. "Come on."

I don't know how long we walked through the ash garden. There was no way to measure time or distance or direction. But Hamakina seemed to know for certain where we were going.

Then the garden was gone and it seemed I was back in the cramped, swaying darkness of the Sybil's house again. I looked around for her luminous face, expectant, but my sister led me without any hesitation across a rope bridge above an abyss, while vast leviathans with idiot, human faces swam up out of a sea of guttering stars, splashing pale foam, each creature opening its mouth to display rotting teeth and a mirrored ball held between them. I gazed down through the swinging, twisting ropes and saw myself reflected there on the curving glass.

Somehow Hamakina was no longer with me, but far away, down below, inside each mirrored sphere, and I saw her running ahead of me across featureless and beneath a sand-colored sky. Then each monster sank down in turn and she vanished, and another rose, its jaws agape, and I saw her again.

There were black stars in the sky above Hamakina now, and she ran across the sand beneath them, a gray speck against the dead sky, receding into the black points which were the stars.

And each leviathan sank down and another rose to give me a glimpse of her, and from out of the abyss I caught snatches of a song she sang as she ran. Her voice was still her own, but older, filled with pain, and a little mad.

> *"When I am in the darkness gone,*
> *and you're still in the light,*
> *come lie each day upon my grave;*
> *I'll lie with you each night.*
> *Come bring me gifts of fruit and wine.*
> *Bring them from the meadow.*
> *I'll bring dust and ash and clay;*
> *I'll bring gifts of shadow."*

Without any transition I could sense, I was suddenly on that endless expanse of sand beneath the black stars, and I followed her voice over the low dunes toward the horizon and a black shape that huddled there.

At first I thought it was one of the stars fallen from the sky, but as we neared it the thing resolved itself, and I slowed to a terrified walk when I saw the pointed roofs and the windows like eyes and the familiar dock beneath the house, now resting on the sand.

My father's house – no, *my* house – stood on its stilts like a huge, frozen spider. There was no river, no Reedland at all, as if the whole world had been wiped clean but for this one jumble of ancient wood.

When I reached the dock, Hamakina was waiting for me at the base of the ladder.

She turned her head upward.

"He is there."

"Why did he do all this to you and to Mother?" I said. I held onto the sword and onto the ladder, gripping hard, trembling more with sorrow than with fear or even anger.

Her reply startled me far more than anything the dreamer Aukin had said. Once more her voice was older, almost harsh.

"Why did he do all this to *you*, Sekenre?"

I shook my head and started climbing. As I did the ladder shivered, as if it were alive and felt my touch.

And my father's voice called out from the house, thundering:

"Sekenre, I ask you again. Do you still love me?"

I said nothing and kept on climbing. The trapdoor at the top was barred from the inside.

"I want you to love me still," he said. "I only wanted what was best for you. Now I want you to go back. After all you have done against my wishes, it is still possible. Go back. Remember me as I was. Live your life. That is all."

I pounded on the trapdoor with the pommel of my sword. Now the whole house shivered and suddenly burst into white, colorless flame, washing over me, blinding me, roaring in my ears. I let out a yell and jumped, barely clearing the dock below, landing face-down in the sand. I sat up, sputtering, still clutching the sword. The house was not harmed by the fire, but the ladder smouldered and fell as I watched.

I slid the sword under my belt again and started climbing one of the wooden stilts. Once more the white flames washed over me, but they gave no heat, and I ignored them.

"Father," I said. "I am coming. Let me in."

I reached the porch outside my own room. I was standing in front of the very window through which Hamakina had been carried away. All the windows and doors were barred against me, and flickering with white flames.

I thought of calling on the Sybil. It would be my third and last opportunity. Then, if I ever did so again – what? Somehow she would claim me. No, it was not time for that.

"Father," I said, "if you love me as much as you say, open up."

"You are a disobedient son."

"I shall have to disobey you further."

And once more I began to weep as I stood there, as I closed my hands together and opened them again. Father had beaten me once for attempting this act. *Then* I had gotten no results. *Now* I did, and it was as easy as breathing.

Cold blue flames danced on my outstretched palms. I reached up with my burning hands and parted the white fire like a curtain. It flickered and went out. I pressed my palms against the shuttered window. Blue flames streamed from between my fingers. The wood smoked, blackened, and fell inward, giving way so suddenly that I stumbled forward, almost falling into the room.

I climbed over the windowsill and stood there, amazed. The

most fantastic thing of all was that I was truly in the house where I had grown up, in the room Mother, Hamakina, and I had shared, and in which I had remained alone for half a night at the very end waiting desperately for the dawn. I saw where I had once carved my initials into the back of a chair. My clothes lay heaped over the edge of an open trunk. My books were on a shelf in the far corner, and a page of papyrus, one of my own illumination projects, was still in place on the desk, with pens and brushes and bottles of ink and paint all where I had left them. Hamakina's doll lay on the floor at the foot of the bed. One of Mother's *hevats*, a golden bird, hung from the ceiling, silent and motionless.

More than anything else I wanted to just lie down in that bed, then rise in the morning, get dressed, and resume work at my desk, as if nothing had ever happened.

I think that was my father's last offer to me. He was shaping my thoughts.

I walked out of the room, the floorboards creaking. I knocked on his workroom door. It, too, was locked.

Father spoke from within. He sounded weary.

"Sekenre, what do you want?"

It was a completely astonishing question. All I could say was, "I want in."

"No," he said after a long pause. "What do you truly want, as my son, for yourself."

"I don't know anymore." I drew my sword once more, and pounded on the door with the pommel.

"I think you do. You want to grow to be an ordinary man, to live in the city, to have a wife and family, to be free of ghosts and shadows and sorcery – on this we are agreed. I want that for you too. It is very important."

"Father, I am not sure of anything. I don't know how I feel."
I kept on pounding.

"Then why are you still here?" he said.

"Because I have to be."

"To become a sorcerer is a terrible thing," he said. "It is worse than a disease, worse than any terror, like opening a door into nightmare that can never be closed again. You seek to know. You peer into darkness. There is a certain allure, what seems like unlimited power at first, then glory, then, if you truly delude yourself, vast wisdom. To become a sorcerer is to learn the secrets of all the worlds and of the gods. But sorcery burns you. It disfigures, changes, and the man who becomes a sorcerer is no longer the man he was before he became a sorcerer. He is hated and feared by all. He has countless enemies."

"And you, Father? Do you have countless enemies?"

"My son, I have killed many people in my time, thousands—"

That, once more, astonished me into helplessness. I could only say, "But *why?*"

"A sorcerer must have knowledge, not merely to ward off his enemies, but to *live*. He hungers for more dark spells, more powers. You can only get so much from books. You *need* more. To truly become a sorcerer, one must kill another sorcerer, and another, and another, each time stealing what that other sorcerer possesses, which he, in turn, has stolen by murder. There would be few sorcerers left were it not for the temptations, which recruit new ones. Sorcery goes on and on, devouring."

"Surely some magic can be used for good, Father."

I stopped pounding. I looked down at my hands, where they had been marked, where the flames had arisen so effortlessly.

"Sorcery is not magic. Do not confuse the two. Magic comes from the gods. The magician is merely the instrument. Magic passes through him like breath through a reed pipe. Magic can heal. It can satisfy. It is like a candle in the darkness. Sorcery, however, resides in the sorcerer. It is like a blazing sun."

"I don't want to be a sorcerer, Father. Truly. I have . . . other plans."

Now, I think, there was genuine sadness in his voice.

"Beloved Sekenre, my only son, you have looked upon the *evatim* and been marked by them. Throughout your life you will be scarred from their touch. You have conversed with the Sybil and you bear her mark also. You have journeyed among the ghosts, in the company of a corpse, through the realm of *Leshé*, the place of dreams. You have drunk of the waters of vision and have seen all that is in *Tashé*, the land of death. And, at the last, you burned your way into this house with flames summoned from your hands. Now I ask you . . . are these the deeds of a *calligrapher?*"

"No," I said weakly, sobbing. All my resolve drained away. I let the sword drop to the floor and I slid down, my back to the door, and sat there. "No," I whispered. "I just wanted to get Hamakina back."

"Then you are a disappointment to me, son. You are a fool," he said with sudden sharpness. "She does not matter."

"But *she is your child too*. Didn't you love her also? No, you never did. Why? You owe me that much, Father. You have to tell me why . . . about a lot of things."

He stirred within the room. Metal clinked. But he did not come to the door or touch the bolt. There was a long silence. I could see my mother's *hevat*, the golden bird, through the open doorway of my own room, and I stared at it with a kind of distracted intensity, as if I could discern all the answers to all my questions in the intricacies of its design. I felt cold. I clutched my shoulders hard, shivering. The slashes the *evatim* had made in my sides and back pained me again.

After a while, Father resumed speaking.

"Sekenre, how old do you think I was when I married your mother?"

"I – I—"

"I was 349 years old, my son. I had been a sorcerer for a long time by then. I had wandered through many lands, fleeing death, consumed by the contagion of sorcery, slaughtering my enemies, raging in my madness against the gods, whom I considered to be at best my equals. But I had a lucid interval. I remembered what I had been, long before. I had been . . . a man. So I pretended I was one again. I married your mother. I saw in you . . . all my hopes for what I had once been. In you, that ordinary man lived again. If I could cling to that hope, I too, in a small way, would remain human. So *you* were special. I loved *you*."

"But *Hamakina*—"

"– is mere baggage, a receptacle and nothing more. When I felt the weight of my death on me at last, when I could no longer hold off my enemies, I planted the seed of Hamakina in her mother's womb, and I raised her as a prize specimen, for a specific purpose. I brought her here to *contain my death*. The seed of her was something wrought in my laboratory. I placed her inside her mother with a metal tube, while her mother lay in a drugged sleep. So, you see, her life did *not* come from the River, from the dreams of Surat-Kemad, but from *me*. I offered this new life to the Devouring God in exchange for my own. It is a bottle, filled with my own death. So I am still a sorcerer, and a great lord in the land of the dead, because I am neither truly living nor truly dead. I am not the slave of Surat-Kemad, but his ally. And so, my son, your father has outwitted all his enemies, evaded all dangers. He alone is not wholly consumed by sorcery. He *continues*. There is a certain beauty to the scheme, you must admit –"

I rose to my feet, numb beyond all sorrow now. I picked up the sword.

"Sekenre," Father said, "now that I have explained everything – you were right; I did owe you an explanation – you must go away. Save yourself. Be what I wanted to be. You are a good boy. When I was your age, I too was good. I only wanted to do what was right. But I changed. If you go now, you can remain as you are—"

"No, Father. I, too, have changed."

He screamed then, not out of fear, but despair. I stood before the door, sword under one arm while I folded my hands together, then opened them.

Once more, it was as easy as breathing.

The flames leapt from my hands, red and orange this time. They touched the door, spreading over it. I heard the metal bolt on the inside fall to the floor. The door swung open.

At first my eyes could not focus. There was only darkness. Then faint stars appeared, then an endless black plain of swirling sand. I saw hundreds of naked men and women dangling from the sky on metal chains, turning slowly in the wind, mutilated, their faces contorted with the idiocy of hate.

The darkness faded. The stars were gone. Father's room was as it had been before the priests had cleaned it out. All the books were there, the bottles, the shelves of jars, the charts, the strange shapes muttering in jars.

He lay on his couch dressed in his sorcerer's robe, as I had last seen him, his eyes gouged out, sockets covered with golden coins. He sat up. The coins fell into his lap. Fire burned within his eye-sockets, white-hot, like molten iron.

And he said to me, "This is your last warning, Sekenre. Your very last."

"If you are so powerful, Father, where is your power now? You have not resisted me, not really. You only give me . . . warnings."

"What would I have to do then, my son?" he said.

"You would have to kill me. It is too late for anything else."

His voice began to fade, to become garbled, to disintegrate into a series of hisses and grunts. I could barely make out his words.

"Now all my preparations are undone. You disobeyed me to the last. You did not heed my many warnings, sorcerer, son of sorcerer—"

He slid off the couch onto the floor, wriggling toward me on all fours, his whole body swaying from side to side, his terrible eyes blazing.

I almost called on the Sybil then. I wanted to ask simply, *What do I do now? What now?*

But I didn't. In the end, I alone had to decide what was right, the correct action. Anything I did would please the Sybil. She would weave it into the pattern. Surat-Kemad did not care –

"My son . . ." The words seemed to come from deep within him, like a wind from out of a tunnel. "To the very end I have loved you, and it has not been enough."

He opened his huge, hideously elongated mouth. His teeth were like little knives.

At that final moment, I did not fear him, nor hate him, nor did I sorrow. I felt only a hollow, grinding sense of duty.

"No, it was not enough, Father."

I struck him with the sword. His head came off with a single blow. My arm completed the motion almost before I was aware of it.

It was as easy as breathing.

Blood like molten iron spread at my feet. I stepped back. The floorboards burned.

"You are not my father." I said softly. "You cannot *have been* my father."

But I knew that he had been, all the way to the end.

I knelt beside him, then put my arms around his shoulders and lay with my head on his rough, malformed back. I wept long and hard and bitterly.

And as I did, dreams came to me, thoughts, visions, flashes of memories which were not my own, and terrible understanding, the culmination of long study and of longer experience. My mind filled. I knew a thousand deaths and how they had been inflicted, how a single gem of knowledge or power was wrested from each. I knew what every instrument in this room was for, the contents of all the books and charts, and what was in each of those jars and how it could be compelled to speak.

For I had killed a sorcerer, and if you kill a sorcerer you become all that he was.

This was my inheritance from my father.

In the dawn, Hamakina and I buried our father in the sand beneath the house. The black stars were gone. The sky was dark, but it was the familiar sky of *Eshé*, the Earth of the living. Yet the world was still empty, and we dug in the sand with our hands. When we had made a shallow grave, we rolled him into it, placing his head between his feet in the way a sorcerer must be buried. For a time, Mother was with us. She crawled into the grave with him and we covered them both up.

The sky lightened into purple, then azure. Then water flowed beneath the dock and I watched the first birds rise from among the reeds. Hamakina stood among the reeds for a little while, gazing back at me. Then she was gone.

Suddenly I began to shake almost uncontrollably, but merely from cold this time. Though it was early summer, the night's chill lingered, and I was almost naked. I climbed up into the house by means of a rope ladder I'd dropped through the trapdoor and put on trousers, a heavy shirt, and a cloak.

Later, when I came down again with a jug to get water for washing, I saw a man in a white robe and a silver mask walking toward me across the water. I stood up and waited. He stopped a distance off, but I could hear what he said clearly enough.

At first he spoke with my father's voice.

"I wanted to tell you the rest of the story of the Heron Boy. There is no ending to it, I fear. It just . . . continues. He was not a heron and he was not a boy either, but he looked like a boy. So he dwelt among men pretending to be one of them, yet confiding his secret to those who loved him. Still, he did not belong. He never could. He lived out his days as an impostor. But he had help, because those he confided in did love him. Let me confide in you, then. Sekenre, when a boy becomes a man his father gives him a new name which is known only between the two of them, until the son gives it to his own son in turn. Therefore take the name your father had, which is *Heron*."

And he spoke with the voice of the Sybil.

"Sekenre, you are marked with my mark because you are my instrument. All men know that out of the tangle of the world I divine the secrets of their lives. But do they also know that out of the tangle of their lives I divine the secrets of the world? That I cast them about like bones, like marbles, and read the patterns as they fall? I think not."

And, finally, he spoke with the voice of Surat-Kemad, god of death and of the river, and the thunder was his voice; and he took off the mask and revealed his terrible face, and his jaws gaped wide; and the numberless, fading stars were his teeth; and the sky and the earth were his mouth; and the river disgorged itself from his belly; and his great ribs were the pillars of the world.

He spoke to me in the language of the gods, of *Akimshé*, the burning holiness at the heart of the universe, and he named the gods yet unborn, and he spoke of kings and of nations and of worlds, of things past and things which are to come.

Then he was gone. The city spread before me now. I saw the foreign ships at anchor in the river, and the bright banners waving in the morning breeze.

I took off the robe and sat on the dock, washing. A boatman drifted by and waved, but then he realized who I was, made a sign against evil, and paddled away frantically.

His fear was so trivial it was somehow incredibly funny.

I fell back on the deck, hysterical with laughter, then lay there. Sunlight slanted under the house. The air was warm and felt good.

And I heard my father whisper from his grave, gently, "My son, if you can become *more* than a sorcerer, I will not fear for you."

"Yes, Father. I shall."

Then I folded my hands, and slowly opened them, and the fire that I held cupped there was perfect and pale and still, like a candle's flame on a breezeless summer night.

NO. 252 RUE M. LE PRINCE

Ralph Adams Cram

Ralph Adams Cram (1863–1942) was an architect, but an architect with style. He was a champion of the Gothic revival and from 1890 onwards, when he opened his first office in Boston, he helped design and oversee the construction of churches, cathedrals, and academic institutions and some of his greatest legacies are at West Point Military Academy and Princeton University. So what's an architect doing in a book of sorcerers' tales? Ah, that's because Cram was an architect with imagination. In his early days he somehow found the time, when he wasn't designing churches, to write stories. He only wrote a handful and these are collected in Black Spirits and White *(1895), one of the undeniable classics of weird fiction. Every story – and there were only five – is a miniature gem. Take the following about a house in Paris once occupied by an ancient sorcerer.*

W hen in May, 1886, I found myself at last in Paris, I naturally determined to throw myself on the charity of an old chum of mine, Eugene Marie d'Ardeche, who had forsaken Boston a year or more ago on receiving word of the death of an aunt who had left him such property as she possessed. I fancy this windfall surprised him not a little, for the relations between the aunt and nephew had never been cordial, judging from Eugene's remarks touching the lady, who was, it seems, a more or less wicked and witchlike old person, with a penchant for black magic, at least such was the common report.

Why she should leave all her property to d'Ardeche, no one could tell, unless it was that she felt his rather hobbledehoy tendencies towards Buddhism and occultism might some day lead him to her own unhallowed height of questionable illumination. To be sure d'Ardeche reviled her as a bad old woman, being himself in that state of enthusiastic exaltation which sometimes accompanies a boyish fancy for occultism; but in spite of his distant and repellent attitude, Mlle. Blaye de Tartas made him her sole heir, to the violent wrath of a questionable old party known to infamy as the Sar Torrevieja, the "King of the Sorcerers." This malevolent old portent, whose gray and crafty face was often seen in the Rue M. le Prince during the life of Mlle. de Tartas had, it seems, fully expected to enjoy her small wealth after her death; and when it appeared that she had left him only the contents of the gloomy old house in the Quartier Latin, giving the house itself and all else of which she died possessed to her nephew in America, the Sar proceeded to remove everything from the place, and then to curse it elaborately and comprehensively, together with all those who should ever dwell therein.

Whereupon he disappeared.

This final episode was the last word I received from Eugene, but I knew the number of the house, 252 Rue M. le Prince. So, after a day or two given to a first cursory survey of Paris, I started across the Seine to find Eugene and compel him to do the honors of the city.

Every one who knows the Latin Quarter knows the Rue M. le Prince, running up the hill towards the Garden of the Luxembourg. It is full of queer houses and odd corners – or was in '86 – and certainly No. 252 was, when I found it, quite as queer as any. It was nothing but a doorway, a black arch of old stone between and under two new houses painted yellow. The effect of this bit of seventeenth century masonry, with its dirty old doors, and rusty broken lantern sticking gaunt and grim out over the narrow sidewalk, was, in its frame of fresh plaster, sinister in the extreme.

I wondered if I had made a mistake in the number; it was quite evident that no one lived behind those cobwebs. I went into the doorway of one of the new hotels and interviewed the concierge.

No, M. d'Ardeche did not live there, though to be sure he owned the mansion; he himself resided in Meudon, in the country house of the late Mlle. de Tartas. Would Monsieur like the number and the street?

Monsieur would like them extremely, so I took the card that the concierge wrote for me, and forthwith started for the river, in order that I might take a steamboat for Meudon. By one of those coincidences which happen so often, being quite inexplicable, I had not gone twenty paces down the street before I ran directly into the arms of Eugene d'Ardeche. In three minutes we were sitting in the queer little garden of the Chien Bleu, drinking vermouth and absinthe, and talking it all over.

"You do not live in your aunt's house?" I said at last, interrogatively.

"No, but if this sort of thing keeps on I shall have to. I like Meudon much better, and the house is perfect, all furnished, and nothing in it newer than the last century. You must come out with me tonight and see it. I have got a jolly room fixed up for my Buddha. But there is something wrong with this house opposite. I can't keep a tenant in it – not four days. I have had three, all within six months, but the stories have gone around and a man would as soon think of hiring the Cour des Comptes to live in as No. 252. It is notorious. The fact is, it is haunted the worst way."

I laughed and ordered more vermouth.

"That is all right. It is haunted all the same, or enough to keep it empty, and the funny part is that no one knows *how* it is haunted. Nothing is ever seen, nothing heard. As far as I can find out, people just have the horrors there, and have them so bad they have to go to the hospital afterwards. I have one ex-tenant in the Bicêtre now. So the house stands empty, and as it covers considerable ground and is taxed for a lot, I don't know what to do about it. I think I'll either give it to that child of sin, Torrevieja, or else go and live in it myself. I shouldn't mind the ghosts, I am sure."

"Did you ever stay there?"

"No, but I have always intended to, and in fact I came up here today to see a couple of rake-hell fellows I know, Fargeau and Duchesne, doctors in the Clinical Hospital beyond here, up by the Parc Mont Souris. They promised that they would spend the night with me sometime in my aunt's house – which is called around here, you must know, 'la Bouche d'Enfer' – and I thought perhaps they would make it this week, if they can get off duty. Come up with me while I see them, and then we can go across the river to Véfour's and have some luncheon, you can get your things at the Chatham, and we will go out to Meudon, where of course you will spend the night with me."

The plan suited me perfectly, so we went up to the hospital, found Fargeau, who declared that he and Duchesne were ready for anything, the nearer the real "bouche d' enfer" the better; that the following Thursday they would both be off duty for the night, and that on that day they would join in an attempt to outwit the devil and clear up the mystery of No. 252.

"Does M. l'Américain go with us?" asked Fargeau.

"Why of course," I replied, "I intend to go, and you must not refuse me, d'Ardeche; I decline to be put off. Here is a chance for you to do the honors of your city in a manner which is faultless. Show me a real live ghost, and I will forgive Paris for having lost the Jardin Mabille."

So it was settled.

Later we went down to Meudon and ate dinner in the terrace room of the villa, which was all that d'Ardeche had said, and more, so utterly was its atmosphere that of the seventeenth century. At dinner Eugene told me more about his late aunt, and the queer goings on in the old house.

Mlle. Blaye lived, it seems, all alone, except for one female servant of her own age; a severe, taciturn creature, with massive Breton features and a Breton tongue, whenever she vouchsafed to use it. No one ever was seen to enter the door of No. 252 except Jeanne the servant and the Sar Torrevieja, the latter coming constantly from none knew whither, and always entering, *never leaving*. Indeed, the neighbors, who for eleven years had watched the old sorcerer sidle crabwise up to the bell almost every day, declared vociferously that *never* had he been seen to leave the house. Once, when they decided to keep absolute guard, the watcher, none other than Maître Garceau of the Chien Bleu, after keeping his eyes fixed on the door from ten o'clock one morning when the Sar arrived until four in the afternoon, during which time the door was unopened (he knew this, for had he not gummed a ten-centime stamp over the joint and was not the stamp unbroken?) nearly fell down when the sinister figure of Torrevieja slid wickedly by him with a dry "Pardon, Monsieur!" and disappeared again through the black doorway.

This was curious, for No. 252 was entirely surrounded by houses, its only windows opening on a courtyard into which no eye could look from the hôtels of the Rue M. le Prince and the Rue de l'Ecole, and the mystery was one of the choice possessions of the Latin Quarter.

Once a year the austerity of the place was broken, and the denizens of the whole quarter stood openmouthed watching many carriages drive up to No. 252, many of them private, not a few with crests on the door panels, from all of them descending veiled female figures and men with coat collars turned up. Then followed curious sounds of music from within, and those whose houses joined the blank walls of No. 252 became for the moment popular, for by placing the ear against the wall strange music could distinctly be heard, and the sound of monotonous chanting voices now and then. By dawn the last guest would have departed, and for another year the hôtel of Mlle. de Tartas was ominously silent.

Eugene declared that he believed it was a celebration of "Walpurgisnacht," and certainly appearances favored such a fancy.

"A queer thing about the whole affair is," he said, "the fact that everyone in the street swears that about a month ago, while I was out in Concarneau for a visit, the music and voices were heard again, just as when my revered aunt was in the flesh. The house was perfectly empty, as I tell you, so it is quite possible that the good people were enjoying an hallucination."

I must acknowledge that these stories did not reassure me; in fact, as Thursday came near, I began to regret a little my determination to spend the night in the house. I was too vain to back down, however, and the perfect coolness of the two doctors, who ran down Tuesday to Meudon to make a few arrangements, caused me to swear that I would die of fright before I would flinch. I suppose I believed more or less in ghosts, I am sure now that I am older I believe in them, there are in fact few things I can *not* believe. Two or three inexplicable things had happened to me, and I had a strong predisposition to believe some things that I could not explain, wherein I was out of sympathy with the age.

Well, to come to the memorable night of the twelfth of June, we had made our preparations, and after depositing a big bag inside the doors of No. 252, went across to the Chien Bleu, where Fargeau and Duchesne turned up promptly, and we sat down to the best dinner Père Garceau could create.

I remember I hardly felt that the conversation was in good taste. It began with various stories of Indian fakirs and Oriental jugglery, matters in which Eugene was curiously well read, swerved to the horrors of the great Sepoy mutiny, and thus to reminiscences of the dissecting room. By this time we had drunk more or less, and Duchesne launched into a photographic and Zolaesque account of the only time (as he said) when he was possessed of the panic of fear; namely, one night many years ago, when he was locked by accident into the dissecting room of the Loucine, together with several cadavers of a rather unpleasant nature. I ventured to protest mildly against the choice of subjects, the result being a perfect carnival of horrors, so that when we finally drank our last *crème de cacao* and started for "la Bouche d'Enfer," my nerves were in a somewhat rocky condition.

It was just ten o'clock when we came into the street. A hot dead wind drifted in great puffs through the city, and ragged masses of vapor swept the purple sky; an unsavory night altogether, one of those nights of hopeless lassitude when one feels, if one is at home, like doing nothing but drink mint juleps and smoke cigarettes.

Eugene opened the creaking door, and tried to light one of the lanterns; but the gusty wind blew out every match, and we finally had to close the outer doors before we could get a light. At last we had all the lanterns going, and I began to look around curiously. We were in a long, vaulted passage, partly carriageway, partly footpath, perfectly bare but for the street refuse which had drifted in with eddying winds. Beyond lay the courtyard, a curious place rendered more curious still by the fitful moonlight and the flashing of four dark lanterns. The place had evidently been once a most noble palace. Opposite rose the oldest portion, a three-story wall of the time of Francis I, with a great wisteria vine covering half. The wings on either side were more modern, seventeenth century, and ugly, while towards the street was nothing but a flat unbroken wall.

The great bare court, littered with bits of paper blown in by the wind, fragments of packing cases, and straw, mysterious with flashing lights and flaunting shadows, while low masses of torn vapor drifted overhead, hiding, then revealing the stars, and all in absolute silence, not even the sounds of the streets entering this prisonlike place, was weird and uncanny in the extreme. I must confess that already I began to feel a slight disposition towards the horrors, but with that curious inconsequence which so often happens in the case of those who are deliberately growing scared, I could think of nothing more reassuring than those delicious verses of Lewis Carroll's:

> Just the place for a Snark! I have said it twice,
> That alone should encourage the crew.
> Just the place for a Snark! I have said it thrice,
> What I tell you three times is true.

which kept repeating themselves over and over in my brain with feverish insistence.

Even the medical students had stopped their chaffing, and were studying the surroundings gravely.

"There is one thing certain," said Fargeau, "*anything* might have happened here without the slightest chance of discovery. Did ever you see such a perfect place for lawlessness?"

"And *anything* might happen here now, with the same certainty of impunity," continued Duchesne, lighting his pipe, the snap of the match making us all start. "D'Ardeche, your lamented relative was certainly well fixed; she had full scope here for her traditional experiments in demonology."

"Curse me if I don't believe that those same traditions were more or less founded on fact," said Eugene. "I never saw this court under these conditions before, but I could believe anything now. What's that!"

"Nothing but a door slamming," said Duchesne, loudly.

"Well, I wish doors wouldn't slam in houses that have been empty eleven months."

"It is irritating," and Duchesne slipped his arm through mine;

"but we must take things as they come. Remember we have to deal not only with the spectral lumber left here by your scarlet aunt, but as well with the supererogatory curse of that hellcat Torrevieja. Come on! let's get inside before the hour arrives for the sheeted dead to squeak and gibber in these lonely halls. Light your pipes, your tobacco is a sure protection against 'your whoreson dead bodies'; light up and move on."

We opened the hall door and entered a vaulted stone vestibule, full of dust, and cobwebby.

"There is nothing on this floor," said Eugene, "except servants' rooms and offices, and I don't believe there is anything wrong with them. I never heard that there was, anyway. Let's go upstairs."

So far as we could see, the house was apparently perfectly uninteresting inside, all eighteenth century work, the façade of the main building being, with the vestibule, the only portion of the Francis I work.

"The place was burned during the Terror," said Eugene, "for my great-uncle, from whom Mlle. de Tartas inherited it, was a good and true Royalist; he went to Spain after the Revolution, and did not come back until the accession of Charles X, when he restored the house, and then died, enormously old. This explains why it is all so new."

The old Spanish sorcerer to whom Mlle. de Tartas had left her personal property had done his work thoroughly. The house was absolutely empty, even the wardrobes and bookcases built in had been carried away; we went through room after room, finding all absolutely dismantled, only the windows and doors with their casings, the parquet floors, and the florid Renaissance mantels remaining.

"I feel better," remarked Fargeau. "The house may be haunted, but it don't look it, certainly; it is the most respectable place imaginable."

"Just you wait," replied Eugene. "These are only the state apartments, which my aunt seldom used, except, perhaps, on her annual 'Walpurgisnacht.' Come up stairs and I will show you a better *mise en scène*."

On this floor, the rooms fronting the court, the sleeping rooms, were quite small – ("They are the bad rooms all the same," said

Eugene) – four of them, all just as ordinary in appearance as those below. A corridor ran behind them connecting with the wing corridor, and from this opened a door, unlike any of the other doors in that it was covered with green baize, somewhat moth-eaten. Eugene selected a key from the bunch he carried, unlocked the door, and with some difficulty forced it to swing inward; it was as heavy as the door of a safe.

"We are now," he said, "on the very threshold of hell itself; these rooms in here were my scarlet aunt's unholy of unholies. I never let them with the rest of the house, but keep them as a curiosity. I only wish Torrevieja had kept out; as it was, he looted them, as he did the rest of the house, and nothing is left but the walls and ceiling and floor. They are something, however, and may suggest what the former condition must have been. Tremble and enter."

The first apartment was a kind of anteroom, a cube of perhaps twenty feet each way, without windows, and with no doors except that by which we entered and another to the right. Walls, floor, and ceiling were covered with a black lacquer, brilliantly polished, that flashed the light of our lanterns in a thousand intricate reflections. It was like the inside of an enormous Japanese box, and about as empty. From this we passed to another room, and here we nearly dropped our lanterns. The room was circular, thirty feet or so in diameter, covered by a hemispherical dome; walls and ceiling were dark blue, spotted with gold stars; and reaching from floor to floor across the dome stretched a colossal figure in red lacquer of a nude woman kneeling, her legs reaching out along the floor on either side, her head touching the lintel of the door through which we had entered, her arms forming its sides, with the forearms extended and stretching along the walls until they met the long feet. The most astounding, misshapen, absolutely terrifying thing, I think, I ever saw. From the navel hung a great white object, like the traditional roe's egg of the Arabian Nights. The floor was of red lacquer, and in it was inlaid a pentagram the size of the room, made of wide strips of brass. In the center of this pentagram was a circular disk of black stone, slightly saucer-shaped, with a small outlet in the middle.

The effect of the room was simply crushing, with this gigantic red figure crouched over it all, the staring eyes fixed on one, no matter what his position. None of us spoke, so oppressive was the whole thing.

The third room was like the first in dimensions, but instead of being black it was entirely sheathed with plates of brass, walls, ceiling, and floor – tarnished now, and turning green, but still brilliant under the lantern light. In the middle stood an oblong altar of porphyry, its longer dimensions on the axis of the suite of rooms, and at one end, opposite the range of doors, a pedestal of black basalt.

This was all. Three rooms, stranger than these, even in their emptiness, it would be hard to imagine. In Egypt, in India, they would not be entirely out of place, but here in Paris, in a commonplace hôtel, in the Rue M. le Prince, they were incredible.

We retraced our steps, Eugene closed the iron door with its baize covering, and we went into one of the front chambers and sat down, looking at each other.

"Nice party, your aunt," said Fargeau. "Nice old party, with amiable tastes; I am glad we are not to spend the night in *those* rooms."

"What do you suppose she did there?" inquired Duchesne. "I know more or less about black art, but that series of rooms is too much for me."

"My impression is," said d'Ardeche, "that the brazen room was a kind of sanctuary containing some image or other on the basalt base, while the stone in front was really an altar – what the nature of the sacrifice might be I don't even guess. The round room may have been used for invocations and incantations. The pentagram looks like it. Any way it is all just about as queer and *fin de siècle* as I can well imagine. Look here, it is nearly twelve, let's dispose of ourselves, if we are going to hunt this thing down."

The four chambers on this floor of the old house were those said to be haunted, the wings being quite innocent, and, so far as we knew, the floors below. It was arranged that we should each occupy a room, leaving the doors open with the lights burning, and at the slightest cry or knock we were all to rush at once to the room from which the warning sound might come. There was no communication between the rooms to be sure, but, as the doors all opened into the corridor, every sound was plainly audible.

The last room fell to me, and I looked it over carefully.

It seemed innocent enough, a commonplace, square, rather lofty Parisian sleeping room, finished in wood painted white, with a small marble mantel, a dusty floor of inlaid maple and cherry, walls hung with an ordinary French paper, apparently quite new, and two deeply embrasured windows looking out on the court.

I opened the swinging sash with some trouble, and sat down in the window seat with my lantern beside me trained on the only door, which gave on the corridor.

The wind had gone down, and it was very still without – still and hot. The masses of luminous vapor were gathering quickly overhead, no longer urged by the gusty wind. The great masses of rank wisteria leaves, with here and there a second blossoming of purple flowers, hung dead over the window in the sluggish air. Across the roofs I could hear the sound of a belated *fiacre* in the streets below. I filled my pipe again and waited.

For a time the voices of the men in the other rooms were a companionship, and at first I shouted to them now and then, but my voice echoed rather unpleasantly through the long corridors, and had a suggestive way of reverberating around the left wing beside me, and coming out at a broken window at its extremity like the voice of another man. I soon gave up my attempts at conversation, and devoted myself to the task of keeping awake.

It was not easy; why did I eat that lettuce salad at Père Garceau's? I should have known better. It was making me irresistibly sleepy, and wakefulness was absolutely necessary. It was certainly gratifying to know that I could sleep, that my courage was by me to that extent, but in the interests of science I must keep awake. But almost never, it seemed, had sleep looked so desirable. Half a hundred times, nearly, I would doze for an instant, only to awake with a start, and find my pipe gone out. Nor did the exertion of relighting it pull me together. I struck my match mechanically, and with the first puff dropped off again. It was most vexing. I got up and walked around the room. It was most annoying. My cramped position had almost put both my legs to sleep. I could hardly stand. I felt numb, as though with cold. There was no longer any sound from the other rooms, nor from without. I sank down in my window seat. How dark it was growing! I turned up the lantern. That pipe again, how obstinately it kept going out! and my last match was gone. The lantern, too, was *that* going out? I lifted my hand to turn it up again. It felt like lead, and fell beside me.

Then I awoke – absolutely. I remembered the story of "The Haunters and the Haunted." *This* was the Horror. I tried to rise, to cry out. My body was like lead, my tongue was paralyzed. I could hardly move my eyes. And the light was going out. There was no question about that. Darker and darker yet; little by little the pattern of the paper was swallowed up in the advancing night. A pricking numbness gathered in every nerve, my right arm slipped without feeling from my lap to my side, and I could not raise it – it swung helpless. A thin, keen humming began in my head, like the cicadas on a hillside in September. The darkness was coming fast.

Yes, this was it. Something was subjecting me, body and mind, to slow paralysis. Physically I was already dead. If I could only hold my mind, my consciousness, I might still be safe, but could I? Could I resist the mad horror of this silence, the deepening dark, the creeping numbness? I knew that, like the man in the ghost story, my only safety lay here.

It had come at last. My body was dead, I could no longer move my eyes. They were fixed in that last look on the place where the door had been, now only a deepening of the dark.

Utter night: the last flicker of the lantern was gone. I sat and waited; my mind was still keen, but how long would it last? There was a limit even to the endurance of the utter panic of fear.

Then the end began. In the velvet blackness came two white eyes, milky, opalescent, small, far away – awful eyes, like a dead dream. More beautiful than I can describe, the flakes of white flame moving from the perimeter inward, disappearing in the center, like a never ending flow of opal water into a circular tunnel. I could not have moved my eyes had I possessed the power: they devoured the fearful beautiful things that grew slowly, slowly larger, fixed on me, advancing, growing more beautiful, the white flakes of light sweeping more swiftly into the blazing vortices, the awful fascination deepening in its insane intensity as the white, vibrating eyes grew nearer, larger.

Like a hideous and implacable engine of death the eyes of the unknown Horror swelled and expanded until they were close before me, enormous, terrible, and I felt a slow, cold, wet breath propelled with mechanical regularity against my face, enveloping me in its fetid mist, in its charnelhouse deadliness.

With ordinary fear goes always a physical terror, but with me in the presence of this unspeakable Thing was only the utter and awful terror of the mind, the mad fear of a prolonged and ghostly nightmare. Again and again I tried to shriek, to make some noise, but physically I was utterly dead. I could only feel myself go mad with the terror of hideous death. The eyes were close on me – their movement so swift that they seemed to be but palpitating flames, the dead breath was around me like the depths of the deepest sea.

Suddenly a wet, icy mouth, like that of a dead cuttlefish, shapeless, jellylike, fell over mine. The horror began slowly to draw my life from me, but, as enormous and shuddering folds of palpitating jelly swept sinuously around me, my will came back, my body awoke with the reaction of final fear, and I closed with the nameless death that enfolded me.

What was it that I was fighting? My arms sunk through the unresisting mass that was turning me to ice. Moment by moment new folds of cold jelly swept round me, crushing me with the force of Titans. I fought to wrest my mouth from this awful Thing that sealed it, but, if ever I succeeded and caught a single breath, the wet, sucking mass closed over my face again before I could cry out. I think I fought for hours, desperately, insanely, in a silence that was more hideous than any sound – fought until I felt final death at hand, until the memory of all my life rushed over me like a flood, until I no longer had strength to wrench my face from that hellish succubus, until with a last mechanical struggle I fell and yielded to death.

Then I heard a voice say, "If he is dead, I can never forgive myself; I was to blame."

Another replied, "He is not dead, I know we can save him if only we reach the hospital in time. Drive like hell, *cocher!* twenty francs for you, if you get there in three minutes."

Then there was night again, and nothingness, until I suddenly awoke and stared around. I lay in a hospital ward, very white and sunny, some yellow *fleurs-de-lis* stood beside the head of the pallet, and a tall Sister of Mercy sat by my side.

To tell the story in a few words, I was in the Hôtel Dieu, where the men had taken me that fearful night of the twelfth of June. I asked for Fargeau or Duchesne, and by and by the latter came, and sitting beside the bed told me all that I did not know.

It seems that they had sat, each in his room, hour after hour, hearing nothing, very much bored, and disappointed. Soon after two o'clock Fargeau, who was in the next room, called to me to ask if I was awake. I gave no reply, and, after shouting once or twice, he took his lantern and came to investigate. The door was locked on the inside! He instantly called d'Ardeche and Duchesne, and together they hurled themselves against the door. It resisted. Within they could hear irregular footsteps dashing here and there, with heavy breathing. Although frozen with terror, they fought to destroy the door and finally succeeded by using a great slab of marble that formed the shelf of the mantel in Fargeau's room. As the door crashed in, they were suddenly hurled back against the walls of the corridor, as though by an explosion, the lanterns were extinguished, and they found themselves in utter silence and darkness.

As soon as they recovered from the shock, they leaped into the room and fell over my body in the middle of the floor. They lighted one of the lanterns, and saw the strangest sight that can be imagined. The floor and walls to the height of about six feet were running with something that seemed like stagnant water, thick, glutinous, sickening. As for me, I was drenched with the same cursed liquid. The odor of musk was nauseating. They dragged me away, stripped off my clothing, wrapped me in their coats, and hurried to the hospital, thinking me perhaps dead. Soon after sunrise d'Ardeche left the hospital, being assured that I was in a fair way to recovery, with time, and with Fargeau went up to examine by daylight the traces of the adventure that was so nearly fatal. They were too late. Fire engines were coming down the street as they passed the Académie. A neighbor rushed up to d'Ardeche: "O Monsieur! what misfortune, yet what fortune! It is true *la Bouche d'Enfer* – I beg pardon, the residence of the lamented Mlle. de Tartas – was burned, but not wholly, only the ancient building. The wings were saved, and for that great credit is due the brave firemen. Monsieur will remember them, no doubt."

It was quite true. Whether a forgotten lantern, overturned in the excitement, had done the work, or whether the origin of the fire was more supernatural, it was certain that "the Mouth of Hell" was no more. A last engine was pumping slowly as d'Ardeche came up; half a dozen limp, and one distended, hose stretched through the *porte cochère*, and within only the façade of Francis I remained, draped still with the black stems of the wisteria. Beyond lay a great vacancy, where thin smoke was rising slowly. Every floor was gone, and the strange halls of Mlle. Blaye de Tartas were only a memory.

With d'Ardeche I visited the place last year, but in the stead of the ancient walls was then only a new and ordinary building, fresh and respectable; yet the wonderful stories of the old *Bouche d'Enfer* still lingered in the quarter, and will hold there, I do not doubt, until the Day of Judgment.

THE BONES OF THE EARTH

Ursula K. Le Guin

Ursula Le Guin (b. 1929) is one of the world's foremost fantasists. She's been writing science fiction and fantasy for over forty years for both adults and children. Her best known work is almost certainly The Wizard of Earthsea *(1968), which won her the first of nearly twenty awards. The world of Earthsea intrigued her enough so that even though she completed the original trilogy with* The Tombs of Atuan *(1970) and* The Farthest Shore *(1972) she returned to it twenty years later with* Tehanu *(1990) and* The Other Wind *(2001) plus a collection of stories,* Tales from Earthsea *(2001).*

If you have read The Wizard of Earthsea, *you may recall that at the start, when news spread of how young Ged had saved Armouth from the Kargish warriors, he is visited by a wizard, Ogion the Silent, whom the townsfolk remember as "the one who tamed the earthquake". We had to wait over thirty years for the story of Ogion, but here it is.*

I T WAS RAINING AGAIN, and the wizard of Re Albi was sorely tempted to make a weather spell, just a little, small spell, to send the rain on round the mountain. His bones ached. They ached for the sun to come out and shine through his flesh and dry them out. Of course he could say a pain spell, but all that would do was hide the ache for a while. There was no cure for what ailed him. Old bones need the sun. The wizard stood still in the doorway of his house, between the dark room and the rain-streaked open air, preventing himself from making a spell, and angry at himself for preventing himself and for having to be prevented.

He never swore – men of power do not swear, it is not safe – but he cleared his throat with a coughing growl, like a bear. A moment later a thunderclap rolled off the hidden upper slopes of Gont Mountain, echoing round from north to south, dying away in the cloud-filled forests.

A good sign, thunder, Dulse thought. It would stop raining soon. He pulled up his hood and went out into the rain to feed the chickens.

He checked the henhouse, finding three eggs. Red Bucca was sitting. Her eggs were about due to hatch. The mites were bothering her, and she looked scruffy and jaded. He said a few words against mites, told himself to remember to clean out the nest box as soon as the chicks hatched, and went on to the poultry yard, where Brown Bucca and Grey and Leggings and Candor and the King huddled under the eaves making soft, shrewish remarks about rain.

"It'll stop by midday," the wizard told the chickens. He fed them and squelched back to the house with three warm eggs. When he was a child he had liked to walk in mud. He remembered enjoying the cool of it rising between his toes. He still liked to go barefoot, but no longer enjoyed mud; it was sticky stuff, and he disliked stooping to clean his feet before going into the house. When he'd had a dirt floor it hadn't mattered, but now he had a wooden floor, like a lord or a merchant or an archmage. To keep the cold and damp out of his bones. Not his own notion. Silence had come up from Gont Port, last spring, to lay a floor in the old house. They had had one of their arguments about it. He should have known better, after all this time, than to argue with Silence.

"I've walked on dirt for 75 years," Dulse had said. "A few more won't kill me!"

To which Silence of course made no reply, letting him hear what he had said and feel its foolishness thoroughly.

"Dirt's easier to keep clean," he said, knowing the struggle already lost. It was true that all you had to do with a good hardpacked clay floor was sweep it and now and then sprinkle it to keep the dust down. But it sounded silly all the same.

"Who's to lay this floor?" he said, now merely querulous.

Silence nodded, meaning himself.

The boy was in fact a workman of the first order, carpenter, cabinetmaker, stonelayer, roofer; he had proved that when he lived up here as Dulse's student, and his life with the rich folk of Gont Port had not softened his hands. He brought the boards from Sixth's mill in Re Albi, driving Gammer's ox team; he laid the floor and polished it the next day, while the old wizard was up at Bog Lake gathering simples. When Dulse came home there it was, shining like a dark lake itself. "Have to wash my feet every time I come in," he grumbled. He walked in gingerly. The wood was so smooth it seemed soft to the bare sole. "Satin," he said. "You didn't do all that in one day without a spell or two. A village hut with a palace floor. Well, it'll be a sight, come winter, to see the fire shine in that! Or do I have to get me a carpet now? A fleecefell, on a golden warp?"

Silence smiled. He was pleased with himself.

He had turned up on Dulse's doorstep a few years ago. Well, no, twenty years ago it must be, or twenty-five. A while ago now. He had been truly a boy then, long-legged, rough-haired, soft-faced. A set mouth, clear eyes. "What do you want?" the wizard had asked, knowing what he wanted, what they all wanted, and keeping his eyes from those clear eyes. He was a good teacher, the best on Gont, he knew that. But he was tired of teaching, didn't want another prentice underfoot. And he sensed danger.

"To learn," the boy whispered.

"Go to Roke," the wizard said. The boy wore shoes and a good leather vest. He could afford or earn ship's passage to the school.

"I've been there."

At that Dulse looked him over again. No cloak, no staff.

"Failed? Sent away? Ran away?"

The boy shook his head at each question. He shut his eyes; his mouth was already shut. He stood there, intensely gathered, suffering: drew breath: looked straight into the wizard's eyes.

"My mastery is here, on Gont," he said, still speaking hardly above a whisper. "My master is Heleth."

At that the wizard whose true name was Heleth stood as still as he did, looking back at him, till the boy's gaze dropped.

In silence Dulse sought the boy's name, and saw two things: a fir cone, and the rune of the Closed Mouth. Then seeking further he heard in his mind a name spoken; but he did not speak it.

"I'm tired of teaching and talking," he said. "I need silence. Is that enough for you?"

The boy nodded once.

"Then to me you are Silence," the wizard said. "You can sleep in the nook under the west window. There's an old pallet in the woodhouse. Air it. Don't bring mice in with it." And he stalked off towards the Overfell, angry with the boy for coming and with himself for giving in; but it was not anger that made his heart pound. Striding along – he could stride, then – with the sea wind pushing at him always from the left and the early sunlight on the sea out past the vast shadow of the mountain, he thought of the Mages of Roke, the masters of the art magic, the professors of mystery and power. "He was too much for 'em, was he? And he'll be too much for me," he thought, and smiled. He was a peaceful man, but he did not mind a bit of danger.

He stopped then and felt the dirt under his feet. He was barefoot, as usual. When he was a student on Roke, he had worn shoes. But he had come back home to Gont, to Re Albi, with his wizard's staff, and kicked his shoes off. He stood still and felt the dust and rock of the cliff-top path under his feet, and the cliffs under that, and the roots of the island in the dark under that. In the dark under the waters all islands touched and were one. So his teacher Ard had said, and so his teachers on Roke had said. But this was his island, his rock, his dirt. His wizardry grew out of it. "My mastery is here," the boy had said, but it went deeper than mastery. That, perhaps, was something Dulse could teach him: what went deeper than mastery. What he had learned here, on Gont, before he ever went to Roke.

And the boy must have a staff. Why had Nemmerle let him leave Roke without one, empty-handed as a prentice or a witch? Power like that shouldn't go wandering about unchanneled and unsignaled.

My teacher had no staff, Dulse thought, and at the same moment thought, the boy wants his staff from me. Gontish oak, from the hands of a Gontish wizard. Well, if he earns it I'll make him one. If he can keep his mouth closed. And I'll leave him my lore-books. If he can clean out a henhouse, and understand the Glosses of Danemer, and keep his mouth closed.

The new student cleaned out the henhouse and hoed the bean patch, learned the meaning of the Glosses of Danemer and the Arcana of the Enlades, and kept his mouth closed. He listened. He heard what Dulse said; sometimes he heard what Dulse thought. He did what Dulse wanted and what Dulse did not know he wanted. His gift was far beyond Dulse's guidance, yet he had been right to come to Re Albi, and they both knew it.

Dulse thought sometimes in those years about sons and fathers. He had quarreled with his own father, a sorcerer-prospector, over his choice of Ard as his teacher. His father had shouted that a student of Ard's was no son of his, had nursed his rage, died unforgiving.

Dulse had seen young men weep for joy at the birth of a first son. He had seen poor men pay witches a year's earnings for the promise of a healthy boy, and a rich man touch his gold-bedizened baby's face and whisper, adoring, "My immortality!" He had seen men beat their sons, bully and humiliate them, spite and thwart them, hating the death they saw in them. He had seen the answering hatred in the sons' eyes, the threat, the pitiless contempt. And seeing it, Dulse knew why he had never sought reconciliation with his father.

He had seen a father and son work together from daybreak to sundown, the old man guiding a blind ox, the middle-aged man driving the iron-bladed plough, never a word spoken. As they started home the old man laid his hand a moment on the son's shoulder.

He had always remembered that. He remembered it now, when he looked across the hearth, winter evenings, at the dark face bent above a lore-book or a shirt that needed mending. The eyes cast down, the mouth closed, the spirit listening.

"Once in his lifetime, if he's lucky, a wizard finds somebody he can talk to." Nemmerle had said that to Dulse a night or two before Dulse left Roke, a year or two before Nemmerle was chosen Archmage. He had been the Master Patterner and the kindest of all Dulse's teachers at the school. "I think, if you stayed, Heleth, we could talk."

Dulse had been unable to answer at all for a while. Then, stammering, guilty at his ingratitude and incredulous at his obstinacy – "Master, I would stay, but my work is on Gont. I wish it was here, with you –"

"It's a rare gift, to know where you need to be, before you've been to all the places you don't need to be. Well, send me a student now and then. Roke needs Gontish wizardry. I think we're leaving things out, here, things worth knowing . . ."

Dulse had sent students on to the school, three or four of them, nice lads with a gift for this or that; but the one Nemmerle waited for had come and gone of his own will, and what they had thought of him on Roke Dulse did not know. And Silence, of course, did not say. It was evident that he had learned there in two or three years what some boys learned in six or seven and many never learned at all. To him it had been mere groundwork.

"Why didn't you come to me first?" Dulse had demanded. "And then go to Roke, to put a polish on it?"

"I didn't want to waste your time."

"Did Nemmerle know you were coming to work with me?"

Silence shook his head.

"If you'd deigned to tell him your intentions, he might have sent a message to me."

Silence looked stricken. "Was he your friend?"

Dulse paused. "He was my master. Would have been my friend, perhaps, if I'd stayed on Roke. Have wizards friends? No more than they have wives, or sons, I suppose . . . Once he said to me that in our trade it's a lucky man who finds someone to talk to . . . Keep that in mind. If you're lucky, one day you'll have to open your mouth."

Silence bowed his rough, thoughtful head.

"If it hasn't rusted shut," Dulse added.

"If you ask me to, I'll talk," the young man said, so earnest, so willing to deny his whole nature at Dulse's request that the wizard had to laugh.

"I asked you not to," he said. "And it's not my need I spoke of. I talk enough for two. Never mind. You'll know what to say when the time comes. That's the art, eh? What to say, and when to say it. And the rest is silence."

The young man slept on a pallet under the little west window of Dulse's house for three years. He learned wizardry, fed the chickens, milked the cow. He suggested, once, that Dulse keep goats. He had not said anything for a week or so, a cold, wet week of autumn. He said, "You might keep some goats."

Dulse had the big lore-book open on the table. He had been trying to reweave one of the Acastan Spells, much broken and made powerless by the Emanations of Fundaur centuries ago. He had just begun to get a sense of the missing word that might fill one of the gaps, he almost had it, and – "You might keep some goats," Silence said.

Dulse considered himself a wordy, impatient man with a short temper. The necessity of not swearing had been a burden to him in his youth, and for thirty years the imbecility of prentices, clients, cows, and chickens had tried him sorely. Prentices and clients were afraid of his tongue, though cows and chickens paid no attention to his outbursts. He had never been angry at Silence before. There was a very long pause.

"What for?"

Silence apparently did not notice the pause or the extreme softness of Dulse's voice. "Milk, cheese, roast kid, company," he said.

"Have you ever kept goats?" Dulse asked, in the same soft, polite voice.

Silence shook his head.

He was in fact a town boy, born in Gont Port. He had said nothing about himself, but Dulse had asked around a bit. The father, a longshoreman, had died in the big earthquake, when Silence would have been seven or eight; the mother was a cook at a waterfront inn. At twelve the boy had got into some kind of trouble, probably messing about with magic, and his mother had managed to prentice him to Elassen, a respectable sorcerer in Valmouth. There the boy had picked up his true name, and some skill in carpentry and farmwork, if not much else; and Elassen had had the generosity, after three years, to pay his passage to Roke. That was all Dulse knew about him.

"I dislike goat cheese," Dulse said.

Silence nodded, acceptant as always.

From time to time in the years since then, Dulse remembered how he hadn't lost his temper when Silence asked about keeping goats; and each time the memory gave him a quiet satisfaction, like that of finishing the last bite of a perfectly ripe pear.

After spending the next several days trying to recapture the missing word, he had set Silence to studying the Acastan Spells. Together they finally worked it out, a long toil. "Like ploughing with a blind ox," Dulse said.

Not long after that he gave Silence the staff he had made for him of Gontish oak.

And the Lord of Gont Port had tried once again to get Dulse to come down to do what needed doing in Gont Port, and Dulse had sent Silence down instead, and there he had stayed.

And Dulse was standing on his own doorstep, three eggs in his hand and the rain running cold down his back.

How long had he been standing here? Why was he standing here? He had been thinking about mud, about the floor, about Silence. Had he been out walking on the path above the Overfell? No, that was years ago, years ago, in the sunlight. It was raining. He had fed the chickens, and come back to the house with three eggs, they were still warm in his hand, silky brown lukewarm eggs, and the sound of thunder was still in his mind, the vibration of thunder was in his bones, in his feet. Thunder?

No. There had been a thunderclap, a while ago. This was not thunder. He had had this queer feeling and had not recognised it, back – when? long ago, back before all the days and years he had been thinking of. When, when had it been? – before the earthquake. Just before the earthquake. Just before a half mile of the coast at Essary slumped into the sea, and people died crushed in the ruins of their villages, and a great wave swamped the wharfs at Gont Port.

He stepped down from the doorstep onto the dirt so that he could feel the ground with the nerves of his soles, but the mud slimed and fouled any messages the dirt had for him. He set the eggs down on the doorstep, sat down beside them, cleaned his feet with rainwater from the pot by the step, wiped them dry with the rag that hung on the handle of the pot, rinsed and wrung out the rag and hung it on the handle of the pot, picked up the eggs, stood up slowly, and went into his house.

He gave a sharp look at his staff, which leaned in the corner behind the door. He put the eggs in the larder, ate an apple quickly because he was hungry, and took up his staff. It was yew, bound at the foot with copper, worn to satin at the grip. Nemmerle had given it to him.

"Stand!" he said to it in its language, and let go of it. It stood as if he had driven it into a socket.

"To the root," he said impatiently, in the Language of the Making. "To the root!"

He watched the staff that stood on the shining floor. In a little while he saw it quiver very slightly, a shiver, a tremble.

"Ah, ah, ah," said the old wizard.

"What should I do?" he said aloud after a while.

The staff swayed, was still, shivered again.

"Enough of that, my dear," Dulse said, laying his hand on it. "Come now. No wonder I kept thinking about Silence. I should send for him . . . send to him . . . No. What did Ard say? Find the center, find the center. That's the question to ask. That's what to do . . ." As he muttered on to himself, routing out his heavy cloak, setting water to boil on the small fire he had lighted earlier, he wondered if he had always talked to himself, if he had talked all the time when Silence lived with him. No. It had become a habit after Silence left, he thought, with the bit of his mind that went on thinking the ordinary thoughts of life, while the rest of it made preparations for terror and destruction.

He hard-boiled the three new eggs and one already in the larder and put them into a pouch along with four apples and a bladder of resinated wine, in case he had to stay out all night. He shrugged arthritically into his heavy cloak, took up his staff, told the fire to go out, and left.

He no longer kept a cow. He stood looking into the poultry yard, considering. The fox had been visiting the orchard lately. But the chickens would have to forage if he stayed away. They must take their chances, like everyone else. He opened their gate a little. Though the rain was no more than a misty drizzle now, they stayed hunched up under the henhouse eaves, disconsolate. The King had not crowed once this morning.

"Have you anything to tell me?" Dulse asked them.

Brown Bucca, his favorite, shook herself and said her name a few times. The others said nothing.

"Well, take care. I saw the fox on the full-moon night," Dulse said, and went on his way.

As he walked he thought; he thought hard; he recalled. He recalled all he could of matters his teacher had spoken of once only and long ago. Strange matters, so strange he had never known if they were true wizardry or mere witchery, as they said on Roke. Matters he certainly had never heard about on Roke, not had he ever spoken about them there, maybe fearing the Masters would despise him for taking such things seriously, maybe knowing they would not understand them, because they were Gontish matters, truths of Gont. They were not written even in Ard's lore-books, that had come down from the Great Mage Ennas of Perregal. They were all word of mouth. They were home truths.

"If you need to read the Mountain," his teacher had told him, "go to the Dark Pond at the top of Semere's cow pasture. You can see the ways from there. You need to find the center. See where to go in."

"Go in?" the boy Dulse had whispered.

"What could you do from outside?"

Dulse was silent for a long time, and then said, "How?"

"Thus." And Ard's long arms stretched out and upward in the invocation of what Dulse would know later was a great spell of Transforming. And spoke the words of the spell awry, as teachers of wizardry must do lest the spell operate. Dulse knew the trick of hearing them aright and remembering them. When Ard was done, Dulse had repeated the words in his mind in silence, half-sketching the strange, awkward gestures that were part of them. All at once his hand stopped.

"But you can't undo this!" he said aloud.

Ard nodded. "It is irrevocable."

Dulse knew no transformation that was irrevocable, no spell that could not be unsaid, except the Word of Unbinding, which is spoken only once.

"But why——?"

"At need," Ard said.

Dulse knew better than to ask for explanation. The need to speak such a spell could not come often; the chance of his ever having to use it was very slight. He let the terrible spell sink down in his mind and be hidden and layered over with a thousand useful or beautiful or enlightening mageries and charms, all the lore and rules of Roke, all the wisdom of the books Ard had bequeathed him. Crude, monstrous, useless, it lay in the dark of his mind for sixty years, like the cornerstone of an earlier, forgotten house down in the cellar of a mansion full of lights and treasures and children.

The rain had ceased, though mist still hid the peak and shreds of cloud drifted through the high forests. Though not a tireless walker like Silence, who would have spent his life wandering in the forests of Gont Mountain if he could, Dulse had been born in Re Albi and knew the roads and ways around it as part of himself. He took the shortcut at Rissi's well and came out before midday on Semere's high pasture, a level step on the mountain-side. A mile below it, all in sunlight now, the farm buildings stood in the lee of a hill across which a flock of sheep moved like a cloud-shadow. Gont Port and its bay were hidden under the steep, knotted hills that stood inland above the city.

Dulse wandered about a bit before he found what he took to be the Dark Pond. It was small, half mud and reeds, with one vague, boggy path to the water, and no tracks on that but goat hoofs. The water was dark, though it lay out under the bright sky and far above the peat soils. Dulse followed the goat tracks, growling when his foot slipped in the mud and he wrenched his ankle to keep from falling. At the brink of the water he stood still. He stooped to rub his ankle. He listened.

It was absolutely silent.

No wind. No birdcall. No distant lowing or bleating or call of voice. As if all the island had gone still. Not a fly buzzed.

He looked at the dark water. It reflected nothing.

Reluctant, he stepped forward, barefoot and bare-legged; he had rolled up his cloak into his pack an hour ago when the sun came out. Reeds brushed his legs. The mud was soft and sucking under his feet, full of tangling reed-roots. He made no noise as he moved slowly out into the pool, and the circles of ripples from his movement were slight and small. It was shallow for a long way. Then his cautious foot felt no bottom, and he paused.

The water shivered. He felt it first on his thighs, a lapping like the tickling touch of fur; then he saw it, the trembling of the surface all over the pond. Not the round ripples he made, which had already died away, but a ruffling, a roughening, a shudder, again, and again.

"Where?" he whispered, and then said the word aloud in the language all things understand that have no other language.

There was the silence. Then a fish leapt from the black, shaking water, a white-grey fish the length of his hand, and as it leapt it cried out in a small, clear voice, in that same language, "Yaved!"

The old wizard stood there. He recollected all he knew of the names of Gont, brought all its slopes and cliffs and raviness into his mind, and in a minute he saw where Yaved was. It was the place where the ridges parted, just inland from Gont Port, deep in the knot of hills above the city. It was the place of the fault. An earthquake centered there could shake the city down, bring avalanche and tidal wave, close the cliffs of the bay together like hands clapping. Dulse shivered, shuddered all over like the water of the pool.

He turned and made for the shore, hasty, careless where he set his feet and not caring if he broke the silence by splashing and breathing hard. He slogged back up the path through the reeds till he reached dry ground and coarse grass, and heard the buzz of midges and crickets. He sat down then on the ground, hard, for his legs were shaking.

"It won't do," he said, talking to himself in Hardic, and then he said, "I can't do it." Then he said. "I can't do it by myself."

He was so distraught that when he made up his mind to call Silence he could not think of the opening of the spell, which he had known for sixty years; then when he thought he had it, he began to speak a Summoning instead, and the spell had begun to work before he realised what he was doing and stopped and undid it word by word.

He pulled up some grass and rubbed at the slimy mud on his feet and legs. It was not dry yet, and only smeared about on his skin. "I hate mud," he whispered. Then he snapped his jaws and stopped trying to clean his legs. "Dirt, dirt," he said, gently patting the ground he sat on. Then, very slow, very careful, he began to speak the spell of calling.

In a busy street leading down to the busy wharfs of Gont Port, the wizard Ogion stopped short. The ship's captain beside him walked on several steps and turned to see Ogion talking to the air.

"But I will come, master!" he said. And then after a pause, "How soon?" And after a longer pause, he told the air something in a language the ship's captain did not understand, and made a gesture that darkened the air about him for an instant.

"Captain," he said, "I'm sorry, I must wait to spell your sails. An earthquake is near. I must warn the city. Do you tell them down there, every ship that can sail make for the open sea. Clear out past the Armed Cliffs! Good luck to you." And he turned and ran back up the street, a tall, strong man with rough greying hair, running now like a stag.

Gont Port lies at the inner end of a long narrow bay between steep shores. Its entrance from the sea is between two great headlands, the Gates of the Port, the Armed Cliffs, not a hundred feet apart. The people of Gont Port are safe from sea-pirates. But their safety is their danger: the long bay follows a fault in the earth, and jaws that have opened may shut.

When he had done what he could to warn the city, and seen all the gate guards and port guards doing what they could to keep the few roads out from becoming choked and murderous with panicky people, Ogion shut himself into a room in the signal tower of the Port, locked the door, for everybody wanted him at once, and sent a sending to the Dark Pond in Semere's cow pasture up on the Mountain.

His old master was sitting in the grass near the pond, eating an apple. Bits of eggshell flecked the ground near his legs, which were caked with drying mud. When he looked up and saw Ogion's sending he smiled a wide, sweet smile. But he looked old. He had never looked so old. Ogion had not seen him for over a year, having been busy; he was always busy in Gont Port, doing the business of the lords and people, never a chance to walk in the forests on the mountainside or to come sit with Heleth in the little house at Re Albi and listen and be still. Heleth was an old man, near eighty now; and he was frightened. He smiled with joy to see Ogion, but he was frightened.

"I think what we have to do," he said without preamble, "is try to hold the fault from slipping much. You at the Gates and me at the inner end, in the Mountain. Working together, you know. We might be able to. I can feel it building up, can you?"

Ogion shook his head. He let his sending sit down in the grass near Heleth, though it did not bend the stems of the grass where it stepped or sat. "I've done nothing but set the city in a panic and send the ships out of the bay," he said. "What is it you feel? How do you feel it?"

They were technical questions, mage to mage. Heleth hesitated before answering.

"I learned about this from Ard," he said, and paused again.

He had never told Ogion anything about his first teacher, a sorcerer of no fame even in Gont, and perhaps of ill fame. Ogion knew only that Ard had never gone to Roke, had been trained on Perregal, and that some mystery or shame darkened the name. Though he was talkative, for a wizard, Heleth was silent as a stone about some things. And so Ogion, who respected silence, had never asked him about his teacher.

"It's not Roke magic," the old man said. His voice was dry, a little forced. "Nothing against the balance, though. Nothing sticky."

That had always been his word for evil doings, spells for gain, curses, black magic: "sticky stuff."

After a while, searching for words, he went on: "Dirt. Rocks. It's a dirty magic. Old. Very old. As old as Gont Island."

"The Old Powers?" Ogion murmured.

Heleth said, "I'm not sure."

"Will it control the earth itself?"

"More a matter of getting in with it, I think. Inside." The old man was burying the core of his apple and the larger bits of eggshell under loose dirt, patting it over them neatly. "Of course I know the words, but I'll have to learn what to do as I go. That's the trouble with the big spells, isn't it? You learn what you're doing while you do it. No chance to practice." He looked up. "Ah – there! You feel that?"

Ogion shook his head.

"Straining," Heleth said, his hand still absently, gently patting the dirt as one might pat a scared cow. "Quite soon now, I think. Can you hold the Gates open, my dear?"

"Tell me what you'll be doing—"

But Heleth was shaking his head: "No," he said. "No time. Not your kind of thing." He was more and more distracted by whatever it was he sensed in the earth or air, and through him Ogion too felt that gathering, intolerable tension.

They sat unspeaking. The crisis passed. Heleth relaxed a little and even smiled. "Very old stuff," he said, "what I'll be doing. I wish now I'd thought about it more. Passed it on to you. But it seemed a bit crude. Heavy-handed . . . She didn't say where she'd learned it. Here, of course . . . There are different kinds of knowledge, after all."

"She?"

"Ard. My teacher." Heleth looked up, his face unreadable, its expression possibly sly. "You didn't know that? No, I suppose I never mentioned it. I wonder what difference it made to her wizardry, her being a woman. Or to mine, my being a man . . . What matters, it seems to me, is whose house we live in. And who we let enter the house. This kind of thing – There! There again—"

His sudden tension and immobility, the strained face and inward look, were like those of a woman in labor when her womb contracts. That was Ogion's thought, even as he asked, "What did you mean, in the Mountain?"

The spasm passed: Heleth answered, "Inside it. There at Yaved." He pointed to the knotted hills below them. "I'll go in, try to keep things from sliding around, eh? I'll find out how when I'm doing it, no doubt. I think you should be getting back to yourself. Things are rightening up." He stopped again, looking as if he were in intense pain, hunched and clenched. He struggled to stand up. Unthinking, Ogion held out his hand to help him.

"No use," said the old wizard, grinning, "you're only wind and sunlight. Now I'm going to be dirt and stone. You'd best go on. Farewell, Aihal. Keep the – keep the mouth open, for once, eh?"

Ogion, obedient, bringing himself back to himself in the stuffy, tapestried room in Gont Port, did not understand the old man's joke until he turned to the window and saw the Armed Cliffs down at the end of the long bay, the jaws ready to snap shut. "I will," he said, and set to it.

"What I have to do, you see," the old wizard said, still talking to Silence because it was a comfort to talk to him even if he was no longer there, "is get into the mountain, right inside. But not the way a sorcerer prospector does, not just slipping about between things and looking and tasting. Deeper. All the way in. Not the veins, but the bones. So," and standing there alone in the high pasture, in the noon light, Heleth opened his arms wide in the gesture of invocation that opens all the greater spells; and he spoke.

Nothing happened as he said the words Ard had taught him, his old witch-teacher with her bitter mouth and her long, lean arms, the words spoken awry then, spoken truly now.

Nothing happened, and he had time to regret the sunlight and the sea wind, and to doubt the spell, and to doubt himself, before the earth rose up around him, dry, warm, and dark.

In there he knew he should hurry, that the bones of the earth ached to move, and that he must become them to guide them, but he could not hurry. There was on him the bewilderment of any transformation. He had in his day been fox, and bull, and dragonfly, and knew what it was to change being. But this was different, this slow enlargement. I am vastening, he thought.

He reached out towards Yaved, towards the ache, the suffering. As he came closer to it he felt a great strength flow into him from the west, as if Silence had taken him by the hand after all. Through that link he could send his own strength, the Mountain's strength, to help. I didn't tell him I wasn't coming back, he thought, his last words in Hardic, his last grief, for he was in the bones of the mountain now. He knew the arteries of fire, and the beat of the great heart. He knew what to do. It was in no tongue of man that he said, "Be quiet, be easy. There now, there. Hold fast. So, there. We can be easy."

And he was easy, he was still, he held fast, rock in rock and earth in earth in the fiery dark of the mountain.

It was their mage Ogion whom the people saw stand alone on the roof of the signal tower on the wharf, when the streets ran up and down in waves, the cobbles bursting out of them, and walls of clay brick puffed into dust, and the Armed Cliffs leaned together, groaning. It was Ogion they saw, his hands held out before him, straining, parting: and the cliffs parted with them, and stood straight, unmoved. The city shuddered and stood still. It was Ogion who stopped the earthquake. They saw it, they said it.

"My teacher was with me, and his teacher with him." Ogion said when they praised him. "I could hold the Gate open because he held the Mountain still." They praised his modesty and did not listen to him. Listening is a rare gift, and men will have their heroes.

When the city was in order again, and the ships had all come back, and the walls were being rebuilt, Ogion escaped from praise and went up into the hills above Gont Port. He found the queer little valley called Trimmer's Dell, the true name of which in the Language of the Making was Yaved, as Ogion's true name was Aihal. He walked about there all one day, as if seeking something. In the evening he lay down on the ground and talked to it. "You should have told me. I could have said goodbye," he said. He wept then, and his tears fell on the dry dirt among the grass stems and made little spots of mud, little sticky spots.

He slept there on the ground, with no pallet or blanket between him and the dirt. At sunrise he got up and walked by the high road over to Re Albi. He did not go into the village, but past it to the house that stood alone north of the other houses at the beginning of the Overfell. The door stood open.

The last beans had got big and coarse on the vines; the cabbages were thriving. Three hens came clucking and pecking around the dusty dooryard, a red, a brown, a white; a grey hen was setting her clutch in the henhouse. There were no chicks, and no sign of the cock, the King, Heleth had called him. The king is dead, Ogion thought. Maybe a chick is hatching even now to take his place. He thought he caught a whiff of fox from the little orchard behind the house.

He swept out the dust and leaves that had blown in the open doorway across the floor of polished wood. He set Heleth's mattress and blanket in the sun to air. "I'll stay here a while," he thought. "It's a good house." After a while he thought, "I might keep some goats."

THE CLOSED WINDOW

A. C. Benson

*I doubt that many people realise it but I suspect all of you know
one of the works of A.C. Benson almost word perfect and quote
it at every opportunity. Yes you do. Because it was A. C.
Benson (1862–1925), brother of the better known E. F.
Benson (creator of the Mapp and Lucia books), who wrote
the words to Edward Elgar's* Pomp and Circumstance *march
we all know as "Land of Hope and Glory". It's always struck
me as strange that the man who could write such a rousing song
spent most of his life with near terminal depression. And most
of this time he spent closeted behind the walls of academe as a
Master first at Eton and then at Magdalene College, Cam-
bridge. He wrote prodigiously, mostly essays and reflections on
life, but he produced two collections of strange stories during his
life time,* The Hill of Trouble *(1903) and* The Isles of
Sunset *(1904). Most of the stories are archaic or antiquarian
but just once or twice he hit the right note. As in the following
story, modelled on the medieval heroic romances, about the
mystery of an ancient Tower.*

T HE TOWER OF NORT stood in a deep angle of the downs;
formerly an old road led over the hill, but it is now a green
track covered with turf; the later highway choosing rather to cross
a low saddle of the ridge, for the sake of the beasts of burden. The
tower, originally built to guard the great road, was a plain, strong,
thick-walled fortress. To the tower had been added a plain and
seemly house, where the young Sir Mark de Nort lived very easily

and plentifully. To the south stretched the great wood of Nort, but the Tower stood high on an elbow of the down, sheltered from the north by the great green hills. The villagers had an odd ugly name for the Tower, which they called the Tower of Fear; but the name was falling into disuse, and was only spoken, and that heedlessly, by ancient men, because Sir Mark was vexed to hear it so called. Sir Mark was not yet thirty, and had begun to say that he must marry a wife; but he seemed in no great haste to do so, and loved his easy, lonely life, with plenty of hunting and hawking on the down. With him lived his cousin and heir, Roland Ellice, a heedless good-tempered man, a few years older than Sir Mark; he had come on a visit to Sir Mark, when he first took possession of the Tower; and there had seemed no reason why he should go away; the two suited each other; Sir Mark was sparing of speech, fond of books and of rhymes. Roland was different, loving ease and wine and talk, and finding in Mark a good listener. Mark loved his cousin, and thought it praiseworthy of him to stay and help to cheer so sequestered a house, since there were few neighbours within reach.

And yet Mark was not wholly content with his easy life; there were many days when he asked himself why he should go thus quietly on, day by day, like a stalled ox; still, there appeared no reason why he should do otherwise; there were but few folk on his land, and they were content; yet he sometimes envied them their bondage and their round of daily duties. The only place where he could else have been was with the army, or even with the Court; but Sir Mark was no soldier, and even less of a courtier; he hated tedious gaiety, and it was a time of peace. So because he loved solitude and quiet he lived at home, and sometimes thought himself but half a man; yet was he happy after a sort, but for a kind of little hunger of the heart.

What gave the Tower so dark a name was the memory of old Sir James de Nort, Mark's grandfather, an evil and secret man, who had dwelt at Nort under some strange shadow; he had driven his son from his doors, and lived at the end of his life with his books and his own close thoughts, spying upon the stars and tracing strange figures in books; since his death the old room in the turret top, where he came by his end in a dreadful way, had been closed; it was entered by a turret-door, with a flight of steps from the chamber below. It had four windows, one to each of the winds; but the window which looked upon the down was fastened up, and secured with a great shutter of oak.

One day of heavy rain, Roland, being wearied of doing nothing, and vexed because Mark sat so still in a great chair, reading in a book, said to his cousin at last that he must go and visit the old room, in which he had never set foot. Mark closed his book, and smiling indulgently at Roland's restlessness, rose, stretching himself, and got the key; and together they went up the turret stairs. The key groaned loudly in the lock, and, when the door was thrown back, there appeared a high faded room, with a timbered roof, and with a close, dull smell. Round the walls were presses, with the doors fast; a large oak table, with a chair beside it, stood in the middle. The walls were otherwise bare and rough; the spiders had spun busily over the windows and in the angles. Roland was full of questions, and Mark told him all he had heard of old Sir James and his silent ways, but said that he knew nothing of the disgrace that had seemed to envelop him, or of the reasons why he had so evil a name. Roland said that he thought it a shame that so fair a room should lie so nastily, and pulled one of the casements open, when a sharp gust broke into the room, with so angry a burst of rain, that he closed it again in haste; little by little, as they talked, a shadow began to fall upon their spirits, till Roland declared that there was still a blight upon the place; and Mark told him of the death of old Sir James, who had been found after a day of silence, when he had not set foot outside his chamber, lying on the floor of the room, strangely bedabbled with wet and mud, as though he had come off a difficult journey, speechless, and with a look of anguish on his face; and that he had died soon after they had found him, muttering words that no one understood. Then the two young men drew near to the closed window; the shutters were tightly barred, and across the panels was scrawled in red, in an uncertain hand, the words CLAUDIT ET NEMO APERIT, which Mark explained was the Latin for the text, *He shutteth and none openeth*. And then Mark said that the story went that it was ill for the man that opened the window, and that shut it should remain for him. But Roland girded at him for his want of curiosity, and had laid a hand upon the bar as though to open it, but Mark forbade him urgently. "Nay," said he, "let it remain so – we must not meddle with the will of the dead!" and as he said the word, there came so furious a gust upon the windows that it seemed as though some stormy thing would beat them open; so they left the room together, and presently descending, found the sun struggling through the rain.

But both Mark and Roland were sad and silent all that day; for though they spake not of it, there was a desire in their minds to open the closed window, and to see what would befall; in Roland's mind it was like the desire of a child to peep into what is forbidden; but in Mark's mind a sort of shame to be so bound by an old and weak tale of superstition.

Now it seemed to Mark, for many days, that the visit to the turret-room had brought a kind of shadow down between them. Roland was peevish and ill-at-ease; and ever the longing grew upon Mark, so strongly that it seemed to him that something drew him to the room, some beckoning of a hand or calling of a voice.

Now one bright and sunshiny morning it happened that Mark was left alone within the house. Roland had ridden out early, not saying where he was bound. And Mark sat, more listlessly than was his wont, and played with the ears of his great dog, that sat with his head upon his master's knee, looking at him with liquid eyes, and doubtless wondering why Mark went not abroad.

Suddenly Sir Mark's eye fell upon the key of the upper room, which lay on the window-ledge where he had thrown it; and the desire to go up and pluck the heart from the little mystery came upon him with a strength that he could not resist; he rose twice and took up the key, and fingering it doubtfully, laid it down again; then suddenly he took it up, and went swiftly into the turret-stair, and up, turning, turning, till his head was dizzy with the bright peeps of the world through the loophole windows. Now all was green, where a window gave on the down; and now it was all clear air and sun, the warm breeze coming pleasantly into the cold stairway; presently Mark heard the pattering of feet on the stair below, and knew that the old hound had determined to follow him; and he waited a moment at the door, half pleased, in his strange mood, to have the company of a living thing. So when the dog was at his side, he stayed no longer, but opened the door and stepped within the room.

The room, for all its faded look, had a strange air about it, and though he could not say why, Mark felt that he was surely expected. He did not hesitate, but walked to the shutter and considered it for a moment; he heard a sound behind him. It was the old hound who sat with his head aloft, sniffing the air uneasily; Mark called him and held out his hand, but the hound would not move; he wagged his tail as though to acknowledge that he was called, and then he returned to his uneasy quest. Mark watched him for a moment, and saw that the old dog had made up his mind that all was not well in the room, for he lay down, gathering his legs under him, on the threshold, and watched his master with frightened eyes, quivering visibly. Mark, no lighter of heart, and in a kind of fearful haste, pulled the great staple off the shutter and set it on the ground, and then wrenched the shutters back; the space revealed was largely filled by old and dusty webs of spiders, which Mark lightly tore down, using the staple of the shutters to do this; it was with a strange shock of surprise that he saw that the window was dark, or nearly so; it seemed as though there were some further obstacle outside; yet Mark knew that from below the leaded panes of the window were visible. He drew back for a moment, but, unable to restrain his curiosity, wrenched the rusted casement open. But still all was dark without; and there came in a gust of icy wind from outside; it was as though something had passed him swiftly, and he heard the old hound utter a strangled howl; then turning, he saw him spring to his feet with his hair bristling and his teeth bare, and next moment the dog turned and leapt out of the room.

Mark, left alone, tried to curb a tide of horror that swept through his veins; he looked round at the room, flooded with the southerly sunlight, and then he turned again to the dark window, and putting a strong constraint upon himself, leaned out, and saw a thing which bewildered him so strangely that he thought for a moment his senses had deserted him. He looked out on a lonely dim hillside, covered with rocks and stones; the hill came up close to the window, so that he could have jumped down upon it, the wall below seeming to be built into the rocks. It was all dark and silent, like a clouded night, with a faint light coming from whence he could not see. The hill sloped away very steeply from the tower, and he seemed to see a plain beyond, where at the same time he knew that the down ought to lie. In the plain there was a light, like the firelit window of a house; a little below him some shape like a crouching man seemed to run and slip among the stones, as though suddenly surprised, and seeking to escape. Side by side with a deadly fear which began to invade his heart, came an uncontrollable desire to leap down among the rocks; and then it seemed to him that the figure below stood upright, and began to beckon him. There came over him a sense that he was in deadly peril; and, like a man on the edge of a precipice, who has just enough will left to try to escape, he drew himself by main force away from the window, closed it, put the shutters back, replaced the staple, and, his limbs all trembling, crept out of the room, feeling along the walls like a palsied man. He locked the door, and then, his terror overpowering him, he fled down the turret-stairs. Hardly thinking what he did, he came out on the court, and going to the great well that stood in the centre of the yard, he went to it and flung the key down, hearing it clink on the sides as it fell. Even then he dared not re-enter the house, but glanced up and down, gazing about him, while the cloud of fear and horror by insensible degrees dispersed, leaving him weak and melancholy.

Presently Roland returned, full of talk, but broke off to ask if Mark were ill. Mark, with a kind of surliness, an unusual mood for him, denied it somewhat sharply. Roland raised his eyebrows, and said no more, but prattled on. Presently after a silence he said to Mark, "What did you do all the morning?" and it seemed to Mark as though this were accompanied with a spying look. An unreasonable anger seized him. "What does it matter to you what I did?" he said. "May not I do what I like in my own house?"

"Doubtless," said Roland, and sate silent with uplifted brows; then he hummed a tune, and presently went out.

They sat at dinner that evening with long silences, contrary to their wont, though Mark bestirred himself to ask questions. When they were left alone, Mark stretched out his hand to Roland, saying, "Roland, forgive me! I spoke to you earlier in a way of which I am ashamed; we have lived so long together – and yet we came nearer to quarrelling to-day than we have ever done before; and it was my fault."

Roland smiled, and held Mark's hand for a moment. "Oh, I had not given it another thought," he said; "the wonder is that you can bear with an idle fellow as you do." Then they talked for awhile with the pleasant glow of friendliness that two good comrades feel when they have been reconciled. But late in the evening Roland said, "Was there any story, Mark, about your grandfather's leaving any treasure of money behind him?"

The question grated somewhat unpleasantly upon Mark's mood; but he controlled himself and said, "No, none that I know of – except that he found the estate rich and left it poor – and what he did with his revenues no one knows – you had better ask the old men of the village; they know more about the house than I do. But, Roland, forgive me once more if I say that I do not desire Sir James's name to be mentioned between us. I wish we had not entered his room; I do not know how to express it, but it seems to me as though he had sat there, waiting quietly to be summoned, and as though we had troubled him, and – as though he had joined us. I think he was an evil man, close and evil. And there hangs in my mind a verse of Scripture, where Samuel said to the witch, 'Why hast thou disquieted me to bring me up?' Oh," he went on, "I do not know why I talk wildly thus"; for he saw that Roland was looking at him with astonishment, with parted lips; "but a shadow has fallen upon me, and there seems evil abroad."

From that day forward a heaviness lay on the spirit of Mark that could not be scattered. He felt, he said to himself, as though he had meddled light-heartedly with something far deeper and more dangerous than he had supposed – like a child that has aroused some evil beast that slept. He had dark dreams too. The figure that he had seen among the rocks seemed to peep and beckon him, with a mocking smile, over perilous places, where he followed unwilling. But the heavier he grew the lighter-hearted Roland became; he seemed to walk in some bright vision of his own, intent upon a large and gracious design.

One day he came into the hall in the morning, looking so radiant that Mark asked him half enviously what he had to make him so glad. "Glad," said Roland, "oh, I know it! Merry dreams, perhaps. What do you think of a good grave fellow who beckons me on with a brisk smile, and shows me places, wonderful places, under banks and in woodland pits, where riches lie piled to-gether? I am sure that some good fortune is preparing for me,

Mark – but you shall share it." Then Mark, seeing in his words a certain likeness, with a difference, to his own dark visions, pressed his lips together and sate looking stonily before him.

At last, one still evening of spring, when the air was intolerably languid and heavy for mankind, but full of sweet promises for trees and hidden peeping things, though a lurid redness of secret thunder had lain all day among the heavy clouds in the plain, the two dined together. Mark had walked alone that day, and had lain upon the turf of the down, fighting against a weariness that seemed to be poisoning the very springs of life within him. But Roland had been brisk and alert, coming and going upon some secret and busy errand, with a fragment of a song upon his lips, like a man preparing to set off for a far country, who is glad to be gone. In the evening, after they had dined, Roland had let his fancy rove in talk. "If we were rich," he said, "how we would transform this old place!"

"It is fair enough for me," said Mark heavily; and Roland had chidden him lightly for his sombre ways, and sketched new plans of life.

Mark, wearied and yet excited, with an intolerable heaviness of spirit, went early to bed, leaving Roland in the hall. After a short and broken sleep, he awoke, and lighting a candle, read idly and gloomily to pass the heavy hours. The house seemed full of strange noises that night. Once or twice came a scraping and a faint hammering in the wall; light footsteps seemed to pass in the turret – but the tower was always full of noises, and Mark heeded them not; at last he fell asleep again, to be suddenly awakened by a strange and desolate crying, that came he knew not whence, but seemed to wail upon the air. The old dog, who slept in Mark's room, heard it too; he was sitting up in a fearful expectancy. Mark rose in haste, and taking the candle, went into the passage that led to Roland's room. It was empty, but a light burned there and showed that the room had not been slept in. Full of a horrible fear, Mark returned, and went in hot haste up the turret steps, fear and anxiety struggling together in his mind. When he reached the top, he found the little door broken forcibly open, and a light within. He cast a haggard look round the room, and then the crying came again, this time very faint and desolate.

Mark cast a shuddering glance at the window; it was wide open and showed a horrible liquid blackness; round the bar in the centre that divided the casements, there was something knotted. He hastened to the window, and saw that it was a rope, which hung heavily. Leaning out he saw that something dangled from the rope below him – and then came the crying again out of the darkness, like the crying of a lost spirit.

He could see as in a bitter dream the outline of the hateful hillside; but there seemed to his disordered fancy to be a tumult of some kind below; pale lights moved about, and he saw a group of forms which scattered like a shoal of fish when he leaned out. He knew that he was looking upon a scene that no mortal eye ought to behold, and it seemed to him at the moment as though he was staring straight into hell.

The rope went down among the rocks and disappeared; but Mark clenched it firmly and using all his strength, which was great, drew it up hand over hand; as he drew it up he secured it in loops round the great oak table; he began to be afraid that his strength would not hold out, and once when he returned to the window after securing a loop, a great hooded thing like a bird flew noiselessly at the window and beat its wings.

Presently he saw that the form which dangled on the rope was clear of the rocks below; it had come up through them, as though they were but smoke; and then his task seemed to him more sore than ever. Inch by painful inch he drew it up, working fiercely and silently; his muscles were tense, and drops stood on his brow, and the veins hammered in his ears; his breath came and went in sharp sobs. At last the form was near enough for him to seize it; he grasped it by the middle and drew Roland, for it was Roland, over the window-sill. His head dangled and drooped from side to side; his face was dark with strangled blood and his limbs hung helpless. Mark drew his knife and cut the rope that was tied under his arms; the helpless limbs sank huddling on the floor; then Mark looked up; at the window a few feet from him was a face, more horrible than he had supposed a human face, if it was human indeed, could be. It was deadly white, and hatred, baffled rage, and a sort of devilish malignity glared from the white set eyes, and the drawn mouth. There was a rush from behind him; the old hound, who had crept up unawares into the room, with a fierce outcry of rage sprang on to the windowsill; Mark heard the scraping of his claws upon the stone. Then the hound leapt through the window, and in a moment there was the sound of a heavy fall outside. At the same instant the darkness seemed to lift and draw up like a cloud; a bank of blackness rose past the window, and left the dark outline of the down, with a sky sown with tranquil stars.

The cloud of fear and horror that hung over Mark lifted too; he felt in some dim way that his adversary was vanquished; he carried Roland down the stairs and laid him on his bed; he roused the household, who looked fearfully at him, and then his own strength failed; he sank upon the floor of his room, and the dark tide of unconsciousness closed over him.

Mark's return to health was slow. One who has looked into the Unknown finds it hard to believe again in the outward shows of life. His first conscious speech was to ask for his hound; they told him that the body of the dog had been found, horribly mangled as though by the teeth of some fierce animal, at the foot of the tower. The dog was buried in the garden, with a slab above him, on which are the words:—

EUGE SERVE BONE ET FIDELIS

A silly priest once said to Mark that it was not meet to write Scripture over the grave of a beast. But Mark said warily that an inscription was for those who read it, to make them humble, and not to increase the pride of what lay below.

When Mark could leave his bed, his first care was to send for builders, and the old tower of Nort was taken down, stone by stone, to the ground, and a fair chapel built on the site; in the wall there was a secret stairway, which led from the top chamber, and came out among the elder-bushes that grew below the tower, and here was found a coffer of gold, which paid for the church; because, until it was found, it was Mark's design to leave the place desolate. Mark is wedded since, and has his children about his knee; those who come to the house see a strange and wan man, who sits at Mark's board, and whom he uses very tenderly; sometimes this man is merry, and tells a long tale of his being beckoned and led by a tall and handsome person, smiling, down a hillside to fetch gold; though he can never remember the end of the matter; but about the springtime he is silent or mutters to himself; and this is Roland; his spirit seems shut up within him in some closed cell, and Mark prays for his release, but till God call him, he treats him like a dear brother, and with the reverence due to one who has looked out on the other side of Death, and who may not say what his eyes beheld.

DISILLUSIONED

Lawrence Schimel and Mike Resnick

*I could easily write an introduction about these two writers
which would end up longer than the story, so I had better curb
my enthusiasm. Lawrence Schimel (b. 1971) is a prolific
writer of short and gay (in all senses of the word) fantasies
some of which will be found in his collection* The Drag Queen
of Elfland *(1997). Amongst his many anthologies are* The
Fortune Teller *(1997), with Martin H. Greenberg, and a
haunting volume of magic realism,* Things Invisible to See
*(1998). He is currently resident in Spain writing mostly books
for children.*

*Mike Resnick (b.1942) has produced a bewildering array of
books and novels, most notably his multi-award winning series
about native Africans who colonise the planet Kirinyaga and
establish a culture as it once was on Earth. Their stories will be
found in, for starters,* Kirinyaga *(1998). Resnick has won four
Hugos, a Nebula and other major and minor awards in the
USA, plus awards in France, Japan, Poland, Croatia and
Spain. His work has been translated into twenty-two languages.*

*Their combined talents produced this clever little story which
questions the nature of reality.*

T HEY WERE GATHERED IN the Great Hall when Edward looked
up with an expectant smile on his face. An instant later it
started raining toads *inside* the castle.

As the guests began screaming, Edward waved his hand, and
suddenly the rug itself became a thousand mouths, each gobbling

up one or more toads. But as the last of the toads were eaten, the mouths became insatiable, and started gnawing upon the furniture.

Another wave of Edward's hand, and the furniture turned to solid gold. Teeth cracked against it, mouths withdrew, and, sprouting wings, the furniture began hovering a few inches above the rug daring it to test its strength once again. The mouths vanished, the furniture gently came to rest upon it, and golden legs metamorphised into wood as Edward grinned and bowed deeply for his applauding audience.

Vivian sighed, wishing she were elsewhere, but she displayed no outward sign of her boredom, laughing along with the other assembled members of the Thirteen Families. She tried to recall when it was that the magic had faded from her and Edward's relationship. There was a time when his every trick delighted her, simply because they were *his*. Now, when they made love, she murmured cantrips she pretended were moans of ecstasy to disguise his appearance with that of another man, *any* other man – she didn't care.

Somewhere along the way, things had come undone.

Her heart, which once had felt as buoyant as the Emperor's sailships, now felt as if it were a splintered wreckage of silken sails and ebony timber, as if the spells which had kept it aloft had malfunctioned, now that Edward's sorceries no longer amused her. He seemed to send the craft hurtling Earthward once again, into the mud. All of Constantinople looked muddied to her now, the bright and glittering splendour eclipsed by her mood, as if the sun had become blotted out by a cloud of dust, or had simply stopped shining altogether.

An intricately-patterned python engulfed Edward from behind his chair. He opened his mouth wide enough to accommodate the snake's thick body and swiftly consumed it as the assembled elite erupted once more into laughter, like giddy schoolgirls over some titbit of gossip. Vivian was so tired of it all, and of Edward in particular. Something was lacking in him, something which she desperately craved from him, though she could not pinpoint precisely what was wanting. She wondered, not for the first time, what he was truly like beneath his illusions and spells – if perhaps, accidentally, she might once have seen the true Edward even as she gave him other men's faces to wile the time away, might have seen the man he was beneath his young and virile exterior. Vivian herself augmented her looks, retarding the vagaries of aging with spells and illusions, but she imagined the true Edward to be a void, as if he were nothing more than his elaborate and powerful sorceries.

Though young, and not merely young-seeming, he was unquestionably the most powerful magic-maker in the city, and therefore the most celebrated member of the Thirteen Families, who were Constantinople's most accomplished magicians and who enforced that status with a swift and iron fist (although always from afar, and via their magic, so as never to sully their own fingers). It had been a coup for Vivian to attract his attentions and even more so to have kept them this long. Although, knowing Edward as she did, Vivian found the task simplicity itself. For all his sorceries, Edward seemed lacking in all artifice in life, easily swayed and manipulated by her cunning. Vivian spent long hours concealing his naïveté, protecting him, and her own position as his consort and lover, from others who would exploit him. That was reserved for Vivian alone.

But even that privilege had long since paled in its thrill, and was now more of a chore than anything else – defending her throne from any and all assailants, petty and overt.

Of a sudden, Vivian's chair dropped through the floor, which had opened a hole as quickly as a champagne bubble bursting up from the glass's bottom to crack the surface with fizz. She idly wondered whether to cast about for some spell to save her life, lest she fall to her death from the heights of the castle they'd been visiting, but she trusted Edward would spare a moment's thought for her and save her (if this were not in fact another of his own pranks).

Vivian took the moment to enjoy her respite from the society of her fellow members of the Thirteen Families, who in their aggregate sum she found quite tedious and sadly droll. She stared down at the city from her aerial vantage: the Grand Concourse, hub of Constantinople and gate through which all visitors passed, the golden globe that shined down from above its dome an earthly sun; and a short ways to the left, the Cathedral, equally majestic in its non-magical splendour of stone and human construction that rivalled, nay, dwarfed, the magical fabrications which had sprung up along and beyond the road that stretched between the Grand Concourse and the Cathedral, puny and insubstantial flights of fancy.

Her reverie was interrupted by Edward wrapping his arms about her from behind the chair. "Were you not even the slightest bit concerned?" he asked, burying his face in her long, curly black locks and running his hands up along her belly to her breasts. "You looked so ravishing up there, I couldn't help stealing you away. Let's make love in mid-air," he whispered into her ear.

"For the world to see? Like some common sailor and his whore."

"We're invisible," he said, fumbling at the laces of her dress, and Vivian knew that in that moment he had indeed made them so.

"Please, Edward, you know it's not that I don't trust your spells to keep us aloft, but I really do prefer the comforts of solid ground beneath my feet, and a bed, and – " Vivian had a long catalogue of her preferences, hoping she might thereby be able to put him off, but they were suddenly back in Edward's terrestrial palaces. For all his sorcerous might, he had constructed his home of natural substances, though equally elaborate and plush as the wholly-dreamed airborne castles of his peers. If Vivian needed to suffer the emotional discomforts of making love to him, she would rather it occur among the creature comforts she had grown accustomed to as his consort. Edward lifted her in his arms and placed her upon the thick, feathered comforter of the bed they shared, climbing atop her. The words to the spell which would change Edward's appearance began running through her mind, and at the first opportunity she uttered them, her fingers clawing Edward's back as she twisted them to form the proper signs. Edward mistook the signs as Vivian goading him, and was further aroused. He no longer bothered with the clasps and stays of her clothing, but made the entire contraption disappear in an instant, leaving her body naked beneath him. Mercifully, it was over in a few minutes, and Edward fell promptly asleep.

The moment he began to snore, Vivian extracted herself from beneath him and pushed away from the bed. She went into the bathroom, locking the door behind her, though she knew such a safeguard meant little to Edward, or practically any of Constantinople's inhabitants for that matter. In this city of magicians, it was simplicity itself to cause a lock to undo itself with a spell most children learned before they had stopped wetting their pants. Still, it was something Vivian felt compelled to do, an emotional signal to herself that she was locking him and them out. She let the illusions fall from her body, and stood regarding herself in the mirrored wall before stopping to run hot water into a basin and scrub his scent from her skin with sponges and soaps. It was a long time before she again felt clean.

Vivian towelled herself dry, though she might as easily have spelled herself so. It was not that she disdained magic, or its benefits; like all the other inhabitants of Constantinople, Vivian's life was thoroughly saturated with magic. She practiced it daily, casting spells and illusions almost before thinking; and that was why she preferred to dry herself, and to perform a hundred other tasks manually, lest she become so dependent on magic that she lose herself to it. It kept her alert to consciously not use her magic to handle the minor details of life, and it was that alertness of mind and attention to detail which was how she had been able to attract and keep Edward's infatuation all these years.

Staring at her image in the mirror, Vivian had to ask herself if the effort was worthwhile. Not the honing of her consciousness, that she would not forsake even for all of Edward's powers – but Edward himself. True, while she lived in Constantinople, his presence in her life gave her access to a society and privilege to which she could not otherwise hope to aspire. But, having now climbed her way all the way to the top, up, even, to their airborne palaces which floated high above Constantinople's towers, Vivian found herself bored.

Life was too easy.

That was perhaps what bothered her about Edward; because of him, there was no longer any sense of competition in her life, no challenge for anything. Edward could by force of magic do or give her anything she desired. And, since he was so easy for her to manipulate, he did. Vivian had nothing left to stimulate her, and her frustration was driving her to distraction. Though she was free to roam throughout Constantinople, she was trapped by her relationship.

She looked at herself in the mirror, saw how she was getting so much older, despite the care she took with her body. Her once raven-dark hair was now heavily greying beneath her illusions. How much longer could she live like this? Vivian felt she would die, suffocated by the tedium of this life and illusion. She almost thought she would have been more content to have stayed far from the city, to have become some farmer's wife, the two of them forever battling with nature to eke out a living for themselves and their family. Vivian knew, of course, that such positing was idle, especially surrounded by such pampering splendour as she was right then, but she would at least have felt alive every day in such a life, she thought. Bitter perhaps, but she felt bitter now, and with less reason.

But could she give it all up? Relinquish her status, the power at her command through Edward . . . the feeling of overwhelming boredom and discontent she felt of her life.

Vivian wasn't quite sure. All her life her mind had been set to climbing to this pinnacle. To climb down now seemed too much like a defeat – and besides, she had no new goal to replace this one.

She sighed, and left her bathroom, hurrying quickly through the bedroom where Edward still snored beneath the rumpled blue comforter. In her closet, she put on a light dressing robe, and was about to leave their apartments and find some more secluded part of the castle, perhaps overlooking the ever-changing mosaic of the city, to ponder further her dilemma – when she spied herself in a small wall mirror and noticed she had forgotten to put on her illusion of her younger self. The words to the spell leapt immediately to her lips as she reached for the door handle, but Vivian paused. She wondered what it might be like to walk about as her true self, to discard her despised life in this small trial. It was not as if she would be seen by anyone of import: just a few servants, if anyone at all.

Pleased with herself, Vivian revelled in the sensation of being free of cloaking illusions as she walked through the familiar halls of Edward's palace. These walls, too, were authentic in their substance. The stone floor was cold beneath her feet. Hardly any other palace in Constantinople could boast the same; they were all fabrications. Her naked foot would tread upon illusions of soft rugs or stones that were always the proper warmth. But Edward, as a show of ostentation, had foregone a magic-made palace, and instead used his magic to command a vast wealth of natural substance into his abode. The other members of the Thirteen Families thought it eccentric, and odd that he chose to remain so terrestrial, while all of them had set their palaces drifting among the clouds . . .

But its simplicity, its genuineness, not to mention the incredible magic it took to construct it, manipulating that which already existed rather than summoning from nothing what was desired, were what had attracted Vivian to Edward in the first place. She stared from a window at the city spread below her, and all the cluster of fanciful and impossible buildings illuminated by the golden globe which hung above the Grand Concourse. She had loved him once, that she couldn't deny; but something had happened, and that love had simply vanished, like one of his illusions. Pop, and it was gone. As if, Vivian thought, staring at the shining golden globe, as if one day it simply vanished.

And, as if in mute response to Vivian's thoughts, the golden globe did just that.

Vivian blinked against the sudden dimness, and wondered, awed, what had happened. Had she caused it to go out? How furious everyone would be! She felt a momentary giddy delight as she surveyed the city, now cast into twilight. There was still light coming from somewhere . . . ah, yes, the sun. How easy to have forgotten that it still shone, eclipsed by the brighter, magical sub that had been created ages ago, and which was held in place by the collective unconscious of Constantinople. Vivian was awed that she, by herself, had been able to counteract that force of will, which all these years had kept the golden globe in place . . .

And suddenly, staring at the city in the dimness, Vivian realized that it had not been her at all. The fanciful and impossible buildings which had clogged the streets were gone. In their place stood sordid, dilapidated constructions of plain wood and brick. As she watched this diminished city, a sailship fell from the sky, and splintered into rubble.

Vivian tried to cast a spell, to bring her customary illusions into place, a spell that was so ingrained into her mind that she could maintain it even when unconscious. But her body would not grow younger and her hair stayed grey, picking up what little light there was.

It had not been Vivian at all, which extinguished the golden globe, but rather the fact that throughout the City the magic had been used up!

The thought delighted her. She imagined the airborne castles of the Thirteen Families plummeting like the sailship she had seen, in great, disastrous wreckages.

And Edward? Now he was just an ordinary mortal, like everyone else. All his powerful sorceries were gone, vanished on the winds. Vivian could not help wondering what he truly looked like without his disguises, if there was any substance to him at all. She hurried back along the corridors, feeling along the walls with her fingers since the magical lights which once had illumined them were absent now. Their bedroom, at least, would still be lit from the large windows that looked out over the gardens.

Vivian paused before the door, savouring the moment, delaying it. She had wondered for so long what Edward truly looked like, she did not want to diminish her discovery by rushing through it. She imagined how he would look as her fingers turned upon the knob, positing some obese and slobbering old man in her mind, the way the grand and fanciful buildings had reverted to rundown tenements without the magic to support them. How much easier it would be to hate him, knowing his true and repulsive form!

Vivian thought she was braced for anything he might seem, any repulsive, disgusting form that she found lying in her bed, a form that she knew she had made love to hundreds and hundreds of times. She had thought she was braced for anything, but what she found took her completely by surprise.

Edward had not changed at all!

The sheets only partially covered his finely-sculpted naked body. Even his teeth were perfectly straight. She could not resist pulling back the covers, to learn that even there, his endowment was no illusion, but his natural-born manhood.

And suddenly Vivian understood what was wrong with their relationship; Edward was all surface. With him there was nothing else, nothing deeper, no soul. He had the thin veneer of society, with which he had been born; good looks, good breeding, and that was it.

She laughed out loud, but softly, not wanting to wake him. She wondered how he would feel, suddenly helpless, when moments before he had been the most powerful person in the city. He would be crippled with out his sorcery, she was certain, like a month-old baby.

Vivian did not know how long she stood, staring down at him, pitying both him and herself. She made plans, now that Constantinople had crumbled, and was grateful that Edward had constructed his palace rather than imagining it. They would likely have been killed by the fall, had he followed the fashion of the other members of the Thirteen Families. Vivian wondered how many of them still survived. She could not say she regretted their imagined deaths. And Edward's physical palace would provide the means to establish a life elsewhere; she would take certain objects with her when she left, items that were portable yet valuable: the silver, a gold vase. But even the thought of sudden poverty did not dismay Vivian. She was brimming over with excitement, and stayed only for the pleasure of watching Edward's face when he awoke and discovered that he was powerless.

Then, suddenly, light flooded the room. The globe was back, and so was the city, restored to its original ostentation of imagination. As Vivian watched, reassembled palaces climbed slowly back into the sky as her plans and hopes sunk.

Behind her, Edward woke and, dreamy-eyed, reached for her. Vivian found herself suddenly, magically, in bed with him, cuddling beneath the covers. "I had the most awful dream," Edward whispered in her ear, running his hand down her back and along her buttocks. "I dreamed that the magic had gone away." He laughed, and began kissing her neck.

The magic had returned. But staring at Edward, who held her in his strong and powerful arms, Vivian knew that the magic was still gone.

IN THE REALM OF DRAGONS

Esther M. Friesner

As with John Morressy, mentioned earlier, I have reprinted several stories by Esther Friesner (b. 1951) in my anthologies of comic fantasy, and though she is best known for her wickedly humorous stories and novels – just check out for example Here be Demons *(1988),* Gnome Man's Land *(1991) or* Majyk by Accident *(1993), each of which are starts of series – she has written much more besides.* The Psalms of Herod *(1995), for instance, is a very dark dystopian post-holocaust novel, and several of the stories in her collection,* Death and the Librarian *(2002), including the following, explore the darker side of life.*

T HE BUS FROM PHILLY to New York was hot as hell. The air conditioning had broken down thirty miles out of the city. Not the best turn of events on a late September day that felt more like high August. Ryan Lundberg sat back limp in his seat without so much as a silent curse to spare for the sweltering air or the stink of urine from the tiny onboard bathroom. He had strength to save, a calling to heed. His eyes closed, dragged down by a weight of scales.

The little clay dragon in his hand smoldered and pulsed with the heat. He held it to his heart and told it to lie cool and still. Time enough for fire when they found Uncle Graham's murderers. Plenty of time for fire then. He drowsed, lapped in thoughts of flame. He was not even a little startled when his head nodded forward and he felt the sting of spiny barbels as his chin touched his chest.

He had not brought the dragon with him on the bus – he knew that with the same certainty that he knew his own name – yet here it was. *Here.* Not where his hands had placed it, tucked away safe in his top drawer at school, keeping watch over photographs, condoms, dryer-orphaned socks he never got around to throwing away. He'd found it in his wasn't-it-empty pocket after the bus left the rest stop on the turnpike. He did not try to understand how it had come to be there; that was to invite madness.

"I just draw the castles," Uncle Graham used to say. "People who ask me when they can move into them and if the rent includes unicorns, *they're* the ones who've got problems." And he would laugh.

Problems . . . The echo of the long-since spoken word faded into the far-and-far behind Ryan's eyes. *Yeah, Uncle Graham, there's more than a few of us around with problems now.* He flexed his hand and felt claws gouge deep chasms into the cheap plastic armrests. *Insanity is not what you see, but what you admit to seeing.* The litany he'd composed to hold onto some sliver of control warmed his mind. *Craziness is the compulsion to explain. The dragon that's suddenly, solidly here when I know I never brought – Let it be here unchallenged. And what I feel closing over me . . . let that come for me unchallenged too. Just accept the apparitions and no one needs to question if I'm numbered among the sane.*

You must do more than accept, the thin, sharp voice hissed in his head. *If you would have the reward I've promised, you know you must do more.*

A reward? Ryan repeated, wasting irony on the echoes in his skull. *A world!*

The key to Uncle Graham's apartment was also in his pocket, but at least he knew there was no magic connected with its presence. He had taken it himself, stolen it from Mom's dressing table last night, while she and Dad lay sleeping, after he awoke from the dream. The key had arrived with Uncle Graham's body, in a small envelope entrusted to the funeral director's care by his uncle's landlady. Included with the key was a friendly note urging Ryan's mother to come to New York as soon as possible to see about the disposal of Uncle Graham's possessions. That was the word she used: *disposal.* When Ryan read it, he thought of a hungry hole in the universe, devouring even the memory of a life that had been – honestly, now – an inconvenience and an embarrassment to so many, even to those who owed it love.

Ryan leaned his head against the window, feeling a film of sweat form between flesh and glass. The black kid in the seat ahead of him lost another battle with the window catch and cursed it out with a fluency one of Uncle Graham's graybeard wizards might have envied, stolen, but never improved. Ryan sighed, a hot gust of breath that only added to the bus's burden of muggy air.

He hadn't known deceit could be so exhausting. His parents had no idea where he was, what he intended to do once he got there. They thought he was back at college. The day after Uncle Graham's funeral, back home in Clayborn, Ryan's father had put him on the bus almost before it was light. When it reached Philadelphia he had only stayed in the city long enough to get some things from his dorm and give his folks a call to tell them that he had arrived safely. Then he went right back to the terminal and took the next bus to New York.

What would they say if they knew? Mom would have a cat-fit, most likely, and Dad . . . Dad would look at him *that* way again. *Why does Uncle Graham matter so to you? He's dead now, safely dead, but you – Why, Ryan? Why care? You're not—?*

And the question, even in thought, would die away, withered by the chill fear Ryan saw in his father's eyes, the fear should his only son give him the answer he could not stand to hear.

No, Dad, Ryan responded to his father's phantom face as the heat drank him further into sleep. *I'm not, don't worry, I'm not like him. Remember last year, the time old man Pitt showed up on our porch, mad as hell, yelling for you to keep me off his daughter? God, I don't think I ever did anything in my life that made you happier, not even the scholarship. Just the hint that I was screwing a girl, some girl, any girl –!* He shifted his shoulders against the rough fabric of the seat back. *So now is it okay with you if I care about Uncle Graham? If I'm not gay, is it safe for me to love him now that he's dead?*

In his cupped hands, the little clay dragon stretched out a single paw and dug into his flesh with the talons of dreams.

So you're Ryan. Graham's told me all about you.

Slim and dark and exotic looking, only just into the beauty of his twenties, Uncle Graham's lover offered a hand that closed around the little clay dragon and cupped it in transparent flesh long since returned to earth. Through the milky prison of those ghostly fingers, Ryan could still see the dragon swirled round-about with Christmas snow.

Ryan patted the last handful of snow into the dragon's side and smoothed it down, embedding jagged holly leaves for teeth, clusters of the bright red berries for eyes. His hands were damp and cold, even through his mittens. Mom was on the porch, holding her sweater tight around her, calling him home. Uncle Graham stood beside her, laughing at what his eleven-year-old nephew had done.

You know, most kids make snowmen.

Ryan shrugged. *I like dragons.*

Uncle Graham put his arm around Ryan's shoulders. *Watch out, kid. If you're any good at it, you get to leave this town.*

Ryan grinned. Eleven years old, he was just waking up to the possibility that he might want to live out his life somewhere else besides Clayborn.

Christmas in Clayborn. Christmas in a place where there were still things like corner drugstores with real working soda fountains, and big autumn bonfires down by the lakeshore, and pep rallies, and church bake sales where everyone knew how each housewife's brownies were going to taste even before they bit into one. There were still such things as high school sweethearts here, and special pools of warm, sweet, private darkness, down the shady orchard lanes, between the rolling Pennsylvania farmlands, where a boy could take his best girl and see how far she'd let him go.

And this was where Uncle Graham brought his New York lover. Even without people *knowing*, Bill would have drawn stares. On Christmas morning he sat right up close beside Uncle Graham, resting his chin on Uncle Graham's shoulder while the presents were unwrapped, softly exclaiming the proper oohs and aahs of wonder and feigned envy as each gift was brought to light.

Ryan watched, fascinated. Whatever Mom had said about Uncle Graham's way of life, the reality was infinitely stranger. He sat on the floor, like Uncle Graham and Bill, and felt as if he were peering through an overgrowth of jungle vines at bizarre creatures never before seen by the eyes of civilized man. Bill's low laugh sent peculiar chills coursing over Ryan's bones. His mind blew a glass bell jar over Uncle Graham's lover and held him there, safely sealed away for observation.

Outside there was snow, crusted over, hugging blue shadows to every curve of the slumbering land. It threw back the brilliant sunlight in harsh assaults of dazzling whiteness. Ryan sat at his father's feet and looked up to see a taut jawline, a gaze fixed and fastened on Uncle Graham and Bill. Ryan felt his father's hands come to rest on his shoulders many times that morning – more times than felt right, when right means usual. The sunlight struck a wall of darkness cast by the shadow of the wings that Ryan's father called up out of empty air to mantle over his son. *This is mine; you won't touch him* hung across the room like a fortified castle wall that Ryan's father made and maintained and walked guard on from that moment until the day Uncle Graham and his lover left to go back to the city.

Ryan's father was not invisible and Uncle Graham was not blind.

There were no letters from Uncle Graham the rest of the winter, no calls, no more news than if New York were really a cloud kingdom full of so many sweet, glorious pastimes and amusements that the souls lucky enough to live there lost all track of time as it was reckoned on the earth. No one said anything, not even when Ryan's birthday came and went without a card from Uncle Graham, without a word.

And then, in late November, the telephone shrilled. Ryan answered. "Hello?"

"Chessie?" The voice was broken, shattered, and around the shards it sobbed the nickname Uncle Graham had always used for his beloved sister.

"Uncle Graham?" Ryan's cheeks flamed. His voice was changing. It was a sharp humiliation every time someone mistook him for his mother on the telephone. "It's me, Ryan."

"For God's sakes, Ryan, get your mom!" Uncle Graham's words stumbled through tears, his breath rags of sound torn out of his chest.

"What's the matter?"

"Just get her. Please."

So Ryan did as he was told, and when his mother got over the surprise of hearing from her brother after so long, there was worse to come. "How are you?" was slashed off into, "Oh, my God! Oh, Graham, I'm so sorry! When did he—?"

The little dragon shuddered in Ryan's hand, breaking the spell. His mother's face froze, then crackled into void, the shattering of ice over black water. Bill's death seized Ryan and roughly shoved him from the haven of his home, sending him lurching forward through the gateway of the hours, bright and dark. Bill's hand faded from ghostly essence to purest air, a cool breath across hot clay that shivered like an egg about to bring forth monsters, mysteries. Ryan's eyelids fluttered, but when he shifted his weight again, instead of the rasp of cheap seatcovering against his jeans he heard the genteel creak of fine leather as he settled onto the green couch in Uncle Graham's apartment.

Bill's funeral was over. Ryan didn't remember too much about it. Mostly he recalled the hot, angry eyes of hard-faced strangers in black. They scowled at him and Mom and Uncle Graham where the three of them stood huddled together on the far side of the open grave. He never found out who they were. The minister read through the service for the dead and Uncle Graham cried. Ryan saw one of the hot-eyed people – an old woman with blue-rinsed hair – writhe her red mouth around an ugly word before pressing a wadded lace handkerchief to her wrinkled lips and bursting into tears.

Mom drove Uncle Graham back to his place in Manhattan, a down-town loft in what had once been an old factory. It was like having one big room for everything – eating and sleeping and watching TV. The only fully cut-off spaces were the bathroom and the kitchen.

There was also a space where Uncle Graham worked, a drafting board and an easel, the floor beneath both liberally freckled with paint. Some men left Clayborn on their wits, some on their brawn. Uncle Graham had soared free of the town on dreams of fantastic beings given life by brush and pen. The loft walls were hung with Uncle Graham's paintings, commissioned illustrations for books – wonderful, terrible, entrancing books, the kind of books that people back in Clayborn pronounced *cute* and bought, if they bought them at all, for their children.

The couch creaked again.

She's making tea.

Uncle Graham's ghost sat at the far end of the couch, head cradled back against the butter-soft upholstery, arms outflung, eyes fixed on the ceiling. He had his feet up on a coffee table that looked as if it had calved from a glacier.

"What?" Ryan's voice barely scaled above a whisper.

"I said your mother's in the kitchen, making tea." And Uncle Graham was suddenly no more a ghost than the twelve-year-old self through whose eyes Ryan now saw everything.

"Oh." Ryan rested his palms on the couch and felt perspiration seep between flesh and leather. They sat there that way for a long time. Ryan heard the shrilling of the kettle and the sound of traffic from outside and the familiar, comforting clanks and clinks of Mom fumbling about in a kitchen not her own. He knew she would sooner die than ask Uncle Graham where he kept things. Dad called it the female equivalent of how a man refuses to ask directions when he's lost on the road.

"Ryan?" Uncle Graham's voice came so loud, so abruptly, that Ryan jumped at the sound of his own name. "Come here, Ryan." Uncle Graham was sitting slumped forward now, his big hands linked and dangling between his knees. Ryan hesitated, fearing the great grief he saw in his uncle's eyes. Uncle Graham could see only that Ryan remained where he was. "Don't worry; I won't touch you," he said.

Ryan did not move.

"I'm clean, you know," Uncle Graham said. "Negative. Bill used to make fun of me, call me paranoid, but—" Some phantom sound escaped his chest, laugh or sob or cough quickly forced back down. "Anyway, like I said, I won't touch you. I promise. Your father wouldn't like that."

Suddenly Ryan wore his father's absence like horns. "Couldn't get off work to come up here with us for the fun'ral," he mumbled.

"Of course not." Uncle Graham was too done out, too indifferent to challenge the lie.

Ryan . . .

Ryan saw the green glow cupped in Uncle Graham's palm, the sheen of a perfectly applied glaze, the ripple of tiny, incised scales like feathers lying sleek on a bird's wing. He sidled nearer on the couch, the cushions squeaking and whispering under his thighs. He craned his neck to see what wonder his uncle held out as an offering.

"It's a dragon," Uncle Graham said, letting the small clay figurine tumble from his palm. Ryan's hands shot out automatically, catching it in midair. Uncle Graham laughed. "Nice fielding. You must be a star with the Little League."

A shrug was Ryan's answer. He was too busy rolling the dragon from hand to hand, feeling its weight, its slick finish, the cold beauty of its eyes.

"Hematite," Uncle Graham said, pointing out the gleaming shapes like silvered almonds imbedded beneath the creature's brow ridges. "It's supposed to center you, keep you calm, let you see all things with tranquility." He closed his eyes and passed one hand over his forehead, brushing away a flutter of black wings.

"It's beautiful," Ryan said. Here, alone with his uncle, he could say such things. At home, with Dad watching – so closely now, so carefully – he would have limited his comments to "Cool."

"It's yours. I made it for – I want you to have it." He opened his eyes and managed a weak smile. "Late birthday gift. Sorry I missed it."

"'S okay." Ryan stroked the dragon's back. The beast was curled in around itself as if for sleep, wings folded back, forepaws demurely resting beneath the barbelled chin. The scaly lips were closed, except where the two most prominent fangs could not possibly be contained. But the eyes were open and saw all.

"Here we are!" Mom burst from the kitchen, triumphant, an assortment of steaming mugs on the tray she carried before her. She sandwiched Ryan in between herself and Uncle Graham, weaving her own spells of strength and militant normalcy from the clatter of teaspoons and the hush of sugar crystals cascading into tea. There were even some cookies on a plate.

"Mom, look what Uncle Graham gave me," Ryan said, holding out the dragon for inspection. "He made it himself."

"It's wonderful, Graham," Mom said sincerely. "Is this something new for you? Are you branching out from painting?"

"I am definitely making some changes," Uncle Graham said.

They drank their tea. That was the last time Ryan saw his uncle alive.

That year at Christmas time Uncle Graham didn't come to visit. He never came to visit them again. There were no letters and no telephone calls, although once, on Ryan's thirteenth birthday, a flat, oblong package arrived for him from New York City.

It was a book, a book enclosed between boards embossed with swirling gold and silver letters that eddied over depths of royal blue and green. "*In the Realm of Dragons*," he read aloud, wondering why his uncle had sent him a picture book clearly meant for little kids. Then he saw the artist's byline and understood: Uncle Graham had done the illustrations. He let the book fall open in his lap.

Page after page of dragons mounted the purple skies of evening, beating wings of gold and green and scarlet. ("The dragon is a nocturnal beast. He loves the hours of darkness.") Youngling dragons peeped from shattered eggshells, stripling worms engaged in mock battles to establish territory and dominion. ("The dragon when it is grown chooses its company with care.") Maidens wreathed with flowers were led forth from villages paved with mud and manure to be offered up to the magnificent beasts, only to be spurned, or simply overlooked. ("It is a false tale that claims dragons desire the flesh of fair maidens, for what mere mortal beauty could hope to equal their own?")

And in the end, there were the pictures of knights – so proud, so arrogant in armor – swords bloodied with the lives of dragons. Here a warrior lurked like the meanest footpad to slay a dragon when it came to drink at a twilight stream. There the severed heads of many worms dangled as obscene trophies from the rafters of a great hall where lords and ladies swilled wine and grew brutish in revelry. The unseeing eyes of the dead were mirrors that hung in silent judgment over their supposed conquerors, each silvery globe giving back an image of man to make the skin crawl and the soul weep. ("Men slay dragons because they fear them, or do not understand them, or because other men tell them that this is what men do. And some destroy them because of how they see themselves captured in the dragon's eyes.")

The last page was an enchantment of art. A single dragon's eye filled it, infusing mere paper with a silver splendor reflecting Ryan's awestruck face. The boy reached out, fingers hovering a hairsbreadth above the sheen that pulled him heartfirst into the dragon's all-knowing gaze.

That night he dreamed dragons.

He woke into dreams, rising naked from a pool of waters silvered by twin moons burning low in a verdant sky. Drops of water fell from his wingtips, trembled at the points of his claws. Far away, over the hills where golden grasses nodded and bent beneath the wind's kiss, came the sound of hoarse voices mangling music.

He climbed the hills, his wings dragging the ground behind him. The air was sweet, heavy as honey. He shook away the last vestiges of human thought and opened his dragon mind to a universe unfolding its most secret mysteries. That was when he knew at last that he could fly.

The air was his realm; he laid claim to it with the first surge of his emerald-keeled breastbone against the sky. Its warmth bore him up from beneath with the steady love of his father's hands. His great head swerved slowly from left to right, his breath glittering with frost in the higher atmospheres, showering the bosom of the land with diamonds.

Below him he saw them, the villagers with their mockery of musical instruments, their faces upturned like so many oxen startled by lightning. The maiden was among them. They had dressed her in white, though even from this height he could see the thin cloth of her gown dappled brown with mud at the hem. Her arms were smooth and bare, her golden hair almost obscured by roses.

He felt hunger burn the pit of his cavernous belly. He stooped to the earth, wings artfully angled to ride the edges of only those air currents that would bring him spiraling down to his waiting prize. His mouth gaped, and licks of flame caressed his scaly cheeks like the kiss of mist off the sea.

And then air before him turned from native element and ally to enemy. The crystalline road solidified, a giant's hands molding themselves from emptiness. He slammed into the immobile lattice of their interlaced fingers, and the impact exploded into a sheet of dazzling pain, an echoing wave of light that hurled him back down the sky, back into the waters of the lake, back into the shuddering boy's body waking in its bed to the dark and loneliness and loss.

All that was left was a whisper: *Not yet. I give you this power, but you must earn its reward.*

Ryan hugged the sheet and blanket to his chest, cold with sweat, and asked the shadows for meaning. Then he became aware of something more than sweat making his pajamas cling to the skin between his legs. In silence, face burning, he stripped them off and stuffed them down the laundry chute, some part of his mind pretending that the gaping black slide into the basement would really send them falling into oblivion.

He did not like to think of the dream after that. He took the book from Uncle Graham and put it away in the attic.

The pulldown ladder to the attic's trove of dust and willfully forgotten memory was springloaded tight. The dangling rope that raised and lowered the hatch, improperly released, closed with a bang to jerk Ryan awake in time to bark his shins against the packing-crate coffee table in a friend's dorm room. He was waiting for someone. He had nothing to do while he waited. He glanced down at the table and picked up a magazine.

He didn't notice that it was a gay men's magazine at first. It was folded open to a beer ad. He picked it up out of boredom and thumbed through it out of curiosity. Uncle Graham's name leaped to his eyes from a photo spread covering the most recent Gay Pride march in Manhattan.

It was not Uncle Graham. Not with that face paint, not with that gaunt, ferocious grin like a wolf's skull. He wore clothing that was ill-considered plumage, meant to startle. It only put Ryan in mind of how old whores were typed in older movies: spotty, papery, raddled skin beneath the monster's pathetic mask of carnival. Uncle Graham marched with arms around two other men, one in amateurish drag, the other sheathed in neon pink hotpants and a T-shirt cropped to leave his midriff bare. Across his forehead he had painted the letters H.I.V.

When Ryan went home for Christmas, he told Mom about the photograph. All she said was, "I know." She showed him the letters she'd written to her brother, every one returned unopened, refused. Only once had he sent her words back accompanied by his own, a piece of lined paper torn from a spiral-bound notebook and stuffed into a manila envelope with the rejected letter. *You never liked cemeteries, Chessie, it said. Why hang on the gate pretending you understand the business of the dead? You need magic to look through my eyes, and you were born fettered to the world. But there is magic, Chessie. It lives and walks at our backs, beautiful and deadly, and when it gets hungry it takes its sacrifice. If one of us had to make that payment, to have our heart betrayed, I'm glad it was me. Leave it so.*

Mom asked Ryan if he remembered Bill; he nodded. "He's trying to die," she said. "He's running after his own death. Even after what Bill did to him – How the hell do you argue with *that* kind of proof you've been cheated on? – even now he still loves him." Mom sighed. "If he finds what he's looking for, do you think he'd call to let us know? I can't bear the thought of him dying like that, without—" She began to cry.

Her tears were for nothing and for everything.

The little clay dragon sighed in dreams, rumbled with ill-banked fires. The rumbling rose up, but by the time it reached Ryan's ears it had become the urgent ringing of a telephone.

He was only half awake when he answered it, a towel swaddling his waist, up at a godawful-hour of the morning because he'd had to sign up for godawful-hour courses in this, his second year of study. The tooth-brush was still dripping in his hand while he heard his father's voice telling him that Uncle Graham was dead. Uncle Graham's head was shattered on the pavement in front of the old factory where he lived. The cops had called Mom even earlier that morning with the news. There was more that the police had told Ryan's father because they didn't think Mom could stand to know the other things that had been done to her brother. He shared it all willingly with Ryan because he thought his son was man enough to know, and because it was too much horror for one man to bear knowing alone.

And maybe too he shared it as a warning.

The closed casket under its blanket of roses blocked most of the aisle on the bus. Everyone from church was there, saying over and over again how talented Graham was and how wonderful his paintings were and how sad, how very sad that he was dead so young. Mrs. Baumann from the drugstore perched on the armrest of the black kid's seat and told Mom that at least Graham was at peace now. Comfort cloyed the air worse than the mingled reek of all the flower arrangements people had sent. Everyone was there, saying all the right things, leaving all mention of murder outside, with the dogs.

The black kid finally managed to jimmy the window enough so that it dragged in its track but slid open. The inrush of fresh air blew away Mrs. Baumann, the roses, the closed black box, blew Ryan all the way back into his old bed at home, the night after the funeral.

He lay there unsleeping, painting the ceiling with endless fantasies of should-have-told-thems. Drowsing at last, he rolled over onto his side and felt something jab him in the hip. He reached between the mattress and the box spring and pulled out Uncle Graham's book.

"I thought I put this away, up in the attic," he said aloud. The silver and gold letters on the cover glowed with their own light. Ryan licked his lips and tasted lake water. He opened the book and read it again, after all the years.

There was a page he found that might have slipped from memory, if memory could ever lose hold of images that clamored to be recalled. Two young men – squires, not knights – laid up a snare of marvelous cunning and cruelty outside a dragon's vine-hung lair. One peered from ambush, knotted club in hand, while the other stood at the cave mouth holding out a sapphire of untellable purity and fire. He was fair, the one who played the lure, his eyes the rival of the sapphire meant to cozen the venerable worm from sanctuary. Already a single green-scaled paw crept into the dappled sunlight. The lure smiled, cold and exquisite as a lord of elven. Behind a fall of rocks, his confederate readied the dragon's death.

Both their faces were plain to see. Not a line could be forgotten. Ryan closed his eyes, and still their faces were outlined against his sightlessness as if with wires burning white-hot. He threw the book across the room and bolted for his bedroom door.

He stepped from bare wood onto naked air. His wings snapped open without the need for any conscious command to reach them. His head-long fall became a naturally graceful glide that carried him down, down to the vast sea of forest and the piteous, defiant roars of a dying dragon and the face of a maiden, lovelier than any girl he had ever known, wreathed with roses.

I give you this power, but you must earn its reward.

He awoke knowing what he must do.

He awoke half choked by the stink of exhaust fumes as the bus pulled into the Port Authority terminal in New York.

Ryan did not have enough money for a cab so he took the bus down-town. He got off at the wrong stop, got lost, wandered in sullen pilgrimage through streets where crumpled newspapers blew like tumbleweeds. Finally he broke down and asked directions.

It was sunset when he found Uncle Graham's address. A flimsy strip of black-and-yellow tape flapped wearily from the hinges of the big entry door to Uncle Graham's building. Ryan's taloned paws moved grandly, daintily overstepping the dull red-brown stains spattering the threshold and the sidewalk before it. Silence sang a hymn of welcome as he entered the loft, the last of the sunlight adding its own wash of color to the row of paintings Uncle Graham had left behind.

The girl from upstairs came down to see what was going on, alerted by the noise of a slamming door. Ryan told her, "I'm here to dispose of my uncle's things." He showed her the key and told her enough about Uncle Graham to convince her of his legitimate right to be there.

She shrugged, thin shoulders sheathed in stretch jersey glimpsed through thin brown hair. "Save it, okay? I couldn't tell if you're making it up or not anyway. I hardly knew anything about the guy. I mean, sure, I knew he was, like, gay, and he painted. I was scared for awhile after he got killed, but—"

"I really am his nephew," Ryan insisted, clutching the doorpost until he imagined he must have driven his talons inches deep into the wood.

"Hey, no argument. You got the key." Another shrug, welcoming him to help himself to the apartment and all found so long as he did not trespass on her well cultivated indifference.

She wasn't pretty. She was what the fashion world would call a waif. Ryan was more attracted to girls whose breasts were larger than orange pips. Still he invited her in. At first she declined, but she called herself an artist too. She had never had the chance to study Uncle Graham's work up close before. She might have come downstairs anytime while Uncle Graham was still alive and asked to see his paintings; she never did. She admitted to Ryan that the idea had never crossed her mind.

"Why not?" he asked.

Again that shifting of the shoulders to let a person slide safely out from beneath uncomfortable questions. "I didn't want to intrude. I thought, you know, what if he's got someone over?"

He found tea to serve her. She drank in short, dull slurps, her eyes forever darting sideways to keep him under surveillance. She wasn't pretty and she wasn't his type and he wasn't attracted to her at all.

What'samatter, Lundberg, doncha like girls?

He gave her all the charm he had, the way he'd done with Karen Pitt, the way he'd perfected with all the college girls he'd ever sweet-talked into bed, the way that proved to everyone who never asked for proof that he wasn't like his uncle. Before she left, he got to kiss her and buy back his peace.

Uncle Graham's bed was made of pale pine with a bowed headboard, the kind you order from L.L. Bean catalogs. One of great-grandma Ruth's handsewn quilts lay across it, a bearpaw design in red and blue. Ryan lay down on the bed, quilt and all, fully clothed, and rested the little clay dragon on his chest. He gazed into its silvery eyes until he felt the lake waters rolling off his flanks and the alien moons of the dragons' realm welcomed him home.

He circled the skybowl once, his scent marking air as his hunting ground and his alone. Below, he dreamed the peasants singing for him to descend and accept the sacrifice. *Later*, he thought, and the power of his mind rumbled across the sky like thunder. *When I have earned it.*

The thunder of his thoughts rolled back to overwhelm him, knocking him sideways into a spin. When he righted himself he saw that the green land had vanished, the crude songs of the rustics thinned into the braying of traffic, the shriek of sirens. The stone forest of the city stood stark against the moon. He dipped into the canyons, following a trail of vision.

It was easy hunting; he knew the prey. He found them with his mind, not with his eyes. They were in a bar, drinking beer, laughing and talking and sometimes trying to get the attention of the women. The lure was loudest, telling the women what he'd like to do to them, telling them how grateful they'd be, telling them they were frigid, bitches, bull-dykes when they turned away. The killer with the club only smiled, and sometimes one of the women would smile back. That made the lure scowl and call her a whore.

"Hey! What you starin' at?"

Ryan gasped with surprise as the lure's hand shot out and closed around the collar of his shirt, yanking him forward. Stale beer stank in his nostrils and sprayed saliva dotted his cheeks as the lure shouted, "What, you see something you *like*, faggot?"

"Get your fucking hands off me!" Teeth like steak knives ground against each other as Ryan smacked the lure's grip away. By chance one talon scored the skin of the lure's forearm, a long, shallow cut. Sapphire eyes widened in childlike awe to see the blood go trickling down.

"Shit, he pulled a knife on me!" he yelled.

"What knife? Where?" the killer drawled, glancing at Ryan's empty hands. "You're crazy, Ted, you know that?"

"Stinking fag *knifed* me," the lure insisted. "Goddamn it, this whole neighborhood's crawling with 'em, like roaches."

"Who are you calling a fag?" Ryan asked quietly. Being what he was, he did not need to raise his voice to make the menace heard.

The killer gave Ryan a slow and easy grin. "Don't pay attention to him. He's been drinking. He don't know what he's saying."

"No shit." Ryan readjusted the lay of his shirt, sounding so calm he astonished himself. He had no idea of how he had become real in this place, how these two, his quarry, had gone from being part of a dragon's vision to tangibility. He did not know why he felt the dragon's body on him so surely that he wanted to grab these men, shake them, and demand, *Can't you see what I am?*

"What the hell are you doing, talking to this guy?" the lure cried stridently, tugging at the killer's sleeve. "You see what he *did* to me?" He stuck his bloodied arm out for inspection.

"With *what?*" the dark one replied. He sounded bored. "A fuckin' fingernail? You see he don't got a knife, so with what? Jesus, grow up. You probably did it to yourself."

"With *what?*" the lure mimicked, spreading empty hands.

"Asshole," the other muttered and turned his back.

Ryan walked out of the bar. The air was cooler than it had been all day and there was the promise of rain. He walked to the corner to check the street signs. The bar was only two blocks away from Uncle Graham's apartment. *This is where it began*, he thought. He wondered which way they would walk when they finally left the bar. He hoped they would walk together at least part of the way. He needed them to be in the same place at the same time. Then, one fiery breath, one slash of his claws, one short snap of jaws that could sever the body of a full grown stag—

It is a well-known fact that dragons do not forget those they love. Their love is always loyal, sometimes blind. This is perhaps a failing.

He took to the sky again to scout his place of ambush. He was fortunate: The area was rich in alleyways. He landed lightly on the roof of the building across the street from the bar, warm tar underfoot making his paws itch, his toes curl. He set his silver eyes high, telling the hours by the slow journey of the moon.

His prey emerged when midnight was two hours gone. A woman was with them, holding fast to the arm of the killer while the lure tagged along behind, head down, shoulders hunched forward. Her hair was the color of lemon-yellow paint and just as lifeless, her face crumpled with rude laughter. She clung to the killer's broad shoulders, her stumbling feet scraping the sidewalk. The lure stared at her, disgust very plain on his face.

The three of them wove their way across the street, tracing the pattern of the drunkards' pavane. High on his perch, the dragon could still snuff up the reek of beer, sour wine, sweat, and old perfume. He flapped his wings once to lift himself into flight, taking care to do it so that the sound remained as muffled as possible. He wondered whether the men intended to share the woman and whether the woman wanted that. He knew that if they desired it, her wants would be nothing.

He hovered over them as they walked, a shadow on the pavement in their wake, a dark shape gliding over rooftops, safe from detection in a city whose inhabitants so seldom raised their eyes to heaven. He watched them stop at street corners to laugh; he saw them stop in the middle of the street to argue.

"What the hell you doin', Ted?" The dark one glanced over his shoulder, the woman wrapped around him like a cape. "You still here? You wanna take a left back there on that last block if you wanna get home."

"I know how to get home." The lure's chin rose, daring his companion to contradict him. "I thought maybe you could use some help with her. You know, in case she pukes all over you before you get her back to your place."

The killer laughed. "Okay, come on."

"I'm not gonna puke," the woman objected. Her eyes narrowed as she glared at the lure. "You're just pissed 'cause you couldn't find someone to go home with you."

"Like I'd want to screw what comes into that bar," the lure replied loftily.

"Yeah?" The woman looked canny. "What *kind* of bars do you like, baby?" She made it mean things.

"Shut up, bitch," he snapped. He would have hit her if his friend were not there. The dragon knew this. As it was, the woman turned to the dark one, squawking indignantly.

"Hey, baby, it's okay, that's just him, he's a little nuts, you know?" the killer said. "Don't push his buttons, okay? And don't go saying shit like that about my buddy." Something in his voice tightened by an almost imperceptible degree. Drunk as she was, the woman sensed it. The dragon saw her cringe.

"I didn't mean nothing," she said.

"Like hell," the lure snarled. "'What *kind* of bars?' Like I don't know! Stupid damn—"

"She don't know you, Ted, that's all," the killer said. "If she did, she'd never even think of saying something like that about you." He showed his teeth, and the lure returned the gesture, a look too sharp to be just a smile. The dragon saw them exchange the secret of a crime in a single glance.

The dragon came to earth. By rights, the walls of the alley it chose should have been too narrow to accommodate its wingspan, yet they did. This place was perfect, only a few yards ahead on the prey's path, on a street whose emptiness was a gift. It waited. The argument was over. They would all continue down the street in this direction now. The dragon had decided on fire. Fire was quick and clean, if indiscriminate. It was too bad about the woman.

Footsteps rang on the pavement. The dragon's eyelids, smooth as shell for all their scales, drew back until the darkness filled with the silver light of its eyes. It heard the woman say, "What the hell's that in there?" and the killer answer, "Who gives a—?"

Then he had them. No deer was ever so transfixed by the headlights' glare. The brilliance of his gaze washed over them, a stark light to shear away everything but the truth. He gathered his breath for the flame.

And in a distant room a dreamer held a book open to its last page, falling into the silver eye of a dragon and seeing only truth. *I can't.*

The fire died in his throat. He felt the dragon's form, the dragon's power slip from him. The image of the rose-wreathed maiden blew away like dust. The splendor of his eyes dimmed and vanished, leaving the alley lit only by the spill of the streetlamp. Rain began to fall, mizzling, penetrating. He felt cold.

"Who's in there? Come out!" the killer shouted. The spell was broken. Ryan crept forward because he didn't know what else he could do. "It's the kid from the bar!" The dark one sounded genuinely surprised.

Not too surprised to seize Ryan's arm and squeeze it hard as he jerked him forward. "What d'you think you're doing, following us?" The fingers drove deeper into soft flesh. "You some kinda pervert?"

"I *told* you what he is!" the lure cried stridently. "I can *smell* 'em."

"Yeah, maybe you can," the killer muttered. His grip shifted to Ryan's shirtfront. "You were right the last time."

"Honey, let him go; he's just a kid," the woman pleaded.

"This *kid*—" he gave Ryan a shake to make his teeth clatter "—was in the bar before, trying to start something. What d'you wanna start, *kid*?"

"Watch out for him; he's got a knife on him," the lure piped up.

"Big deal." The killer reached into the pocket of his jeans. "So do I."

The blade snicked silver in the shadows. Ryan saw the reflection of his eyes along the shining edge. He remembered all the things that had been done to Uncle Graham, the things the police told Dad, the things Dad only hinted at to him, shaking. These two had only smashed his uncle's skull after they had done everything else they wanted. He heard a plaintive voice inside him say, *They killed me without a moment's hesitation, Ryan. I know I was looking to die, but like that? As less than a man, less than an animal, just a toy for willful, sadistic children? They'll kill you without a single regret. It will shatter Chessie's heart. Why didn't you destroy them when you had the power?*

And Ryan's heart answered, *Because that would make me one of them.*

"Jesus, let him go," the woman whined. "You're not gonna cut him, are you?"

"You don't wanna see, close your eyes," the killer instructed her.

"Oh, shit, you're crazy too." With a shake of her head she tried to bolt, but the lure grabbed her and held her fast.

"You don't wanna go running for the cops, *do* you?" he hissed in her ear. "Nah, I bet you don't." He seized her straggly hair and punched her hard in the face before she could scream. She groaned and folded to the ground.

"Hey! What'd you do to the bitch?" The killer spoke with the same heat reserved for street punks caught putting scratches on a new car.

"Ah, so what?" The lure shrugged. "Like you can't do what you want with her now?"

The knife rose, a straight line of cold blue across Ryan's sight. He shut his eyes. A fist slammed into his shoulder.

"Uh-uh, pervert," the killer told him. "You gotta see it coming. I wanna see you see. Open 'em." Another violent shake of Ryan's shirtfront. "*Open* 'em!"

So Ryan opened his eyes.

Screams.

Screams not his, screams that battered his ears as the pure white light flooded the alleyway again. They jarred him free of his captive body, throwing him skywards into the rain. He gasped to feel chill droplets pattering over skin still human, then turned in wingless mid-flight to look down at what this release had left behind.

He expected to see the two men staring up after him, mouths

agape like the lowest wonderstruck peasant of the dragons' realm. Instead he saw them crouching in the alleyway, on their knees in filth, hands trembling before their faces. He realized that they were trying not to look, trying to shield their eyes from the assault of sight. He let go his tenuous hold on the air and touched the ground behind them, beside the fallen woman.

He saw the dragon's eyes.

It was a great beast, huge, splendid, grander by far than the youngling worm that once housed Ryan's soul. The alley walls strained, bricks and mortar crumbling under the pressure of containing it. It lay with paws folded under its jagged chin, its gleaming eyes regarding the two men almost casually, in after-thought. There was no intent of a killing in its attitude. It only looked at them, slumbrous, steadily.

They tried to look away and could not, tried to close their eyes and found the lids frozen wide, tried to make screens of their hands and knew a strange paralysis that withheld that mercy. They had to look. They had no choice but to see.

And some destroy them because of how they see themselves in the dragon's eyes.

In one eye's curved and shining surface, the killer crouched in a dark place, jabbing sticks at phantoms, wailing with fear. His naked body was covered with lesions, his limbs skeletal, his face all blades of bone beneath a patchwork of bare, purple-veined scalp and pitiful tufts of hair.

In the other eye, the lure clung to the killer's arm, pressed himself against that towering, healthy body. He let his mouth wander at will, his eyes holding all the ecstasy of long-deferred fulfillment. His hands were everywhere, touching, caressing, claiming all he desired for his own. *I want this*, his image mouthed in the monster's mirrored gaze. *I've always wanted this . . . I've always wanted you.*

The dragon raised his head and blinked once, shuttering away the vision. When he opened them again, he disappeared.

The two men turned to stare at each other, the rain running down their faces. The woman stirred and whimpered, waking. They did not hear her. Ryan stooped to murmur in her ear, "Get up. We've got to get out of here." She cursed and shoved him aside.

So he ran away. He ran alone, stumbling down the rainwashed street, wondering how far he would be allowed to go before the spell of the dragon's gaze broke, before the others came after him. He thought he could hear them behind him, coming up fast. His breath burned in his chest. He did not dare to look over his shoulder. His hunters were as certain a presence as the night. He could almost feel the icy breath of the knife on his flesh.

He ran harder, and the harder he ran, the thicker the air around him became. He needed to fight a passage through it. His feet were weights instead of wings. The wet pavement turned to tar, sucking him down, holding him back against his will, keeping him prisoner. There were more enchantments loose in this world than the magic of dragons. Dark things commanded more servants here than things of light. Ryan opened his mouth to scream for help and no sound came. Again and again he filled his lungs, again and again only black silence packed his chest and throat and mouth like wool. The tar hardened to stone, holding his feet; he could not move at all. He gathered his breath for a last cry before the hunters had him—

—and woke screaming in his uncle's bed.

He was sitting upright, stiff as a doll. His clothes stuck to his skin. The waterlight that came before the dawn whitened the windows. He swung his feet out of bed and heard a crunch underfoot when they touched the floor.

Beside the bed, the little clay dragon lay shattered. He picked up all the pieces, glad to see that they were fairly large. Some glue should fix it. He assembled it dry on the coffee table and studied the results. All that was missing was the eyes.

He made himself some instant coffee and locked up the apartment when he left. The street was damp and cool from the rain. Puddles of oil in the gutter gave back rainbows. He stood in the doorway, looking down. The threshold stains did not stand out at all now that the concrete was wet. Soon who would know what had happened here? He fingered the tattered end of black and yellow tape still caught in the door hinge and tore off as much of it as he could.

He wondered whether he should call the police when he reached Penn Station and give them an anonymous tip about who had killed his uncle and where to find them. He could describe them exactly, send the police to the bar that was their hangout—

– if the police would take the time to listen to a caller who refused to admit how he knew so much. And if he explained? They'd believe it when the sky between worlds split open. But he had to do something. This was all he could think of to do.

He decided that the first thing he should do, even before he made the call, was to go and see whether there really was a bar where his vision had placed it. He began to walk.

The police cars were there when he turned the corner. Two of them were pulled up at the curb in front of the alleyway, blue and red lights flashing. The ambulance was sandwiched in between them. It wouldn't be going anywhere in a hurry, but there was no need for speed. The stretcher slipping away into the back held a zippered bag.

The killer glowered and shouted obscenities at the yellow-haired woman talking to the cops. His hands were manacled behind his back, but there was nothing to stop his mouth. Passersby on their way to work or homeward bound from a life between sunset and dawn stopped to listen. The man did not care for the rights he had been read, it seemed. He was willing to tell the world what he'd done. He didn't think of it as crime, but a service. He had cleansed, purified, rescued society from a monster. He was a hero, a knight, a slayer of unnatural horrors! How dare they call it murder, even when the victim had once been his friend?

"Honest, I don't know why," the yellow-haired woman was saying as the man was forced into one of the police cars. "We was all going along here, real late, and all of a sudden—"

She turned and saw Ryan. For an instant her bruised face flushed, then bloomed, its unmarred beauty embraced by roses.

Then the policeman said, "Ma'am?" She shuddered and shook off all seeming. She went back to telling the officer what she had witnessed.

Ryan stooped at the barricade of black-and-yellow tape. The rose was red without holding memories of blood or fire. It had no thorns. He breathed its fragrance all the way to the train station, all the way home.

FOREVER

Tim Lebbon

Tim Lebbon (b. 1969) has exploded on the fantasy scene during the last few years. He has won two British Fantasy Awards and a Bram Stoker Award for his short fiction and his work has been optioned for the screen on both sides of the Atlantic. His books include the novels Mesmer *(1997),* Face *(2001),* The Nature of Balance *(2001), and* Until She Sleeps *(2002) and the collections* White and Other Tales of Ruin *(1999),* As the Sun Goes Down *(2000), and* Fears Unnamed *(2004).*

The following story, which was specially written for this anthology, is set in the same world as his as yet unpublished dark fantasy novel Dusk. *In this world, magic has withdrawn itself after misuse by the mages (Angel and her brother S'Hivez). Since magic has gone, the land itself is in decline and the populace of the huge island of Noreela is apathetic and passive. Far to the north of Noreela lies a large, frozen island. The mages and the remains of their army were driven here after the Cataclysmic Wars a century before "Forever" takes place. And here they remain, awaiting their chance at revenge, awaiting the return of magic.*

O N DANA'MAN THE cold bit hard, ice informed thought, frost froze dreams of freedom, and duty and supplication were the way. On Dana'Man there was preparation for a war long in coming, with no sign of its beginning yet in sight. On Dana'Man – island of the damned, natural home only to glaciers and snow demons and the ice people – life was hard, but death was harder.

The mages needed every man and woman for their army; death was unpardonable.

From a distance the island seemed huge and barren, a desert of ice and snow with a few silent volcanoes protruding like the fingertips of buried giants. It stretched east and west farther than the curves of the world, and its widest point north to south would take twenty days to traverse. Occasionally a localised melt would occur when the island's only active volcano erupted, and the resultant floods would rearrange its geography for generations to come.

Closer in there were settlements, scattered across the low-lying plains at the foot of the volcanoes, staggered along the seashore, a few further inland. Some were long-deserted, others appeared to be thriving. Smoke rose high from countless fires, boats bobbed between ice floating at the coast, and occasionally a hawk would drift down out of the constant cloud cover, disgorge its passenger and then rise up again to its customary heights. There were even a few farms where snow and ice had been painstakingly removed and the ground given over to sparse greenery.

Closer still, one settlement clung to a slip of rock that protruded half a mile out to sea, curving around and forming a natural breakwater and harbour. It was here at Newland that the mages and the remains of their army had landed over a century before, driven out of Noreela far to the south and sent into exile. Fitting, then, that their new Krote army called this place their home. Boats and ships of all sizes rested here, most of them small fishing sloops, a couple of transports for carrying materials and people around Dana'Man, and two larger vessels brimming with tools of war. The harbour was a busy place. It stank of freshly-landed fish – much of it rank and inedible, gone to rot – and echoed to the sound of metal on metal from glowing metal-smiths at its very tip. One of the warships was moored at the breakwater, and once each day a giant trolley was pushed back and forth, the ship weighed down with more weapons.

At the landward end of the breakwater, on a slope where Newland spread and cast its roots into Dana'Man proper, a collection of timber and ice buildings was laid out in a regular, monotonous design. Pennants floated above some buildings, others were bare. Some were well maintained, others less so, given over more to evidence of violent times than careful tending. Hundreds of men and women walked in and out of the barrack complex, sometimes in groups or pairs, more often alone. They wore furs and leathers, wrapped against the cold, and they all carried weapons of some kind attached to their belts or strung across their backs. But there was no fight in the air today. Dana'Man was their island, and theirs alone. The fight they existed for would come later.

In one of the rows of barracks there was a tent made of whalebone and cured horse skin, and in that tent sat a man named Nox. He was a big man and, like most of the Krote warriors he shared the encampment with, his clothing bristled with weaponry; knives, stars, maces, slide-shocks and throwing spikes. His hair was long and braided, more to keep it out of his eyes than for decoration. His skin was dark as leather, weathered by his four decades living on Dana'Man, and his eyes were as cool blue as the oldest glacier. He sat alone. Those sharing his quarters had gone for food. Had anyone entered, they would have seen instantly that something was wrong. Nox was slowly, deliberately slicing grooves into his arm, letting the blood well and flow from each cut before raising the knife to his face, scraping away a line of rough stubble and running the knife through each wound again. He was breathing hard and fast, swaying on the end of his cot, shaking his head slowly as if to spread and dilute the pain.

The stubble dug into the raw flesh of his wounds, stung him there, promising to keep them open and bleeding. When his wounds were noticed, he would be sent to the hospital barge moored at the end of the breakwater.

And from there, escape from Dana'Man – and the mages – was so much closer.

"How the hell did you do that?" Serville said. She was staring at Nox's arm with frank fascination. She had always been one for blood.

This is it, thought Nox. *This is the lie that changes me forever.* "Foxlion cub," he said. "I went down to the beach looking for crabs, and it was hiding behind a float of ice."

"A cub did that?" Serville leant in closer, removing her glove and reaching out. Nox pulled away, wincing as his arm flexed and the wound gaped. More blood ran. Serville licked her lips.

"You'll have none of me!" Nox said. He was sitting on his cot, furs splashed with blood, waiting for the words that may set him free. He thought it unlikely that they would come from Serville – she had been here much longer than him and was of the Western tribes, wild and hard even for a Krote – but the others would be back soon. He had to be ready.

"Did you kill it?"

"No, it swam away. Dived as soon as it took a swipe at me."

Serville glared at him. "A cub bettered you?"

Nox shrugged. "I wasn't there looking for trouble. I was looking for crabs. I wanted something different from that shit they serve in the mess."

"We eat to live, not for pleasure," she said, looking at his bloodied arm once again.

"You Westerns are so backward," he said, and Serville threw back her head and laughed. Nox glanced at her belt in the second she looked away, marking her weapons. Just in case. She was part of his troop, but they had never really been friends.

Jaxx and Morton came into the tent, belching and laughing, and a gust of cold air and snow followed them in.

"Nox had a fight with a foxlion cub and lost," Serville said.

Morton sat on his bunk, unconcerned. Serville went to him – they were together sometimes, these two, and Nox only hoped that they did not start right now.

"That looks painful," Jaxx said. He stood over Nox and stared down at the wounds. "It'll scar well. Better than mine!" He displayed a fleshy knot on his own arm.

"You're welcome to it," Nox said. "And yes, it does hurt."

"You should get to the hospital barge," Jaxx said. "Foxlions carry contagion. And no offence, Nox, but I don't want to catch anything you may have."

There they are, Nox thought, *the words that set me free*. "You think so? It's not that bad. The bleeding's almost stopped and—"

"How long ago did it happen?"

"Just after you went to eat."

"It should have stopped by now," Jaxx said. "Krote's don't bleed for long, you know that. Something's keeping your blood thin and your wound open. And I say again, I don't want to catch it." He stepped back, giving Nox room to stand. Serville and Morton were looking over now, sensing the threat of violence in Jaxx's voice.

"A warm bed and the attention of those medics!" Morton said. "Don't pretend you don't want to go!"

Nox did not risk a response. *Give myself away*, he thought, *they'll know I intend never to see them again. Serville and Morton I'll not be sorry to leave, but Jaxx has been something of a friend.* So he shrugged his weapon belt over one shoulder, held his bleeding arm beneath his outer jacket and exited into the open air.

Nox took in a deep breath and let it out. Somewhere in that stew of stenches, freedom.

Nox had been caught by the Krote armies when he was a child. He knew nothing but his past existence, even though there were sometimes dreams that he could never truly know or understand. Then, he saw the faces of kindly people, green fields, a village working for survival, not war. He had no idea what had happened to that place, nor those people, and mostly he pretended not to care. He was as much a Krote warrior now as those born here, and he lived, as did every Krote, to serve the mages. His upbringing and training had made sure of that.

Newland, the only named settlement on Dana'Man, was where the mages had landed after being driven out of their rightful home on Noreela. So it was told, so it was true. They had landed here, nursing wounds driven into their flesh by the arrogant Noreelan armies, and they and their surviving Krote warriors had made the place their home. The harbour had welcomed them in with its long, curved breakwater, protecting them against the storms that had raged for all their weeks at sea, allowing them a gentle landing on this place of snow and ice. And now, though the mages were rarely seen away from their volcano lair miles inland, this harbour was still a special place.

Nox had lived here all his life, venturing away only to train on the mountain slopes inland, or to join a raiding party to the islands far to the east and west of Dana'Man. He ate here, trained for the promised war to come, slept, screwed, drank, made friends and lost them. He returned here to nurse occasional wounds suffered on raids. He relaxed here on those days given over to leisure, hunting sea snakes with his friends, wrestling and sparring on the harbour front. He called it home. And yet . . . there were those dreams. Fields of green, not white. Striving for survival and peace, not war. And Nox had begun to wonder more and more just where those dreams could lead.

He walked out of the barracks and headed down the gentle slope into Newland. From here he could see the whole expanse of the natural harbour, curved out into the sea like the arm of Dana'Man itself. Boats were docked all along the breakwater, but it was the two warships that stood out. Five times larger than any other vessel, they sported huge masts and furled sails, ready for sailing at a moment's notice. Snow and ice made surreal sculptures of their rigging. From this distance Nox could barely make out individual people walking along the harbour, but there was a sense of continuous movement about the port which made him yearn, briefly, for the relative calm of the barracks.

But his arm throbbed, and the stubble in the wounds kept them open and leaking. He withdrew it from the cover of his jacket and was surprised at the amount of blood still running from the cuts. How ironic it would be to die from blood-loss, now that he had finally found the nerve to attempt escape. After all these years, all those vague notions of fleeing, no one would know. He would slump down here in the snow and, dreaming of green fields, his life would filter away into the ice of ages. They would find his corpse frozen into the hillside, thaw him and feed him to the trained hawks that came down on occasion from above the clouds. Killed by a foxlion cub, they would say, probably mocking him. And in weeks or days, he would not even be a memory.

Nox shook his head and bit his lip, the pain stinging him into action. He hurried on toward the harbour. He could make out the hospital barge now, right at the end of the breakwater past the weapons workshops. And beyond that there was open sea, and freedom.

When he was seventeen Nox already knew the meaning of faith. The subjects of his faith were the mages – sinister, elusive S'Hivez; beautiful, terrible Angel – and his belief was strong and profound. He had faith in the fact that he was there to serve them, and nothing else. Those brief memories of childhood were dream fragments frozen by the snows and ice of Dana'Man, their meaning lost, any emotion conjured by them scorched away by the frost. The mages were his masters, and everything he was, everything he *would* be, was because of them. He was a soldier, and one day they would call on his services to take revenge on the people far to the south that had driven them away. They owned his mind and, most of the time, his heart.

Most of the time. Because even pure faith is fickle. And one evening, lying in a sweaty tangle with a female Krote warrior, sated, sharing body warmth against the freezing air outside, he uttered a brief, illicit sentence. "One day, maybe we'll get out of here." The Krote mumbled something and shifted, her hands searching for the hottest part of him, and within minutes Nox had forgotten the thought that had conjured those words.

But above them, in shadows cast between the ceiling and wall of the tent, something blinked out of existence. It was a nothing, not even blackness; a shade, a ghost of a soul yet to be born. It too served the mages, though it had no mind to doubt, nor a heart to debate. It skimmed away beneath the surface of reality, back to its masters. And though the words meant nothing to the shade, the mages heard and stored them for the future.

Nursing his bleeding arm, Nox entered the outskirts of the harbourside. The iced road had been powdered with volcanic ash to make the going easier. Snow had been cleared from the rooftops, icicles hacked away from windows, and animal hides hung heavy across doorways. All the timber used in construction was brought in from other places, and along with the materials came slaves to do the building. There were dozens of them in the streets. Nox paid them as much attention as he did snow goats and sea gulls. They were below his contempt. Human, yes, but beyond that there was little to compare the slaves to the Krote masters they served. The mages used some arcane chemicala to drive down any rebellion in the imported slaves, and they strolled through the streets like dim-witted goats, heavily muscled and vacant. Nox met their gazes occasionally and saw no intelligence there. Instinct kept them out of the Krotes' paths, and interaction was unheard of.

He stepped aside to let some burden-beasts pass, ex-slaves that had been transformed even further by the mages' chemicala. It had taken time and interbreeding, but over two or three generations the mages had created large, strong beasts out of previously man-sized, weak slaves. These things had lost their sexuality, their humanity, and any remnants of dignity or pride that often still existed deep in a slave's mind. Their skins were sometimes stretched and split by accelerated growth, and the dusted roads showed trails of dried blood where burden-beasts had passed by. Nox watched these four snort and strain as they hauled a sled of food out of the harbourside and up towards the barracks on the hill. A Krote rode the sled, sitting casually amongst the crates, smoking and staring absently over the beasts' heads. He glanced down as the sled passed by, looked at Nox's bloodied arm and away again. None of his business, his attitude said, and Nox could only agree.

He walked further into Newland, and the closer he came to the harbour, the busier it became. The whole point of the Krotes' existence was to go to war; the fabled Great Return of which the mages spoke whenever they emerged from their solitude, a return to Noreela and vengeance upon the peoples that had made them outcasts before magic had withdrawn itself from humanity. Yet though the Great Return was their sole reason for being, generations of Krotes had been waiting for a long time. Over a century since the mages had landed on Dana'Man – so it was told, so it was true – still the war seemed no closer, the final order to prepare and launch as distant as ever. In darkened taverns and the dead of night, some whispered that it was because the mages had lost their magic. They had their chemicala, they had their *rage*, but without magic they were powerless against the land that had driven them out. Others said it was because the mages were too old. Most that spoke bad of them rarely did so more than once. Punishment was silent, and swift.

Nox felt suddenly dizzy, and he had to lean against a wall to gather his strength. He glanced inside his jacket and saw the weak sun reflecting from fresh blood. *Maybe I've killed myself*, he thought, and smiled grimly. *Maybe that is an escape of sorts.*

At the age of twenty Nox went on his first raid. He and his troop of thirty Krotes took a coastal sloop and travelled east for three days, dodging icebergs, whirlpools and giant cold-whales until they reached the far end of the isle of Dana'Man. Here they came ashore overnight before heading out across the sea. The small boat was not built for the swells and storms of the open ocean, and on more than one occasion Nox was certain that they would capsize. He knew very well that to be tipped into these waters meant certain death, either from the intense cold, or the things that lived beneath the waves. They saw them sometimes, white movement in the depths like wraiths floating by at twilight, and though the Krotes were not cowards, they *could* feel fear. Fear keeps you alive, the female mage Angel once said at a gathering. And it was fear that saved Nox and his fellow Krotes that day. Close to being swamped they took up oars, rowing all day and night and into the next day until they reached their destination.

Then, after days travelling without sleep, freezing, hungry and weak, the Krotes had to fight.

The tribe they went against were not warriors. Perhaps decades before they had held some semblance of organisation and civilisation, but after a century enduring regular Krote raids their society had regressed to something base and pitiful. Some had fled, but most stayed because their island was all they knew. And though they were all but resigned to the regular pillage, some still fought. They used rocks and sharpened whalebone, fiery blubber bombs and fists, and to begin with the Krotes toyed with them, giving the islanders a brief sense that victory was possible. After an afternoon of running, hiding and fighting, however, the mages' warriors' exhaustion took over. They stormed the islanders' stronghold, slaughtered anyone who offered resistance and took what they had come all this way to steal.

They returned to Dana'Man with their hold filled with food, spices, and seedlings for the farms on Dana'Man's volcano's flanks. Also in the hold were several men and women from the island, and each Krote, man and woman alike, took turns pleasuring themselves.

"There has to be more than this," Nox whispered to himself that night. It was not guilt or shame, but a hollowness that seemed to fill him as he lay on the deck, staring up at a sky so filled with stars, it seemed to be snowing. It was not a sensation he was familiar with, and he put it down to post-fight fatigue. But he felt empty, wanting, and perhaps then more than any time before he perceived a fraction of the potential his life could have borne. "*Has* to be."

As he slept he dreamed of green fields.

And a Krote that had been lying near him remembered his words, sensed their rebellious potential, and pledged to confer them to her superior.

In Dana'Man, anything out of the ordinary had a way of making itself known to the mages.

"Nox, you snow goat's cock. Where are you off to in such a hurry? Am I missing a fight?"

"No Sir," Nox said. *Of all the luck*! The woman standing before him was at least two hands taller than Nox, wider, heavier, older, and scarred from countless fights and battles. A Krote took pride in his or her scars, displaying them whenever possible, and despite the cold this Lieutenant wore only bands of hide around her chest and hips. Her bare stomach was a network of livid red disfigurements, and her shoulders, though broad, had great chunks of flesh missing, as if burned away by a white-hot iron. *Of all the bloody luck*! Lieutenant Lenora was something of a legend amongst the Krotes of Newland.

"What have you done there, cut yourself shaving?" She nodded at the bloody patch on Nox's jacket, her bald head shimmering with frost.

"Foxlion, Sir," Nox said, changing his story slightly. He had to impress her now, pass her by, go on his way. If she thought he'd come out worse in a fight with a foxlion cub, she was likely to take a knife to him herself.

"And that's all you have? I'm impressed, Nox. I'll bet you cut the thing's head off as a trophy, eh?"

"Absolutely, Sir. It's back at the barracks. Serville is boiling it up for me even now. I'm off to the hospital barge to make sure I didn't catch anything from the shitting thing, then it's foxlion stew all round."

"Hah!" Lieutenant Lenora clapped him on his bad arm and laughed at the sky. They said she had the ear of the mages. Some even said she was one of the Krotes that had survived the rout from Noreela, immortal now, the ultimate killer. "So let me smell your sword!"

"My sword?"

"The blood of victory smells sweet, Nox, and it's months since I've bloodied mine in battle. A foxlion's a worthy opponent, that's for sure. Even though you shouldn't have been down at the beach on your own, eh?" She leaned in close and smiled.

"I . . . I was looking for—"

"Something better to eat. Yes, I know Nox. Can't blame you. The shit they serve you Krotes is enough to drive anyone to fend for themselves."

I'm being tested here, Nox thought. *She's probing, she smells something wrong; maybe it's my eyes, my guilty eyes*. The way she referred to Krotes as if she were not one disturbed him greatly. Far from sounding disrespectful to the mages, it showed that she thought herself above a mere Krote, a true warrior of the mages with countless scars to prove it. He had heard that her shoulder wounds were caused by a hawk gone berserk. It had grabbed her and flown so high with her in its claws, that when she finally burst its stomach with her sword it took her a whole afternoon to fall. Foolish legends. But her eyes held a cool, dark humour, as if challenging him to doubt.

"Well, you don't have to agree with me, Nox, even though I know you do. So, your sword! I trust you didn't polish it clean, what with your arm half off?"

"Polish? No. No . . ." He felt suddenly faint. His arm began to burn where the blood still pumped through, and Lieutenant Lenora grew higher, wider, as he sank to his knees on the ice road.

When Nox came to, he knew that he was caught. Lieutenant Lenora had known from the second she saw him that he had escape on his mind. It was obvious from the way he walked, the look in his eyes, the tint of his skin, and now he was being held somewhere awaiting punishment.

He had never, ever heard of a Krote trying to escape Dana'Man. He had never heard of anyone even entertaining the thought. It was bred out of them, and though he knew he was abnormal even considering fleeing, he did not waste time questioning why. Perhaps it was the grass-green dreams . . . but really, he did not care. Actions had meaning; musing upon such mysteries did not.

He had sometimes wondered whether there was a place on Dana'Man where attempted escapees were held. Now he opened his eyes, not knowing what to expect.

"You've lost a lot of blood," Lieutenant Lenora said. She was sitting on a bench before him, holding him upright. The muscles in her arms were knotted and hard. Even if he wanted to fall away, she would not let him.

"I'm flying," he muttered, and for a brief instant he thought he'd said, *I'm fleeing*.

"Nasty bastards, foxlions. They carry something in their spit that stops blood clotting. Helps them drink from their prey easier. You say you were scratched, not bitten?"

Nox only nodded. To elaborate would be to open his story up to scrutiny, and he was not level-headed enough for that.

Lenora frowned. "Hmm. Well there's *something* in there keeping you flowing like a holed goat." She twisted Nox's arm up out of his lap and licked across his wounds, slowly, her tongue fat and grey. She cleared a path through his blood, glanced up at him, smiling grotesquely. "Tasty," she said.

Nox looked away, unnerved. He had often seen Krotes blooding themselves after a battle – had done so himself – but he had only ever heard of cannibalism second-hand. *The immortal ones do it*, Serville had told him one drunken evening. *Those that came back from Noreela with the mages. They never die, so it doesn't matter if they're eating infected flesh drinking bad blood. Imagine being like that . . .*

"Strange," Lenora said. She turned Nox's arm this way and that, examining the wounds. They began to seep and Nox was certain she was going to lick them again, and he was not sure he could stand it, that sandpaper tongue scraping across the pouting lips of his gashed arm—

"What?" he said, trying to draw her attention. "What's strange?"

"Something in there," she said, running her tongue around her mouth. "Gritty. We'd best get you where you were going, what do you say?"

Nox nodded, and his gratitude and relief were not feigned.

Lieutenant Lenora – allegedly immortal and over a hundred years old already – swung his right arm around her shoulders and held him upright. His feet could only just touch the floor, such was her height, but to begin with it seemed not to matter. She walked quickly towards the harbour, a path clearing naturally before her, and for a few seconds Nox began to believe his own lie. A few Krotes glanced at them, and he saw admiration in their expressions. Wounded in battle, he thought, and he wanted to tell them about the foxlion he had fought and defeated. But of course there had been no foxlion, there had been only his knife. And if Lenora asked again to smell the vanquished beast's blood on his sword, then his ruse was over.

He looked down at his feet trailing across the dirty ice. *Did I really believe I could get away?*

Yes, he had. And he may yet.

They reached the harbour, and Nox suggested that he walked himself to the hospital barge. "It's not fit for a warrior to be carried into hospital," he said. "Not unless he's missing legs and arms. Then, maybe, there's no shame in having a lift."

Lenora smiled and set him down, and Nox knew that he had impressed her. That was good. Perhaps it would ensure that she would ask no more about his foxlion-blooded sword.

"You're a brave Krote," she said.

"I'm surprised you even knew me, Sir."

Lenora raised her eyebrows. "I'm a Lieutenant. You think it's my duty to not know those under my command?"

"Of course not, Sir. It's just that you've never called me by name before."

"I never had cause to. You never impressed me before." She stared frankly at him, her eyes intelligent and filled with the cool threat of imminent violence.

Nox smiled weakly, and his genuine pain and faintness helped him on his way. "I hope this will not be the last time," he said.

Lenora laughed and clapped him on the shoulder, sending him staggering sideways into a mound of fishing baskets piled on the breakwater. She stepped after him and held him steady, still laughing.

"I'm sure it won't," she said. "When the time comes and we

sail to Noreela, I expect you to be at the head of your troop. There'll be plenty of blood to spill there. Plenty of Noreelan women to be stung by your sword. The wait for revenge is cold, but its fulfilment is hot as blood."

Nox forced himself to smile. *Maybe I'll even be living in Noreela then*, he thought. How ironic that would be. "And when will that be?" he said. Asking questions like this was usually frowned upon, but he seemed to have gained Lenora's respect. And, truth be told, the idea that he may well be away from this place and on his way to freedom by nightfall made him more daring.

Lenora raised her eyebrows. "Keen, are we?"

"Of course," Nox said, suddenly afraid that he had gone too far.

"Good. That's good, Krote. Because whenever the mages call on us, we need to be ready to make them proud." She turned to walk away, and through his queasiness Nox felt a warming sense of relief. And then she turned back to him. "Magic," she said. "That's what they await, the re-emergence of magic. When the time comes they'll want it, and isn't that right? Isn't it proper that those who used magic to its full extent before should have it for themselves?"

"Of course," Nox said. "Yes."

Lenora glanced around at the bustling harbour-front, leaned in close, whispered in his ear. He smelled her breath – cool, stale, like a ruptured air pocket in a shifting glacier – and and he could not help but draw back.

"They still have it, you know," she said. "Not true magic, but means. Methods. Knowledge. They know more than we can imagine. Now . . . here . . . they probably even know that we're together. They can see us. They'll smell us. And when I say this to you – when I tell you that the mages are your gods, and any god you betray will give you an eternity of pain – then they hear what I say. You hear, Mistress? You hear, Master?" Lenora stared into Nox's eyes as if looking way deeper than her own reflection. "Oh yes," she whispered. "They hear." And then she turned and walked away.

Nox watched her go. Faint from loss of blood, sick with terror, he waited until she was out of sight on the harbourside. Then he turned and started to make his way to the hospital barge. It was almost half a mile away along the breakwater. Every step of that journey, he imagined the mages watching.

When he was twenty-eight, Nox fell in love.

She was another Krote, a warrior from a troop stationed at a remote village way along the coast. When they visited Newland to attend a training exercise run by the mages themselves, Lucie caught Nox's eye. Hours after first introducing himself he was screwing her behind a storage hut on the harbour-front, and hours after that he knew that this was something different. She did not seem to realise, but his devoted attention was for more than the physical, his comments to her over the next few days held far more substance than simple sex-talk. They screwed every night and fought every day, but when they returned to their barracks – bloodied, exhausted, confident as ever in their abilities to fight for the mages – Nox would always fall in step with Lucie. She would smile at him hungrily, and he would smile back, silent, unable to speak, painfully aware of her presence, her warmth, her smell. Her talk was of the day they had spent slaughtering slaves brought in from the north and given ice-swords to spar with; his own words sang her praise. Lucie heard nothing of it, or if she did, she smothered it with her sexual abandon.

Nox could not tell her what he felt. Love encouraged weakness and gave its victims over to mindlessness. Though not punishable, those who claimed love were often sent away to live in the northern mountains for a year or more. If they returned, they invariably found their way back to normality. If not, then their love was frozen into infinity along with their weak flesh.

One night, as she lay sleeping after sex, Nox laid his head beside Lucie's and whispered into her ear. "It can't always be like this," he said. "We can escape. You and I, we'll go away. There must be somewhere I can tell you the truth." She stirred and uttered a dreaming growl, and Nox turned on to his back and sought sleep.

Behind him, beneath the skins insulating them from the icy ground, a worm the size of a thumb squirmed its way northward. It had listened. It had heard. It had not understood, but knowledge was not its purpose, only delivery of what it had heard to the mages. The tone of voice it had been programmed to find had been here. The intent it was made to discover was evident in the man's voice, his words, the way he breathed and sweated and finally slept.

The worm's journey to the mages' redoubt took almost a year. That did not matter; a year was nothing. And once its message was delivered, its reward was Angel's teeth tearing it in half for the cool juice of its insides.

The hospital barge was far from refined. It was a large coastal sloop, stripped bare of its superstructure and covered by a simple timber and animal skin roof. It had glassless windows, a few doors, a couple of chimneys smoking lazily in the still afternoon air. Inside there was no pretension to comfort. Those that came here always left very soon after, either back on their feet again, or dragged to the end of the breakwater and given to the carrion creatures that lived in the cold sea. There was never a long stay; once wounded or taken ill, patients would either recover quickly to fight again, or they were no longer of use. There was as much treatment by the sword as by medicine.

Nox stepped on to the barge. He paused for a second, glanced down at his bleeding arm, felt the slight shifting of the boat beneath his feet. And here he was, one step closer to freedom.

Several medics glanced up as he went inside, but none of them rose to aid him. He was walking, his wound looked minor, and the pride of a warrior was precious. He found himself a bed – only a few were occupied – and sat down heavily. Closing his eyes, he could not decide whether his queasiness was due to the boat's movements, or his own blood loss.

"Cut yourself shaving?" a medic asked.

Nox glanced up at her and smiled. "Argument with a foxlion."

The woman raised her eyebrows, mildly impressed, and held his arm. "How long ago?"

"This morning."

"Should have stopped bleeding by now. You look pale. I'll have to flush the foxlion's poison from the wounds." She paused and looked Nox in the eye. "It'll hurt."

"I didn't expect anything less."

As the medic went to gather some equipment, Nox looked around at the few other patients. Most of them sat on their beds or lay propped up, conscious and alert, eager to leave as soon as possible. A few were prone, moaning softly in whatever sleep had taken them. One of them was dead. Blood pooled under their bed, and Nox could see a chipped sword glistening nearby. One more free meal for the sea creatures.

When the medic returned Nox felt a sudden stab of fear and doubt. He began to wonder whether his plan had held any sanity after all, or whether the cold had finally driven him mad.

"Lay down," she said.

Nox did not move. "Are you sure?"

She smiled, but it held little humour. "Scared, Krote?"

Nox shook his head, lay down and held out his arm.

The medic was right. It hurt.

Later, at night, in the quiet, Nox kept himself awake. The medic had given him a chemicala powder to help him sleep and regain his strength, but he had retained it beneath his tongue and spat it out when she left. Dregs of it had found its way into his system. Shadows of sleep crowded in. But every few minutes he tensed his dressed arm, and the pain brought him back.

His wounds were flushed and had stopped bleeding, but the process had hurt more than putting them there in the first place.

The hospital barge was never completely quiet. There were a few snores from his fellow patients, and one of them moaned in her sleep, haunted by sleep demons. Nox was glad of this. He used a heavy snore as cover for sitting up. When a man cried out in his sleep, Nox stood from his cot. When the nightmaring woman muttered some ancient curse at whatever troubled her, he paced quickly to the windows and moved a curtain aside. The harbour was much quieter than during the day, but there was still movement here and there, torches flaring along the breakwater, shadows slipping through shadows. He had always known that there would be people around, but his plan was brazen enough to have a chance. Or so he thought. If he was wrong, then he would be dead by dawn. Floating in the icy seas. Fodder for the carrion creatures cruising its dark depths.

"Never seen the mages!" someone cried out, and Nox froze. Moonlight cast his shadow back into the barge. Anyone opening their eyes would see him silhouetted against the starlight, but there were no more words. It had sounded like the woman. Perhaps it was the mages that haunted her sleep.

Nox lifted himself slowly on to the windowsill and stepped outside. The edge of the barge was just wide enough to walk around, but any missed footing would send him into the water. That would be the end of him. Night was a time for foxlions. How ironic it would be to fall victim to one now.

He worked his way to the end of the barge and back up on to the breakwater. At its very tip were moored some old fishing sloops. They had been there for years, and their ragged sails and abandoned appearance had planted the seed of his plan. He would steal one, sail it away from Newland and Dana'Man, never trying to hide. If anyone glanced out at the moonlit scene they would see a sailing boat heading confidently out to sea. They would assume that there was nothing wrong and go back to sleep. Or, they would raise the alarm and follow his stolen boat with a hail of arrows and bolts.

The more he thought about his plan, the more Nox realised how crazy he was. But in a way that gave him comfort, because it was that very craziness that would offer his greatest chance of success. No one had ever heard of a Krote escaping the mages' island. No one had ever heard of anyone even *trying*. And the simple reason was that it was suicide. Even if they could escape, to truly be free of the mages' influence they would have to sail a thousand miles south to Noreela.

Standing at the end of the breakwater, Nox looked out at the dark sea that would be his home for the next few weeks. He planned to fish for food and gather rainwater to drink. A thousand miles . . .

No, he thought, *I can do it. It will work! It's so simple and foolish and impossible, it* has *to work*. He climbed down a rusted ladder on to the deck of one of the boats, untied its mooring ropes, used a paddle to shove it away from the breakwater, hoisted the sail, held the tiller and smiled as a breath of wind seemed to rise from nowhere, helping him on his way to freedom. *The breath of fate*.

And he was right. Fate breathed down his neck that night.

When he was thirty-five, Nox took part in a raid on a settlement to the north. The Krotes knew of the ice people, bands of rovers that wandered across the snow fields, killed birds for food, eking out a sparse existence. They were undeveloped, wild people, all but cultureless, spending every minute of their waking time embroiled in a battle of survival against the elements. The one talent they did possess was speed. It could have been due to their long legs, grown strong and thin over time to enable them to step through deep snow. Or maybe it was a gift born of the need to flee the many predators that hunted them for food. Whatever the cause, it provided for excellent target practice for Krote crossbows.

The fight was ferocious. The surface of the glacier was left stained red with the blood of the ice people, redder than any blood the Krotes had ever seen, and the few that escaped became an enjoyable distraction for the next couple of hours. Nox and his companions followed the escapees through the snow, using refined skills of tracking and stalking that had been honed through many other such hunts. The ice people knew their territory well; they were adept at hiding, they could blend in with the snow-scape, so pale was their skin. But they were no match for the Krotes, and in truth it was simply sport.

Nox ran down one ice woman, finally bringing her legs from under her with a bolt to the back of the knee. He stood over her, panting, watching her blood seep into the snow and turn it a deep red. She stared up at him, rapid breaths condensing in the air and floating across the glacier like frozen screams. She spoke, but he did not know her language. He decided to slit her stomach open and let her insides out. A slow, cruel way to kill her. But she had led him on a long chase and now he was sore and tired, and his blood was up.

For a second as he bent down, the idea flashed across his mind that this was wrong.

He glanced at the woman's face and was amazed at the change there. She had gone from terrified to enraged, fearful to ferocious. Shock made him plunge his sword into her chest. She gasped, arched her back, and he pushed harder, twisting the handle and feeling ribs snap under the pressure.

She hissed blood. He did not know the words but their meaning was clear. He could see the hate in her eyes.

Nox withdrew the sword and brought it down on to her neck, severing her head. Then he stood and walked away.

The woman died. Her wraith rose up, colder than the freezing wastes that had been her home. And using a talent that the Krotes would never know, she looked into her killer's mind and saw his greatest, most secret wish.

And she knew how vengeance could be hers.

Leaving the bloody wreck of her body behind, the ice woman's wraith drifted south with a message for the mages.

They let him think he had escaped.

He spent that whole night sat at the tiller, sailing hard, aware of every boat length he put between himself and Dana'Man. His whole life was falling behind, and he felt nothing for it. No loss, no sadness, no sense of the version of himself he was leaving. Ahead, in the dark, the promise of something new loomed like the sun waiting to rise. The weight of all his bad deeds sailed with him, but they were lighter by the second. It was as if putting distance between himself and the mages was also diluting the evils he had performed at their behest.

And then as the sun peered over the horizon, he heard the screech of something diving down from above. Even before Nox had turned to look, the voice came down to slaughter all his hopes and dreams.

"Going somewhere?" Lenora shouted.

He thought to reach for his sword. But how could he fight this flying thing? The hawk was huge, tentacles trailing as it plummeted, wicked curved beak catching the first rays of sunlight. It would crush him.

The creature pulled up short and hovered above his head. The stink of its exhausts thrust down at him, billowing the boat's sails and forcing him to his knees, retching. When he looked up again he saw who else rode the beast's back . . . and hope left him forever, purged by the sight of the mage.

"Mistress Angel wants your help!" Lenora shouted down.

Nox could only stare, hands limp by his side, unable to tear his gaze away from this sorceress. Though bereft of magic for a century still she exuded malevolence, a sense of dread like sweat seeping from her pores. She was beautiful, but awful to behold. She looked down on him without expression. Lifeless. And he wished for all the world that she would speak, because her silence was most terrifying of all.

"Will you help?" Lenora said.

"You're toying," Nox said. "Just kill me and get it over with."

"*Kill* you?" Lenora said. "Of course not, Nox. What a waste!"

Nox could not begin to imagine the punishment he would receive.

He reached quickly for his sword. He would drag the keen blade across his own throat and gasp one last bloody laugh at this mage. Perhaps a century ago she would have been able to torture his departed soul, but now in a magic-less world dead was dead.

Goodbye, he thought.

The crossbow bolt passed clean through his palm. He dropped the sword and it fell into the ocean with hardly a splash.

"No," Angel said, her voice like a rumble in the ocean depths.

Lenora whistled and the hawk came down, its claws outstretched, and grabbed Nox from the boat. Its talons passed through his thigh and shoulder and he screamed, the mage's laughter a ghastly accompaniment.

"Mistress Angel *demands* your help!" Lenora shouted. The hawk rose swiftly, and Nox saw his own blood spattering the deck of the boat. Part of him may find freedom, at least.

The hawk rose high and flew fast, and Nox's petty attempt to flee was belittled by the short time it took them to reach Newland.

He hung from the creature's talons trying not to scream, weathering the pain, certain that there would be far worse to come. Pain is imaginary, he had been told. Control it as you control your imagination. But the feel of the thick talons scraping against his bones was real enough, and each change in direction brought a screech from his throat. Above him, out of sight on the hawk's back, Angel's Lieutenant laughed every time.

"Where are we going?" Nox asked. There was no answer, and he was not surprised. The mage would not deign talk to him unless she so desired. And when she did, it would doubtless be to tell him of some awful fate.

From high up, Nox saw that Newland was deserted. The usually bustling harbour had been left to the bobbing boats and scavenging sea birds, and the only movement in the barrack fields was the flutter of flags. *Where has everyone gone?* he thought. *And why?*

As if passing from above sea to land was a signal, one of the hawk's huge tentacles suddenly whipped around his waist. Its claws uncurled and Nox screamed as he was tugged from them. He struggled and tried to fall, but the tentacle held him tight, crushing his stomach and lifting him up, depositing him in the saddle on its back. The hawk let go, but Nox could not move. Before him, Lenora held the reins and guided the creature inland. And behind him, her breath hot on his neck, her presence like a hole that could swallow him up, Angel.

"I've known for years that you would flee," Angel whispered. Her voice was a shard of ice penetrating his skull. "My brother and I have been watching, waiting. We decided a long time ago that we'd make an example of you."

"Why?" Nox said, having to shout into the air disturbed by the hawk's flight. Angel's voice did not sound raised at all, and yet he heard her words clear and heavy.

"Because we wished it," Angel said. She rested her hand on his wounded shoulder and squeezed gently. "You have no friends, Nox. They've betrayed you. You have no comrades or lovers on your side. No one. You're quite unique. The others that try to escape we simply kill. Cut up. Eat. But time is moving on, things change. I want everyone to see what happens to you."

Nox pressed his hands flat against the saddle and pushed hard. He would tumble to the side and fall away, and for every second of his descent he would relish those last few moments of freedom. But Angel's hand pressed him down, she whispered, "No," and Lenora whistled to the hawk to begin its descent.

"We're not warriors!" Nox shouted, directing his words at Lenora. To address the mage was too terrifying. "We're slaves! No better than the fodder we eat, the slaves we capture and kill. Lenora! What will this gain you?"

Lenora did not answer, but Angel did.

"You're right," she said. "The slaves we control with chemicala, you Krotes with promises and fear. You're all slaves to us."

Lenora laughed, her shoulders shook, and Nox looked down.

They were descending rapidly, and now he could see long columns of people marching up through the snow. There were thousands down there, all of Newland making its way into the mountains. A few Krote pennants waved shadows on to the snow. He wondered where his own troop would be, and whether any of them would care.

Nox suddenly felt his fear transmuting into something else. Not hope, nothing so limitless. But peace. He realised that Angel was helping him on his way. However terrible his manner of death, once gone he would be beyond the mages' reach.

"I'll still escape," he said, and Angel's hand left his shoulder.

"I'm sure you're right," she said, and Nox felt her smiling. "Even I can't see forever."

They landed on the glacier. It was a bright morning, no snow showers, and the cold air was sharp and clear. There were already a thousand Krotes and slaves there, huddled around hastily lit fires, cooking fish, drinking, already entering into something of a festival atmosphere. *And why not?* Nox thought. *They're here to see a killing, and killing is what they love.*

Lenora slipped down the side of the hawk. The assembled throng grew silent, watching her. She looked up at Nox and motioned him down.

"Don't make me come up there and get you," she said quietly.

Nox considered the weapons he carried. His sword was gone, but he still had throwing spikes, the slide-shock on his belt, maces strung along both legs. He could surely reach them before Lenora made it back on to the hawk, but Angel still sat behind him. And even if the mage did nothing to prevent him – he guessed she may enjoy the sport of seeing Lenora and him enter into combat – Lenora herself was more than his match.

At least it would be an honourable death.

He fell sideways, right hand reaching to his belt for a throwing spike, left held out to roll himself across the hard packed snow. He saw Lenora tense, and then smile, and then he felt a hand close around his ankle.

Angel stood on the hawk's back and held him high. He drew back his own hand, throwing spike ready.

He heard the familiar whistle before the slide-shock snapped off three of his fingers at the second knuckle. The crowd cheered and Lenora grinned. Nox screamed, instantly ashamed at his pain.

"Here he is," Angel said. "The escapee! He didn't get far. Noreela is that way, Krote!" She swung him southward and jerked him back, blood from his fingers spattering a line across the glacier.

"We're all slaves!" Nox shouted, but the crowed cheered and jeered, and he wondered where he had ever found hope.

"My brother and I are slaves also," Angel said, and the shouting suddenly ceased. She dropped Nox to the ice and jumped down, feet landing either side of his head. He could see her mottled skin, smell her age, sense the power she still possessed. "Slaves to the magic that tore itself from us. Slaves to this place, our banishment. Slaves to revenge."

"Kill him!" someone shouted. Other voices rose in support. Nox turned and scanned the assembled crowd of Krotes for a familiar face, but they were all strangers to him now. He had left them less than a day before but already he no longer belonged. He had changed.

"Bless you," Angel said, as if talking to a thousand children. "Death is all you know." She reached down and gathered Nox to her chest, lifting him as easily as she would a baby.

Nox stared up at her face. Was she growing? Was he shrinking? He should be able to move, to struggle and fight. But each message he sent his limbs was translated into another pathetic whimper from his mouth. *Just let it end*, he thought. *Please, just kill me*. The mage glanced down, smiling as if hearing his thoughts.

"Lenora!" Angel shouted. "You know what to do."

Nox did not see, but he heard. The hawk shifted on the ice, clumsy out of the air. Its great feet crashed down, once, twice, three times. And then came a blast of heat, a gasp from the crowd, and clouds of steam formed an unnatural mist around them.

"All ready, Mistress."

"All ready," Angel echoed, looking down at Nox. "Betrayer," she whispered. She looked up again at the ever-growing crowd.

"This is a warning," she said, her voice carrying across the slope. "Anyone who tries to flee my brother and I will suffer a similar fate, or something worse. We may not have magic, but we still have knowledge. Ways and means. And chemicala. This is Nox! See him alive now! And see him live forever."

Angel dropped Nox to the ice and straddled his chest. Her long hair fell either side of her face and there, hidden from the crowd, he saw her true madness for the first time. Her eyes glowed with something more than reflected sunlight. Her mouth hung open, tongue lolling, and her lips were twisted into a grotesque sneer.

"Have this," she said, forcing a pellet of something into his mouth, "and this." She thrust a knife through his clothes and into his chest just above the heart. He whined and tried to jerk himself upward, urging the blade to penetrate further, but Angel withdrew the knife and probed inside his clothing, pressing something cold and hard into the wound.

She sat back and punched him in the face. His jaw slammed shut on the pellet and crushed it, releasing a foul-tasting fluid across his tongue.

"Put him in," Angel said, standing and stepping away.

Lenora approached, walking slowly. The crowd started to roar again, but their voices rose as if from miles away, starting low and deep and building relentlessly to a climax that never came. Looking up, Nox saw fresh snowflakes hanging in the air above him, just hanging.

What is this? he thought.

"I will see you again," Angel said. And her words sounded forever.

They buried him in the glacier.

Lenora had formed a cavern deep down, just large enough for Nox to lay out flat or stand up. The ice they piled in above him was melted with a blast of chemicala heat. The whole process seemed to take days. Lenora moved so slowly, and Nox never saw those snowflakes land.

His mind . . . that kept its speed.

Inside the glacier was not a silent place. It growled. It roared. Every few years, it moved. And when the sun hit it just right, on the last day of winter each year, its ancient ice glowed like unending fields of green.

Nox spent the first century trying to relive his dreams.

THE WIZARD OF ASHES AND RAIN

David Sandner

Besides his occasional stories and poems David Sandner (b. 1966) is also an expert on children's fantasy and has written The Fantastic Sublime *(1996), a scholarly study of nineteenth-century fantasy. Sandner teaches literature at California State University, Fullerton. He is also the editor of the forthcoming,* Fantastic Literature: A Critical Reader. *The following story may show some influence of the great Victorian fantasist George Macdonald. If he were alive today and living in San Francisco, this may be just what he would produce.*

CRUNCHING ON HER SKATEBOARD, Sarah zoomed downhill into a white fog rolling into the City off the Pacific and the San Francisco Bay. Last night's rain had washed the streets clean, leaving rainbow oil slicks under parked cars, white streaks on windows, dew on leaves and park benches, and silver-shiny-wet glinting on the streetcar tracks running away over the hills. The sunlight made the fog luminous white, somehow morning-bright and twilight-soft at once. Her headphones played loud, holding her in her own world. While everything else stood still, she raced past waiting cars and through strings of red lights. She sped up, fog condensing cold on her face and hands as she leaned hard into turns, her arms opening like wings. She had been looking for the Wizard of Ashes and Rain all morning with no luck at all. She had been looking for him ever since she had talked to her sister about her sister's dream, the dream she had been having over and over for three days.

Today was Sarah's sister's birthday. Thirteen.

"Did you have the dream again?" Sarah had asked, standing on the top step of the stairs in her mother's house. Amanda had stood in the upstairs hallway looking at herself in the full-length mirror.

Sarah could never just talk to her sister, not anymore. Her sister wouldn't respond, or, when she did talk. Sarah could never figure out what she really meant.

"Come on, Amanda," she said. "Talk to me."

Amanda walked on tiptoe, twirling around in their mother's favorite blue sequined evening dress, holding the loose sides out away from herself like a cape.

"Mom's going to kill you if she sees you in that."

"It's my birthday," Amanda said.

Amanda swayed from side to side, eyeing herself from different angles in the mirror.

"Yesterday, sister, darling," Amanda said, with a slight fake Southern drawl, "the handsomest boy in school asked me out, just like that." She turned around so she could see herself from behind. "Kyle was going to break up with his girlfriend, the ever popular Margie Stevens, just to ask me out, can you believe it?"

"Amanda, cut it out."

Amanda had just started Junior High School. Sarah knew it was bad, but she hated to tell her sister that in High School, things just got worse.

"I told him, Kyle, I do believe I want to stand on my own just now. I'm afraid you'll just have to go out with Margie Stevens after all."

"I hate it when you're like this."

"Margie never even knew, and she being the most popular girl school and all, she would have been devastated, just completely. Sometimes I even surprise myself by my generosity."

"Amanda, did you have the dream again? It's serious."

Amanda let the sides of the dress fall from her hands.

"I saw myself today," she said. "Another me."

"What do you mean?" Sarah asked.

"After having the dream again, I woke up and went to the window and there I was, waving at myself to come down and follow."

"Amanda, are you just funning around? Well, don't."

Bad. Not just a dream, a hallucination. Or worse. Things were always getting worse.

Amanda stared at herself in the mirror, expressionless.

"I'm not," she said.

"Mom sent me up here to tell you to get dressed, people will be arriving for your party soon. Look." Sarah made a decision. "Look, I'm going to find the Wizard and ask him about your dream, O.K.? I've been hoping to run into him since your dreams started, but I haven't – and I should talk to him. I'll be back soon. I'll ask him about you seeing yourself, O.K.? Just have your party. And don't tell Mom anything. And take off that dress. And I'll be back soon, I promise."

Sarah went back downstairs, picking up her skateboard in the entranceway. She slipped out the door unnoticed. If her mother caught her, there'd be yelling: it's your sister's birthday, why don't you ever do anything for this family, why can't you think of anyone besides yourself? She was doing this for her sister. But she could never talk to her mother anymore, either.

Sarah skidded her skateboard to a stop. The Wizard of Ashes and Rain pushed his shopping cart – piled with bundles wrapped in plastic bags, and discarded clothing marked by oil smears, and a grimy sleeping bag, and aluminum cans and plastic bottles – up to the doughnut shop on the street corner. The clouds darkened above him, that's how he had gotten part of his name. The rain seemed to follow him everywhere, a low drizzling starting whenever he stayed in one place too long. The Wizard usually hung out in Golden Gate Park, walking through the arboretum, tending flowers until the gardeners chased him away, or sitting on the steps of the museum panhandling, or checking the garbage cans for deposits, or sleeping on the benches.

"Hey, Wizard," she called, putting one hand up. He didn't turn.

Sarah slid the headphones – playing loudly the endless guitar solo of "The Daedel Wings of Madness" by Lord Percy – off her ears; the volume dropped to a tinny, insistent whine, the headphones hanging around her neck. It always made her feel self-conscious when she realized that no one else heard what had been everything to her, pulsing inside her head, vibrating in her body to the grate of her wheels on the street, absolutely filling the sky; she felt as if suddenly shaken up out of a dream, asking herself, was it real? And realizing, no, what I know, no one else does, so they wouldn't understand, so I have to act normal, like I didn't have the dream, like I didn't hear the music. Sarah wasn't very good at acting normal. Sometimes that bothered her.

Two weeks ago Sarah had found the Wizard sitting cross-legged in a cardboard box by the old greenhouse in the park, sickly sweet incense wafting out of a small ceramic bowl beside his ragged backpack. The Wizard had motioned her to kneel down beside him, and in a whiskey-throated whisper had predicted the dream her sister began having three days ago. Sarah hadn't believed it at the time, but she knew enough about the Wizard to remember what he said. Besides, the Wizard had called Sarah's sister by name and described the thing that would appear in her dream, right down to the long corkscrew nose and the two eyes facing away on either side of its head, and the two mouths where the eyes should have been. And the way it scratched at the window, and under the floorboards and behind the walls, wanting to be let in. The Wizard had known all about it.

The Wizard stood in front of the doughnut shop and looked down the cross street at something Sarah couldn't see. Sarah put her foot down to push toward him when three O-boys came around the corner in black derby jackets, brown Bens and black waffle-stomper boots. One pushed at the Wizard and another pawed into the Wizard's shopping cart, idly pulling a plastic-wrapped bundle from the Wizard's junk pile. The Wizard pulled a short oak staff from the bottom rack of the shopping cart. There was a flash.

Sarah wasn't worried about the Wizard. The O-boys had made a mistake. But she didn't want to deal with them herself. She turned around only to see two more O-boys coming up the street behind her. What were they doing here? They hung out by the beach and rarely came this far up the avenues. Now there were five.

"Hey you," one of the O-boys said. "C'm'ere."

Surprised, she realized she knew him. His name was James.

She had gone to seventh grade with him – what? – was it three years ago already? He had been her friend. Things had changed for the worse, obviously. He had red hair and braces, and then the uniform: black jacket, brown work pants, the heavy boots. And now he had the usual O-boy's red eyes that glowed and shimmered; she didn't know how they got contacts to burn like that. Sarah had once sat with James in the closet at one of Laura Willard's parties during a game of truth or dare. They had giggled, and he had been pretty cool about it and not tried anything. Then he had gone to a different High School. And something must have gone terribly wrong. Everything seemed to be going terribly wrong today.

The O-boys ran toward her. She flipped her skateboard up into her hands. She stood before a sushi place and a used bookstore. Neither offered much protection. That left only the Elves. Sarah hated the Elves. A group of street kids who had read too many fantasy trilogies, they lived in an abandoned warehouse across the street. Not directly across the street. But there was a door, one of many around the neighborhood, that led down a narrow passageway, past the businesses up front, and somehow ended up at the abandoned warehouse. She never could make the spaces fit together right in her mind and figure out where the warehouse was exactly, somewhere in the middle of the block somehow, behind everything else.

The O-boys came upon her sooner than she expected. They spread apart, trying to hem her in before she could run. They had their arms out to catch her, they loomed up close.

James used a racial epithet for someone Chinese. He didn't know what he was talking about. Sarah's great-grandparents on her mother's side had been Korean, on her father's side, Irish. She had heard it all before, but it still shocked her, coming from someone she once knew.

"James, man, it's me. Sarah," she said, looking into his burning eyes as if saying: is there anybody still there at all? Anything worth a damn?

James stopped, confused. He had a mustache of fine dirty blonde hair on his upper lip, pimple scars along his cheeks and greasy hair dropping to his shoulders. He still had a kind face, though he looked hurt somehow, cornered. He dropped his arms to his sides. She hit his friend with her skateboard just below his knee. It was a kindness for an old friend; she could have hit the knee. James's friend buckled over with a cry, clutched his shin, fell into a parking meter, then straight down. He would have a bad bruise. She dodged between two parked cars and out into the street.

Someone, an adult, came out of the bookstore, looking to see what the problem was. That would slow them down, she thought. But James was after her sooner than she expected. And the others, the ones on the corner with the Wizard, they were now running down the street toward her, mad and wanting to take it out on someone, the Wizard nowhere to be seen. A streetcar stopped short, horn blaring, as she ran out in front of it. On the far sidewalk, she pushed past a woman carrying two full shopping bags who cursed at her.

A peeling, hand-painted sign on the plain white door read simply **Elves**. She pushed at the door and it opened into a long dark corridor. She'd never known any of the doors to be locked. But no one ever seemed to notice the sign or bother the Elves. She ducked through the door and ran down the corridor. The door swung closed behind her. Large pipes ran close over her head, puddles splashed under her feet. She tripped in the darkness, landing on concrete, skinning her hands, wetting the knees of her jeans. She heard the O-boys push the door open behind her, saw the light shine in and throw her shadow out before her. She struggled quickly to her feet.

Up ahead, she knew the passageway would lead to a large open courtyard sunk into the middle of the block, surrounded by high walls, sunlight leaking down from high above, past windows with plants and pigeons perched on their ledges, past the murals painted by the Elves showing their "history," their arrival at the warehouse, musicians and trees. She could see the dim, filtered light up ahead. A figure stepped into the doorframe at the end of the passage.

"Who?"

Her heart caught, in her throat. The Elves scared her too, somehow, that's part of why she avoided them, aside from the fact that they were freaks, quoting long passages of heroic poetry to one another, or dialogue from Monty Python, or acting out whole scenes from Star Wars, or comparing home-made chainmail. Sarah swallowed hard.

"Damn," Sarah muttered. She hated this part. "Elf-friend," she said. This was no time to tease them about their lame need to playact at being something that didn't exist.

"Orcs?" the voice said.

"O-boys," she said in agreement.

Hands reached out to support her. She struggled at first but saw the Elves around her, coming out of the darkness. They had been in the corridor all along. She let them lead her into the courtyard, where they sat her on a bench beside the door.

Aladuniel, the Elf who had challenged her, gave orders to the others. Many ran down the passageway. Sarah couldn't understand anything they said. They spoke their own language, Elvish. They named themselves, airy, overlong names they spoke with fake British accents. They dressed like refugees from a renaissance faire, in loose shirts with billowing sleeves, leather breeches, and high lace-up boots. But their clothes were old, badly patched, and stained. They were skinny like all street kids. But they also had knives at their belts, and she had seen them fight. Better than expected. More than that, really, but she didn't want to admit it. The O-boys, if they had any sense, would already be running for it. The O-boys weren't known for sense.

The Elves left her alone for a while, until Aladuniel emerged from the corridor and handed her back her baseball cap, which must have fallen off when she had tripped. It was wet. She looked down at herself. She wore an overlarge army surplus jacket with the sleeves rolled up. The left knee of her jeans hung open: it must have ripped when she fell. She wore black hightop sneakers, now soaked through, and held her skateboard across her lap. She clutched the cap tightly in her hands. Her hands shook. Had it been that close? She supposed it had. She wrung her cap out and stuck it in her pocket.

"Thanks, Al," she said.

Aladuniel had long hair feathered to his shoulders. He had a red sash across his chest and had a drinking horn on his belt beside his knife. He had red cheeks dotted white and black with pimples and a large nose. His body was long and bony, awkward even at rest.

"The Lady has been expecting you."

He took her hand and led her past the murals and into the warehouse, then up a long staircase and through a large open storage area littered with piles of old TVs and computers, broken glass and cables on the floor, all covered over with dust; finally, he led her to a small, neat room at the back, the floor painted bright red with neon trees on the walls reaching into a psychedelic sky; Lady G, the matriarch of the Elves, waited there for her.

Lady G was an obese woman, older than any of the other Elves, her black wispy hair streaked premature grey. She sat in a chair before a computer set up on a work table. The chair squeaked loudly as she pushed herself away from the table. Rolls of fat lay over the arms of the chair, hung from her arms and pushed up under her large, wide-set breasts. She had a flat face and nose, loose cheeks and jowls and overlarge black eyes that seemed to look in two directions. She radiated enormous calm and power.

Before he left, Aladuniel knelt beside Sarah, still holding her hand.

"You are a true Elf-friend," Aladuniel said.

Sarah shook her head. "Thanks." What could she say?

Aladuniel bowed his head solemnly to her, putting his hand on his heart, and she couldn't help but smile. Who were they kidding? Didn't they give a damn about what everyone else thought of them? She thought that at least she tried not to be lame, whatever everyone in school thought of her anyway. But of course they didn't go to school, the Elves. They didn't have homes either. As bad as things were with her mother, she always had a place to go back to, a home. This was their home, this old, drafty warehouse with its fading murals. She tried to remember that and not laugh. Aladuniel stood and quietly departed.

"The Wizard was just here," Lady G said. "He wanted me to tell you that he's leaving. He wasn't sure he'd have a chance to see you."

"When's he coming back?"

"We'll have to get along without him for a while. He's going home."

"Where to?"

"Under the sea."

Sarah stared, uncomprehending.

"What do you mean?"

"He's tired, and he wants to go home."

The screensaver on the computer came on, slowly filling in a red lidless eye dot by dot. She shook her head, thinking, all right, let me try this again.

"How's he going to go home?"

"He's just going to wade into the sea."

"He's going to kill himself?"

"No, not at all. Or, well, not exactly."

Sarah stared again. She couldn't seem to find anyone who would have a straight conversation with her, not her sister, not Al, not Lady G, and she couldn't even find the Wizard at all.

"I needed to talk to him." Sarah looked down at her hands, uncertain where to put them, absently rolling the wheels of her skateboard. Lady G made her feel too young.

"Maybe I can help." Lady G waved to another chair, inviting Sarah to sit down. She remained standing.

"My sister had a dream. The Wizard predicted it."

"What kind of dream?"

"She saw a monster." Sarah described it: tall, maybe ten feet tall, gaunt, stick-thin, the long corkscrew nose, almost a foot long, the fish eyes on either side of its head, the mouths where the eyes should have been, the scratching to be let in.

Lady G nodded. "She saw Old Shadow. He's come back." She motioned toward the computer screen. "Always he watches and waits for his chance."

"What is it?"

"Always, we must be ready for it. Though we are weaker than we were the last time, perhaps than we have ever been. And no wizard this time. We have stories going back a long way, telling us to be ready, to look for the signs. Again, there will be the story to be told, and all must play their parts."

This was too fast. Sarah didn't understand.

"Why does he come to my sister?" Sarah's heart was in her throat again. She didn't exactly believe Lady G. She didn't disbelieve her either.

"She's the dreamer. The one who is strong enough to open a way between place and place, between This and The Other. She will dream him into being, unless she resists. You must bring her to me. We will explain it to her, help her resist it."

"Yes," Sarah said, daring to look into Lady G's wide eyes. Why not believe her? She had come to believe in the Wizard. "Yes," she said more decisively. "I'll bring her here to you."

Only after she left did she realize she had forgotten to mention that her sister had seen herself, out the window, in the street, beckoning herself to come down. What did that mean?

When Sarah came through the door, her mother was in the front hallway on the phone. Her mother put her hand up flat to stop her. Sarah could hear Amanda's party out in the backyard past the kitchen door, laughter and shouts.

"What do you mean you don't want to live there anymore, mother?" Sarah's mother was talking to Sarah's grandmother. Sarah's mother sounded shrill, exasperated, worried. She put her hand over the phone. "Where's Amanda? I thought she was with you," she said to Sarah.

"She's not here?"

"What's that, mother? What do you mean you're going to live in the park? What are you talking about. It's ridiculous."

"What's going on?" Sarah asked.

"Grandma Rebecca doesn't want to live in the house she's lived in with Grandpa George for the last twenty years. She says now that he's dead, the house doesn't feel like hers anymore. Look, mother, you're just trying to get me to ask you to live here. Yes, you are. You know I can't. This is emotional blackmail. Mother, you can't do this."

"And Amanda's gone?" Sarah asked.

"Yes. I thought I asked you to get her ready this morning? Hello? The line's dead."

"I'll find them," Sarah said, opening the front door again. "I'll find them both."

"Wait, where are you going? I can't go with all these kids in the yard. I need you to watch them. Sarah. *SARAH!*"

Sarah took the front steps two at a time, dropped her skateboard and jumped on, already rolling downhill.

Two years ago, Sarah had run away from home. She had slept for two nights in the park under a bush beside a chainlink fence. The third day, cold, hungry, she walked down to the beach, rummaging through garbage cans along the way. She had woken up that morning shivering, and it hadn't stopped the whole day. As evening dimmed in the sky and on the water, the glistening spray of the waves becoming shadows thrown up against the sky, Sarah saw the Wizard of Ashes and Rain. She walked to him where he sat cross-legged before a small fire, looking out to the sea. He wore three ragged sweaters and a heavy black skirt over grey sweatpants, no shoes.

She knew who he was, but at the time she didn't know him very well. He was another crazy street person, nice enough, harmless, who sometimes hung around the Elves. Still, she felt so alone, and so cold. She no longer cared, felt she might never care again and that scared her. She looked down at him, shivering, not knowing what to say. Wanting desperately for him to say something to make it all better. It started drizzling, of course. The clouds darkened as she waited.

"You need a reading," he said.

"I ran away from home." She hugged herself tight.

He reached into his pack and handed her a plastic bag filled with trail mix. She sat down and ate it hungrily. He handed her a thick plastic bottle with water inside.

"My mother has rules for everything. Not just about studying, but what I can wear. What I can say."

She had to keep the reasons before her because they didn't seem convincing anymore even to her.

The Wizard removed a small bronze plate from his pack. The plate had unfamiliar symbols carved around an elaborately ornamented border.

"What's that."

"It is a tynka, a reading wheel, where I can see the future and the past."

The Wizard put his staff in the fire and sifted the ashes. It was the day she learned about the other part of his name, why they called him the Wizard of Ashes and Rain. He knocked some of the ash out of the fire and into the cold sand. He scooped up the ashes and some dirty sand mixed with old wrappers and broken plastic toy parts, and poured it on the wheel. He set the tynka between them. She had heard that he could divine, but she had never seen him do it. He took her hand and held it over the plate. Uneasy, she resisted, but not strongly. He spoke words she did not understand, then released her hand.

"What are you doing?"

He picked up the plate and jiggled it, letting the ashes and sand crumble into pieces and spread across the plate. Water droplets splashed on the wheel, scarring the ash.

"The way the ashes fall across the symbols, the way the water runs, the creases and breaks in it tell a story. Everything tells a story."

Sarah leaned forward to look.

"Yes," the Wizard said. "I see."

"Did it tell you about my mother? What should I do?"

The Wizard looked up into her eyes.

"Your father's sorry. He's sorry he had to die."

Her father had died the year before.

The Wizard dumped the ashes back into the sand and sat humming to himself until she left. For a long time Sarah watched the waves push out and beach themselves, then run back into the sea. A light drizzle soaked her hair. Then she went home and negotiated rules that both she and her mother could live with.

Sarah found her sister and her Grandmother Rebecca on a park bench near Stow Lake, eating cucumber and cream cheese sandwiches. Her grandmother had on her nice pink party dress with the ruffles, and black shiny shoes. Her grandmother wore a blue sweatsuit made of synthetics. By the time she found them, the sun had passed overhead and was already tangled in the treetops as it descended toward the sea.

It was still hours before sunset, though. The late afternoon duck feeders with their bags of bread were just being joined by the afterwork joggers and dog walkers. The winds had started up, blowing off the ocean, already pushing in the fog that would arrive with nightfall. The trees swayed, gathering around the edge of the lake in milling crowds, or standing alone, seeming to shift from foot to foot. The ducks complained as the bread ran out and the wind ruffled their feathers.

"Why, hello, dear," her Grandmother Rebecca said, scooting closer to Amanda so Sarah could sit down, patting the bench.

"Do you want part of my sandwich?"

"I brought the sandwiches," Amanda said with her mouth full.

"Yes, certainly you did. They're my favorite."

"I have one for Sarah in the bag." Amanda pointed at her feet without reaching down.

"What are you doing here, grandma?"

Sarah came closer, stood before her grandmother.

"Oh, the house, it's too big. It's filled with George's books, crowding me out. I couldn't breathe. It was his house, really. I just stayed there with him."

Sarah didn't believe her grandmother, but thought she understood. "It all reminds you of him."

Sarah's grandmother nodded. "Yes, I suppose that's part of it."

"Are you really going to sleep out here?"

Her grandmother picked up the bag, reached in and produced another sandwich.

"Yes, right on this bench."

"It's dangerous."

"You're beginning to sound like your mother."

Sarah sat down. She accepted a cucumber and cream cheese sandwich. Benches lined the asphalt walkway around the lake. At night, the benches would be claimed one by one. Her grandmother might even get pushed out by someone stronger.

"Besides," her grandmother said. "You have friends out here, right? That Wizard, he's out here. Maybe he could look out for me."

"He's gone," Sarah said. "He's not coming back."

"Oh, I'm sorry, dear."

"He knew about my dream," Amanda said with her mouth full.

"What dream? You didn't tell me you had a dream. Your sister," Grandmother Rebecca said to Sarah, "doesn't tell me anything anymore. She has just been sitting there, eating, refusing to answer my questions. She just makes comments about the things *she* wants to talk about, what people are wearing, the dogs." Grandmother Rebecca shook her head.

"I can't talk to her anymore, either," Sarah said.

Amanda, chewing, looking forward, pretended not to hear.

"I had a dream about a monster," Amanda said, "over and over the same dream.''

Grandmother Rebecca looked stricken.

Sarah described the monster again.

"I used to have that dream,'' Grandmother Rebecca said. "I used to have that same dream. But I told it to leave you alone. If I said yes it was supposed to leave you alone. Your mother, all of you. I told it.''

Sarah looked at her grandmother, hard. Her grandmother fretted with the zipper of her jacket. Only Amanda seemed undisturbed by their grandmother's revelation.

"When was this?'' Sarah asked.

"When I was a little girl, so of course none of you existed, but he said he'd come for you unless I said yes. He wanted in to this world. My mother warned me. It had come to her. It said if I said no, it would come for my daughters, and my daughter's daughters. I had to. I thought I had to.''

"Wasn't there anyone to help you? The Elves?''

"Elves? There are still Elves in the world? I thought they'd all left. Under the sea or something like that.''

"Here comes mom,'' Amanda said.

They all looked. Sarah's mother walked fast, taking short steps, her arms crossed on her chest.

She stopped before them, distracted. They could see it on her face. They had all failed her. She didn't know where to start.

"Do you want a sandwich?'' Amanda said. "There's one in the bag for you.''

"Amanda it's your birthday.'' Sarah's mother's voice trembled. "Your party is ruined.'' Her face looked pinched, her mouth small and drawn down, her shoulders tight. She wore a long dark print dress and a blue sweater.

"You know I work so hard for this family. Why won't any of you do anything? Why won't any of you even try?''

Sarah's mother put her hands on her hips.

"Mother,'' she said to Sarah's grandmother, "you know this is just your way of getting what you want. I told you I can't let you stay with us. You know I have two kids to raise alone. I'm trying so hard.''

She shook. Sarah thought of herself on the beach beside the Wizard two years ago.

"Sarah," her mother faltered. She looked away. "Sarah, I told you to stay home. Take your sister home. I need to talk to your grandmother alone."

Sarah stood, taking Amanda's hand and pulling her up. Sarah's mother sat down, slumping, beginning to cry, her shaking becoming sobbing heaves. Her mother cried a lot since her father's death three years ago. Grandmother Rebecca put her arm around her daughter.

Sarah walked away with her sister, but not toward home. She took her sister to the Elves.

Sarah walked her sister through the park, past the Japanese Tea Gardens, the Asian Art Museum and the Academy of Sciences, holding her skateboard in one hand and her sister's hand in the other. Just before they left the park, two O-boys stepped onto the asphalt path ahead. One of them was James, the contacts in his eyes smoldering red in the twilight. She wondered again how they made them glow like that. His derby jacket seemed a size too big on his skinny frame. The other O-boy looked even younger, and bow-legged, with a ripped white t-shirt and no jacket. The younger one kept looking around nervously, pulling at his shirt, straightening and unstraightening it, unable to stand still, his red eyes shifting in the gloom. Beyond them, the City streets opened out and cars sped by behind the trees.

"Where're you going?" the younger one said.

"She can pass," James said. He wouldn't meet her eyes. His pock-marked face sullen, he shoved his hands in his pockets and stepped out of the way.

"No one in or out," the younger one said, pointing at Sarah.

"Shut up," James said. The lines on his face drew tight as he clenched his jaw, staring down the younger one.

The younger one stepped out of the way.

Sarah led her sister on, pausing when she passed James.

"Thanks," she said.

"Fuck you," he said. "Get out of here."

Sarah sneered, pulling Amanda past.

"Yeah, nice contacts," she said, "so scary."

It did unnerve her. That's why she mentioned it.

"They're not contacts," James said.

Sarah didn't look back.

"What does he mean by that?" Amanda asked.

"Quiet," Sarah said.

"What are they?"

"Quiet."

Two blocks out of the park, Sarah and Amanda ran into a group of Elves led by Aladuniel.

"You're lucky you didn't run in to any O-boys," Aladuniel said. "They are everywhere. They're gathering in the long shadow again. We've been sent to look for you. Lady G said you would bring your sister."

Aladuniel knelt beside Amanda.

"Any sister of Sarah's is a sister of ours," he said. "I name you Elf-friend." He bowed his head. The other Elves put their hands over their hearts. "Elf-friend," they said together.

Sarah looked around, embarrassed. No one on the street, running errands or heading out for a late lunch, seemed to notice. No one ever did seem to notice the Elves. Maybe they just thought they were geeks and ignored them. Amanda giggled.

"We don't have time for this, Al," Sarah said, not knowing if that was true. "Take me to Lady G."

When Aladuniel ushered Sarah and Amanda in to see Lady G on the second floor of the Elves' warehouse, the Lady was not alone. The Wizard of Ashes and Rain sat in a rolling ergonomic chair.

"I heard you were looking for me," the Wizard said to Sarah. The Wizard wore layers of ragged unbuttoned sweaters and a pair of grimy jeans. He was shoeless, and his salt and pepper hair hung past his shoulders. His face had the sunburnt and leathered look of steetpeople who slept outside too much. He had a long scar near his right ear. His staff, gnarled and black, sat across his knees. Behind the Wizard and Lady G, the screensaver on Lady G's computer was on, filling in the red lidless eye dot by dot.

"Oh, it's good to – I thought you were—"

Sarah wanted to hug the Wizard, though they had never hugged before. Except for the time he had held her hands over the tynka plate, they had never even touched.

"You were looking for me, so I came back to help you," the Wizard said. "I guess I still have a part to play," he sighed. "The story can be so demanding."

Sarah told Lady G and the Wizard what her grandmother told her. Neither looked at all surprised. The Wizard just nodded his head.

Lady G leaned forward toward Amanda.

"It's all right. You couldn't have known."

Then Sarah noticed that Amanda was crying.

"What is it?" Sarah said. "Amanda?"

"She already said yes," Lady G said. "Sometime this morning."

"I read it myself," The Wizard said, "in the wheel."

"I'm sorry," Amanda said. She spoke in a rush. "The other me, the one from the dream, led me into the park, after you left, before I saw grandma. To the wooden bridge by the lake in the arboretum. The other me was the monster, or from the monster, or something. And if I said yes it wouldn't bother me anymore, so I did." She took Sarah's hand again. "Please don't go away again. I'm sorry. I know I was supposed to wait for you."

"The monster is resting," Lady G said, "waiting for the night to move against us."

"I'm sorry," her sister said again. "Please."

"You've hardly even talked to me in the past year," Sarah said, "now you're worried I'll leave you?"

"Amanda," the Wizard said, "I've seen this sort of thing before, many times, and for all the dreamers, I've only known one to say no. One. It's all right. The story tells itself. It always does. It didn't let me go home, did it? So, you played your part. It's all right. We all do."

Amanda did not look away from Sarah. "Please."

Sarah sighed, touching the tears on Amanda's cheek. "Of course I'm staying." Would she ever understand her sister? She supposed she never would. She hugged her.

Amanda, still holding Sarah around the waist, looked back at Lady G. "Am I still an Elf-friend?" she asked.

"Of course."

Oh, God, Sarah thought, don't hang with the Elves. Please, no.

"Come on," Lady G said. "There's not much time before nightfall. We have to be ready to head into the park, to the arboretum."

"To the bridge?" Sarah asked.

"Yes, where we should find the O-boys gathering. And then the story will be finished."

The Elves set out into the park after nightfall, fanning out in small groups. They met groups of O-boys almost immediately. There was fighting reported, though Sarah didn't see it where she was, in the back of the main group with her sister, Lady G and the Wizard. But mostly, the O-boys fell back as the Elves advanced, as if wanting them to come in, almost showing them where to go. They entered the arboretum about midnight. The open area of the arboretum covered two fenced-in miles. Except for the O-boys and Elves, the park was quiet and empty of people. The O-boys must have chased the other homeless people away. Amanda had to help her sister over the fence. She didn't see how Lady G made it in.

"Mom's going to kill us for staying out so late," Amanda had said, jumping down on the other side.

"Unless the monster kills us first," Sarah said.

Her sister just looked at her.

"It was a joke."

Near the entranceway to the arboretum, an old tree stood in a large field. The Elves regarded it as sacred. Each one touched the trunk and spoke a word of Elvish before moving off toward a path across the field which sloped down to a lake where they found the O-boys massing on the far side, their eyes bright red in the moonlight. They seemed to be chanting something in a low guttural tone. It made Sarah's skin crawl. She couldn't stop watching their eyes, darting, blinking out or staring across at the Elves.

A wooden bridge spanned the lake at a narrow point in its middle. The Elves gathered on one side, the O-boys waited on the other, shouting taunts. The number of Elves was pitifully few, not even half the number of the black-booted O-boys. The ducks in the pond flew off as the O-boys began to throw rocks. The Elves backed out of range of the missiles, which hit the ground before them with loud thumps. The moon was full, shining behind the fog, making everything seem to glow, dimly luminous. The trees over them seemed to be holding up their arms and swaying in a slow-motion dance, crowding over them to see what would happen.

Sarah scanned the O-boys for James, but she couldn't spot him in the gloom. She was surprised when her grandmother came up behind her.

"What—?"

"I wouldn't miss this."

"How did you get rid of mom? She let you just stay in the park?"

"Oh, I agreed to stay at your house, for her sake."

"Yes." Sarah looked down, embarrassed.

"But I slipped out when she wasn't looking. I haven't seen Elves in an age. Aren't they wonderful?"

"They are," Amanda said.

Sarah looked at them. Not really, she thought. Though they did stand bravely in their overlarge shirts with the billowing sleeves, seemingly unafraid of the much larger body of O-boys. But still.

"But where's the monster?" Sarah asked the Wizard who sat nearby on an old stump.

"Under the bridge," the Wizard said. He smiled at Sarah's grandmother. "Hello, Rebecca."

Sarah's grandmother smiled back. She had on an overcoat, but Sarah could see she had slippers on her feet, and the edge of her nightgown peeked below the long coat. How had she gotten over the fence?

The Wizard laughed as a bare drizzle started to fall. He caught some drops on his tongue.

"I think it's time to end this," the Wizard said, sighing. He stood. "Goodbye, Amanda, Rebecca." He shook their hands. "Goodbye, Sarah. If you need me again, look for me in the West, in the far place."

"What are you going to do?"

"You'll see." The Wizard took her hands in both of his and squeezed.

The Wizard turned and headed toward the bridge. He'll be hit by rocks, Sarah thought. But instead the O-boys became quiet, no longer shouting or moving, just watching. The rain increased. It seemed to cow the O-boys.

The Wizard looked older and more tired than Sarah had ever seen him. He leaned heavily on his staff, and picked his way carefully down the path that led on to the bridge. He waited on the bridge with his head bowed, almost fallen against his staff. His sweaters sagged off him, becoming heavier and heavier with rain.

It was not long before the monster emerged from under the bridge. A long, bony hand reached out and clasped the edge, then the monster pulled itself up and peeked over with one fish eye. Amanda took Sarah's hand as the monster put another hand up on the railing and hauled itself out of dream and into the world. It stood for a moment outside the railing, regarding the wizard, before leaping over in one bounce and landing on the bridge. Sarah took a step back involuntarily. It was ten feet tall and had a long, impossible and grotesque corkscrew nose. Its two mouths where its eyes should have been gnashed and grimaced. Sarah couldn't breathe or move.

The Wizard looked horribly small and over-matched before the monster. In his torn rags, barefoot, leaning on his staff as if he might collapse, the Wizard looked up at the monster towering above him. The monster reached out with its long bony fingers – sharp claws emerged as from a cat's paw. This had come in her sister's dream. Sarah thought, if it had come to me, I would have said yes to get rid of it too.

The monster approached the wizard cautiously, reminding Sarah that the Wizard had power of his own, though it did not always show itself. The Wizard raised his staff, and the winds picked up, seemed to blow about wildly and then focus in on the monster, buffeting it back. It clawed the air, then leapt forward. Landing unsteadily before the Wizard, it slapped at him, knocking the Wizard from his feet. The Wizard touched the monster's foot with his staff and there was a flash. Everyone had to look away, blinded.

The O-boys had begun to shout, calling for blood. And the Elves, who had been grimly silent, began to chant in Elvish, and the tune, sung in high pitched voices, chilled Sarah. She knew they too called for blood, and would not back down.

When Sarah could see again, the monster and the Wizard were locked together in an embrace, struggling, inside a small maelstrom that surrounded only them, leaves, water, dirt and small rocks circling them in the air, then with a lurch, both of them fell into the railing, then over it, tumbling. They hit the water with a loud splash and the hiss of steam. Again, they were lost from view. The winds calmed. The ruffled waters calmed. The steam cleared. Even the rain became a drizzle, then stopped. Nothing.

The O-boys stopped shouting first. Then the Elves stopped chanting. A few ducks had returned to the far side of the pond, and they quacked loudly. That was all.

"What happened?" Amanda asked.

"They went back through the hole in dreams," Lady G said, "under the bridge."

Lady G called out and the Elves advanced, crossing the bridge to attack the O-boys. The O-boys still outnumbered them, but their hearts weren't in it anymore. A few had come to the water's edge to peer in. Some threw stones as the Elves advanced in a tight formation. But most took off running, many leaving their derby jackets behind.

The Elves chased the O-boys out of the arboretum easily, whacking some with sticks, capturing others. They did not even have to draw their knives. Sarah waited with her sister and grandmother beside Lady G, who ran the Elves in a tight military fashion, barking orders, gathering prisoners. At one point, two Elves came up to Sarah with an O-boy. It was James.

"He says he's your friend," one elf said.

Sarah looked at him. James had a bloody lip, and he was covered in dust and leaves from being rolled on the ground. And his eyes had dimmed, the red in them losing luster, burning out. He looked almost human again, she thought.

"Yes," she said. "Let him go."

"We're even," James said sullenly, wiping his lip, his eyes darting to the Elves.

"Yes," She paused. "James, if you—"

James turned and stalked away, straight-armed, his hands balled into fists. One of the Elves left to follow and give him safe passage.

"What will happen to the O-boys?" Sarah asked Lady G.

"They're finished. Some will become Elves."

"Really?"

"Yes, maybe even your friend."

Sarah looked after James.

"I don't know."

"It may take time." Lady G shrugged. "That I have plenty of."

Sarah's grandmother squeezed her hand. "It's over," she said. "Time to get you two home to bed."

Hand in hand, they walked home through the cool San Francisco night, laughing, recounting their adventures.

"The Wizard," Sarah asked her grandmother soberly. "What will happen to him?"

"Did you ever read the book the Elves love so much?"

"Yes," she said.

"Do you remember what happens to the Wizard in that one?" She nodded.

"I wouldn't worry about him," Grandmother Rebecca said. "The story always repeats itself."

When they arrived home, the lights were still on, though Sarah's mother did not hear them come in. They could hear her in the kitchen, rattling jars in the cupboards. The clock in the entryway read four a.m.

"I'd better go tell her we're O.K." Sarah said.

"And I'd better go to sleep," Grandmother Rebecca said. "I don't think she knew I was gone. I'll tuck Amanda in to bed."

Amanda was almost asleep on her feet, but was happy. She would sleep dreamless tonight. Grandmother Rebecca led her up the stairs by the hand. Sarah took a deep breath and entered the kitchen.

"Hi, Mom."

Sarah's mother was bent into an emptied cupboard. She stood up.

"I'm sorry we were out so late. Amanda's fine."

"It's O.K."

Sarah blinked.

"It's O.K.?"

"Your grandma explained what was happening. I know you had to go."

Sarah stared, dumbfounded.

"I cleaned out all the cupboards, put down new contact paper, and labeled all the jars."

"Mom, it's four a.m."

"I'm a little nervous, all right? I'm – I'm – I'm so happy you are all all right."

Her mother fidgeted, rubbed her hands together compulsively.

"I wish you could have told me," her mother said. "I really do."

"Mom, you don't make it easy."

"I do everything I can for this fam—" She stopped, clasped her hands together to stop them from moving, pursued her lips. "O.K., O.K., I know it's not easy, but could you try?"

Sarah saw her mother was trying so hard.

"Yes," Sarah said. "I will. I promise."

"Your grandmother's moving in."

"Really?" Sarah glanced over her shoulder. Her grandmother was long gone upstairs.

"For a little while, yes. Just a short time."

"O.K.," Sarah said.

"You know I'm just – just doing the best I can."

"Sure," Sarah said. "I just wish you could see that everyone else is, too."

"O.K." her mother said. She bit her lip. "I'm proud of you, do you know that? You are becoming a fine young woman."

Sarah smiled. "Thanks."

"I'm sure you'll have a fine adventure to tell me about, tomorrow, after you've rested."

Sarah stepped forward, picking up one of the jars scattered about the kitchen counters.

"I should finish this," Sarah's mother said.

"Mom, it's late. Go to bed."

"I'm too nervous."

"Well," Sarah said, "let me help you."

"Oh, O.K., good, you can tell me about what happened tonight."

"O.K.," Sarah said, "but you surprise me. Mom. How come you know about this stuff?"

"Sarah," her mother looked at her, smiling. "I'm the one who said no. The only one, I think the Wizard said."

My mother, the dreamer, Sarah realized, who would have thought it? They talked all night, even after finishing up with the kitchen chores.

And in the morning they made a large breakfast for everyone.

THE WALKER BEHIND

Marion Zimmer Bradley

Although she'd been selling short fiction since 1953 and had her first book, The Door Through Space, *published in 1961, Marion Bradley, (1930–1999) shot to stardom with her perceptive recreation of the Arthurian world,* The Mists of Avalon *(1982), which remained on the New York Times bestseller list for over four months. Bradley's early work was in the form of planetary adventures, much in the spirit of Leigh Brackett and C.L. Moore, and included the long running Darkover series, set on an alien planet where a form of magic works. With the success of* The Mists of Avalon, *Bradley wrote further historical fantasies including* The Firebrand *(1987), set during the Trojan War, and* The Forest House *(1993), which dealt with the British at the time of the Roman conquest. It was later incorporated into an Avalon series as* Forests of Avalon, *continued by* Lady of Avalon *(1997) and* Priestess of Avalon *(2000).*

In all of this Bradley's short fiction has perhaps been overlooked, but she wrote a series of stories about a female adept, Lythande, some of which were collected in the volume Lythande *(1986), but that doesn't include the following.*

> *As one who on a lonesome road*
> *Doth walk in fear and dread*
> *And turns but once to look around*
> *And turns no more his head*
> *Because he knows a frightful fiend*
> *Doth close behind him tread . . .*

L YTHANDE HEARD THE FOLLOWING footsteps that night on the road: a little pause so that if she chose, she could have believed it merely the echo of her own light footfall. Step-pause-step, and then, after a little hesitation, step-pause-step, step-pause-step.

And at first she did think it an echo, but when she stopped for a moment to assess the quality of the echo, it went on for at least three steps into the silence:

Step-pause-step; step-pause-step.

Not an echo, then; but someone, or some *thing*, following her. In the world of the Twin Suns, where encountering magic was rather more likely than not, magic was more often than not of the evil kind. In a lifetime spanning at least three ordinary lifetimes, Lythande had encountered a great deal of magic; she was by necessity a mercenary-magician, an Adept of the Blue Star, and by choice a minstrel; and she had discovered early in her life that good magic was the rarest of all encounters and seldom came her way. She had lived this long by developing very certain instincts; and her instincts told her that this footfall following her was not benevolent.

She had no notion of what it might be. The simplest solution was that someone in the last town she had passed through had developed a purely material grudge against her, and was following her on mischief bent, for some reason or no reason at all – perhaps a mere mortal distrust of magicians, or of magic, a condition not all that rare in Old Gandrin – and had chosen to take the law into his or her own hands and dispose of the unwelcome procurer of said magic. This was not at all rare, and Lythande had dealt with plenty of would-be assassins who wished to stop the magic by putting an effective stop to the magician; however powerful an Adept's magic, it could seldom survive a knife in the back. On the other hand, it could be handled with equal simplicity; after three ordinary lifetimes, Lythande's back had not yet become a sheath for knives.

So Lythande stepped off the road, loosening the first of her two knives in its scabbard – the simple white-handled knife, whose purpose was to handle purely material dangers of the road: footpads, assassins, thieves. She enveloped herself in the gray cloudy folds of the hooded mage-robe, which made her look like a piece of the night itself, or a shadow, and stood waiting for the owner of the footsteps to come up with her.

But it was not that simple. Step-pause-step, and the footfalls died; the mysterious follower was pacing her. Lythande had hardly thought it would be so simple. She sheathed the white-handled knife again, and stood motionless, reaching out with all her specially trained senses to focus on the follower.

What she felt first was a faint electric tingle in the Blue Star that was between her brows; and a small, not quite painful crackle in her head. *The smell of magic*, she translated to herself; whatever was following, it was neither as simple, nor as easily disposed of, as an assassin with a knife.

She loosened the black-handled knife in the left-hand scabbard and, stepping herself like a ghost or a shadow, retraced her steps at the side of the road. This knife was especially fashioned for supernatural menaces, to kill ghosts and anything else from specters to werewolves; no knife but this one could have taken her own life had she tired of it.

A shadow with an irregular step glided toward her, and Lythande raised the black-handled knife. It came plunging down, and the glimmer of the enchanted blade was lost in the shadow. There was a far-off, eerie cry that seemed to come, not from the shadow facing her on the dark road, but from some incredibly distant ghostly realm, to curdle the very blood in her veins, to wrench pain and lightnings from the Blue Star between her brows. Then, as that cry trembled into silence, Lythande felt the black handle of the knife come back into her hand, but a faint glimmer of moonlight showed her the handle alone; the blade had vanished, except for some stray drops of molten metal that fell slowly to the earth and vanished.

So the blade was gone, the black-handled knife that had slain unnumbered ghosts and other supernatural beings. Judging by the terrifying cry, Lythande had wounded her follower; but had she killed the thing that had eaten her magical blade? Anything that powerful would certainly be tenacious of life.

And if her black-handled knife would not kill it, it was unlikely it could be killed by any spell, protection, or magic she could command at the moment. It had been driven away, perhaps, but she could not be certain she had freed herself from it. No doubt, if she went on, it would continue to follow her, and one day it would catch up with her on some other lonesome road.

But for the moment she had exhausted her protection. And . . . Lythande glowered angrily at the black knife handle and the ruined blade . . . she had deprived herself needlessly of a protection that had never failed her before. Somehow she must manage to replace her enchanted knife before she again dared the roads of Old Gandrin by night.

For the moment – although she had traveled too far and for too long to fear anything she was *likely* to encounter on any ordinary night – she would be wiser to remove herself from the road. Such encounters as a mercenary-magician, particularly one such as Lythande, should expect were seldom of the likely kind.

So she went on in the darkness, listening for the hesitating step of the follower behind. There was only the vaguest and most distant of sounds; that blow, and that screech, indicated that while she had probably not destroyed her follower, she had driven it at least for a while into some other place. Whether it was dead, or had chosen to go and follow someone safer, for the moment Lythande neither knew nor cared.

The important thing at the moment was shelter. Lythande had been traveling these roads for many years, and remembered that many years ago there had been an inn somewhere hereabouts. She had never chosen, before this, to shelter there – unpleasant rumors circulated about travelers who spent the night at that inn and were never seen again, or seen in dreadfully altered form. Lythande had chosen to stay away: the rumors were none of her business, and Lythande had not survived this long in Old Gandrin without knowing the first rule of survival, which was to ignore everything but your *own* survival. On the rare occasions when curiosity or compassion had prompted her to involve herself in anyone else's fate, she had had all kinds of reason to regret it.

Perhaps her obscure destiny had guided her on this occasion to investigate these rumors. She looked down the black expanse of the road – without even moonlight – and saw a distant glimmer of light. Whether it was the inn of uncanny rumor, or whether it was the light of a hunter's campfire, or the lair of a were-dragon, there, Lythande resolved, she would seek shelter for the night. The last client to avail himself of her services as a mercenary-magician – a man who had paid her well to dehaunt his ancestral mansion – had left her with more than enough coin for a night at even the most luxurious inn; and if she could not pick up a commission to offset the cost of a night's shelter, she was no worse off. Besides, with the lute at her back, she could usually earn a supper and a bed as a minstrel; they were not common in this quarter.

A few minutes of brisk walking strengthened the vague light into a brilliantly shining lantern hung over a painted sign that portrayed the figure of an old woman driving a pig; the inn sign read the Hag and Swine. Lythande chuckled under her breath . . . the sign was comical enough, but it startled her that for such a cheerful sign there was no sound of music or jollity from inside; all was quiet as the very demon-haunted road itself. It made her remember again the very unsavory rumors about this very inn.

There was a very old story about a hag who had indeed attempted to transform random travelers into swine, and other forms but Lythande could not remember where she had heard that story. Well, if she, an Adept of the Blue Star, was no match for any roadside hag, whatever her propensity for increasing her herd of swine – or perhaps furnishing her table with pork – at the expense of travelers, she deserved whatever happened to her. Shouldering her lute and concealing the handle of the ruined knife in one of the copious pockets of the mage-robe, Lythande strode through the half-open door.

Inside, it was light, but only by contrast with the moonless darkness of the outdoors. The only light was firelight, from a hearth where a pale fire flickered with a dim and unpleasant flame. Gathered around the hearth were a collection of people, mere shapes in the dim room; but as Lythande's eyes adapted to the darkness, she began to make out forms, perhaps half a dozen men and women and a couple of shabby children; all had pinched faces, and pushed-in noses that were somehow porcine. From the dimness arose the tall, heavy form of a woman, clad in shapeless garments that seemed to hang on her anyhow, much patched and botched.

Ah, thought Lythande, *this inn-keeper must be the hag. And those wretched children might very well be the swine*. Even secretly the jest pleased her.

In an unpleasant, snuffling voice, the tall hag demanded, "Who are you, sir, going about on the road where there be nowt but hants an' ghosts at this season?"

Lythande's first impulse was to gasp out, "I was *driven* here by evil magic; there is a monstrous Thing out there, prowling about this place!" But she managed to say instead, peacefully. "Neither hant nor ghost, but a wandering minstrel frightened like yourselves by the dangers of the road, and in need of supper and a night's lodging."

"At once, sir," said the hag, suddenly turning deferential. "Come to the fire and warm thyself."

Lythande came through the jostling crowd of small figures – yes, they were children, and at close range even more unpleasantly piglike; their sounds and snuffles made them even more animal. She felt a distinct revulsion for having them crowding against her. She was resigned to the "sir" with which the hag-innkeeper had greeted her; Lythande was the only woman ever to penetrate the mysteries of the Order of the Blue Star, and when (already sworn as an Adept, the Blue Star already blazing between her brows) she had been exposed as a woman, she was already protected against the worst they could have done. And so her punishment had been only this:

Be forever, then, had decreed the Master of the Star, *what you have chosen to seem; for on that day when any man save myself proclaims you a woman, then shall your magic be void and you may be slain and die.*

So for more than three ordinary lifetimes had Lythande wandered the roads as a mercenary-magician, doomed to eternal solitude; for she might reveal her true sex to no man, and while she might have a woman confidante if she could find one she could trust with her life, this exposed her chosen confidante to pressure from the many enemies of an Adept of the Blue Star; her first such confidante had been captured and tortured, and although she had died without revealing Lythande's secret, Lythande had been reluctant ever to expose another to that danger.

What had begun as a conscious masquerade was now her life; not a single gesture or motion revealed her as anything but the man she seemed – a tall, clean-shaven man with luxuriant fair hair, the blazing Blue Star between the high-arched shaven eyebrows, clad beneath the mage-robe in thigh-high boots, breeches, and a leather jerkin laced to reveal a figure muscular and broad-shouldered as an athlete, and apparently altogether masculine.

The innkeeper-hag brought a mug of drink and set it down before Lythande. It smelled savory and steamed hot; evidently a mulled wine with spices, a specialty of the house. Lythande lifted it to her lips, only pretending to sip; one of the many vows fencing about the powers of an Adept of the Blue Star was that they might never be seen to eat or drink in the presence of any man. The drink smelled good – as did the food she could smell cooking somewhere – and Lythande resented, not for the first time, the law that had often condemned her to long periods of thirst and hunger; but she was long accustomed to it, and recalling the singular name and reputation of this establishment, and the old story about the hag and swine, perhaps it was just as well to shun such food or drink as might be found in this place; it was by their greed, if she remembered the tale rightly, that the travelers had found themselves transformed into pigs.

The greedy snuffling of the hog-like children, if that was what they were, served as a reminder, and listening to it, she felt neither thirsty nor hungry. It was her custom at such inns to order a meal served in the privacy of her chamber, but she decided that in this place she would not indulge it; in the pockets of her mage-robe she kept a small store of dried fruit and bread, and long habit had accustomed her to snatching a hurried bite whenever she could do so unobserved.

She took a seat at one of the rough tables near the fireplace, the pot of ale before her, and, now and again pretending to take a sip of it, asked, "What news, friends?"

Her encounter fresh in her mind, she half expected to be told of some monster haunting the roadway. But nothing was volunteered. Instead, a rough-looking man seated on the opposite bench from hers, on the other side of the fireplace, raised his pot of ale and said, "Your health, sir; it's a bad night to be out. Storm coming on, unless I'm mistaken. And I've been traveling these roads, man and boy, for forty years."

"Oh?" inquired Lythande courteously. "I am new to these parts. Are the roads generally safe?"

"Safe enough," he grunted, "unless the folks get the idea you're a jewel carrier or some such." He needed to add no more; there were always thieves who might take the notion that some person was not so poor as he sought to appear (so as to seem to have nothing worth stealing), and cut him open looking for his jewels.

"And you?"

"I travel the roads as my old father did; I am a dog barber." He spoke the words truculently. "Anyone who has a dog to show or to sell knows I can make the beast look to its best advantage." Someone behind his back snickered, and he drew himself up to his full height and proclaimed, "It's a respectable profession."

"One of your kind," said a man before the fire, "sold my old father an old dog with rickets and the mange, for a healthy watchdog; the old critter hardly had the strength to bark."

"I don't sell dogs," said the man haughtily. "I only prepare them for show—"

"And o'course you'd never stoop to faking a mongrel up to look like a purebred, or fixing up an old dog with the mange to look like a young one with glossy topknots and long hair," said the heckler ironically. "Everybody in this county knows that when you have some bad old stock to get rid of, stolen horses to paint with false marks, there's old Gimlet the dog faker, worse than any gypsy for tricks—"

"Hey there, don't go insulting honest gypsies with your comparisons," said a dark man seated on a box on the floor by the fire and industriously eating a rich-smelling stew from a wooden bowl; he had a gold earring in his ear like one of that maligned race. "We trade horses all up and down this country from here to Northwander, and I defy any man to say he ever got a bad horse from any of our tribe."

"Gimlet the dog barber, are ye?" asked another of the locals, a shabby, squint-eyed man. "I been looking for you; don't you remember me?"

The dog barber put on a defiant face. "Afraid not, friend."

"I had a bitch last year had thirteen pups," said the newcomer, scowling. "Good bitch; been the pride and joy of my family since she was a pup. You said you'd fix her up a brew so she'd get her milk in and be able to feed them all—"

"Every dog handler learns something of the veterinary art," said Gimlet. "I can bring in a cow's milk, too, and—"

"Oh, I make no doubt you can shoe a goose, too, to hear you tell it," the man said.

"What's your complaint, friend? Wasn't she able to feed her litter?"

"Oh, aye, she was," said the complainer. "And for a couple of days, it felt good watching every little pup sucking away at her tits; then it occurred to me to count 'em, and there were no more than eight pups."

Gimlet restrained a smile.

"I said only that I would arrange matters so the bitch could feed all her brood; if I disposed of the runts who would have been unprofitable, without you having to harrow yourself by drowning them—," Gimlet began.

"Don't you go weaseling out of it," the man said, clenching his fists. "Any way you slice it, you owe me for at least five good pups."

Gimlet looked round. "Well, that's as may be," he said. "Maybe tomorrow we can arrange something. It never occurred to me you'd get chesty about the runts in the litter, more than any bitch could raise. Not unless you've a childless wife or young daughter who wants to cosset something and hankers to feed 'em with an eyedropper and dress 'em in doll's clothes; more trouble than it's worth, most folks say. But here's my hand on it." He stuck out his hand with such a friendly, open smile of good faith that Lythande was enormously entertained; between the rogue and the yokel, Lythande, after years spent traveling the roads, was invariably on the side of the rogue. The disgruntled dog owner hesitated a moment, but finally shook his hand and called for another pot of beer for all the company.

Meanwhile the hag-innkeeper, hovering to see if it would come to some kind of fight, and looking just a little disappointed that it had not, stopped at Lythande's side.

"You, sir, will you be wanting a room for the night?"

Lythande considered. She did not particularly like the look of the place, and if she spent the night, resolved she would not feel safe in closing her eyes. On the other hand, the dark road outside was less attractive than ever, now that she had tasted the warmth of the fireside. Furthermore, she had lost her magical knife, and would be unprotected on the dark road with some *Thing* following.

"Yes," she said, "I will have a room for the night."

The price was arranged – neither cheap nor outrageous – and the innkeeper asked, "Can I find you a woman for the night?"

This was always the troublesome part of traveling in male disguise. Lythande, whatever her romantic desires, had no wish for the kind of women kept in country inns for traveling customers, without choice; they were usually sold into this business as soon as their breasts grew, if not before. Yet it was a singularity to refuse this kind of accommodation, and one that could endanger the long masquerade on which her power depended.

Tonight she did not feel like elaborate excuses.

"No, thank you; I am weary from the road and will sleep." She dug into her robe for a couple of spare coins. "Give the girl this for her trouble."

The hag bowed. "As you will, sir. Frennet! Show the gentleman to the south room."

A handsome girl, tall and straight and slender, with silky hair looped up into elaborate curls, rose from the fireside and gestured with a shapely arm half concealed by silken draperies. "This way, if ye please," she said, and Lythande rose, edging between Gimlet and the dog owner. In a pleasant, mellow voice, she wished the company good night.

The stairs were old and rickety, stretching up several flights, but had once been stately – about four owners ago, Lythande calculated. Now they were hung with cobwebs, and the higher flights looked as if they might be the haunt of bats, too. From one of the posts at a corner landing, a dark form ascended, flapping its wings, and cried out in a hoarse, croaking sound:

"Good evening, ladies! Good evening, ladies!"

The girl Frennet raised an arm to ward off the bird.

"That accursed jackdawl Madame's pet, sir; pay no attention," she said good-naturedly, and Lythande was glad of the darkness. It was beneath the dignity of an Adept of the Blue Star to take notice of a trained bird, however articulate.

"Is that all it says?"

"Oh no, sir; quite a vocabulary the creature has, but then, you see, you never know what it's going to say, and sometimes it can really startle you if you ain't expecting it," said Frennet, opening the door to a large, dark chamber. She went inside and lighted a candelabrum standing by the huge, draped four-poster. The jackdaw flapped in the doorway and croaked hoarsely, "Don't go in there, Madame! Don't go in there, Madame!"

"Just let me get rid of her for you, sir," said Frennet, taking up a broom and making several passes with it, attempting to drive the jackdaw back down the staircase. Then she noticed that Lythande was still standing in the doorway of the room.

"It's all right, sir; you can go right in. You don't want to let her scare you. She's just a stupid bird."

Lythande had stopped cold, however, not so much because of the bird as because of the sharp pricking of the Blue Star between her brows. *The smell of magic*, she thought, wishing she were a hundred leagues from the Hag and Swine; without her magical knife, she was unwilling to spend a minute, let alone a night, in a room that smelled evilly of magic as that one did.

She said pleasantly, "I am averse to the omens, child. Could you perhaps show me to another chamber where I might sleep? After all, the inn is far from full, so find me another room, there's a good girl?"

"Well, I dunno what the mistress would say," began Frennet dubiously, while the bird shrieked, "There's a good girl! There's a clever girl!" Then she smiled and said, "But what she dunna know won't hurt her, I reckon. This way."

Up another flight of stairs, and Lythande felt the numbing prickling of the Blue Star, *the smell of magic*, recede and drop away. The rooms on this floor were lighted and smaller, and Frennet turned into one of them.

"Me own room, sir; yer welcome to the half of my bed if ye wish it, an' no obligation. I mean – I heard ye say ye didn't want a woman, but you sent a tip for me, and –" She stopped, swallowed, and said determindedly, her face flushing, "I dunno why yer traveling like a man, ma'am. But I reckon ye have yer reasons, an' they's none of me business. But ye came here in good faith for a night's lodgin', and I think ye've a right to that and nothin' else." The girl's face was red and embarrassed. "I swore no oath to keep my mouth shut about what's goin' on here, and I don't want your death on my hands, so there."

"My death?" Lythande said. "What do you mean, child?"

"Well, I'm in for it now," Frennet said, "but ye've a right to know, ma'am – sir – noble stranger. Folk who sleep here don't come back no more human; did ye see those little children down yonder? They're only halfway changed; the potions don't work all that well on children. I saw you didn't drink yer wine; so when they came to drive you out to the sty, you'd still be human and they'd kill you – or drive you out in the dark, where the Walker Behind can have ye."

Shivering, Lythande recalled the entity that had destroyed her magical knife. That, then, had been the Walker Behind.

"What is this – this Walker Behind?" she asked.

"I dunno, ma'am. Only it *follows*, and draws folk into the other world; thass all I know. Ain't nobody ever come back to tell what it is. Only I hears 'em scream when it starts followin' them."

Lythande stared about the small, mean chamber. Then she asked, "How did you know that I was a woman?"

"I dunno, ma'am. I always knows, that's all. I always knows, no matter what. I won't tell the missus; I promise."

Lythande sighed. Perhaps the girl was somewhat psychic; she had accepted a long time ago that while her disguise was usually opaque to men, there would always be a few women who for one reason or another would see through it. Well, there was nothing to be done about it, unless she were willing to murder the girl, which she was not.

"See that you do not; my life depends on it," she said. "But perhaps you need not give up your bed to me either; can you guide me unseen out of this place?"

"That I can, ma'am, but it's a wretched night to be out, and the Walker Behind in the dark out there. I'd hate to hear you screamin' when it comes to take you away."

Lythande chuckled, but mirthlessly. "Perhaps instead you would hear *it* screaming when I came to take *it*," she said. "I think that is what I encountered before I came here."

"Yes'm. It drives folk in here because it wants 'em, and then it takes their souls. I mean, when they's turned into pigs, I guess they don't need their souls no more, see? And the Walker Behind takes them."

"Well, it will not take me," Lythande said briefly. "Nor you, if I can manage it. I encountered this thing before I came here; it took my knife, so I must somehow get another."

"They's plenty of knives in the kitchen, ma'am," Frennet said. "I can take ye out through there."

Together they stole down the stairs, Lythande moving like a ghost in that silence that had caused many people to swear that they had seen Lythande appear to disappear into thin air. In the parlor most of the guests had gone to rest, she heard a strange grunting sound. Upstairs there were curious grunting noises; on the morrow, Lythande supposed, they would be driven out to the sty, their souls left for the Walker Behind and their bodies to reappear as sausages or roast pork. In the kitchen, as they passed, Lythande saw the innkeeper – the hag. She was chopping herbs; the pungent scent made Lythande think of the pungent drink she had fortunately not tasted.

So why had this evil come to infest this country? Her extended magical senses could now hear the step in the dark, prowling outside: the Walker Behind. She could sense and feel its evil circling in the dark, awaiting its monstrous feast of souls. But how – and why? – had anything human, even that hag, come to join hands with such a ghastly thing of damnation?

There had been a saying in the Temple of the Star that there was no fathoming the depths either of Law or of Chaos. And surely the Walker Behind was a thing from the very depths of Chaos; and Lythande, as a Pilgrim adept, was solemnly sworn to uphold forever and defend Law against Chaos even at the Final Battle at the end of the world.

"There are some things," she observed to the girl Frennet, "that I would prefer not to encounter until the Final Battle where Law will defeat Chaos at world's end. And of those things the Walker Behind is first among them; but the ways of Chaos do not await my convenience; and if I encounter it now, at least I need not meet it at the end of the world." She stepped quietly into the kitchen, and the hag jerked up her head.

"You? I thought you was sleeping by now, magician. I even sent you the girl—"

"Don't blame the girl; she did as you bade her," Lythande said. "I came hither to the Hag and Swine, though I knew it not, to rid the world of a pigsty of Chaos. Now you shall feed your own evil servant."

She gestured, muttering the words of a spell; the hag flopped forward on all fours, grunting and snuffling. Outside in the dark, Lythande sensed the approach of the great evil Thing, and motioned to Frennet.

"Open the door, child."

Frennet flung the door open; Lythande shoved the grunting thing outside over the threshold. There was a despairing scream – half animal but dreadfully half human – from somewhere; then only the body of a pig remained grunting in the foggy darkness of the innyard. From the shadowy Walker outside, there was a satisfied croon that made Lythande shudder. Well, so much for the Hag and Swine; she had deserved it.

"There's nothing left of her, ma'am."

"She deserves to be served up as sausages for breakfast, dressed with her own herbs," Lythande remarked, looking at what was left, and Frennet shook her head.

"I'd have no stomach for her meself, ma'am."

The jackdaw flapped out into the kitchen crying, "Clever girl! Clever girl! There's a good girl!" and Lythande said, "I think if I had my way, I'd wring that bird's neck. There's still the Walker to deal with; she was surely not enough to satisfy the appetite of – that thing."

"Maybe not, ma'am," Frennet said, "but you could deal with her; can you deal with it? It'll want your soul more than hers, mighty magician as you must be."

Lythande felt serious qualms; the innkeeper-hag, after all, had been but a small evil. But in her day, Lythande had dealt with a few large evils, though seldom any as great and terrifying as the Walker. And this one had already taken her magical knife. Had the spells weakened it any?

A long row of knives was hanging on the wall; Frennet took down the longest and most formidable, proffering it to her, but Lythande shook her head, passing her hand carefully along the row of knives. Most knives were forged for material uses only, and she did not think any of them would be much use against this great magic out of Chaos.

The Blue Star between her brows tingled, and she stopped, trying to identify the source of the magical warning. Was it only that she could hear, out in the darkness of the innyard, the characteristic step of the Walker Behind?

Step-pause-step.

Step-pause-step.

No, the source was closer than that. It lay – moving her head cautiously, Lythande identified the source – the cutting board that lay on the table; the hag had been cutting her magical herbs, the ones to transform the unwary into swine. Slowly, Lythande took up the knife; a common kitchen one with a long, sharp blade. All along the blade was the greenish mark of the herb juices. From the pocket of her mage-robe, Lythande took the ruined handle – the elaborately carved hilt with magical runes – of her ruined knife, looked at it with a sigh – she had always been proud of the elegance of her magical equipment, and this was hearth-witch, or kitchen-magic at best – and flung it down with the kitchen remnants.

Frennet clutched at her. "Oh, don't go out there, ma'am! It's still out there a-waiting for you."

And the jackdaw, fluttering near the hearth, shrieked, *"Don't go out there! Oh, don't go out there!"*

Gently, Lythande disengaged the girl's arms. "You stay here," she said. "You have no magical protection; and I can give you none." She drew the mage-robe's hood closely about her head, and stepped into the foggy innyard.

It was there; she could feel it waiting, circling, prowling, its hunger a vast evil maw to be filled. She knew it hungered for her, to take in her body, her soul, her magic. If she spoke, she might find herself in its power. The knife firmly gripped in her hand, she traced out a pattern of circling steps, sunwise in spite of the darkness. If she could hold the Thing of darkness in combat till sunrise, the very light might destroy it; but it could not be much after midnight. She had no wish to hold this dreadful Thing at bay till sunrise, even if her powers should prove equal to it.

So it must be dispatched at once . . . and she hoped, since she had lost her own magical knife, with the knife she had taken from the monstrous Thing's own accomplice. Alone in the fog, despite the bulky warmth of the mage-robe, Lythande felt her body dripping with ice – or was it only terror? Her knees wobbled, and the icy drips seemed to course down between her shoulders, which spasmed as if expecting a knife driven between them. Frennet, shivering in the light of the doorway, was watching her with a smile, as if she had not the slightest doubt.

Is this what men feel when their women are watching them?
Certainly, if she should call the Thing to her and fail to destroy
it, it would turn next on the girl, and for all she knew, on the
jackdaw, too; and neither of them deserved death, far less soul-
destruction. The girl was innocent, and the jackdaw only a dumb
creature . . . well, a harmless creature; dumb it wasn't; it was still
crying out gibberish.

"Oh, my soul, it's coming! It's coming! Don't go out there!"

It was coming; the Blue Star between her brow was pricking
like live coals, the blue light burning through her brain from the
inside out. Why, in the name of all the gods there ever were or
weren't, had she ever thought she wanted to be a magician? Well
it was years too late to ask that. She clenched her hand on the
rough wooden handle of the kitchen knife of the kitchen hag, and
thrust up roughly into the greater darkness that was the Walker,
looming over her and shadowing the whole of the innyard.

She was not sure whether the great scream that enveloped the
world was her own scream of terror, or whether it came from the
vast dark vortex that whirled around the Walker; she was enveloped in a monstrous whirlwind that swept her off her feet and into
dark fog and dampness. She had time for a ghostly moment of
dread – suppose the herbs on the blade should transform the
Walker into a great Hog of Chaos? And how could she meet it if
it did? But this was the blade of the Walker's own accomplice in his
own magic of Chaos; she thrust into the Thing's heart and,
buffeted and battered by the whirlwinds of Chaos, grimly hung on.

Then there was a sighing sound, and something unreeled and
was gone. She was standing in the innyard, and Frennet's arms
were hugging hard.

The jackdaw shrieked, *It's gone! It's gone! Oh, good girl, good
girl!*

It was gone. The innyard was empty of magic, only fog on the
moldering stones. There was a shadow in the kitchen behind
Frennet; Lythande went inside and saw, wrapped in his cloak and
ready to depart, the pudgy face and form of Gimlet, the dog faker.

"I was looking for the innkeeper," he said truculently. "This
place is too noisy for me; too much going on in the halls; and
there's the girl. You," he said crossly to Frennet. "Where's your
mistress? And I thought you were to join me."

Frennet said sturdily, "I'm me own mistress now, sir. And I ain't for sale, not any more. As for the mistress, I dunno where she is; you can go an' ask for her at the gates of Heaven, an' if you don't find her there – well, you know where you can go."

It took a minute for that to penetrate his dull understanding; but when it did, he advanced on her with a clenched fist.

"Then I been robbed of your price!"

Lythande reached into the pockets of the mage-robe. She handed him a coin.

"Here; you've made a profit on the deal, no doubt – as you always do. Frennet is coming with me."

Gimlet stared and finally pocketed the coin, which – Lythande could tell from his astonished eyes – was the biggest he had ever seen.

"Well, good sir, if you say so. I got to be off about my dogs. I wonder if I could get some breakfast first."

Lythande gestured to the joints of meat hanging along the wall of the kitchen. "There's plenty of ham, at least."

He looked up, gulped, and shuddered. "No, thanks." He slouched out into the darkness, and Lythande gestured to the girl.

"Let's be on our way."

"Can I really come with you?"

"For a while, at least," Lythande said. The girl deserved that. "Go quickly, and fetch anything you want to take."

"Nothing from here," she said. "But the other customers—"

"They'll turn human again now that the hag's dead, such of 'em as haven't been served up for roast pork," Lythande said. "Look there." And indeed, the joints of ham hanging along the wall had taken on a horrible and familiar look, not porcine at all. "Let's get out of here."

They strode down the road toward the rising sun, side by side, the jackdaw fluttering after, crying out, "Good morning, ladies! Good morning ladies."

"Before the sun rises," Lythande said, "I shall wring that bird's neck."

"Oh, aye," Frennet said. "Or dumb it wi' your magic. May I ask why you travel in men's clothes, Lady?"

Lythande smiled and shrugged.

"Wouldn't you?"

THE LAST WITCH

James Bibby

James Bibby (b. 1953) is best known for his series of humorous fantasy novels featuring Ronan the Barbarian which began with, uhm, Ronan the Barbarian *(1995). Bibby has been experimenting with other ideas recently of which this is his latest story. It has a neat sting in its tail.*

P AUL INKMAN TOOK ANOTHER drag on his cigarette and then leant on the worn sandstone parapet of the old bridge and stared down at the smoothly-flowing river below. Outlined against the image of the bright blue sky, his reflection stared morosely back.

"What the hell are you doing *here*, you loser?" it seemed to be saying to him. "Upton-upon-Dee . . . a place with less going on than Bournemouth on a Monday night. What the hell has happened to your career?"

For most of his life, Paul had wanted to be a television war reporter. As a child, he couldn't imagine anything more exciting than to be one of those super-cool, casually-dressed heroes speaking earnestly to camera from beside some dusty, foreign track whilst soldiers scurried purposefully about, tanks rumbled by and refugees shuffled dejectedly past. So when he had joined regional television at the age of twenty-two as a local reporter, it was to be just the first, purposeful step onto the career escalator that would sweep him up to the heights of national TV journalism. Cats stuck up trees and award-winning sausages were to be mere stepping-stones to fame, fortune and instant recognition wherever he went.

And so it was all the more galling to find that, six years later, the escalator had not budged one inch. Paul Inkman was still just a minor name on regional television, still covering the marathon-running octogenarians and the motor-biking vicars, still being sent to obscure little hamlets like Upton-upon-Dee to cover non-existent village poltergeists. For some reason, he had never stumbled across that big story, the one that would make the national news and give his career the boost it needed. And something told him he wasn't going to find it today, either. Sighing, he flicked his cigarette away and watched as it spiralled down to land in the water and be swept to oblivion beneath the bridge.

"This is going to be a complete bust. I can feel it," he said to Tony, his cameraman and sound operator.

"Oh, I don't know," replied Tony. He was peering through the eyepiece of the steadicam, swinging it round and zooming in and out on whatever caught his fancy. "This place is dead pictur-esque. Good sound, too. Cows, birds, the river, the church bells . . ."

"But what use is that?" complained Paul. "We haven't found a trace of a hint of a sniff of a story! I've interviewed eight people about this so-called poltergeist and they've all said exactly the same thing." His voice took on a mock-rustic accent. "Oi've seen nothing myself, but there's definitely summat *odd* going on."

"Maybe you just need to dig around a bit."

"Maybe I just need a miracle. Ah, what the hell! I might as well go and dig around in the village store. I need some more ciggies, anyway. I'll see you in the pub for lunch."

The road over the bridge dipped down, running between pictur-esque grey stone cottages for a couple of hundred yards before meeting the main A441 at a crossroads in the centre of the village. It was quiet and deserted as Paul walked along, the peace being broken only by the occasional car passing through in the direction of Hereford, and Paul found himself wondering yet again what the hell people found so attractive about living in the countryside. It would have driven him mad inside a week.

He reached the crossroads and paused outside the village store. He could hear the increasing rumble of a diesel engine, and a faint tremor in the ground told him that some massive lorry was passing through the village. After a few seconds it appeared, swerving round the corner by the church and travelling too fast, roaring between the houses like some rogue, runaway monster in pursuit of its prey.

And then, before Paul had time to react, it happened. A cat tore across the road in front of the lorry with a small dog yapping excitedly in pursuit. The cat had timed its run well; it had reached the far pavement before the lorry drew level. But the dog was not so lucky. Realisation arrived a fraction of a second before nemesis and the dog jerked its head towards the massive juggernaut that was about to strike. And then the dog was flying through the air and the lorry was rushing past, the turbulence of its wake ruffling Paul's hair, its horn bellowing a belated warning, roaring onwards down the road past *The White Hart* before vanishing round another corner.

Paul stared in disbelief as the roar of the lorry dwindled, unable to accept what he had just seen. For the dog hadn't been smashed to a pulp by the juggernaut. It hadn't even been touched. A fraction of a second before the lorry struck, the dog had been snatched up, yanked sideways through the air and deposited safely on the pavement as though by some giant, invisible hand.

It sat there for a few moments, visibly shaking, before turning and bolting back between the houses from where it had come. And then Paul realised that he wasn't the only witness. Twenty yards further down the road was a small girl of nine or ten who was gazing at him with a horrified expression on her face. Briefly, Paul wondered whether it was her dog, but then realisation hit him and professionalism took over. He had just seen something completely inexplicable. He had a story, and now he had a witness.

"Did you see that?" he called urgently, taking a couple of steps towards the girl. She began to back away, and he realised that the expression on her face wasn't just horror. There was something else there, something furtive . . . yes! Guilt! She looked as guilty as a kid who had just been caught shoplifting. Then she turned away and raced off down the road, scrambling over a stile near the church to disappear behind the hedge.

Paul watched her go, a little knot of excitement in his stomach.

He knew, without a shadow of a doubt, that whatever it was he had just witnessed, the little girl had been responsible for it. There was substance behind the poltergeist rumours after all. This was a story, all right. This was a big one.

Smiling, he pushed open the door of the village store and went inside. He had some serious questions that needed answering.

Sarah lay motionless in the long grass like a fawn hiding from a wolf and tried to hold back the tears. *You idiot!* she told herself. *Now you've done it! Now you've* really *gone and done it!* And after all the promises she had made to her parents, too. They would be *soooo* cross with her! No chance of tonight's sleep-over at Emma's now. But what had she been supposed to do? She couldn't have let Mrs Lambert's dog get run over!

Rolling on to her stomach, she peered through the roots of the hawthorn hedge, expecting to see that horrible rat-faced man following her down the road. But instead, she was just in time to see the door of the village store closing behind him. Sarah drew back, puzzled. He *must* have seen what she'd done to the dog . . . of course he had, he'd started to ask her about it. But he'd asked her if she'd *seen* it . . . Yes, that was it! He had no idea it was anything to do with her! Sarah had already learned that most adults, when faced with what they thought of as inexplicable events, never connected her with them. Not for the first few times, anyway . . .

She'd got away with it! Relieved, Sarah leapt up and began to trot home. And as she did so, she repeated the same little mantra to herself, over and over again. *No more witchcraft . . . no more witchcraft . . .*

Ever since she could remember, Sarah had known that she was a witch. No, that wasn't strictly true. She'd always had the abilities, but it had taken her a while to learn that no-one else shared them or that the rest of humanity (if they had known) would have called her a witch. Some innate sense of caution had caused her to keep her talents hidden from the outside world most of the time, but she was a kind-hearted child who liked to please others, and every now and then she just couldn't help herself. And, boy, had that caused trouble!

She had never forgotten the first serious incident, when she was four years old. Invited for the umpteenth time round to her friend Kylie Smith's house for tea, and having nagged, pleaded and cried until her parents had given way, she had been dropped off with their urgent warnings and cautions ringing in her ears. But Kylie's mum had been tired and stressed, and Sarah had heard the sincerity in her voice when she had shouted, "No, we're not going down to the playground! I've got far too much to do and I haven't got two pairs of hands, I only wish I had!" That day, Sarah had learned the hard way that grown-ups don't always mean exactly what they say. Even now, lying in bed at night, she sometimes thought she could still hear Mrs Smith screaming.

They'd moved to another town almost immediately afterwards. Since then, Sarah had tried to keep her abilities secret, but things would keep on happening, and there had been two more major incidents which had necessitated a rapid relocation of the family. But now she really did seem to be able to control herself and it had been two years since the last move. It would have been such a shame if that unpleasant-looking man had caught on to her . . .

With a smile on her face and a happy heart, Sarah headed for home totally unaware of the vast surprise that fate held in store for her.

"No, I haven't found a bit of posh totty!" Paul Inkman flicked another cigarette end into the river and desperately tried to keep hold of his temper. "Believe me, Andrew, nothing would induce me to spend one minute longer in this boring, inbred wilderness than I have to. But there's a story here, a real story. This is going to be big."

"More than just a one-off news item?" came the reply, and Paul could sense the quickening of interest in the news editor's voice.

"Far more," he stated. "Several news items, investigative coverage, a one-off special . . . and far more than just local interest. We're talking international here."

"Right." Andrew's voice paused, and Paul could hear a strange noise emanating from the phone that sounded vaguely like someone tapping their teeth with a pencil. "This could be good timing," the news editor continued after several seconds. "Sue is looking for another programme topic. She's had to drop the eighty year old prostitute after the old dear died of a heart attack whilst entertaining a client. I'll send her straight down there. See you."

The phone went dead. Paul stared at it in fury for a few seconds and came within an ace of hurling it against a nearby stone wall.

Sue Perrigo! That self-obsessed bitch! He swore dully and repetitively to himself. He'd already lost two of his best stories to that over-made-up, empty-headed bimbo, and now it was threatening to happen again. Well, not this time. Not if he could help it . . .

Paul thought quickly. He'd have to move fast and find out as much as he could. Then he needed to get Tony on his side, although that would be easy as Sue always used her own pet cameraman whose main talent lay in making her look wonderful on a TV screen. When she turned up, it shouldn't be too difficult to convince her that she'd been sent on a wild goose chase, although it wouldn't be pleasant; Sue Perrigo's volcanic temper was legendary. And then when the dust had settled, he and Tony could slip back down here and make their own detailed report, a report that would make headline news.

Paul smiled hungrily to himself. That little girl didn't know it, but she was about to provide him with the boost that would propel him to fame and fortune.

"A sleep-over? After what happened last time?" For a brief moment Sarah thought her father might actually explode.

"But Dad, I was only seven then! And, anyway, I thought I was doing the right thing. You and Mum said I should always do what I was told."

Lost for words, Mr Parker spluttered like an old-fashioned kettle coming to the boil, and his wife took over hurriedly.

"Sarah, when a harassed adult tells two boisterous children to disappear, they just want them to go away."

"Well, I know that *now*! But . . ."

"Poor Mrs Harris has never been the same since!" Her father had managed to get his vocal chords working again. "And as for that other trick you pulled . . ."

"But Tracy was my best friend! And she really wanted it to snow!"

"Yes, dear," answered her mother, "but outside would have been better. It took her father two hours to shovel that drift out through the bedroom window."

"I *said* I was sorry! But, Mum, that was ages ago! There's been no trouble at all since we came to Upton, has there?"

"Er, no. Not really. Nothing that anyone can *prove* was you."

"Well, then!"

Mrs Parker looked at her daughter for a moment, then sighed.

"Sweetheart, why don't you go and tidy your room? Your father and I need to talk."

Sarah hadn't been in this world very long before Mrs Parker had realised that her baby girl had abilities which were, to say the least, unusual. But whereas most mothers would have been deeply disturbed by levitating feeding bottles or nappies that changed themselves, Sarah's mother had been half expecting something out of the ordinary. She had very strong childhood memories of her own grandmother, a small, secretive, plump old lady who had been able to do some remarkable things, and who had seemed deeply disappointed that neither her daughter nor her grand-daughter had shared this ability. And there were some very strange family stories about Great Great Grandmother Pritchard, who had been born in Pendle . . .

Sarah's father had been far less willing to face facts, but eventually the evidence had become too overwhelming to discount. And since then, the Parkers had devoted their lives to . . . well, they were never sure whether they were simply protecting Sarah from the world or if they were also protecting the world from Sarah. They both knew that, in this modern age, if television or newspaper journalists got hold of her story her life would be ruined, but they felt that to isolate her completely from the rest of the world would also ruin her life.

And so they had trodden a middle line. On the whole it had worked, although on three separate occasions Sarah had done something which couldn't be explained away and they had been forced to leave the area quickly. The last time they had moved, Mrs Parker had thought that it would help if they could have settled close to someone else who had the same ability, but when she had suggested this to her daughter, Sarah had been adamant.

"There *is* no-one else, Mum. I just know it. If there was, I'd be able to . . . sense them. I could when I was little. There was a comforting feeling at the back of my mind, a sort of glow, old and shaky but always there. But I woke up one morning and it had gone. Whoever it was must have died and now I'm alone. I'm the last witch, it's as simple as that."

Since then, Mr and Mrs Parker had done their best to shield their daughter whilst hammering home the need for rigid self-discipline. At first, Sarah had tended to slip up, but the incidents had only been minor and had easily been explained away. But in recent months it looked as though Sarah had at last learnt to keep her ability secret, and Mrs Parker felt that an increase in responsibility should be rewarded by an increase in freedom.

She looked up at her husband, who had risen from the couch and was pacing restlessly up and down, fulminating about the danger to Sarah herself and to the rest of the world of allowing her outside the house for even a moment. This wasn't going to be easy.

"Darling," she said, uttering the words that would change things for ever, "I really think we should let Sarah go on this sleep-over . . ."

Paul Inkman sat in the chair opposite Dr Phillips with an expression of polite interest pasted firmly in place and tried to contain his mounting excitement. The more he talked to people about events in Upton, the more convinced he became that he was on to something sensational.

This interview with the local G.P. was typical. Taken by themselves, her comments weren't that startling, but when added to all the other stories Paul had heard, the body of evidence was overwhelming.

"So let's see if I've got this right," he said to the doctor. "Are you saying that people in Upton are never sick?"

"Oh, no, I wouldn't go that far. People still get ill. But there seems to be much less of it round here, for some reason. I hardly ever see locals with colds or 'flu. And the children at the local school must be the healthiest kids in Britain. We haven't had a case of chicken pox for ages."

"And this is well out of the ordinary?"

The doctor leant back in her chair and fiddled with a pencil as she considered the question.

"I'd say so, yes. It's been enough to make me wonder whether the powers that be have been using the village as a living laboratory . . . antibiotics in the water supply, or something like that."

Paul nodded before casually asking the most important question.

"How long would you say this has been going on?"

"Difficult to say. But I'd guess that it began about two years ago now . . ."

Sarah clattered down the stairs with her overnight bag in her hand to find her father waiting for her in the hall. At first, from the serious look on his face, she thought that he must have changed his mind and her heart sank. But then he forced a smile into place and she knew that everything was alright.

"Now you be careful, young lady," he said. For the first time today she noticed that his voice sounded husky and his nose was a little blocked. "Make sure that you don't do anything . . . ah . . . ah . . . *atishoo!*"

He sneezed noisily. Sarah put down her bag, took hold of his hand and probed. Immediately she could sense the thousands upon thousands of microbes clustered in the membranes lining his nose and throat. She concentrated, her lips moving faintly as she muttered the necessary commands and sent them all away.

"There you go, Dad," she grinned. "You'll feel much better now."

Her father nodded almost tiredly.

"Thanks, love." His voice sounded sad. He rubbed his chin thoughtfully and then sat down on the bottom stairs. "Sarah," he added, "there's something I've always meant to ask you."

"What's that, Dad?"

"Well, whenever you see witches casting spells in films or books, they're always brewing up magic potions in vast, bubbling cauldrons. I've always half expected that I'd come in from work one day to find you in the kitchen, mixing up a load of bats' wings and frogs' noses in one of your Mum's best Le Creuset pans. But you've never seemed to need all that . . . hocus pocus stuff. Why is that?"

"I don't know, Dad." Sarah settled herself down on the stair next to her father and thought about it. "I guess maybe in the old days, their customers demanded it. I mean, take love potions. If you were paying a witch for a spell to make Mum fall in love with you, you'd probably want to have something definite for your money. Like a nice little bottle full of magic potion. Otherwise, if you just gave the witch some money and then found that Mum was suddenly mad about you, you might think that it was all down to you and nothing to do with the witch." Sarah paused and then laughed. "Or maybe they just weren't very good at being witches and needed help. But I don't." She looked up at her Dad, smiling confidentially. "I'm really good at it, you know."

"I know."

He looked at her with a strange, crinkly sort of smile and for one awful moment she thought he was going to start crying, but then he put his arm around her and hugged her tightly.

"Just . . . just be *careful* out there," he said.

"Don't worry, Dad," she told him inaccurately, "nothing is going to go wrong . . ."

The words poured out of Paul Inkman like a torrent as he paced excitedly up and down. Nearby, Tony the cameraman sat on a wooden picnic bench, listening doubtfully and hugging his camera to himself for comfort. They were in Upton's only public car park, a gravel-surfaced area cut out of a field behind the church that lay huddled in a bend of the river and was ringed by picnic tables and waste bins.

"*Everything* began two years ago," said Paul. "And you know the kid I told you about? Sarah Parker? You know when she and her family moved here? *Two years ago!* All we need to do now is find out where they came from and check the place out for strange occurrences. Once we confront her parents with what we know, they won't have any option but to cooperate."

He stopped pacing and appealed directly to the cameraman.

"This is a hell of a story, Tony. And it's *ours*. We've just got to put Sue off the trail first."

"Yeah . . . right," said the cameraman, doubtfully. "Only . . .

well, she's got a bloodhound's nose for a story, Paul. And you know what she's like with people who cross her! I talked to Gareth Murray after he sent some film of her picking her nose to that out-takes show. He said it was like being savaged by a Chanel-drenched rottweiler!"

"She won't know until it's too late, and we'll have made our name by then."

Paul paused as his mobile phone began trilling and hauled it out of his pocket.

"Hello?" he said. "Oh, hi, Sue. Yes, we're waiting for you. We're in the car park behind the church. You can't miss it." He paused and winked at Tony. "Only I'm afraid we've got some rather bad news for you . . ."

Sarah rang the front doorbell and grinned as the door shot open almost immediately. Emma Williams was standing there, a flurry of excitement on legs.

"You're late!" she squealed. "I thought you weren't coming! Come in! Mum says take your bag upstairs, then we can go out for a bit. But you'll have to say hello to Mum first . . ." Her voice dropped dramatically to a whisper. "And to *Matt*."

"Who's Matt?" Sarah whispered back.

"His Dad works with my Dad at the university. He's *American*. They've just moved over here and Dad said it would be nice for him to have someone to play with, so we're *stuck* with him for the weekend. Come on!"

Emma led the way along the hall and into the living room, where Mrs Williams was sitting on the couch, sipping coffee from a Scorpio mug and reading the paper. Beside her, controller in hand and thumbs a blur, a tousle-headed boy of about ten was concentrating on a computer console game on the television.

"Hello, Sarah," smiled Mrs Williams. "I'm glad you could come to stay at last. This is Matt."

The boy pressed the pause button on the controller and then grinned at Sarah.

"Hi there," he said.

"Why don't you . . ." Mrs Williams began, but then the phone beside her rang. "Just a minute," she said as she picked it up. "Hello . .? Yes, she is. Hold on."

She held the phone out to Emma. "It's Tracy."

"Tracy?" said Emma, disdainfully. (Tracy was not currently on her best-friends list.) "What does *she* want?"

She put the phone to her ear and listened, and her whole attitude changed visibly.

"What? *Where?* She isn't! Really? Okay! See you!" Emma almost threw the phone back to her mother and was hopping up and down with excitement. "That was Tracy! She says there are TV cameras in the car park, and *Sue Perrigo* is there! She's going to film something. We've got to go and watch! We could be on *television!* Come on, Sarah!"

"Emma!" There was a warning note in Mrs Williams' voice. "Aren't you forgetting someone?"

"Oh. Right. Er, do you want to come along too, Matt?"

"Yeah. Great!" He stood up and grinned at Sarah again. Emma raised her eyes to heaven wearily.

"Okay then," she said. "Come on."

"I don't believe you!" Sue Perrigo hissed at Paul Inkman. "I've only been in this village for half an hour but I can tell there's a story here. I can smell it!"

She turned and began to advance on Tony the cameraman. Her face was calm and she was smiling, seeming to the forty or fifty onlooking locals just like the attractive, sparkling television star that they knew so well, but Tony could see the flint-like hardness in her eyes and he began to back away. It was like being confronted by a life-size Barbie doll in kill mode.

"So tell me, Andy . . ."

"Tony."

"Whatever. Tell me what the story is."

"I . . . er . . . I mean, I don't . . ."

Tony found that he had backed up against a picnic table and was trapped. Sue laid a hand on his shoulder and stared into his eyes from a foot away. A single perfectly-manicured, crimson fingernail stroked his neck just below the corner of his chin, and for a brief second he had a horrible foreboding that it would suddenly burst through the skin and plunge into his jugular.

"We don't want to disappoint all these people, do we?" Sue whispered, indicating the watching locals. "They're expecting to see me filming a story. I *hate* disappointing people. And I *hate* being disappointed . . ."

Tony closed his eyes and swallowed.

"Apparently there's this little girl . . ." he began.

From her position at the back of the crowd of onlookers, Sarah couldn't see a thing. Emma, Tracy and Matt had pushed their way through to the front, but some innate sense of self-preservation had told her that this wasn't a very sensible place for her to be and she had kept to the rear. Bored, she turned away and began to stroll across the car park towards the river. And that was when she caught sight of little Tim Griffiths.

Tim had somehow managed to escape the attentions of his Mum (who was a big Sue Perrigo fan) and was toddling in pursuit of a butterfly as fast as his two-year-old legs could carry him. The trouble was that the butterfly had fluttered out over the river.

Sarah threw a quick glance towards the crowd but everyone was still preoccupied by the television people. She started to run, but it was too late.

Tim snatched at the butterfly, missed, and toppled into the river with the softest of splashes. Sarah reached the edge of the bank but Tim had already been swept downstream. Anxiously, she glanced again at the crowd but no-one was watching. It was up to her. She took a deep breath and concentrated.

She was Concentrating so hard that she barely noticed the scream of "TIMOTHY!" that suddenly rang out. She stood on the bank of the river, hands raised slightly and trembling a little (for Tim was heavy), and she lifted him out of the water thirty feet downstream. Then she lifted him across to the bank nearby and deposited him safely on the grass.

And that was when she became aware that, save for Tim's whimpering, everything had gone deathly quiet. She turned to find fifty pairs of eyes staring at her in wonder. For several seconds no-one moved, and then Mrs Griffiths rushed forward, picked up little Tim and cuddled him to her.

Sue Perrigo threw a look of triumph at Paul Inkman and then began to walk towards Sarah.

"I saw what you did!" she said. "It was you, wasn't it? How did you do it?"

Sarah gazed round at the faces staring at her and saw the astonishment and wonder on them. Suddenly she realised that, this time, she really had done it. This time there was no going back, no running away. Everyone knew. Her secret was out.

Then she looked up into Sue Perrigo's eyes and the expression she saw there frightened her. She began to back away, but Sue followed.

"Go away!" Sarah cried. "Leave me alone!"

And screwing her eyes tight shut she slumped to the ground and clamped her hands over her face.

"Please!" she begged. "Just leave me alone!"

It was quiet. Too quiet. The only sound she could hear was her own panting. Oh, God, what had she done now? She didn't dare to look. And then a voice spoke.

"Gee! How dumb was that?"

She opened her eyes. Matt was standing there staring down at her almost angrily.

"Using magic in front of all those people!" he continued. "I mean, duh-urrh!"

Sarah stared round. The whole crowd had frozen like statues. Sue Perrigo was the nearest, her hand static in the act of reaching out to touch Sarah, her eyes staring sightlessly at the place where Sarah had been moments before. For a second she tried to work out what had happened, but then she saw a bird hanging motionless in the act of flight and realised that the river wasn't moving.

"You!" she gasped to Matt. "You did this! But you can't have . . . you *can't* be a witch! I'm the only one left, I know I am!"

"Of course I'm not a witch!" he said, almost scornfully. "Don't you know anything? Witches are female. I'm a warlock, or wizard, or sorcerer. Whatever. It's different."

"How do you mean, different?"

"You witches, your power is all to do with people and plants and animals. Oh, what did Grampa call it? Organic, that's it. My power is more . . ." Matt groped for the word." . . . elemental. Yeah. To do with earth and fire and time and stuff."

Sarah thought about that. Maybe it was the reason she'd never sensed Matt's Presence. She reached out and there it was, clearly obvious now that he was so close, a cold blue fire in her mind that contrasted sharply with the warm, red, fuzzy glow of her own Presence.

"Here." Matt held out a hand and helped her to her feet. "We need to talk."

They strolled to a picnic table and sat down with their backs to the eerie ranks of motionless people. Sarah had never known such a silence.

"About two years ago," Matt began, "I discovered your Presence. There had been other witches, but I guess they died. Anyway, I could sense that you were the last one. And after my Grampa died I was the last warlock. It seemed like a good idea for us to get together. But it's taken me two years to manoeuvre my parents into moving over here without them catching on."

"Don't they know about you?" Sarah asked.

"Hell, no! My parents are fundamentalist Christians. If they found out I had these powers, they'd think I was, like, Satan or something. They'd probably feel they had to sacrifice me or have me exorcised or stuff. No, Grampa looked after me when I was little and made sure they never caught on."

"And your Grampa was a . . . warlock . . . too?"

"Yep. It ran in the family. All the way back to a great great great great grampa who came from Salem. But my Grampa was the first one who combined it with modern science. He went to university and did a whole load of research. And guess what he found?"

"What?"

"It's genetically inherited!"

"Jenny who?"

"No, I mean the power gets passed down from parents to children. But it gets weaker if only one parent has it. Grampa said that after all those witch hunts they had years ago, we all got separated and the power has waned. He said that if I found a witch and married her, we'd pass on stronger power to our kids."

"So what do we do?"

"Well, we're the last ones. I guess that means we're gonna have to make some babies together."

"What, now?"

"Jeez, no, not right away! I mean, I'm eleven and you're ten! We'd get into real bad trouble with our parents, right? No, I mean when we're older. For the moment, we just need to hang out together and look after each other."

"Like friends?" suggested Sarah.

Matt looked at her and grinned again. "Yeah. Friends."

Sarah was suddenly aware of how alone and empty she'd felt for the past ten years. All at once, that feeling had completely disappeared. She grinned back.

"Come on," she said. "You'd better do something about all these poor people."

They turned and looked at the motionless crowd.

"If I just fix their memories slightly," Matt said, "they won't remember a thing about today. That should do."

Sarah looked at Sue Perrigo then switched her gaze to Paul Inkman. He was looking at Sue and there was a twisted scowl of pure hatred on his face.

"It's a shame about these two," she told Matt. "They hate each other so much. I wish I could change that and make them like each other."

"Well, why don't you? You've got the power."

And so Sarah reached into the minds of Paul and Sue and changed their emotions just a touch. And then Matt did something that was far beyond her own abilities, and all of a sudden everything was normal. The river flowed, the birds flew and the people moved. And every one of them paused for a moment and looked around, puzzled, all thinking exactly the same thing. *What was I doing? I can't remember a thing . . .*

But then Paul Inkman looked at Sue Perrigo and she looked back at him. Something between them ignited, flared and then exploded, and they ran at each other, meeting in a passionate clinch and locking instantly into an intense, hungry kiss.

Matt stared as Sue began to rip Paul's clothes off.

"Whoa!" he muttered to Sarah. "You made them like each other all right! I don't think you realise quiet how strong your power is."

He gazed at her in open admiration and she looked away, embarrassed and yet pleased.

"Come on," she said. "Let's get out of here. I'll race you!"

She leapt up and hared off across the car park, and Matt raced after her, grinning from ear to ear.

And so it began. Nobody knew it yet, but the events necessary for the next step upwards in human evolution had just taken place. *Homo neanderthalis* had come and gone 30,000 years ago, and now *Homo sapiens* was about to follow him into the dustbin of history. And blissfully unaware of their place in evolutionary history, the two sole providers of the gene pool for *Homo magicus* raced home laughing.

LAST RITES

Louise Cooper

Thirty years ago I was bowled over when I stumbled across Louise Cooper's first novel The Book of Paradox *(1973). I couldn't find anything else by her or about her, even though a few years later another astonishing novel,* Lord of No Time *(1977), appeared. It wasn't until 1985, with the start of her Time Master series, with* The Initiate, *that Louise became better known in fantasy circles, though she had also written several horror novels, including* Blood Summer *(1976) and* In Memory of Sarah Bailey *(1977). Fortunately, since 1985, Louise Cooper (b. 1952) has produced a steady flow of fine fantasy novels including the Indigo series,* starting with Nemesis *(1988), the Chaos Gate series, starting with* The Deceiver *(1991) and the Star Shadow series. That began with* Star Ascendant *(1994) and the following is the opening segment to that book which stands alone as a short story and serves as a reminder of what a powerful and potent series that was.*

"**B**ENETAN LISS."

The flat, toneless voice speaking his name penetrated through the layers of a bizarre dream, and he turned in his bed, instinctively pulling the heavy covering up over his ears.

"Benetan. Stir yourself; wake up."

This time it wasn't a whisper but a command, and urgent. The two-mouthed thing that had been crawling across Benetan's dream landscape shivered and faded, and he awoke to blackness broken only by a small, unsteady pinpoint of light. Above the light two eyes gleamed in the darkness; then as his own pupils dilated he made out the indistinct shape behind the eyes; a ghost of a human figure.

"Wh . . ." Benetan swallowed the question unasked as his mind began to function. A hand loomed out of the dark to cup the candle; the flame reflected on thin fingers, then his visitor blew gently on the flame and it burned brighter, illuminating a narrow face etched in black and silver shadow.

"Savrinor . . ." The last traces of sleep fell away and Benetan Liss was suddenly wide awake. "What is it? What's the hour?"

"Second moonrise." Savrinor, whose official title was historian but whose functions ranged much further afield, moved towards the window and drew back the curtain. Cold grey light slanted in, turning the ragged strands of his long, fair hair to grey and sharply defining the hawkish profile with its narrow, handsome nose, and he touched the candle to the small lamp at Benetan's bedside.

"You'd better get dressed, my friend. There'll be no more sleep for any of us tonight." His eyes, pale blue and feline, met Benetan's in the gloom that the lamplight and moonlight did little to relieve. "The First Magus is dying at last."

Benetan sat up. "Tonight? How can you be sure?"

Savrinor shrugged, the gesture spare but eloquent. "I have ears, and I use them. There's movement below; the castle's bones are shifting, and there are already rumours of the Chaos Gate being opened from the far side. Something's coming through uninvited, and you know as well as I do that that can only mean one thing."

"An emissary?"

"To take his soul." Savrinor smiled a small, unemotional smile that didn't extend as far as his eyes. "Before dawn, I'd hazard. So you'll please our masters by pre-empting their order and being ready when they send for you."

Benetan started to say, "If you're right –" then thought better of it. Savrinor was never wrong. On the narrow path he trod between one faction and another, he couldn't afford to be.

He swung his legs over the side of the bed and stood up. "I owe you a debt."

"No, no." Savrinor watched with something approaching detached admiration faintly tinged with envy as Benetan reached for his clothes. "I'm still indebted to you for that little dark girl you found for me on your last sortie."

Benetan's head turned sharply, eyes narrowed, looking for sarcasm. "You tired of her in four days."

"Maybe so; but it was a pleasant diversion while it lasted. So this is a favour for a favour, so to speak." The smile again. "To even the slate."

Savrinor maintained a tally of favours granted and favours received and, by his devious and often unfathomable code of ethics, could always be relied on to give or exact payment in kind to a scrupulous degree. Benetan nodded curtly. "Very well. The slate's evened."

He began to dress, grimacing with distaste at the clammy touch of his clothing against bare skin. His ceremonial accoutrements were slung carelessly on a chair; he clipped the heavy silver flashes with their seven quartz pendants to the shoulders of his tunic, then cinched the tunic with a wide black leather belt on which seven more gems of differing colours glowed like bizarre eyes in the dark. As he secured the complex buckle, Savrinor said, "Our masters will want an extra tally tonight, I think."

Benetan paused and looked up, but Savrinor's face gave nothing away beyond that small, sly smile, which was beginning to irritate him.

"Extra?" His voice was terse. "Why?"

Savrinor shrugged. "You know who the chosen successor is?"

"No, I don't. I'm not privy to the inner dealings of the magi."

"None of us are. But some of us pick up a snippet here and a snippet there, and when we're alone in our solitary chambers we amuse ourselves by making a pattern of those snippets, and the pattern sometimes forms a picture." The smile became a leer. "Your greatest defect, Benetan my friend, is that you have no curiosity beyond the demands of your duties."

"In this place, it's safer to keep matters that way," Benetan retorted sharply.

"Safer, maybe. But far less interesting." Savrinor picked his way delicately across the cluttered room towards the door as though about to leave, then stopped and looked back. "So your admirable prudence precludes you from wanting to know the name of the man who will step into the shoes of our First Magus. A pity."

He reached for the door latch. Benetan sighed. Games were a favourite pastime with Savrinor; if one wanted more than the most cursory information, one had to learn to become a player and abide by his rules.

"All right," he said wearily. "Tell me."

"Tush!" Savrinor raised a long finger. The weak lamplight barely touched him, and his face looked cadaverous and not quite human. "I wouldn't dream of compromising you against your will."

Not for the first time in their long acquaintance Benetan felt an urge to strike Savrinor. It would have been the work of less than a minute to extort the information he wanted; he was twelve years younger and several inches taller, and the historian was, besides, a notorious physical coward. But whatever Benetan's personal view of the value of Savrinor's friendship, he would make a very dangerous enemy.

He forced his shoulders to relax. "Please, Savrinor. I haven't the time or the skill to fence with you. Tell me."

Savrinor inclined his head with a gracious smile. Then his expression changed, and he met Benetan's gaze and said: "Vordegh."

A cold worm moved in Benetan's gut. He mouthed the syllables of the name, though no sound emerged from his throat, then swallowed. "You're certain?"

"As certain as it's ever possible to be without official confirmation."

"But he's—"

Savrinor held up a warning hand, forestalling him. "Don't say it. Not in jest, not in heat; not under any circumstances." All trace of banter was gone from his voice. "You'd be well advised not to even *think* it again, if you've any concern for your own future."

He was right. Benetan knew Vordegh's skills and temperament, although to his eternal relief he had never been a target for the magus's displeasure.

Yet, said a formless voice within him, and, hardly realising that he did so, Benetan touched the small, star-shaped amulet that hung on an iron chain about his neck.

"So," Savrinor continued, quite softly, "you'll appreciate, I think, my anxiety that all should go smoothly tonight."

"Yes. And I'm doubly grateful to you for forewarning me."

"Ah!" Again the warning gesture, but now the sly humour was back. "Be careful. I might take you at your word and alter the slate of our mutual indebtedness in my favour."

It wasn't always possible to tell when Savrinor was joking and when he was serious. After a moment, learning nothing from the historian's expression, Benetan shrugged, smiled thinly and followed Savrinor out of the room.

In darkness relieved only by the faint eye of Savrinor's candle the two men made their way via the castle's mind-numbing maze of passages and stairways towards the stables. A small door admitted them to the courtyard, and Benetan paused for a moment to breathe the chilly night air and take in his surroundings. He would never become inured to the effect the castle had on him when seen in anything like its entirety; and at night the atmosphere that seemed to ooze from the stones was doubly and unsettlingly enhanced. Grim black walls, their angularity a perverse joke on the part of the architects and their supernatural inspirers, rose foursquare to each side of him, reflecting no light, absorbing the gaze like dark vortices. At the cardinal quarters stood four titanic black spires, spearing savagely into a cloud-wracked sky and lit by fitful shafts of moonlight. Fighting the drag of vertigo to look towards their summits, Benetan saw that a high window in each spire was lit by a dim, uneasy glow, a sign that someone there watched and waited. He looked away again, quickly.

"You see?" Savrinor, at his elbow, spoke softly. "They're preparing. And if you stop still and concentrate, you can feel what moves towards us."

Reluctantly Benetan stilled his breathing, muscles tense. For a moment he could hear only the faint, ominous murmur of the sea far below, pounding the titanic stack on which the castle was built. But then beneath his feet, far down in the foundations, he sensed a steady, pulsing vibration. Not a sound: it was pitched far too low to be audible to the human ear. But a movement, a shifting, something that stirred the marrow in his bones and made the cold sweat break out anew.

He glanced at his companion, his face taut and angry. "I haven't time to waste, Savrinor. I must rouse my men."

"Of course." The historian fell into step beside him again as he set off across the deserted courtyard. The clouds broke, and the first and larger of the two moons hung like a disembodied face in the sky, blotting out the remote glitter of all but the brightest stars. Cold light showered down on the courtyard and the two men's shadows flowed before them over the flagstones. Benetan tried not to shiver: summer waned fast in this northern latitude and he could smell the change in the season on the sharp sea air.

Something flickered across the sky, a brief-lived shimmer like distant lightning. Involuntarily Benetan glanced up, and was in time to see a hissing charge of energy crackle between two of the spires' summits in answer to the celestial signal. His heart stabbed nervously and, unaware of the gesture, he made a quick, reflexive sign with his right hand. Savrinor, whose eyes missed nothing, smiled dryly.

"Yes; there's a Warp storm coming." He glanced heavenwards, speculatively. "More powerful than usual, I'd surmise. It should be an impressive spectacle."

There was a faint glow in the northern sky; a sickly and unnatural radiance that hinted at something alien lurking over the horizon. Trapped lightning sang between the spires again. Unconsciously Benetan quickened his pace, until Savrinor was forced to jog to keep up with him. The stable block loomed in the moonlight ahead; they moved into the shadow of the arched doorway and he felt his tension easing as he heard the muffled stamp of horses in their straw bedding and smelled the warm, mammalian scent of them. Eyes gleamed in the glow of a single lantern, and at the sound of footsteps a shape shook itself from among a stack of haybales in the far corner, rising to its feet with undignified and fearful haste.

"Captain Liss . . ." Relief coloured the voice, and Benetan looked hard at the young sentry, who was hurriedly brushing hay from his clothing.

"Sleeping, Colas?"

"A moment's rest only, sir –" The lie tailed off and the youth swallowed. "I'm sorry, sir."

Aware that Savrinor was watching with lazy interest, Benetan said, "Don't let it happen again, Colas. Another time, you may be interrupted by someone considerably less tolerant than I am."

"Especially once tonight is over," Savrinor put in, stepping forward into the reach of the lamplight.

Colas's face lost all its colour as he saw the historian for the first time, and he made an obeisance. "Master Savrinor! I—"

"Save your excuses for your commander, boy; I'm not interested in reporting such minor breaches of discipline to higher powers." Disdainfully Savrinor turned on his heel, and Benetan nodded to Colas. "It's all right. There's nothing to fear." He felt on firmer ground now, in an element that was familiar to him, and his sapped confidence was returning. "Get the grooms and weaponsmen out of their beds."

"Yes, sir." Colas had potential, Benetan thought: he was learning never to question an order. The youth headed for the inner door that led to the cramped dormitory where the stable servants were housed, then hesitated and looked back.

"Beg your pardon, sir. Should I tell the grooms how many horses you're to need?"

Benetan made to reply, but before he could speak Savrinor laid a light hand on his arm. "I think not," the historian said quietly.

Benetan hesitated, then looked towards the far end of the stable, where an iron door, heavily barred but otherwise unremarkable, gleamed dimly in the shadows. He understood Savrinor's meaning. It was some time since the Chaos riders had been required to make use of their alternative mounts; but this was no ordinary occasion.

Repressing a shudder, he turned again to Colas, who was watching and awaiting a reply.

"We won't be using the horses tonight, Colas. We'll have other requirements."

"Yes, sir." The boy frowned faintly, but the implications were lost on him: he was, Benetan reminded himself, a very new recruit to the elite ranks.

"Promising." Savrinor spoke mildly as the door closed behind Colas's back. "But not castle-bred, I suspect."

"Colas came from a village in the east last year. He's learning."

"As you learned, of course."

"Yes." Their gazes met briefly, and Savrinor saw what he had anticipated in Benetan's eyes: distaste, and a growing tinge of fear. He let his hand close on the captain's arm.

"Take advice from your good friend Savrinor, and don't expend needless energy on thoughts of what has yet to happen." His thin fingers squeezed, a little too familiarly for Benetan's liking, and he withdrew his hand with a final pat. "Dawn will come."

"I don't need –" Benetan began angrily, but before he could say any more a sound from somewhere within the castle silenced his tongue. Slow, sonorous, echoing, it was the voice of a single, deep-tongued bell.

Savrinor's eyes narrowed with quick tension, then flicked to Benetan's face. The historian nodded. "As I thought. We'd best go outside."

The bell's metallic voice continued while they moved towards the courtyard, then as they emerged the tolling abruptly stopped. The quiet in its wake was eerie, and for several minutes the night's stillness remained unbroken. Then a door opened somewhere near the main gate, the sound of the latch carrying loudly and making Benetan start, and three men came hurrying across the courtyard. Others followed, and more doors were opening, dark figures emerging from the castle to converge on the stables. Metal glinted under the moon and Benetan heard the jingle of spurs and belt-buckles.

"I should be elsewhere," Savrinor murmured.

With an effort Benetan gathered his wits. "Thank you, Savrinor. You've done me a service tonight."

The historian's answering smile made his face skull-like in the chilly light. "Good hunting," he said, and moved away as silently as a shadow.

"Captain Liss." The first group of men had reached him, and each touched a hand to the emblem of the Seven-Rayed Star at his breast in salute. "The bell – does it mean that—"

"It does," Benetan replied tersely. "The grooms are being roused now." To his private relief he felt his trained responses beginning to take over, eclipsing the sickness in his stomach.

"Full complement: if we haven't enough fit men, get the unfit out of their beds. I want everyone presented and ready ten minutes from now. Where's your sergeant?"

"Here, Captain." Dark eyes in a white face, the man's rank denoted by a crimson shoulder-flash.

"Ten minutes, sergeant. It's imperative that nothing goes wrong." He added, more quietly, in the man's ear: "The rumour is for Vordegh."

Fear; yes. The same fear he had felt when Savrinor whispered the news. It stirred within him again now as he uttered the magus's name, adding a sour spice to the disquiet. And with good reason, Benetan told himself as the sergeant hastened away.

With good reason.

They were ready when the expected summons came. Forty-nine fully armed warriors – seven times seven – ranged in silent ranks before the stable block. Inside the stable Benetan could hear the horses stamping restively; they had caught something of the pervasive atmosphere and were alerted. But the Chaos riders would have no need of them tonight.

The sky was beginning to agitate now. The spires no longer spat their shivering bolts of energy, but the lightning far to the north was almost continuous and an uneasy spectrum of dim colours marched slowly across the heavens, blotting out the stars. Though the moon still glared down, it was haloed with a pale, ghastly corona; minutes more and its face would be obliterated as the supernatural storm, known to the cowering world as a Warp, gained power.

Benetan's senses were straining involuntarily to catch the first eerie and far-off sounds that would herald the Warp's onslaught. He was sweating again, and the black silk of his shirt and trousers clung to his skin with a cold, faintly repellent touch. He had put on the silver circlet with its ornate embellishments that made a fearsome half-mask around his eyes; it kept his unbraided black hair from blowing across his face but couldn't hold back the perspiration beaded on his forehead. Each time he blinked, droplets of it glittered on his lashes, breaking and refracting the reflections of moonlight on silver wristbands and on the glinting gems at his waist and shoulders. His teeth were clenched

– try as he might he couldn't stop the reflex – as he listened for the first hell-born shrieking out of the north, and waited for the summons that he knew must come at any moment. Then a sound alerted him – the scrape of wood on stone, the creak of hinges – and he looked towards the double doors at the castle's main entrance.

A shadow fell across the steps before the doorway, and a solitary man emerged. Disquieting patterns of light from the moon and other, less discernible sources distorted his figure and made him impossible to identify, but his bearing, and the long, heavy robe that enveloped him, told Benetan that he was no mere servant. For a moment the newcomer surveyed the scene, then a hand rose, gestured; and, heart quickening painfully, Benetan hastened across the courtyard and up the steps.

"Captain Liss." The voice was dry, slightly clipped; old, shrewd eyes regarded Benetan from under hooded lids. In the fine embroidery of the magus's robe, strange shapes writhed and shifted with a life of their own. "You are to be commended for your prompt response."

"Thank you, my lord." Benetan's own eyes were unfocused; he touched a hand to his breast in formal salute, and somewhere overhead felt rather than saw the sky shiver. Footsteps sounded softly on the flagstones as the magus moved back from the steps and into the silent, lofty entrance hall beyond, and Benetan followed at a respectful distance. Then the dusty voice spoke again.

"We require a full harvest tonight. Satisfy that requirement and your diligence will be commended to those whom we all are privileged to serve."

"I'm grateful, my lord. And I will discharge my duties to my utmost ability." Benetan fought a tic that threatened to make his cheek muscles twitch, and silently praised Savrinor.

The magus nodded. "We ask nothing more, and demand nothing less. Now: you have a full complement of riders?"

"Yes, sir."

"Good. Then you are ready to take the sacrament."

"I –" His voice cracked; he forced it back under his control. "I am ready, my lord."

He could hear the first thin, screaming wail far out over the sea as the Warp began to move in towards the peninsula. Ten minutes, perhaps fifteen, no more, and the huge forces unleashed by the magi would come shrieking out of the night in wild and deadly celebration. And he must face the Warp, and lead his riders out into its howling heart . . .

He heard the magus turn away, heard the crisp snap of his fingers, the light, hesitant feet of the servant who had been waiting in the shadows and now came forward at his summons. She held a pewter tray on which were set a pitcher and a tiny chalice carved from a single diamond: averting her gaze she dropped to one knee before the magus and held the tray out.

As the sorcerer filled the cup to the brim, Benetan tried to quiet the pounding of his heart. He could see the faint, darkly phosphorescent gleam of the liquid, and against his will he found himself starting to crave it and the effect it would have on him. It was a bulwark against fear, a shield for his sanity in the face of what was to come. Shrewd, relentless eyes focused on him, seeming to see beyond the physical contours of his skull and into his inner mind. The magus smiled thinly and held out the brimming chalice.

Yandros, greatest lord of Chaos, strengthen my resolve tonight! Benetan shut his eyes as the silent prayer went through his mind, then drank, draining the chalice as swiftly as he could.

The taste of the draught burned his tongue as he swallowed, and he felt its heat pervade to his stomach. Then, his legs not entirely steady, he set the cup back on the tray.

"The Maze stands open and waiting, Captain. I would advise you not to delay." The magus gestured towards the doors. "Search well, and reap a good harvest."

Aware that the last words might be either a blessing or a warning, Benetan repeated his formal salute. The servant stepped forward and handed him the tray; the magus nodded once, satisfied, and walked away as Benetan turned numbly back to the courtyard.

Two sergeants were waiting at the head of the line of men. One took the tray, and Benetan said curtly: "See that each man takes a full draught."

"Sir." The sergeant nodded, understanding. With a queasy sensation that couldn't yet be due to the effects of the narcotic

Benetan watched him carry the pitcher down the line, watched each man drink in his turn. Then he looked over his shoulder and saw Colas waiting, wide-eyed, at the stable door. The boy was too young and too inexperienced for this; better that he be dismissed now rather than risk him before he was ready. Benetan signalled, and Colas hastened forward.

"Captain?"

"Go to your bed, Colas. You'll not be needed again tonight."

"But sir—"

"I said, *go to your bed*. Or you'll face the lash tomorrow for insubordination." He didn't want to be harsh with the boy, but there was no time for explanations. If Colas lingered, his sanity could be in jeopardy without the drug to shield him.

Colas's eyes lost their focus and he touched his hand to his left shoulder. "Yes, sir!" He turned stiffly and strode away, trying to maintain his dignity in the face of stung pride.

Overhead the sky spat crimson lightning, and the distant singing sound swelled like a tidal surge, counterpointed by a far-off rumble of thunder. Without warning the scene before Benetan warped, as though he were viewing it from another dimension. The illusion lasted only a moment but it made him realise that the narcotic was beginning to work. He drew several steady breaths, counting, hearing the air rasp in his throat. The sounds in the sky were augmented now by a singing in his brain, an unholy choir of joyous voices; and an arrhythmic vibration thrummed through him. He felt as though his body was stone, the stone of the castle, and the breaths he took tasted of fire and of wine and of other, subtler things that he couldn't name.

He looked to where his sergeant was administering the magus's draught to the last men in the line. The ranks of riders looked alien, silhouettes etched by the night's feral glow, and the world was turning, turning, the huge, dim spectrum of the Warp gaining strength as it wheeled across the sky high above. Benetan felt laughter shake itself into life deep inside him and he turned, moving in a fluid, dreamlike way to the stable, past the nervous horses and towards the iron door with its heavy bar. The grooms – meaningless shadow-men, not worthy of his notice – backed away from him, and the dimensions of the stable seemed to stretch into impossible distortions, walls rearing and lurching,

floor undulating beneath his feet. Benetan knew he was halluci-
nating, but the earlier dread was leaving him now as the drug took
hold of his mind and body, and he welcomed the illusions, gloried
in them. The door loomed like a mouth; he stopped before it and
from his belt pulled a pair of long, black gauntlets, each finger
tipped with a silver claw. His hands tingled as he drew the
gauntlets over them and smoothed them on his arms; under
the moon the claws glinted and he flexed them, feeling the power
and the control they granted him as they transmuted his hands
into something other than human.

The door's metal bar gave under his grip; he wrenched it aside
and let it fall. Then he bunched his fist and the laughter spilled
from his throat as he pounded on the door's surface. With the
seventh blow the door smashed back on to a black tunnel.
Benetan swayed backwards as a vast breath of air belched out
of the dark: then a heavy, phased clopping echoed in the confined
space, and something huge, blacker even than the tunnel, moved
beyond the door, treading towards the physical world.

Even in his drug-heightened state Benetan couldn't fully
assimilate it. It was a monstrous thing of iron and dark, horse-
like but not spawned by any creature of flesh and blood, quartz
hooves shimmering, cold silver glittering in its eyes, the shadows
of great wings rising from its back. It opened a crimson mouth,
and its breath was like the touch of fire on his face as he reached
up towards it, grasped the mane that writhed like snakes in his
hands, coaxed it, caressed it, urged its sleek, sinuous form out
into the courtyard. Behind it more were emerging; huge silhouettes, things born of Chaos, demonic and powerful. Benetan was
laughing again and his men were joining in as they, too, fell prey
to the sacrament. The laughter, mingling with the voices that
howled their weird harmonies in the sky and in his head, was
tinged with insanity. The entire world was turning to black and
silver as Benetan's perceptions altered; he saw beyond the dimensions that physically held him, into places where other
consciousnesses moved in dark and formless undercurrents,
feeding on his excitement, imbuing him with sensations that
made his blood burn and race in his veins.

In the stable, someone was screaming. A young groom, unprepared for the things that he was witnessing, unprotected by

the narcotic that gripped the minds of the riders and held them steadfast in the face of Chaos. Another Benetan felt pity and regret for the youth's horror, but that Benetan was a stranger, an alien being: the Chaos captain who swung himself up on to the smoke-dark back of his mount could know only contempt for such weakness.

A jolt of raw power slammed into him as the terrible fusion between man and demon-beast engulfed his reeling senses. The courtyard turned and toppled about him and he uttered a high, ululating yell that was taken up by his fellow riders, a hungry and feverish celebration of energy, desire, madness. He raised his left arm high so that the gauntlet's claws caught the angry moonlight and, in his altered, churning vision, seemed to flash five searing bolts that spat upwards into the night. Lightning answered from the heavens, and the northern and eastern spires crackled and sang again. Benetan felt the moment coming, felt the Warp's awesome power building to a crescendo, thrumming through his bones – on the far side of the courtyard the great gates were opening—

A titanic howl smashed against his eardrums, and the sky split open. Blinding light turned the courtyard to an inferno, and, in hideous harmony with the voice of the breaking storm, the Chaos creatures shrieked a wild challenge as the mass of riders surged forward like a black, breaking wave, with Benetan screaming at their head. Possessed, inspired, deranged, his mind was no longer his own; the gates within him had opened, as the Chaos Gate was even now opening far, far below him, and humanity was drowned in the dervishistic joy of the warrior, the hunter, the reaper, as the demonic riders streamed through the gate to be unleashed upon the world.

Savrinor had returned quietly and unobtrusively to his rooms. He knew he would be summoned soon enough; although he wasn't of the magi's ranks, not even a sorcerer, his position as the castle's historian required him to attend and chronicle all major events, and for tonight's ceremony he had no doubt that his presence would be demanded.

He did not watch the Chaos riders leave. Spectacular though their departure might have been, it was nothing he hadn't seen a hundred times before and he was no longer moved or even

especially impressed by it. Instead as the Warp shrieked in from
the north he sat motionless at the ornately carved desk in his
study, elbows on the desk top, hands clasped before his face, pale
eyes unquiet. He didn't care to probe the reason for it but there
was unease in him, a sense of tension and anticipation – not
pleasant anticipation – that even the arrival of the Warp had done
nothing to allay. And when at last he heard the tentative knock at
his door, he wasn't sure whether relief or dread had the upper
hand.

"M-master Savrinor . . .?" The magi had a marked preference
for female servants; this one was probably no more than twelve or
thirteen years old, and any promise of later beauty she might have
had was spoiled by her slack mouth and empty, hunted eyes.
Savrinor doubted if she would last the year out.

"What is it?"

"The . . . l-lord magus Croin, master, he . . . that is, I am to
tell you . . . if you will permit . . ."

Fear and stupidity offended Savrinor in equal measure, and he
made no attempt to hide his irritation. "Speak clearly! Does
Magus Croin wish to see me?"

"He – the lord Croin . . . he is at the b-bedside of the F-f-f . . ."

"Yandros preserve us!" Savrinor hissed the words exasperat-
edly and, as the girl continued to stammer, brushed her aside and
strode away down the corridor. He had made out enough of the
faltering mumbles to surmise the rest of the message, and the
girl's efforts to tell him that Croin was with the First Magus
confirmed it. Croin was the magi's most skilled physician; if he
had issued this summons it must mean that the end was very
close, probably less than an hour away. By now the magi would be
preparing for the final procession. If he valued his skin, Savrinor
couldn't afford to be late.

Tidying his hair and clothes as he went, he reached the First
Magus's private chambers within minutes and found the thin,
aesthetic Croin waiting for him outside the door. The door was
closed, but light swirled beneath it and on the far side Savrinor
could hear the chilly, atonal sound of a dirge as the senior magi
chanted an elegy for their leader.

"My lord." Savrinor's bow was punctiliously formal. "The
First Magus is surely not—"

"No, no." Croin made a negative gesture, rings glinting on each of his seven fingers. "He has not yet left us. But it will be very soon. We are ready to proceed, and of course your presence is required at the time of passing."

"Yes, my lord. I'm only sorry that I must be the chronicler of the castle's loss."

Croin regarded him shrewdly, noting the genuine regret in Savrinor's tone and perhaps interpreting the reason for it all too well. "Our sorrow is the First Magus's joy, Savrinor. He goes to a reward that we all hope to earn in our time."

"Of course, sir." Savrinor averted his gaze.

"And if the gods accept his chosen successor, we will have cause for celebration." Croin's eyes narrowed. "I advise you not to overlook that fact."

"My lord." Savrinor bowed again in a way that conveyed apology and understanding without the need for further words. The physician continued to stare at him for a few moments longer, thinking his own thoughts. Then he turned, lifted the door's heavy latch, and led the way in to the First Magus's chambers.

The last journey of the dying man began ten minutes later. No lamps shone in any of the castle's windows now; shutters were closed and all but those who walked with the procession had retired to their quarters as tradition demanded. The Warp had passed, shrieking into oblivion, and the cortege emerged from the entrance doors under the indifferent eyes of the two moons which now hung in a clear, silent sky.

The first herald of the procession was a cold, glowing green sphere hanging unsupported in the air. It moved slowly from the shadows of the entrance to hover in the courtyard, and behind it came the magi, dressed in flowing robes, their forms ghastly and otherworldly under the eerie light. In their midst, four bearers carried a litter draped with white hangings, on which a still figure lay.

There was no sound: no chanting, no dirge now, not even the shuffle of feet. The magi moved as noiselessly as ghosts, the shining ball of light guiding them as they advanced in slow and stately procession towards the covered walkway of colonnaded pillars on the far side of the courtyard, and the door at the colonnade's end through which they would carry the First Magus to his final earthly encounter.

Savrinor walked behind his masters. Though he knew the form that tonight's ceremony would take, he didn't know precisely what to expect and was reluctant to speculate. He watched the shadows of the colonnade as they passed by, unconsciously counting the pillars; then the procession turned as it reached the door, and passed through it to begin the long, slow descent of the spiral stairs winding down into the foundations. At the foot of the stairs they passed through a vaulted room, dark and silent now, then another door gaped before them and they were on the last stage of their journey, along the sloping corridor that would bring them at last to the Marble Hall.

The Marble Hall, deep beneath the castle foundations, was a place of mist and deception. Its dimensions – if it could truly be said to have dimensions – were shrouded in an uneasy swirl of pastel-shot light and shadow, while the floor from which it took its name was an intricate mosaic of every perceptible shade, a random pattern that drew the eye yet disturbed senses constrained by the limitations of humanity. Centuries ago, when the seven lords of Chaos spoke to the sleeping minds of the world's greatest artisans, inspired them with dreams of terror and glory and guided their hands to cut the massive foundation-stones on which this castle was built, Yandros himself, highest of all the seven, had created the Marble Hall and with it the Chaos Gate. The Gate was a link between this world and the realm of Chaos, which no man still cloaked with the trappings of mortality dared enter; and as the procession moved across the shimmering floor Savrinor felt the deep-rooted thrill of awe and fear that no amount of familiarity could ever erode. The Gate lay at what was believed to be the hall's exact centre, and when closed it was marked by nothing more than a black circle in the mosaic pattern of the floor. Now, however, the mists about the circle were agitating, their pastel hues shot through with dark and dangerous colours. As he took his appointed place Savrinor saw a wavering column of intense blackness flickering close to the limits of perception, and felt the pulse of the forces held but barely in check under his feet. Chaos was stirring.

The bier was lowered with reverential care to the floor of the hall, before the Gate. The First Magus's eyes were open and aware; but if he recognised the faces that surrounded him, or the nature of what lay ahead, he gave no sign of it. A paralysing weakness had overtaken him that morning together with the final loss of his powers of speech, any last benisons he might have wished to grant to old friends would never now be uttered.

Savrinor watched the dying man, whilst seeming to keep his gaze focused on the floor. A good master, in his own way; vain and self-seeking, yes, but who wasn't in these times? Such faults, if faults they were, had their uses, as Savrinor knew very well. A good servant to the seven gods from whom he took his power? Perhaps; though that was not for any but the gods to say. Better, certainly, than the one who would come after him.

At that thought Savrinor's gaze slid surreptitiously to the members of the innermost coterie of magi who had taken up their positions at the head of the bier, and to one man in particular.

Vordegh. In late middle age now, but still retaining the strength and musculature of youth in his massive build. Black-haired, swarthily handsome, dark eyes calm as he regarded the Chaos Gate and waited with his peers. A sorcerer of rare skill, a demon-master, ascetic, sadist . . . and the word he had stopped Benetan Liss from uttering came unbidden into Savrinor's mind.

A madman.

Efficiently, Savrinor quashed the thought. With Vordegh as First Magus he would do well to take his own advice to Benetan and not even allow such concepts to enter his mind. Croin had echoed that same warning back to him, though not in so many words, and Savrinor hadn't missed the brief flicker of unease in the physician's eyes as he spoke. From now on he would guard even his innermost thoughts with the utmost care. Whichever way the wind blew there would still be room for him to man-oeuvre, if he kept his wits about him.

A stirring in the group's midst alerted him and he looked up quickly. The First Magus on his litter was trying to speak. Words were beyond his power now, but a guttural croaking issued from his throat, like the last cry of an old, sick raven. The other magi hastened to his side, and Vordegh leaned over the bier and took hold of the old man's hand as though to offer comfort or a last farewell. The First Magus's fingers fluttered feebly; he held something bright in his failing, arthritic grasp, and the artefact passed from his hand to Vordegh's before the arm fell back limply to his side.

Vordegh straightened, and a cold, proud smile touched his mouth. Then he raised his arm, and Savrinor saw the thin, metallic wand that the First Magus had placed in his palm. A chilly blue-white radiance spilled from the wand; bands of shadow moved slowly along its length, and Savrinor sucked in a quiet breath as he recognised it. The ultimate symbol of the power granted to the magi by the gods, and one whose use lay solely in the charge of the castle's undisputed master – the key to the Chaos Gate.

The First Magus had named his successor.

Vordegh turned to face the Gate, and raised the key high above his head. As his arm reached its full extent the wand's white radiance changed suddenly and shockingly to black, and it began to pulse like an unstable, earthbound star. The shivering column of the Gate took up the rhythm of the pulse, until the two meshed in perfect synchrony.

The old man on the bier stirred again. A crazed smile split his seamed features, and a spark of fire lit up the failing eyes as, with many hands supporting him, he raised his head a few inches from its pillow. The pulsing black light intensified in a ferocious flare – and the column of darkness seemed to invert, twisting in on itself and opening like a gigantic eye as the Chaos Gate yawned wide.

Savrinor looked into the eye and through it, to a black road that arrowed from the Gate towards a horizon so vast that he bit his tongue in shock. He could never habituate himself to this: to the vastness, the vertigo, the impossible, alien madness of the world that assailed his senses. Wild colours spun across dizzying spectra, shapes that defied comprehension shifted in constantly alternating patterns of gloom and livid brilliance, figures that were not quite tangible, and held their form only for the space of a heartbeat, moved like restless wraiths on the periphery of vision. And the Marble Hall vibrated with the anticipation of something titanic, that breached dimensions, approaching.

The magi were still again. Even the shrunken old man on the

pallet had ceased his efforts and lay passive once more, waiting, only his eyes animated and eager. Then came a sound like measured footsteps or a lethargic heartbeat, felt in the marrow rather than heard. Tension became palpable; somewhere – it seemed to emanate from the vastness beyond the Gate but that might have been illusory – a low humming vibrated in the bones behind Savrinor's ears.

The Gate shuddered and for a moment seemed to collapse back in on itself. Then a massive flash of brilliance, scarlet shot with searing white, turned the Marble Hall briefly to a blaze of light and fire, blinding the watchers and forcing them to turn their heads aside. When Savrinor, teeth clamped down on an invo-luntary oath, was able to look again, Chaos's emissary stood in the shadows of the portal.

The being, which was half again as tall as any of the magi, had the body of a man and the head of a scaled, gape-jawed reptile. Colossal wings rose from its shoulders, the flight feathers fash-ioned from white-hot metal that spilled molten fragments about its feet. A phantasmic, golden corona of flames burned around the figure; flanking it, two eyeless and monstrously distorted chimeras strained at their chains, snakes' tongues licking at the air, dogs' claws scraping and scrabbling for purchase on the mosaic. The emissary opened its jaws, and the stench of a charnel-house made Savrinor's nostrils flare. He forced himself not to flinch from it – discourtesy would be dangerous – and watched as the being's eyes, which were a warm amber-brown, calm and intelligent and beautiful, slowly scanned the gathering, their gaze resting at last on the now quiescent First Magus.

The silence was profound. Blood pounded in Savrinor's ears and he held his breath, not daring to move a muscle. The emissary gazed down at the pallet; then its unencumbered hand came up, and a finger, tipped with a curving claw the colour of old bronze, pointed at the First Magus's heart.

The old man smiled, and in the smile was the joy and triumph of achievement. He reared up as though to meet and embrace the Chaos being – then the hiss of his last breath echoed hollowly through the silent hall, and his empty husk fell back on to the bier.

Hastily following the lead of the magi, Savrinor dropped to one knee and traced the Seven-Rayed Star over his own heart as a mark of respect for the First Magus's passing. Only Vordegh didn't kneel or make the sign; he merely stood erect, unmoving, gazing steadily into the quiet eyes of the demon before him, and waiting. The emissary's reptilian head inclined once, and Vordegh extended his hand, displaying the darkly glowing wand on his palm. The claw reached out, plucked; and in the demon's grasp the wand turned white-hot. The monstrous jaws gaped again in a parody of a smile. Then the emissary touched the tip of the wand to the exact centre of Vordegh's forehead, and held it there.

Savrinor almost gagged at the reek of charring flesh, and some of the magi looked away. Vordegh, however, did not flinch. The tendons of his neck stood out like whipcord, but he stayed his ground, eyes staring straight ahead, though unfocused now with the strain of absorbing and withstanding the agony he must have felt. He would not recoil, he would not plead for cessation. The will of the man, Savrinor thought with an inward shudder, was beyond belief.

Suddenly it was over. The demon's arm fell to its side, and Savrinor saw the puckered and near-black stigma of a ferocious scar on Vordegh's brow; a scar that would never heal. Vordegh's gaze dropped – the only sign of relief that he would permit himself to show – and the emissary held out the wand, no longer blazing with heat, for the new First Magus to take. The two eyeless chimeras opened toothless mouths and shook their chains, and the emissary stepped back a pace. Once more, briefly, it scanned the assembly with something resembling cool speculation in its eyes. Then the molten wings rose high, clashed together, and with an enormous, silent concussion, the black eye of the Chaos Gate closed and the emissary was gone.

Through the silence of the darkest hours Savrinor sat at the table in his room, committing the night's events to parchment as his duty compelled. He couldn't stop shivering. The window was heavily curtained, and the airlessness together with the heat from the built-up fire made the chamber stifling, but the cause of the bone-numbing cold in him was the unpleasant and unnerving track of his own thoughts.

There had been something wrong with the ceremony. He had

not dared to consider it at the time, but now the memory echoed in his mind like a recalled nightmare. On the surface, everything had gone well enough. The old First Magus's soul had been gathered to the realm of Chaos and had made its last journey gladly; his successor had undergone trial and had not been found wanting. But there were anomalies. The emissary sent by the Chaos lords had been a demon of no great rank; Chaos was perverse, and its higher beings tended to favour less bizarre manifestations than their lower brethren. Though Savrinor had never been privileged to witness such an event, he had heard that Yandros himself took the form of an ordinary man on the rare occasions when he deigned to make himself known to his human worshippers. All well and good; the emissary had been of an order warranted by such an occasion as this. But there had been no shout of fanfares, no violent assault on the senses, none of the ceremonial that usually accompanied the arrival of the lesser demons. The emissary hadn't spoken a single word, had demanded no praises or psalms in its turn. And Vordegh's trial had been simplicity itself.

It didn't fit the accepted pattern. Despite its erratic nature, Chaos maintained a certain predictability in its dealings with the mortal world; without that stability its worshippers couldn't hope to function. And by those rules, such anomalies as Savrinor had witnessed tonight simply shouldn't have existed. They suggested, to his uneasy mind, an ambivalence on the part of Yandros and his six brothers. But ambivalence towards what? The old First Magus? The new? Or something that, as yet, he couldn't even begin to guess at?

Savrinor shook sand over the last of his parchments. He had no time for false modesty and knew that his work tonight had excelled even his usual high standard. Every detail of the ceremonial was there, and woven in among the facts was a sober tribute to the wisdom and nobility of the late First Magus, carefully balanced by several subtle paragraphs in respectful but emphatic praise of his successor. Even Vordegh couldn't possibly find fault with this. And no one, Savrinor hoped and prayed, would ever know of the other document, the few brief but succinct notes in his own shorthand code that now lay secreted in an inner drawer, and which told a different story.

Feeling faintly queasy with the relief of having shed an unpleasant burden, Savrinor set the completed document aside. Fastidiously he turned down the cover of his bed, then moved to extinguish the lamp by which he had been working. A gaunt shape moved in the gloom beyond the lamplight, and he started nervously before realising that it was nothing more than his own shadow disturbed by a flicker within the lamp's chimney. Jinking at shadows. It was a trait he mocked in others, for twilight, literal or metaphorical, had always been his natural habitat. But suddenly he felt uneasy in its embrace. And the thoughts that had been troubling his mind were still there, and they would not let him alone.

Forcing down the tension within him Savrinor sought refuge in his bed, for once not troubling to shed his clothes. It would be dawn soon enough, and the new day would see a good many changes if he and his bones were any judge. Better to be ready at a moment's notice, in case of . . . what? He didn't know. Perhaps nothing; perhaps not. He, like all of them, would have to wait and see.

He reached out to extinguish the lamp – then let his hand fall away from it and instead left it burning, a small pool of brightness in the dim room. It was irrationally comforting, and there was no one else here to witness his small show of weakness.

Savrinor did not sleep that night.

THE ETERNAL ALTERCATION

Peter Crowther

If ever there is a present day British writer who succeeds in capturing the essence of American fantasy it's Peter Crowther (b. 1949). I'd go so far as to say he is the modern-day British Ray Bradbury. He can create a believable everyday setting and imbue it with an unsettling sense of strangeness. You'll find that in his novel Escardy Gap *(1996), written with James Love-grove, and in his many stories, some of which are collected in* The Longest Single Note *(1999) and* Lonesome Roads *(1999). Crowther has also edited anthologies and runs PS Publishing, the small press with big ideas. The following story just had to be the final story in the collection because it reaches such a breathless pace that nothing can follow it. So, brace yourself.*

Q. "The railroads are doing pretty well are they not?"
A. "Some of them are. The old ones are. Yes."

J. P. Morgan,
at a Congressional Hearing in late 1912

A BOUT 20 MINUTES AFTER abandoning the gas-dry hulk of his trusty Trans Am by the roadsign, Paul Abbott reasoned that he'd taken a wrong turn. Or maybe he'd just mis-read the route signs because they happened on the fold of his road atlas. Or maybe – and more than likely – he was just tired, completely fucked-in-the-head and road-weary after hundreds and hundreds of miles along shimmering gray ribbons stretched out between seemingly endless cornfields.

But whatever the reason, Nashville had not appeared.

Hell, maybe even Tennessee hadn't appeared.

What had appeared was a rusted sign explaining that Madrigal – and what the hell was that, pray tell? wasn't it some kind of old-time dance? – lay four miles ahead, with a population of . . . how many? The number had either been chipped off or worn down by the elements.

And now, here he was, gas can in hand, standing on the town's edge, looking along its wind-blown Main Street at a clumsy array of buildings that owed more allegiance to an old black-and-white Randolph Scott western than to anything even vaguely reminiscent of the Brave New World promised by the turn of the millennium.

And there was not a single person to be seen.

And not a single car.

At the first albeit casual glance – and Abbott suspected that the same impression would hold true for many more in-depth glances to come – Madrigal was a ghost town. And one that had surely never featured in the *National Geographic* or appeared even as a sideways reference in even the most offbeat travel book.

Certainly, it was a far cry from any of the towns Larry McMurtry had encountered when he drove his beloved Inter-states like a blacktop surfer in search of the perfect wave for his *Roads* book. And it was a world away from the smalltown eccentricities uncovered when Bill Bryson returned to his native America to rediscover his roots in *The Lost Continent*. Hell, it even made the backwoods shanty communities of William Least Heat-Moon's *Blue Highways* seem like bustling Metropolises by comparison.

Down the street, an Esso sign creaked in the wind and a skeletal tumbleweed trundled across to lodge itself against the door of a barber's shop, the shop's candy-striped pole faded by many years' sunshine . . . or simply many years' disinterest.

Abbott hoisted the can into his other hand and set off for the filling station.

Every building he passed was empty.

No, they were more than empty: they were dead. Was that right? Could a building actually be dead?

He reached the filling station with less than optimism. The

door of the little kiosk across from the pumps stood ajar so Abbott walked across and banged his can on the wood panelling.

"Anybody there?" he yelled.

There was no response.

He walked over to one of the pumps and pulled the lever, praying for the tell-tale hum that promised gasoline.

No hum. Just the wind.

"Shit!"

He stepped back into the street and looked further along.

A little way down, on the boardwalk, was a wide sign pointing off to the right. He squinted into the sun, unsure of what to make of the sign: RAIL DEPOT, the letters read.

"Rail depot? What the hell is a place like this doing with a rail depot?" he asked the wind. If it knew the answer, it was keeping quiet about it.

Abbott looked around some more.

For that matter, where were the rails? He didn't recall seeing any back on the road . . . but then he had been more intent on watching the faltering needle on the fuel gauge than in checking for local amenities.

Abbott tossed the can over to the pumps and set off for the sign. Hell, maybe he could catch a train to Nashville, pick the car up another time . . . call the Auto Club to come along and tow it away.

He wasn't surprised to find the rail station was deserted.

He walked along banging doors loudly and shouting but the wind caught the sounds and took them up to wherever the wind takes sounds that it doesn't want to linger . . . and doesn't want anyone to hear.

The silence was thick and inhospitable.

The ticket window gave out his own reflection, staring at him in incredulity . . . presumably just as fascinated to see a living person in the town as he was to see a place so bereft of life.

Abbott walked around the side of the building, stepped down on to the hard-packed ground and went in search of the tracks.

He found them – or what was left of them – in a long ditch that stretched into the distance in each direction, curving into town from the west and curving back out, again to the west . . . which explained why he hadn't seen them on the way in.

As he stood on the bank of the ditch and followed the tracks –
saw the sun on the distant horizon, a thick bruise shot through
with gold and scarlet – he heard something that sounded for all
the world like a throaty chuckle.

Abbott span around and looked back at the station building. It
was still deserted. Must have been the wind.

When he turned around and faced north, straight across the
ditch, he saw an old man sitting on the bank at the far side, a
lopsided grin on his face. As Abbott watched, the man seemed to
be mouthing something, his lips drifting from smirk to grimace,
all the time peppered with muttered catechisms and oaths, as he
rubbed the side of his face with the stump of his left arm, from
which a thin and dirty streamer of bandage wafted in the hot
breeze.

"Hey," Abbott shouted across the track. "Where is everybody?"

The old man sniggered and nodded, then spat into the dust by
his side. Even from here, Abbott could see that the spit was dark.

The man held something in his right hand, something that
looked like tiny breadsticks. Then, shielding his eyes against the
late afternoon sun's glare so that he might see with more clarity,
Abbott realized that the breadsticks were in fact the last surviving
fingers of the man's other hand. As though reading Abbott's
thoughts, the man nodded and held up the grisly collection like an
offering of straw-picking . . . short straw loses. He mouthed
something more, sniggered and spat again, curling the fingers
into his good hand and placing it between his belly and the two-
fingered claw of his other.

"Shit," Abbott whispered, and the wind took the word and
sent it scurrying across the track and the arroyo alongside it . . .
where once water had surely run but where now only dust and
dirt prevailed.

The old man pulled his knees up to his belly and wrapped his
arms around them, glaring off into the distance down or up the
track – Abbott didn't know which. He turned to face in the same
direction.

The breeze which ran along the shallow-sided arroyo cooled a
little, as though perhaps remembering the water that once
streamed there. The fall was maybe a drop of only a few degrees

but it was noticeable. Abbott glanced across and saw the old man straining forward, his hands now resting at either side of his emaciated body as he affected the stance of an artist's model.

The man grunted and shook his head, lifting a hand to smooth down strands of wiry hair. It was a monosyllabic grunt, a single surprised word that could have been "rain", though Abbott did not believe the drop in temperature heralded anything more than a temporary glitch in meteorological aerodynamics and the promise of more excesses in the days ahead. He looked up into the marbled sky and tried to imagine the sensation of rain falling on to his upturned face. It seemed like an old memory . . . something he had experienced in another life.

The old man grunted again, this time even more anxiously.

It could have been "pain" that he was saying, for the man's face, Abbott now saw, had become a mask of seemingly exquisite agony. Perhaps he had suffered another loss – a toe, perhaps, or a foot . . . that even now lay sideways-on to the ankle to which it had so recently been attached.

But no, it did not look like either of these, for the man hunched himself closer to the distance before him, anxiously straining towards it. The wind grew cooler, markedly cooler, and Abbott moved to the edge of the platform, glancing down at the littered corpses of small rodents before turning his full attention to the arid plains that stretched out from Madrigal like the pavements of Hell.

The old man grunted a third time, and Abbott felt a sudden surge of cool wind against his face.

"*Train!*" Abbott said. That was what the old man was saying: a train was coming. He didn't know where it was coming from not where it was traveling to . . . nor even who might be riding it. None of these factors seemed to carry any consequence. The only thing that mattered was that a train was coming to Madrigal station.

Abbott watched and saw a shape forming out of the heat haze in the far distance, over where the sky met the earth and the two of them plotted new and undreamed of mischief to amuse and frustrate mankind. The shape loomed as though out of a sea mist, like a fabled galleon of bulwark and figurehead, mast and sail, rigging and plank . . . only this was no schooner ploughing the waves, its boards creaking in the wind: this was an automotive monster of gleam and smoke, glass and metal, a steaming engine pulling behind it a string of carriages, the last one of which boasted bulbous sides that hung far out over the track on each side, like insect wings partly folded against the sunlight.

His mouth open in something resembling astonishment, Abbott glanced across at the old man. The man nodded enthusiastically and then pointed down at the wide ditch that separated him from Abbott. The man chuckled to himself, almost folding over in mirth, and then pointed again, this time waving his hand over towards the approaching train, still pointing downwards.

Abbott frowned and looked down into the ditch, his eyes searching for the cause of the old man's amusement. But there was nothing, at least nothing obvious.

"What?" Abbott shouted over the sound of escaping steam and revolving pistons, a mournful mechanical wail carried towards them by the breeze coursing the arroyo. "What's so goddam funny?"

The old man leaned back, his mouth wide in laughter that Abbott could not hear. And he pointed again, jabbing the bandaged stump violently at the ditch and again moving it to his left and towards the approaching train.

A whistle blew . . . a shrill outpouring of pain and frustration – or was it anger? Then came the sound of collision, of massive impact and a high-pitched squeal like a giant's fingernails being dragged across a monolithic blackboard. An explosion sounded and Abbott hunched forward.

When he glanced across the ditch, he saw the old man trying to get to his feet.

Abbott looked up and out to the train again, shaking his head.

A thick plume of smoke-topped fire now filled the distance, and Abbott saw that the back carriage of the train had swung out, out over the side of the track and on to the concrete aprons which formed a goods yard where trucks had maybe once carried produce and equipment to towns and cities many miles away.

The carriage had collided with a small filling station and then what must once have been a dispatching shed, carrying on, weaving madly, stretching the other carriages with it – Abbott counted seven in all. One of the middle ones was pushing before it an old car which itself was on fire. As he watched, the car impacted with a building side, hesitated for a second and then caromed backwards as the carriage compressed it further against the building before demolishing the wall and continuing onwards, swinging crazily back towards the track while the car turned top over tail several times and dropped over the rail of a highway overpass.

The train was off the track!

Abbott looked back into the ditch and stared in sudden realization at the twin lines of metal, sometimes in place and sometimes askance . . . and still other times not there at all.

He followed the pieces of metal, saw that in one section they were actually laid across themselves like a metallic tic tac toe board . . . and in another section they had been inserted into the uneven dirt of the ditch bottom like the flagpoles of an army long since departed from the field of battle, their pennants taken – or buried – with them.

Abbott backed slowly away from the ditch.

Across from him the old man had managed to get to his feet – or foot, as Abbott now observed . . . the man's left leg ending just below his knee where a thick bandage which might once have been white trailed in the dust. He was shuffling across to the edge of the concrete block which clearly had once served as a platform.

"Get back!" Abbott shouted.

The man looked up and across at him.

This time Abbott waved his arm at him. "Get back from the edge!"

The old man laughed and nodded. He took another lopsided limp – he was actually walking on his shin stump, Abbott realized – and reached the very edge of the concrete where he stopped for a few seconds and swayed drunkenly.

Abbott looked to his right and saw that the train's engine was now approaching the small station at an angle, the cowcatcher bars on the front raking through dilapidated fencing and taking down the occasional telegraph pole it encountered. The poles fell some to the left of the track, away from it, and others to the right, lying temporarily across the ditch before being snapped like firewood as the train caught them and swept them up.

A sound of scraping and complaining metal and distant explosions from somewhere out of sight filled the air. The train's whistle screamed once more, and then again . . . this time a bovine bellow that rattled Abbott's bones beneath his skin.

When he glanced across the ditch that separated him from the old man he saw that the man was nowhere to be seen. And then he saw a frail figure pull itself to its full height – surely no more than five feet, and possibly much less – in the ditch. The old man had climbed down and was now staggering forward to meet the oncoming train.

The chain of carriages had now whiplashed back across the track, the final carriage – the wider one – out of sight . . . though Abbott had a good idea as to exactly where it had gone. Three wire-less telegraph poles across the track folded over with sharp snapping sounds and tumbled to the ground, felled like trees in an old logging camp.

The train whistled again.

The old man shouted and lifted his arms in supplication. Abbott saw the mummified fingers cast carelessly on to the dirt beside and beneath the askew rails.

Abbott jogged along the platform, quickly coming up alongside the man, shouting . . . but the man paid no heed.

The train hit the old man side on, the width of the engine and its shimmering spinning wheels gathering him up on to it, spread-eagled like a bug on a windscreen, and then it lurched sideways, the front momentarily catching Abbott in the sightless eyes of its twin lamps as it lunged across and rattled slowly and laboriously through a series of thick wooden supports which held up the old station's roof. Abbott looked up in time to see planks disengage themselves from their once collective canopy structure and cascade in shards of varying size, one of the more sturdy examples narrowly missing his head. There was a hoarse scream suddenly cut off and Abbott saw that although there was still a torso lodged amidst the chrome and silver bars that criss-crossed the black metal of the engine, the old man's legs had disappeared, severed by the engine's impact with a low holding wall that ran across the end of the platform.

He turned and started to run, the sound of cracking wood and collapsing timbers filling the air behind him. At the end of the platform he dodged sideways into the thick scrub grass that now festooned most of the gravelled car park, home in these dim days of Madrigal's history to nothing more than a few tyres piled haphazardly in one corner.

With a triumphant *horrrrrnk!*, the engine emerged from the remnants of the station house like the mythical white whale, resplendent with the lifeless body of the old man – its very own Ahab – caught in the gleaming framework of its muzzle. It must have been the shucking, side-to-side movement of the train . . . but the old man looked like he was waving. And was that a smile on his face?

Looking down, Abbott could see that the wheels were not like any other train wheels he had ever seen. They were like the wheels on a car – albeit much wider – encased in what appeared to be thick rubber and cross-hatched with a myriad slender spokes which erupted from the raised hub. Moreover, the wheels seemed to change direction independent of each other, with the first on the set of six running beneath the engine first twisting outwards – while the wheel behind it remained straight and the one behind that seemed to bend in – and then it twisted back again, with the others assuming their own rogue directions.

How on earth could whoever was driving this thing – Abbott glanced up at the side of the engine, at the misted window, where he could make out the hunched form of someone presumably fighting with the controls – keep it in any sense of a straight line?

As though emphasizing the sheer impossibility of such a task, given the difficulties imposed by the system of wheels, the train suddenly swerved back towards the track-ditch and Abbott saw the ripple move through the carriages that followed. He knew what was going to happen. It would have a snapping effect, the carriages swinging out and moving forward side-on, a thick and impenetrable wall of wood and metal taking down everything in its path. He looked around and, sure enough, the back carriage exploded from a small group of outbuildings at the far side of the station house, pushing before it a bellowing cloud of dust and debris, moth-eaten units of furniture . . . and the other carriages could now be seen through the holocaust, claiming their own victims in the process.

He looked to the side and saw a wall between him and the road. No time to run alongside the wall to the opening, and no time to turn the other way and try to outdistance the renegade engine and cut across its path to the space beyond.

There was only one solution.

With the back carriage now scraping along the wall and the engine seemingly powering forward to produce what would be a whip-crack effect once the bellied-out line straightened to its maximum, Abbott ran towards the driver's cab and leapt for the rail, managing to get one foot on the narrow platform and grabbing hold of a gold coloured handle. Seconds later, he was slammed back against the paintwork.

The engine let out another bellow and the train smashed forward through the track-ditch, bucking like a wild horse, thundering across the road where, a few miles outside town, Abbott's Pan Am lay waiting for sustenance and straight for a nest of wooden leantos lazing in the dappled, watery sunlight.

Gasping for breath, Abbott pulled himself around and grasped a piece of silver rail with his free hand. Then he edged forward and fell into the gap between the engine and the cab. It wasn't too soon. Almost immediately, the train hit the lean-tos and a rain of timber and who knew what else fell on to the cab roof and the overhang like an apocalyptic hailstorm. The train lurched, swerved sideways, lurched again – lifting Abbott momentarily into the air and then crashing him down again on to the dimpled metallic platform – and then ploughed a deep furrow into a barren field, throwing curtains of sun-bleached soil out on each side.

The platform he was standing on at the front of the cab was barely a foot wide and, without decent hand-holds, maintaining any kind of balance at all required Abbott to lean across the gap over the rusted coupling attaching the cab to the engine. A sudden jolt could easily topple him and his fear was of not being thrown clear but of tumbling through the gap to be torn up beneath the wheels.

Then he saw the recessed handle.

As he grappled the handle bar away from its recess and pulled, the train swung wildly to the left and Abbott felt himself lift from the platform. He folded his fingers tightly around the handle and felt something twang in his shoulder, immediately giving way to a kind of cold tingle that travelled down his arm and into his fingers. Any minute – any *second* – feeling and, more importantly, control, was going to go from that hand and he would fall . . . and now that the train had straightened off a little, he would fall through into the path of the wheels. Face it, with the way the driver was handling the controls, anywhere at all beneath the train would be in the path of at least *one* of the wheels.

Abbott pulled the handle and the door gave way. With the last vestiges of his strength, he reached with his other arm, grabbed the door jamb and pulled himself through. Almost immediately, the train seemed to pirouette and Abbott fell forward into the cab, rolled over and was thrown to the side wall, all breath being forced from him.

He slid down the wall, grateful for the momentary calm, and looked for something to hold on to while he gasped for air.

A deep voice spoke above the roar of steam and gears and pounding wheels. "You okay?"

Abbott looked around.

The engine compartment was gloomy, lit only by a couple of lanterns – Abbott presumed they were some kind of oil or fuel lanterns, seeing as they were not connected to anything – hanging from levers on the roof and swinging crazily. The walls were festooned with all manner of dials and steering wheels, huge levers and knobs, buttons and flashing lights. Oil ran over and between everything, pooling on the metal floor. At either side of a thick column which looked like a chimney breast, two small windows looked out through grime and dust on to a shuddering landscape of trees and field, the perspective changing virtually by the second, lurching first one way and then the other, and suddenly seeming to jump into the air or drop into some unforeseen chasm without warning.

"I said, you okay? Took quite a pounding back there."

Abbott squinted and part of the darkness in front of the chimney breast shifted to one side until the outline of a head, topped with some kind of cap, obliterated the view from the right hand window.

"I'm . . . okay," Abbott said. Speaking was difficult and he tried just to wave a hand, but the pain shot down his side and touched his right hip.

The figure turned around again, moving back into the dark

obscurity between the windows. "Don't worry about the old guy," the disembodied voice said. "He'll be okay."

"Okay?" Abbott was incredulous. "You hit him with the fucking train, for crissakes."

"Yeah, well . . . he'll be okay. He always is."

"Always is? You mean this has happened before?"

"Oh sure," the man said matter-of-factly. "It's Madrigal."

Abbott was reminded of the closing lines in Roman Polanski's *Chinatown* movie . . . the old man mentioning the town's name like it explained everything that was shitty with the world.

"What's that got to do with anything?"

"Nothing . . . everything. Who knows any more." The man seemed to be busy working something. Then he said, "He show you his fingers?"

Abbott didn't answer.

"He's always doing that . . . taking them off, putting them back again." He chuckled. "He'll be okay. He's an angel – he'll fix things up."

"What exactly will he fix up?"

"The town. Madrigal. For when I hit it again. That's what he does. Like I said, he's an angel." He chuckled. "Anyways, you sure you're okay?"

Abbott could tell from the voice that the man had turned away from him but he couldn't bring himself to consider what the man might be doing. The pain was now travelling down his right leg and his foot was going numb.

"Cos otherwise, you sure don't talk much," the man added. "Now, there's some folks think that's a plus factor – me, I could use a little conversation, you know what I'm saying here?"

The pain was subsiding a little now and Abbott shuffled to his left until he wedged himself into the corner of the engine compartment. He rested his head back against the wall, placed a hand behind it to minimize the damage from it being repeatedly banged against the metal structure and opened his eyes.

The light was either getting a little better or his eyes were simply getting more accustomed. Now Abbott could make out the man's shape; he was small – around 5–5, maybe 5–6 – stocky, wearing a set of striped overalls which looked creased and covered in oil and grease. From his back pocket, some kind of rag was caught in the act of overflow, one pointed corner jiggling back and forth as the man fought at a massive steering wheel attached to the central area. The hat was a baseball cap, dark in colour – maybe blue, or dark green: Abbott couldn't make out – and it covered a thick thatch of wiry hair, grey-white, worn unfashionably long so that it exploded into tiny ringlets plastered by sweat and grease against the man's bulbous neck.

The steering wheel looked to be a complex affair: one wide rim – which the man held with one hand – and three others, each progressively smaller in diameter, raised up in tiers and fastened to a central column by ornate metal bars. Alongside it, a nest of long gear levers protruded like bullrushes from a circular socket.

Abbott watched for a while, enjoying the sensation of the pain gradually diminishing. He kept shifting his attention between the man's activities and the view of the outside, which could be seen through the two side windows. At first it was just somewhere to move his eyes, and then he noticed something.

The field of vision through the windows, at least from Abbott's position on the floor, was limited to clouds. The man wrenched the wheel first one way and then the other, thrust this lever forwards, churned that one in a circular motion to rest almost horizontal with the floor.

"Quite a ride," Abbott shouted above the noise.

"Yep," came the reply.

"Is she . . . is she out of control?"

"Who?"

Abbott smiled. "The train."

"Oh, the train." He spun one of the wheels suddenly with one hand in an almost ballet flourish, pushing one of the levers upwards with the other and then smacking the side of the wheel to maximize the speed of the revolution. Then he caught hold of it and twisted one of the others in the opposite direction. The train lurched drunkenly and Abbott slid away from his corner.

"No, I'd say I've got it pretty much under control right now."

Now Abbott saw that the man was not even looking out of the windows at all. He seemed to be staring at the chimney breast wall directly in front of him.

"Where you headed?" Abbott said as he continued to look around the compartment.

"Everywhere. And nowhere," the man added. "Just travelling."

Abbott nodded. "What I mean to say is, where can I get off?"

"Get *off*?" He chuckled. "Well, now, you can get off any time you've a mind to." He pulled down on a piece of knotted string and the whistle blew a shrill screech. "Makes no odds to me."

"But where do you stop?"

The man pulled on the wheel, tugging it to the right with all of his might, and sent a lever screeching to one side. "I don't," he grunted.

"You don't *stop*?"

"That's what I said."

Watching the man's back, Abbott said, "You're not steering to avoid things are you? You're steering to *hit* them."

The man opened a rectangular metal door in front of him exposing a blazing furnace. He reached down into the large tub alongside him and fished out what looked like a handful of empty polythene bags which he threw on to the flames. As the fire burst with renewed ferocity, the man slammed the metal door and took hold of the wheel again.

Accepting that he wasn't going to get an answer to that one – though, of course, it could be that the man hadn't even heard him . . . which was all too possible given the noise – Abbott said, "What kind of fuel is that?"

Now the man turned around and smiled.

"Dreams," he said.

The face was a mixture of sadness and gentleness, self confidence and humility . . . with an underlying edge of something darker. The man looked to be around 65 or 70 years old. He had a round face fringed with grey sideburns that ran all the way to his jawline, a couple of intercrossed deep furrows across the bridge of his nose and eyes that were half-lidded . . . as though Abbott were looking at a photograph that had been taken mid-blink.

"Dreams." It was all Abbott could do simply to repeat the word, though he did so without any inflection of doubt. If the man said the fuel was dreams then it was dreams. Abbott didn't know how that could be but, if this guy said it, it must be so. He immediately felt that there would be many things that this man could tell him – or even ask of him – that Abbott would accept without so much as the hint of argument.

The man turned around and spun the big wheel like a demonic conductor, one chubby arm shooting towards the compartment's roof as soon as it left the wheel . . . and then dropping to take hold of one of the other wheels, turning it quickly back while the man leaned forward and studied whatever it was in front of him. Abbott felt suddenly freed.

"So," he said as he struggled to his feet. "We're in a train that doesn't stop anywhere and that's fuelled by dreams." Hearing it now, spoken by his own voice, Abbott wondered how he could ever have considered such an answer as being anything other than the lunatic ramblings of an old man.

"That's it. Got it in one."

Abbott moved forward holding on to a series of small levers protruding from the roof and stood alongside the man. Great . . . he'd hitched a ride out of Nowheresville on a car-wheeled train – driven by some old fart who spoke riddles – which had just killed a man in broad daylight and caused more damage (even though that damage was to downtown Madrigal, which could surely use a little spring-cleaning) than all the *Lethal Weapon* movies put together. And the man the old fart had killed looked like he was a leper, for crissakes: and where in the world do lepers still exist? Abbott looked out on to the countryside and saw that it was a blur.

"Jesus, how fast we moving?" He glanced to the piece of wall in front of the man for some kind of instrument panel. There was nothing . . . except for what appeared to be a flickering television screen protected on all four sides by extended panels. Abbott couldn't see what the screen was showing, and there didn't seem to be any sound coming from it . . . though with all the background noise he couldn't be sure.

The man shrugged. "No idea. Pretty fast, I'd guess."

"We in some kind of rush?"

"Not particularly."

"So why're we going so fast?"

The man yanked a protesting lever towards him and spun the wheel again, stomping a couple of times on a wide pedal at the base of the wall. The train juddered a couple of times and slewed wildly to one side, knocking Abbott off balance. He fell back but managed to avoid hitting the wall.

"I said, why we—"

"To keep up our speed."

Abbott was about to say something else when the man looked at him – just a glance, and a smile – and then turned his attention back to his little screen. Abbott felt his frown melt and *yeah, right . . . to keep up our speed . . . obvious . . .* he looked back out of the window and watched countryside shoot by in a dizzying succession of groves of trees, columns of houses, rows of vehicles . . . some of them moving, others just parked up in endless aisles – and wasn't it strange that there wasn't a single person to be seen anywhere? Wouldn't they hear the noise and come out to see what the hell was happening?

Hey, Mabel, come look – there's a goddam train slewing its way through the neighbourhood even though we ain't got no tracks right here in the suburbs . . . and it's carving everything up as it goes. And isn't that an old man lying spreadeagled across the engine? Looks to me like he's waving . . .

The scenery didn't simply go by, it frequently shifted to one side and then to the other, sometimes slowing almost to a halt before speeding up again. What the hell kind of train *was* this?

And there was something else.

Thick clouds of debris flew up against the window and rattled over the engine housing, clattering down its sides and back to the ground . . . building materials, furniture, cars, telegraph poles, streetlights . . . all of them fell beneath the careering engine and its maniac driver. And yet, when Abbott looked out of the window he saw that everything they had seemingly destroyed was still in place.

"How do you do that?"

"What?"

Abbott nodded at a delivery truck which upended against the cab but which was in exactly the position it had started in as soon as they had passed by. "That."

The old man shrugged and span the wheel. "They're just soul debris."

"Soul debris?" Great, Abbott thought. I'm having a conversation on metaphysics with an old fart driving a renegade train through the countryside. "Trucks and cars and buildings have souls?"

"Everything has a soul, young feller," the old man said. "Everything stays pretty much the way it was once I've passed through."

"What about the people?"

"They don't see me," the old man snapped as he swerved to the right.

"I saw you," Abbott said.

"Yep, you did that."

"So what does that mean in the great scheme of things?"

"Maybe it's just you got better eyesight than most," the old man said. "And maybe it's cos you got a job to do."

"Well, I do have a job to do," Abbott said. "I have to write a whole series of articles on just how far the heartland of America is drifting from the overall corporate structure of the country in the new millennium."

"Sounds a whole lot of fun," the old man said softly as he shifted a lever forwards and gave the wheel a sharp turn.

Abbott watched as the scenery shifted yet again and the cab sliced through an apartment building. "It wasn't that way back where you picked me up. In . . . Madrigal? The buildings sure took a pounding there."

"Yeah, well . . . that's Madrigal. And, like I keep telling you, they'll get fixed up. That old man . . . he's—"

"Yeah, I know . . . he's an angel."

The old man nodded without turning around. "Now you're getting it."

The train lurched to the left and Abbott bounced against the side. And he was supposed to *jump* from this? No way! Maybe when the guy got tired . . . maybe then he'd have to pull over.

"When do you take a break?"

"I don't."

"You don't take a *break*? Don't you have a . . . an assistant?"

"Uh uh."

"So when do you sleep?"

"Don't sleep." The old man pulled a lever, held it and wound it to the side. "Don't sleep, don't eat. Don't do no toilet neither."

Abbott blinked, assessing the information. *Don't do no toilet neither*? If that were true, then the guy had to have a bowel as big as a zeppelin . . . and a bladder as big as the shed that housed it. He was obviously a complete fruitcake . . . but Abbott had dealt with fruitcakes before.

But then there was the not-so-small matter of the fact that the train seemed to be smashing through everything apparently without causing any damage. Maybe there was some kind of closed-circuit playback fed into the windows . . . something showing lots of carnage, and with a hydraulic system patched into the undercarriage. Maybe they weren't even moving at all. But then Abbott had seen what the train had done coming into town.

yeah, well . . . that's Madrigal

The trick was humouring him.

Managing to keep the incredulity out of his voice, he asked, "How long –" He pointed to the steering wheel and waved his arm around the driving compartment. "– how long you been driving this—"

The man turned around and smiled again. "Long time," he said. "I been driving all the time you been driving around writing your articles. I know everything. I know your name and your every breath . . . felt it in my circuits –" He laughed and thumped his chest. "– heard it from the engine."

Abbott listened.

It was the sound of whispered voices, a multitude of accents and words, a sibilant rush of packed vowels and consonants, rising and falling, surging and retreating like waves on a beach. It was both a part of the engine noise and something else entirely, a complement as well as a distraction.

"You know my name?"

"That's what I said."

"So what is it?"

"Abbott." The old man shot him a *fuck you* smile and returned his attention to the wheel.

"How'd you know my name?"

"Oh, I know *lots* of stuff. Hear it all from here . . ." He patted the chimney breast. "Listen:"

Abbott frowned, trying to discern coherence from the chaos. Here and there he thought he could hear phrases, questions, statements and pleas, some in English and others in other languages, other tongues.

"What is it?" he asked the old man.

"It's the Sound."

"*Which* sound?"

The old man spun one of the wheels and jammed a foot on the pedal. Spinning another wheel in a different direction, he pulled a lever and said, "It's *the* Sound. Every sound that ever was . . . every cat's fart and every baby's cry . . . every lover's promise and every corpse's first and last breath . . . the breath that escapes in that wondrous fraction of a second when the body has ceased to function. It's every murderer's gasp of panic and the beat of every airborne wing as it flaps against and through the currents. It's the drumbeat of every hoof and the swish of every fish's tail. And it's every word that has ever been said, some to other folks and a lot – more than you'd think – spoken only in the silence of mirrored rooms or against the feigned softness of lonely pillows, or into endless glasses whose promise of oblivion is always just another drink away."

Abbott was suddenly aware that he was nodding, caught up in the hypnotic meter of the old man's words.

"Those are the dreams. Once I throw them on the fire, they keep burning . . . cos dreams never end – anybody knows that, right?"

"Right."

Hello, 911? Could you send a team around to someplace in Tennessee . . . there's a train rampaging the countryside and an old man driving it has just flipped over into Never Never Land. And bring your nets!

Abbott would have agreed with anything the old man said. "But if they keep burning, how come you have to keep adding more?"

"They get smaller. They keep burning, and they get real small –" He held up his hand and made a pincer shape with the thumb and forefinger – the space between them was infinitesimal. "– but they never burn away. A dream is something lasts forever, yeah?"

Yeah! Hell, why *not* right? Anybody knew *that*. Stuck in an out-of-control steam train chatting with the ghost of Carlos

Casteneda while he threw dreams into the furnace . . . pretty much anything at all made perfect sense.

"And they talk about *me*, these dreams? Call me names?"

The old man laughed and stamped his foot. "Heh, they don't call you names, they speak of you. And not all of them do even that," he said as he slowly pitched the train to the left and then spun the uppermost wheel, the smallest, back to the right. The train pitched and tossed like a lost ship on a midnight ocean, screaming soundlessly to the stars and an uncaring night sky. "But a lot do . . . and not all of them ever knew you."

"That doesn't make any sense."

"Nothing much does," came the response. He waited a few seconds, staring intently at the chimney breast, and then said, "I listen to them all day every day."

"What do they say about me?"

"Can't say."

"Can't or *won't?*"

"Won't. Can't. What does it matter?"

"It matters to me."

"Tough titties, Sergeant. You don't count diddly." The man rested his elbows on the wheels and tugged the handkerchief out of his back pocket. He wiped his face and looked closer at the chimney breast. "No . . . you . . . don't –" he said and, taking the second-largest wheel, he twisted his arms around fast, like a martial arts punch, and swiped at the nest of levers. The train lurched. The old man looked back at the chimney breast. "That's better," he said, and spun the wheel again, but less frantically this time, managing to return the handkerchief to his pocket at the same time.

Abbott got to his feet and sidled towards the wall in front of the man.

"What is it that you keep looking at?"

Without looking around, the old man said, "This?" He tapped what appeared to be a small screen set in the wall just above the column of steering wheels. "This is why I have to keep the train moving . . . and keep it moving in anything but a straight line." He waved Abbott over. "Come see."

It was a television screen.

"You're watching TV?" He didn't know whether to laugh or

cry. "You're watching television while you plough a couple hundred tons of metal through civilization?"

"Uh uh," the old man said. "Not TV. Watch with me a while."

Abbott watched.

It was some kind of fight . . . a conflict between what appeared to be two huge and completely naked . . . figures: Abbott couldn't decide whether they were men or women for, though they appeared to have no breasts, there was also an absence of any obvious genitalia or pubic hair. In fact, the creatures had no hair anywhere . . . be it on their heads, on their faces or beneath their arms., their bodies shiny and glistening with sweat. Just two sleek, enormous bodies that, at first glance, seemed to be bulbously fat. Closer examination, however, showed no rippling of flesh but only taut muscle.

One of the creatures – there was no way to differentiate between them – had pulled itself away from the corner and was padding around the far wall of the large room while the other figure stood its ground in the centre. Both of them had their arms outstretched, their fingers folded over into a grasp, their knees bent as they strived to maintain their balance.

"Hold on!" The old man spun the wheel to the left.

Abbott shot his left arm out and grabbed a hold of a fluted rail that ran at head height across the chimney breast.

At the same time, the figure in the centre of the room pictured on the screen toppled backwards and slid to the wall. The other figure pitched sideways in another direction.

The old man turned the wheel again, this time to the right, while, with his other hand, he shifted one of the levers and then twisted one of the other wheels.

One of the figures stayed against the wall while the one in the middle of the floor slid backwards. They were now at opposite sides of the room.

Abbott looked up and looked behind him, half expecting to see the things fighting right behind him. "They . . . they're here, aren't they? Here on on the train."

"That's right."

"Who are they? What are they doing?"

"They're altercating."

"They're *what*?"

"Altercating . . . disagreeing."

"What are they disagreeing about?"

The man sniggered. "Everything!" he snapped. And he sniggered again.

Abbott watched the figures on the screen pacing around each other menacingly while they were thrown first one way and then the other, bouncing across the floor and against the walls, seemingly with little or no adverse effect. No blood, no apparent pain or even discomfort. "And just who – or *what* – are they?"

"Those, young fella, are Hope and Despair. And as for why they're altercating, well . . . they've always done it. Nothing else matters to them. Why, I figure they wouldn't want to take a break or get off of the train . . . even if they could." He turned to face Abbott and added, "Which they can't." He turned back. "They're natural enemies, each one a contradiction of the other. Can't exist in harmony by the simple definition of what they're about."

Abbott watched the old man's profile as the man concentrated on spinning the wheels, jabbing a foot occasionally on to one or other of the large pedals, shifting one of the levers in an apparently random fashion and throwing another handful of dreams into the furnace . . . which, Abbott noted, threw no heat when the door was opened.

"That's their names? Hope and Despair?"

The old man shook his head. "They don't have names. Hope and Despair is what they *are*." He straightened his back for a second and shot Abbott a smile before returning his attention to the wheels and the screen. "Been altercating forever. What I got to do is make sure neither of them wins. In fact, I got to make sure neither of them even gets hands on the other one."

"How do you know which one is which?" Abbott asked, ignoring a whole slew of other questions.

"Don't know that. It don't matter."

"What happens if one of them *does* win?"

"They won't . . . leastways, not on my shift."

"When does your shift end?"

The old man shrugged.

"When did it begin?"

Another shrug. "Don't rightly recall. Long time ago. Been doing this ever since I can remember."

"You've always been driving a train around the countryside try—"

"Uh uh. Not around the countryside. I been driving the train but hardly anybody's seen it, and nobody's *ever* been on it . . . 'cept me, of course. And –" He nodded to the screen. "– them two. But now . . . now that everything's *changing* –" He emphasized the word. "– things aren't the same. There's a lot of things folks can see now they never saw before." He turned and held Abbott's eyes with his own. "These are bad times, Sergeant," he said. "Bad times."

The old man turned back and spun a couple of wheels, sending the two figures on the screen somersaulting across the floor in different directions. "Hope wins, folks get complacent," the old man said matter-of-factly. "They think everything's gonna work out just fine and dandy. Ain't nothing to get all perturbed about, nothing to strive for.

"On the other hand, Despair wins and folks don't think *anything*'s gonna work out . . . they lose that spirit of determination, that feeling of being positive. So what I gotta do is keep the two of them fit and healthy, the one inspiring the other – the despondency providing a healthy shadow for the complacency . . . and the optimism throwing just a little light on to all that negativity. Maintaining the balance, preserving the status quo."

"*Ain't nothing to get all perturbed about*" and ". . . *the despondency providing a healthy shadow for the complacency*"?

The man's voice and words were a curious amalgam of tones, dialects and vernacular. Sometimes it was a down-home folksy drawl and others it sounded intelligent and laced with profundities. Abbott couldn't decide which one was the man's real voice and which one was the affected one . . . if *either* of them was affected.

"Who are you?" He paused, thinking about what he was about to ask . . . and then went right ahead and asked it. "Are you God?"

The old man's laugh sounded more like a horse's bray. "Hah . . . *God*? *Me*? No way, Sergeant. I'm just the driver." He laughed some more. "Me . . . God! That's a good one."

On the screen, one of the figures caught hold of the other's arm and held fast.

"Damn!" The man jammed a foot on the pedal, the sudden pitch of the train slamming Abbott against the chimney breast.

Then he spun the wheel to the left. Abbott came away from the wall at an angle, pulling a piece of the rail with him. He was unable to stop himself from stumbling forward, his arms pinwheeling, one hand still holding the piece of rail.

The rail hit the old man across the side of his face and opened a gash down his cheek – which, to Abbott's astonishment, drew no blood. But the old man's eyes opened wide in surprise and then rolled back on themselves. He took a couple of faltering steps, lifted one hand to his head . . . and then slid to the floor in a heap.

Abbott quickly knelt down by the man and took hold of his shirt front. "Hey, you okay?" He threw the piece of rail to the floor and slapped the driver on the face. "Hey . . . talk to me . . . tell me some more of –" He stopped and stared at the gash in the old man's cheek.

"What?"

Abbott didn't respond. He lifted his hand and touched the man's face. It was cold. And hard. He moved his hand up to the gash . . . up to where he saw the dark gray beneath the skin.

"Your face . . ." Abbott began.

"What's the matter with it?"

Abbott gently prodded a finger between the torn pieces of flesh and felt metal. He pulled the hand back and looked the old man square in the eyes.

"What's the matter with my face?"

Maybe he had a steel plate in it . . . yes, that's what it must be. Abbott nodded at the thought.

"I said—"

"You cut yourself," Abbott said weakly.

The man's eyes opened. "I need . . . I need to repair myself," he said, his voice sounding strange . . . like a record moving between speeds.

"You got something metal there . . . there in your cheek."

"Metal in my cheek?" the old man said, pronouncing the words "mett-al" and "cheee-eeek". "Hell, I'm metal everywhere, Sergeant. It's what I'm made out of. You think I was flesh and blood like you?" He laughed raucously when he saw Abbott striving to answer. "Hell, how d'ya think I don't need to sleep or to eat, or

even to take a pee every once in a while?" He laughed again and
Abbott thought he saw a brief flicker of sparks down the old
man's throat.

"So all those stories—"

"They're not . . . stories."

Abbott looked up. On the screen, the two figures were now
locked together. And the train was slowing.

"The train's slowing down!"

"Hey, full marks, Sergeant," the man said as he pulled himself
to his feet. He nodded to the wall. "There . . . stomp your foot on
the pedal."

Abbott looked at two pedals

this isn't going to work, this is not *going to work*

at the foot of the steering column. "Which one?"

"Which foot?"

"Which *pedal*?"

"Don't matter which pedal – one's the brakes and the other's
the fuel. We either jerk to a stop or we jerk forward. Either way,
we may be able to break them up."

Abbott spun around, thrust out his right foot and

*it was going to be okay . . . What the hell was all the fuss about –
everything was going to be A-okay*

jammed it down hard.

The train stopped in its tracks.

A high pitched squeal came from beneath them, the sound of
grinding metal. Then from somewhere behind them, they heard a
series of collisions, loud crashes and explosions.

"She's jackknifing," the driver said as he pulled himself up.
"Hit the other pedal."

Abbott moved his foot across and

*shit, the train's jackknifing . . . he said it was jackknifing – what
does that mean, exactly? It means we're going to die . . . it means
"tough titties, Sergeant", we're going to*

jammed it down again, this time on the second pedal. The train
lurched forward and he fell back, away from the pedals.

The man stepped to the steering column, shook his head, and
stomped on the fuel pedal again, this time keeping it pressed.

Abbott came to a stop against the back of the room and

. . . it's the end . . . that's it . . . we're finished . . . we're going to

die . . . I'm going to die . . . what will that last gasp of breath be like? how will it feel?

immediately put his head in his hands.

"Jesus, Jesus, Jesus, Jesu—"

"Shut up!"

"That's it," Abbott shouted over the noise of the engine and the steam and the pounding of the wheels. "I've had it with this. *We've* had it. *Every*one's had it."

And he started to sob.

He hadn't cried in years . . . in fact, he couldn't remember when he *had* cried. Then came a flood of memories . . . a hallucinatory kaleidoscope of faces, some old, some not so old and some young . . . some of whom he knew were friends, some lovers and some

mothers? fathers?

relatives . . . but all of them different colours and wearing different styles of clothing . . . and each of their faces stared at him from the recesses of his mind, like pictures on a badly-tuned TV screen, pictures trying to get through . . . staring through the static at him and trying to get through.

"You have to go back."

Abbott shook his head at the imagined – remembered? – faces.

Who were all these people? Why did he recognize them? They were all shaking their heads at him in his myriad memories . . . turning their faces from him, disowning him for what he had done. He could hardly breathe, the sobs coming in spastic gulps, tearing his throat and his chest.

"Ohgodohgodohgodohgo—"

The old man spun around and kicked Abbott in the shins. "I said, you have to go back . . . you have to go back and break them up."

Abbott wheezed and coughed saliva onto his hands. "Have to . . . have to go *back*? You said you never stopped the train?"

"I don't." The old man turned back and nodded to the screen. "I mean you have to go back to the last carriage. You have to break them up."

Abbott started to moan and shake his head. Then

. . . he remembered sunshine . . . and laughter – he remembered dark days that turned out not to be so dark after all

he stopped.

"There's no need to do *anything*," he shouted triumphantly, waving his hands in the air. "We're going again . . . you've got it under control again. There's no worry . . . don't you *see*!"

"Now you listen to me." The word "me" split into a series of elongated "ee" syllables and the old man thumped a fist against the side of his head causing one of his eyes to plop out on a long, coiled spring. "Shit!" he snapped. "Pardon my French but now look what I gone and done." He pushed the eye back into its socket and twisted it around until it made a dull *click* . . . but not before Abbott saw what was in there. Flickering lights and more metal.

"The two of them are locked together," the old man said, nodding to the screen. "I can't break them up. First Despair gets the upper hand and then Hope . . . that's what's happening – can't you hear yourself? That's what's *happening*. I can't break them apart and I can't risk stopping the train or entrusting it to you. The only way is for you to go back."

Abbott laughed at the sudden flood of elation coursing through his head. "Boy, you sure are a worr—"

Then the flood withdrew and in its place came a wave of doom drifting across his mind . . . a thick black cloud of death and destruction, the promise of decay in the silent sanctity of the grave, the three-in-the-morning thoughts of loss and disease and failure, the certainty of that final breath . . . his body reaching upward with every last ounce of determination and energy, but all to no avail. Determination and energy didn't count for anything in this game.

A tear rolled down his cheek.

"We're finished, aren't we?"

The driver pulled off his baseball cap and threw it to Abbott. "Put that on."

"Huh?"

"Put on the cap. It'll help."

Help? Will it stop me from dying? Will it keep away tumours and growths, liver failure and embolisms? Will it make people love me? Will it keep my heart beating? Will it stop my bones crumbling? Will—

The old man spun around and, in one fluid motion, lifted the cap from Abbott's lap and pushed it on to Abbott's head. Then he spun back and grabbed the steering wheels again, spinning them wildly, his feet jabbing the pedals ferociously, first one and then the other, his other hand shifting levers, first forward and then back, the train spinning, jolting, pirouetting.

"What's happening?" Abbott felt conflicting waves washing over him, some – like regular waves – pushing him forward and upwards, and others pulling him back . . . bringing him down. But it was manageable now. Now he was able to ride the currents and tread the water.

"They're kicking the shit out of each other . . . if you'll pardon my French," the old man said breathlessly. His voice had changed and Abbott watched the man's back, noting with sadness – and the tiniest frisson of fear – that he appeared to be crying. But what happened when a man made out of metal cried? Abbott didn't like to think. In fact, Abbott would have preferred not to think about any of it. "Oh god," the driver said, the words coming out in a soft voice that somehow carried above the sound of the train. "Ohgodohgo—"

Abbott pulled the cap tighter and stood up. "I'm on my way."

Once out of the cab, Abbott made his way across the space between the platforms, smelling the air as it buffeted him, sending his coat tails spiralling up and out around him. Trying hard not to think about the nearness of freedom, he stepped across and forced his way into the first carriage.

At one time, the carriage may well have been the last word – or, going by what the old man had said, perhaps the first – in luxury, with ornate hangings and chandeliers glittering from walls and ceiling, and plush drapes, gathered with sashes, relieving the blur of outside glimpsed through dusty windows. But not any more.

Now the floor was a veritable battleground of debris and rotting cloth, mildewed timber and rusty pipes of metal, rolling languidly to and fro to the movement of the train.

He stepped across the piles of junk and rubbish, almost losing his footing one time as the train pitched suddenly sideways, and made his way through the carriage to the door at the far end.

For a few minutes, Abbott thought that he was not going to be able to open it. And then it gave, creaking open on hinges that had lain immobile perhaps for millennia. As he took what he hoped would not be a last look around the place, he wondered how *anything* on the train worked. He glanced back at the dusty floor and the cobwebbed walls and tried to equate their obvious aged and dilapidated condition with the old man's story of a train that had always run . . . presumably since the days when the world was still only a formless mass of unfettered energy, on through the times of the dinosaurs and on past the crucifixion and ever onwards to the present day.

He didn't know what made him do it – one of those automatic things when the body seems to assume its own motivation – but he placed a hand over his heart and pressed. For a long time, there was nothing . . . and then a thick and solitary beat pounded once against his palm. Then nothing again.

He felt for his pulse. But it was only after waiting several minutes that he was rewarded with a single *blip* beneath the fingertips pressed against his wrist.

So that was it. Time had been slowed down. That was how the train had managed to keep even its present shambling condition, roaming around the . . .

cosmos? dimensions? heavens?

when it should long ago have crumbled to dust and flakes of rust.

As he began to squeeze through the doorway on to the second platform between the carriages, he realized that even that information brought with it a sense of foreboding: the brutal fact remained that not even the train – this artefact presumably from the very dawn of time – was to be spared the process of deterioration. One day, it would fall apart . . . no matter how successful he was today.

And when it fell apart, the train would come to a stop.

And when the train came to a stop, nothing would be able to keep apart the two battling figures in the last carriage.

And then—

He pushed through the gap and stepped across on to the next platform.

All of the carriages were the same as the first . . . each of them strewn with cloth and wood and dirt, pieces of metal and glass littering the floors. Halfway along the fifth carriage, he turned back and saw his footprints in the dust of centuries: facing front again, there was nothing. Everything was as it had been since . . . since *when*? And what had it been like before the train set off? Where were Hope and Despair then?

The train jackknifed sideways and Abbott flew forward, arms outstretched. He hit the floor with his left shoulder and slid to the end corner, near the door. Pieces of glass from a long-ago smashed lantern dug into his face and neck but the pain was limited and short-lived.

He got to his feet and dusted himself down, bending his knees as though he were riding a surfboard to weather the sudden changes in direction.

When he stepped though the door and on to the platform, he came face to face with the last carriage . . . much wider than the others.

From inside came the sound of thunder.

The sides of the carriage thudded – Abbott fancied that he saw the thick-looking wooden planks shudder a time or two, and then the thunder seemed to move away slightly.

It was now or never.

He pulled the baseball hat tightly down around his head and stepped across the gap, over the thick coupling links that forever tethered the last carriage to the eternal train, and he grasped the rail.

On either side of him, fields flashed by, and buildings, a wall, some houses . . . the wind blowing his hair and trailing his coat tails like a kite. But he kept facing forward.

On the wall in front of him was a recessed handle set into a door.

He took hold of it, pulled it outwards and pushed the door.

It slid open on to the thunder.

It was a place of shadows, a place of darkness lit only by laser-light beams streaming from the hundred thousand cracks and splintered knotholes that dotted and criss-crossed the wooden walls.

The sound was deafening.

It was a herd of dinosaurs rampaging the Jurassic plains.

It was the everlasting electrical storm that fuelled the sun.

It was the sound of conflict, an endless fight between tireless armies on a field of blood . . . a battlefield so big that the sun never truly set on it, for the armies were so vast that they spread across entire time zones.

It was all of these and much, much more.

The two figures seemed to be locked together.

One had the other by the wrist and by the back of the neck.

The other, one arm taken up by its opponent's hand-hold, had its hand clasped around a piece of neck, pulling it ever nearer, stretching it like a turkey's wattle . . . and with each step it took backwards, clearly pulled from behind by the hand on its own neck, its opponent followed, the two of them stumbling, staggering . . . soundlessly fighting for foothold and traction on a floor that had been smoothed by constant footwork into something more resembling dusky marble than the wood it truly was.

Abbott sidled into the room and thought for a moment of preventing the door from closing . . . in case he was forever trapped in here, striving to keep out of the way of the two leviathans rampaging around the carriage. Then he saw that there was a handle on the inside of the door. He grasped it and turned, watching the door's edge – the lock went back and came forward: back, forward. He frowned.

Then why hadn't they left the train?

Then the old man's words

. . . *nothing else matters to them . . . why, I don't figure they'd want to take a break or get off of the train . . . even if they could* came back to him.

That was why.

They existed, these things, only to fight. To fight each other and *win*. Watching the creatures stagger around the carriage, Abbott wondered if even *that* summary were sufficiently accurate. He wondered if it were simply the fighting that counted . . . and that, maybe, if one of them were to be defeated, it would be a Pyrrhic victory for the other.

"Hey!" He waved his arms like he was about to take off. "Hey, break it up, okay?"

The things caromed to one side as the train lurched, but their holds didn't waver. Abbott grabbed the door handle as he pitched forward and swung to the side with it, his legs pinwheeling until he hit the wall and lay against the open door.

And there it was, gaping at them.

The outside.

The light from outside flooded through the doorway and into the carriage, illuminating fully the chaos in which the two things had existed for so long. And, as luck would have it – though Abbott thought that maybe luck didn't have the ante to sit in on *this* game – the combatants were caught in profile, the light spilling down the length of their bodies, catching the bones and musculature.

And they looked around, as one entity, ceasing for the most infinitesimally small fraction of time. Their faces were bizarre contradictions of emotion and personality, awesome and gentle at the same time . . . even within the same furrow of hairless brow.

Without a second's thought or hesitation, Abbott pulled himself to his feet and threw himself at them.

And he screamed.

The creatures seemed to frown – was it wonder? fear? amusement? It didn't matter. In that split of a split second, their holds relaxed.

Abbott hit the thing on the right and slid off into its opponent, his coat wafting behind him like the cloak of an avenging angel or one of the creatures of the night, the do-gooders he used to read in the comic books in simpler times.

simpler lives?

so long ago.

And as he hit them, the train ground to a halt, then started again, then lurched around. Wheels screeched and hissed, the train's whistle blew into the world filling it with just the one thing: noise.

The fighters staggered, slipped, fell, coming apart.

One of them scrabbled to its knees while the other turned in its prone position on the floor and reached out a grasping hand.

There was no emotion on their faces.

They did what they did because that was what they did. No hate, no fear . . . no intelligence.

The train spun.

Abbott rolled across the floor to the back of the carriage.

The door swung shut and everything became gloom again.

Now the train spun around the other way, speeded up, stopped almost dead in its tracks – if it had have been on tracks – and then shot off again, slewing in the opposite direction.

The creatures had rolled apart, one against the side wall and the other already getting to its feet against the door.

Abbott pulled himself to a sitting position and started to shuffle.

Both of the creatures were now on their feet, pacing each other in a wide circle, hands outstretched, knees bent for maximum spring.

He shuffled along the side wall as they tried to lurch at each other, and the train leant over madly, sending one body flailing against the wall only a few feet from Abbott's shoulder.

Oblivious of Abbott, the figure spun around and tried to grab its opponent, and the train shifted again, sending it spinning down to the back wall. The other scrabbled on its hands and knees in pursuit but already the centre of gravity was shifting again, and the creature fell backwards.

Abbott got to a semi-kneeling position and scurried towards the door.

Behind him the thunder had abated.

Now there was only the silence of intent.

The storm had passed. For now.

He turned the handle and crawled out on to the tiny platform, pulling the door closed behind him.

They were passing fields.

A sea of corn waved in the late afternoon sunshine.

The sky above it shone clear blue.

Abbott caught sight – briefly – of a road sign before it sped past into memory. It was a road sign he had seen before.

The air, blasting now into Abbott's face, tasted of cotton candy.

Abbott pulled himself to his feet and looked up.

And somewhere down the train, in the tiny cabin, the old man turned a wheel or maybe stepped on the other pedal . . . or maybe the train just hit something . . . and Abbott lost his hold.

He flew through the air, through the gap between the last carriage and the one in front of it, and then the train was moving past him, the last carriage with its eternal altercators . . . and he was still flying . . .

A huge ploughed wave of grass and soil swept behind the carriage like a brown and green-flecked curtain. And then it was gone, the engine's mournful wail like the distant sound of a storm drifting away.

Abbott hit the ground on his side, grunted loudly, rolled over, head over heels, bounced up and pistoned his legs with a gasp, winded, gulping for air. His feet touched the edge of the cornfield and he bounced again, flying forward, face down into the yellow stalks. His chest exploded in pain, his head gashed open on a protruding rock . . . and his eye felt as though someone had jabbed a long needle straight through the iris.

But his momentum was slowing.

He rolled over and over, sideways now, twisting his right shoulder and hearing – *feeling* – something twang in his side.

And then he was still.

Everything hurt . . . nothing hurt.

A stillness was coming over him. Without moving, he regrouped inside of himself, consolidated . . . effected a damage report the way they did it on intergalactic spaceships after a meteor shower.

He lifted one arm slowly from the ground, flexed his fingers. Seemed okay. Then the other. Then his left leg. His right.

He blinked. One eye didn't seem to be working too well but when he closed the other one, he could still see.

He placed a hand on his chest and felt.

His heart was hammering like a rock drummer.

Forcing himself to breathe slowly, he pulled himself upright, grimacing at the flashes of pain that signalled from a hundred places. But, amazingly, nothing seemed to be broken.

Or maybe it wasn't so amazing. For beside him, amidst the crushed stalks of corn and flattened soil, lay the filthy baseball cap. It must have stayed on his head until he came to a stop.

Abbott reached over to retrieve it but as his fingers touched the brim the thing crumbled to dust and blew away in the direction the train had gone.

He looked over into the distance, shielding his eyes from the sun, and fancied he could see a column of smoke drifting and spiralling up into the sky like Pecos Bill's tornado steed . . . fancied he could see, in his mind's eye, the old man – like Pecos

Bill himself – twisting and turning his steering wheels and pounding his pedals

Yeeeh hahhhhh!

grinding down anything that got in his way. While behind him, a few carriages back, the embodiments of Hope and Despair faced each other in their endless and bitter struggle during these strange days. Abbott wondered if the old man were wasting his time and his energy . . . wondered whether the die in *this* crap shoot had already been rolled.

But maybe it hadn't. Maybe *everything* was worth a fight.

"God's speed, old man!" Abbott shouted. And then, his voice softer, he added, "Whoever made you did a good job."

And way way off in the distance, a whistle blew.

He twisted around until he was on his knees and then stood up. He was shaky but intact. Everything that should bend *did* bend, and everything that shouldn't didn't. He dusted down his coat and looked around.

A pick-up honked at him from the road. He nodded and acknowledged the waving arm extended from the window.

"That your car back there?" a voice shouted. "The Trans-Am?"

"That it is," Abbott said as he approached the pick-up.

A young man leaned out of the window and nodded back up the road he'd just travelled. "Old fella back there said you might need help so I drove slow until I saw you. Taking a lie-down?"

Abbott frowned. "Old fella?" He looked back along the road and saw only settling dust.

"Yeah, real old guy – I mean real old . . . looked enough to be a hunnerd – he was sitting on the side of the road." The man held his hand up and wiggled his fingers. "Didn't have but a finger and thumb on his hand," he added, shaking his head. "Damnedest thing . . . like a claw."

Abbott looked back through the shimmering heat but couldn't see anything.

"You know him?"

Abbott patted the dust from his trousers. "Heard of him, I guess you could say."

"Yeah?" The man seemed to wait for more information. When Abbott didn't provide any, the man said, "How'd he get his hand like that?" He held out his own hand, the fingers bunched up into a two-pronged claw, and tried to move them up and down.

Abbott shrugged. "Making things," he said. "I hear he used to be pretty good at it."

The man nodded, looked Abbott up and down before glancing back up the road. When he turned back to face Abbott he said, "Well, you want a lift into town?"

Abbott nodded. "I need gas is all."

The man gestured Abbott to move around the cab. "Well hop in. There's a filling station a mile or two ahead."

"In Madrigal," Abbott said.

"Pardon me?"

He slipped alongside the man. "The town up ahead. Madrigal."

"No sir. Town up ahead is Hobbes Corner." The man rubbed his chin and frowned as they moved off. "Can't say I ever heard of anyplace around here name of Madrigal."

"Well, anywhere will do for me . . . so long as I can get some gas."

"Right enough there," the man said. "It's a fine day."

Abbott nodded. "A fine day," he agreed.

From somewhere far off out of sight, came a shrill call that sounded for all the world like a train's whistle. Abbott looked across at the driver but the young man didn't seem to have heard anything.

He faced front again and listened, closing his eyes to concentrate. But there was only the throaty purr of the engine . . . and the wind . . . and the hum of the tyres eating up blacktop in the late afternoon.